STEPHEN JONES lives in London, England. A Hugo Award nominee, he is the winner of four World Fantasy Awards, three International Horror Guild Awards, five Bram Stoker Awards, twenty-one British Fantasy Awards and a Lifetime Achievement Award from the Horror Writers Association. One of Britain's most acclaimed horror and dark fantasy writers and editors, he has more than 150 books to his credit, including *The Art of Horror Movies: An Illustrated History*; the film books of Neil Gaiman's *Coraline* and *Stardust*; *The Illustrated Monster Movie Guide* and *The Hellraiser Chronicles*; the non-fiction studies *Horror: 100 Best Books* and *Horror: Another 100 Best Books* (both with Kim Newman); the single-author collections *Necronomicon* and *Eldritch Tales* by H.P. Lovecraft; *The Complete Chronicles of Conan* and *Conan's Brethren* by Robert E. Howard, and *Curious Warnings: The Great Ghost Stories of M.R. James*; plus such anthologies as *Horrorology: The Lexicon of Fear, Fearie Tales: Stories of the Grimm and Gruesome, A Book of Horrors, The Mammoth Book of Halloween, The Lovecraft Squad* and the *Zombie Apocalypse!* series and twenty-nine volumes of *Best New Horror*. You can visit his web site at *www.stephenjoneseditor.com* or follow him on Facebook at *Stephen Jones-Editor*.

BEST NEW HORROR
VOLUME №29

Front cover illustration by Howard Nostrand.
Originally published in *Chamber of Chills #20,* November 1953.
Back cover illustration attributed to Al Avison.
Originally published in *Witches Tales.*

This trade paperback edition published in April 2019
by Drugstore Indian Press, an imprint of PS Publishing Ltd.,
by arrangement with Stephen Jones.

2 4 6 8 10 9 7 5 3 1

ISBN 978-1-786363-92-3

Design and Layout by Michael Smith
Cover design by Smith & Jones

Printed and bound in England by T. J. International

PS PUBLISHING
Grosvenor House, 1 New Road
Hornsea HU18 1PG, England

editor@pspublishing.co.uk
www.pspublishing.co.uk

BEST NEW HORROR

#29

BEST NEW
HORROR

#29

*Edited and with
an Introduction by*

STEPHEN JONES

DIP

BEST NEW HORROR

#29

BEST NEW
HORROR

#29

Edited and with
an Introduction by

STEPHEN JONES

DIP

BEST NEW HORROR
VOLUME №29

This trade paperback edition published in April 2019
by Drugstore Indian Press, an imprint of PS Publishing Ltd.,
by arrangement with Stephen Jones.

2 4 6 8 10 9 7 5 3 1

ISBN 978-1-786363-92-3

Design and Layout by Michael Smith
Cover design by Smith & Jones

Printed and bound in England by T. J. International

PS PUBLISHING
Grosvenor House, 1 New Road
Hornsea HU18 1PG, England

editor@pspublishing.co.uk
www.pspublishing.co.uk

CONTENTS

ACKNOWLEDGEMENTS

THE EDITOR WOULD like to thank Kim Newman, David Barraclough, Mandy Slater, Andrew I. Porter, Amanda Foubister, Ellen Datlow, Gordon Van Gelder, Robert Morgan, Lydia Gittins, Rosemary Pardoe, R.B. Russell, Andy Cox, James D. Jenkins, Michael Kelly, David Longhorn, Jason V. Brock, John Landis, Grete Kotryna Domarkaite, Robert T. Garcia, Angela Slatter, Michael Dirda and, especially, Peter and Nicky Crowther, Mike Smith, Marie O'Regan and Michael Marshall Smith for all their help and support. Special thanks are also due to *Locus, Ansible, Classic Images, Entertainment Weekly, ISFDB* and all the other sources that were used for reference in the Introduction and the Necrology.

This one is for my old pal
Bill Nolan,
like Logan, he's still running!

INTRODUCTION

HORROR IN 2017

I T WAS REPORTED in 2017 that physical books were making a comeback in the UK, with sales of e-books forecast to fall for the first time. With sales of physical books predicted to grow by 6% and e-reader sales set to fall by 1%, it was said that readers "appeared to be showing a new appreciation for the traditional print format".

This was borne out by a 31% rise in the sale of hardcovers to £97 million, although sales of audiobooks also increased 25% to £31 million and income from overseas sales rose 8% to £3.4 billion.

Meanwhile, funding for English libraries was down for the fifth year in a row, with local authorities cutting a further 5% on spending, wiping around £37 million off the library budget.

In July, Pearson sold a 22% stake in its publishing company, Penguin Random House, to Germany's Bertelsmann for £776 million, while Canongate bought the independent Severn House imprint from founder Edwin Buckhalter, who remained on as a consultant.

Chaosium, Inc., the company behind the popular *Call of Cthulhu* role-playing game, announced that it was relaunching its Lovecraftian fiction line in 2018 under new fiction editor James Lowder, however the American horror imprint Samhain Publishing closed down at the end of February due to "declining sales" and the "changing market".

Forbes updated its annual guesstimates about what the top authors earned for the twelve months ending May 31, 2017. With new books, a West End play and futher movie adaptations, J.K. Rowling returned to the top of the list with an estimated $95 million. James Patterson was second with $87 million and then, some way behind, came Dan Brown at fourth with $20 million and Stephen King at fifth with a measly $15 million. *Percy Jackson* author Rick Riordan tied with Danielle Steel at 10th place with $11 million.

The cumulative estimated earnings of the top authors rose to $311 million—up from the 2016 total, but down from the consecutive four years before that.

No.2 on that list, James Patterson, continued to donate $1.75 million to US school libraries as part of his School Library Campaign started in 2015, while George R.R. Martin (who didn't even make the *Forbes* list!) announced in April that he would fund the "Miskatonic Scholarship" to a writer of Lovecraftian fiction for the annual Odyssey Writing Workshop held every summer in Manchester, New Hampshire.

Women all over the world suddenly dozed off in cocoons, leaving the men to sort things out in *Sleeping Beauties*, a hefty, high-concept collaborative novel between Stephen King and his youngest son, Owen King. The authors named their sleeping sickness "Aurora"—after the Disney princess in *Sleeping Beauty* (1959).

King also collaborated with Richard Chizmar on *Gwendy's Button Box*, a new novella about temptation set in the author's Maine town of Castle Rock during the early 1970s. It was published by Chizmar's Cemetery Dance imprint with cover art by Ben Baldwin and interior illustrations by Keith Minnion. A custom slipcase was also available, which could be additionally ordered for $49.95.

After a seventeen-year wait, Philip Pullman returned to the "His Dark Materials" universe with *The Book of Dust: Volume One: La Belle Sauvage*, the first in a new prequel trilogy inspired by the English poet and painter William Blake and illustrated by Chris Wormell.

Neil Gaiman's *Norse Mythology* contained the author's retellings of fifteen myths for a new audience.

The Silent Corner and *The Whispering Room* were the first two books in Dean Koontz's "Jane Hawk" series, and *Ramses the Damned: The Passion of Cleopatra* by Anne Rice and Christopher Rice was a belated sequel to Anne Rice's 1989 novel *The Mummy, or Ramses the Damned*.

Broken Glass and *Shattered Memories* were the second and third volumes in the "Mirror Sisters" series, which was still being credited to the long-deceased V.C. Andrews'.

In Naomi Alderman's *The Power*, women and teenage girls suddenly found themselves enabled with lethal electric powers. It came with a glowing cover blurb by Margaret Atwood.

Written in alternating first-person chapters, Sarah Pinborough's *Behind Her Eyes* told its story from the perspective of two women—the wife and secretary of a rich and handsome doctor—before it took an unexpected turn into lucid dreaming and a surprise twist ending.

Kerri Maniscalco's murder mystery *Hunting Prince Dracula*, the author's sequel to her #1 best-seller *Stalking Jack the Ripper*, was presented by James Patterson, which probably gave a clue to its quality.

In Joanne Harris' novella *A Pocketful of Crows*, a young girl took her revenge on a squire's son and the family that wronged her.

Irish film director and screenwriter Neil Jordan's novel *Carnivalesque* could have been inspired by Ray Bradbury, as a teenage boy found himself trapped in a Hall of Mirrors when a creepy carnival visited the Irish coastal town where he lived.

All of a Winter's Night was the fourteenth volume in Phil Rickman's popular "Merrily Watkins" series.

The undead Geneviève Dieudonné found herself exiled to Japan by Count Dracula and on the trail of a vicious murderer in *Anno Dracula: One Thousand Monsters*, the latest novel in Kim Newman's best-selling alternate vampire mythology.

A group of holidaymakers found themselves trapped in a strange world in John Ajvide Lindqvist's *I Am Behind You*, the first in a trilogy, while *Night Shift* was the third and final installment in Charlaine Harris' "Midnight Texas" trilogy.

A group of mercenaries investigated a New Mexico kidnapping cult and were forced to confront something much more monstrous in *Little Heaven* by Canadian author Nick Cutter (Craig Davidson), and *Rhyming Rings* was a previously unpublished serial killer novel by the late fantasy writer David Gemmell (who died in 2006), which came with an Afterword by Stan Nicholls.

Marcus Sakey's thriller *Afterlife* was set in an alternate world, as a pair of murdered FBI agents were hunted by the serial killer responsible for their deaths.

An American criminology student discovered an underground black market for high-priced arcane artefacts in Tim Lebbon's *Relics*, the first volume in a new trilogy, and Adam Nevill's *Under a Watchful Eye* followed on from the author's short story 'Yellow Teeth'.

It Devours! was a sequel to the novel and podcast *Welcome to Night Vale* by Joseph Fink and Jeffrey Cranor and found the small desert town menaced by the Smiling God and its Joyous Congregation. Jessica Hayworth supplied the illustrations.

In Daniel Kehlmann's *You Should Have Left*, a screenwriter and his family found the world around them changing while staying at a wintry Alpine retreat, and Andrew Michael Hurley's *Devil's Day* was a slice of folk horror set around a Lancashire farm where tradition was important,

Paul La Farge's *The Night Ocean* featured H.P. Lovecraft himself as a character—along with other historical writers and editors in the genre—before lifting the lid on Lovecraft's (fictional) gay relationship with his teenage protégé, Robert Barlow, who possibly didn't commit suicide in 1951.

Eric Flint and Mike Resnick teamed up for the Lovecraftian SF novel *The Gods of Sagittarius*, which featured a race of aliens known as the "Old Ones", and an FBI agent and one of two survivors of Innsmouth teamed up in 1949 in Ruthanna Emrys' *Winter Tide*.

James Lovegrove's *The Cthulhu Casebooks: Sherlock Holmes and the Miskatonic Monstrosities* was another literary mash-up nobody needed, while *Black Goat Blues* was the second volume in Levi Black's contemporary "Mythos War" series.

There was also an echo of Lovecraft in Caitlín R. Kiernan's novella *Agents of Dreamland*, as secret agents combated an alien fungus plague.

The grown-up members of the Blyton Summer Detective Club reunited after thirteen years to confront the suppressed horrors they witnessed during their final case unmasking the "Sleepy Lake Monster" in Spanish writer and cartoonist Edgar Cantero's *Meddling Kids*, a postmodern homage to everything from Scooby-Doo to Lovecraft.

Alison Littlewood's Victorian horror novel *The Crow Garden* involved an obsessed asylum doctor, while a woman locked in a psychiatric hospital revealed the tragic history of a dilapidated haunted house in *The Silent Companions* by Laura Purcell.

Three friends unearthed something horrific beneath an old mansion's outhouse in Jeffrey Ford's novella *The Twilight Pariah*, and a teenager connected with his Native American roots in his own house in Stephen Graham Jones' ghostly novel *Mapping the Interior*.

A young dead girl found herself still trapped in the world of the living in Seanan McGuire's novella *Dusk or Dark or Dawn or Day*, while *Into the Drowning Deep* was the second in the "Rolling in the Deep" series by the same author writing under the name "Mira Grant".

Corpselight was the second volume in Angela Slatter's "Verity Fassbinder" series, and *In the Still of the Night*, David L. Golemon's sequel to *The Supernaturals*, found the TV ghost-hunting team trying to save the President.

A group of characters in present-day Portland discovered that something evil was planning to invade this dimension through the Internet in Benjamin Percy's *The Dark Net*.

Ezekiel Boone's *Skitter* was a sequel to the author's spider-horror novel *The Hatching*.

Scientists in Antarctica reawakened a deadly, dormant organism in Michael McBride's *Subhuman*, the first book in the "Unit 51" series, and a mining operation awakened something nasty underground in Kurt Anderson's *Resurrection Pass*.

A teacher having visions of missing students was drawn back to an ancient woodland, the site of a mysterious disappearance a decade before, in *Hekla's Children* by James Brogden, and a street musician discovered that his former girlfriend had unusual psychic powers in Rio Youers' *The Forgotten Girl*.

Mysterious events occurred around a writers' and artists' retreat in Wendy Webb's *The End of Temperance Dare*, and paranormal investigator Jenny Logan was faced with a possible werewolf killing at a writers' retreat in Lincoln Child's *Full Wolf Moon*.

Victorian artifacts awakened a killer in modern-day California in Robert Masello's *The Jekyll Revelation*, while Dr. Jekyll's daughter Eliza investigated another mystery in *The Dastardly Miss Lizzie*, Viola Carr's follow-up to *The Diabolical Miss Hyde*.

Molly Tanzer's *Creatures of Will and Temper* was inspired by Oscar Wilde's *The Picture of Dorian Gray*.

M.R. Carey's novella *The Boy on the Bridge* was set in the same zombie post-apocalyptic Britain as *The Girl with All the Gifts*.

The Burning World was the second book in Isaac Marion's zombie post-apocalypse "Warm Bodies" series, while Scott Kenemore's *Zombie-in-Chief: Eater of the Free World* was a satirical spoof on the 2016 American presidential election.

A woman could communicate with the dead in Sara Flannery Murphy's debut novel, *The Possessions*, and a reporter investigated an Appalachian snake-handling cult in Kristi DeMeester's first novel, *Beneath*.

In Emily Bain Murphy's first book, *The Disappearances*, aimed at the young adult market, everyday things began to vanish every seven years.

A former mummy-turned-vice cop and his undead partner investigated an attempt to upset the relationship between vampires and humans in Michael F. Haspil's first novel, *Graveyard Shift*, which could perhaps have done with a more original title.

The New Annotated Frankenstein celebrated the forthcoming 200th anniversary of Mary Shelley's 1818 novel. Edited and annotated by

Leslie S. Klinger, the book included around 200 illustrations, an Introduction by Guillermo del Toro and an Afterword by Anne K. Mellor.

With a Foreword by Dacre Stoker and an Afterword by John Edgar Browning, *Powers of Darkness: The Lost Version of Dracula* from Overlook Press reprinted Valdimar Ásmundsson's 1901 Icelandic translation/reinterpretation of Bram Stoker's novel (*Makt Myrkranna*), translated back into English with notes and annotations by Hans Corneel de Roos, who speculated in his Introduction that Ásmundsson's version may have been based on an earlier, unpublished draft of *Dracula*.

Harper's "Collins Chillers" series continued with a new anthology of neglected vampire stories, *Dracula's Brethren*, edited by Richard Dalby and Brian J. Frost, along with the reprint collections *In the Dark* by E. Nesbit, *The Black Reaper* by Bernard Capes and *Three Men in the Dark* by Jerome K. Jerome, Barry Pain and Robert Barr, all edited with revised Introductions by Hugh Lamb.

Selected with an Introduction by Mark Gatiss, *Ghost Stories* collected nine tales by E.F. Benson, while the British Library published *Out of the Deep and Other Supernatural Tales*, which reprinted thirteen stories by Walter de la Mare, along with an Introduction by Gary Buzwell.

The Best of Richard Matheson appeared as part of the Penguin Classics series. It contained thirty-three stories first published between 1950-2010, with an Introduction by editor Victor LaValle.

The Horror on the Links and *The Devil's Rosary* were the first two volumes in Night Shade Books' handsome hardcover series "The Complete Tales of Jules de Grandin", reprinting Seabury Quinn's tales of the dapper occult detective from *Weird Tales*. Edited by George A. Vanderburgh, the first volume was introduced by Vanderburgh and the late Robert E. Weinberg and the second by Stefan Dziemianowicz. Both books featured terrific cover paintings by Donato Giancola.

Edited with an Introduction by Stefan Dziemianowicz, *Great Supernatural Stories: 101 Horrifying Tales* ran to more than 700 pages and featured classic fiction by H.P. Lovecraft, M.P. Shiel,

William Hope Hodgson and many others. Dziemianowicz also edited the companion volume, *Great Thrillers: 101 Suspenseful Tales*.

A 50th Anniversary reprint of Ira Levin's *Rosemary's Baby* came with a new Introduction by David Morrell.

Playwright Erik Forrest Jackson's *Muppets Meet the Classics: The Phantom of the Opera* was a mash-up of Gaston Leroux's original and the puppet characters.

The young protagonist thought her life was more mundane than most until she discovered an ancient machine that converted evil into energy, some talking mushrooms and that her grandfather had been friends with the Devil for more than 150 years in Michael Marshall Smith's inventive young adult novel *Hannah Green and Her Unfeasibly Mundane Existance*.

Teen Frankenstein was the first volume in the "High School Horror" series by Chandler Baker. It was followed by *Teen Hyde*.

Amy Ross' *Jek/Hyde* was a contemporary reworking of Robert Louis Stevenson's book, while A.G. Howard's *RoseBlood* was inspired by Gaston Leroux's *The Phantom of the Opera* and Michelle Gagnon's *Unearthly Things* was an updated version of *Jane Eyre* given a supernatural twist.

A teenage girl was haunted by deadly powers in Jennifer Bosworth's *The Killing Jar*, and a girl traded her heart to a demon in Emily Lloyd-Jones' *The Hearts We Sold*.

Another teenager was possessed by the spirit of a bear in Frances Hardinge's YA historical horror *A Skinful of Shadows*, while Mary Downing Hahn's ghost novel *One for Sorrow* was set during the 1918 influenza outbreak.

A young Romany girl collected body parts from the four men who raped her and killed her friend so that she could bring him back to life again in Hilary Monahan's *The Hollow Girl*.

Jenna Black's *Night Magic* was a sequel to *Nightstruck*, about a girl enjoying the dark magic of Philadelphia at night, and *Hellfighters* and *Hellwalkers* were the final two books in Alexander Gordon Smith's "The Devil's Engine trilogy".

Libba Bray's *Before the Devil Breaks You*, the third volume in the

"Spectral Diviners" series, was set in New York City during the Jazz Age.

Jonathan Stroud's "Lockwood & Co." series came to a conclusion with the fifth and final volume, *The Empty Grave*, as the members of London's smallest detective agency finally discovered the origin of the supernatural threats attacking the city.

It was a busy year for R.L. Stine with the new "Fear Street" novels *The Dead Boyfriend* and *Give Me a K-I-L-L*, which were also packaged together in the omnibus *Fear Street Super Thriller: Nightmares*.

Fear Street Saga: Cursed was an omnibus of three 1996 "Fear Street" novels by Stine: *A New Fear, House of Whispers* and *Forbidden Secrets*, while the *Goosebumps 25th Anniversary Retro Set* featured five of the author's most popular books reissued in their original covers and packaged in a purple tin.

Harry Potter and the Prisoner of Azkaban was the third volume in J.K. Rowling's series given an artistic makeover by Jim Kay.

British publisher Sanrio created an unlikely mash-up line of books, art prints and clothing that brought together the late Roger Hargreaves' Mr. Men children's characters and the BBC's *Doctor Who*.

In Laura Ellen Anderson's *Amelia Fang and the Barbaric Ball*, the young vampire's pet pumpkin "Squashy" was kidnapped by a spoilt prince.

Sharon Gosling's werewolf novel *Fir* from Stripes Publishing/Red Eye was described as a "chilling scandi *noir* YA horror". It dealt with the Scandinavian version of the myth, the "Varulv".

A teenage boy found himself caught up in a war between good werewolves and evil witches in *The Black Wolves of Boston*, the first volume in a new series by Wen Spencer.

Poe: Stories and Poems was aimed at the YA market and featured Gareth Hinds' graphic adaptations of four stories and three poems by Edgar Allan Poe.

The collection *Anno Dracula 1899 and Other Stories* was basically a "best of" Kim Newman, with seventeen reprint tales spanning a period of nearly thirty years, along with a short play and an excerpt from the author's new novel *Anno Dracula: One Thousand Monsters*.

Strange Weather collected four novellas (or "four short novels" as it claimed on the cover) by Joe Hill, while *You Should Come With Me Now: Stories of Ghosts* was the first new collection of short fiction from M. John Harrison in fifteen years.

Redder Than Blood collected nine fairy tale-inspired stories by the late Tanith Lee, three original.

The Complete Sookie Stackhouse Stories included the contents of the 2009 collection *A Touch of Dead* plus five more recent stories by Charlaine Harris, who also supplied a new Introduction and story notes.

The debut volume from Manchester's Cōnfingō Publishing, a new imprint specialising in contemporary fiction and poetry, was Nicholas Royle's *Ornithology: Sixteen Short Stories*. This collection of often dark and surreal tales was based around the theme of birds, and two of the stories were previously unpublished.

Published by Penguin Random House's Blumhouse Books/Anchor Books imprint, *Haunted Nights: A Horror Writers Association Anthology* was edited by Ellen Datlow and Lisa Morton and featured sixteen original Halloween-themed stories by HWA members Stephen Graham Jones, Garth Nix, Kelley Armstrong, Paul Kane, Pat Cadigan and John Langan, amongst others. Co-editor Morton also supplied an Introduction.

Mad Hatters and March Hares: All-New Stories from the World of Lewis Carroll's Alice in Wonderland, edited by a solo Datlow, featured eighteen stories and poems by Priya Sharma, Richard Bowes, Stephen Graham Jones, Jeffrey Ford, Angela Slatter and Jane Yolen, amongst others.

Ellen Datlow also edited and introduced *Black Feathers: Dark Avian Tales: An Anthology* for Pegasus Books. It contained fifteen stories (two reprints) and a poem by some of the same contributors, along with Nicholas Royle, Paul Tremblay, Joyce Carol Oates, Alison Littlewood, M. John Harrison and Pat Cadigan.

Created by Stephen Jones, *The Lovecraft Squad: Waiting* was the first in a trilogy of "mosaic novels" from the same publisher, based around a super-secret worldwide organisation dedicated to battling the eldritch monstrosities given form in H.P. Lovecraft's fevered imagination. It featured contributions from Angela Slatter, Brian Hodge, Reggie Oliver, Michael Marshall Smith, Steve Rasnic Tem, Peter Atkins, Richard Gavin, Jay Russell, Thana Niveau, Stephen Baxter and Kim Newman.

The Lovecraft Squad: All Hallows Horror was a spin-off novel by John Llewellyn Probert that also tied in to Jones' earlier *Zombie Apocalypse!* series.

The first in a welcome new original anthology series edited and introduced by Mark Morris for Titan Books, *New Fears: New Horror Stories by Masters of the Genre* featured nineteen tales by a stellar line-up of writers that included Alison Littlewood, Stephen Gallagher, Angela Slatter, Chaz Brenchley, Ramsey Campbell, Adam L.G. Nevill, Muriel Gray, Conrad Williams, Kathryn Ptacek, Stephen Laws and Christopher Golden.

For the same imprint, Golden edited and introduced *Dark Cities*, an original anthology of nineteen urban horror stories by Tim Lebbon, Helen Marshall, M.R. Carey, Amber Benson, Simon R. Green, Paul Tremblay, Nathan Ballingrud, Tanarive Due, Ramsey Campbell, Sherrilyn Kenyon, Nick Cutter and others, including the editor himself.

Jonathan Maberry and the late George A. Romero were credited as co-editors of *Nights of the Living Dead*, yet another anthology set in Romero's iconic zombieverse. It included stories by, amongst others, Maberry, Joe R. Lansdale, David J. Schow, Mike Carey, John Skipp, Brian Keene and Jay Bonansinga, along with original filmmakers John A. Russo and Romero himself.

Published to tie in with Worldcon 75, the first Finnish World Science Fiction Convention, Johanna Sinisalo and Toni Jerrman edited *Giants at the End of the World: A Showcase of Finnish Weird*. The give-away paperback contained eleven stories (two original) in English, with a Foreword by Sinisalo.

Edited by the busy Ellen Datlow for Night Shade Books, *The Best Horror of the Year Volume Nine* included twenty-one stories, along with the usual Summation of the previous year by the editor and Honorable Mentions, while *The Year's Best Dark Fantasy & Horror:*

2017 edited by Paula Guran for Prime Books included thirty-seven stories.

Published by Canada's Undertow Publications, *Year's Best Weird Fiction Volume Four* guest-edited by Helen Marshall and series editor Michael Kelly featured fifteen stories along with introductory material by the editors.

The Datlow and Guran anthologies shared the same stories by Gemma Files and Livia Llewellyn, and different contributions by Brian Hodge and Steve Rasnic Tem. There was no overlap between the Datlow and Marshall/Kelly volumes, but both the Guran and Marshall/Kelly compilations included the same story by Jeffrey Ford.

Best New Horror #27 edited by Stephen Jones appeared from PS Publishing and featured seventeen stories and novellas from 2015, along with the usual long Introduction and Necrology. It was available in both trade paperback and as a 100-copy signed and slipcased hardcover.

Co-edited by Sean Wallace and Silvia Moreno-Garcia, the monthly online magazine of *The Dark* featured "dark and strange" original fiction by Lisa L. Hannett and Kristi DeMeester, and reprints from Ray Cluley, Helen Marshall, Angela Slatter and Robert Shearman.

Meanwhile, John Joseph Adams' electronic *Nightmare Magazine* showcased new stories monthly from, amongst others, Carrie Vaughn, Jessica Amanda Salmonson, Nick Mamatas, Silvia Moreno-Garcia and Adam-Troy Castro (who also contributed a new quarterly book and media review column). There were also reprints by Lynda E. Rucker, Robert Shearman, Helen Marshall, Stephen Graham Jones, V.H. Leslie, Nalo Hopkinson, John Skipp, Brian Everson and Lisa Morton.

Anya Martin, John Langan, Nathan Carson, Gemma Files, S.P. Miskowski and Kristi DeMeester contributed non-fiction pieces, and there were interviews with Seanan McGuire, Norman Prentiss, Stephen Graham Jones and Richard Kelly.

As always, Jeani Rector's electronic 'zine *The Horror Show* presented plenty of fine reading on a monthly basis, with contributions from Brent Monahan, Graham Masterton, Joe R. Lansdale,

Tim Lebbon, Nancy Kilpatrick, P.D. Cacek, Simon Clark, Lisa Morton, Aaron J. French, Deborah LeBlanc, Piers Anthony and the editor herself, amongst many others.

The "Doctor Who Bot" on Skype allowed users of the app to listen to new adventures of the Time Lord, voiced by Peter Capaldi, in "binaural sound".

The eleven-episode podcast *Spooked* from WNYC Studios/Snap Judgment featured short "real-life" supernatural experiences recounted by the people who experienced them.

The seventh volume of editor Michael Kelly's print-on-demand (PoD) anthology series, *Shadows and Tall Trees*, from Undertow Publications presented nineteen original stories from an impressive line-up of contributors that included Brian Everson, M. Rickert, V.H. Leslie, Rosalie Parker, Conrad Williams, Simon Strantzas, Steve Rasnic Tem, Robert Shearman, Alison Moore and Nicholas Royle. It was available in both trade paperback and hardcover formats, with variant cover artwork, as well as an e-book edition.

I Will Surround You was a welcome collection from Undertow of fourteen stories (two original) by Conrad Williams, while from the same on-demand imprint, *The Dream Operator* collected eleven stories by Welsh writer Mike O'Driscoll, three of them original to the book.

The third annual compedium of editor C.M. Muller's *Nightscript* from Chthonic Matter featured twenty-three literary "strange and darksome tales" by, amongst others, Simon Strantzas, Daniel Braum, Clint Smith, Adam Golaski, Rebecca J. Allred and John Howard.

Issued under the Electric Pentacle Press imprint, *The Persistance of Geraniums and Other Worrying Tales* collected ten linked Edwardian-styled strange stories (four original) and a novel extract by British author John Linwood Grant. Alan M. Clark supplied the Introduction and Paul Boswell contributed a number of black and white illustrations. Unfortunately, as with so many PoD books these days, this one had no idea what running heads are used for.

Another volume that had the same problem was the otherwise solid anthology *The Beauty of Death II: Death by Water*, produced in English by Italian imprint Independent Legions Publishing. Co-edited by Alessandro Manzetti and Jodi Renée Lester, it contained thirty-nine stories (ten reprints) set around water by, amongst others, Lucy Taylor, Eric J. Guignard, Simon Bestwick, Peter Straub, Ramsey Campbell, Caitlín R. Kiernan, Dennis Etchison, John Palisano, Edward Lee, Tim Waggoner, David J. Schow, Michael A. Arnzen, Adam L.G. Nevill, John Langan, Clive Barker and Lisa Morton, along with both editors.

Eric J. Guignard was also the new editor of *Horror Library Volume 6* for Cutting Block Books, taking over from R.J. Cavender. It featured twenty-seven stories by Tom Johnstone, Bentley Little, Jeffrey Ford, J.G. Faherty, Jay Caselberg and Carole Johnstone, amongst others.

Edited by Doug Murano and D. Alexander Ward, *Shadows Over Main Street Volume 2* contained seventeen small-town Mythos stories (two reprints) by Lucy A. Snyder, William Meikle, Erinn L. Kemper, Damien Angelica Walters, Joe R. Lansdale, Gary A. Braunbeck, Joyce Carol Oates and others. Laird Barron supplied the Introduction.

Cutting Block Single Slices Volume 1 edited with a Foreword by Patrick Beltran was another on-demand anthology from Cutting Block Books, featuring nine novellas (three reprints). Contributors included Jason A. Wyckoff, Felice Picano, Tom Johnstone, Kristin Dearborn and John F.D. Taff.

Edited with an Introduction by Vince A. Liaguno for on-demand imprint Evil Jester Press, *Unspeakable Horror 2: Abominations of Desire* was an attractive trade paperback anthology of twenty horror stories (three reprints) from the LGBT and horror communities. Contributors included Lisa Morton, Martel Sardina, Helen Marshall, David Nickle, Stephen Graham Jones, Norman Prentiss, Gemma Files and the editor himself.

Edited by Steve J. Shaw for his own Black Shuck Books imprint, *Great British Horror 2: Dark Satanic Mills* was a print-on-demand hardcover containing eleven original stories by Paul Finch, Cate Gardner, Angela Slatter, John Llewellyn Probert, Marie O'Regan, Gary Fry, Penny Jones, Gary McMahon and others.

With an Introduction by Lynda E. Rucker and published by Black Shuck in a hardcover edition of just fifty copies, *A Suggestion of*

Ghosts: Supernatural Fiction by Women 1854-1900 edited by J.A. (Johnny) Mains collected fifteen incredibly obscure stories from around the end of the 19th century which had never been anthologised since their original publication. Mains was able to attribute the correct authorship of 'The Closed Cabinet'—a tale which has been continuously published under the byline "Anon" since its original appearance in *Blackwood's Edinburgh Magazine* in January 1895—to Lady Gwendolyn Gascoyne-Cecil. The book was signed by the editor and cover artist Les Edwards.

British horror and fantasy author Paul Kane added a middle initial "B." to his byline for *Nailbiters: Tales of Crime and Psychological Terror.* The PoD paperback collected twenty-three stories (three original), along with an Introduction by Paul Finch.

The Life Cycle, featuring a quartet of stories (one original) in Paul Kane's series about his werewolf hero Neil, and Thana Niveau's *Unquiet Waters* containing four new stories based around liquids, were both part of the "Black Shuck Shadows" series of inexpensive micro-collections, presenting the best of classic and modern horror.

From Cycatrix Press, *Disexistence* collected twenty stories (six original) and a poem, along with story notes by author Paul Kane and an Introduction by Nancy Holder. The trade paperback included a trilogy of the author's "Hooded Man" tales.

Boasting a cover painting by Les Edwards and an Introduction by A.K. Benedict, *Death* was a PoD hardcover collection from Sinister Horror Company containing ten stories (two original) and a play script by the extremely productive Paul Kane.

Lynn M. Cochrane took over the editing of *Weird Ales: Last Orders*, the final book in the anthology trilogy from Quantum Corsets and publisher Theresa Derwin. It featured eleven stories (two reprints) by James Newman, Josh Reynolds, Gav Thorpe and others, along with an Introduction by Charlotte Bond and an Afterword by Derwin.

Under the Terror Tree Books imprint, editor Theresa Derwin's *Mummy Knows Best* featured fifteen original stories about mummies from all over the world by Pauline E. Dungate, Christine Morgan, Rhys Hughes, Lyn M. Cochrane and others. The PoD paperback also featured an impressive cover illustration by Luke Spooner.

A bookshop assistant's best friend was pregnant with the Antichrist and being hunted by religious fanatics trying to prevent the End of Days in Anne Billson's latest satirical novel, *The Coming Thing*, which was available as an on-demand paperback.

The exemplary Valancourt Books imprint published *Offbeat*, which collected twelve stories by Richard Matheson with a new introduction by David J. Schow, along with reprints of Michael McDowell's superb southern Gothic serial *Blackwater* for the first time in a single volume (with an Introduction by Nathan Ballingrud), *The Travelling Grave and Other Stories* by L.P. Hartley (with an Introduction by John Howard), *The Happy Man* by Eric C. Higgs (with a new Introduction by the author) and *The Other Passenger* by John Keir Cross (with a new Foreword by J.F. Norris).

Originally published under the byline "Jessica Hamilton" in the 1970s, Valancourt also reissued the novels *Elizabeth*, *Hell Hound* (aka *Baxter*) and *Childgrave* by Ken Greenhall.

The Valancourt Book of Horror Stories Volume Two edited by James D. Jenkins and Ryan Cagle collected twelve obscure reprints by such Valancourt authors as Bernard Taylor, R. Chetwynd-Hayes, Robert Westall, Russell Thorndike, Michael McDowell and Basil Copper, along with two previously unpublished ghost stories by Nevil Shute and Stephen Gregory.

Edited with an Introduction by Allen Grove, *The Valancourt Book of Victorian Christmas Ghost Stories, Volume Two* featured fifteen tales by a number of obscure Victorian authors, including three from the prolific "Anonymous".

Edited by S.T. Joshi and Martin Anderson for Hippocampus Press, *The Ghost in the Corner and Other Stories* was an important new volume of fiction by the Anglo-Irish author Lord Dunsany (1878-1957), based around an untitled collection the writer had assembled in 1956, but which was never published. The PoD volume contained the definitive texts of fifty stories, including ten previously unpublished tales discovered amongst manuscripts at Dunsany Castle in County Meath, Ireland.

From the same imprint, *The Dark Sea Within: Tales & Poems* was a substantial collection of the work of Jason V. Brock that included a number of new poems and a story collaboration with Sunni K. Brock and William F. Nolan.

The Doom That Came to Dunwich from Endeavour Press collected nine Lovecraftian stories by Richard A. Lupoff with an Introduction by Philip Harbottle.

Revenge of the Vampir King was the first volume in Nancy Kilpatrick's "Thrones of Blood" series of vampire novels published by Macabre Ink/Crossroad Press.

Hersham Horror Books' "Primal Range" series of short paperback novellas continued with *Bury Them Deep* by Marie O'Regan, *Perfect Darkness Perfect Silence* by Richard Farren Barber and *Monstrous* by Charlotte Bond.

Paul Dale Anderson's *The Girl Who Lived: Megan's Story* was a serial-killer novel from 2AM Publications.

From Spectral Press, Dan Weatherer's novella *Crippen* was based on an unproduced stage play and purported to offer fresh insights into the notorious British serial killer. The author's own biographical notes ran for ten pages at the back of the book!

Jordon Greene edited *Down with the Fallen: A Post-Apocalyptic Horror Anthology* for North Carolina PoD imprint Franklin/Kerr Press. The trade paperback contained sixteen stories by Jessica Clem, Toby Alexander and Marvin Brown, amongst others.

Co-edited with an Introduction for Dark Mind Press by James Everington and Dan Howarth, *Imposter Syndrome* was an anthology of ten original doppelgänger stories from Gary McMahon, Neil Williamson, Stephen Bacon, Phil Sloman and others. Shame about the typo in the title.

What if Henry James, Bram Stoker and Arthur Conan Doyle had founded an exclusive dining club in London where the cost of a seat at the table was a story? This was the inventive premise behind *The Ghost Club: Newly Found Tales of Victorian Terror* from Crystal Lake Publishing. With fourteen original stories, Scottish writer William Meikle cleverly mimicked the styles of those three authors, along with Robert Louis Stevenson, Rudyard Kipling, H.G. Wells, Oscar Wilde, Jules Verne and others.

J.S. Breukelaar's supernatural thriller *Aletheia*, also from Crystal

Lake, was about an island on a remote lake that nobody remembered.

Brendan Deneen and David G. Barnett edited *Chopping Block Party*, a PoD anthology of fourteen original stories from Necro Publications, set on the small-town street of Golden Elm Lane. Contributors included Paul Kane, John Everson, Richard Chizmar, Damien Angelica Walters, Gerard Houarner, Jeffrey Thomas, Tim Waggoner and co-editor Deneen, while *Friday the 13th* scriptwriter Victor Miller supplied a brief Introduction.

From the same imprint, *In the Country of Dreaming Caravans* was a novel about a girl lost in the desert by Gerard Houarner and GAK, while Charlee Jacob's *Containment: The Death of Earth* was an apocalyptic horror novel involving an abused boy and angels.

Published by JournalStone, *Behold the Void* was a debut collection of nine stories (six original) by Hollywood screenwriter Philip Fracassi with an Introduction by Laird Barron, while *Sacculina* from the same author was a fast-paced novella about the crew of a fishing boat fighting off mutated ocean creatures.

Aaron J. French's debut novel *The Time Eater* was about the ritual summoning of a vast supernatural entity, and Michael Griffin's *Hieroglyphs of Blood & Bone* was another first novel from the same imprint.

Curtis M. Lawson's *Black Pantheons: Collected Tales of Gnostic Dread* from Wyrd Horror contained ten short stories and a novella (eight original) along with a brief Forward [*sic*] by the author and a preview of what appeared to be a novel.

Tales of Blood and Squalor from Dark Cloud Press was an anthology of fourteen "sordid, wretched, seamy, seedy" stories edited by Lee Allen Howard.

Despite its title, Gehenna & Hinnom Books' *Year's Best Body Horror 2017 Anthology* edited by C.P. Dunphey featured forty-two mostly new stories (seven reprints) by James Dorr, Kurt Newton, Gary Power and others, along with an Introduction by film-maker Shane Ramirez.

From the same PoD imprint and also edited by Dunphey, the first three perfect-bound issues of *Hinnom Magazine* featured interviews with S.T. Joshi, T.E. Grau and Philip Fracassi, along with fiction by Kurt Newton, G.A. Miller, John Leahy, Joanna Costello and others. The second volume was a double-sized "H.P. Lovecraft Birthday Edition".

The first issue of editor-in-chief Tara Blaine's perfect-bound *Decidious Tales: Tales of Darkness and Horror* from Black Thunder Press featured seven stories and six poems, including reprints from Lovecraft, Charles Baudelaire and Clark Ashton Smith.

Issue #27 of Perpetual Motion Machine Publishing's Patreon-funded *Dark Moon Digest* featured ten original stories, and two articles, plus cover art by Allen Koszowski.

One Night at the Villa Diodati from Shadowridge Press was an attractive paperback to which Peter Atkins, Kelly Dunn and editor Stephen Woodworth contributed short stories in the style of Percy Bysshe Shelley, Mary Wollstonecraft Shelly, John William Polidori and Lord Byron. The contents had originally appeared on an online blog in slightly different form.

Everything That's Underneath was a collection of eighteen stories (three original) by Kristi DeMeester from Apex Publications.

Eric Ian Steele's collection *Nightscape* was published as a PoD hardcover by Parallel Universe Publications. It contained eleven stories (three previously unpublished), while *Parlour Tricks* by Carl Barker contained fourteen stories loosely themed around conjuring tricks, four of them original to the collection. *Shades* collected twenty-two "dark tales of supernatural horror" (eleven reprints) by Joseph Rubas.

Also from Parallel Universe with an Introduction by David A. Sutton, *Radix Omnium Malum* collected sixteen dark stories (two original) by Mike Chinn, and for fans of pulp-hero fiction, Chinn's *Walkers in Shadow* from Pro Se Press contained seven rollicking novellas in which quasi-immortal hero Damian Paladin and adventuress Leigh Oswin pitted their wits and flying skills against demons, zombies and old-world vampires across the length and breadth of 1930s America.

Weinberg Tales from American Fantasy Press/Tattered Pages Press was a tribute to the late writer and pulp collector Robert Weinberg edited by Doug Ellis, Robert T. Garcia and Phyllis Weinberg. It included numerous articles by its subject, and also tributes from such friends and colleagues as Joe R. Lansdale, F. Paul Wilson, Otto Penzler, Will Murray, Stefan R. Dziemianowicz, Stephen Jones, Phyllis and Alex Eisenstein, Randy Broecker, Mort Castle and many others.

From Australia's Oz Horror Con, *The Refuge Collection Volume 1-3: Heaven to Some...* and *The Refuge Collection Volumes 4-6: ...Hell to Others!* were two hefty PoD hardcover volumes that reprinted a number of stories first published as e-books online. Authors working in the shared-world universe included Lee Murray, Paul Kane, Ramsey Campbell and series editor Steve Dillon, and the fiction was illustrated by Will Jacques, Edward Miller, Brian Craddock and others. Unfortunately, despite all profits going to charity, the lack of page numbers and running heads didn't make either book easy to read.

The Empath's Tale: The Complete Story was the latest volume in Dillon's *Hellraiser*-inspired *Refuge Collection* series. Reprinting parts 1-6 of the online series aimed at "helping people who've lived real-world horror stories", all profits from the sale of this collection also went to charity.

Between the Tracks: Tales from the Ghost Train was a PoD hardcover anthology of twenty-three railroad-themed tales (seven reprints) and a comic-strip from Things in the Well publications, edited and introduced by Dillon. Authors included Ramsey Campbell, M.R. James. Christopher Golden, Paul Kane, Lee Murray, Charles Dickens and the editor, while an annotated reprinting of Clive Barker's 'The Midnight Meat Train' merited its own Introduction, accompanying interview and critical essay.

As the title indicated, *Below the Stairs: Tales from the Cellar* was a trade paperback anthology from editor Steve Dillon that contained twenty-one stories (five reprints) set in the basement by, amongst others, David H. Keller, Theresa Derwin, Ramsey Campbell, Paul Kane, Clive Barker, H.P. Lovecraft and, once again, the editor himself.

With an Introduction by Bram Stoker Award-winner Alessandro Manzetti, *When the Night Owl Screams* from MoonDream Press/

Copper Dog Publishing collected more than 100 poems (five reprints) by Michael H. Hanson, with illustrations by Chris Mars.

With mainstream publishers continuing to cut back on their midlist titles—especially when it came to collections and anthologies—the independent presses were busier than ever in 2017, and none so much as Peter and Nicky Crowther's PS Publishing, which also published most of its trade titles in 100-copy signed editions.

In Bruce Golden's pulp-ish *Monster Town*, a private investigator searched for a killer and a missing teenager amongst the classic movie monsters in 1960s Hollywood.

Meanwhile, *Forever Konrad: A Vampire's Vampire* by Martin Goodman featured the titular bloodsucker in a race against time to find a teenager with special powers, and there were more vampires to be found in Ian R. MacLeod's historical novel *Red Snow*.

The lyrics to a pop song reopened dark secrets in R.B. Russell's debut novel, the 1980s-set murder-mystery *She Sleeps*.

When a girl discovered that her superhuman strength came from the Viking god Odin, she travelled to the City where she faced seven challenges in Kim Wilkins' dark fantasy, *Odin's Girl*. Marni Scofidio's *Knucklebones* was set in a run-down North Wales seaside town and involved the escalating feud between two women.

Rough Trade collected twenty-three criminally overlooked crime and mystery stories from the late 1950s and early '60s by Robert Silverberg, who also supplied a fascinating historical Introduction.

Darker Companions, edited by Scott David Aniolowski and Joseph S. Pulver, Sr., was confusingly subtitled *Celebrating 50 Years of Ramsey Campbell*, despite the fact that Campbell's first short story was published in 1962 and his first novel appeared two years later.

It contained twenty stories by, amongst others, Steve Rasnic Tem, John Llewellyn Probert, Alison Littlewood, Marc Laidlaw, Gary McMahon, Gary Fry, Kristi DeMeester, Cody Goodfellow, Jeffrey Thomas, Lynda E. Rucker, Thana Niveau and Adam L.G. Nevill. However, the editors apparently elected not to include any story introductions or author biographies, which might have allowed the contributors to put their work into context within the confines of a tribute anthology. Also, given its subject's insistence on precise spelling and punctuation, it was disappointing that this volume was so carelessly put together.

The sixth volume of editor S.T. Joshi's *Black Wings* series, subtitled *New Tales of Lovecraftian Horror*, featured twenty-one stories and poetry (one reprint) by such authors as Ann K. Schwader, Darrell Schweitzer, William F. Nolan, Caitlín R. Kiernan, Nancy Kilpatrick, Don Webb, W.H. Pugmire, Steve Rasnic Tem, Jason V. Brock and Stephen Woodworth.

There were more Lovecraftian horrors to be found in *Tales from the Miskatonic University Library* edited and introduced by Darrell Schweitzer and John Ashmead. The anthology contained thirteen original stories by Don Webb, Adrian Cole, Harry Turtledove, Will Murray, P.D. Cacek, James Van Pelt, Robert M. Price and others, including co-editor Schweitzer.

Dark Places, Evil Faces was yet another charity anthology, with any proceeds going to MacMillan cancer support. Editor Mark Lumby assembled twenty-five stories (six original) by such genre luminaries as Brian Lumley, Richard Chizmar, Jack Ketchum, Graham Masterton, Peter Crowther, Ramsey Campbell, Adam L.G. Nevill and himself, while Shaun Hutson supplied the Introduction.

A husband was forced to investigate when his wife failed to return home from the titular gathering in Australian author Alan Baxter's novella *The Book Club*, while a man became the person he always wanted to be, but with unexpected consequences, in Stephen Volk's novella *The Little Gift*.

With *The Complete Adventures of Solar Pons* edited by Stephen Jones, PS reprinted revised and corrected versions of all Basil Copper's macabre mysteries featuring the eponymous Sherlockian detective created by August Derleth. Published as 100 sets comprising two hefty signed and numbered hardcovers in a slipcase (£175.00), it also contained a completely new book, *The Solar Pons Companion*. After it sold out prior to publication, *The Complete Adventures of Solar Pons* was reissued as seven inexpensive paperbacks under the Drugstore Indian Press banner.

Also published as a DIP paperback was a welcome reissue of

T.E.D. Klein's epic 1984 Lovecraftian novel *The Ceremonies*, which the author slightly revised for its new appearance.

Under The Pulps Library imprint from PS, artist Pete Von Sholly's excellent "Lovecraft Illustrated" series of hardcover collections continued with *The Festival and Other Abnormalities, Herbert West—Reanimator and Kindred Night Spawn, Dagon and Diverse Monstrosities* and *The Other Gods and Various Ethereal Effusions*. Each volume contained a knowledgeable Introduction by S.T. Joshi and numerous colour illustrations by Von Sholly.

Clive Barker's Next Testament from Earthling Publications was actually the debut novel of comics writer Mark Alan Miller, about a revived entity that claimed to be the multi-coloured Father of the Old Testament.

Christopher Golden and James A. Moore's *Bloodstained Wonderland* from the same publisher was set during the London Blitz, as vampire creatures from Oz attempted to track down two women who possessed a strange green pendant. The book was illustrated by Glenn Chadbourne.

Chadbourne also supplied the illustrations and Moore the Foreword to Josh Malerman's *Goblin*, a novel in six novellas set in the titular town. The thirteenth volume in Earthling's annual "Halloween Series", it was limited to 500 signed and numbered copies and fifteen traycased lettered copies ($400.00).

From Fedogan & Bremer, *Earth, Air, Fire & Water: Four Tales of Elemental Mythos Horror!* featured a new Cthulhu Mythos novella and three reprints by Brian Lumley, illustrated by Jim Pitts.

As if Robert Shearman's clever Introduction alone didn't make it worth picking up, *Holidays from Hell: Fourteen Stories* also featured a selection of relatively recent stories and one original by the inimitable Reggie Oliver, who also supplied the Afterword and the illustrations. It was available from Tartarus Press in a hardcover edition limited to 500 copies.

From the same publisher, *Seven Strange Stories* was another superior collection from Rebecca Lloyd that contained two reprints. It was published in an edition of 300 signed copies.

The Autobiography of Arthur Machen reprinted the memoirs *Far*

Off Things and *Things Near and Far* with a new Introduction by Stewart Lee and four colour plates of the original manuscript. Tartarus also issued a new paperback edition of the 1904 magical text *The House of the Hidden Light* by Arthur Machen and A.E. Waite, who were both members of the Order of the Golden Dawn. Waite scholar R.A. Gilbert provided an explanatory Introduction and fully annotated text.

Holy Terrors was a paperback of five classic stories by Arthur Machen, published in association with the release of Obsolete Films' portmanteau film of the same name, released on DVD.

A man was possessed by the untrustworthy cross-dressing ghost of his twin brother in Magda McQueen's ghost novel *Mirror Dead* which, like Andrew Hurley's second novel *Devil Day*, was available from the publisher in a 300-copy signed edition.

A Country Still All Mystery was a collection of esoteric essays by Mark Valentine, limited to 300 signed copies from Tartarus.

From Subterranean Press, Clive Barker's fix-up novella *Infernal Parade* contained six short pieces originally used as backstories for a series of "Tortured Souls" action figures designed by the author and Todd MacFarlane in 2004. Bob Eggleton supplied the cover art and six interior illustrations. It was available in a signed edition, limited to 500 copies plus a fifty-two copy traycased, leatherbound and lettered edition for $275.00.

Bubba and the Cosmic Blood-Suckers by Joe R. Lansdale was a prequel to *Bubba Ho-tep*, as Elvis and his band of warriors battled vampire-like aliens in New Orleans. It was published in a signed edition of 1,500 copies and a lettered and leatherbound traycased edition of twenty-six copies ($250.00).

Dear Sweet Filthy World collected twenty-nine stories by Caitlín R. Kiernan, most of which were published on the author's online subscription service. A 600-copy leatherbound signed edition came with a bonus chapbook from Subterranean.

From the same publisher, the novella *Final Girls* by Mira Grant (Seanan McGuire) concerned a new psychiatric treatment that involved patients watching scenes from horror movies. It was available in a signed edition, limited to 1,250 copies.

Peter Straub's novella *The Process (is a Process All Its Own)* featured 1950s Midwest serial killer Tillman Hayward and was available from Subterranean in a signed edition limited to 750 copies.

The Weight of Words edited by Dave McKean and William Schafer featured twelve stories written around McKean's sepia paintings by, amongst others, Neil Gaiman, Joe Hill, Joe R. Lansdale, M. John Harrison, Ian Sinclair, Caitlín R. Kiernan and the artist himself. It was published in various states, including a traycased, lettered edition of twenty-six copies ($500.00).

Edited solely by publisher William Schafer, *The Best of Subterranean* reprinted thirty stories from *Subterranean Magazine* by Joe R. Lansdale, Joe Hill, Kelly Link, Robert Silverberg, Ian R. MacLeod and others, along with an unproduced *Twilight Zone* script by George R.R. Martin.

Robert McCammon's 1987 novel *Swan Song* was reissued by Subterranean in a 500-copy signed and slipcased edition illustrated by David Ho. There was also a $400 traycased edition limited to fifty-two lettered copies.

The Slave Tree, from Cemetery Dance Publications, was a novel by the late Alan (Peter) Ryan (who died in 2011), set in the Amazon rainforest.

Brian Hodge's novella *I'll Bring You the Birds from Out of the Sky* was available in a 1,000-copy signed edition illustrated with colour plates by Kim Parkhurst, while Bentley Little's novel *The Handyman* was also published in a 500-copy signed deluxe edition.

It is doubtful that anybody needed yet another edition of Stephen King's *The Shining* but, just in case you did, Cemetery Dance made sure it was packed with extras—the deluxe limited edition included a long-lost forty-page prologue, a section on deleted material from the novel, an Introduction by King and an Afterword by Mick Garris, and full-colour illustrations by Don Maitz. All that didn't come cheap: the 3,000-copy slipcased edition printed in two colours was $95.00, the 750-copy signed by artists Maitz and Glenn Chadbourne cost $275.00, while a fifty-two copy lettered edition of the same "artists edition" would set you back a whopping $1,250.00!

Edited by publisher Robert Morgan, *Darkly Haunting* was a limited and numbered hardcover anthology from Sarob Press featuring five new ghostly tales by James Doig, Colin Insole, Rhys Hughes, Peter Holman and D.P. Watt. As usual, Paul Lowe supplied the dust-jacket artwork, as he also did for *From Ancient Ravens*, which collected three new novellas by Mark Valentine, Ron Weighell and John Howard. The numbered and signed edition was limited to just 300 copies.

Tanith by Choice from NewCon Press featured twelve reprint stories by the late Tanith Lee chosen by, amongst others, editor Ian Whates, Storm Constantine, Stephen Jones, Sarah Singleton, Sam Stone, Freda Warrington and Cecelia Dart-Thornton. The book was also available as a 100-copy numbered hardcover.

With Gray Friar Press having ceased operation in 2016, Telos Publishing continued editor Paul Finch's superior anthology series with *Terror Tales from Cornwall*. It contained sixteen stories (two reprints) by Mark Morris, Reggie Oliver, Mark Valentine, Kate Farrell, D.P. Watt, Adrian Cole, Mark Samuels, Thana Niveau and others, including the editor himself, along with a number of short folk tales and legends. Neil Williams' evocative cover illustration perfectly captured the mythological mysteries of England's most southwest county.

Tales from the Weekend was a slim anthology edited by David J. Howe that contained eight stories (six reprints) by Paul Lewis, Darren Shan, Freda Warrington, Justina L.A. Robson, Sam Stone, Steve Lockley, Simon Morden and the editor himself.

In Paul Lewis' novella from Telos, *Small Ghosts*, a recently-widowed journalist returned to his roots and soon found himself investigating an unsolved murder case.

Nights of Blood Wine: Lush Dark Tales of Vampires . . . and Others collected fifteen stories (four original) by Freda Warrington. The attractive trade paperback was split into two sections, the first containing ten stories set in the author's popular "Blood Wine" vampire universe, and the second part featuring five other tales, including a tribute to Tanith Lee.

Also from Telos, *Cthulhu & Other Monsters* was a collection of sixteen stories (six original) by Sam Stone. Just over half the contents were Lovecraft-inspired.

Edited with an Introduction by Mark Valentine for Ireland's The Swan River Press, *The Scarlet Soul: Stories for Dorian Gray* was a handsome hardcover anthology of ten original stories inspired by Oscar Wilde's classic novella by, amongst others, Reggie Oliver, Lynda E. Rucker, John Howard, D.P. Watt and the late Avalon Brantley. Limited to only 300 copies, the volume came with a colour post-card depicting the cover of the issue of *Lippincott's* magazine (July, 1890) that contained the first publication of 'The Picture of Dorian Gray'.

In *The Greenwood Faun*, poet Nina Antonia speculated about what happened to Lucian Taylor's literary masterpiece after the death of the hallucinated hero of Arthur Machen's *The Hill of Dreams*. It was available from German imprint Egaeus Press in a hardcover edition limited to 420 copies.

From the same publisher, *Buried Shadows* contained ten previously uncollected stories and novellas by John Howard.

Murder Ballads was an anthology of seventeen original stories inspired by the "Penny Dreadfuls" from, amongst others, Alison Littlewood, Helen Marshall, Philip Fracassi, Angela Slatter, Reggie Oliver, Rhys Hughes, Daniel Mills and Lisa L. Hannett. It was limited to 375 copies.

Limited to 250 copies, *The Echo of the Sea & Other Strange War Stories* was the Egaeus Press Keynote Edition III. It contained four novellas by Paul StJohn Mackintosh, three of them connected to form a loose novel.

The House of Silence by Avalon Brantley was a homage to William Hope Hodgson's *The House on the Borderland* from the Zagava imprint. The author tragically died the same month the book was published.

The Prozess Manifestations, the sixth collection from Mark Samuels, contained six linked stories and was limited to 170 numbered hardcover copies from the same publisher.

Zagava also produced the first-ever full facsimile of the first issue (January, 1919) of the German weird magazine *Der Orchideengarten:*

Phantastische Bläter (The Orchid Garden: Fantastic Tales), translated by Helen Grant.

Razor King, David Britton's latest Absurdist fantasy from Savoy Books, was set against real historical events and influenced by Karl May's series of German Westerns and Edgar Rice Burroughs' "Mars" books. The lavishly produced hardcover was illustrated throughout in colour by Kris Guidio.

Looming Low Volume 1: Being an Anthology of Original Weird Fiction was a hefty large-size paperback anthology from Dim Shores edited and introduced by Justin Steele and publisher Sam Cowan. It contained twenty-six stories by, amongst others, Kurt Fawver, Brian Evenson, Daniel Mills, Damien Angelica Walters, Lucy A. Snyder, Simon Strantzas, Lisa L. Hannett, Michael Cisco, Jeffrey Thomas, Richard Gavin and Gemma Files. There was also a deluxe hardcover edition limited to 150 copies.

Centipede Press continued its series of huge retrospective volumes with *In the Realms of Mystery and Wonder: Collected Prose, Poems and Artwork by Clark Ashton Smith* edited with an Introduction by Scott Conners. It contained many full-colour photographs of Smith's sculptures, paintings and drawings, along with a number of memoirs of Smith by George F. Haas and others. The oversized hardcover was available in a 300-copy numbered and slipcased edition signed by the editor.

Originally published as an out-of-print limited hardcover by Centipede, JaSunni/Cycatrix Press produced an affordable paperback edition of the collection *It Only Comes Out at Night* by Dennis Etchison, with the addition of previously uncollected fiction and unpublished appreciations by fellow authors. S.T. Joshi supplied a new Introduction, and there were story notes by the author.

Funded by a Kickstarter campaign, *Tales from the Shadow Booth Vol.1* was a rack-sized paperback edited by Dan Coxon and featuring thirteen stories (two reprints) by, amongst others, Alison Moore, Paul Tremblay, Sarah Read, Richard Thomas and Joseph Sale.

From Dark Regions Press, *Return of the Old Ones: Apocalyptic Lovecraftian Horror* edited by Brian M. Sammons featured nineteen new stories of cosmic horror by, amongst others, Jeffrey Thomas,

Lucy A. Snyder, Tim Curran, Pete Rawlik, Sam Gafford, Christine Morgan and Cody Goodfellow, while *The Children of Gla'aki: A Tribute to Ramsey Campbell's Great Old One* edited by Sammons and Glynn Owen Barrass contained eighteen stories set around the Severn Valley town of Brichester by Nick Mamatas, Robert M. Price, W.H. Pugmire, Thana Niveau, William Meikle, Tim Waggoner and others, including Campbell himself.

From the same imprint, *Nightmare's Realm: New Tales of the Weird & Fantastic* edited by S.T. Joshi featured seventeen original dream-stories by Ramsey Campbell, Gemma Files, Richard Gavin, Caitlín R. Kiernan, Nancy Kilpatrick, John Langan, Reggie Oliver, W.H. Pugmire, Darrell Schweitzer, John Shirley, Simon Strantzas, Steve Rasnic Tem and others, along with reprints from H.P. Lovecraft and Edgar Allan Poe.

Also from Dark Regions Press, Clive Barker's *The Body Book* reprinted the stories 'The Body Politic' and 'In the Flesh', along with exclusive material from Mick Garris' unproduced movie version of the latter story. It was available in a signed and numbered edition.

Issued by the Dark Regions Press imprint Written Backwards, *Adam's Ladder* was a dark science fiction anthology co-edited by Michael Bailey and Darren Speegle that contained eighteen new stories by Chaz Brenchley, Ramsey Campbell, John Langan, Mark Morris, Erin L. Kemper, Lisa Morton, Tim Lebbon, Roberta Lannes, Scott Edelman and Mark Samuels, amongst others.

Angela Slatter's "Sourdough" novella *The Tallow-Wife* was reprinted by Australia's FableCroft Publishing in an attractive hardcover edition illustrated by Kathleen Jennings. The book also included some "Found Fragments", along with Afterwords by both the writer and artist.

In July, Christopher Teague announced the closure of his Welsh-based small press horror imprint Pendragon Press, which was established in 1999. Teague cited lifestyle changes as the reason.

Paymon's Trio, a tale of music and demonology, was originally written in 1949 by Colette de Curzon but remained unpublished until Nicholas Royle's Nightjar Press put it out as one of the imprint's short story chapbooks. Other Nightjar releases were *The Automaton* by David Wheldon, and *Bremen* and *The Unwish* by Claire Dean. All Nightjar chapbooks were limited to 200 signed copies.

From California's Dim Shores imprint came four square-bound chapbooks limited to 200 numbered copies each: *Palladium at Night* by Christopher Slatsky was illustrated by Dave Felton; *The Polite Ones* by Cody Goodfellow was illustrated by Marcelo Gallegos; Edward Morris produced the artwork for *The Resplendent Troswoman Below* by Joseph S. Pulver, Sr., and Gemma Files' *Coffle* was illustrated by Stephen Wilson.

Tom Johnstone's twisted Christmas story *How I Learned the Truth About Krampus* was the third in the Eibonvale Chapbook Line.

Andy Cox's *Black Static* published the usual six bi-monthly issues featuring original fiction by, amongst others, Simon Avery, Mike O'Driscoll, Mark Morris, Helen Marshall, Kristi DeMeester, Rosalie Parker and Ray Cluley, along with regular opinion columns by Lynda E. Rucker and Ralph Robert Moore, film reviews by Gary Couzens, and book reviews by Peter Tennant. Amongst those interviewed were Stephen Volk, Andrew Hook, Richard Chizmar, Gwendolyn Kiste and Daniel Mills. The magazine celebrated its tenth anniversary with issue #60.

Black Static's sci-fi sister title, *Interzone*, also turned out six issues. The March-April edition (#269) featured an editorial, new story and an interview with Steve Rasnic Tem, while Andy Hedgecock contributed a personal recollection of Brian W. Aldiss to #272.

Edited by C.C. Finlay, *The Magazine of Fantasy & Science Fiction* reached its sixty-eighth year of publication with its usual six bi-monthly issues featuring original fiction by Rachel Pollack, Nina Kiriki Hoffman, Marc Laidlaw, Albert E. Cowdrey, Matthew Hughes, Gardner Dozois, Samuel R. Delany, Michael Swanwick, Kate Wilhelm and Larry Niven, amongst others. David Langford contributed half the 'Curiosities' essays along with Mark Esping, Paul Di Filippo and Robert Eldridge, and there were the usual review columns by Charles de Lint, James Sallis, Michelle West, Elizabeth Hand, Kathy Maio, Tim Pratt, Paul Di Filippo and David J. Skal.

John Gilbert's venerable *Fear* magazine managed two more bi-monthly print editions early in the year before apparently disappearing back into the ether again. The brace of full-colour issues included interviews with writers Peter James, Susan Hill, David A. Sutton, Tim Lebbon, Adrian Cole, the multi-author *nom de plume* "Rowan Casey", Christopher Rice and Stella Gemmell, along with actress Nichelle Nichols and literary agent John Jarrold. David J. Howe contributed some media reviews.

Aaron J. French's *Dark Discoveries* included fiction by Brian Lumley, Reggie Oliver, Paul Tremblay, Barbie Wilde and others, along with interviews with Tremblay and Ellen Datlow, plus the usual non-fiction and poetry.

Occult Detective Quarterly was a new, large-size paperback magazine launched via Kickstarter by Electric Pentacle Press. Edited by Sam Gafford, John Linwood Grant and Dave Brzeski, the print-on-demand title featured pastiche fiction from, amongst others, William Meikle, Amanda DeWees, Adrian Cole, Josh Reynolds, T.E. Grau, Brandon Barrows (a "Carnacki" story), Mike Chinn, Tim Waggoner and Brian M. Sammons. There were also articles by Charles Routledge, Danyal Fryer, Bobby Derie and Tim Prasil, and brief interviews with Donald F. Glut and actor Dan Starkey.

Wildside Press' PoD *Weirdbook*, edited by Doug Draa, put out four quarterly issues with new stories and poems from Adrian Cole, Franklin Searight, Frederick J. Mayer, Jason Rubis, Paul StJohn Mackintosh, L.J. Dopp, Darrell Schweitzer, John B. Rosenman, Cody Goodfellow, Lucy A. Snyder, K.A. Opperman, Jessica Amanda Salmonson and Kyla Lee Ward, amongst others. Issue #36 was entirely illustrated by Allen Koszowski.

The title also produced its first *Weirdbook Annual*, devoted to *Witches*. The same pulp-format as the regular issues, it contained twenty-one stories by Adrian Cole, Paul Dale Anderson, Franklyn Searight and others, along with twelve poems from, amongst others, Lucy A. Snyder, Frederick J. Mayer and K.A. Opperman.

David Longhorn's PoD magazine *Supernatural Tales* featured new fiction from Tina Rath, Mark Valentine, Michael Chislett, John Howard, Helen Grant, Paul Lewis, Tom Johnstone and Gary Fry, amongst others, along with a regular reviews column by the editor. Issue #34 included Adam Golaski's lecture notes on Mark Samuels' 2012 collection *The White Hands and Other Weird Tales*.

The British Fantasy Society managed to turn out just one issue of the *BFS Journal* and two issues of *BFS Horizons*. While the former included a number of academic articles along with David A. Sutton's look back at the history of the Society, the latter featured fiction and poetry by Paul Kane, Allen Ashley, Marie O'Regan, Richard Webb, Tim Major, Chris Morgan and others.

The ninth issue of Katushi Makihara's attractive Japanese digest magazine *Night Land Quarterly* included fiction by Edward Lucas White, Lisa Tuttle, Angela Slatter, William Meikle, Manly Wade Wellman, Michael Chislett, Robert Aickman and others, including two Japanese authors, along with art, essays and interviews.

Finnish Weird 4: Call of the Weird was published in English by the Helsinki Science Fiction Society and included short stories by Magdalena Hai and J.S. Meresmaa, along with a novel excerpt by Viivi Hyvönen and interviews with the three authors by Anne Leinonen.

The December 10 issue of *The New York Times Magazine* featured 'The Year in Horror', which was nowhere near as interesting as it sounded and mostly consisted of ten performers (including Andy Serkis, Cynthia Nixon, Daniel Kaluuya, Jake Gyllenhaal and Nicole Kidman) in slightly spooky photographs.

Actors Mark Gatiss, Steve Pemberton, Jeremy Dyson and Reece Shearsmith wrote 'The League of Gentleman's Christmas Ghost Story' for the December 16-22 issue of *Radio Times*.

The Canadian media magazine *Rue Morgue* included interviews with actors James McAvoy, Bill Skarsgård and Doug Bradley, directors Colm McCarthy, M. Night Shyamalan, Paul W.S. Anderson, Julia Ducournau, Jordan Peele, John Hough, Gary Sherman, Clive Barker and Franck Khalfoun, and producers Jason Blum, Roger Corman and Bruan Fuller. The 20th anniversary annual Halloween double issue was devoted to "A Century of Witches".

The British *Scream*, which debuted back in 2010, billed itself as "The World's No.1 Horror Magazine", which may be true. Edited by

Richard Cooper, the colour glossy contained much of the same kind of material to be found in *Rue Morgue*. The 100-page Hallowe'en edition (#45) featured retrospective looks at British witchcraft movies, *A Nightmare on Elm Street 3: Dream Warriors*, the legacy of Leatherface, horror movies released in the first half of 2014, Hammer's *The Revenge of Frankenstein* and DC's Vertigo imprint, alongside interviews with a number of current film-makers and some mostly negative reviews of the latest book and DVD releases.

Having announced that they would no longer be publishing print editions of the magazine, Tim and Donna Lucas managed to squeeze out a final "Farewell Issue" of *Video WatcHDog* thanks to the generosity of several supporters (including Martin Scorsese). The 184th edition featured a number of apparently left-over reviews, along with columns by Ramsey Campbell, Douglas E. Winter and Larry Blamire, and the conclusion of John-Paul Checkett's in-depth look at movies based on or inspired by J. Sheridan Le Fanu's 'Carmilla'.

Classic Images reached its 500th issue in February. The monthly newsprint included fascinating feature articles on the restorations of *The Old Dark House* (1932) and *The Vampire Bat* (1933), Universal's sound serials, and veteran actors George Zucco ('Hollywood Madman') and Robert Shayne, along with interviews with B-movie performers Jan England and Robert Clarke. Tom Weaver's column 'The Sci-Fi Stalwarts' shone the spotlight on Jeff Morrow, Barbara Rush, Marshall Thompson, Mara Corday and John Agar amongst others, while Dr. Robert J. Kiss contributed a terrific meditation on Boris Karloff's involvement with NBC-TV's *Thriller* series (1960-62). The magazine also got a long-overdue design update.

Entertainment Weekly issued a special Halloween double issue that included "Untold Stories" about such movies and TV series as *The Stepford Wives*, *The Night Stalker*, *Little Shop of Horrors* (1986), *The Craft*, *Hocus Pocus*, *Shaun of the Dead*, *Supernatural*, *Psych*, *Hannibal*, *Black Mirror* and other titles, along with a brief interview with Neil Gaiman.

The monthly *Locus* featured interviews with, amongst others, Jane Yolen, John Joseph Adams, Paul Tremblay and Matt Ruff. The April issue was an artist spotlight on Kinuko Y. Craft and other illustrators.

The two issues of Rosemary Pardoe's *The Ghosts & Scholars M.R. James Newsletter* featured the usual mixture of news, non-fiction, stories and reviews. Issue #31 included a story by C.E. Ward, while the following issue not only featured a brief interview with M.R. James from 1923, which had probably never been reprinted before, but also a bonus chapbook of Daniel McGachey's story *Ting-a-Ling-a-Ling*, published under the Haunted Library imprint.

The two issues of Hildy Silverman's *Space and Time: The Magazine of Fantasy, Horror, and Science Fiction* featured the expected mix of fiction and poetry by Scott Edelman, Thomas Canfield, Larry Hodges, Paul Michael Anderson, Gordon Linzner, Jill Bauman and others, along with a couple of author self-portrait articles and poetry reviews by Linda D. Addison.

The first issue of Steve Dillon's annual *Trickster's Treats: Tales from the Pumpkin Patch* appeared in time for Halloween. It was split into six themes and featured thirty-two short short stories (two reprints) by Theresa Derwin and others, including three by the editor.

Written by Grady Hendrix with Will Errickson for Quirk Books, *Paperbacks from Hell: The Twisted History of '70s and '80s Horror Fiction* was a superb compendium of information and images spotlighting many of the authors, publishers and artists working in the genre during the horror boom of thirty and forty years ago.

Sir Christopher Frayling's *Frankenstein: The First Two Hundred Years* was a fascinating look at Mary Shelley's monstrous creation in fiction, media and popular culture, beautifully illustrated with many rare and fascinating images. It also included a facsimile reprint of the earliest-known manuscript version of the creature's creation scene.

Based on a series of columns he wrote for the *Independent on Sunday* newspaper, Christopher Fowler's *The Book of Forgotten Authors* featured insightful mini-essays on ninety-nine forgotten authors and their forgotten books. Although the author's definition of "forgotten" might have been open to question, the attractive hardcover included compact biographies of such genre-related authors as Virginia Andrews, Pierre Boulle, Mary Elizabeth Braddon, John

Dickson Carr, John Christopher, Edmund Crispin, Jack Finney, Graham Joyce, Thomas Nigel Kneale, George Langelaan, Michael McDowell, Richard Marsh, Simon Raven, Thomas Tryon, Edgar Wallace, Dennis Wheatley and T.H. White, amongst many others.

Leo Margulies: Giant of the Pulps: His Thrilling, Exciting, and Popular Journey was written by Margulies' nephew Philip Sherman and published by Altus Press in both softcover and hardcover. During the 1930s and '40s, Margulies was editor of more than seventy different magazine titles.

From the University of Minnesota Press, *Zombie Theory: A Reader* edited by Sarah Juliet Laura contained twenty-three essays about the popularity of the walking dead.

The Written Dead: Essays on the Literary Zombie edited by Kyle William Bishop and Angela Tenga, *Romancing the Zombie: Essays on the Undead and Significant "Others"* edited by Ashley Szanter and Jessica K. Richards, and Chase Pielak and Alexander H. Cohen's study *Living with Zombies: Society in Apocalypse in Film, Literature and Other Media* were all published as part of McFarland's "Contributions to Zombie Studies" series.

In *The Irish Vampire: From Folklore to the Imaginations of Charles Robert Maturin, Joseph Sheridan LeFanu and Bram Stoker* from the same publisher, Sharon M. Gallagher took a critical look at the work of the the three authors in the title.

Thomas Phillips' *T.E.D. Klein and the Rupture of Civilization: A Study in Critical Horror* included an interview with its subject, while James Arthur Anderson's *The Linguistics of Stephen King: Layered Language and Meaning in the Fiction* from McFarland looked at the way King structured his stories.

Clive Barker, Richard Chizmar and Bev Vincent were amongst those who contributed essays about why they loved the author's work to *Reading Stephen King*, edited by Brian James Freeman for Cemetery Dance. It was limited to 1,000 copies signed by most of the contributors, and a twenty-six copy lettered and leatherbound traycased edition ($200.00).

From PoD imprint Hippocampus Press, *Varieties of the Weird Tale* collected nineteen essays (three previously unpublished) by S.T.

Joshi that looked at writers from the "golden age" of weird fiction like Ambrose Bierce, Bram Stoker, E. Nesbit, M.R. James, Lord Dunsany, Sax Rohmer and Irvin S. Cobb, along with more contemporary authors such as Ramsey Campbell, Thomas Ligotti and Caitlín R. Kiernan.

Scholastic's *Harry Potter: A Journey Through a History of Magic* was an official companion to the British Library Exhibition and featured unseen sketches, manuscript pages from J.K. Rowling and illustrations by Jim Kay.

With the third volume in 2016, Phil and Sarah Stokes' The Clive Barker Archive took over from Century Guild as publisher of the stunning *Clive Barker Imaginer: The Visionary Art of Clive Barker* series of oversized hardcovers. *Volume Four: 1993-2012* was limited to 1,000 trade copies and a 100-copy slipcased edition, and included a brief Afterword by the author and painter.

Edited by Douglas Ellis, Ed Hulse and the late Robert Weinberg, *The Art of the Pulps: An Illustrated History* from IDW Publishing was a visual celebration of pulp magazines in all genres—adventure, crime, Western, war, sport, romance, hero, spicy and, of course, horror and science fiction. With a Foreword by F. Paul Wilson, and contributions from Tom Roberts, Mike Ashley and Will Murray, amongst others, the only disappointment was that there was so little original artwork included amongst the more than 400 superbly reproduced magazine covers.

Edited by publisher John Flesk, *Spectrum 24: The Best in Contemporary Fantastic Art* included a profile of Grand Master Award-winner Bill Sienkiewicz.

From Parallel Universe Publishing, *The Art of Jim Pitts: Rolling Back the Years...* featured the work of the veteran British artist and was limited to a numbered and signed edition of just 250 copies. It also included tributes by editor David A. Riley, David A. Sutton, Nick Caffrey, Stephen Jones, Ramsey Campbell, Adrian Cole, Brian Lumley and Peter Coleborn, and pre-ordered copies also came with four signed art prints.

Arcturus published *The H.P. Lovecraft Colouring, Dot-To-Dot and*

Activity Book which was described as containing "sanity-shredding imagery and puzzles from the Cthulhu Mythos". Nigel Dobbyn created the impressive line artwork.

The first nine-issue series of *American Gods: Shadows* from Dark Horse Comics was adapted by P. Craig Russell from the novel by Neil Gaiman, with art by Russell and Scott Hampton.

From the same imprint, *Tarzan on the Planet of the Apes* was a genre mash-up that also threw in Edgar Rice Burroughs' lost world of Pellucidar.

Dark Horse's *Hellboy: Into the Silent Sea* was a welcome collaboration between Mike Mignola and Gary Gianni, inspired by the work of William Hope Hodgson. Flesk publications issued a Kickstarter-funded oversized hardcover "studio edition" signed by Gianni.

Anno Dracula 1895: Seven Days in Mayhem was an original five-issue series from Titan Comics, written by Kim Newman and illustrated by Paul McCaffrey (with a bewildering number of variant covers by McCaffrey, Tom Mandrake, Brian Williamson, Jeff Zornow, Mike Collins and Martin Stiff). In an original story set ten years after Dracula came to power, undead journalist Kate Reed joined up with a secret anarchist group in an attempt to end the vampire's rule. Titan subsequently released the five volumes as a graphic novel, with an additional Foreword by Mike Mignola, a cover gallery, some examples of McCaffrey's sketches and an Afterword by the author.

The first title in Titan's new Hammer Comics imprint was the five-part *The Mummy Palimpsest* by Peter Milligan and Ronilson Freire, which was set in present-day London. It was followed by Dan Abnett and Tom Mandrake's *Captain Kronos*, inspired by the 1974 film.

Some of Titan's other comics included *Penny Dreadful* by writer Chris King and artist Jesús Hervás, which was set directly after the events in the third season of the cancelled TV show, and *Sherlock: The Great Game*, based on the BBC-TV series.

From PS Publishing's PSi imprint, *Some Notes on a Nonentity: The Life of H.P. Lovecraft* was a hardcover graphic novel biography by Sam Gafford, illustrated in black and white by Jason C. Eckhardt.

Emil Ferris' beautifully illustrated debut graphic novel, *My Favorite Thing is Monsters*, was about a 10-year-old girl who loved horror.

With its "Rebirth" line, DC Comics decided to update its key superheroes—Superman, Batman, Wonder Woman, Green Arrow and The Flash—yet again.

Goosebumps creator R.L. Stine took on Steve Gerber's *Man-Thing* for a new series from Marvel, while *Marvel Horror: The Magazine Collection* was a Halloween compilation of reprints from *Marvel Preview*, *Haunt of Horror*, *Monsters Unleashed* and *Bizarre Adventures* that included fiction by Harlan Ellison, Anne McCaffrey, Ramey Campbell and others.

A new series of the classic EC title *Tales from the Crypt* was launched under the Papercutz inprint Super Genius, and writer Nathan Carson and artist Sam Ford adapted Algernon Blackwood's 1907 story *The Willows* over two issues for Floating World Comics.

The movie novelisations for 2017 included *Resident Evil: The Final Chapter* by Tim Waggoner, *Kong: Skull Island* by Tim Lebbon, *The Great Wall* by Mark Morris, *Alien: Covenant* by Alan Dean Foster, *Wonder Woman* by Nancy Holder, *War for the Planet of the Apes* by Greg Cox, *Ghost in the Shell* by James Swallow and Abbie Bernstein, and *Valerian and the City of a Thousand Planets* by Christie Golden.

Edited by Rich Handley and Jim Beard, *Planet of the Apes: Tales from the Forbidden Zone* featured sixteen original stories set in the world of the movie series by Greg Cox, Nancy A. Collins and others.

Meanwhile, *Planet of the Apes: Omnibus 1* contained the 1970s sequel tie-ins *Beneath the Planet of the Apes* by Michael Avallone and *Escape from the Planet of the Apes* by Jerry Pornelle, while *Omnibus 2* comprised *Conquest of the Planet of the Apes* by John Jakes and *Battle for the Planet of the Apes* by David Gerrold, along with William T. Quick's 2001 reboot tie-in, *Planet of the Apes*.

Aliens: Bug Hunt edited by Jonathan Mayberry contained seventeen original stories and *Predator: If It Bleeds* edited by Bryan Thomas Schmidt featured sixteen original stories, both set in their respective cinematic universes.

Greg Cox's *The Librarians and the Lost Lamp* and *The Librarians and the Mother Goose Chase* were both based on the Syfy TV series.

The X Files Origins series featured the young adult novels *Agent of Chaos* by Kami Garcia, about a seventeen-year-old Fox Mulder, and *Devil's Advocate* by Jonathan Maberry, about a fifteen-year-old Dana Scully.

Other TV tie-ins included *Supernatural: The Usual Sacrifices* by Yvonne Navarro, *Robert Kirkman's The Walking Dead: Return to Woodbury* by Jay Bonansinga and *The 100: Rebellion* by Kass Morgan.

Doctor Who: The Pirate Planet was a novelisation by James Goss of Douglas Adams' draft script for the second unproduced "Key to Time" sequence, with notes and Adams' original treatment.

Doctor Who: Plague City by Jonathan Morris, *Doctor Who: The Shining Man*, and *Doctor Who: Diamond Dogs* by Mike Tucker all featured Peter Capaldi's twelfth Doctor.

Doctor Who: Myths and Legends featured thirteen original stories by Richard Dinnick inspired by Greek mythology and set in the Whovian universe, while *Doctor Who: Tales of Terror* was an anthology of twelve original stories by Paul Magrs and others.

Doctor Who: Now We Are Six Hundred: A Collection of Time Lord Verse included fifty-one Whovian poems by James Goss, illustrated by former showrunner Russell T. Davies.

Both *The Flash: Hocus Pocus* by Barry Yga and *Supergirl: Age of Atlantis* by Jo Whittemore were based on The CW superhero shows.

Buffy the Vampire Slayer: The Official Grimoire: A Magical History of Sunnydale was credited to series witch "Willow Rosenberg" (A.M. Robinson) and collected the spells cast during the TV shows' seven seasons, with annotations by the other characters.

Edited by Stephen Jones with a Foreword by John Landis, *The Art of Horror Movies: An Illustrated History* from Applause/Hal Leonard was a companion volume to the award-winning *The Art of Horror* from the same editor and publisher. It featured chapters written by Sir Christopher Frayling, Tom Weaver, Barry Forshaw, David J. Schow, Kim Newman, Jonathan Rigby, Lisa Morton, Anne Billson and Ramsey Campbell, along with more than 600 rare posters, lobby cards, advertisements, promotional items, and tie-in books and maga-zines. Amongst the many artists featured were Ivan Albright, Rolf Armstrong, Vincent Di Fate, Les Edwards, Basil Gogos, Graham Humphreys, Mark Maddox, Dave McKean, Lee Moyer, Doug P'gosh, Sanjulián, William Stout and Drew Struzen.

The Thing Artbook from Printed in Blood celebrated the 35th anniversary of John Carpenter's movie with more than 375 original pieces of art by, amongst others, Gary Pullin, Dave Dorman, Godmachine, Tim Bradstreet and Bill Sienkiewicz. It also featured an Introduction by film director Eli Roth and an Afterword by Carpenter himself.

Kim Newman's Video Dungeon: The Collected Reviews was a hefty paperback from Titan Books that included more than 500 themed movie reviews inspired by the author's *Empire* magazine column of the same name.

Into The Unknown from Headpress was a revised and expanded paperback edition of Andy Murray's biography of Nigel Kneale. It included extracts from interviews with Kneale himself, along with such admirers as John Carpenter, Ramsey Campbell, Grant Morrison, Russell T. Davies, Mark Gatiss and Jeremy Dyson.

Originally set to appear from another publisher, PS Publishing picked up *We Are the Martians: The Legacy of Nigel Kneale* edited by Neil Snowdon. The hefty tome looked at the life and career of the maverick British author and screenwriter with essays by, amongst others, Tim Lucas, Stephen Bissette, Ramsey Campbell, David Pirie, Kim Newman, John Llewellyn Probert, Richard Harland Smith, Jonathan Rigby, Stephen Volk, Jeremy Dyson and Mark Gatiss, who supplied the Foreword.

The PS signed and limited hardcover came in a slipcase with a hardcover edition of Kneale's unproduced 1965 TV script for *The Big, Big Giggle*, which was published under the Electric Dreamhouse imprint.

Limited to 500 hardcover copies apiece and also issued under the Electric Dreamhouse banner, series editor Neil Snowdon's "Midnight Movie Monographs" series of slim hardcovers included *Twin Peaks: Fire Walk with Me* by Maura McHugh and *Death Line* by Sean

Hogan, who at least attempted a different approach with his volume. As always, the one annoying point about the series was that the formatting was not consistent from book to book.

Universal Terrors 1951-1955: Eight Classic Horror and Science Fiction Films from McFarland was the first of a two-volume set by Tom Weaver, with David Schecter, Robert J. Kiss and Steve Kronenberg. It featured in-depth essays on the studio's *It Came from Outer Space, Creature from the Black Lagoon, This Island Earth, Revenge of the Creature, Cult of the Cobra, Tarantula, The Strange Door* and *The Black Castle*.

In *Laird Cregar: A Hollywood Tragedy*, author Gregory William Mank looked at the brief career of the talented Hollywood actor who died at the age of thirty-one, while Robert Michael "Bob" Cotter's *Ingrid Pitt, Queen of Horror: The Complete Career* featured a Foreword by the late Hammer actress herself.

Roberto Curti's *Riccardo Freda: The Life and Works of a Born Filmmaker* looked at the life and career of the cult Italian director best known for his Gothic horror movies starring Barbara Steele and others.

Apocalypse Then: American and Japanese Atomic Cinema, 1951-1967 by Mike Bogue was split into three sections: 'Mutants', 'Monsters' and 'Mushroom Clouds', and featured a Foreword by Allen A. Debus.

Giant Creatures in Our World: Essays on Kaijū and American Popular Culture edited by Camille D.G. Mustachio and Jason Barr included chapters about 'Observations on Religious Elements Seen in *Ultraman*' and 'Narrative and Neutrality in *King Kong Escapes* and *Frankenstein Conquers the World*'.

Count Dracula Goes to the Movies: Stoker's Novel Adapted, Third Edition was an expanded version of Lyndon W. Joslin's reference work, while the first volume of *Midnight Marquee's Classic Horror Movie Scrapbook: 1930s* was filled with rare clippings, articles and images from the period.

Edited by Michele Brittany, *Horror in Space: Critical Essays on a Subgenre* looked at such movies as *Event Horizon, Planet of the Vampires, Ghosts of Mars* and, of course, the *Alien* series.

Rubberhead: Sex, Drugs, and Special FX was the first volume in a five-part Kickstarter-funded autobiography by visual-effects artist Steve Johnson, published by Montauk Publishing.

From BearManor Media, *Monster Squad: Celebrating the Artists Behind Cinema's Most Memorable Creatures*, journalist Heather A. Wixson looked at the careers of twenty special effects pioneers of the 1970s, '80s and '90s, including John Dykstra, Steve Johnson, Bob Keen, Todd Masters, Phil Tippert, Steve Wang and Tom Woodruff, Jr., amongst others. The book also featured hundreds of behind-the-scenes photographs.

In *Hollywood's Pre-Code Horrors 1931-1934*, Raymond Valinoti, Jr. explored the sex and violence in movies from *Dracula* (1931) to *The Black Cat* (1934), before the production code was rigidly enforced.

Tom Weaver's "Scripts from the Crypt" series from BearManor continued with the sixth book, Gary D. Rhodes' informative look at the 1936 sequel *Dracula's Daughter*. As with other volumes in this series, the book contained all kinds of fascinating extras, including earlier treatments and DeWitt Bodeen's 1953 treatment for a version of *Carmilla*, which might have starred Marlene Dietrich!

Scripts from the Crypt volume #7 was dedicated to the obscure 1958-59 anthology TV series *The Veil*, hosted by Boris Karloff. Tom Weaver supplied his usual thorough history of the Hal Roach Studios' production, but as usual the fun was in the extras—including three of the original scripts and a look at a further six that were never made, while Dr. Robert J. Kiss' essay was probably the last word needed on Karloff's various hosting duties on TV.

Mark Frost's *Twin Peaks: The Final Dossier* was told from the point-of-view of agent Tamara Preston's reports, which filled in the years between the two TV series, and Jay Steven Rubin's *The Twilight Zone Encyclopedia* was a guide to the TV show.

Slayers & Vampires was an unauthorised look behind the making of the TV series *Buffy the Vampire Slayer* and *Angel* by Edward Gross and Mark A. Altman, while *The Anatomy of The Walking Dead* was a look at the popular TV show with recaps of each season by journalist Paul Vigna.

Edited by Carey Fleiner and Dene October for McFarland, *Doctor Who: Critical Essays on Imagining the Past* explored how the BBC-TV series engaged with historical events, while *Doctor Who: Dalek: The Astounding Untold History of the Greatest Enemies of the Universe* was written by George Mann, Justin Richards and Cavan Scott, with contributions by Terence Dicks, Paul Magrs and others.

Published by Canadian imprint Spectacular Optical on heavyweight paper, *Yuletide Terror: Christmas Horror on Film and Television* was an anthology of twenty-five critical essays edited by Paul Corupe and Kier-La Janisse. Given the somewhat limited scope of the title, the number of topics covered was eclectic and ranged from the obvious (*A Christmas Carol, Black Christmas, Silent Night Deadly Night* and the M.R. James *Ghost Story at Christmas*) to more esoteric subject matter (Hammer's *Cash on Demand, The Evil Touch, Santa Claus Conquers the Martians* and the "Krampus" myth). Contributors included Stephen Thrower, Amanda Reyes, Kim Newman and the two editors, and there were plenty of photographs (including a colour section) and a useful 'Compendium' of Christmas-related titles.

Both on and off the screen, movies in 2017 were defined by their women and the emerging #MeToo movement. For the first time since 1958, the top three highest-grossing US releases featured female leads—Daisy Ridley in *Star Wars: The Last Jedi*, Emma Watson in *Beauty and the Beast*, and Gal Gadot in *Wonder Woman*.

Meanwhile, Andy Muschietti's *It*, a perfectly serviceable remake of the 1990 TV movie based on the 1986 novel by Stephen King, inexplicably became the most successful horror movie of all time (with a record-breaking $117 million opening weekend in the US), surpassing *The Exorcist*'s lifetime domestic gross of $232.9 million. A horror film for the *Stranger Things* generation, Bill Skarsgård starred as Pennywise, the demonic shape-shifting clown preying on the children of Derry, Maine, during the summer of 1989.

In September, Warner Bros. and Wild Creations teamed up to create "The Pennyplex" interactive immersive experience in a South London cinema for those people who wanted more out of their film-going experience of *It*.

The latest attempt to reboot the Universal Monsters franchise, as part of a larger "Dark Universe" concept (along the same lines as Marvel's *The Avengers* team-ups), unfortunately floundered from the outset. Tellingly, the studio slapped a global review embargo on *The Mummy*, which starred a miscast Tom Cruise as a smug soldier of fortune who found himself under the influence of evil ancient Egyptian Priestess Ahmanet (Sofia Boutella). Russell Crowe turned up as a pompous Dr. Henry Jekyll.

Director Alex Kurtzman's flashy visuals accentuated the adventure aspects over the horror, and the multi-authored screenplay blatantly borrowed from many other—much better—movies. As a result of disappointing box-office returns (a terrible $32.2 million opening in the US) and poor reviews, the studio quickly pulled the plug on its planned "Dark Universe" series, resulting in the cancellation of Bill Condon's *Bride of Frankenstein*, *The Invisible Man* starring Johnny Depp, and yet another misguided remake of *Creature from the Black Lagoon*.

We didn't need it anyway. Set at the height of the Cold War in 1962, *The Shape of Water*, Guillermo del Toro's love-letter to the *Creature from the Black Lagoon*, found Sally Hawkins' mute cleaner falling in love with a captured Gill Man (Doug Jones) being held prisoner at the secret government facility where she worked. The terrific supporting cast included Octavia Spencer, Michael Shannon, Richard Jenkins, David Hewlett, Nigel Bennett and John Kapelos. The movie received the Golden Lion, the top prize at the Venice Film Festival.

Set in 1973 for no apparent reason, story and characterisation took a backseat to the impressive CGI effects in *Kong: Skull Island*, in which a team of scientists (including Tom Hiddleston, Brie Larson and John Goodman) investigated the titular Pacific atoll and discovered a gigantic ape and some nasty, reptilian "Skullcrawlers". The real villain was Samuel L. Jackson's over-the-top army colonel. The ending hinted at a forthcoming match-up between Kong, Godzilla and a bunch of other members of the *kaijū* "MonsterVerse".

It's doubtful that anyone was crying out for a remake of the 1990 Joel Schumacher movie, but Sweden's Niels Arden Oplev gave us

Flatliners anyway, in which Ellen Page's manipulative doctor and a group of medical students (Nina Dobrev, Diego Luna and James Norton) experimented with near-death experiences to get a glimpse of the afterlife. Kiefer Sutherland returned from the original film, but as a different character.

Rupert Sanders' *Ghost in the Shell* was a flashy, live-action version of the cult *manga* comic and *anime* movies, although Scarlett Johansson's casting as a near-future, cyber-enhanced spy, predictably resulted in accusations of "whitewashing".

Dean Israelite's *Power Rangers* was yet another movie reboot of the 1990s TV series, as five high school misfits were given special powers by a buried spaceship. Bryan Cranston played the teenagers' mentor Zordon, while Elizabeth Banks camped it up as the evil Rita Repulsa.

Emma Watson's Belle fell in love with Dan Stevens' majestic motion-captured Beast in Bill Condon's live-action remake of Walt Disney Pictures' animated musical *Beauty and the Beast*. A box-office smash, the classy supporting cast included Kevin Kline, Ewan McGregor, Ian McKellen, Emma Thompson and Stanley Tucci.

Set three years into the American Civil War, Nicole Kidman, Kirsten Dunst and Elle Fanning starred in *The Beguiled*, Sofia Coppola's more gentle remake of Don Siegal's 1971 Southern Gothic that starred Clint Eastwood. For the new version, Colin Farrell played the unfortunate Union soldier who took refuge in a delapidated girls' school.

Predictably, Rian Johnson's overblown eighth episode, *Star Wars: The Last Jedi*, was the most successful movie of the year, as a grumpy Luke Skywalker (Mark Hamill) returned to help his sister Leia (the late Carrie Fisher in a poignant cameo) and her rebel forces escape the fascist First Order. Despite Kelly Marie Tran's annoying resistance fighter, at least it was a lot better than *Rogue One*, and there was solid support from Andy Serkis, Anthony Daniels, Laura Dern, Benicio Del Toro, Frank Oz and Adrian Edmondson.

With a $220 million North American opening and $36.7 million in the UK, *The Last Jedi* took an impressive $450 million worldwide in its first weekend—the fifth highest of all time—and went on to gross more than $620 million in the USA and earn a cumulative $1.332 billion throughout the world.

Ridley Scott's *Alien: Covenant* was certainly better than its lugubrious predecessor, *Prometheus*. This time audiences got a full-on *Alien* movie, as Billy Crudup's colony spaceship captain took a detour to investigate a mysterious signal and the crew ended up fighting for survival on an uncharted planet. However, despite the terrific visuals, fans of the series had seen it all before.

London's Madame Tussauds opened an immersive adventure game in July entitled *Alien: Escape*. Based on the movie franchise, visitors found themselves trapped on the colony spacecraft *USCSS Covenant* overrun by various aliens, from face-huggers to a fully-grown xenomorph.

Coming thirty-five years after Ridley Scott's original, Denis Villeneuve's belated sequel, *Blade Runner 2049*, was actually much better than expected, as Ryan Gosling's LAPD blade runner uncovered a monumental secret that led him to the reclusive Rick Deckard (a returning Harrison Ford). The impressive supporting cast featured Robin Wright and Jared Leto, along with Edward James Olmos and Sean Young from the earlier movie. However, the movie's poor opening weekend ($31.5 million) was blamed by Hollywood analysts on a lack of appeal amongst women and younger audiences.

Pirates of the Caribbean: Dead Men Tell No Tales (aka *Pirates of the Caribbean: Salaza's Revenge*), the fifth entry in the Disney series, was also a definite improvement over the previous entry (*On Stranger Tides*), as Johnny Depp's Jack Sparrow searched for the legendary Trident of Poseidon while being pursued by Javier Bardem's undead sea captain and his ghostly crew. It even included a trio of zombie sharks! Series regulars Geoffrey Rush, Kevin McNally, Orlando Bloom and Keira Knightley were joined by Sir Paul McCartney and Bruce Spence.

Andy Serkis' motion-captured Caesar was back for Matt Reeves' *War for the Planet of the Apes*, the fourth in the rebooted franchise that actually began with Tim Burton's 2001 remake, as the simian leader squared off against Woody Harrelson's power-mad Colonel. Although it opened at #1 in the US, the initial weekend gross was below that of the previous entry, *Dawn of the Planet of the Apes* (2014), which was set two years earlier.

Although Steven S. DeKnight's *Pacific Rim: Uprising* was an unnecessary sequel to producer Guillermo del Toro's 2013 original, it benefitted from a likeable young cast as John Boyega played the son of Idris Elba's character, who led a new team of big CGI battle-bots into kicking the shit out of another *kaijū* incursion.

A slumming Anthony Hopkins added some much-needed class to Michael Bay's bombastic *Transformers: The Last Knight*, the Arthurian-themed fifth entry in the franchise based on a line of Hasbro toys.

New Zealand director Taika Waititi decided to inject some much-needed fun into the all-so-serious Marvel universe with *Thor: Ragnarok*, probably the best superhero movie of 2017.

The eponymous God of Thunder (Chris Hemsworth, who actually looked like he was enjoying himself for a change) found himself battling his older sister Hela, the Goddess of Death (the wonderful Cate Blanchett, camping it up) with a little help from Tom Hiddleston's Loki, Idris Elba's Heimdall, Tessa Thompson's Valkyrie, Anthony Hopkins' Odin, Mark Ruffalo's The Hulk, Benedict Cumberbatch's Doctor Strange and Jeff Goldblum's Grandmaster. The director turned up as a likeable motion-capture rock creature named Korg, and there were a number of surprise cameos.

The movie grossed an impressive $121 million during its US opening weekend, which was around 42% higher than Marvel's *Doctor Strange* took during the same period the previous year.

Despite not being quite as much fun as its 2014 predecessor, Marvel's *Guardians of the Galaxy Vol.2* found the motley crew of reluctant space heroes helping Peter Quill/Star-Lord (Chris Pratt) to bond with his omnipotent father (Kurt Russell). Sylvester Stallone and Michael Rooker also turned up, along with cameos by Rob Zombie, Stan Lee, David Hasselhoff, Gregg Henry, Ving Rhames, Michelle Yeoh, an uncredited Jeff Goldblum, and Seth Green as the voice of Howard the Duck. It also had no less than four teaser trailers at the end!

Hugh Jackman and Patrick Stewart brought a surprising amount of depth and pathos to their apparently final outings as an aging Wolverine and a dying Professor X, respectively, in James Mangold's thoughtful superhero movie *Logan*, which was set in a futuristic version of Marvel's X-Men universe. The movie debuted to an impressive $88.4 million at the US box-office, and it was subsequently re-released in a moody black and white version known as *Logan Noir*, which was also included on the Blu-ray release.

Having taken over the role in *Captain America: Civil War* (2016), Tom Holland's baby-faced webslinger finally got his own movie with Jon Watts' *Spider-Man: Homecoming*, as he faced Michael Keaton's bluecollar villain, the Vulture. Robert Downey, Jr.'s Iron Man, Gwyneth Paltrow's Pepper Potts and Chris Evans' Captain America all showed up to firmly tie it into *The Avengers* universe. It was still a box-office hit, despite dropping more than 60% during its second weekend of release in America.

Gal Godot was the best thing about the overpraised *Wonder Woman*. As DC's Amazonian heroine, she was the heart and soul of director Patty Jenkins' 1940s origin story, and she acted rings around Chris Pine's dumb hero and David Thewlis' pantomime villain. Marvel's *Agent Carter* still did it better though.

A movie that could have done with a lot more fun was Zack Snyder's bloated *Justice League*, based on the DC comics franchise. Attempting—and failing spectacularly—to match the success of Marvel's *The Avengers* blockbuster movie franchise, the movie re-united Ben Afflick's grumpy Batman, Henry Cavill's Superman and Gadot's Wonder Woman with fellow DC heroes The Flash (Ezra Miller), Aquaman (Jason Momoa) and Cyborg (Ray Fisher) in a battle with CGI alien villain Steppenwolf (voiced by Ciarán Hinds). Inspired by Geoff Johns' 2011 reboot of the comic series, it reputedly cost $300 million to make but grossed less than that in the US.

A series of murders pointed to the long-dead John Kramer (Tobin Bell) in *Jigsaw*, Peter and Michael Spierig's cynical and unnecessary attempt to reboot the *Saw* franchise for a new generation. Made for around $10 million, the eighth film in the series opened at #1 with a below-expectation $16.3 million during the worst October US box-office since 2007.

Alexandre Bustillo and Julien Maury's *Leatherface* was an unecessary prequel to *The Texas Chain Saw Massacre* (1974). It featured Stephen Dorff as a vengeful sheriff on the trail of a trio of Texas asylum escapees.

Jennifer Jason Leigh's single mother moved her comotose son into the infamous haunted house in the beleaguered Weinstein Company's *Amityville: The Awakening*, a much-delayed meta-reboot of the franchise that was cut by thirteen minutes to achieve a PG-13 rating and earned just $742.00 after playing a Saturday-only engagement on only ten screens in America. It quickly ended up on Blu-ray and DVD from Dimension Films.

Matilda Lutz and Alex Roe were the young couple who watched a cursed videotape in the unnecessary and also much delayed franchise reboot *Rings*, which featured Johnny Galecki and Vincent D'Onofrio. Meanwhile, Kôji Shiraishi's *Sadako vs. Kayako* pitched the vengeful spirits of *The Ring* and *The Grudge* series against each other.

Matthew Vaughn's lazy sci-spy sequel *Kingsman: The Golden Circle* revived Colin Firth's supposedly dead agent Harry Hart and added Julianne Moore's demented drug-dealer. The supporting cast included Mark Strong, Michael Gambon, Channing Tatum, Halle Berry, Jeff Bridges, Bruce Greenwood, Emily Watson and Elton John as himself.

Possibly even better than the 2014 original, Paul King's *Paddington 2* once again featured the CGI-created bear (voiced by Ben Whishaw) and his adopted family (including Hugh Bonneville and Sally Hawkins) getting involved with more mayhem with support from Julie Walters, Ben Miller, Jessica Hynes, Jim Broadbent, Tom Conti, Peter Capaldi, Brendan Gleeson, Joanna Lumley and a terrific Hugh Grant. There was even a sly homage to one of Vincent Price's best films! More than two decades after the Robin Williams original, the entertaining *Jumanji: Welcome to the Jungle* was described by its makers as a "continuation", as four high school kids were sucked into the titular videogame and found themselves inhabiting the bodies of Dwayne Johnson, Jack Black, Karen Gillan and Kevin's Hart's avatars.

And then there was Tyler Perry's dire *Boo 2! A Madea Halloween*, the ninth movie in the low budget comedy franchise. It was cut for a PG-13 rating.

Jessica Roth's college student was trapped in a time-loop where she had to relive the day of her murder over and over again until she could discover the identity of her baby-masked killer in Christopher Landon's *Happy Death Day*, an inventive horror twist on *Groundhog Day*. The original ending had to be re-shot after test screenings.

Ry Ruso-Young's *Before I Fall*, based on the YA novel by Lauren Oliver, had a similar theme as Zoey Deutch's seemingly perfect teenager relived her last day over and over again and learned to be a better person, and a teenage girl (Joey King) found a magical Chinese box that granted seven wishes—at a price—in the PG-13 *Wish Upon*, which also featured Ryan Phillippe, Sherilyn Fenn and an uncredited Jerry O'Connell.

Daniel Kaluuya's African-American suitor wished he'd never met his white girlfriend's wealthy, seemingly liberal parents (Catherine Keener and Bradley Whitford) in comedian-turned-film-maker Jordan Peele's low budget debut *Get Out*, which became a surprise box-office smash.

The creepy doll from Warner Bros.'s now-franchised "*The Conjuring* universe" got its second stand-alone feature with David F. Sandberg's prequel *Annabelle: Creation*, which told how a girl's orphanage run by a married couple (Anthony LaPaglia and Miranda Otto) was terrorised by their late daughter's demonic plaything.

It was announced that movies set in *The Conjuring* "universe" reached the $1 billion mark at the worldwide box-office as, in July, Warner Bros. opened a pop-up immersive haunted house attraction for two days in east London, inspired by the movie. The purpose-built Victorian mansion was filled with props from *Annabelle: Creation*.

When the eponymous religious teenager (Eili Harboe) suppressed her feelings for a female classmate (Kaya Wilkins), it triggered her psychokinetic powers in Norwegian director Joachim Trier's art house horror *Thelma*.

Seeking revenge for the death of his father, a sixteen-year-old boy

(Barry Keoghan) insinuated himself into the bourgeois family of a respected cardiovascular surgeon (Colin Farrell) in Yorgos Lanthimos' twisty mystery *The Killing of a Sacred Deer*, which also featured Nicole Kidman and Alicia Silverstone.

Jennifer Lawrence and Javier Bardem's married couple found their lives interrupted by uninvited guests (Michelle Pfeiffer and Ed Harris) in Darren Aronofsky's art-house horror *mother!* [*sic*]. The movie received both boos and a standing ovation when it was premiered at the Venice Film Festival.

Casey Affleck's melancholy dead musician wandered around under a white sheet attempting to reconnect with his bereft wife (Rooney Mara) in *A Ghost Story*, writer-director David Lowery's gloomy art-house treatise on love and death.

Katee Sackhoff's sculptor tried to save her estranged daughter (Lucy Boynton) from the urban legend of murderous witch Baba Yaga in Caradog James' Welsh-made *Don't Knock Twice*, and writer/director Alice Lowe starred as a heavily pregnant woman whose unborn child guided her through a homicidal rampage in the black comedy *Prevenge*, also filmed in Wales.

Although also set in Wales, writer-director Liam Gavin's atmospheric folk-horror debut, *A Dark Song*, was actually filmed in Ireland as a grieving mother (Catherine Walker) and an occultist (Steve Oram) used ritual magic to—apparently—contact ancient forces.

A couple (Jasmine Hyde and Richard Flood), grieving for their dead son, took a break in the Lake District with disastrous consequences in Gary Sinyor's low budget psychological thriller *The Unseen*, while in *Totem*, a teenager (Kerris Dorsey) tried to protect her family from a supernatural intruder. It was released directly to TV in the UK and elsewhere.

A family hiding in a remote cabin in the woods from an unspecified pandemic received some unwelcome visitors from the infected world outside in Trey Edward Shults' *It Comes at Night*.

A pair of estranged sisters (Taryn Manning and Clint's daughter Francesca Eastwood) were forced to rob a mysterious bank and unwittingly released a supernatural force in Dan Bush's low budget *The Vault*, which also starred James Franco.

Malcolm McDowell turned up as a devilish character in the Faust-inspired music movie *American Satan*, which also featured Denise Richards.

Based on the novel by Adam L.G. Nevill, Rafe Spall and his friends discovered that they should never have gone down into the woods in David Bruckner's eerily effective *The Ritual*, shot in Romania.

A group of co-workers were trapped in their high-rise corporate office building and forced to kill each other by a mysterious voice in Greg McLean's *The Belko Experiment*, scripted by James (*Guardians of the Galaxy*) Gunn.

Doug Jones portrayed the eponymous urban legend come to life in the delayed low-budget slasher *The Bye Bye Man*, which also featured Michael Trucco, Carrie-Ann Moss and a slumming Faye Dunaway.

Two years after it was made, writer-director Sean Byrne's *The Devil's Candy* finally got a limited release, as Ethan Embry's struggling painter moved his family into a rural Texas dream house beset by Satanic forces.

British actor Jason Flemying made his directing debut with the low budget vampire comedy *Eat Locals*, which featured an impressive cast that included Charlie Cox, Mackenzie Crook, Freema Agyeman, Eve Myles, Dexter Fletcher and Annette Crosbie.

A homicidal New York vampire fan (Eric Ruffin) developed a relationship with an equally troubled young girl (Chloe Levine) in Michael O'Shea's indie debut, *The Transfiguration*. Troma's Lloyd Kaufman and film director Larry Fessenden both turned up in cameos.

Set in 1980s Perth, Australia, Ben Young's disturbing debut, *Hounds of Love*, featured Ashleigh Cummings as a teenage schoolgirl abducted and tortured by a psychopathic couple (Emma Booth and Stephen Curry). It was apparently based on a real incident.

Virginia Madsen was wasted in Chris Peckover's Australian home invasion movie *Better Watch Out*, as Olivia DeJonge's teenage babysitter had to protect her twelve-year-old charge (Levi Miller) from a pair of intruders.

John R. Leonetti's 1960s-set home invasion thriller, *Wolves at the*

Door, was inspired by the infamous Manson family murders, while Katherine Heigl stalked her ex-husband's new fiancée (Rosario Dawson) in *Unforgettable*.

Three kidnapped girls had to escape before James McAvoy's twenty-fourth different personality emerged in M. Night Shyamalan's *Split*, which was set in the same universe as the director's *Unbreakable* (2000) and had an impressive $40 million opening weekend.

Samantha Robinson's young spellcaster used magic to make men fall in love with her in Anna Biller's clever 1970s feminist pastiche *The Love Witch*, and Dane DeHaan's ambitious young executive was sent to collect his boss from a creepy Alpine retreat run by Jason Isaacs' mysterious director in Gore Verbinki's stylish horror mystery *A Cure for Wellness*.

Featuring such veteran Canadian actors as Kenneth Welsh and Art Hindle, *The Void* was set in a rundown hospital under seige from multiple demonic forces, and a veteran war photographer discovered that his photographs predicted imminent death in Aaron B. Koontz's *Camera Obscura*.

Mandy Moore and Claire Holt's vacationing sisters soon found themselves becoming great white shark-bait when their viewing cage sank to the bottom of the Mexican ocean in Johannes Roberts' claustrophobic *47 Meters Down*. The movie was originally intended as a straight-to-video release under the title *In the Deep*.

A teenage vegetarian vetinary student (Garance Marillier) developed a taste for human flesh in Julia Ducournau's French-Belgian-made debut *Raw*, while Kristen Stewart was stuck in Paris trying to make contact with her recently dead twin brother in Oliver Assayas' euro-thriller *Personal Shopper*.

Emilia Clarke played a nurse in 1950s Tuscany, hired to help a mute boy who heard the voice of his deceased mother in the walls of the family home in Eric Dennis Howell's atmospheric chiller *Voice from the Stone*, based on the novel *La voce della pietra* by Silvio Raffo.

In *The Limehouse Golem*, based on the novel *Dan Leno & the Limehouse Golem* by Peter Ackroyd, Bill Nighy (in a role originally intended for the late Alan Rickman) starred as an urbane police detective investigating a series of gory murders in 1880 London, reputed to have been committed by the titular creature.

Michael Fassbender starred as a detective hunting a serial killer through a bleak winter landscape in Tomas Alfredson's *The Snowman*. Despite an eclectic supporting cast that included Charlotte Gainsbourg, J.K. Simmons, Val Kilmer, Toby Jones and Chloë Sevigny, it was a disappointing adaptation of Norwegian author Jo Nesbø's best-selling novel.

The atmospheric Vietnamese movie *The Housemaid* (*Cô Haû Gaî*) was set in 1953, when an orphaned peasant girl (Kate Nhung) went to work at a haunted rubber plantation in French Indochina.

Luc Besson's overlong and totally bonkers *Valerian and the City of a Thousand Planets* was based on a French comic book series set in the 28th century. It may have looked visually sumptuous, but the two leads (Dane DeHaan and Cara Delevingne) shared zero screen chemistry, while singer Rihanna was wasted in a cameo.

As a result of the film's poor performance at the box-office, Edouard de Vesinne—who had only been appointed deputy CEO of Besson's EuropaCorp a year and a half earlier—was ousted from the company.

Dean Devlin's ridiculously entertaining *Geostorm* starred Gerard Butler as an unlikely scientist trapped on an international space station and trying to prevent someone in Washington DC using a network of weather satellites to decimate areas of the Earth. It wasn't much of a stretch to guess who the villain was in a cast that included Jim Sturgess, Abbie Cornish, Andy Garcia and Ed Harris. Danny Cannon was brought in to do extensive re-shoots for a reported budget of $15 million after the movie tested poorly. It apparently didn't help.

Matt Damon's midlife loser agreed to join a community of shrunken people in Alexander Payne's whimsical *Downsizing*, while Anne Hathaway's hard-drinking party girl realised that she was somehow connected to a giant monster destroying Seoul in Spanish director Nacho Vigalondo's offbeat *kaijū*, *Colossal*.

A scientific crew (including Jake Gyllenhaal, Rebecca Ferguson and Ryan Reynolds) aboard the International Space Station learned the hard way that you shouldn't experiment with a rapidly-evolving Martian life form in Swedish director Daniel Espinosa's enjoyable, if clichéd, SF thriller, *Life*.

The first human born on Mars (Asa Butterfield) developed a long-distance relationship with a teenage Earth girl (Britt Robertson) in *The Space Between Us*, which had its release pushed back from 2016. Gary Oldman and Carla Gugino were amongst the adult actors.

Wesley Snipes turned up as a crazy survivalist in *The Recall* (aka *Final Recall*), as five teenagers sharing a remote lakeside cabin found themselves in the middle of an alien invasion.

Alien Invasion S.U.M.1. was a low-budget German SF movie starring Welsh actor Iwan Rheon as the titular soldier sent to rescue a group of survivors.

Lois Smith's 86-year-old widow spent most of her time talking to a younger holographic re-creation of her dead husband (John Hamm) in Michael Almereyda's thoughtful *Marjorie Prime*, which also featured Geena Davis and Tim Robbins.

British model-turned-actress Suki Waterhouse played a young amputee who found herself abandoned in a post-apocalyptic Texas wasteland and menaced by cannibals in the halluciogenic thriller *The Bad Batch*. Writer/director Ana Lily Amirpour somehow convinced Jason Momoa, Keanu Reeves, Jim Carey and Giovanni Ribisi that it would be a good idea to appear in it.

A washed-up 1980s TV detective (co-writer Julian Barratt) used his prop robotic eye to hunt down a serial killer on the Isle of Man in the low budget British comedy *Mindhorn*. Essie Davis, co-executive producer Steve Coogan, Russell Tovey, Simon Callow and an uncredited Kenneth Branagh were also featured, while Ridley Scott was another executive producer.

James Cameron's *Terminator 2: Judgment Day*, made back in 1991, when the franchise still felt fresh, was reissued in movie theatres with added 3-D.

Based on the series of eight epic fantasy novels by Stephen King, Nikolaj Arcel's long-awaited *The Dark Tower* turned out to be a complete mess, as Tom Taylor's troubled teen travelled to an alternate world where he encountered Idris Elba's bland gunslinger and Matthew McConaughey's over-the-top Man in Black. Despite $6 million in re-shoots and the movie opening at #1 during a particularly soft weekend at the US box-office, it quickly ran out of steam.

Matt Damon's miscast mercenary found himself helping to defend the Great Wall of China against a horde of invading mythological monsters in Yimou Zhang's impressive-looking, but hopelessly muddled fantasy epic, *The Great Wall*. At the time, it was the most expensive Chinese movie ever made.

Takashi Miike's 100th movie, *Blade of the Immortal*, found a samurai cursed with immortality (Takuya Kimura) helping a young girl (Hana Sugisaki) avenge the death of her parents. It was based on a *manga* series by Hiroaki Sumara.

Guy Ritchie's re-imagining of *King Arthur: Legend of the Sword* featured Charlie Hunnan as a cocky (and cockney) once and future king and Jude Law as his black-clad uncle (things are kept simple). The supporting cast included Poppy Delevigne, former footballer David Beckham and Katie McGrath (from TV's *Merlin*).

A grieving father (Sam Worthington) received an invitation from God to visit the place where his youngest daughter may have been murdered in *The Shack*, based on the best-selling 2007 novel by William P. Young.

Dan Stevens played a struggling Charles Dickens who had to come up with a yuletide hit in Bharat Nalluri's Irish-Canadian *The Man Who Invented Christmas*, which also featured Miriam Margolyes, Ian McNeice, Jonathan Pryce, Bill Paterson, Donald Sumpter, Simon Callow, and Christopher Plummer as Ebenezer Scrooge.

Angela Robinson's *Professor Marston and the Wonder Women* felt like a bit of a cash-in as it took a look at the unconventional love life of Wonder Woman creator William Moulton Marston (played by Luke Evans).

Three years after the release of the Guillermo del Toro-produced *The Book of the Dead*, Pixar's hyper-coloured 3-D *Coco* covered similar animated ground as a young Mexican boy (voiced by Anthony

Gonzalez) travelled to the skeletal Land of the Dead on Día de los Muertos to find a legendary guitar.

A teenage boy discovered he was was something different in the Mexican children's CGI cartoon *Monster Island*, which was animated in India.

The French/Belgium animated comedy *Zombillénium* was set inside the eponymous Halloween theme park and was based on the graphic series by Arthur de Pins, who co-directed with Alexis Ducord.

Will Arnett, Michael Cera, Rosario Dawson and Ralph Fiennes voiced the animated toy brick versions of, respectively, Batman, Robin, Batgirl and Alfred Pennyworth in *The LEGO Batman Movie*. Arranged against them were an impressive line-up of classic villains, including Joker (Zach Galifianakis), Harley Quinn (Jenny Slate), Scarecrow (Jason Manzoukas), The Riddler (Conan O'Brien), Bane (Doug Benson), Two-Face (Billy Dee Williams), Catwoman (Zoë Kravitz), Clayface (Kate Micucci) and Poison Ivy (Riki Lindhome). Perhaps somewhat more unexpected were also versions of Voldemort (Eddie Izzard), Sauron (Jemaine Clement) and King Kong (Seth Green)!

Based on the children's books by Angela Sommer-Bodenburg, the Dutch-made *The Little Vampire 3-D* featured the voices of Jim Carter, the late Tim Piggot-Smith, Alice Krige, Kevin Otto and Mirian Margolyes.

Alexandre O. Philippe's feature documentary *78/52* was a look behind the curtain at the infamous shower murder scene in Alfred Hitchcock's *Psycho* (1960). The title referred to the number of set-ups and edits in the sequence, and amongst those interviewed were Peter Bogdanovich, Jamie Lee Curtis, Guillermo del Toro, Bret Easton Ellis, Mick Garris, Neil Marshall, Eli Roth, Richard Stanley and Marli Renfro, who was Janet Leigh's body double.

In the feature-length documentary *David Lynch: The Art Life*, the artist and film-maker discussed his early life and his idiosyncratic approach to the creative process.

A 16mm film enthusiast in Scotland discovered a lost British production of Edgar Allan Poe's *The Tell-Tale Heart* while clearing out his loft. The twenty-minute short was made by Adelphi Films in 1953 and starred Stanley Baker as the Poe-like Narrator. Originally purchased for £5.00 in 1984 from a junk shop in Brighton as part of a "bargain box" job lot, The British Film Institute subsequently digitally restored the 16mm reel and added it to the BFI archive.

London's BFI Southbank mounted a retrospective season of "Stephen King on Screen" in September that included showings of *The Dark Half*, *Dolores Claiborne*, *The Night Flier* and *The Mist*, amongst other titles.

The politically correct 89th Academy Awards ceremony in January may have featured an embarrassing mix-up for the award for Best Picture, but at least *Arrival* won Best Sound Editing and *Suicide Squad* received Best Make-up and Hairstyling. The Best Costume Design Oscar went to *Fantastic Beasts and Where to Find Them*, while *The Jungle Book* collected the award for Best Visual Effects. Once again, TV viewing figures were down.

Despite featuring the voice of Brad Dourif as the titular killer doll and Jennifer Tilly as his character's former wife, Don Mancini's *Cult of Chucky*, the seventh entry in the series since the 1988 original, went straight to DVD and Blu-ray.

With Roger and Julie Corman credited as co-producers and featuring Malcolm McDowell, Yancy Butler, and Manu Bennett as racing driver "Frankenstein", *Death Race 2050* was a remake of the original 1975 movie that made its debut on home video.

Basically a rip-off of Joe R. Lansdale's 2012 story 'The Hunt: Before, and After the Aftermath', the low-buget *The Rezort* was set after the zombie apocalypse, when tourists could hunt the walking dead in a safari park. Dougray Scott starred.

Released two weeks before the bigger budgeted *Geostorm*, The Asylum's similar-sounding *Geo-Disaster* featured a family trapped in the midst of a super volcano, a major earthquake and massive twister all destroying Los Angeles at the same time.

Andy Edwards' crass British comedy *Ibiza Undead* (aka *Zombie Spring Breakers*) found a group of typical tourists confronting the walking dead while on holiday in Spain. TV and radio presenter Alex Zane had a cameo.

Given a brief theatrical release before going to DVD, the animated *Batman and Harley Quinn* found the caped crusader (voiced by Kevin Conroy) and Nightwing (voiced by Loren Lester) teaming up with the Joker's sometimes-girlfriend Harley Quinn (voiced by Melissa Raunch).

Meanwhile, original stars Adam West (in his last film role) and Burt Ward recreated their 1960s TV incarnations of Batman and Robin for the animated *Batman vs. Two-Face*. William Shatner voiced Harvey Dent/Two-Face, and various other villains turned up, including both Julie Newmar *and* Lee Meriwether as Catwoman.

Mark Hamill, Jeffrey Combs, Christopher Plummer and Doug Bradley added their voices to Sean Patrick O'Reilly's CGI animated *Howard Lovecraft and the Undersea Kingdom*, an adaptation of a graphic novel and sequel to *Howard Lovecraft and the Frozen Kingdom*.

Flicker Alley's restored and newly-scored Blu-ray of the 1925 *The Lost World* was the most complete version of the movie to date, and included deleted scenes, two short films made by Willis O'Brien and a booklet essay by Serge Bromberg.

Criterion's deluxe restored version of Carl Dreyer's *Vampyr* (1932) came with an additional commentary by film scholar Tony Rayns, a 1966 documentary and a booklet by Mark Le Fanu and Kim Newman.

The Film Detective's re-mastered Blu-ray of the 1933 movie *The Vampire Bat*, starring Lionel Atwill and Fay Wray, featured UCLA Film & Television Archive's 35mm restoration, which recreated the hand-coloured effects done for the initial opening prints by the Danish-born Gustav Brock (who also worked on the release prints of the same year's *The Death Kiss*), and featured an audio commentary by film producer Sam Sherman.

Arrow's Blu-ray/DVD reissue of *Caltiki the Immortal Monster* not only featured a new restoration from the 1959 Italian SF film's original camera negative, but also an audio commentary by Tim Lucas and on-screen interviews with critics Kim Newman and Stefano Della Casa, and film-maker Luigi Cozzi.

Blue Underground's Blu-ray/DVD combo pack of the cult 1972 film *Death Line* (aka *Raw Meat*) was limited to 3,000 copies and came with a host of extras, including commentaries and interviews with, amongst others, director Gary Sherman, producer Paul Maslansky, and actors David Ladd and Hugh Armstrong.

Blue Underground took the same kind of care with its three-disc limited edition of Dario Argento's psycho-sexual thriller *The Stendhal Syndrome*, which included bonus interviews with the director, star Asia Argento, assistant director Luigi Cozzi, and various other people involved in the 1995 movie.

Benedict Cumberbatch and Martin Freeman returned as, respectively, Sherlock Holmes and Dr. John Watson, for a much darker fourth series of BBC's *Sherlock*. The three linked feature-length episodes revolved around the death of Watson's wife Mary (Amanda Abbington) and ended with a series of *Saw*-like challenges and a not all too surprising revelation about a third Holmes sibling. Guest stars included Lindsay Duncan, Toby Jones, Andrew Scott, Art Malik, Timothy Carlton, Wanda Ventham and Siân Brooke.

Meanwhile, *Sherlock* co-creator Steven Moffat pulled out of an appearance in Moscow in January after an online leak of the series finale—a day before the episode was screened in the UK—was found to have originated in Russia.

Released on Netflix two weeks after *It* premiered in theatres, Mike Flanagan's *Gerald's Game* was another adaptation of a Stephen King novel, as Carla Gugino found herself a little tied-up after the unexpected death of her husband (Bruce Greenwood) during a sex game in a remote lake house.

Robert Redford's scientist proved the existence of the afterlife in the Netflix Original movie *The Discovery*, which also featured Mary Steenburgen, Jason Segel and Rooney Mara.

Adam Wingard's *Death Note* starred Nat Wolff as a high school outcast who was egged on by a Shinigami Death God (voiced by Willem Dafoe) to write the names of those he wanted dead in a mysterious notebook. Based on a Japanese *manga* comic and *anime*, the American film-makers were accused online of "whitewashing".

Not all the Netflix Original movies received good reviews, and that was especially true of David Ayer's $90 million *Bright*, in which Will Smith's LAPD cop was teamed with Joel Edgerton's rookie Orc to find a magical weapon. However, despite being panned by the critics, the Max Landis-scripted film attracted an audience of more than 11 million during its first three days of streaming through TV sets in December, according to Nielsen estimates. That loosely translated to a $98.2 million theatrical opening weekend had the movie been launched in a more traditional manner.

iBoy was the first UK original movie on Netflix. Based on the young adult novel by Kevin Brooks, a teenager (Tom Milner) gained superpowers after being shot and waking up with fragments of a smart phone embedded in his brain. Masie Williams, Miranda Richardson and Rory Kinnear co-starred.

Released directly to BBC iPlayer, Simon Amstell's comedy *Carnage* was set in 2067, in which a now-vegan human race struggled to come to terms with its meat-eating past, while Bong Joon Ho's *Okja*, a cautionary satire about genetically modified meat starring Tilda Swinton, went to Netflix.

Set in 2032, after starvation and plague have decimated much of the Earth's population, Richard Madden starred as a Scottish chaplain sent to a new colony on a distant planet in the Amazon pilot movie *Oasis*, based on the novel *The Book of Strange New Things* by Michel Faber.

Following the mysterious disappearance of her husband, a woman gave up her large high-tech home and moved into an isolated tiny house in Lifetime's *Tiny House of Terror*.

Anjelica Huston took over the part played by Bette Davis in the original for Lifetime's atmospheric Halloween remake of Disney's *The Watcher in the Woods*, which was expertly directed by TV's *Sabrina, the Teenage Witch*, Melissa Joan Hart, whose family financed the movie. Benedict Taylor, who co-starred in the 1980 version, returned for the "re-imagining" of Florence Engel Randall's young adult novel.

The partially crowdfunded *The Carmilla Movie* was set five years after the original 2014-16 web series, as the now-mortal vampire

(Natasha Negovanlis) began to revert to her blood-sucking ways and her partner, Laura (Elise Bauman), started having ghostly dreams.

Thumbing its nose at the laws of diminishing returns, Anthony C. Ferrante's *Sharknado 5: Global Swarming* on Syfy found Ian Ziering's put-upon hero Fin Shepard and Tara Reid as his bionic wife April Wexler travelling around the world to save their young son from the ludicrous CGI flying sharks. The usual long list of cameos by C-list "celebrities" included Chris Kattan, Clay Aiken, Samantha Fox, Katie Price, Tom Daley, David Naughton, Nichelle Nichols, Geraldo Rivera, Downtown Julie Brown, Fabio, Margaret Cho, Kathie Lee Gifford, Al Roker, Gilbert Gottfried, Dolph Lundgren and Olivia Newton-John!

Alan Moore's crowdfunded anthology of three stories, *Show Pieces*, was set in an otherworldly Nighthampton [*sic*] gentleman's club and was belatedly streamed on the new horror/thriller service Shudder.

Susan Lacy's epic HBO documentary *Spielberg* was an in-depth examination of one of the most influential film-makers of all time, with input from Steven Spielberg himself, along with such friends and colleagues as Martin Scorsese, Richard Dreyfuss, John Williams, J.J. Abrams, George Lucas, Francis Ford Coppola, Brian De Palma, Tom Hanks, Harrison Ford, Robert Zemeckis, Tom Cruise and many others.

Okay, there are now officially too many genre shows on television/online for anyone to possibly keep up with and still have a life!

In the opening episode of Season 7 of HBO's *Game of Thrones* (which consisted of seven delayed episodes instead of the usual ten), pop star Ed Sheeran turned up in an embarrassing cameo as a singing soldier. Despite that small mis-step, a record 16.5 million US viewers tuned in to the finale, making 'The Dragon and the Wolf' the most-watched episode in the show's history. Finally, having moved beyond George R.R. Martin's source novels, most of the series' major characters came together to confront the approaching threat of the army of the dead as fans were treated to the sight of a zombie dragon!

Following a year's hiatus, the tenth season of the BBC's revived

Doctor Who found Peter Capaldi's Doctor teaming up with companions Nardole (Matt Lucus) and gay university student Bill Potts (the remarkable Pearl Mackie) to confront an alien puddle, futuristic emojibots, a giant monster living in London's River Thames, a haunted house, zombies in outer space, a demonic book, alien monks, fake news, Martian Ice Warriors (scripted by a busy Mark Gatiss), and a vanished Roman Legion. Steven Moffat's two-part season finale found poor Bill converted into a Cyber-person, and the double-jeopardy of Missy (Michelle Gomez) and The Master (a returning John Simm with requisite beard) playing very different incarnations of the same character.

Capaldi finally bowed out as the twelfth incarnation of the Doctor, along with showrunner Moffat, with the *Doctor Who* Christmas special 'Twice Upon a Time'. The actor's Time Lord teamed up with his brusque first incarnation (David Bradley) and a First World War captain lifted out of frozen time (the ubiquitous Mark Gatiss again) in a talky and sometimes mawkish valediction of Capaldi's ambitious tenure in the role.

There were squeals of delight from fans when Capaldi's Doctor finally regenerated into Jodie Whittaker's first regular female Doctor, although former Doctor Who actor Peter Davison had been forced to come off Twitter when he criticised "the loss of a role model for boys" after the gender-transformation was originally announced back in July.

Thank the gods for Ian McShane and Ricky Whittle, who basically held the first season of *American Gods* together as the enigmatic Mr. Wednesday and former thief Shadow Moon, respectively. Based on co-executive producer Neil Gaiman's epic fantasy novel, the eight-episode road trip on Starz! featured such guest stars as Crispin Glover, Chris Obi, Orlando Jones, Cloris Leachman, Corbin Bersnen and Gillian Anderson in several roles, including TV's Lucy Ricardo.

Having defeated the British Men of Letters and saved Lucifer's nephilim son Jack, Sam and Dean Winchester (Jared Padalecki and Jensen Ackles) headed into the twelfth season of The CW's *Supernatural* with Crowley and Castiel apparently dead and their mother, Mary (Samantha Smith), trapped in an apocalyptic alternate universe. After Jack quickly grew into a teenager (Alexander Calvert), the brothers helped him control his powers as Lucifer (the wonderful Mark Pellegrino) escaped his imprisonment and started searching for his extremely powerful offspring.

After Nick (David Giuntoli) and his allies finally defeated the power-mad Renard (Sasha Roiz), the sixth and final season of NBC's *Grimm* ended on a confusing note and then added on a coda set twenty years later that angered some viewers and baffled others.

Following the shocking death of his detective partner (Nicole Beharie) at the end of the previous series, Tom Mison's Ichabod Crane found himself working out of Washington DC in the fourth and final series of the Fox Network's *Sleepy Hollow*. Despite having a new mystical library to work out of, and a couple of young assistants at his disposal, this attempt to turn what was once a clever and fun show into just another formulaic fantasy series fell decidedly flat, despite a downbeat dystopian climax.

The ten-part second and final season of Fox's *The Exorcist* found Father Thomas Ortega (Alfonso Herrera) and Father Marcus Keane (Ben Daniels) leaving Chicago to investigate demonic possession at an island foster home run by John Cho's foster father.

Cinemax's tedious *Outcast* was also inexplicably back, as Patrick Fugit and Philip Glenister's demon-hunters tried to prevent their West Virginia hometown of Rome being overrun by the possessed. The entire second season was shown on the Fox channel in the UK more than a year before it aired in America.

After the nuclear explosion that ended the first season, the second series of AMC's *Preacher*, based on the Vertigo comic book by Garth Ennis and the late Steve Dillon, was extended to thirteen episodes. It found Jesse (Dominic Cooper), Tulip (Ruth Negga) and vampire Cassidy (Joseph Gilgun) on the road searching for a missing God and being pursued by a cursed gunslinger (Graham McTavish). They all ended up in New Orleans, where Jesse discovered he was being groomed to become the new Messiah. Meanwhile, Arseface (Ian Colletti) managed to escape Hell with the help of Adolf Hitler (Noah Taylor) in a (so far) completely unrelated plot strand.

When psychic hustler Manfred Bernado (François Arnaud) arrived in the titular small town, he didn't expect to encounter witches, vampires, werewolves, angels and demons in NBC's ten-episode *Midnight Texas*, based on the novels by Charlaine Harris.

The eighth and thankfully final series of The CW's *The Vampire Diaries* ended with brothers Stefan (Paul Wesley) and Damon (Ian Somerhalder) working together to save the town of Mystic Falls, while original co-star Nina Dobrev returned to the show after a two-year hiatus.

The fourth season of companion series *The Originals* found Marcel (Charles Michael Davis) once again in control of New Orleans and Klaus (Joseph Morgan) imprisoned and concerned for the safety of his seven-year-old daughter. Eventually an all-powerful new threat, known as "The Hollow", forced the vampires into an uneasy alliance.

The third season of Freeform's *Stitchers* found Kirsten (Emma Ishta) and her team of fellow psychics using the memories of the recently dead to solve more murders.

Following on from the nuclear explosion that ended the previous season, the fourth series of FX Network's *The Strain*, based on the novel trilogy by Guillermo del Toro and Chuck Hogan, found the world plunged into Eternal Night and ruled over by The Master and his undead *strigoi*. Although not all the major characters survived the final ten episodes, the show at least came to an end on an upbeat note.

The seventh season of the Fox Network's *American Horror Story*, subtitled *Cult*, was another step down for Ryan Murphy and Brad Falchuk's once darkly humorous horror show. This time, the eleven-episode series was based around the aftermath of Donald's Trump's surprise election victory, as an upwardly-mobile liberal lesbian couple (Sarah Paulson and Alison Pill) found themselves menaced by a murderous cult of personality, led by Evan Peters' homicidal narcissist. Unfortunately, the satire was as laboured as the script.

The third season of Fox Network's *Lucifer*, based on the DC/Vertigo comics character, opened with the demon detective (Tom Ellis) trying to discover who kidnapped him and gave him back his angel wings.

Tom Welling (*Smallville*) joined the cast as the new police captain who was hiding a secret of his own.

The second series of ITV's *The Frankenstein Chronicles* found Sean Bean's reanimated former police inspector John Marlott escaping the madhouse and using his new-found ability of seeing ghosts to investigate the mutilation murders of local clergymen in 19th century London. Marlott suspected that his old adversary, mad scientist Lord Daniel Hervey (Ed Stoppard), was somehow connected to the killings, and he wasn't wrong in this sumptuously made and acted six-part period melodrama.

The second season of The Duffer Brothers' over-hyped *Stranger Things*, streamed on Netflix, continued its endless plundering of pop culture references as it opened on Halloween 1984, a year after the events in the first season. Will (Noah Schnapp) was having traumatic flashbacks to the Upside Down dimension, while it was revealed that Milly Bobby Brown's telekinetic Eleven had a "sister" named Kali, aka "Eight" (Danish actress Linnea Berthelsen). Sean Astin and Paul Reiser joined the cast as, respectively, a new boyfriend for Winona Ryder's Joyce and an enigmatic government scientist.

According to Nielsen ratings, an impressive 15.8 million viewers tuned into the *Stranger Things 2* premiere episode over its first three days in October, with nearly 11 million of those coming from the all-important 18-49 year-old demographic.

The ten-episode second season of Hulu's *Freakish* found its band of high school students not only battling mutated members of their own community, but also a new group of survivors.

David Lynch and Mark Frost's much-anticipated revival of *Twin Peaks*—a quarter of a century after the show last aired on ABC-TV—pretty much eschewed the norms of series TV. Many of the original characters returned (including Kyle MacLachlan's off-kilter versions of Special Agent Dale Cooper, Sheryl Lee's Laura Palmer and the late Miguel Ferrer's FBI Agent Albert Rosenfield), but the result never lived up to the whole of its parts. The original series was challenging at times, but at least it attempted a coherent narrative structure. Unfortunately, for this new eighteen-episode sequel/re-imagining, Lynch mostly jettisoned such things as storytelling, characterisation and entertainment for frustrating self-absorption. As a result, those viewers who stayed with the Showtime series either loved it or loathed it.

Leaving no cliché in the author's work unturned, Spike's ten-part series based on Stephen King's novella *The Mist* made the mistake of focussing on the dull survivors trapped in the mall instead of the horrors happening outside. It was justifiably cancelled after just one season.

David E. Kelley somehow managed to spin executive producer King's 2014 novel *Mr. Mercedes* into a ten-part limited series for the AT&T Audience Network, as Bredan Gleeson's retired cop played a cat-and-mouse game with a psychopathic killer (Harry Treadaway).

With Max Landis as one of its executive producers, the second season of Syfy's *Channel Zero*, entitled *No-End House*, featured six episodes linked to a mysterious building that showed those who entered its six rooms their greatest fears. The series was based on stories on the *Creepypasta* website.

Based on a series of SF books by James S.A. Corey and set against an intergalactic conflict between Earth and Mars, *The Expanse* turned into another *Star Trek*-style series in its second season as Jim Holden (Steven Strait) and the crew of the *Rocinante* uncovered a plot to release a destructive proto-molecule on the Eros asteroid station.

Somehow the Syfy series *Dark Matter* reached a third season, as the crew of the derelict spaceship *Raza* continued to fight an intergalactic war while having to deal with a *Groundhog Day* plot and being transported 600 years back in time to the 21st century.

The trio of rebel intergalactic bounty hunters found themselves going to war in the equally baffling third season of Syfy's *Killjoys*. The third season of *12 Monkeys* began with the birth of the "Witness" as Cole (Aaron Stanford) and his team travelled back and forth in time to try to prevent the end of the world. Guest stars included Tom Noonan, Rupert Graves, James Callis, and Christopher Lloyd as the villain who wanted to destroy time and reality.

Christopher Meloni's hit-man found himself befriended by his kidnapped daughter's imaginary friend—a tiny cartoon blue-winged unicorn voiced by Patton Oswalt—in Syfy's surreal nine-part series

Happy!, based on a graphic novel by Grant Morrison and Dick Robertson.

Ghost Wars was set in a remote Alaskan town that had been overrun by paranormal forces and featured Avan Jogia, Kim Coates, the busy Vincent D'Onofrio and singer Meat Loaf. Created by Simon Barry, it ran for just one thirteen-episode season before Syfy cancelled it.

Set in a dystopian 1999, Syfy's thirteen-episode *Blood Drive* managed to rip-off a bunch of much better movies as a former cop (Alan Ritchson) and a tough street racer (Christina Ochoa) were forced to team up in a grindhouse version of *Wacky Races*, where the cars ran on human blood for fuel.

The second season of Syfy's *Wynonna Earp*, based on the IDW comic, found the gunslinger's titular great-granddaughter (Melanie Scrofano) and her companions still battling the demonic Revenants, and the second season of *Van Helsing* found the vampire-hunter's distant relative Vanessa (Kelly Overton) and her friends trying to survive against both humans and vampires in a post-apocalyptic world.

As the patriarch of a mysterious family of undertakers, executive producer Mario Van Peebles hung around for just ten of the twelve episodes of Syfy's *Superstition*. The show, which co-starred the actor's appropriately named real-life daughter Morgana, saw the Hastings family battling demons, witches, demonic dolls and recurring villain, "The Dredge".

In the second series of *Zapped* on Dave, hapless office worker Brian (James Buckley) was still trapped in a magical parallel universe and only the Super Solstice could get him home again. Sylvester McCoy turned up as the "Lord Protector".

The small town of Winden was beset by mysterious disappearances and family secrets as the past and present intertwined in the creepy German-made series *Dark*, which ran for eleven episodes on Netflix.

There were more missing children and family secrets in the second season of the Swedish series *Jordskott*, as police detective Eva Thörnblad (Moa Gammel) once again found herself caught up in another otherworldly mystery, and a group of friends staying in a remote, abandoned ski lodge discovered a malign force in the "haunted" cellar in the eight-episode Swedish series *Black Lake* (aka *Svarysjön*).

A woman (Lynn Van Royen) woke up covered in blood and discovered that she had been murdered and was now a ghost in the ten-part Belgian series *Hotel Beau Séjour*.

Following the death of Sonequa Martin-Green's Sasha Williams at the end of Season 7, the eighth season of AMC's *The Walking Dead* began with the show celebrating its 100th episode, as the various bickering human groups banded together to try to defeat Negan (Jeffrey Dean Morgan) and his self-appointed Saviours and Rick's hugely annoying son Carl (Chandler Riggs) was bitten by the zombies.

Meanwhile, the third season of the spin-off show *Fear the Walking Dead* found the equally irritating Clark family still attempting to deal with the zombie apocalypse and their own dysfunctionalism while prisoners of a militia group (a recurring theme of these shows).

Andrew Lincoln, Norman Reedus, Melissa McBride and Jeffrey Dean Morgan were amongst the original cast members who voiced animated versions of their characters in Adult Swim's *The Robot Chicken Walking Dead Special*, which aired in early October.

In the third season of The CW's *iZombie*, Chase Grave's (Jason Dohring) private army of walking dead soldiers prepared to take control of Seattle, while Ravi (Rahul Kohli) continued to search for a cure to the zombie infection.

Drew Barrymore's SoCal realtor woke up one day with a taste for human flesh, while her husband (Timothy Olyphant) and teenage daughter (Liv Hewson) attempted to support her cannibalist cravings in Netflix's inventive ten-episode zom-com, *Santa Clarita Diet*.

A seventeen-year-old boy (Benjamin Papac) and his cyborg pal (Hartley Sawyer) searched for a female survivor to help repopulate the human race after a zombie apocalypse in the six six-minute episodes of *Saving the Human Race: Webisodes* streamed on CW Seed.

The fifth season of the BBC's *Wolfblood* found the pack about to lose their alpha, Jana (Leona Vaughan), until they discovered they had a traitor in their midst, and the sixth and final season of MTV's *Teen Wolf* kicked off with "True Alpha" Scott McCall (Tyler Posey) and his pack searching for the missing Stiles, who was trapped inside the Wild Hunt, while protecting their friends from the Ghost Riders.

The six-episode second season of the Australian *Cleverman* found the mythological "Hairies" being persecuted by a near-future human government.

Adam Scott's nerdy scientist and Craig Robinson's ex-cop were teamed up by the top-secret Bureau Underground, led by Ally Walker's acerbic Captain Lafrey, to battle supernatural and paranormal threats in Fox's *Ghosted*. Adeel Akhtar and Amber Stevens West added solid support to the often silly half-hour comedy show.

John C. McGinley's alcoholic ex-cop and Janet Varney's small-town sheriff continued to battle witches, ghosts and demons while travelling back and forth through time in the second season of the half-hour comedy series *Stan Against Evil* on IFC. Genre veterans Jeffrey Combs and Patty McCormack guest-starred.

The opening episode of Sky Arts' second series of three new *Halloween Comedy Shorts* featured veteran actress Sheila Reid as a woman who claimed to see the future.

To celebrate its twentieth anniversary, the BBC's *The League of Gentlemen* returned for three new episodes in December, as creators Mark Gatiss, Jeremy Dyson, Steve Pemberton and Reece Shearsmith caught up with the decidedly odd inhabitants of Royston Vasey.

Meanwhile, the third series of Shearsmith and Pemberton's *Inside No.9* on BBC2 featured five more off-kilter stories with a twist at the end. Episodes featured the two creators along with such guest stars as Philip Glenister, Alexandra Roach, Tamzin Outhwaite, Keeley Hawes, Muriel Gray, Peter Kay, Felicity Kendal, Montserrat Lombard and Fiona Shaw.

In the second season of Adult Swim's *Neon Joe, Werewolf Hunter*, John Glaser's eponymous one-eyed hero had to save mankind over five half-hour episodes, while Jenna Elfman played a woman whose childhood imaginary friend (voiced by Rachel Dratch) returned when she started dating a divorced dad in the ABC sit-com *Imaginary Mary*. It only lasted nine episodes.

The titular Toronto detective (Yannick Bisson) encountered a teenaged Howard Phillips Lovecraft (Tyler East) in an episode of CBC's cosy *Murdoch's Mysteries*. Other episodes revolved around a murderer who claimed he was possessed and a mysterious youth tonic.

Pop singer Rihanna turned up as the ill-fated Marion Crane (played by Janet Leigh in the 1960 movie *Psycho*) in the fifth and final season of A&E Television Networks' prequel series *Bates Motel*, which ended with Norma Bates (Vera Farmiga) and her lover Alex Romero (Nestor Carbonell) ending up dead, along with serial killer Norman (Freddie Highmore)—a major betrayal of Robert Bloch's novel and Alfred Hitchcock's classic movie.

The seventh and final season of Freeform's *Pretty Little Liars* finally revealed who the real "A.D." was.

Fifty-one years after Gene Roddenberry's seminal SF show debuted on NBC, the prequel *Star Trek: Discovery* followed the crew of the eponymous Starfleet warship. These included rebellious First Officer Michael Burman (Sonequa Martin-Green), mysterious Captain Gabriel Lorca (Jason Isaacs), alien Commander Saru (Doug Jones) and Lieutenant Ash Tyler (Shazad Latif) as they literally went where no crew had been before while battling the Klingon Empire. Rainn Wilson also turned up as "Harry Mudd". The first two-part episode debuted on CBS in September, before the series moved over to the digital subscription service CBS All Access in the US.

More *Star Trek: The Next Generation* than *Stark Trek: Discovery*, the Fox Network's *The Orville* saw Captain Ed Mercer (creator Seth MacFarlane) and his motley crew (including Adrianne Palicki, Scott Grimes and Penny Johnson Jerald) boldly going where everybody had gone before in the titular exploratory starship. Despite such interesting guest stars as Charlize Theron, Rob Lowe, Jeffrey Tambor, Victor Garber, Steven Culp, Brian Thompson and a reportedly uncredited Liam Neeson, this pastiche charted an uneasy course between comedy and drama.

The first season of NBC's *Timeless* featured the time-travelling team encountering such historical figures as Jesse James, Ernest Hemingway and Al Capone in their pursuit of Goran Visnjic's time-tampering villain.

Eric McCormack's FBI special agent led a team comprising some of the last surviving humans from the future, who sent their consciousness back in time to possess recently-dead bodies so that they could correct the problems that created their dystopia in Netflix's *Travelers*.

Based on the 1979 cult movie, *Time After Time* was created by co-executive producer Kevin Williamson and starred Josh Bowman as Jack the Ripper, pursued through time from 1893 to present-day New York by Freddie Stroma's hot young H.G. Wells. ABC ran just five of the twelve episodes before pulling the show from its schedule.

A mother (Paula Patton) travelled back into the past to try to prevent the murder of her eight-year-old daughter by a serial killer in ABC's ten-part *Somewhere Between*.

Although The CW wisely cancelled the ham radio time-travel thriller *Frequency* in January, after just one season, nearly four months later the network released a four-minute epilogue that brought the show to a tidy conclusion.

Elisabeth Moss' fertility surrogate Offred/June found herself living in the home of Joseph Fiennes' creepy patriarch in the Republic of Gilead, a totalitarian, puritan near-future America, in *The Handmaid's Tale*, Hulu's grim ten-episode adaptation of the1985 dystopian novel by Margaret Atwood (who had a cameo in the opening episode).

Previously filmed as a movie in 1990, the book became one of the UK's best-selling fiction paperbacks in 2017 thanks to the popularity of the TV series.

Meanwhile, the BBC's five-part series *SS-GB* was based on Len Deighton's 1978 novel, set in an alternate 1941 London where the Nazis had won the Battle of Britain. Sam Riley played a Scotland Yard detective forced to work for his German masters.

The second season of the USA Network's *Colony* started with a look back to the first day of the invasion before returning to the present timeline, where Will and Katie Bowman (Josh Holloway and Sarah Wayne Callies) discovered they were on opposite sides of the struggle as they attempted to keep their family safe after a near-future alien occupation.

Following the revelation that their town was under attack from thawed prehistoric insects in Season 1, Dennis Quaid starred in the second series of Sky Atlantic's *Fortitude*, which found the remote Arctic community plunged into the middle of another series of gory murders as Dan Anderssen (Richard Dormer) went through a disturbing transformation.

First shown on Japanese TV in 2016, the incredibly gory six-episode *Crow's Blood* involved some questionable scientific experiments in regeneration based around pupils at the International Dolly Girls' College.

Having come to a natural conclusion at the end of Season 2, CBS' *Zoo* returned for a completely unecessary third season set in a dystopian near-future, as an army of mutated "hybrids" threatened to wipe-out an already sterilised humankind.

Season 2 of AMC's *Into the Badlands* found its characters still trying to survive in a feudal, post-apocalyptic America.

The second season of BBC America's *Dirk Gently's Holistic Detective Agency* found Dirk (Samuel Barnett), Todd (Elijah Wood) and Farah (Jade Eshete) reunited again and teaming up with the unpredictable Amanda (the wonderful Fiona Dourif) to solve a cold case that led them all into a magical realm.

BBC America's fan favourite *Orphan Black* ended after five seasons, as Sarah and her #CloneClub "sestras" (all portrayed by Tatiana Meslany) finally made their stand against the sinister Neolution movement and its 170-year-old founder (Stephen McHattie).

Executive produced by actor Bryan Cranston, *Electric Dreams* was an hour-long anthology show inspired by the stories of Philip K. Dick. Despite an ensemble cast that included Cranston, Steve Buscemi, Geraldine Chaplin, Timothy Spall, Anna Paquin, Greg Kinnear, Juno Temple, Maura Tierney, Liam Cunningham, Julia Davis, Vera Farmiga, Lara Pulver and Tuppence Middleton, the results were a decidedly mixed bag, although when it was good it was *very* good. The first six episodes were shown on Channel 4 in late 2017, with the remaining four scheduled for the following year.

The second Netflix series of Charlie Brooker's dystopian anthology series *Black Mirror* featured an unexpected *Star Trek* parody, robot dogs, a tribute to the Amicus horror anthologies and an episode directed by Jodie Foster.

Hulu's six-part anthology series *Dimension 404* was narrated by Mark Hamill and apparently inspired by the 1980s *Twilight Zone* with appearances by Tom Noonan, Charles Fleischer, Ken Foree, Joel McHale, Megan Mullally and Adrienne Barbeau.

Created by Jay and Mark Duplass, HBO's anthology series *Room 104* featured twelve offbeat stories set in the same motel room.

The Netflix fan favourite *Sense8*—about a number of chracters connected mentally with each other around the world—was cancelled after the second season.

The inhabitants of Arkadia had to deal with an apocalyptic radiation death-wave in The CW's thirteen-part, fourth season of *The 100*, which had now developed well beyond its original concept, and the Earth had just six months before it was destroyed by an asteroid in CBS' thirteen-episode conspiracy series *Salvation*.

Shades of *Voyage to the Bottom of the Sea*! Having saved America at the end of Season 3, Commander Tom Chandler (Eric Dane) and the crew of the *Nathan James* found themselves dealing with another global threat, this time from Peter Weller's mad scientist, in TNT's redundant fourth season of *The Last Ship*.

The finale of Dave's twelfth series of *Red Dwarf* found hologram Rimmer (Chris Barrie) and his fellow crew members experiencing a tear in time, thus allowing Norman Lovett to return as "Holly", eighteen years after he last played the role, and Mac McDonald to reprise the part of "Captain Hollister" for the first time since 1999. Comedian Johnny Vegas guest-starred in an earlier episode.

In the half-hour ITV2 comedy series *Timewasters*, a struggling jazz quartet from South London was transported by an elevator back in time to 1926. Guest stars included Nigel Havers and Nigel Planer.

In the fourth season of Fox's half-hour comedy series *The Last Man on Earth*, the apocalypse survivors travelled to Mexico, while Josh Hutcherson's janitor by day and gamer by night found himself recruited by visitors from the future to travel back and forth through time to save humanity in Hulu's half-hour comedy series *Future Man*. Ed Begley, Jr, and the late Glenne Headley co-starred, and Seth Rogan co-directed three of the thirteen episodes, including the pilot.

Season 3 of The CW's *The Flash* concluded with a member of Team Flash sacrificing themselves so that Barry (Grant Gustin) could prevent Savitar (voiced by Tobin Bell), his vengeful doppelgänger from the future, from killing Iris (Candice Patton). The fourth season introduced a new villain, DeVoe aka "The Thinker" (Neil Sandilands), and Hartley Sawyer joined the team as Ralph Dibny aka The Elongated Man. Danny Trejo also turned up as a bounty hunter from an alternate Earth.

The sixth season of the same network's increasingly grim *Arrow* ended with Stephen Amell's Oliver Queen teaming up with a group of old foes to finally take down whiny villain Prometheus/Adrian Chase (Josh Segarra). That threat was soon replaced in Season 7 by an alternate Earth's Black Siren (Katie Cassidy) and computer genius Cayden James (Michael Emerson), who wanted to hold Star City to ransom.

The second season of The CW's *Supergirl* found the Girl of Steel (Melissa Benoist) battling such super-villains as Livewire (Brit Morgan), Metallo (Frederick Schmidt), Mr. Mxyzptik (Peter Gaidot) and Music Meister (Darren Kris). Calista Flockhart's Cat Grant returned for a couple of episodes, Tyler Hoechlin was back as Superman, and the inspired stunt casting included 1990s TV Lois Lane Teri Hatcher (*Lois and Clark: The New Adventures of Superman*), Kevin Sorbo (*Hercules: Hercules: The Legendary Journeys*) and Lynda Carter (*Wonder Woman*).

Season 3 of *Supergirl* introduced a new threat in the form of "World Killer" Reign (Odette Annable) and another TV Lois Lane, Erica Durance, turned up in several episodes as Supergirl's Kryptonian mother.

DC's Legends of Tomorrow still refused to take itself seriously, as the disparate team of time travellers finally managed to defeat the Legion of Doom with the help of a young J.R.R. Tolkien (Jack Turner) and the Spear of Destiny at the end of Season 2 on The CW. The third season opened with the Legends falling foul of the Time Bureau for breaking time, and in a later episode they were on the trail of a time-travelling vampire in 1895 London.

All The CW shows based on DC Comics characters included cross-over episodes, including the epic four-part 'Crisis on Earth-X' (featuring all the heroes from the various shows and a cameo by William Katt from *The Greatest American Hero*).

Edward Nygma (Cory Michael Smith) finally became the Riddler in the third season ('Heroes Rise') of *Gotham*, the Fox Network's *Batman* prequel series, as the Court of Owls planned to destroy the city and Alexander Siddig joined the cast as Ra's al Ghul.

NBC's *Powerless* was a half-hour workplace comedy also set in the DC universe. The staff of a Wayne Corp. subsidiary created products to prevent innocent bystanders from being injured by super-heroes and villains. The twelve-episode series included guest appearances by Adam West, Corbin Bernsen and Marc McClure, before the network pulled the final three episodes from airing and cancelled the show.

The Fox Network's *The Gifted* was set at an indeterminate time in the *X-Men* universe, as a couple (Stephen Moyer and Amy Acker) discovered that their two children had mutant power. They soon found themselves on the run from a distrustful government's Sentinel Services and teaming up with a super-powered Mutant Underground.

The utterly bonkers *Legion* was to Marvel what *Preacher* was to DC, as Dan Stevens' schizophrenic patient discovered that his often psychedelic visions were manifestations of his mutant powers. The FX Network's eight-episode series was based on an *X-Men* spin-off by Chris Claremont and Bill Sienkiewicz.

A group of teens got back together to investigate a friend's death and discovered that their privileged parents were all members of a sinister resurrection cult in Marvel's *Runaways* on Hulu. Based on the comic book series created by Brian K. Vaughan and Adrian Alphona, *Buffy*'s James Marsters turned up as a sinister scientist named "Victor Stein".

Having successfully escaped an AI parallel universe where Hydra ruled, and with the help of Ghost Rider having thwarted renegade robot Aida's plans to destroy the world, the fifth season of ABC's convoluted *Agents of S.H.I.E.L.D.* unwisely moved the action into outer space, as Phil Coulson (Clark Gregg) and his team found themselves trapped with the remnants of humanity on a far-future spaceship controlled by the alien Kree.

And then there was the *S.H.I.E.L.D.* spin-off *Inhumans*, which thankfully lasted for just eight turgid episodes before it was cancelled. Based on the Marvel comic series created by Stan Lee and Jack Kirby, a group of superhumans living on the dark side of the Moon and led by their dull king Black Bolt (Anson Mount) were teleported by a big dog to Hawaii after his evil brother Maximus (Iwan Rheon, channelling his *Game of Thrones* character) seized power. A month before the show debuted on ABC, the first two episodes were released as a movie in selected IMAX theatres across America.

Over on Netflix, Finn Jones' billionaire Danny Rand used mystical martial arts to fight New York's criminal underworld in *Iron Fist*, based on the 1970s Marvel comics character created by Roy Thomas and Gil Kane.

Jones was back on Netflix later in the year for Marvel's eight-episode *The Defenders*, which teamed Rand up with Daredevil (Charlie Cox), Jessica Jones (Krysten Ritter) and Luke Cage (Mike Colter) to battle an evil underworld organisation led by Sigourney Weaver's villainous Alexandra.

Meanwhile, Jon Bernthal spun his anti-hero Frank Castle from *Daredevil* off into Netflix's sixteen-part series *The Punisher*, as the ruthless vigilante confronted his past.

The second season of *Stan Lee's Lucky Man* on Sky 1 saw police detective Harry Clayton (James Nesbitt) encountering a mysterious woman (Thekla Reuten) with an identical magic Chinese bracelet which she used for selfish reasons, no matter what the consequences were.

Amazon Prime's revival of *The Tick* starred Griffin Newman as an average accountant who teamed up with the eponymous blue-suited hero (Peter Serafinowicz) to battle supervillain The Terror (Jackie Earle Haley).

The OA was a Netflix Original. The eight mismatched episodes (with various running times) began with a blind girl (Brit Marling), who had been missing for seven years, turning up older and able to see. Only her name was now "the OA" ("Original Angel"), and that was only the first of many mysteries surrounding her. Guest stars included Scott Wilson, Alice Krige, and Jason Isaacs as a creepy scientist.

The approaching anniversary of the "Sudden Departure" heralded a global apocalypse in the third and final season of HBO's The Leftovers, which ran for just eight episodes and was mostly set in Australia, three years after the previous series.

Following a lacklustre sixth season that featured a musical wedding episode and saw ratings fall, ABC's Once Upon a Time went through something of a reboot for Season 7 as the story picked up six years later with a grown-up Henry (Andrew J. West) living under a curse in the new neighbourhood of Hyperion Heights. Although most of the original cast had departed following the natural conclusion to the previous season, Colin O'Donoghue's Hook, Lana Parrilla's Regina and Robert Carlyle's Rumplestiltskin were all still around in new personas.

NBC decided to give L. Frank Baum's classic Wizard of Oz books another misguided make-over with Tarsem Singh's ten-episode re-imagining Emerald City, as Adria Arjona's troubled millennial set out on a journey of self-discovery with the help or hindrance of, amongst others, Glinda the Good (Joely Richardson), the Wicked Witch of the West (Florence Kasumba) and the Wizard himself (Vincent D'Onofrio).

After Eve's betrayal and the storming of The Library by General Cynthia Rockwell and her black ops team at the end of Season 3, TNT's The Librarians was quickly back to normal for its fourth season, as Flynn (Noah Wyle) and his companions set out to prevent a secret sect of the Vatican Church from locating the seven corner-stones of the Library of Alexandria, amongst other magical threats.

Following the 2004 movie starring Jim Carrey, Neil Patrick Harris took over the role of scheming master of disguise Count Olaf in Netflix's eight-part *A Series of Unfortunate Events*, based on the popular YA book series by "Lemony Snicket" (Daniel Handler). Barry Sonnenfeld directed four episodes and co-executive produced.

The second season of Freeform's *Shadowhunters: The Mortal Instruments*, based on the YA books by Cassandra Clare, found its cast of young demon-hunters discovering a traitor in their midst while confronting a possible uprising by the Downworlders.

The second, ten-part season of *The Shannara Chronicles*, based on the series of books by Terry Brooks, moved over from MTV to Spike and was set a year after the War of the Forbidding.

Syfy's *The Magicians*, adapted from Lev Grossman's YA book series, returned for a more adult-themed, thirteen-part second season as Quentin (Jason Ralph) and his magical friends had to come to terms with Julia's (Stella Maeve) deal with "The Beast", aka Martin Chatwin (Charles Mesure).

In a surprising Season 1 finale, the selfish Eleanor (Kristen Bell) discovered that she and her new friends Chidi (William Jackson Harper) and Tahani (Jameela Jamil) were actually in The *Bad* Place in NBC's smart fantasy comedy *The Good Place*. The second season opened with the duplicitous Michael (Ted Danson) erasing everyone's memories of that hellish fact.

Fashioned around the making of a 1978 documentary, FX Network's eight-part *Feud: Bette and Joan* was Ryan Murphy's semi-fictional look at the on- and off-screen rivalry between Hollywood superstars Joan Crawford (Jessica Lange) and Bette Davis (a perfectly cast Susan Sarandon), set against the making of such movies as *What Ever Happened to Baby Jane?*, *Strait-Jacket*, *Hush . . . Hush, Sweet Charlotte* and, incredibly, *Trog*. The terrific supporting cast included Judy Davis (Hedda Hopper), Alfred Molina (Robert Aldrich), Stanley Tucci (Jack Warner), Dominic Burgess (Victor Buono), Kathy Bates (Joan Blondell), John Rubinstein (George Cukor), Sarah Paulson (Geraldine Page), David A. Kimball (Freddie Francis) and John Walters (William Castle).

Unfortunately, despite having been made a Dame Commander of the Order of the British Empire in the Queen's 2017 Birthday

Honours list (the oldest-ever person to achieve the distinction), 101-year-old screen legend Olivia de Havilland decided to sue over Catherine Zeta-Jones' portrayal of her in the series. The case was subsequently thrown out by both a California appeals court and the US Supreme Court on first amendment grounds.

What Ever Happened to Baby Jane? was also the basis for one of a trio of scary stories told in the by-now-traditional Hallowe'en episode of the BBC daytime soap opera, *Doctors*, in which three of the surgery staff revealed their greatest fears to each other. The other two tales involved a cannibal revenge and a deal with the Devil. In another episode of the show earlier in the year, a security guard apparently encountered a ghost in a reputedly haunted building on campus.

Robert Patrick's team of geniuses took on a case where they investigated the existence of ghosts on the *Queen Mary* in the Halloween episode of CBS' *Scorpion*. The Christmas episode was yet another variation on *It's a Wonderful Life*, set in a dream-world where Team Scorpion never existed.

Mark Williams' genial clergyman investigated the murder of a member of a pagan community, the supposed ghost of a 300-year-old alchemist and an alien invasion of Kembleford in the fifth season of the BBC's *Father Brown*, which by now had strayed a long way from G.K. Chesterton's original.

On Christmas Eve, BBC4 hosted "Ghost Story Night", which included repeats of Mark Gatiss' disappointing version of M.R. James' *The Tractate Middoth* (2013), such other recent James adaptations as *A View from a Hill* (2005) and *No.13* (2006), two episodes of *Christopher Lee's Ghost Stories for Christmas* ('The Stalls of Barchester' and 'A Warning to the Curious'), along with Gatiss' documentary *M.R. James: Ghost Writer* and the 1976 version of Charles Dickens' *The Signalman* starring Denholm Elliott.

The anthology series *Creeped Out* was a surprisingly spooky UK/Canadian co-production created by Bede Blake and Robert Butler and aimed at young children. Linked by a genuinely unnerving bobble-headed figure known as "The Curious", each episode was like a juvenile *Black Mirror*, as youngsters fell foul of an evil Punch

and Judy show, a legendary monster living across the road, a posses-
sive mobile phone, a mysterious well and other teenage terrors.

Bella Ramsey starred as the accident-prone magic student in the
UK/German co-production *The Worst Witch*, which aired over thir-
teen episodes on CBBC. The cast also included Clare Higgins, Wendy
Craig, Amanda Holden and Anita Dobson.

Netflix's four-part animated *Castlevania* was based on the
Nintendo video game of the same name, as vampire-hunter Trevor
Belmont (voiced by Richard Armitage) took on a vengeful Dracula
(voiced by Graham McTavish) and his army of demonic creatures.

David Tennant was the voice of "Scrooge McDuck" in Disney
XD's revival of the 1980s cartoon series *DuckTales*. His old *Doctor
Who* companion, Catherine Tate, voiced the vengeful "Magica De
Spell" over several episodes.

Michael Jackson's Halloween was about a pair of teenagers (voiced
by Lucas Till and Kiersey Clemons) who experienced a magical
adventure in a mysterious hotel. The animated CBS special also
featured Christine Baranski, Alan Cumming, Lucy Liu, Jim Parsons
and a dancing cartoon version of the late Michael Jackson.

Meanwhile, over at NBC, Tom Hanks voiced the titular character
he created for a silly *Saturday Night Live* sketch in the animated
The David S. Pumpkins Halloween Special, as the pumpkin-suited
mystery man and his two dancing skeleton sidekicks showed a young
boy and his sister the true meaning of Halloween. Peter Dinklage
narrated.

In *The Simpsons*: 'Treehouse of Horror XXVIII', Lisa discovered
a button-eyed version of her family in a clever reworking of Neil
Gaiman's *Coraline*, Maggie was possessed by Pazuzu the demon in
a segment inspired by *The Exorcist*, and a hungry Homer canni-
balised himself. Gaiman, actor Ben Daniels and director William
Friedkin were the guest voices.

In other episodes of the animated Fox show, Bart was haunted
by a ghostly manifestation of his guilty conscience, there was a
medieval spoof of *Game of Thrones* and *Harry Potter*, Lisa looked
back on her life from the future, and Stan Lee and Norman Lear
turned up as themselves.

The sixteenth season Christmas episode of Fox's animated *Family Guy* was yet another variation of *A Christmas Carol*, as Peter Griffin (Seth MacFarlane) was visited by the ghosts of Christmas past, present and future. Carrie Fisher and Don Swayze (voicing his late brother Patrick) were featured.

The fourth and final season of the animated *Star Wars Rebels* on Disney XD started out with two two-part episodes as Sabine Wren (voiced by Tiya Sircar) and the rest of the Rebel Alliance continued their resistance against the Empire.

Meanwhile, Disney XD's series of 2-D animated shorts, *Forces of Destiny*, was narrated by Lupita Nyong'o's sage Maz Kanata and focussed on such female characters in the *Star Wars* universe as Rey (Daisy Ridley), a youthful Princess Leia Organa (Shelby Young) and Jyn Erso (Felicity Jones). To balance things out, Mark Hamill and Anthony Daniels voiced their original movie characters. Predictably, there was also a series of related Hasbro figures.

When werewolf teenager Luke (voiced by Tyger Drew-Honey) and his family were moved to their titular new home by the Government Housing of Unusual Lifeforms (G.H.O.U.L.), he soon found himself hanging out with some monstrous new friends in the animated CBBC series *Scream Street*.

"Vee" Hauntley (voiced by Isabella Crovetti) was a young vampire girl whose family moved from Transylvania to Pennsylvania in the Disney Junior cartoon series *Vampirina*. The voice cast also included Wanda Sykes, James Van Der Beek and Patti LuPone.

The late Anton Yelchin voiced the young hero of the second season of the Guillermo del Toro-created animated series *Trollhunters Part 2* on Netflix. The impressive list of guest-voices included Clancy Brown, Mark Hamill, Anjelica Huston, Lena Headey, David Bradley, James Purefoy and Wallace Shawn.

A Gizmonic Institute employee (Jonah Ray) and his robot pals were forced to watch bad movies by the daughter (Felicia Day) of a mad scientist in *Mystery Science Theater 3000: The Return*, a Kickstarter-funded revival of the 1980s geek favourite on Netflix. The fourteen episodes included asinine commentary on such movies as *Reptilicus*, *The Time Travelers*, *The Beast of Hollow*

Mountain, Starcrash, The Land That Time Forgot (1974) and *At the Earth's Core*.

Denis O'Hare was cast as the troubled author in PBS' *American Masters: Edgar Allan Poe: Buried Alive*, a drama-documentary that attempted to correct many of the common misrepresentations surrounding the writer's life (and death).

Paul Kaye portrayed the late fantasy author, who died in 2015, in the BBC's *Terry Pratchett: Back in Black*, much of which was related in the writer's own words, with contributions from Stephen Briggs, Neil Gaiman, Eric Idle, Paul Kirby, Val McDermid and Pratchett himself.

Harry Potter: A History of Magic on BBC2 tied in to a special exhibition at the British Library, with a little help from J.K. Rowling, David Thewlis, Evanna Lynch, Warwick Davis, Miriam Margolyes and Mark Williams.

The first episode in a new series of the BBC's *Imagine . . .* featured Alan Yentob talking to Canadian author Margaret Atwood about her life and work.

AMC's six-part documentary series, *Robert Kirkman's Secret History of Comics*, looked at the people and events that shaped the medium with the help of actresses Lynda Carter, Gal Gadot and Lucy Lawless, amongst others.

Aaron Mahnke's horror podcast *Lore* premiered as a live-action show on Amazon in October with six episodes based on supposedly true historical events.

BBC Radio 4 kicked off the year with Hatti Naylor's hour-long dramatisation of Ann Radcliffe's 18th-century Gothic novel *The Mysteries of Udolpho*, while Richard Kurti's adaptation of *Isaac Asimov's I, Robot* ran over five nights as part of *15-Minute Drama*.

As part of "Mars Week", Melissa Murray's two-part dramatisation of H.G. Wells' *The War of the Worlds* starred Blake Ritson, and in the five-part *Following the Martian Invasion*, author Francis Spufford and such guests as Roger Luckhurst, Darryl Jones, Ian McDonald and Stephen Baxter, followed the path of the Martian invasion in Wells' book, from the Basingstoke Canal to London's Primrose Hill.

Recorded in front of a live audience at London's Science Museum, *Cells and Celluloid: Aliens on Film* found host Francine Stock and "space geek" presenter Adam Rutherford talking about science fiction movies with a number of special guests.

The three-part series *I Was…*, which looked at encounters between members of the general public and famous personalities, concluded with 'I Was Philip K. Dick's Reluctant Host', as Michael and Susan Walsh explained to Andrew McGibbon how the SF author shared their Vancouver home after his wife left him.

The short drama series *To the Ends of the Earth* consisted of two-part adaptations of Jules Verne's *Journey to the Centre of the Earth*, featuring Stephen Critchlow as Professor Otto Lindenbrock, and H. Rider Haggard's *King Solomon's Mines*, with Tim McInnerny as Allan Quatermain.

To the Ends of the Earth: Lost Worlds, New Worlds found Alex Clark talking to writers Fay Weldon and Tom Holland about fictional imaginary worlds and "boy's own" adventures.

Stephen Wyatt's drama *The Shadow of Dorian Gray* was about the poet John Gray (Blake Ritson), who is believed to be the inspiration for Oscar Wilde's *The Picture of Dorian Gray*.

Beatrice Colin's darkly comic drama *The Ferryman's Apprentice* found a human rights lawyer (Rosalind Sydney) being transported across the river Acheron to Hell by a curmudgeonly Charon (Gary Lewis), while her sympathetic son Thomas (Chris O'Reilly) encouraged his mother to reassess her morals.

The Hauntening featured two fifteen-minute ghost stories written and starring Tom Neenan as a tech blogger haunted by modern technology, while Alexandra Roach's Ms. Sherman searched for her tower block's missing thirteenth floor in Sam Burns' *Floor 13*.

Adapted into two one-hour episodes by Roy Williams for Graeae, a theatrical company for disabled performers, *Graeae's Midwich Cuckoos* was a re-telling of John Wyndham's 1957 novel, and Matthew Graham's psychological thriller *Jayne Lake* featured partially-sighted stand-up comic Georgie Morrell as a blind woman forced to face unknown terrors in a Cornish holiday cottage.

BBC Radio 4's annual "Dangerous Visions" stream featured an

hour-long dramatisation of Arthur Koestler's totalitarian future novel *Darkness at Noon* starring Matthew Marsh as the doomed prisoner Rubashov.

Al Smith's *Culture* starred Pippa Nixon as a doctor working in a dystopian future Britain where antibiotics had stopped working and access to NHS treatment was judged on percieved lifestyle or worth. Adrian Penketh's three-part *Siege* was set in 2020, when Joseph Millson's charismatic French National Front candidate became mayor of a traditionally left-wing city.

As part of the same series, Alan Harris gave Franz Kafka's *Metamorphosis* a darkly comic modern twist. Tom Basden starred as call-centre worker Gregor Samsa, who woke up one day to find he had turned into a giant insect.

Alex Jennings read a ten-part adaptation of Ray Bradbury's 1953 novel *Fahrenheit 451* as part of Radio 4's *Book at Bedtime: Dangerous Visions*.

In February, Tristan Sturrock read Richard Hamilton's three-part abridgement of Daphne du Maurier's *The Birds* over three nights in the same slot while, later in the year, Rosie Cavaliero and Tracy Wiles read Sarah Pinborough's psychological thriller *Behind Her Eyes* over ten nights, abridged by Jeremy Osborne.

Radio 4 celebrated a Philip Pullman week in October with *Book at Bedtime: The Book of Dust: Part One: La Belle Sauvage*, the first in a three-book prequel to *His Dark Materials* read by Simon Russell Beale, and *Book of the Week: Daemon Voices*, in which the author himself read five essays about the art of storytelling.

For Hallowe'en, Mark Gatiss co-scripted and directed the feature-length radio drama *Unmade Movies: The Unquenchable Thirst of Dracula*. Lewis MacLeod played the Count and Meera Syal was his evil High Priestess in Anthony Hinds' unproduced 1970s Hammer script, *Kali: Devil Bride of Dracula*, set in 1930s India. Michael Sheen narrated.

Miles Jupp used Jonathan Harker's journey in Bram Stoker's 1897 novel as a train timetable to plot a route across Europe by rail in *The Trainspotter's Guide to Dracula*.

To commemorate the unveiling in November of an eight-foot high bronze statue of George Orwell outside the New Broadcasting

House in London, *George Orwell Back at the BBC* was a half-hour documentary that included an interview with 100-year-old Annie Oliver Bell, to whom the widowed author once proposed.

Dirk Maggs' six-part adaptation of Neil Gaiman's 2005 novel *Anansi Boys* debuted on Christmas Day on Radio 4. The cast featured Jacob Anderson and Nathan Stewart-Jarrett as long-lost brothers Fat Charlie and Spider, Lenny Henry (for whom the book was written) as the trickster god Anansi, and a cameo by Gaiman himself.

Meanwhile, over on BBC Radio 4 Extra, Maggs' adaptation of Gaiman and Terry Pratchett's *Good Omens* from 2014 was repeated in six half-hour episodes.

Also on Radio 4 Extra, Paul Magrs' *Doctor Who—Serpent Crest* featured Tom Baker's fourth Doctor and Susan Jameson as Mrs. Wibbsey. The half-hour audio productions comprised five two-part stories, 'Tsar Wars', 'The Broken Crown', 'Aladdin Time', 'The Hexford Invasion' and 'Survivors in Space'.

Colin Baker and Nicola Bryant starred in Brian and Paul Finch's two-part stories 'Leviathan', 'Paradise 5', 'Point of Entry' and 'The Song of Megaptera' as part of *Doctor Who—The Lost Stories*.

As usual, Radio 4 Extra grouped various repeated readings and dramas under various series titles: Thirty-two years after Radio 4 first ran a series of supernatural dramas under the title *Spine Chillers*, Radio 4 Extra resurrected three episodes—Don Webb's 'Witch Water Green', Jill Hyem's 'Origami' and Peter Redgrove's 'Dracula in White'.

From 1983, *The Price of Fear* found the late Vincent Price introducing William Ingram's stories 'Goody Two Shoes', 'To My Dear, Dear Saladin', 'The Family Album', 'Out of the Mouths', 'Not Wanted on the Voyage' and 'Is Anybody There?'.

Under the umbrella title *Thou Shalt Not Suffer a Witch*, Tamara Kennedy read five stories from Scottish writer Dorothy K. Haynes' 1996 collection: 'Gas', 'The Gay Goshawk', 'Pentecost—A Flashback', 'The Memory' and 'Windfall', while *Haunting Women* featured five supernatural tales by Dermot Bolger.

A Sting in the Tail featured Brony Glassco's 'Myrtle, Mamonia and Rue', Philip Martin's 'Voices from Another Room' and Natalia Powers' 'Sally Go Round the Moon', while Edward de Souza introduced a half-hour adaptation of Denise Sims' 'Dark Feathers' for *Fear on Four*.

Ruth Gemmell read 'The Transfer' and Matthew Marsh read 'Keeping His Promise', 'The Land of Green Ginger', 'The Man Who Lived Backwards' and 'The Kit Bag' for *Algernon Blackwood's Ghost Stories*, while Phlip Madoc's unabridged reading of Blackwood's 1927 werewolf story, *Ancient Sorceries*, was repeated from 2005 over four evenings in March.

The half-hour radio series *Haunted* included 1980s adaptations of Rosemary Timperley's 'Listen to the Silence' and Bram Stoker's 'The Judge's House' in May; 'The Inexperienced Ghost' by H.G. Wells, 'The Emissary' by Ray Bradbury, 'Mists of Memory' and 'Channel Crossing' by Rosemary Timperley, and 'Esmeralda' by John Keir Cross in May, and Agatha Christie's 'The Lamp', R. Chetwynd-Hayes' 'The Liberated Tiger' and 'Which One?', J.B. Priestley's 'The Grey Ones' and the anonymously-authored 'The Dead Man of Varley Grange' in December.

In May and early June, *Ray Bradbury's Tales of the Bizarre* featured 'The Jar', 'The Fruit at the Bottom of the Bowl', 'I Sing the Body Electric' and 'Skeleton'.

Richard E. Grant read 'All Hallows', Toby Jones read 'Seaton's Aunt', Kenneth Cranham read 'Crewe', Anthony Head read 'A Recluse' and Julian Wadham read 'The Almond Tree' for *Ghost Stories of Walter de la Mare*, while Paul Danemen read the 1852 mystery 'A Terribly Strange Bed' for *Mysterious Tales by Wilkie Collins*.

The fifteen-minute *Charles Dickens—Tales of the Supernatural* included 'The Trails of Murder', 'Chips Bargains with the Devil', 'The Signalman', 'Madman's Manuscript' and 'The Queer Chair'.

Radio 4 Extra also presented a forty-five minute adaptation of Dickens' festive 1848 tale *The Haunted Man and the Ghost's Bargain*, which was originally broadcast in 1990.

The Ghost Stories of H.G. Wells featured David McAlister reading 'The Moth', 'The Temptation of Harringay', 'The Inexperienced Ghost', 'The Stolen Body' and 'The Door in the Wall', and *The Darker Side of the Border* adapted stories by Sir Arthur Conan Doyle, Robert Louis Stevenson and James Hogg.

Angela Thorne read 'I'll Never Know' and Stephen Tompkinson read 'The Game' in September, and in November Keith Drinkel read 'The Dress', Jill Graham read 'The Paradise Garden' and James Bolam read 'You Have to Laugh', all by A.L. Barker, from the 1992 series *Five Strange Stories*.

Through the Wardrobe featured three fifteen-minute readings by Kerr Logan, Michelle Fairley and David Troughton of, respectively, Lucy Caldwell's 'The Belle Dress', Glenn Patterson's 'Tilly's Tale' and Frank Cottrell Boyce's 'The Rosy Rural Baby' in tribute to the work of C.S. Lewis.

Sherlock Holmes with Carleton Hobbs featured Michael Hardwick's half-hour adaptations of Sir Arthur Conan Doyle's short stories 'The Man with the Twisted Lip', 'The Beryl Coronet', 'The Blanched Soldier', 'The Copper Beeches' and 'The Noble Bachelor', all featuring the now-forgotten British stage and screen actor who received an OBE for his services to drama.

Originally broadcast in 1978, Anna Massey starred in an adaptation of Neville Teller's *The Horror at Bly*, a reposte to Henry James' *The Turn of the Screw*, and James Laurenson, Jennifer Piercy and Patrick Troughton starred in Wally K. Daly's three-part science fiction thriller *Before the Screaming Begins*, from the same year.

BBC Radio 4 Extra aired a welcome repeat of Robert Holmes' six-part drama *Aliens in the Mind* from 1976, starring Vincent Price and Peter Cushing and set on a remote Scottish island. It would have made a terrific movie or TV series.

Katie Hims' 'Enoch's Machine', about a Victorian scientist who created a mechanism to record the voice of his dead daughter, was featured in *Listening to the Dead*, and Graham Padden and Natasha Pyne starred in a repeat of Trevor Walker's supernatural thriller *And When You Sleep You Remind Me of the Dead*, from 1987.

Jon Strickland's adaptation of Susan Hill's novel *The Woman in Black* was repeated over four half-hour episodes from 1993 featuring Robert Glenister, John Woodvine and Jane Marlow.

David Wade's adaption of Alan Garner's *The Weirdstone of Brisingamen* from 1989 was also repeated in four half-hour segments, while Wendy Baxter starred in a five-part repeat of Wally K. Daly's *The Children of Witchwood*.

A ninety-minute version of Horace Walpole's 1764 novel *The Castle of Otranto*—widely considered the first Gothic novel—from 1996 featured the voice talents of David Burke, Gerrard Murphy, Alfonsia Emanuelle and Sylvestra La Tousel, and Tim McInnerny, Mia Soteriou and Ben Onwukwe starred in Hattie Naylor's two-part adaptation of H. Rider Haggard's 1887 novel *She*.

To tie in with the three-episode TV revival, *The League of Gentlemen Night* from 2005 featured co-creator and star Reece Shearsmith presenting the original radio series from 1997.

David March starred as M.R. James in a revival of the 1989 drama *The Lodestone*, based on the story by Sheila Hodgson. On New Year's Eve, Radio 4 Extra repeated a 1993 version of Jonathan Miller's *Oh, Whistle and I'll Come to You*, based on the story by James and starring Michael Horden, who was also in the 1968 TV production.

BBC Radio 3 celebrated the centenery of Anthony Burgess' birth in October with a live, two-hour production of the author's own stage musical adaptation of *A Clockwork Orange*, starring Samuel Edward-Cook as "Alex".

In the lead-up to the Christmas episode, the two-hour *Jo Whiley—Access All Areas Doctor Who Special* on BBC Radio 2 featured the radio presenter talking with actors Peter Capaldi, Pearl Mackie, Matt Lucas and David Bradley, along with showrunner and executive producer Steven Moffat.

Mike Redman's independent label Redrum Recordz of Rotterdam, the Netherlands, described itself as "Beneath the mainstream, on top of the underground".

Many of its vinyl and CD releases were of interest to horror fans, including Deformer's *The Living Dead Deformed*, a limited-edition homage to George A. Romero's *Night of the Living Dead* (1968) with cover art by Graham Humphreys, and *Full Moon Deformed*, presented by singer/musician Redman and movie producer Charles Band.

Redrum's other releases included The Travel's *Nyctophobia*, another

Redman project, while Mü and Mike Redman's *Mentalmorphosis* from PRSPCT Recordings featured apparently Lovecraft-inspired sleeve art.

Waxwork Records issued Jed Kurzel's soundtrack to the 2014 Australian horror film *The Babadook* on deluxe vinyl in a package that included old-style tip-on gatefold jackets and pop-up Mister Babadook, heavyweight printed inserts featuring all new artwork by Jessica Seamans of LandLand.

The late movie composer Roy Budd created a new score for Lon Chaney's 1925 *Phantom of the Opera*, which was performed by the Docklands Sinfonia Orchestra at a screening of the movie on October 8 at the English National Opera's London Coliseum.

Successful stage shows such as *Harry Potter and The Cursed Child* helped increase London theatre audiences past the 15 million level for the first time since records began more than thirty years ago, with 2017 being a banner year as box-office revenues topped £700 million.

In January, the Charing Cross Theatre presented the European premiere of Thom Southerland's musical version of *Death Takes a Holiday*, which was first staged Off Broadway in 2011.

Based on the classic 1977 record album by Meat Loaf, *Jim Steinman's Bat Out of Hell: The Musical* had its world premiere at the Manchester Opera House in February and transferred to the London Coliseum in June.

Nigel Harman's *Big Fish*, based on the novel by Daniel Wallace and Tim Burton's surreal 2003 movie, was a sentimental musical production at Andrew Lloyd Webber's 312-seat venue, The Other Place. Making his London stage debut, Kelsey Grammer took over Albert Finney's role as the dying father who told his son (Jamie Muscato) fantastical stories about mythical creatures.

Following sold-out runs at the Southwark Playhouse and Edinburgh Festival Fringe, a revival of David Bryan and Joe DiPietro's *The Toxic Avenger: The Musical* moved to The Arts Cafe in London's West End for a strictly limited three-month season in September. Based on the 1984 cult movie, The *Edinburgh Evening*

News called it "Blatant, bonkers and brimming with brio", while *The Telegraph* newspaper said it was "Gloriously silly, perfectly executed".

Mel Brooks brought a slimmed-down revival of his 2007 *Young Frankenstein* Broadway musical to London's Garrick Theatre in September. It starred Hadley Fraser, Summer Strallen, Lesley Joseph, and comedian Ross Noble as Igor, while Shuler Hensley played the tap-dancing Monster.

As a follow-up to their stage production of *Attack of the Giant Leeches* in 2016, four-person comedy troupe The Lampoons opened a parody version of William Castle's 1959 movie *House on Haunted Hill* at London's Leicester Square Theatre on Hallowe'en.

Sean Mathias' 2016 stage production of William Peter Blatty's *The Exorcist* finally transferred to London's Phoenix Theatre in November. Rated 18+ for containing material "which may shock and offend", the critically-acclaimed production starred Jenny Seagrove, Peter Bowles, Adam Garcia, Clare Louise Connolly as Regan, and the pre-recorded voice of Ian McKellen (whose name mysteriously disappeared off the advertising) as the demon Pazuzu. Illusionist Ben Hart created the head-turning special effects.

From December 3 through to January 27, 2018, London's acclaimed Almeida Theatre presented the world premiere of Richard Jones' skilfully staged production of *The Twilight Zone*, which blended adaptations of eight episodes written by Rod Serling, Charles Beaumont and Richard Matheson into a single narrative. At once both funny and poignant, the production concluded with not only a wonderful validation of the original CBS-TV series, but also the whole field of imaginative fiction itself. The souvenir booklet included a brief article by Neil Gaiman.

Louis Maskell portrayed the hideously-deformed Grinpayne in *The Grinning Man*, Tom Morris' stage musical based on Victor Hugo's 1869 novel *L'homme qui rit* (aka *The Man Who Laughs*), which premiered in Bristol before transferring to London's Trafalgar Studios.

Matthew Kelly starred as the mysterious magician Cole Hawlings in the first stage adaptation of John Mansfield's 1935 Christmas-themed novel *The Box of Delights* at London's Wilton's Music Hall.

Also aimed at Christmas audiences was the first revival of Andrew Lloyd Webber's *The Woman in White* at the Charing Cross Theatre. Based on Wilkie Collins' 1859 Gothic mystery novel, Thom Southerland's new production was a newly revised version of the troubled 2004 musical and featured Greg Castiglioni as the villainous Count Fosco.

Another revival was *Gaslight* at Birmingham's New Alexandra Theatre. Kara Tointon, Rupert Young and Keith Allen starred in this new production of Patrick Hamilton's 1938 psycholigical chiller.

Brother Wolf's production of Kim Newman's first full-length dramatic work, *Magic Circle*, had a limited run at Harrogate Theatre from July 25. Directed by Phil Lowe, the two-handed mystery play was set in the early 1970s—the Dawn of the Age of Ophiuchus—and starred James Hyland and Michael Shon.

Producers of the New York production of George Orwell's *1984* considered hiring a nurse after audiences reacted badly to the torturing of Winston Smith (Tom Sturridge) during performances at Manhattan's Hudson Theatre. There was already an age restriction policy, barring children born after 2004 from seeing the play.

Meanwhile, following Donald Trump's Counselor Kellyanne Conway's use of the phrase "alternative facts" during an interview in January, Orwell's original book went back into the best-seller charts in the UK.

Game of Thrones: The Rock Musical—An Unauthorized Parody opened in February at the Macha Theater in Los Angeles and had a run of eight shows in San Diego before enjoying a three-week run at the Off Broadway Jerry Orbach Theater at the Theater Center in Manhattan in October. Created by Steven Christopher Parker and Steven Brandon, who previously worked together on a musical based on *Lost*, the show revisited the first season of the TV series.

Andy Karl recreated Bill Murray's role in the Broadway production of *Groundhog Day*, based on the 1993 movie about a weatherman trapped in the same day of the year.

For Hallowe'en, Hammer created its own immersive theatrical experience at a former London music hall with *Hammer House of Horror Live*. 'The Soulless Ones', co-written and co-directed by Oscar

Blustin and Anna Söderblom, allowed up to 200 audience members each night to follow the undead Queen Carmilla and her thirteen vampire followers.

Following on from its new *Harry Potter* attraction *The Forbidden Forest* in March, the Warner Bros. Studio Tour in London presented a temporary *Hogwarts After Dark* exhibition for Hallowe'en.

On November 10, "Even Stranger Things: A Night for Robert Aickman" was held at the British Library in London to mark the arrival at the Library of the author's literary archive. Introduced by author and editor Richard T. Kelly, the evening featured readings and discussion with Ramsey Campbell, Jeremy Dyson, Reece Shearsmith, Aickman's literary agent Leslie Gardner and his US editor Victoria Nelson.

Phil and Sarah Stokes' ongoing The Clive Barker Archive launched "The Clive Barker Playscripts" series with *The Magician: A Farce in the Style of the Commedia Dell'arte* (1978) and *The History of the Devil or Scenes from a Pretended Life* (1980). Both of the attractively produced and keenly priced paperbacks featured cover paintings by Barker, along with photographic histories of the original stage productions and other bonus material.

In early July, Warner Bros. and the estate of J.R.R. Tolkien finally resolved their long-running £62 million rights dispute over the digital exploitation of *The Hobbit* and *The Lord of the Rings* in video games and apps. Terms of the settlement were not disclosed.

Based somewhat loosely on Tolkien's mythical world, Monolith's *Middle-Earth: Shadow of War* was the follow-up to the 2014 hit *Shadow of Mordor*, as the player controlled an army of orcs in the war against Sauron.

Capcom's first-person perspective *Resident Evil 7: Biohazard* was set in a creepy Louisiana farmhouse and was a distinct improvement over the survival horror franchise's previous installment. The company opened a forty-five minute pop-up immersive experience for four days in an empty house in London's Shoreditch to promote the new game.

Bathesda Softworks' third-person sequel game *The Evil Within 2* returned to the virtual world created by psychopathic serial killers, as Sebastian Castellanos had to rescue the daughter he thought dead from the digital framework.

MachineGames' *Wolfenstein II: The New Colossus* was a sequel to the 2014 reboot set in a Nazi-occupied world, which allowed the player to "Make America Nazi-Free Again" in an alternate version of 1961.

A mercenary's attempt to rescue a kidnapped girl went disastrously wrong in The Farm 51/Bandai Namco's realistic-looking *Get Even*, which featured a haunting musical score composed by Olivier Derivière.

Players had to take on alien abilities to survive in an interstellar research facility over-run by extraterrestrials in *Prey*, while players hunted giant robot dinosaurs in a world reclaimed by nature in Guerrilla Games' *Horizon: Zero Dawn*.

Celebrating the game's tenth anniversary, Ubisoft's *Assassin's Creed: Origins* moved the action to ancient Egypt.

EA's *Star Wars: Battlefront II*, a sequel to the 2015 reboot video game series, featured both a single-player and multi-player campaign that was set after *Return of the Jedi* and followed Imperial special-forces squad leader Iden Versio (voiced by Janina Gavankar) and her Inferno Squad avenging the death of the Emperor.

Marvel vs Capcom: Infinite was the sixth incarnation of the 2-D console game, in which the player could control characters from Capcom franchises like *Resident Evil*, *Nemesis* and *Street Fighter* to slug it out with Marvel superheroes such as Iron Man, Doctor Strange and Rocket Raccoon.

The *Stranger Things* Ouija Board could have put you in touch with the Upside Down, while around fifty fans queued up in a rainy London in October for the launch at Topshop of a new fashion range based on the Netflix show.

Fright Rags released T-shirt and mask boxed sets of R.L. Stine's *Goosebumps* characters "The Haunted Mask" and "Night of the Living Mummy" in limited editions of 500 units each.

The Wand Company, who started up with a remote-control replica

Harry Potter wand, released The Twelfth Doctor's Sonic Screwdriver universal remote, which allowed you to change TV channels while pretending to be Peter Capaldi's Time Lord. From the same manufacturer, the *Star Trek* Original Series Communicator connected to a mobile phone thanks to its bluetooth technology.

For Halloween, Target stores in America partnered up with Universal Studios for the usual selection of masks, costumes, door greeters, make-up kits, vampire teeth, and home decor items all themed around the Universal Monsters. These included a talking animatronic head of The Mummy and plastic-domed animated cloches of the Burning Windmill and the Monster and his Bride from *Bride of Frankenstein*.

From the Narragansett Brewing Company came the H.P. Lovecraft-inspired Unnamable Black Lager—"a roasty and robust Black Lager with notes of toffee, caramel, coffee and chocolate," finishing with a slightly juicy hop bite.

£42,000 was paid for a French poster of *King Kong* (1933) during Sotherby's inaugural online auction in September, which was the highest amount for a movie poster sold by the London auction house. The event also included a one-of-a-kind British poster for *The Wizard of Oz* (1939).

A convicted drug lord's collection of movie figures was sold at a Belfast auction house in October under the Proceeds of Crime Act. Martin Fillery kept his collection of life-size figures—from *Star Wars*, *E.T.*, *Terminator 2*, *Gremlins*, *Back to the Future II*, *Iron Man*, *Battlestar Galactica*, *Doctor Who*, *Batman* and many other movie and TV series—in a former Cold War nuclear bunker in the south of England, which he also used to grow cannabis. Although the collection cost Fillery more than £1 million to accumulate over two decades, it sold for just £340,000.

In November, a rare "Style-A" one-sheet poster for Universal's *Dracula* (1931) set a new world record when it sold at auction in Dallas, Texas, for $525,800. It was one of only two examples of the poster known to exist. At the same auction, a "Style-L" poster for the same studio's *The Phantom of the Opera* (1925) realised $95,600, a six-sheet for *The Day the Earth Stood Still* (1951) went for $38,240, and Albert Kallis' original gouache painting for the poster for AIP's *Invasion of the Saucer-Men* (1957) sold for $107,550.

At the "TCM Presents... Out of This World!" auction, held at Bonhams auction house over November 21-22, the original seven-foot tall Robby the Robot suit and jeep from MGM's *Forbidden Planet* (1956) sold for $5.375 million (£4 million). It was a new record for classic movie memorabilia, beating the $4 million paid for the original *Maltese Falcon* statuette in 2013. At the same New York event, a lobby card for *Bride of Frankenstein* (1935) went for $9,375.00, while director Tod Browning's dog's ashes and his dog-related scrapbook realised $1,187.00!

That same month, a copy of *Harry Potter and the Philosopher's Stone*, inscribed and signed by author J.K. Rowling, sold for a record £106,250 at a Bonhams sale in London. The previous record for the book was £60,168, which had been set earlier in the year in Texas.

An incredibly rare British edition of the October 1912 issue of *The All-Story* pulp magazine, which featured Edgar Rice Burroughs' complete novel *Tarzan of the Apes*, was sold by a UK auction house for £9,000 (before fees). The money went to charity.

To mark the 40th anniversary of the first *Star Wars* movie, Japanese jewellery store Ginza Tanaka created a 24-karat gold life-size mask of Darth Vader, which went on sale in Tokyo for $1.38 million (154 million Japanese yen). They also offered a solid gold commemorative coin, which was available in just seventy-seven sets of three for $11,000 apiece.

Britain's Royal Mail issued a set of eight first-class *Star Wars* stamps to tie in with the release of *Star Wars: The Last Jedi*.

From June to September, the prestigious Tate Britain gallery in London featured "The Art of Ray Harryhausen", an exhibition showcasing the late special effects expert's models, bronzes and drawings from such movies as *Jason and the Argonauts*, *The Golden Voyage of Sinbad* and *Clash of the Titans* alongside artwork by John Martin, Gustave Doré and Joseph Gandy.

Over the same period, London's Barbican Art Gallery centre hosted an exhibition entitled "Into the Unknown: A Journey through Science Fiction". Curated by historian and writer Patrick Gyger, the display of art, design, film and literature consisted of more than 800 items (including works by H.R. Giger and Ray Harryhausen), many of which had never been seen in the UK before.

The British Library's record-breaking "Harry Potter: A History of Magic" exhibition featured items from J.K. Rowling's personal archive—including handwritten drafts and annotated sketches—along with items that inspired the series. 30,000 tickets were sold prior to the opening on October 20. According to the Great British Pride Index survey in June, the fictional boy wizard instilled more pride in the UK's 16-24 year olds than either the Queen or William Shakespeare.

Guillermo del Toro's "At Home with Monsters" exhibition, which opened at the Los Angeles County Museum of Art in 2016 and featured the movie director's own exhibits and art from the horror genre, toured the Minneapolis Institute of Art and the Art Gallery of Ontario in 2017, before finishing up in Mexico City. The similarly themed "El Mundo de Tim Burton" also opened in Mexico in December.

The rural Oxfordshire farmhouse where J.R.R. Tolkien lived until his death in 1973 went on the market in January for £2 million.

The historic *Queen Mary* ocean liner, permanently docked at Long Beach, California, was the inspired location for the The Horror Writers Association's second annual StokerCon, held over April 27-30. The bewildering line-up of guests included Guests of Honour George R.R. Martin, Elizabeth Hand, Chuck Wendig, Peter Crowther, Tananarive Due, Gretchen McNeil and Stephen Graham Jones. Bill Bridges was Gaming Guest of Honour, Becky Spratford was Librarian Guest of Honour, and Nancy Holder was Toastmaster [*sic*].

Almost as bewildering were the number of Bram Stoker Awards for "Superior Achievement" (there are no "winners" in the HWA) handed out on the Saturday night Banquet by regular Awards MC Jeff Strand. The Poetry Collection award went to Stephanie M. Wytovich's *Brothel*, Non-Fiction went to *Shirley Jackson: A Rather Haunted Life* by Ruth Franklin, and Thomas F. Monteleone and Olivia F. Monteleone's *Borderlands 6* received the Anthology award.

Joyce Carol Oates' *The Doll-Master and Other Tales of Terror* received the award for Fiction Collection, Robert Eggers *The Witch* was given the Screenplay award, and convention co-chair Kate Jones's *Omnium Gatherum* picked up the Specialty Press Award.

Oates also received the Short Fiction award for 'The Crawl Space' (in *Ellery Queen Mystery Magazine*), Tim Waggoner's *The Winter Box* got the award for Long Fiction, and Dennis Etchison and Thomas F. Monteleone were the Lifetime Achievement Award recipients.

The Graphic Novel award went to *Kolchak: The Night Stalker: The Forgotten Lore of Edgar Allan Poe*, Maria Alexander's *Snowed* received the award for Young Adult Novel, Tom Deady's *Haven* picked up the award for First Novel, and John Langan's *The Fisherman* collected the award for Superior Achievement in a Novel.

Various other HWA awards went to James Chambers, Caren Hanten and Linda Addison for their services to the organisation.

The British Fantasy Society's FantasyCon 2017 was held over September 29-October 1 in Peterborough. The Guests of Honour were writers Nancy Kilpatrick, Ben Aaronovitch and Pat Cadigan. The British Fantasy Awards were presented at a banquet on the Sunday afternoon.

The Sydney J. Bounds Award for Best Newcomer went to Erika L. Satifka for *Stay Crazy*, Best Film/Television Programme was *Arrival*, Best Independent Press was Grimbold Press, and Daniele Serra was voted Best Artist. The Best Non-Fiction Award went to Kameron Hurley's *The Geek Feminist Revolution*, Jan Edwards was the recipient of The Karl Edward Wagner Special Award, and Marjorie Liu and Sana Takeda's *Monstress Vol.1: Awakening* was voted Best Comic Graphic Novel.

The British Fantasy Award for Best Magazine/Periodical went to Tor.com, Best Short Fiction was 'White Rabbit' by Georgina Bruce, Best Anthology was *People of Colour Destroy Science Fiction* edited by Nalo Hopkinson and Kristine Ong Muslim, Best Collection was *Some Will Not Sleep* by Adam L.G. Nevill, and Victor LaValle's 'The Ballad of Black Tom' won Best Novella.

The Robert Holdstock Award for Best Fantasy Novel went to *The Tiger and the Wolf* by Adrian Tchaikovsky, and The August Derleth

Award for Best Horror Novel went to *Disappearance at Devil's Rock* by Paul Tremblay. David Sutton and Sandra Sutton were named as Legends of FantasyCon.

The 43rd World Fantasy Convention was held over November 2-5 in San Antonio, Texas. The theme was "Secret Histories", and the guests of Honour were Tananarive Due, Karen Joy Fowler, Gregory Manchess, David Mitchell and Gordon Van Gelder, with Toastmistress Martha Wells.

The World Fantasy Awards were presented at a Banquet on the Sunday afternoon, and, unfortunately, this was the year that the convention's administration boards finally decided to bow to minority pressure and replaced Gahan Wilson's iconic Lovecraft bust with an anodyne award designed by artist Vincent Villafranca.

Special Award, Non-Professional went to Neile Graham, for fostering excellence in the genre through her role as Workshop Director, Clarion West, and Special Award, Professional was won by Michael Levy and Farah Mendlesohn's *Children's Fantasy Literature: An Introduction*.

Jeffrey Alan Love was voted Best Artist, Jeffrey Ford's *A Natural History of Hell* won Best Collection, and editor Jack Dann's *Dreaming in the Dark* received the award for Best Anthology.

Best Short Fiction was 'Das Steingeschöpf' by G.V. Anderson (from *Strange Horizons*), Best Long Fiction went to *The Dream-Quest of Vellitt Boe* by Kij Johnson, and Claire North's *The Sudden Appearance of Hope* won the Best Novel award.

Lifetime Achievement Awards were presented to Terry Brooks and Marina Warner.

There is a dichotomy in publishing at the moment. As noted at the beginning of this column, book sales are on the increase. This is particularly true of ghost and horror fiction which, according to Nielsen Bookscan, in 2017 saw its highest sales in four years, up almost a third in value to £4.2 million.

The reasons given for this increase are given variously as the popularity of horror in the media—from a new generation discovering Netflix's *Stranger Things* and the remake of Stephen King's

It—to the increase in reprint anthologies (really?), the exploration of gender and sexuality by new female writers exploring the #MeToo movement, or as a reaction to the "scary" state of world events and politics—with concerns over everything from Brexit to Donald Trump's unpredictable presidency of the US driving readers to the relatively "safe" scares of horror fiction.

As a result, Stephen King's sales in the UK went up an impressive 59%, while sales of Shirley Jackson's work soared an incredible 654%.

However, at the same time, according to ALCS (Authors' Licensing and Collecting Society) research, the median annual income of professional writers in the UK dropped to below £10,500 ($13,300), down by 15% since 2013 (putting an author's hourly rate well below minimum wage level).

The research stated that the median earnings of a "professional" writer—that is defined as someone who dedicates over half their working hours to writing—had fallen by 42% in real terms since 2005, and by 15% since 2013. At the same time, it was estimated that the profit margins of the five big publishers in the UK increased by around 13%, with shareholders receiving up to three times the amount paid to authors.

This will come as no surprise to those writers (and editors) who are not in the top tier of "best-sellers"—the annihilation of the publishers' "midlist" over the past decade has led to lower advances and royalties at a time when more and more people are attempting to build a career as an author.

It is therefore inevitable that, as earnings have fallen, so have the number of full-time writers. In 2005, 40% of professional writers earned their income solely from writing. By 2017, that figure had fallen to just 13.7%. As writing earnings decline, authors have been forced to work much harder to supplement their income by taking secondary careers, such as teaching or freelance editing. Despite that, at a time when book sales are increasing, figures show that the earnings of many authors continue to decline on both sides of the Atlantic.

The question has to be where all of this will end? Except for a lucky few, is the future of the full-time fiction writer doomed to extinction, or is it time that the way in which authors are paid needs to be re-evaluated? If not, then there is a real danger that writing will once again become the profession of the wealthy elite—just as it was with the "gentlemanly" writers of the 19th century.

And none of us want that . . . do we?

The Editor
January 2019

HELEN MARSHALL

SURVIVAL STRATEGIES

H ELEN MARSHALL is a Senior Lecturer of Creative Writing and
Publishing at Anglia Ruskin University in Cambridge, England.
She is also the general director of the Centre for Science Fiction and
Fantasy there. Her debut novel, *The Migration*, is released by
Random House Canada and Titan Books in the UK in 2019.

"I wrote this story after I took a research trip to the United States
in 2016 to look into the publishing history of Stephen King's first
novel, *Carrie*," explains the author. "My own first novel, *The
Migration*, had just been bought by Random House Canada, and it
made me interested in the writing life of one of my favourite
authors—those pivotal years that propelled his career forward.

"Much of the research I had done for my PhD in medieval
literature has focused on long-dead authors, and so I was excited by
the prospect of access to those who had been alive during those days,
particularly Bill Thompson, King's original editor.

"But as the trip progressed, I found myself increasingly
uncomfortable by the fact that I was prying into someone's life, a life
filled with texture and detail and relationships that I didn't really
have any right to.

"The story took on the proportions of a ghost story when I was
told by more than one person that Thompson had passed away (he
hadn't!). Rather than publishing an article, I wrote a short story that

captured the uncanny mood of the trip and the destabilising politics of the period in which it was written."

B ARRON ST. JOHN must have been nearing his seventies by that point. The pictures I'd copied from magazine covers and newspapers charted his rise from a rake-thin tower of a man, nearly six-three, clad in a badly fitting white wool jacket with a thick crop of black hair cut like a bowl around his ears to his older self: hair grey but still as thick as it had ever been, fine laugh lines etching the curve of that grinning, maniac mouth. In his heyday people had taken him to calling him the King of Horror, a real scaremeister—that term always made me laugh—but the man I saw in those later pictures had the look of a grandfather, which I suppose he was, one who could spin a yarn, sure, but not the kid who'd posed with a shotgun for his university paper under the headline "Vote dammit!"

My university had given me a small grant for my research project into St. John's career. I had planned to stay in Hotel 31, the cheapest place Luca and I had agreed we could afford. He had wanted me in midtown so I could walk most places. He was a worrier, had never been to New York and the idea of me riding the subway right then made him uneasy.

"It'll be fine," I told him, "nothing will happen. It isn't like that anymore. It hasn't been since the '90s." We both knew that wasn't exactly true. The situation was different now, but scarier in other ways. There were journalists being stopped at the borders, asked invasive questions. Not everyone was allowed in. And Luca, for all his woolly sweetness and soft English manners, had a serious stubborn streak. He was protective, I knew, and didn't like the idea of me travelling on my own, not after I'd reacted so badly to the procedure, and certainly not "abroad" as he called it in that charmingly old-fashioned way of his.

But "abroad" was what I had wanted. Even if it wasn't home for me, which lay four-hundred miles north across the border in Toronto where my sister lived, New York still felt more familiar than the still-drizzly streets of London in the summer. Besides, I suppose there was a part of me that wanted to see how bad things had got.

And St. John was a new obsession of mine, one I'd taken up in my recovery. Luca had been reading his pulpy looking paperbacks for years but I'd never touched them. They were too scary, I'd thought, too low brow. I remembered the garish paperbacks though, the ones that showed off his last name in huge embossed letters. They'd been ubiquitous when I was a kid. Each had a plain black cover with a silhouette cutaway so you had to turn the page to get the full effect. *Rosie* was the first I ever saw, his debut, the starting point for his surprising upward trajectory. It featured a small New Hampshire town—eerily similar to the one where I'd grown up, what had once been a small farming community until the petroleum processing plants transformed it. The town was engulfed in a crackling lightning storm. *Gory and horrifying,* read the cover, *you can't put it down!!!*

St. John didn't live in New York, but his former editor did: Lily Argo.

I'd found her e-mail address online. Like St. John she must have been in her seventies, but was still working freelance. There were no pictures. The best I could find was a black and white shot of her and St. John at the signing of his fourth book, *What Is Mine,* the last they worked on together. Lily Argo was an inch or two taller than St. John, glorious, an Allison Janney look-alike, which meant the two of them towered over the line of moist-lipped teenage girls who were clustered around the table. That was back in '79.

When I first approached one of my friends—an anthology editor named Dylan Bone (real name or not, I never knew)—about the possibility of an article on the publication of *Rosie,* he told me Argo had died. Dylan had even written up her obituary for *Locus*—but in retrospect he couldn't remember how he'd first found out. She'd been one of the few female editors at Doubleday back then, mostly due to her lucky discovery of St. John. When I mentioned I'd been in contact with her, that she'd agreed to meet me, Dylan had stared at me thoughtfully.

"Just be careful," he said.

"About what?"

He'd just waved his hand. "You know," he said before lurching off to the bar to fetch another round.

I didn't have any problems with the border guards. The customs line was tense, but I'd always had that feeling whenever I entered the States. Once I'd swallowed two painkillers before a flight back to London and the random swipe they'd done on my hands had registered a false positive for explosives or drugs. I'd been taken to a small backroom where a dark-haired woman in a uniform demanded to know why I had been in the country. I kept apologising, I don't know why. She had to search me by hand and the process was brusque and businesslike. She asked me to remove my bra. Then someone else came in, a heavy-set man with a broad forehead. He didn't look at me. Neither of them did. Afterwards they let me go but ever since I'd been stopped for "random" checks whenever I boarded a plane. This time though the guard took one look at me and waved me through. I must have looked harmless to him.

Hotel 31 was as old as the Overlook, mostly derelict with a walk-in elevator whose grille door you had to close yourself. The room was sparse, but by that point exhaustion had sunk into my skin. I called Luca to tell him I'd arrived and then collapsed under the thin covers.

All night I could hear animal sounds in the walls. The bodies of whatever moved beyond the peeling wallpaper hummed like batteries. Still, I slept. And in the morning I felt better than I had in weeks. Not mended, but stronger.

I was still in that dusky phase of grieving so that sometimes when I slept it felt as if I had fallen through a hole in the world. Each morning I woke up as a different person, discovered new wrinkles at the corners of my eyes, wires of thick, unrecognisable, grey hair. The doctor warned me of changes in my body, cramping, small clots of blood between my legs. I had expected my breasts to shrink but they'd only gotten larger. I read online the best thing to do was to bind them tightly with a snug towel and apply ice for ten minutes on, twenty minutes off. He hadn't told me how old I would feel after.

where his face seems to be receding into the folds of flesh around his neck. In the past couple of months I'd seen it on social media from time to time and reprinted in the papers.

"It's made things a bit hard for me," Benny told me as we sat sipping margaritas in The Lantern's Keep, a classy place near Times Square where the cocktails cost four times what they would at home. There had been a teary week before Luca and I made our decision when I'd given up alcohol, and even after we changed our minds I still hadn't felt like touching the stuff. This was the first drink I'd had in eight months.

"How do you mean?"

"Well it's brought me lots of attention, sure, but not the good kind, you know? Trump supporters *hate* that picture. Trump does too, which is why it gets recycled so often."

Benny's face looked strained and he fidgeted with his glass. He wasn't quite how I remembered him. Benny was always a big man, a corn-fed Iowa type whose Baptist parents had taught him to shun dancing and drink. When I'd met him at orientation he'd been shy, a bit overwhelmed. But after those first awkward weeks he'd just thrown himself into everything. He had this irrepressible love of the new, and he'd taken to those things he'd missed out on most: booze, women—then men, dancing late into the night with this kind of unselfconscious clumsiness which made you want to join in.

He was much thinner now, that kind of thinness that didn't look healthy. "I'm worried about Emmanuel," he said, "worried about . . . well. Anyway. People can be absolute shits, can't they?"

I agreed that they could.

"But you're looking good," Benny said, and I caught his eyes skimming over my breasts. Even though it didn't mean anything coming from him I still blushed and pulled at the cardigan. "But not . . . I don't know, maybe not entirely good?" he was going on. "Hell. I don't know what I'm trying to say."

I took his hand gently and told him not to worry about it.

As The Lantern's Keep started to fill up eventually we wandered out into the street. It was hot and swampy, that kind of early August weather that makes you feel as if you've been wrapped in a damp blanket and beaten. We headed south towards the West Village by foot so I could see the sights. North was Central Park and Trump Towers, which were all basically off limits now. New York hadn't changed so much, not in terms of that strange and beautiful blend of architecture and anger, but there were bits that alarmed me. Like all the police cars all had stickers listing the reward for information on cop-killers with a number you could call.

When I told Benny about the project I was working on, It turned out he'd read St. John as a kid, which surprised me, given his background.

"What I remember about him was that my parents were reading him. They never read *anything* like that otherwise. Murder and cannibalism and demons and all that stuff. But *Faction of Fire*, you know, it was all about faith, wasn't it? In that book there was no getting around it: The Devil was real. And I suppose that's what my parents thought anyway. Good and evil weren't abstract concepts to them. There were good folk and there were bad folk. And it wasn't just that the bad folk made bad decisions. They were … *bad*. It was something more fundamental. Badness worked through them. It was something tangible, real. And St. John, well, his books were all about that, weren't they?"

Benny grinned at me and for a moment I could see his younger self peering out, that kid who'd never touched a drop of liquor in his life before I met him.

"How're your parents doing?" I asked him because that was the kind of thing we were supposed to ask one another now that we weren't kids anymore.

"Dad had a stroke two years ago," Benny said with a shrug. "I go back when I can to help her out. She's lonely, I know, but whenever I do go we just end up fighting."

I didn't ask him about Emmanuel, about whether his parents knew. I figured probably they did. There were enough profiles floating around about Benny's photos so you could only avoid knowing if you really tried.

"How are you and Luca doing?"

"Good."

"He didn't want to come with you?"

"Couldn't get away. You know how it is with these NGOs. Anytime he leaves he feels like he's letting people down."

"It's good what he's doing," Benny told me. "We need more people like him right now." After a moment he stretched and I heard the joints in his shoulders pop. "It must be hard writing horror stories now, you know? It seems like that's all we've got these days. I can't bear to watch the news anymore."

I didn't sleep well that night. When I'd glanced at the papers they were filled with stories about tensions escalating, something to do with the South China Sea islands and whether the U.S. was being too aggressive. John McCain was trying to dial things back but you could tell he was getting tired of it. His eyes looked sharp and a little bit scared.

I'd had panic attacks all throughout the October leading up to the election. There'd been Brexit, of course, our own particular mess. At a conference last summer an American colleague had told me, "What we're seeing is radical politics. People stopped believing that they mattered to the system—but all that's different now. It's exciting, isn't it? Anything could happen." Trump had seemed funny back then, dangerous but still avoidable. They called it all a horror show but you could tell there was fascination underneath it all. How close could we come to disaster? But Hillary was ahead in the polls. Some of the Republicans were denouncing Trump, trying to put a little distance between themselves for when the eventual shellacking came on November 8th.

But it didn't come. For weeks after, all throughout the Christmas break, whenever I heard Trump's name it was as if there was a loud gong echoing in my head. My feed was filled with anguish, betrayal, heartbreak. But I had seen all that already. I felt immured, resilient— and besides I still didn't believe, not really, that it would happen. Then eventually the cold hard truth settled in when I watched the inauguration with Luca. As Trump walked to the podium I burst out laughing, I don't know why, the sheer cognitive dissonance of the whole thing. I felt hysterical. My palms were sweating.

Afterwards I learned St. John had written a novel about something similar, *Answering the King*, about a madman who cheats his way to becoming the President of the United States. Eventually it comes down to a fifteen-year-old girl tormented with visions of the past and the future to stop him. The question at the heart of it is: if you could go back in time to stop Hitler, would you? They had made a movie about it with Steve Buscemi. I don't remember who played the girl, only how wide her eyes were, how she captured that world-weariness so well for someone so young. She was a Cassandra. No one would listen to her.

That was the night when the whole thing with Luca happened. Normally we were very careful. I hadn't been in my job for very long and he'd just moved across the country to live with me. We had talked about having kids one day but . . . We weren't careful enough. Disaster crept in the way it always does.

I called Argo the next day. It was the first time I'd spoken to her and her voice was thin and cagey with a flat Ohio accent. It sounded as if it were coming away from much further away than the Upper East Side.

It felt strange to be listening to her voice and I thought about what Dylan Bone had told me. I'd read the obituary in fact, half as a joke and half because I knew Dylan didn't make mistakes very often. He'd cut his teeth in the '80s horror boom and still made most of his money by convincing writers like St. John and Clive Barker to give him new material. It might sound mercenary but it isn't, not really: Bone was a believer, a horror fanatic. He loved the stuff and even when the market dropped out of it in the nineties he had kept at it, putting out anthology after anthology with cheesy hand-drawn skeletons or zombified hands reaching out of the grave. Argo had been part of that, someone who'd *made* the genre in its heyday.

One the phone Argo was polite and she agreed to meet me for lunch the next day at a café. "It'll have to be close to my apartment," she told me, "I can't move very well now."

I told her I understood, and could meet her wherever she wanted.

"What's this about then? Really?" Her tone wasn't querulous, but wondering. "You know I wrote a chapter about working with St. John for some anthology twenty years ago, *Devilish Discussions* or something like that."

I hesitated because I didn't really have an answer. Yes, I knew the story about how she'd been sent St. John's first manuscript by mistake. It had been meant to go to her boss but he'd been on vacation. She'd liked it but her boss wouldn't touch it, and she didn't have enough support inside Doubleday to push it through, not then, a low-level assistant. But they'd kept in touch, writing letters when the mood took one or the other. Then when *Rosie* had come along it had been "a day of glory"—so she called it.

I gave her the answer I gave most of my colleagues. St. John had changed the genre, really changed it. For one brief moment horror hadn't been the red-haired stepchild of fiction. Horror had been *king*. And I wanted to know how that had happened. Part of my answer was true. I'd always been fascinated by the way books were made, the countless decisions that went into them. But if I were really honest it was simply because I'd become a fan, a real fan—maybe not Dylan Bone level—but my admiration for St. John was genuine.

It was more than that though. The real reason was one I couldn't quite put my finger on, but it had something to do with stories of chance—which St. John's certainly was. And that underneath every story is a pivotal moment when things changed. I wanted to know what that looked like. I needed to know if Argo had understood when that manuscript crossed her desk what it would mean, if she'd felt a chill when he opened the envelop. Like someone had walked on her grave.

That afternoon Benny took me out to the Cloisters for old time's sake, and it was beautiful, just like he'd promised it would be. The place was a mishmash of architecture taken from a series of medieval abbeys in France, Catalan and the Occitan, simultaneously peaceful and surreal, liminal, a sliver of another world transplanted into New York.

"I thought you'd like it," Benny told me. We were staring at a tree that had been shaped to fit one of the alcoves in the garden. Its branches curved unnaturally like a menorah to fill the space. I couldn't help but wonder how it had been manipulated, what sort of subtle violence had pressurised the wood to assume the shape it had.

"I do," I told him, shivering despite the mid-day heat.

"So, tomorrow. The editor, what's her name again?" He snapped his fingers. "Argo, right? Lily Argo. You're going to interview her. What about St. John then? Any chance you'll get to speak to him?"

I didn't think so. St. John lived in New Hampshire and I had no idea what kind of relationship the two of them still had. If they kept in touch. If Argo would even like me.

"Of course she will. You're—well, you're the *makeles quene*, aren't you?" He smiled. "You are without blot."

"Someone back home said she was dead," I told him uneasily. I still didn't like that part of the story. Why would Dylan have thought that?

"Huh," Benny said. "It sounds like the beginning of a ghost story, doesn't it? Like she'll bestow her wisdom on you, settle her unfinished business, and vanish into the night."

"It sounds exactly like that."

"But maybe you're lucky, not seeing St. John."

I asked him what he meant.

"You know. He's bound to be pretty weird, isn't he? I mean he's been writing that stuff for more than forty years now. You can't keep that close to the darkness without some of it sticking to you."

It wasn't the first time I'd heard something like this. I was used to getting it myself sometimes at the university. But the horror writers I'd met were amongst the most well-adjusted people I knew, certainly they were much calmer than the other writers I tended to deal with. Some people said it was because there wasn't much money in horror writing these days. But I thought it was something else: writers were good at channelling their anxieties into something productive. We all have those nasty thoughts, those worries that maybe we don't love our partners as much as we should, or maybe they don't love us. Fears that maybe something awful will happen tomorrow. The phone will ring and it will be the police. An accident somewhere. Or a fight escalated, a button pushed.

"When I studied the Middle Ages," I told him, "it always seemed like it must have been so difficult for those people. I mean, the Black

Death wiped out 40% of the population. Imagine whole villages lost, your family—everyone you've ever met—wiped out."

"I know," he said, "I just couldn't take living like that. I'd, I dunno. I'd go crazy, I guess."

I wondered if he really would go crazy. Or if he was going crazy right now, waiting for that call about Emmanuel. Waiting for Trump to finally get around to signing a new Executive Order. I had always liked Benny because he had a sense of outrage, a keen abhorrence of injustice. I knew he had marched in those early protests and knew that he wasn't marching anymore. He didn't want to draw attention to himself. Benny was strong but he was adaptable. He was finding ways to survive, to keep making his art—but doing it so it didn't hurt Emmanuel.

Luca was the same way. Most nights he didn't come home until close to midnight. There was always more he felt he could be doing. For a while I'd felt really proud of him. And then when things got bad I'd just felt resentful, angry at him for spending so much time saving other people when what I really wanted was for him to save me.

In the gift shop I chose a postcard for him, a picture of the Flemish tapestry called *The Hunt for the Unicorn*. It showed five young men in aristocratic clothing with their spears and their dogs. If it weren't for the title you wouldn't have been able to tell what they were doing there. I wanted to choose one with the unicorn but all of them looked too violent or depressing. Something about the unicorn in captivity, collared, in a fence that can barely hold her, reminded me of *Answering the King*, and how the girl had been taken to prison after she shot the president. There had been a coda at the end of the novel, the little girl twenty years later, grown up, in solitary confinement. They had thought she had gone mad because she wouldn't stop hurting herself.

But St. John showed the real reason. The girl had had another vision, one worse than what she'd stopped all those years ago. But this time there was nothing she could do about it.

I couldn't get hold of Luca that night. He wasn't answering his e-mail and when I tried him at home—and then at work—the phone just rang and rang. It wasn't that unusual. Sometimes there were emergencies, and Luca would become so totally absorbed in them he would forget everything else.

There were emergencies like that, I knew, one every few days it seemed. So eventually I left a message saying I loved him. I tried the TV but got nothing but static. Eventually I settled down to read. It was another story from *Strangers and Friends*, but this one was about a haunted house called 'Question the Foundations'. It was a twist on the trope: the houses weren't haunted by people so much as the people by houses. In St. John's world each person had a tiny space within them, an impression of the place where they had been born. And it remained there, like a scar, or a memory. And everyone else could see it too, who you were and where you came from. Except there was this young boy who didn't have a place like that. He had nothing. He had come from nowhere. And because he had nothing he scared people.

I put the book down, confused and unsure of myself. The story bothered me but I didn't know why. It was different from the others, softer, sadder. There was no real horror in the story. It had been about loneliness. How it felt to be hollow, an outsider. Rootless.

Maybe it was just those constellations of images, emptiness and violence. Luca had told me a story once about how his family used to keep chickens. He had lived in the middle of a wood. One day a fox broke into the henhouse and tore open all the chickens. He'd found their bodies, or what was left of them, the next morning. Inside their bodies he had found strings of growing eggs, like pearls.

After he told me that I couldn't sleep and it was the same feeling now. I didn't have any regrets. Luca and I had talked, and he had left the decision to me. There had been no pressure, none from him anyway. But I'd been watching the news. And when the first bomb exploded in Paddington Station it had been like a warning sign. Not now. It wasn't safe. Things would settle down soon, they had to. And then we could try again.

I put the book down and touched my stomach gently, tentatively. Beneath my fingers all I could feel was my own thick flesh.

Three times I passed the café before I finally had the courage to meet Lily Argo. I could see her—at least I thought it was her—sitting in the courtyard with her walker folded up beside her. She had long white hair and a red-and-grey printed dress with long sleeves. I knew her because of how tall she was, even a little stooped over. She still had at least six inches on me.

"Ms. Argo?" I asked her and she nodded politely while I pulled up a seat.

"So you're the one who's come asking about Barron St. John."

"That's right." I tentatively launched into my pitch: an article on St. John's early publication history, documenting her involvement in acquiring and editing his first title. She stopped me with a wave of her hand.

"Sure, honey," she said with a wide, generous smile, "you don't need to go on like that. I'm happy to talk about those days though I confess they seem a while ago now. You know I got that manuscript by accident, don't you?"

I nodded and she seemed relieved.

"Good, so we're not starting from scratch. What you want is the story, I take it, of how Bear—that's what I always called him—and I got along in those early days? Where the horror came from?" I nodded again and took out my phone but she eyed it warily. "I'll tell it as best I can and you can make of it whatever you will—but no recordings, okay? You can listen and you can write down what you get from it but you only get to hear it once."

What was I supposed to say? Already I could feel a kind of strange buzz around her, the magnetic pull of her charisma. I had wanted her story and here she was, ready to give it to me.

"I was pretty young in those days," she began, "when I first started working for Doubleday. I'd grown up in Ohio which I never liked very much in part because it didn't seem like I was much use to my parents. I was a reader, even then, but they had wanted me to go to one of the nursing schools but I knew I'd never be happy with something like that, taking care of people all the time. So when I was seventeen I ran off to New York City.

"Publishing was still very much a gentleman's sport back then and if you were a woman you were either someone's secretary or you were publishing feminist pamphlets and burning your bra. I was the former." She paused and took a delicate sip from her Coke. Her lipstick remained unsmudged though it left a trace of red on her straw. "Most of us at the time wanted to be writers. I suppose I did as much as anyone, and so we'd spend our days editing and we'd spend our nights writing. What was funny was that we knew all the people we were sending our drivel to, we'd met them at luncheons or for after hours drinks. I was embarrassed. I was a good editor and *because* I was a good editor I knew I wasn't a very good writer. I thought, how on earth will these men take me seriously if they see what I'm coming up with?

"So I did what most women did at the time, or anyone who wasn't Daphne du Maurier anyway, and I made up a name. Mine was Victor Wolf, which today seems so damned fake I don't know why no one thought anything of it. Or maybe they did but they just didn't care. Anyway I may have been writing garbage but eventually the garbage got better and I started getting some of it published. It was what they called Kooks and Spooks stuff, I suppose, sort of crime fiction but with some other bits thrown in, monsters sometimes, and ghosts. Possession—or Russian spies using hypnosis to control young American teenagers, that sort of thing. There was a real taste for that sort of thing back then. By the early seventies the papers were going crazy, telling us the irrationalism of our reading was helping the Commies and we had to get back to old-fashioned American literature. But *Rosemary's Baby* was an absolute hit, and then there was *The Exorcist* and people just wanted more of it.

"That was when Bear's first manuscript came across my desk. The two of us call it an accident but it wasn't that, not really. See, I was used to reading submissions for Donnie Rogers and when I finished Bear's first one I knew there was magic in it; raw, maybe, but magic nonetheless. And I knew Donnie was slated for laparoscopic gallbladder surgery. He was going to be off for at least a week recovering. That was when I tried to pitch the manuscript.

"Of course, I got laughed out of the offices. No one took me seriously and when Donnie came back he heard what I'd done and he bawled me out in front of the whole crew. Jesus, he took a strip off one side of me and then the other. After that I didn't dare try anything like that for a good long while.

"Still, Bear had appreciated the support. He was poor as a church mouse and he and Mya had a second little one on the way. He tried me with this and that a couple of times but it never really made it anywhere. I guess it was while he was sending me his stuff that I sent him one of mine. God, the nerve I had!" she chuckled and I couldn't help but chuckle along with her. "Well Bear wrote back and said it was pretty good, and I said it was better than pretty good, that *Playboy* had taken it. Bear had been trying to crack *Playboy* but hadn't managed it by that point.

"For six months Bear went silent after that and I guess I thought maybe I'd offended him. Men don't like being shown up; not then, not now. That's why there's all the craziness there is today. Women are afraid of violence, but men? Men are afraid of humiliation. Humiliation to them is like dying over and over and over again. And speaking of humiliation I had just about survived mine. Donnie Rogers had moved over to New American Libraries and I was covering for him while they looked for a replacement. That was when the next manuscript crossed my desk."

"That was *Rosie*?" I asked her.

"Indeed it was, though it was called *Revenge of the Stars* at the time which was a godawful title, I have to say."

"And this time it stuck?"

"Not right away it didn't. The ending was clunky. It had Rosie transforming into this giant radioactive slug thing and devouring the town that way. Pure St. John, you know. He always loved the EC comics stuff. People want to say he's got literary chops, and sure he does, but a part of him is pure pulp and is perfectly content to stay that way, thank you very much."

"So what happened?" I wanted to know.

"Oh, that's the easy bit. Some good luck, I suppose. Ira Levin was big and Bear's book was enough like that for me to pull together an advance for him. Small, you know. The real success came later with the paperback sales and that wasn't me, not exactly. But I suppose if what you're after is who found Barron St. John then it's me as much as it was anyone."

She paused there to take another long drag of her Coke. While she'd been talking she seemed so animated, so full of vigour but as the seconds stretched on I could see how old she was now, how time had etched fine lines around her lips. Her wrists were thin and frail, the skin bunching and slack at the same time.

She moved then, pulled up a black leather handbag and began to dig around in it. Eventually she came up with a Christmas card. "Look at that," she said, her eyes sharp. The paper was old and creased in several places. When I opened it there I found a simple hand-written note. *To Lilian*, it said, *a real wolf in sheep's clothing. We owe you so much. Love, Bear and Mya St. John*

Lily was smiling slightly as she showed it to me, smiling and watching to see my reaction. I tried to smile back but there was a part of me that felt disappointed. Most of the story was what she had published in that chapter. Little of it really surprised me. It felt rehearsed, the way you keep old memories by telling yourself the story behind them again and again. Whatever I was looking for, it wasn't there.

I was getting restless and it seemed like she was finished when she cocked her head to the side. "That's not what you wanted to hear, was it?"

I tried to tell her it was great, wonderful stuff. It would certainly make it into the article.

"Sure it will," she said, "but you didn't need any of it. Certainly you didn't need to fly over here from England just to get this story, did you? I could've told you that over the phone. You didn't need to come."

I shrugged.

"What you wanted was him, wasn't it? You wanted Bear."

"Maybe," I told her wearily. The heat was starting to get to me, making me a touch queasy.

"It isn't easy, you know," she said, "to try to tell your story when the best parts are about someone else." She sighed. "You know, I had to give up writing once I found St. John. It wasn't like it had been before. We were so busy all the time. St. John could write like a madman, he was *fast*. There was always another book. And then things got tricky with the contracts. You must know about this?"

I did. Everyone did. St. John had left Doubleday after a series of well-publicised contract disputes. Doubleday had been keeping most of the profits on the paperback sales and he felt he deserved a bigger cut. Doubleday wouldn't budge and eventually he left.

"There wasn't much I could do for him. They wouldn't give him a better deal and they wouldn't listen when I told them how serious he was about leaving. When he finally did switch publishers all those men at the top said it was *my* fault. I got parked for a while editing books on what types of music you can play to help your plants grow, that sort of kooky trash. After a year or so they fired me."

I fiddled with my own straw, unsure how to react to any of this.

"Bear didn't take me with him, see. I told him not to. I told him I had enough status in the company—but I was wrong. When you're on top you always think you're going to stay there forever, that there aren't sharks circling beneath. But I guess Barron knew about those sharks. The one thing he knew about was the sharks. He could be one himself when he needed to."

"You didn't want to go back to writing?"

"Nah, I felt I'd spent my chance by that point. I think I had one lucky break in me—and it went to St. John. There wasn't going to be another. I got by after that. I moved over to another house for a little while and convinced St. John to come do a book for us. But by that point things were different. He was a superstar and I felt spent. I had had enough of horror. It was the '80s. Despite everything it still felt as if the world was falling apart. There was the banking crisis, the AIDS epidemic. The people weren't reading the news though. They were reading Bear.

"I did write one more story though. I tried to sell it myself but no one would buy it. Victor Wolf had been forgotten. Bear liked it though. And he knew I was in danger of losing my mortgage. So he sent it out for me, under his name. When it sold to the *New Yorker*—his first real literary sale though God knows he deserved others and got them eventually—he gave me the profits." Her smile then was bitter. "I was grateful, you know. At the time he said it was only fair. I had made his name after all. I should get the use of it whenever I wanted.

"And I was grateful at the time. I kept my brownstone, paid it off eventually. When he sold the collection he gave me the whole advance. For a while I thought about going back to Ohio but I still couldn't admit to my parents I hadn't been able to last in New York. So instead I stayed."

She stared at me for a moment or two after that and I could feel the cool ripple of sadness passing over me like a shadow.

"Someone told me you died," I said, just to break the spell of her silence.

"Of the two of us, Barron was always the shark, you see?" she told me wryly, "No, I didn't die. I just learned something he never figured out: how to stay alive when you stop moving."

That evening I collected my things from Hotel 31.

Benny offered to drive me to the airport but I told him he didn't need to do that. I could get a taxi. The university had given me a budget for that. When he said okay it sounded like there was relief in his voice, and I wondered if that meant Emmanuel was home. Or maybe it was just that he didn't want to get so close to the airport. There were regular protests still going on. People were angry about the deportations but no one knew how to stop them.

"Did you get what you wanted from Lily Argo?" Benny asked me. "She wasn't just a ghost?" I told him I hadn't really known what I wanted but I was certain, despite everything, I had met Lily Argo. But probably I was going to scrap the story. My Head of Department would be pissed but that was how these things went. Sometimes you thought you had something and you didn't.

What she had told me felt too invasive to write about. What I had wanted, I realised, was not just her story but a glimpse of her secret self. I didn't have a right to it. And that's what had made me want it even more. Maybe we all have a secret self: some of us keep it chained in the basement of our minds while others like St. John learn how to feed it.

"Well," he said, "it was good to see you anyway. Give my love to Luca. You tell him to take proper care of you."

I promised I would.

While I waited for my flight to board I watched the news. We were all watching the news. We couldn't help it. Tense security officers patrolled the hallways with machine guns at the ready, just in case. There were fewer travellers those days, fewer coming in, fewer getting out. But I felt a kind of solidarity with the others as my eyes were glued to the screens. We were liminal people moving from one reality to another. We were going home.

So we watched the footage of explosions in Yemen. Pleas from refugees who had found themselves trapped in abandoned tenements, living in filth. It was only when I saw the story about the bomb that had gone off on a train along the Victoria Line that I remembered Luca still hadn't called me back.

I was watching them pulling survivors out of the rubble and the blood gelled to ice in my veins. I couldn't move. It had happened then. It had happened. Time seemed to slow. Luca mostly worked from Cambridge but the NGO had offices in London. He went there from time to time. When had I last heard from him? Who could I call to check? But by that point the attendant was calling me forward. I didn't move. She called me again and the people behind me began to murmur. I must have had a dazed expression on my face, a look they didn't like. The attendant called me a third time as an officer drew near. It was only then I was able to move. I showed them my passport and made my way down the ramp.

Inside the plane most of the seats were empty. The air was canned, stale tasting in my mouth. I wondered if I might have a panic attack but out on the runway I didn't dare check my phone again. The hostesses were murmuring to each other. I could tell they were twitchy. But already a strange calm was taking hold of me—a sense of icy horror. There was something inevitable about what was happening. There was nothing I could do to stop it. Whatever had happened had happened.

And this feeling? It wasn't the same as all those St. John books I had read. There I could find purpose, structure—meaning in all the bad things that had happened. But outside there was only chaos. The unravelling of beautiful things into violence. It signified nothing.

As the plane taxied down the runway I settled back in my chair and tried to sleep.

CONRAD WILLIAMS

CWTCH

CONRAD WILLIAMS is the author of nine novels: *Head Injuries*, *London Revenant*, *The Unblemished*, *One*, *Decay Inevitable*, *Loss of Separation*, *Dust and Desire*, *Sonata of the Dead* and *Hell is Empty*. His short fiction is collected in *Use Once Then Destroy*, *Born with Teeth* and *I Will Surround You*. He has won the British Fantasy Award, the International Horror Guild Award and the Littlewood Arc Prize and has been a finalist for the Shirley Jackson Awards and the Crime Writers' Association Daggers. He lives in Manchester with his wife and three sons. He is currently working on a new novel.

'Cwtch'—which has also recently been reprinted in *Best British Short Stories*—was inspired by a family walk through the countryside while camping in the Lake District. "There was a section of the walk through knee-high grass," recalls Williams. "I looked back at the tracks I'd made and immediately had a vision of another set of tracks added later, giving a suggestion of casual pursuit. It gave me the creeps, and I knew I'd have to find a way of incorporating it into a story.

"Sometimes that's how it happens. You see a scene play out in your mind and you know it's a keeper. The fun starts when you have to build a beginning and an end around it."

S ALTER WOKE IN the night and this time the screams were real. Raw, lusty, the kind of scream only an infant can make. It seemed so close as to be just the other side of the canvas. This was his first night on the campsite. The family had turned up to their pitch late: Salter had eaten dinner and was reading by torchlight as a middle-aged man in shorts and a waterproof coat cursed over a jumble of poles and pegs. His partner switched on a radio tuned to old pop songs despite the camp rules stipulating no music at any time. Salter had purposefully selected this campsite because it was not child friendly, it didn't allow pets and it placed a premium on silence. Why couldn't people adhere to simple rules? Why was there this constant flouting of regulations? It might seem trivial to them—*it's only OMD, lighten up, Grandpa*—but this was his holiday, a rare chance to enjoy some rest and recuperation before returning to the grind.

And now this infant, shrieking [greeting, skriking]. Salter checked his watch. Just shy of 5:00 a.m. He rolled off his mattress and flexed the muscles complaining in his back before pulling open the tent flaps and sticking out his head. Folds of drizzle [mizzle, Scotch mist], colour low in the sky: green and pale gold where dawn threatened. Opposite, screaming miles of black. The cries became muffled, as if the parents had noticed his appearance and were trying their best to soothe the child. The poor thing might be teething, or suffering a cold. Well... they could have chosen to not bring it here, he thought, knowing that for a few pounds more he could have stayed in a B&B and not been disturbed at all. But part of the reason for this holiday— for these holidays—was because it was what he had done as a young boy. Abersoch, Dolgellau, Port Eynon. Each summer his mum and dad had loaded up the old Austin Princess with tents and fishing rods and they'd follow the M56 to Wales, him in the back seat with a *Beano* and a quarter of aniseed twists, specially for the trip. *Save one for Mo,* Dad would say. And he did, every time. His mum and dad would bicker good-naturedly about what they listened to on the cassette player and it was usually his mum who prevailed. Everyone she liked seemed to be called Joan or Joni and all of the songs seemed to be happy and sad at the same time.

At the end of all this road there'd be the usual bellyaches [gripes, protests, whinges] about pitching the tent in the wrong place, or getting the groundsheet pinned down incorrectly...but the bad tempers didn't last long. He would find a nice spot and bury that final sweet for Mo, Mum would get some pasta going on the camping stove and Dad would tuck into a couple of cans of McEwan's. There would be rain, and complaints about bad backs. Fish would be caught or, more likely, wouldn't. They played cards. They told jokes. He had loved these holidays.

Now he rolled up his night things knowing that he wouldn't be able to catch hold of the tail of sleep [shuteye, kip, slumber] so there was no longer any point in trying. He dressed quickly and reached for his raincoat, unzipping the tent at speed in order to make as much noise as possible. The violent sound of it was close and waspish in the dark. He would have words with the owner when the office opened at 9:00. He needed rest and no distractions. So much of his normal everyday life was riddled with noise that he craved these oases in the year, rare and precious holidays that allowed him to reflect and, yes, heal [repair, recover, mend]. He believed he was still coming back from that childhood insult—the shock and the unacknowledged pain; a grief that would not hatch in him—and only silence could provide the environment in which he might achieve that release.

He walked to the far edge of the campsite where a perimeter fence gave access to a track through the woods. Beyond those trees Craig y Cilau rose like a sheer grey wave. Pockets of golden light opened up on the rock face as breaks appeared in the cloud that had clung to the base of the mountain all night. Already there were climbers arranged upon the limestone.

Crossing the track he entered the woods at their thinnest point. Sunlight was filtering through here too, gilding the whitebeam and adding varnish to the boughs of rowan and hawthorn. He had no idea where he was going. Away was enough: he could still hear the child's agonised, red cries rising in the trough behind him. Three hours until Davis, in his self-important tweeds and his moisturised beard, came down from his nice stone cottage to open the office and treat everyone with an air of amused indifference.

The crack of a twig underfoot highlighted the depth of quiet he had stumbled into. He could no longer hear the child; its shrieks had been replaced by the soft suck and blow of a breeze sifting through the limbs. It was as if the wood had lungs and he had detected the rhythms of its breathing. He could smell moss and fungus, a mix of the clean and the corrupt, and, he was sure, the mineral aroma of the warming rock face. He felt the tension of the last few hours lift a little.

The family must have been unaware of the regulations, as unlikely as that sounded. Salter was not a father, but he tried to put himself in the shoes of those people now. They'd be more stressed than him, that was for sure. At least he could have a nap this afternoon when fatigue [lassitude, enervation] inevitably caught up with him. They would undoubtedly be asked to move their pitch to one of the neighbouring camps where families were tolerated. He'd help them relocate if that was the case. Everything would be fine.

He was a little out of breath by the time he broke through the far stand of trees into full sunlight. Since observing the climbers on Craig y Cilau Salter had seen no other people. He craved that sense of being alone, the illusion of the last man on Earth, to the extent that he felt cheated and disappointed [crestfallen, despondent] whenever he spotted a figure clinging to rock, or a car winding along the A465, or the peal of a distressed child in a badly constructed tent. Now though, he was here for a different reason. Mo. Though he couldn't work out the impulse for it. Could it just be as simple as a need to tidy up the strands of his life now that he was closer to the end than the beginning? For so many years he had avoided coming to the Brecons, but why? It was not as if he could remember much about his sister. He felt that those memories he did have of her were informed by the photographs in his parents' old albums; Kodacolor prints he had picked through only once since their death. Invariably, the photographs of Mo displayed a toddler with long, fine blonde locks (from birth until her death, they had not cut her hair), her hands outstretched, begging a hug, or for someone to pick her up. Salter was never in these pictures, which was another reason why he felt a buffer between himself and his grief, if grief was what it could be called. How could you grieve for what you had never consciously known? How did you love a sister who had been in your life for only two years?

He stood at the edge of the trees and opened his arms, opened himself to a feeling that would not come. They had been twins, but there was never any of that rumoured synergy. No telepathic communion. No phantom muscle recollection. The breath in the trees intensified as if in sympathy. He watched the canopy wave. The moment moved on; he came to his senses, feeling self-conscious, foolish.

Three sheep paused in their cropping to watch as he picked a route across stony ground. He angled through another field, though a sign on the gate asked that ramblers restrict themselves to the edges. Lines of blue mould in a cracked plastic bathtub drew a map of a world he didn't understand. He'd always felt apart, on the edge of things, as if life was filled with codes he didn't have the key to access. He resented his parents for that, believing their withdrawal from the public eye in the wake of Mo's death had included him too. Their protection of him became smothering, but he never felt it was motivated by true love, more out of guilt, or some misplaced effort to atone [expiate, recompense]. His father had slapped him across the face when he suggested it was a little too late for that.

They used Mo as a stick with which to beat him. So many times over the years to the point where they no longer had to use euphemisms to suggest that if any child should die, it ought to have been him. It was in the cast of their faces; the language of their ever more stooping bodies.

Salter had trained to become a teacher, anticipating that spending time with children might help him cope with his suite of insecurities, but all it did was trap him in a prison of "what if?". He daydreamed elaborate fantasies in which he somehow managed to rescue Mo, prevent her from falling into the pond rather than being the one to find her. He set his class exercises and then watched as they frowned over their books, wondering if Mo might have grown up to talk like Susan Webb, or laugh like Debra Barker, or would she have been naughty, like Kathy Bowden?

He mythologised the discovery of her body, unable to remember what had happened, conscious [aware, sentient] only that he had discovered her because of second-hand stories, heavily censored by parents who did not want him to have to deal with the trauma. Instead he internalised it, torturing himself with any number of death scenes. It was a wonder he didn't drown too; the pair of them were little older than two, relatively new to the task of walking.

The image that stuck in his mind more than any—which persuaded him to believe it was authentic [*bona fide*, genuine]—involved the slow roll of Mo's head in the blue/black water of the pond as her face returned to the surface. Her fine hair was arranged around her like glass noodles left too long to soak. Her mouth and eyes were open, and he always recoiled from that part of his recollection, the infant part of his mind upset that she was swallowing dirty water and would get a poorly tummy. Her arms were outstretched; even in death she was keen for a cuddle.

Salter exhaled in the silence and it was a ragged, unnerving sound. He gazed back in the direction of the campsite and saw the route he had carved through the deep grass, a dark green oblique bisecting the field. Beyond that he could just make out the small parallelogram tents peeking over the tops of the trees. He could see now that his quickening breath was as much to do with the gradual incline he was ascending, as any delayed childhood shock. The early morning sunlight persisted, but grey cloud, like the edifices of stone they towered over, was gathering. He would walk as far as the river and then return for breakfast and a reckoning with Davis. He shook his head clear of unpleasantness; enough thinking about Mo for now.

He stretched his legs and strode hard along a path under the rock-face, enjoying the heat building at his back. Muscles in his legs sang; he knew they would ache later, but it would be a good ache, telling of honest exercise. His thoughts returned to the classroom. He'd brought a little marking with him that he would enjoy: stories by his pupils written without fear, something he found common to primary school

children in the main. Something that sadly would be unlikely to last
as self-consciousness kicked in and distractions mounted. There were
some children who had natural skill [expertise, adroitness], a real feel
for words, as he had done as a boy. He remembered being teased for
taking a dictionary with him on a school trip. His peers nicknamed
him "The 'Saurus" because he was constantly getting his pupils to
come up with synonyms, a habit that he couldn't shake himself; he
was often consulted in the staff room regarding a crossword clue, or
a letter that needed to be precisely worded.

He reached a stile almost fully concealed by bright green lichen.
Over that, a field of what looked like stubbled barley dipped away to
a barn in the far corner. By the time he reached the building—little
more than a weather-thrashed lean-to built from asbestos cement
and corrugated iron roofing—it had begun to rain. Now he could see
a series of single-storey outbuildings hopscotched amid the green
beyond. Salter pulled up his hood and watched the thick grey clouds
spend themselves. Black nets of rain hung across the sky like dirty
curtains in a terrace filled with secrets. The only sound was a stippling
against his waxed jacket. It felt as if he was at a moment of poise, or
pause. It felt as if something would develop imminently: he was
tensed for the explosion of wings as a heron broke through the tree
line or a rabbit shot out of clover. Nothing like that transpired, but the
feeling remained and his heart rose to meet it.

The sound of running water turned his head. For a moment he
thought the downspout from the gutter was blocked with hair, but it
was only water, hurtling from the mouth in a shock of white. Thin
veils of cloud sank from the top of the mountain and removed sense,
softened edges. A cow despondently chewing its cud became a sepia
stain on blotting paper. Cold found its way past the toggles of his
jacket; he wished he'd taken the time to prepare a flask of coffee, but
anger had ushered him from his tent. It was time to go back. The sun
had threatened enough and retreated quite possibly for the rest of the
day given the thickening shroud and the absence of any breeze to
shift it along.

A single magpie ducked and fluttered, washing itself in a dip in the
barn's concrete apron. The ancient shadow of an oil-puddle. Rust

ghosts in the wall told of machinery grown old, defunct, removed. There was an old wheel-barrow inside the barn, and a tyre torn through to its steel belts. Dead nests of things long gone. Water lipped troughs and gutters. It spanged off the metal roofs.

Salter did not drink water; not in its purest state, not any more. It had to be blended with some other beverage: tea or coffee, an ice cube in his gin and tonic. His parents had to fool him into imbibing water by disguising it in a cordial of some kind, or topping up his cocoa from the kettle. They had always shielded him from the truth, perhaps believing that to protect him in this way gave them licence to take their anger, frustration and guilt out on him. Not that they would ever admit as much. How could they? How could any parent acknowledge such an egregious transfer? He trudged back, raking the burning embers of his resentment; every little spiteful episode. The pointed fingers. The heated asides.

His route took him alongside the river, now swollen and fast, groaning under the weight of itself. It was unlikely to remain clear for much longer as the muddy banks were encouraged to became part of the flow. For now, though, he could see into the heart of the river, and the reeds trapped there, like slender arms waving in the current.

She could not say his name. *Trevor.* He seemed to remember her trying, but she got the name twisted in her mouth. *Rover,* she used to say. That was it. *Rover.* "Mo," he said now, in response to that memory, and the simplicity of it, the stark snap of it in the relative quiet shocked him. He had not uttered her name in twenty years, at least. The trees murmured again, as if he'd spoken too loud. Already he suspected he might have done. His breathing would not settle; he could feel, see, even, the torment of his heart in the materials layered across his chest. That sense of imminence. Perhaps he was anticipating thunder in some lizard chamber of his back brain, as other animals were able. But there was no such rumour in the colour or shape of these clouds. Panic gnawed at him. Heart attacks were a shadow in his bloodline. He had stumbled upon a dead rabbit on one camping trip, its splintered [fragmented, spillikin] ribs splayed to allow access to the soft vitals within; it was too easy to imagine himself become much the same. Perhaps under the beak of that magpie, and whatever else hunkered in the undergrowth with a nose for carrion. *Please don't let me die out here, alone.* The hiss of the trees. Had he spoken aloud again? Despite everything, he laughed.

He came back along the bank until he could avoid it no longer and strode into the stand of trees. Gloom and sullen silence under the canopy now. Odour of petrichor. He felt swaddled, but there was no comfort in it. When he reached the edge of the trees he saw his tracks in the field again, those deep green furrows, but now they had been supplemented by another set of narrower tracks, weaving in and around his determined pattern like those of a dog, or a small child. The rain intensified and he couldn't understand if it was the hiss of that he was hearing or those incessant trees. A sharp intake of breath at the witnessing of atrocity. The cusp of something. It was like that game he had played as a child. When someone hid something and you went looking for it. Warm, warmer, colder, cold. Hot now. Very hot. Boiling.

Nothing had ever been cut and dried in his life. There was always doubt [uncertainty, confusion, hesitancy]. It might have had something to do with his never marrying. He didn't feel comfortable taking that risk with someone, a person he could never know as well as himself. And the fact he didn't know himself all too well meant that any chance of intimacy was stymied from the start. "Buggered every which way", as his dad had been fond of saying.

He stumbled into a clearing. He knew this place. This arrangement of wood and water. The peculiar sweep of land. He saw the pond and cried out at the pale oval turning slowly within it. But it was only a soft glancing of light finding its way between the cradle of branches. He heard the cry of the child again, and knew there was no such thing. There was no child on the campsite.

"Dad," he said, and steadied himself against the bole of a tree. It was as if, viewing it all again, fifty years on, a match had been made in his head, like a copy on tracing paper aligned with the original. "Mum."

Dead a dozen years now. He was the last of the Salters. And their name would die with him.

He crouched and placed his hand in the cold water, wishing his infancy back, a crucial few seconds in which he might have made a difference. Everything could have changed since that pivot in time. All of those holidays he remembered since Mo's death. The sham of their routines. The jokes. The games. They were told and played behind masks. Nobody was who they had been before. He had hated these holidays. Yes, he had hated them. The last sweet for Mo? He had eaten them all.

He thought of the way his parents regarded him as he grew up. That barely concealed mixture of revulsion and guilt. Laced with something else, he thought now. Fear, was it? What if? What if?

He heard movement in the undergrowth. That moment opening up again. That bubble of imminence. He dredged his hand through the water, ruining the calm of the pond. He fancied he felt something winding itself around his fingers, but when he pulled them clear, there was nothing to see. He stood up. All his life he had been pushing people away. Always pushing people away. Always pushing. He didn't have a word for what he had done.

The trees hissed as he closed his eyes and Mo coalesced there, reaching out for him as he had done for her half a century ago. The arms that tried to encircle his body were much too short for the task.

GEMMA FILES

LAGAN

G EMMA FILES was formerly a film critic, journalist, screenwriter and teacher, and has been an award-winning horror author since 1999. She has published two collections of short work (*Kissing Carrion* and *The Worm in Every Heart*), two chapbooks of speculative poetry (*Bent Under Night* and *Dust Radio*), a Weird Western trilogy (the "Hexslinger" series—*A Book of Tongues, A Rope of Thorns* and *A Tree of Bones*), a story-cycle (*We Will All Go Down Together: Stories of the Five-Family Coven*) and an award-winning stand-alone novel (*Experimental Film*).

The author has two new story collections from Trepidatio (*Spectral Evidence* and *Drawn Up From Deep Places*), one upcoming from Cemetery Dance (*Dark Is Better*), and a new poetry collection from Aqueduct Press (*Invocabulary*).

She is currently working on a book of essays about horror culture as comfort food in an age of fear.

"In maritime law, the terms 'flotsam', 'jetsam' and 'lagan' describe specific and distinct kinds of wreckage," explains Files. "'Jetsam' describes goods voluntarily cast into the sea (jettisoned) by the crew of a ship, usually to lighten it in an emergency. 'Flotsam' describes goods left floating on the water by accident, often after a shipwreck. Both may generally be salvaged, reverting to the original owner only if explicitly claimed.

"'Lagan', on the other hand, is the term for goods that have been marked, most often by a buoy, so the previous owner can retrieve it later. Lagan therefore remains that owner's property, and cannot be salvaged unless it can be legally proven that the owner is either dead, or abandoned it under circumstances which assured they could not possibly have ever held out any real hope of recovering it.

"It's oddly amusing to me to recall that at one point, I was known for writing specifically erotic horror—I sold five stories to Ridley and Tony Scott's blood-and-nudity anthology cable TV series, *The Hunger*, after all, and two of my earliest placements were in Michael Rowe's seminal anthologies *Queer Fear* and *Queer Fear II*. Writing the "Hexslinger Series" also gave me a bit of a reputation, I suppose, or at least enough of one to get a lot of irate Amazon reviews from users who hadn't expected any hot gay sex in their Weird Western with Aztec gods and black magic.

"These days, however, I just don't get to flex those muscles much anymore . . . not unless somebody like Vince Liaguno comes along, at least.

"So here was Vince, asking me to write something specifically erotic, specifically queer, and specifically horrifying. The three components that immediately popped into my head were the fetish known as *vore* (a fantasy of deriving sexual satisfaction from consuming and/or being consumed, from *Hannibal*-style cannibal cookouts to feeding yourself to some overpowering animal). The general dread and mystery of the sea (they're always finding stuff that's new down there, and it's often awful!—the sea is like an endless, deceptively gorgeous stew of parasitism and predation!— except for all the parts of it we humans have fucked up beyond repair, because that's just the sort of garbage-spreading eco-terrorists we are!); and the sort of chimeric, combinative, alchemical body horrors that rest securely somewhere between David Cronenberg's *The Fly* and John Carpenter's *The Thing*.

"How does the thing they pull from the sea in 'Lagan' work, exactly? Don't ask me, mate—I'm no scientist. I just know what scares me, and what I like, and how what I like scares me. And here's the result.

"Enjoy."

The sea is so much deeper than the grave.
                    —Robyn Hitchcock.

"YOU LOOK LIKE shit," Sean said. "Seriously, mate. Like you haven't slept in yonks."

Draped across the rail, Ric didn't bother to shake his head. "That's 'cause I haven't."

Barely gone noon, the air even below-decks so hot everybody felt mildly feverish. Not that Sean'd be able to tell, really, barring recourse to the 'Net; though he'd bluffed his way on board (with Ric's connivance) by mis-representing his summer job at Auntie Di's veterinary clinic as some sort of pre-med internship, all he'd had to do thus far was dole out dramamine, ibuprofen, Polysporin and Band-aids. Oh, and stitch up a few shallow wounds here and there, but that's where a strong stomach and Mum's sewing lessons came in handy.

"Best go down, then," Sean suggested. "Knock a few back, have a bit of a zizz . . ."

"Can't do that, mate." Ric looked at him full on, then—face haggard under its tan, eyes bruise-set, like they'd been boiled. "I do that, I'll have the dream. And then . . . yeah, better not."

Which dream's this, again? Sean thought of saying, but didn't.

But Ric was already deep into monologue-mode: ". . . like I'm drowning, or . . . remember the one about cats sitting on babies' faces, stealing their breath? Like I'm being pressed down by something, so hard I'm paralysed, and it covers my face so I can't breathe, all warm and moist but not furry at all, it's *skin*, flat as a bag, and wrinkled, and naked. Like . . . somebody else's bloody scrotum."

"Ah, Jesus, now I *know* you're not serious."

"You're the one fuckin' asked, you prat."

To which Sean simply shrugged and leant back against the rail, arms crossed to ward off a vague, creeping discomfort. "That's just a night-hag, Ric; bloody sleep apnoea, dressed up like the Late-Night Fright Show. Sure you're not speeding again?"

"Been out going on a week, so no." But even total exhaustion couldn't completely root out the essential Ric-ness, same eyebrow-waggling comic charm which'd originally fished Sean in, at least halfway. "S'pose a quick blowie's out the question, then?"

"And that'd pay back for me how, exactly?"

"Fresh protein?"

Without wanting to, Sean found himself hovering on the verge of laughter before biting it back, hard. "Thanks, but no thanks. How's about a few aspirins and a massage, and we call it even?"

"Prick-tease."

"Well, you know me."

Ric shot him a dark look from under equally dark lashes, genuinely too knackered to take further offence. Just as well: six-two of enraged Melbourne Greek was nothing to sneeze at, the best of times, and Sean really didn't feel up to doing yet another *piss-off-out-of-my-personal-space* Macarena with the fucker, below-decks or above-. He one-eightied to look out over the water instead.

Sometimes the ocean seemed a bright-burnt skin they could crawl upon blindly, persuading themselves it was impenetrable, but this wasn't one of those days. The usual salt-haze had boiled off, discovering all too clearly the near-endless soup of part-degraded garbage and haphazard death they floated in: the Great Pacific Garbage Knot's outermost gyre, folding all manner of entropised crap in towards the centre, where it could hit, stick, grow by incredibly slow degrees into the loose trash-conglomerate "island" that rumours now reckoned at roughly half the size of Texas.

Around them, "Captain" Shaftoe's folly let out a chorus of groans, like small animals were being pinched between its joints. Dougray Shaftoe himself having only the barest interest in boats for their own sake, it was nameless except for its maritime registry code; between themselves, Ric and Sean had taken to calling it the *Bad Idea*, persisting long after the joke stopped being funny. A full-displacement hull outrigger shrimp trawler from New Guinea, Shaftoe had had it converted to salvage-hauler by removing the refrigeration equipment, freeing up storage space for that legendary cargo harvest he was sure would drift into their laps if they only camped out by the Knot long enough. Chief amongst many things he hadn't really reckoned on, though, was the lingering stench of a million hauls past, which made sleeping on the *Idea* a fairly disgusting exercise in itself, nightmares notwithstanding.

Neither the actual smell nor the general stench of idiocy hovering 'round this venture had seemed quite so obvious back in Port Moresby, where Sean had been stupidly content to stand by as a blind-drunk Ric threw both their oars in with Shaftoe's crew. Still, ridiculous as this all seemed in hindsight—especially from his current perspective, bobbing like a tin-can in the middle of arse-end nowhere with a bunch of similarly delusional losers—at least he hadn't compounded the mistake by giving it up to Ric later on, considering what a berk he'd since turned out to be. And it was the rancid aftertaste of that not-quite-relationship, in fact—liberally cut with five weeks of too-close quarters, and Ric's increasing craziness throughout—which now kept Sean securely at arm's length, unwilling to dole out even a perfunctory clap on the shoulder (*Cheer up, mate! Could be worse . . . somehow*), lest it be misconstrued as a come-on.

"We're all in the same boat, though, aren't we?" Ric demanded, breaking Sean's train of thought. "Like, literally."

"You're right there," Sean agreed. But felt his gaze drawn further down, towards the hatch, where that all-important first piece of flotsam they'd picked up still lay discarded—a dark green, plastic-blend hull-chip marked with the centre-set yellow letters EEN and PHOE.

Green Phoenix.

Experimental craft, whole thing's made out of recyclables, Sean had told Shaftoe, running three searches at once, while the rest of the tiny crew loomed angrily 'round them. *They launched, uh . . . two years back, off of California; big idea was to surf currents all the way here, tracing the gyre's path and taking samples of all the garbage that went along with 'em. Been out of contact for . . . nine months, looks like.*

Private venture?

Corporate—ReVive, a subset of Grummacher Pan-Oceanic. WikiLeaks says they set it up as a PR dodge, to shift attention off those dumping scandals.

So . . . they'd pay to find out what happened to it, yeah?

Yeah, sure. Probably.

Which gave them a plan, at long last. That little piece of drift was the best "catch" they'd had since pushing off, one way or the other— and it'd certainly stopped that potential mutiny in its tracks, for which Shaftoe'd privately declared himself grateful. As he bloody well should be.

Trouble had started a fortnight back, when Arjit and Sam-I-Am went poking 'round in the hold, only to discover half the crates down there were empty rather than supply-packed—meant for that endless flood of three-year-old jetsam Shaftoe'd been shit-sure would flock their way, they only made it to the Knot and camped out in its orbit. So far—as one might only expect, given the original plan's intensely un-researched laziness—it hadn't exactly panned out; the stuff they did rake from the water tended to be either damaged or worthless, with an occasional side-order of resale-unfriendly randomness. (An entire crate of little party balloons that blew up into funny animal shapes, for example, seemed virtually designed not to attract big eBay bidders, unless one of them turned out to be a nostalgic Nicolas Cage.)

What are we gonna do for food, then? Arjit'd demanded, understandably.

Fish? was Shaftoe's grand suggestion. *Ship's already set up for it, right?*

Yeah. Except that the area was *contaminated*, as befit a fucking two hundred and fifty thousand square mile dump, a rummage-bin toxin-patch culled from here to China; every catch they brought up was half corpses, scales dull and lifting, gills deformed, their bloated stomachs stuffed with degrading plastic leaching fluorocarbons. Sam-I-Am took to sharpening his clasp-knife, while Arjit spoke darkly of how easy it would be to signal pirates, if not simply give Shaftoe (who'd holed himself up in his cabin, where he kept at least two guns) the stealthy heave some night, and become them.

Then Sean found the *Green Phoenix* drift while flushing out the bilges, done some satellite uplink-grade asking 'round, and made his pitch. Radar and hard work did the rest—hadn't taken much past forty-eight hours, in the end: a media event, just waiting to happen. The whole of the wreck, or what was left, plus an arse-load of lagan clearly marked with reVive's eco-friendly tramp stamp. Plus, inside one of them, something even Sean could've never foreseen . . .

. . . a survivor.

Above water-level, the garbage piles together in shoals, mortared with its own melt; pollution becomes cement, suture, cobbling a crazy-quilt that daily grows more dense. Beneath, the underside spirals down in tails like kelp, great interlocking daisy-chains of current like inverted tornadoes: Turning and turning, an endless fishline loop, to scrape at the sea-bottom.

Under the water, down in the dark; where light fades as it diffuses, where things become slimy and inappropriate, unreadable as some alien alphabet. The mimic-octopus on the off-reef floor, masquerading as either what it eats or fears—burying itself until only two or three limbs are visible, a coiled knot of mock sea-snakes, poison-banded. The sponge angler, further down and dimmer, rooting itself amidst anemone-forests and great shell-shelves—flicking one long spine out and back, out and back into the oncoming current, to reel in unwary prey. The glass-headed barrel-eyes, prowling restless at Immeasurable Depths—swivelling its nostrils in two different directions at once, negotiating by its nude brain's light, mouth wide for whatever it chances to blunder against.

None of us are what we seem below a certain depth, where narcosis' inevitable prospect transmutes to one immense, all-over kiss, suffocation a blissful blessing. Caught up in this joyful sub-tide, we forget our original forms, grow fluid and slippery, like drowned men's flesh. We degrade by degrees, scatter our bones at random in a broken necklace, and watch them turn to coral.

Even further down, bones are a luxury, far too easily crushed. Here we become elastic, infinitely supple; we drift, exerting no unnecessary effort, reshaping ourselves to whatever comes along. Gelid, we spin ourselves out like ropes, chains of stomachs inside stomachs. We digest, and are digested, in turn.

Thus hunger in itself becomes a form of selflessness, a form of worship. A form of love.

Sean still couldn't figure if it'd been blind luck, seat-of-the-pants cunning, or maybe a fortuitous combo of the two. When they'd first dredged it up, the rig looked like half a car-wreck fused with found-object sculpture—mucky scribble of knotted-up lead line cross-knit with weed, an American flag reduced to sodden ribbons lashing half a trimaran pontoon to one side of a rickety, semi-compacted shipping crate, whole thing stoppered by a massive, partially-cracked rainwater cycling tank they only later realised had been haphazardly patched with sail tape, from the inside. Just a random conglomeration of garbage, or so they'd thought, 'til they tried to lift it: Impossibly heavy, shadowed internally, sloshing with who knew what. When Shaftoe gave the order, the crate's sodden remnants prised up and away on three, like husking a coconut.

And there *he'd* been, inside: curled foetal, skin a too-soft mess of salt and burn—like he'd been steeping in his own filth for weeks, poached egg-style under that relentless sun. Try to pull him out now, and Sean could already see his hide ruck, bones ground like marbles in a sock from bobbing through twenty-foot waves, meat beneath just a rancid stew. That bright thatch of hair slipping off beneath prying fingers, an ill-glued skullcap.

Sean caught his breath at the very idea, deep. Then gasped, almost retching, as he seemed to feel the whole cobbled-together escape pod's funk come in at his eyeballs, ream him from stem to stern; not so bad, really, once you got used to it. Not *so* very bad, at all.

Which was when the man in question had opened his eyes, green-guileless as the sea itself, and looked at him.

They got him down to "sickbay" (ie, Sean's storage-closet of a bunk), sent Sam-I-Am and Ric back up for a gallon jug of fresh, and started the process—cut away what was left of his clothes, sluiced him down, sponged away the shed. What emerged was sallow yet weirdly fresh-looking, free of scars and hair alike, cool and firm to the touch. No detectable pulse at neck or wrist, so Sean was forced to search further afield: brush his torpid tackle aside, snoozing oyster-slack in the shadow of his equally blond groin's half-shell, and feel for the femoral. Which did indeed respond, albeit sluggishly, as though still underwater.

Then: *Aussie,* his patient'd suddenly observed, mouth not even sounding dry after what had to be days of drifting, and not seeming concerned at all about a stranger's hand in his crotch; it was a soothing voice with vowels worn flat, classic SoCal drawl up-climbing towards the sentence's end, familiar from any one of a hundred TV commercials. *'M I... near there, now?*

Closer to Papua the one side, Indonesia the other.

So... still in th' Knot, then.

Still, yeah. Don't try to talk.

Then Sean scooped two fingertips' worth of water, let the guy suck it back, and felt his tongue's unexpected heat lave the prints; immediately, his cheekbones burnt hectic, saliva-scoured nerves firing raw, nape sweat-damp. To fend off a blush, he contradicted himself, asking: *You're Grinnage, right? Simon? Navigator, did all the IT work... I saw your Photo Stream on Flickr.*

... 'f you say so.

Look, you either are or you aren't, mate. It's not multiple bloody choice.

The guy made a sketchy attempt at a shrug, which worked out more like a ripple. He seemed limp, leached, like all his minerals were gone.

Could be, he allowed, finally.

A cough. Sean looked up to find Shaftoe in the doorway, arms crossed, frowning. Demanding: *What's that even mean, son?*

Means... I could be this... whoever you said. Or not. Could be you, or him...

(nodding here at Sean, who coloured again, obliquely embarrassed)

... or anybody.

Nemo, Sean'd thought, at the time, same as cyclops Polyphemus in his cave: curse of a Classical education, though it did make reading MedicalWiki entries a fair bit easier. *No Man. I will eat No Man last, as my guest-gift. Come quickly and help me, brothers, for No Man has put my eye out!*

Shaftoe shrugged once more, like he was throwing off flies. *Well. Whoever you are, you should be grateful, eh? 'Specially to* this *one. He's the bloke found you—your ship, anyhow. Man saved your bloody life.*

Sean gave a dismissive headshake, mumbled something down into his neck, but those mild eyes—washed clean, tide-abraded, like sea-glass—had already turned back his way. They caught him up without prejudice, neat as a flounder's sand-plus-prey suction, and swallowed him whole.

Thank you, the man from the sea told him. To which Sean could only reply—

. . . you're welcome.

And now Sean finds himself once more sunk deep in his own dreams— no Freudian rape-fantasies here, no flesh-bag settling over him, sliding a proboscis down his throat and digesting him from the inside. These visions are all numbing cold and softness, dark on dark, the gloom he floats in only further obscured by a silken mesh of movement: Narcosis, shipwreck-hypnotism, the endless waves, amniotic. The lure of the drift. The lure of letting go.

Because: What do I have to keep me here, after all? What did I ever have?

This stinking boat, Shaftoe's folly. These awful people, him very much included. Just crap and garbage, a tainted, tainting mess of air-breathers' detritus. Trash in a soup of trash, under which something else lurks, unrecognised—something tempted slowly upwards by the scent of change, of possibility. Unrealised hungers revealed, made suddenly attainable, the same way bodies fruit, decay sliding fast from waste to potential.

In his marrow, Sean simply knows these aimless loops of sleep-thought are nothing to fear; quite the opposite, really. Weirdly pleasurable, in a purely perverse way: Circuitous skull-spirals, itch-scratchingly slow, which clear him out so completely he often looks forward to returning to them in progress, even while awake . . . some-times feels he'd gladly sleep all fuckin' day to do so, he only could . . .

(but don't tell Ric that, mate)

Like back when he was twelve, travelling the Great Barrier Reef with his mum and dad, and he side-stroked without looking first right into the middle of a Lion's Mane jellyfish bloom: that clench of recognition, filaments already wrapping 'round him from every side in streamers, pale poison-full vermicelli, just beginning to sting him with their multitudinous fine hairs. A caress on its way to becoming a wound.

There at the edge of the shelf, the last clump of brain and cup and stone before the drop-off: clear shading to blue shading to black, going down down down into nothing. He'd hung above an abyss, spun sugar-caged by luminous mucus, watching the jellies' stomachs pulse like hearts through their sides, and contemplated—in one skipped beat, one breathless no-scream—the utter end of the world.

What's down there, Dad?

Things you've never seen, son. Things you never will see.

(Things you never want to.)

But separate, always, kept down by pressure, gravity versus its lack. No place in our world for their eddying, porous likes, and barely any room in theirs for us: fragile in a different way, clumsy, blundering in our bathyspheres and our pressurised suits, subject to the bends. Go down too fast, we rupture; come up too fast, we burst. Never the twain shall meet, for long…

But we do strew our leavings everywhere we go, and each bit of garbage left behind is a seed, a potential grit-pearl. The ocean adapts to our corrupting influences, shaping itself to what it assumes is a new system of prey-or-be-preyed-upon.

Look, Sean, *Mum said, pointing, her mask-voice a tinny buzz in his ear.* Here's a stonefish, looks like a rock. A skate, trying to look like an old shoe. A sponge grown into the shape of a slipped carburetor—is that rust, or protective colour?

And there, where the bombies meet, a jumble of far more intimate human litter… is that somebody's femur, somebody's splintered tibia? Or just a thousand-generation anemone colony bleached white sand-on-calcium grey, trying to fit itself into the hole where somebody's trapped and weighted corpse once used to lie?

All this, or none of it, or something else entirely—something new, unknown, unseen. For there is far more sea to pore through, waiting unexplored, than there ever will be land.

Sean came back up gasping, sweat-wet, in darkness. Felt his dreams shrug aside to let him free, silky-smooth and sandpaper by turns, an affectionate quilt of flocking rays—their cartilaginous wings sliding away quick down every limb, a peeled cocoon. An extra pulse seemed to hammer at his breast-bone, where the female ray's pectoral disc would lie; when he checked himself in the cabin mirror, sure it was purely psychosomatic, he thought he saw a bruise just beginning to raise, a wine-dark birthmark kiss. As though something trawling sleep's deepest levels had bit down on him, hard, before trying to slide its fertilising claspers in.

Up on deck, the moon hung low and huge in a star-crammed sky, its outline sketched in burnt-retina heat-haze orange. The planks still held most of the day's heat, beating up right through his flip-flops' rubber soles; sweat had already stuck pits to sleeves before he'd even climbed the ladder, warm as blood and glue-heavy, 'til he could barely tell ass-crack from shirt-tail.

When he sucked down a long gulp, straining in search of relief, all he got was more of the same, but salt-flavoured, mildly decayed. Like he was breathing air from his own corpse's lungs.

"Hey," the man from the sea said, from behind him.

Sean turned, blinked stupidly, blood pounding in his face and pelvis—instinctively made to back up, and rocked against the railing. Might've fallen, even, if somebody hadn't laid their big American hand (dusted with gold hair on the back, palm still rough with broken blisters) on his, and pulled.

"Should watch out; it's pretty dark. You fell, sharks'd find you a damn sight faster'n we would."

"Too right. Smell bring you up?"

"Nah, that's about the same—just stop noticing it, eventually, I guess. I thought..." He gave a cursory look 'round: a bit too quick, barely a headshake. "Thought I might check the rig out again, that thing you found me in. See if anything pops."

"And?"

"Nope."

"That's normal, mate. Given the circumstances."

Another eye-flick, tracing the same static path. "I'm not even trying to *remember*, so much, now—just to, you know, figure it out. How it all must've happened."

"The wreck..."

"Sure, and after. Like when your captain asked me: *That how it went?*" He shrugged. "I don't know. I just—woke up, inside that thing. I mean, I *think* I woke up..."

"Yeah, well. What else would you've done?"

"...I don't know."

Sean didn't, either. So he looked away again, studied what he could see of the waves instead, until his head began to hurt. Thinking, all the while, how immature his long-expired crush on Ric now seemed in the face of *this* yearning—an all-encompassing draw, deepwater pull, stronger than any undertow.

Desire as a devouring force, as loss of self, as death-wish. The crazy urge to somehow submerge himself inside this ghost of a man he "knew" only from Google, apparently better than the guy knew himself; to dive in head-first, let all that sun-kissed Yank-ness wrap 'round him and sink 'til he either came out the other side, or smothered.

"Crazy" is right, Jesus.

"Smart to get yourself in there, though, in the first place," he heard himself say, numbly. "Shows presence of mind, and all that. I mean ... you couldn't've known anybody'd be coming for you, not really."

The guy nodded. "Yeah, that makes sense, what you're saying. But I think ... I must've hoped they'd come for the ship, anyhow. Cost a lot of money. Not the kind of thing you'd just ... throw away."

"No," Sean agreed.

"It's yours now, though, I guess. Me, too."

All at once, that pulse was back, hammering twice as hard.

He can't mean what you think.

But: "What do you mean?" Sean found himself incapable of stopping himself from asking, shamefaced. To which the guy simply smiled, gently.

"Well . . . you found me. So, I guess—"

(you get to keep me)

Speech? Thought? Those five small words seemed to stone-skip through him like a bullet-fragment ricochet, cascading from ear to brain and straight back out again. Exiting through the lips, already opened wide, as they collided with the guy's own and stuck fast: passing the same lust-flavoured breath back and forth, back and forth, like sharing an air-bubble.

Oh God, let go. Oh God, don't.

Don't let me go.

Oh God.

They were the same height, give or take; pretty much the same build, 'specially after all that time on Shaftoe's cargo-before-crew starvation diet versus all that time—how long, exactly?—adrift. Even their hand-span a near-exact match, just wide enough for each to clasp the other's wrists without strain. Yet the contact alone was enough to sap Sean's reserves, dip the empty he'd apparently already been running on low enough he could feel himself vibrate; he clutched at the guy for dear life, tongues twining, holding on. Holding tight.

Because: *If you let me go, I'll fall. And . . . if I fall . . .*

. . . *I'll drown*, Sean thought, feeling his eyes roll back, his temples throb and sing. Practically goddamn *swooning*.

And time must've passed, without either even noticing. For a moment later he glanced back up to find Ric, looming large—already halfway lunged forward into their all-too-closely-shared personal space, raw eyes bugged 'til his lids started to slant the wrong way.

Uh oh.

A warning seemed in order, but his mouth was otherwise engaged. Besides, the juggernaut was well on its way; all they could do was make room. So Sean side-stepped, tried his best to swing the guy along with him, but only succeeded in turning him so he and Ric could lock gazes: glazed and crazed to amiably mild, almost stoner-calm, swimming in endorphins. Should've gone over like a bong-hit, defusing the situation, and yet—

Ric simply froze, rigid, riveted. Neither angry nor jealous, anymore, but terrified.

What is he seeing? Not what... who... I am.

A rush and a push and the deck was cleared: Ric went past at high speed, *Demeter* first-mate style, and folded over the rail as if he'd been stomach-punched. Sean grabbed for Ric's shoulder but felt it slip by, sweat-greased; felt the guy reaching down as well, yet saw Ric twist mid-plunge to avoid that grasping, offered hand. A strange cunning lit both irises, made them flash in recognition. Like:

I know you, now—don't see how I couldn't see it, before.

But you won't bloody get me, too.

Letting go, perfectly deliberate, Ric fell into darkness, hit the unseen water below with barely a splash. Sean made to follow, hollering:

"Ric, *fuck*, swim, you idiot! Grab for the Knot! Grab *hold*, you bloody fool!"

No reply, save the lapping waves. And a whisper that might've come from the guy whose strong arms were even now holding him back, making sure he wasn't going after poor, sleep-deprived idiot Ric... Ric, whose misfiring synapses had sent him off and running so hard he'd thrown his entire life away like trash, all to escape a damn dream...

Nothing out here to grab hold of, Sean. Just garbage soup, and plenty of it.

"Sharks'll get him," Sam-I-Am said from the wheelhouse door, with peculiar satisfaction. Like he'd just been waiting, all this time, for the pleasure of eventually getting to make *that* call.

Behind him, further down the staircase, Sean glimpsed both Arjit (pausing to spit, derisively, while perhaps wondering if he should join this impromptu all-hands-on-deck funeral) and Shaftoe (knuckling sleep from his eyes, dazed and confused, having apparently left his six-guns behind in his cabin), both staring upwards. Then everyone cringed at once, top-lit by the glare, as a flare split the night to illuminate a pair of small, sleek craft coming in dark off either bow, armed to the teeth. Didn't have to be sporting the Jolly Roger to know what *their* game was, either, way the hell out here, where there was nothing worth stealing but the trawler out from under them.

Sean did a double-take Shaftoe's way, wondering if he looked a bit like Ric had, before blurting: "No way in hell even *you'*d've been stupid enough to e-mail reVive already, you stunned fucking cunt."

Shaftoe gulped. "I...just asked 'em if they wanted their property back," he managed. "Before the media got hold of it, and him..."

"Oh yeah. 'Cause there's absolutely *nothing* dicey-looking 'bout an eco-boat that bloody *sinks*, is there? Nothing that reeks of corner-cutting, nothing that says: *I don't* really *give a toss so long's they stop telling me where not to dump, so please just make sure to drift off-radar when your rig falls apart, and stay there—*"

The guy nodded, slightly, like this was happening to somebody else entirely. "Does kinda seem that way, doesn't it? Man, Sean, you should be in GPA-Marine, or something."

Two steps saw Arjit up on deck next to Sam-I-Am, Shaftoe left wibbling in the gloom behind; he gave Sam a friendly cuff to the shoulder: *You 'n' me, eh? Only two brown boys on a ship of crazy whites!*

Sam-I-Am just shifted stance to ask out one side of his mouth: "You *in* on this, man?"

Arjit shrugged. "They get the ship, we're home in a month, find a real damn job. Told ya it'd be better, this way."

"Oh, you think? Can't trust pirates, fool! We ain't worth the chain to sink us, to them scallawags."

"Chill, mate. Everything be fine. Just gotta...take care of a few things, first—"

Shaftoe, three steps behind as usual, seemed at last on the ragged brink of reacting to Arjit's confession when his former second-in-command pivoted to empty the *Bad Idea*'s own flare-gun—conveniently holstered nearby, for easy distress access—into his face. Though the flare's velocity was far too slow to penetrate anything, the effects were nonetheless startling: A bright red nitrate-magnesium flash, all hiss and burst, bouncing off-centre to crush in Shaftoe's beak with a satisfying, gluey *crack* before ricocheting further, skipping down the hallway like a lit phosphorus-brick.

The "Captain" fell back, hair a-smoke, and out of sight—possibly dead, but Sean supposed that didn't much matter either way, now the rocket-exhaust trail had below-decks safely caught on fire. And at this answering signal, a volley of shots rang up from the starboard boat, along with a spatter of cheers.

Sam-I-Am clapped both hands over his mouth, and heaved. "Fuck *me*, up, down and sideways—"

Sean contemplated cutting and running, just for a second, but there weren't a whole lot of places left to go. Besides which, the guy— *Grinnage*, goddamnit—

(Simon?)

—seemed spot-rooted, studying Arjit as though he were less threat than vaguely interesting problem, simply one more oddity in a days-long string.

"Got one of those handy for us, buddy?" he inquired, mildly.

Arjit shook his head and pulled a Glock from his waistband, advancing. "Nothing personal, man," he replied. "I mean, you already had the short end, what with that wreck 'n' all. But, see...those out there, they only got berth enough for two."

And here it's as though the dream drops back over him, a wall of water slopping down to place five fathoms' worth of highly-welcome waves between himself and what happens next: how the guy, glancing back at him, raises a faint gold brow...

...and Christ-well sheds himself somehow, flips inside-out, opens wide as a bifurcated cloak of lip, unwrapping a slimy heap of bones and muck that clatters to the boards and lies there steaming, an awful surprise gift. What's left launches itself at Arjit, tumbling from axis to axis, like it can't tell which way is up. As though it's used to dealing with a different grade of gravity, entirely,

(but that can't happen)

(*can't* happen, not like that, not like)

(any of it, impossible, no no goddamn *no*)

And: Are there eyes in those sockets, that same hypnotic green gone shucked and nude, unblinking? What the hell can it have left to see its way with now, if so?

Arjit's a bastard, not dumb—pumps his whole clip into it, but nothing slows it down. Sam-I-Am, on the other hand, takes one look, and slams the wheelhouse door on 'em both. After's a second's hammer-

ing and cursing, Arjit turns right back into the thing, which hits him like
a pizza-dough facial: submerges him completely, quick-digesting him
from the outside in. Sean can hear him, muffled, through wads of flesh
and cartilage, a kitten swung in a bag against unforgiving walls.

Drowning would be a fucking mercy, by comparison.

Eventually, the sounds stop. Sean looks up again, just in time to see
whatever-it-is detach from—never mind, some grotesque hybrid of
corpse and turd, like what you get when you peel a snake. Then tumble-
splat, tumble-SPLAT as it heads for the wheelhouse, targeting that
thread-sized crack under the door and squishing itself flat, flatter, so
thin its molecular bonds almost separate. The privileges of bonelessness,
caught in action.

From inside, Sean hears Sam-I-Am start to scream. But that doesn't
last too fucking long, at all.

(oh god, I think it's coming back out)

Re-emerging, the creature flows back over its original sticky core-
dump mess and reassembles itself, wetly; everything moves back into
place with a series of clicks and pops, "the guy" re-emerging whole from
an unrecognisable lump of goo—skin reversed and mainly blood-free,
pinky-blond hair only slightly out of place. Those naked eyes pop back
into their orbits, open, crinkle slightly.

"Hey," he—it—says.

Sean coughed, wrackingly, mouth gone drier than he'd been in a
month. "Are you...gonna kill me?"

"Don't think so, no. You want me to?"

"...not like that."

A fresh rush of yells from the pirate peanut gallery—might be they
saw what happened to Arjit; might be they didn't like it—proved
weirdly easy to ignore, 'specially as Sean's brain raced to fill in the
spaces, ever newer and dumber questions just rolling straight off his
tongue with gumball-machine precision. "You're not...him, then.
Simon Grinnage. Never were."

"No. I thought I was, but..." A shrug. "Guess it doesn't much
matter now, really, what I thought. Or didn't."

"So—you just attached yourself to his corpse, that what happened?

Grew into the shape of the hole he left, somehow?" Without waiting for a reply: "Is there anything of him still in there at all, in you?"

"Shit, Sean, I don't know. You saw, when I—back there—" Sean nods. "—well, much as I'd like to think I'm at least some sort of composite, what came out . . . it felt like bones, to me."

"Looked like 'em, too."

"There you go, then."

Fresh flares went up, spotlighting this odd little triptych: Sean, Arjit's leavings. The thing, unnecessary clothes discarded—Sean couldn't remember where they'd gone—and now clad only in its own smeared blood-tracery, a pattern of red tattoos. More yells from the pirates followed, urgent-fearful, as though they somehow recognised it.

"Don't s'pose you could take 'em all," Sean suggested, only half-joking.

"Unlikely. But . . . " It glanced over at the *Green Phoenix* rig. "Could just get back inside that, and hit the water. Did okay, last time."

"*You* could, mate. Simon didn't come off quite so well, though, did he?"

Swapping banter in the face of death, or worse . . . much worse. Yet Sean still can't find it in him to fear, not completely; every breath he draws seems to say it means no harm to him, if no one else. Something chemical, probably, borne on the hot and stinking wind—something it probably doesn't even need, underwater. Pheromones, designed to attract land-bound prey by making the thing seem loveable? Or spores drifting up his nose to root in his cortex, then bloom and puppet him consumption-wards, the way Brazilian zombie fungi turn ants into living seeders?

"*I still want to touch you," he tells it, helplessly. "Even now."*

"*Me too."*

"*Why?"*

"*I don't know, Sean—how do I know anything? I just do. Everything Simon knew, most of what you know . . . what Arjit knew, and Sam-I-Am. And Ric."*

"*So that was you, then? The dream?"*

It shapes that easy, white-toothed SoCal smile. "Who else?"

On the port boat, someone raises an ArmaLite's massive barrel, bracing it against their shoulder: the Bad Idea's *off-limits now, apparently, not worth salvaging. Infected, possibly infectious. And they'll get the contract fee either way, Sean can only think, so long as what's left of the* Phoenix *goes down with the rest.*

"Too late," the thing confirms, stepping closer. "But...I really do want you to come with me, Sean. I want you. I think...I kinda want to be you..."

(oh)

(oh God, me too)

... is what Sean replies, in that last second before the rocket ignites. Or maybe he only thinks he does.

The explosion cracks the deck in half; the prow goes up, stern down, Titanic *in reverse. And as they fall together Sean grabs his long-drowned demon lover by both elbows—its arms come up like a toddler, like a trap. It latches on.*

Together, they step down, holding fast, joined at the lips. Until the trash-strewn waters close, kiss-warm and -soft, over both their heads.

Falling and falling and falling, forever, with nothing left to break against. With no hope of an impact, an ending.

Sean and the thing—heavier than it looked, by far—rode cold currents torn from the ocean's floor, winding upwards to capture the Knot's turnover, its increasingly brisk gyre. They nudged past confused sharks, kicked aside scraps of Ric, barely escaped being grazed or brained by various pressure-driven trawler-bits. They sank through fathoms, sharing air, light and air narrowing together in one last spasm—then winking out, the same way each synapse inside Sean's brain had already begun to flare and crisp and die, like bone-jarred fireflies.

Thinking: *I'll be him, I guess, or he'll be me; close enough. Too close for even him to tell. So it'll be as though one of us survives, anyhow...*

... as his grip kept on steadily tightening, pulling it ever-closer, bruising it 'til the skin-suit folded back and all he held were Simon Grinnage's bones, before heaving to enwrap him once more...

smothering him in a heat that was fever and spice and slime alike, pulsing organs fluttering like mouths against every part of him as its spiny heart suckered fast to his breastbone, eating its way inside… the mere unfiltered scent of it enough to make his own blood boil in his haemorrhaging eyes, his gouting ears screech like dolphins before they popped and his trouser-caught cock to finally explode, perhaps even literally…

Praying, all the while: *Don't let me go, please. Never let me go. Don't let me drown.*

(I don't want to drown, not now)

(not like this)

(not)

(without you)

Down there, in the deep and dark, where everything blended with everything else. Down where trash became treasure, and vice versa. Where flesh was eaten, over and over again, in endless communion; where prey and predator alike became bone, fossil, sand. Where currents bore him away in every direction at once, hoping against hope that nothing was ever lost, only changed. That the ocean, though a cornucopia of miracles and horrors—like death, like love—

(for all that it *had* a floor, one which he might never reach)

—might yet prove to have no real bottom.

ALISON LITTLEWOOD

THE ENTERTAINMENT ARRIVES

ALISON LITTLEWOOD's latest novel is *The Crow Garden*, a tale of obsession set amidst Victorian asylums and séance rooms. It follows *The Hidden People*, a Victorian tale about the murder of a young girl suspected of being a fairy changeling.

The author's other novels include *A Cold Season*, *A Cold Silence*, *Path of Needles*, *The Unquiet House* and *Zombie Apocalypse! Acapulcalypse Now*. She is currently working on her next book, a folkloric winter ghost story. Her short fiction has been collected in *Quieter Paths* and *Five Feathered Tales*, and she is a winner of the Shirley Jackson Award for Short Fiction.

She lives with her partner, Fergus, in Yorkshire, England, in a house of creaking doors and crooked walls. She has inky fingers and a growing collection of fountain pens, and is often to be found wandering the hills and dales in the wake of two hugely enthusiastic Dalmatians.

"When I was asked to contribute to the *Darker Companions* anthology celebrating the work of Ramsey Campbell, I was delighted," says Littlewood, "not only because Ramsey is one of the foremost talents in our field, but because he's a welcoming presence at events, a great supporter of new writers and a friend.

"I always loved his short story 'The Entertainment', a macabre affair of a man who stumbles into a run-down seaside hotel and is mistaken for the mysterious "entertainment". I started wondering . . . what happened to the real entertainment that night? Where did that end up, and what was its purpose?

"This is the result. I'd really like to thank Ramsey for the inspiration, and for his generosity in allowing me to venture into his world."

THE PROFESSOR DROVE slowly down the rain-lashed promenade, passing sign after dispirited sign that marked the boarding houses still clinging to whatever sorry living this place could afford. Westingsea in early May, and the angry sky flung handfuls of rain at its houses and pavements and the battered old black Wolseley he drove, drowning out any other sound. He could see the sea, black and heaving to his right, shifting in as surly a fashion as it always did, but only the rain was listening to any murmur it made. He knew without looking that the belligerent clouds, fierce as he'd ever seen them, were indifferent to whatever lay beneath. Of humanity there was no sign, unless it was the mean slivers of light trying to escape the windows of the blank-faced, three storey properties along the front.

None of it mattered to the Professor. In fact, it was probably better this way; there was no one to see him arrive and no one to see him leave. He required no witnesses, no applause; there would be enough of that later. He knew where he was going and he knew what he would find when he got there, since it was always the same. The jaded, the worn out and the mad: that was who he had come for. Momentarily, he closed his eyes. *After the strife*, he thought, *after the rain, the entertainment.* He could almost smell their clothes, redolent of over-boiled potatoes and their own unloved skin. He could almost feel the texture of it on his hands, and his fingers, resting on the steering wheel, twitched—though sometimes it seemed to him that the car responded to his thoughts, or someone else's, rather than his touch.

He suddenly wanted to look over his shoulder at the things on the old and clawed back seat, but he didn't need to look. He could feel them, as if their eyes were fixed on his shoulder blades, boring into him. Punch had woken, then. He must be nearly there; he saw the spark of irritation from a neon sign to his left, HO EL, it said, the "T" too spent to play its part any longer, and he spun the wheel, or it spun under his hands; he wasn't sure which. The even movement of wheels on road gave way to the jolt and judder of potholes and the car drew to a halt facing a crumbling brick wall, drenched and rain-darkened. He stared at it. He still didn't want to turn around, though he never eluded what he did; it was his—what? Duty? That seemed too mild a word, for duty could be shirked. It's who he *was*. He was the entertainment, and he was here to entertain, and entertain he would. *After the rain . . .*

But for now the rain showed no sign of ceasing. It hammered on the roof and spat at the windows, and he switched off the engine and thus the wipers, and the deluge blurred the world entirely. He realised he hadn't even looked for the name of the hotel, but he had no need to do so; it had called him here and he had answered, just as he always did, even when the day wasn't special, as this one was.

He pushed open the car door, his right sleeve soaked through at once, but that didn't give him pause. Rain seemed to follow him even in the height of summer, and at least this smelled right: of ozone and tarmac and, peculiarly, of dust. He stepped out, retrieving the heavy duffel bag from the back seat before heading for the hotel entrance. He heard the cackle of the neon sign and turned to see that the "O" had also given up the ghost. A matching spurt of electricity ran down his spine, and he savoured it; he hadn't felt anything like it for a long time. It was a special night indeed. The shadow of an echo of a smile tried and failed to touch his lips, and he reflected that such a thing hadn't happened for a long time either.

The glass doors slid aside at his approach—unusual for the establishments he frequented—and the rain was suddenly cut off and other sounds, human sounds, returned. From an opening to one side came the clink of glasses. Somewhere someone was vacuuming, which made him frown, and he stared down at the dust-free carpet. His shoes were as wet as if he'd emerged from the sea and he shifted them, watching the moisture darken the floor with something like satisfaction. Then a voice, a cheery voice, said: "Can I help you, sir?"

A young woman with sleek hair pulled back against her head was seated behind a reception desk, smiling at him with reddened lips. The desk was grey, as was her uniform, and the wall behind her, and indeed that too-clean carpet. It looked anonymous; the hotels he frequented were often shabby and dirty, but they were never anonymous. The Professor frowned in answer, but he felt a sudden jolt of—what? Hunger? Eagerness?—from within his bag, and the contents shifted as if they were settling, or perhaps its opposite. He walked towards the girl and simply said, "Snell?"

His voice was dry and cracked. In truth he was unused to using it; his real voice, anyway. Sometimes he used his clown voice, or his jolly comedian voice, but not today. Generally, until it was time, he didn't need to; he certainly didn't like to.

"Welcome, Mr. Snell. One night, is it?" She wrinkled her nose as if she could smell something unpleasant, then covered her expression by parting those red-painted lips once more. It wasn't quite a smile.

"No." He leaned in closer until he could sense her wanting to recoil, *needing* to recoil, and he stared at her and he did not blink. "The manager. Snell. Booked the entertainment. Snell."

Her forehead folded into wrinkles. "Our manager—Miss Smith—she's not on tonight, I'm afraid sir, but I don't—"

"Snell."

His voice was implacable, and she knew it was implacable, he could see it in the way her eyes struggled to focus when she raised them to meet his. "Of course. I'll get someone for you, sir. I'll only be a moment."

She was as good as her word, trotting into the room from whence he'd heard the sound of glasses and returning a few seconds later with a gangling lad in dark, ill-fitting trousers and a waistcoat with grey panels down the front. He looked puzzled, was muttering something to her, but he fell silent when he stood in front of the Professor, who stared at the pock-marks in his skin until he was forced to look away.

"I'm sorry," the lad began, but suddenly another voice rang out behind him, so bright and full of excitement and somehow *pure* that they all turned to look.

"Punch!" the voice cried. It belonged to a small boy of maybe six or seven, his hair curling and golden, and he grinned and pointed at the Professor's bag.

The Professor looked, though as soon as he saw the shadow of a hand reaching across the carpet towards the child he knew what he would see. The crimson sugarloaf hat with its jolly green tassel had escaped the fastening and was poking from the top of the bag, along with the beaked nose, the hooked chin, the single avaricious eye, staring and endlessly blue.

"Mr. Punch!" the boy said again, his voice disturbing the very air, which seemed to reconfigure itself around them. "Is there a show? Is Judy in there? Can we go, Mummy, can we?"

The child looked up at the slender woman with the fond gaze who was holding his hand, and she smiled back at him. "We'll see."

"We will," the Professor said, but it was like being in the car, that odd feeling that he wasn't always the one steering, the one forming his lips into words. It was better when he had the swazzle in his mouth. Everything he said felt right then, even though the sound emerged as a series of shrieks and rasps and vibrations, words that no one else could understand. He realised he didn't know if Judy was in the bag, as the boy had asked. Sometimes it was the earlier one, the older one: Joan. Sometimes it was the newer one—the one he never quite knew where she came from: Old Ruthless.

The waist-coated lad who'd only managed to say *I'm sorry* drew a sigh. "I suppose we could—in a corner of the bar, if it's just a booth."

The Professor answered him with a look.

"Just the one show, is it? Just one? Because we're kind of busy."

"And dinner."

The boy looked puzzled. "I'm afraid service just finished. Chef might be able to plate something up for you, before he goes."

The Professor scowled. "I'll be fed."

He nodded in relief. "Our manager—she left no information about paying you—"

"I'll be paid." The Professor started to walk across that grey, too-smooth carpet, leaving the youth to follow in his wake. A special night, and nothing was ready: he did not suppose his theatre would be set up waiting for him, as it usually was, nor his watery soup turning tepid upon the table. It was lucky he always carried his booth; and his puppets—his special puppets—were always at hand, as they should be, or he wouldn't deserve the name Professor, or Punchman, or, as some were wont to call the entertainment, Beach Uncle. And without such a name, what would he be? He supposed, once, he had borne some other moniker, but if he had, he could no longer remember it.

The space opened around him, larger than he had expected; perhaps the night was special after all. The walls were painted a slightly paler grey, too bright, but it was flaking in the corners and the edges of the sofas were scuffed. The bar was grey too, and the high ceiling, lost to the dim lighting, was a deeper shade. He saw at once where he would set up his booth. There was a little nook off to one side, too small to be of use for anything else, where he knew the floors would not have been swept and the dim corners would have been abandoned to the spiders or whatever else cared to take up residence there. Yes: that was the way to do it.

He did not look at the faces of the occupants of the room, not yet. It wasn't time. But his gaze went towards the wall of windows, which were dark, reflecting back the interior of the bar and the deeper shadow where he stood. He nodded with satisfaction. The rain, finally, had stopped.

In the long pause, in the silence and the darkness, the Professor waited. He was on his knees, his back bent; the bag was at his feet with Mr. Punch still supine, half-in and half-out of the opening. Above the Professor's head was the little waiting stage and beyond that was the bar, entirely stilled, its patrons gathered in to a row of chairs hastily brought forward by the lad who'd said *I'm sorry*.

Outside the booth nobody spoke, but he could picture their faces, all turned expectantly to the little rectangular opening draped in fabric that had once been brightly striped in red and white. Without looking, the Professor slipped the swazzle from his pocket and into his mouth, tasting the old, cold bone, and he held it in position with his tongue. He could still sense the excitement creeping from the bag and towards his hands. It was *the* night. Early in May on the seafront, and not just any day in May: it was the 9th, the evening that was recognised throughout the land as Mr. Punch's birthday.

In answer to that thought a faint wheezing, a little like a laugh, emerged into the quiet. He was not sure if it came from his own breath passing through the swazzle or the bag on the floor or from the air around him. It didn't matter. Soon they would begin and everything else would end. It was almost time. He reached down, his fingers seeking out Mr. Punch's hat, passing over the soft nap of its fabric and finding the opening into which he would slip his fingers. He couldn't see it but he pictured the soft brown substance; its touch felt like skin against his hand as he pulled it home.

He closed his eyes. *That's the way to do it.*

He pictured the little boy's face. *Is Judy in there?* He knew, despite his excitement, the child would not be watching. He was too new, too fresh for any of this. The show wasn't meant for the likes of him. He knew who would make up his little audience: ladies in voluminous chintzy skirts, their face powder clogging the wrinkles beneath; old men, tired from years of stale marriages and disappointing jobs, disillusioned and spent; the worn out, the mad and the lost. That's who would be waiting for him, who was always waiting for him.

In the next moment, he had poked Mr. Punch's head up over the stage and an odd sort of sigh rose from the audience. With his other hand he stretched down and rummaged in the bag, finding another soft, leathery opening. As Mr. Punch began to shout for his wife, he slipped it on. It wasn't Judy, he felt that at once. It was the original: it was Joan, though he knew the people watching wouldn't know the difference. Sure enough he heard a call of "Judy, Judy!" as he used her little hands to grab her baby from within the bag's innards and sent her up to join her irascible husband.

He spoke through the swazzle, every word and gesture coming as if from somewhere miles distant, the show drifting over him as if he wasn't the one in control at all, and yet it was the same as always; a sense of being in the very right place at the very right moment, though he felt discomfited at that, and an image of that hotel sign rose before him, flashing its maimed sign as a woman's voice said: *Mr. Snell. Mr. Snell...*

As he thought of it, Mr. Punch dropped the baby, Joan screamed, and the couple set to, her beating him with her hands, he fighting back with his stick until the sound the swazzle made rose to a scream. Joan fell, though within reach, as she always did; he pulled her into the dark with the tip of his shoe. He knew that she was waiting; she was only ever waiting. And then he realised that no one had yet laughed.

He listened, hearing only silence on the other side of the booth, and felt the stillness creeping from that side of the grimy fabric and into the dark, and the little twist of discomfiture inside him grew a little. But of course all was still; nothing was happening, and he grasped in the bag for the policeman and sent him up to make his arrest until Mr. Punch beat him too and flung him into the void.

At last there came a titter, too high and too clear, but there was no time to think of it. The words were forming, the next puppet fitting itself slick and snug onto his hand.

"It's dinnertime." The words were clear, even swazzle-distorted as they were, but as he said them the Professor thought *No, it's not, I haven't had my dinner*, and he knew something was wrong even as Joey the Clown entered stage right and waved his string of sausages at the onlookers. Punch descended once more into the dark and nestled in close. He didn't speak in words, not exactly, but the Professor heard him anyway: *Hungry.*

I know. I know you are.

It's my birthday. I want cake.

The Professor swallowed, carefully, around his swazzle. Punchmen had been known to die that way, choking on the thing that made them what they were: when their time was up. He felt suddenly very tired. His time would never be up, he knew that. The characters were all there, in his bag, waiting: Scaramouche and the Skeleton; the Hangman; the Ghost; the Lawyer; Jim Crow; the Blind Man. The Crocodile, who would soon go up and wrestle the clown for his sausages. All had made their appearance in his show so many times, appearing in the very right place at the very right time. Old words ran through his mind:

With the girls he's a rogue and a rover
He lives, while he can, upon clover
When he dies—only then it's all over
And there Punch's comedy ends.

As if in answer, laughter finally came from the other side of the curtain, as the sausages and then the clown went to join Mr. Punch's wife in the nothingness beyond the booth. It wasn't the right kind of laughter though, he knew that, *felt* that, and he found himself wondering if tonight was the night and an odd kind of hope rose within him. Tonight, the Devil might come, the one character from the show who never did; the Devil might come and take them all.

That's the way to do it, he thought but didn't say, because it wasn't yet time: he always knew when it was time. First Punch went back to dispose of the crocodile and then the doctor tried to treat him only for Punch to beat him with his slapstick—"Take that!" said the swazzle—and he too was thrown into space, emptied and wrinkled without the enlivening force of the Professor's hand, nothing but an empty skin.

Another delve into the bag and a jolt of that same electricity he'd felt earlier crackled through him. Jack Ketch, the Hangman, was soft yet cold against his hand. Suddenly, he knew he had to look. He didn't know why but he felt almost sick with the need to do it, and he used Ketch's arm to draw the awning back, just a slit.

The breath seized in his throat. The golden-haired boy he'd seen earlier was there after all, sitting in the front row, his smiling mother on one side and a man who must be his father on the other, all of them smiling, not used up, not worn out, not *ready*. It wasn't right. None of it was right, and he realised he'd known it when the steering wheel had turned in his hands and he'd felt the greed rising from the back seat where Mr. Punch lay, watching with his blank blue eyes and hungering, always hungering, but especially today.

I want cake.

The Professor closed his eyes. He knew suddenly it was not the right time; it wasn't the right time and it wasn't the right place. It never had been. Snell was waiting, he knew that too. Mr. Snell had called him and booked him, the entertainment to follow the strife, to follow the rain, but Mr. Snell wasn't here.

The Professor opened his eyes and saw Punch's blue orbs staring back.

"I don't know how to do it," he said, except it came out in a series of wheezing growls, the words lost, because this was what he did: a duty that could not be shirked. Mr. Punch whipped his head back up onto the stage and Jack Ketch chased him with his noose, Punch pointing at it, condemned but not ready to go quietly, not yet. "I don't know how to do it." The words, this time, were clear.

Here, the Professor knew, was where the Hangman would put his own head in the noose to show Punch how to do it, only to be kicked off the stage and hung himself. That's what was supposed to happen. It wasn't what happened in his show, however, because Joan was back, taking Ketch's place, holding the noose herself and looking about, shading her painted eyes with one hand.

"I need a volunteer," she said, every word crystal-sharp despite the swazzle, the old bone that was cold in the Professor's mouth. He recalled that it was sometimes called a *strega*. The word meant "witch". He had never known why, not properly, and yet somehow he had always understood and had felt strangely proud of the fact, because it showed that he belonged: he was the Professor, the Punchman, the Beach Uncle.

He realised the boy was staring directly at the slit in the curtain, looking straight at him. He nudged it back into place even as the child pushed himself to his feet.

"A volunteer!" Joan shrieked, waving her little hands in excitement, jangling the noose, beckoning him on, and the Professor heard footsteps approaching, too soft and light.

For a moment there was silence. Then Joan made prompting noises, little wheezy nudging sounds, and she waved the noose, and he heard:

"I don't like it," spoken softly and with a little breathy laugh at the end, and the same footsteps retreated, and Joan shrieked more loudly than she had ever shrieked, so loudly that it hurt the Professor's ears.

Then came another voice, a louder, smoother voice, which said "Don't worry, it's fine, I'll show you," and louder, more tappy footsteps approached, and the Professor knew without looking that the child's mother was coming forwards; that she was going to show him the way to do it.

Joan showed her the noose. She slipped it over the woman's head. And then there was a pause because Mr. Punch wanted a souvenir; he always wanted a souvenir. He bobbed down and reached his camera from the bag—an old, heavy, Polaroid camera, and he bobbed up and had her pose, trying this angle and that before there was a loud bang and a flash drowned the world in light, just for an instant, and the woman's son caught his breath.

The camera whirred and spat its picture onto the floor. The Professor could just see it, below the old tangled fringe that ran around the bottom of the booth. Faintly, like a ghost, the woman's grin was appearing in the photograph: only that, her lips parted in the strained semblance of a smile, revealing teeth a little less white than the paper.

Then Mr. Punch stepped forward and hit her with his slapstick. There was another bang, this time so loud that everyone would be forced to close their eyes, just for a moment, just as long as it took, and the woman was hung, her body limp and falling, emptied of enlivening force; nothing but an empty skin.

"I don't know how to do it," said Mr. Punch.

"I need a volunteer," said Joan.

A rough shout came from the other side of the booth, of mingled surprise and awe, followed by loud clapping, albeit from a single pair of hands. The Professor peeked out to see the woman's husband looking impressed, grinning and clapping. They always grinned and clapped. And he realised that the child and his father were the only ones watching the show. There were no worn-out old ladies, no tired and ancient men. The boy wasn't grinning and clapping, however. He was peering to left and right of the booth at the blank grey walls and the grey floor, no doubt wondering when his mother was going to appear again, laughing at his surprise and perhaps, too, his fright.

But his mother didn't appear. Instead his father was coming forward, his smooth-soled shoes making hardly any sound on the carpet. Joan placed the noose over his head. There came a *bang—flash—whirr*, and a photograph drifted to the floor, the ghost of another fixed smile already beginning to form.

"Dad," the boy said from his place in the front row. "I don't like it."

"Come on, son!" his dad replied, his voice full of humour. "It's all jolly good fun!"

The words didn't sound right, even to the Professor who didn't know the man, who should never even have seen him, and yet Joan tightened the noose about his neck and held him steady for Mr. Punch, who grasped his slapstick in both little hands and spun, and the man slid to the floor, as empty and used up as his wife.

This time there was no laughter; there was no applause. There was only a pensive little boy looking up at the stage, waiting for his mum and dad to come back.

"I need a volunteer!" said Joan.

The boy shook his head. The Professor peeked once more through the curtain and thought he saw, in the dim light, the glisten of a tear on his cheek. *Don't*, he thought, *don't you do it, that's not the way*, and something in the child sagged and he pushed himself to his feet, as weary as any old lady in chintzy skirts, as any man waiting to use up his retirement, and he stepped forward.

The Professor felt his hands carry out the motions as Joan slipped the noose over the boy's golden head. He felt it as she tightened the rope. He heard the bang and the whirr but he didn't see the flash because his eyes were already pressed tightly closed. He realised he hadn't felt much at all in a very long time. He wasn't certain he ever wished to again. There was only the darkness behind his eyes and then Mr. Punch said, "That's the way to do it!" and it was so full of excitement, so full of triumph, and the Professor opened his eyes to see another little square of white, a photograph of a child's clean smile. He knew the boy hadn't been smiling, that he would never smile again, but Mr. Punch's camera had caught it anyway, just as it always did.

He lowered his hands, feeling the strain in his elbows and shoulders, feeling suddenly very old. He caught only disjointed words as he started to thrust the puppets, without looking at them, back into their bag. Soon he would be on the road again. He would be driving somewhere else, anywhere, and he knew that it would be raining, and that the rain would smell inexplicably of dust.

Dinnertime, said Joey the Clown.

Birthday, said Joan.

Cake, said Mr. Punch, and his voice was the most contented of all: *Cake*.

The Professor slipped his hands under the booth's fringe and felt for the puppets that had fallen. He grabbed Joey and the Crocodile and the Doctor, feeling the old, cold skin, and then he grabbed the new ones, those who had fallen. He paused when he felt their touch on his hands.

The skin was still warm, and it was supple, and smooth, and soft. He drew them towards him and picked them up, holding them to his chest, then stroking them against his cheek. He *felt* them and their warmth went into him. It awakened parts of him he had rather hadn't awoken because it was wonderful, conditioned by their love, seasoned by their life. They weren't used up and they weren't jaded. They weren't mad or spent or lost. They were fresh and new and something inside him stirred in response.

Cake, Punch murmured again, and the hard unyielding surface of his face pressed up close to the Professor's. *Cake*.

The Professor pressed his eyes closed, though he could see everything anyway. There were beaches outside, not just rain-tossed promenades. There were hotels limned in sunlight. There were roads he had not yet taken. All he had to do was see where the Wolseley wished to go, and grip the wheel, and force it to go somewhere else.

The entertainment would arrive, and he did not suppose they would welcome him in. He had a sudden image of Mr. Snell, thin and bent and grey, twitching the dingy curtains of a faded boarding house and waiting, fruitlessly waiting. The Professor decided he did not care. He had tasted cake, the only kind he wanted, but he had not had his dinner; and he found he was very, very hungry indeed.

One day, he supposed the Devil might come and take them all. Until then, he would find them: the golden little boys and girls who did not laugh and did not clap. He would find every one of them. He whispered under his breath as he emerged from the booth into the empty and quiet bar. He began to dismantle the stage, his whisper sounding different as he slipped the swazzle into his pocket, speaking in his own voice at last the words that were always waiting there for him: *That's the way to do it.*

JOHN LINWOOD GRANT

HIS HEART
SHALL SPEAK NO MORE

JOHN LINWOOD GRANT lives and works in West Yorkshire, England. Widely published in anthologies and magazines, he writes both contemporary weird fiction and dark stories of the late Victorian and Edwardian period. His extended "Last Edwardian" series—tales of murder, madness and the supernatural—occasionally features Mr. Edwin Dry, the Deptford Assassin, described by one reviewer as: "One of the most evocative presences in modern dark fiction—precise, relentless, inexorable."

Recent period works include the collection *Persistence of Geraniums* and his new Mr. Dry novel, *The Assassin's Coin*, set in the Whitechapel Autumn of Terror. The "Last Edwardian" series also covers the Mamma Lucy tales of 1920s hoodoo, and a fair bit of new Holmesian fiction, such as the real canonical answer to Arthur Conan Doyle's 'The Musgrave Ritual'.

Grant's contemporary fiction can be found in magazines such as *Vastarien*, *Weirdbook* and *Lackington's*, and ranges from unsettling weird horror to serious explorations of Lovecraftian themes. Plus stories of Mr. Bubbles, a slightly psychotic pony with attitude who stalks the Yorkshire Wolds. He is also senior editor of *Occult Detective Quarterly*, including the anthology of new longer fiction, *ODQ Presents*.

Forthcoming projects include *Hell's Empire*, an anthology

concerning the incursion of the Prince of Darkness' forces into Victorian Britain; an interleaved novel, *13 Miller's Court* (with Alan M. Clark); a further collection of weird fiction, and a book on the mysteries of St. Botolph-in-the-Wolds, a village which channels both Enid Blyton and H.P. Lovecraft.

"'His Heart Shall Speak No More' was conceived whilst walking the long, lonely sands of the Holderness coast, not so different from those of Suffolk," recalls Grant. "Sometimes, by the low cliffs, little more than a scramble of mudstone and sand, you wonder if you see a figure in the distance, and you remember the many drowned settlements of that coastline. A gull shrieks, a cormorant rises, and then there is no one there.

"The Dark Heart of Dunwich is, of course, a genuine legend, and so I set off with a nod to M.R. James, and a dash of my own Last Edwardians. I knew that the redoubtable Aunt Beatrice would try to face whatever the tide brought in, real or illusory."

I T HAD LONG been my habit to spend at least a fortnight each autumn with my friend, Emilia Rawkins, the wife of a successful wine-merchant in Suffolk. The countryside there was charming, with the advantage that their house was only some ten miles from the coast, not that far from the towns of Southwold and Dunwich. Emilia herself had a passion for the natural history of marine life, which inevitably involved numerous enjoyable trips to the long Suffolk shoreline.

I was disconcerted, therefore, to find that just before my next planned visit, I was unexpectedly placed in charge of my nephew Philip, a young man reading Law at Oxford. Philip had suffered a fearful blow that summer, having been jilted by his fiancée only days before his wedding. Neither his spirits nor his studies had recovered from the blow, and so my ailing sister appealed to me, long widowed and unencumbered by other duties as I was, to take him in hand.

Whilst I will not say that I had maternal feelings for Philip, I was sufficiently fond of him to see that something had to be done.

Accordingly, I agreed, and wrote to Emilia to enquire if an additional guest would be an inconvenience. I received a card by return saying that it would be no bother at all, and so I informed a diffident Philip that he should pack his cases.

The railway journey to Halesworth, by way of Ipswich, was quiet. A slight, shy fellow, given to too much reading, Philip stared out of the railway carriage window throughout, answering questions politely but with no sense of engagement.

Isaiah Rawkins himself was at Halesworth Station with their large, two-horse wagonette. He was a short, portly man, with red cheeks which came more from his own wares than from any sea breeze.

"Beatrice, good to see you again." Isaiah kissed my glove. "And, um, young Philip, yes."

They shook hands formally as a porter placed our cases in the carriage.

During the journey Isaiah and I engaged in empty conversation about London these days, the weather and his trade, while Philip once again stared at the countryside. With the Adnams Brewery doing well at Southwold, Isaiah had secured business supplying wines and spirits to all their public houses, and he was busier than ever.

"Emilia will be delighted to see you," he said. "The wagonette will be yours for the week, as I have my automobile. She has many ideas to entertain our young . . . to entertain anyone who wishes to take, um, advantage of this mild October."

Little need be said of our being installed at Bitterns, the Rawkins' large, comfortable place just outside Halesworth. Emilia was not given to fuss, and so left Philip to arrange his room to his liking, pointing out that Isaiah had a small library downstairs which was open to all. I had warned her of my nephew's circumstances in a letter the day before.

"Remind me, Beattie, how old is he?" Emilia poured tea for the two of us in the drawing room, dismissing the maid as soon as the tray had arrived.

"Twenty-three," I sighed. "The arrangement was ill-starred, the two of them with such different expectations, but they would hear nothing against it from those around them. With Philip's allowance from his grandfather, he was keen to marry. She was taken by his earnestness at first, drawn in by his plans, I believe, but near the end, well, she saw only the limitations which marriage would impose."

"We did not do so badly, did we?"

I smiled. "No, indeed, but perhaps we were fortunate. Now Philip's girl has fled to an aunt in Scotland, breaking his heart, and he has been reluctantly attached to an aunt in England..."

"Yourself." Emilia laughed, her brown curls their usual tangle. "Well, a change of air may do him some good, so the coast it will be."

After a light dinner, Emilia insisted on taking us to see her study. I had been many times before of course, but it was always an experience. The smell, for example, was never the same. One week she had garlands of seaweed drying on a ceiling rack; the next, a fox hide curing by the window. Had she continued her schooling, I think that Emilia might have been counted a considerable natural historian. As it was, she was known as a slightly eccentric enthusiast, and rarely published at all.

Her study contained shelves of books and pamphlets in disorder, along with far more shelves displaying relics of her trips around Suffolk, most of them as yet unlabelled. The jumbled nature of the room seemed to intrigue Philip, who examined item after item.

"Aunt Beatrice, what's this?" He held up a Kilner jar full of murky brown liquid. I peered over my glasses as he swirled the jar, but could see nothing else.

"Emilia?"

She clapped her hands together.

"Goodness, you've found my foetal pig. How marvellous."

Philip and I abandoned the jar to examine other, more recent finds of hers. A small Chinese table stood by the door, its lacquer peeling. The surface was littered with pale, delicate shells of a type I had not seen before.

"Sea potatoes," she said, pleased at our attention. "The heart urchin, *Echinocardium cordatum*. They burrow in the beaches here, rarely seen alive. These are what we call their tests, or shells."

She passed some around, letting us examine the fragile shells, which were indeed almost heart-shaped. The largest was three inches from top to bottom, the shell dotted with rows of tiny holes.

"They have flexible spines in life, you see," she pointed out. "Harmless, but no doubt part of their burrowing equipment. We might find more tomorrow at Dunwich."

The wagonette ride to Dunwich the next afternoon was pleasant, Emilia chatting as she drove. We disembarked in the fields by the remains of Greyfriars Priory, a tumble of walls and arches which seemed perilously close to the beach.

"Most of Dunwich has gone, of course, washed away by centuries of storms. It's a haunted coast, in its way. There are supposed to be a dozen churches out there, under the sea."

"Really?" I gazed out over the grey water, imagining spires and stained glass windows being stared at by the fish, pews and stalls which now harboured only crabs and lobsters.

"Mmm. They say you can hear the bells ringing some nights, far below the waves." She handed each of us a small hessian sack for anything interesting we might find.

An easy slide brought us down the crumbling cliffs to the stretch of beach. A line of shingle, a line of sand nearer the water. I had waxed and treated my boots, knowing what Emilia would have us doing, and was pleased enough to stroll along with her while Philip ranged ahead. He had not been communicative that morning and was lost, I supposed, in the doldrums of his own thoughts.

"Now, Beattie, tell me about the captain who was bothering you at the Sutherland's dance … "

And we walked, discussing life, the latest gossip, and of course Captain Martins, who I had threatened to shoot if he pressed his attentions further. My late husband had been an army man, and I did know how to load and aim a revolver, after all.

"So after the next waltz, we—"

"Aunt Beatrice!"

A hundred yards away, Philip was waving to us. My nephew stood near the lapping waves of the outgoing tide, tips of foam on the long lines of dark water. Around him were shells, not only razor clams and the little tellins, but at least half a dozen tests, as I had learned to call them, of heart urchins.

Emilia was delighted. "Quite a high tide earlier this morning. It seems these were discarded in its wake. Let's see what we have."

We spent some hours exploring the lower beach, popping anything to which we took a fancy into Emilia's sacks, and the sea was coloured with the first pink tinges of sunset by the time we abandoned our beach-combing to return home. Even Philip seemed more animated than usual.

At Bitterns we washed, ate a cold collation (Isaiah was in Ipswich on business), and examined our finds. Most were akin to Emilia's existing collection, but she had found a large tellin, the two halves of its shell spread in the manner of a perfect rose-coloured butterfly. Some of the urchin tests were broken, the material like fine porcelain. She discarded those as Philip went though his own sack.

"Mrs. Rawkins . . . " He stared at the rounded object in his hand. It was crusted with sand, the crude shape of a heart and some three and a half inches across.

She took it from him gently, and frowned. Her hand-brush took the sand away, to reveal something which was clearly not an urchin.

"Wood," she said, peering through an eyepiece she had been using to identify crustacea. "It appears to be a wooden carving."

"Of a heart urchin?" he asked, though I thought that one would hardly need to make an effigy of these common animals.

"No, of an actual heart I think, Philip. Quite a curio. A sailor's carving, perhaps, from a dull voyage."

She threw it back to him, and went about her work.

"I shall keep it as a memento of this afternoon." He cradled it oddly in his hands, as if it were delicate, then slid it into his jacket pocket. I forbore from saying the cloth might stain—at least his attention had been dragged from his own unhappiness.

Isaiah returned not long after, and a pleasant late supper ensued, punctuated by Isaiah's tales of dim-witted shipping agents and watered whisky. Emilia and I laughed or nodded as appropriate, used to his stories. Philip picked at his food, saying little but offering the occasional faint smile.

"Emilia tells me you found a rather unusual 'urchin,'" said Isaiah, wiping his fingers on a napkin. "Might I have a look?"

My nephew took the carving out of his pocket, though at first he seemed reluctant to hand it over. Isaiah turned the object in his thick fingers, examining it.

"Amazing what gets washed up around here. Emilia found, um, part of a figurehead once, half-buried in the sands after a storm."

"Because of a shipwreck?" I asked.

"Or an incompetent carpenter who had not affixed his work securely." Isaiah laughed. "This wooden thing, however, reminds me of something I once read, long ago. A local bit of, um, nonsense. You could try my library, young man."

"Thank you, Mr. Rawkins." Philip took the carving back, slipping it into his pocket once more. I had to wonder why the boy was still carrying it around. There was something about it which was not to my taste.

The Rawkinses and I played cards for an hour or two, leaving Philip, at his request, to follow Isaiah's suggestion and investigate the library. I did not see him again that night.

Our second visit to Dunwich was at Philip's request. As Emilia thought his interest to be healthy, I acquiesced. The trip was without note, excepting one seemingly unimportant incident.

I had settled by the cliffs, which were little more than dunes in places, and was polishing a pebble on the coarse grass. Emilia was further down the beach, inspecting wrack from the last tide. I scanned the horizon for my nephew, and saw him on the shingle, holding the wooden heart in one hand and talking, as it seemed, to the air. I had to suppose that he was talking to himself, or reciting poetry perhaps, as the lovelorn do, and I said nothing when we reunited.

The afternoon was overcast. Philip chose to cloister himself in the library again, whilst I helped my friend to put some order into her linen stores. Emilia was not enthusiastic about domestic duties, but occasionally interfered with the work of her maids as a token gesture.

The full-time housemaid, Sarah, was already folding bedsheets which had returned from the laundry.

"If I may, ma'am..." She bit her lower lip, obviously feeling awkward in my presence.

"Yes, Sarah. Say whatever it is." Emilia smiled.

"The young man, ma'am. Did he get very wet, yesterday?"

"What might you mean, dear?" I asked before Emilia could speak, trying to sound gentle.

The maid looked at the toes of her boots.

"It's just that, me and Lucy were wondering, with you two ladies seeming dry, and so much water in the young gentleman's room this morning... we thought as he might have fell in or the like."

"Water?" I pressed her for more details.

According to Sarah, there had been wet patches on the carpet of Philip's room when she cleaned it, and his armchair had been quite damp, as if someone had sat in it after a ducking. They had had to coerce the gardener into taking the chair outside to air it.

"There was some spray on the beach," I said quickly. "That must be it."

I slipped her sixpence, to share with Lucy, and her pleasure at that seemed to dismiss the matter.

Emilia and I abandoned the linen for a walk in the garden. The armchair was there, by the gravel drive, and indeed, the upholstery was damp. I could think of no explanation, knowing that we had kept quite dry all day.

I ventured to inspect the library myself that evening. A book was open on the table by the window. I lifted the cover without fully closing the book. Leather-bound and somewhat foxed, it bore the title *Curiosities of Old Suffolk, Being a Collection of Sundry Tales*, by one Josiah Smith, Rvnd.

I sat down and turned to the open section.

> In the Parish of Dunwich they have a number of such stories, including that of a young woman who killed herself after being abandoned by her sailor lover. It is said that the girl, being without that Mercy which God might have

granted, may be encountered as a restless spirit on the sands. Some believe that those creatures known as sea potatoes are shaped in a reminder of her lost heart.

Others, more fantastically, report that she tore the organ in question from her own bosom and cast it to the sea. Old folk say that her heart may yet be found on Dunwich sands, hardened by grief, and that if found it should be consigned to the waves, for ill-fortune will otherwise follow.

The general tone of the book made it clear that the Reverend Josiah Smith placed little faith in the folk legends he had recorded.

This must be the tale which Isaiah had vaguely remembered at dinner. Philip had indeed found a heart-shaped object in the sand. I did not for one second believe that it was any organ of the lost girl's, hardened or otherwise, but nor did I have any sure notion as to why someone would carve such a thing. If it were not a sailor's discarded toy, then had it been made to keep an ageing legend fresh, to attract those who took pleasure in the macabre? Was what remained of Dunwich Town (a grand word for those houses which had not been washed away) eager for additional revenue?

Whatever the truth, I was hardly pleased at this discovery. I feared that it might play upon my nephew's mind, abandoned as he too saw himself.

As the next day brought a smatter of rain, we undertook a train journey down the branch line to Southwold, where we had lunch in a respectable hotel called Masons. The food was palatable and a good view could be had of the harbour.

"Rather dull for you in here, Philip," I said, knowing that in Oxford there were many more lively establishments catering for student tastes. "Perhaps we might call in at a local hostelry afterwards?"

In our youth, Emilia and I had undertaken many dares, not the least of which was going into a Camden public house and ordering a half-pint of porter each. The denizens of that establishment had been too surprised to do anything other than stare as we finished our drinks and left to collect our reward from a friend.

The hotel waiter recommended The Quay as "tolerable". We admired the Southwold lighthouse which stood, rather disconcertingly, in the centre of the town and had only been erected a decade earlier. The Quay, a tall, narrow tavern, was to be found a short distance beyond that landmark, near the new pier.

The beer was Adnams, as I had expected, and we could see a case of spirits bearing Isaiah's import mark by the bar. I had acquired a taste for ale from my husband, and Philip was used to drinking it at his college, but Emilia only sipped, declaring it "a trifle sharp". She and Isaiah favoured a mellow, aged sherry at home.

The tavern was busy but not crowded. As Philip went to fetch a second glass of ale for the two of us, he lurched to one side without apparent reason, almost falling. In the process he jostled a man in an oilskin coat.

"Sir, I do apologise—" began my nephew, regaining his balance.

The fisherman (I assumed) was not looking at Philip. He was staring at an object on the floor. It was the carved heart we had found the day before, kept in Philip's jacket ever since.

"That yers, bor?" The man pointed at the carving.

"Er, yes." Philip picked it up, shoving it back into his pocket hastily.

"If Oi was yer, Oi'd hull e back, 'fore next tide is gorn."

Philip looked nonplussed, but the fisherman had walked away. My nephew turned a questioning look on Emilia.

She was frowning.

"He said that you should throw it away, into the sea. I can't imagine why."

The man who had spoken to Philip had lingered by the tavern door, tamping down his pipe. I made my way to him quickly.

"Excuse me, sir."

The look he gave me was one of indifference.

"You said something to my nephew, at the bar." I nodded in the direction of Emilia and Philip. "I wondered, did you recognise what fell from his pocket?"

I saw suspicion growing, but I was, if I flatter myself, a tall, handsome enough woman and practically dressed, not some ribbon-bedecked girl from a seaside charabanc.

"Aye," he said begrudgingly. "Oi sin e, betimes."

Men are men, whatever rank they hold. I improvised what was hopefully a winning smile.

"If you could give me just a little more detail about the . . . item?" I prompted.

The fisherman pushed his pipe-stem into the corner of his mouth. "Jackie Stanley did find e, this las' winter. Kept e, too."

"And could I speak to Mr. Stanley?"

"Not unless yer swim well an' deep-loik, lady. Oi see him drown an' gorn, not a se'enday after that, off Lower-stoff."

"You believe that the carving brought bad luck?"

He stared at me from under dark, unkempt eyebrows.

"Jackie found e, and no good come after, if that be what yer want t'hear, lady."

There was no more to be had from that source.

On the train journey back I felt something pressing at the back of my mind.

"Did you trip on something, Philip, in that tavern?" I asked. "When you almost fell."

"Trip? Oh, no. I was trying to avoid the girl."

"What girl was that?"

"You know, Aunt Beatrice, the one with the tangled hair. She was right in my way."

Emilia and I exchanged a glance. There had been no one between my nephew and the bar save the man in oilskins. I knew my friend well, and with that glance we agreed to leave the matter there.

That night, I slept badly. It was windy outside, and I could swear that I could smell the sea, even that far inland. The air felt damp, my bedclothes felt damp, and I went to the window to see if it was actually raining.

It was not, but there on the front lawn, illuminated by the lantern at the main door, stood Philip. That carving was in his left hand; with his right he was gesticulating, as if illustrating a point to someone. The lantern shifted in the breeze, and for a moment I thought that I did indeed see a slender figure before him, then it was gone.

I examined the lawn that morning, on the pretext of admiring

Emilia's rather random approach to gardening. It was easy enough to see the prints of Philip's boots in the grass, but were those other prints beyond his, less defined?

"An early frost, it seems," said Emilia. I looked to where she pointed, a faint line of white across the lawn. As she walked on, I bent down. Touching the whiteness, which was cold enough, I brushed my fingertips to my lips. It was not frost.

It was salt.

I did not understand how that could be, but we rationalise in the oddest ways. A gardener, I told myself, had spilled rock salt stored against the winter, or something he used on the abundant slugs.

In the end I feigned admiration of an old cedar tree and said nothing to Emilia.

I was less than enthusiastic when Philip suggested that we went again to Dunwich, but there were no obvious excuses to be made. We took the wagonette to Greyfriars, with a picnic lunch in a hamper, and with some reluctance began our beachcombing.

Philip, as before, was well ahead of us, following the low cliffs. Given the circumstances I kept a closer eye on his whereabouts, and Emilia was left to wander the shingle on her own, collecting shells, semi-precious stones and those pieces of sea-weathered glass that so often delight. I found it difficult to concentrate on the beach itself, picking up the occasional piece of weed or interesting pebble out of duty.

Calling to Emilia that we might soon go back to the carriage for our lunch, I turned to check on my nephew. He was talking to someone in the shadow of the cliff, presumably another beachcomber.

"Philip!" I shouted. "Lunch-time."

Emilia scrambled to my side, struggling with her sack.

"I found a rather large cuttlefish bone," she said, face flushed. "Look..." She parted the hessian, lifting out a chalky oval.

I glanced at it, and turned to Philip. He was on his own again, a hundred feet away. His acquaintance must have climbed the cliff, which was easily scaled in these parts.

"Come on now. We're hungry."

He came slowly, his face pale.

"Are you all right, dear?" I took one of his hands, which was wet, as if he had been dipping into pools.

His eyes were clear enough when he looked up at me.

"I . . . yes, thank you, aunt. The girl distracted me, she seemed so sad."

"Girl?"

"The one with the long wet hair, the one we saw in Southwold. I think she lacks company."

I felt strangely faint, seeing Reverend Smith's book as if it were there before me at Dunwich. *A restless spirit on the sands.*

"What . . . what did she say to you, Philip?" I managed to ask.

Emilia looked puzzled, the cuttlefish bone still in one hand.

He shrugged. "She didn't really say anything. She was waiting for me, I think, but she seemed so lonely that I showed her the heart, which—"

"What did she do when she saw it?" I spoke more sharply than I had intended.

"Aunt Beatrice, we were only talking." He flushed. "She reached towards me, and then you shouted. You must have startled her, for when I looked back she had gone."

I had heard enough.

"We must get back to Halesworth." I gave Emilia a hard glance.

"Yes," she said. "I do think it might rain, and we're hardly dressed for it today. October rain can be so cold. Let's have lunch back at the house, instead."

I could see that Philip wanted to argue, but between us we bustled him away from the beach, making empty chatter as we went. I engineered it that he should see to the horses, taking his linen jacket from him while he checked the traces. The wooden heart was there, easily taken. I handed the jacket to Emilia.

"I'm just going to check if I dropped a hair-pin on the way up," I said.

The army does not breed weak women. At a moment when Philip was involved in settling one of the mares, I took up the carving and hurled it across the shingle, hearing the faint dull sound of it landing at the edge of the incoming tide. Innocent or not, let someone else find it.

There was no wind that night, but the house had a compelling odour of mud-flats and fish which had passed their best. Emilia had all the windows thrown open, and she ejected certain bags from her study, claiming that some specimens must have gone bad.

I did not entirely believe her.

I think that at that point, God help us, Emilia and I still wished to pass this matter of the heart and the mysterious girl off as a fancy caused by my nephew's recent distress, a fancy which had unnerved us through association. I could not offer an immediate solution to Philip's woes, but at least with that carving gone, an unhealthy focus had been removed.

By the following morning guilt had wormed its way into me. I resolved to tell my nephew what I had done with his find, and why, however ridiculous it might seem. Perhaps we might even broach the subject of his fiancée, and how he now felt, though I doubted I could find a way to introduce the topic easily. I had no idea how to play the amateur alienist, having always been of a somewhat robust temperament myself.

He was in his room, reading *Curiosities of Old Suffolk*.

"Quite a bit of poppycock in there," I tried to joke, sitting on the edge of his bed. The room held the iodine tang of seaweed from the study below.

He nodded.

"I suppose so. There must be some truth to one or two of these tales, though."

"People make things up, all the time."

I put my hand on the quilt. It was damp, and when I looked around I thought that there were darker patches on the carpet.

"Have you spilled something?"

He looked at the patches, shrugged. "I must have upset my water-glass last night." He tilted his head on one side. "Is something bothering you, Aunt Beatrice?"

"Philip, the wooden thing you found..." I prepared myself to explain why I had disposed of it.

"The heart?" He reached into his jacket, which was on the back of the chair, and held up the same object which I had thrown to the waves not five hours before. "I think it must have got wet at the beach somehow. I mean to dry it with a towel later, before it warps or cracks..."

"May I see it closer?" I managed to keep my voice steady.

"I'd rather..." He pursed his lips. "Perhaps when I've dried it out. Perhaps then."

I did not stay to hear whatever excuses might have followed.

Emilia was in her study. Taking her arm, I poured out what I had read, and what I had done.

She listened as she washed her cuttlefish bone in a small bowl, then put it down. She knew me for a practical woman, whose normal reading was confined to the likes of sewing books and poultry manuals. I had imagination, yes, but not the sort that dwelt upon the psychic or the strange.

"The girl with wet hair." Emilia pulled up a stool. "Philip has been under a lot of strain. Might it have caused, how I can I put it, a peculiarity in his thinking? Temporary, of course," she added hastily.

"I suppose that it might." She was too old a friend to upset me by making such talk. "You remember O'Connor, in David's old regiment? He was never quite the same after he lost his wife."

"Yet the heart found its way back," she said, templing her fingers at her chin. "Listen to me talking like that! I mean, someone must have brought it back."

This I could not explain.

"The girl he mentions," I murmured.

"The girl who may not even exist." Emilia's finger-tips were white, pressed together so tightly. "But we've had no visitors this afternoon, and Sarah's been polishing the hall floor. It would have been nigh impossible to slip in the house. I can't make head nor tale of this, really I can't. Do we require a doctor, a policeman or a priest?"

I had no answer, unless we were over-complicating matters. Had a local girl taken a fancy to him and come in pursuit? If that were the case, what of the incident in the public house?

Emilia and I agreed, after some discussion, that it might be necessary to cut short our stay, for Philip's sake. If Dunwich was bringing him distress, or unhealthy thoughts, then he must be taken from Dunwich's reach. As for tangible threat, a passing fisherman's story and suggestions in an old book were hardly proof that anything dreadful would happen.

But there was one matter I had not mentioned to my friend. If I were pushed, I would have said that the damp patches in Philip's room resembled small, regular footprints, leading to and from the window.

Matters were brought to a head by the arrival of Isaiah that afternoon, home from business in Lowestoft. He bustled in, the antithesis of anything strange or unnatural, but his first words cut into me.

"Who's that odd lass at the end of the drive?" he asked, throwing his gloves onto the hall table. "Have we had callers?"

Emilia dropped the cut flowers in her hands, scattering the last of the dahlias in a red and yellow confusion.

"What sort of lass, Isaiah?" I helped pick up the flowers, squeezing Emilia's arm as I did so.

"Haven't the faintest. Slim, lots of tangled long brown hair, an old-fashioned dress. A gypsy, perhaps. She seemed to be looking up to the house. Didn't look at me, so I drove past her."

He kissed her on the cheek.

"Have we had rain here while I was away?"

"Why?" asked Emilia.

"Oh, just that the lass seemed rather wet," he said, and bustled off to change for dinner.

And then I knew what must be done. At least, I knew what to do next.

That evening we took Isaiah aside, and told him that Philip was a little unwell, that I was considering returning to London. He thought it over, but had noticed the mood at dinner.

"I have to go to Ipswich tomorrow, to the Tollemache brewery. Shall I drive you and Philip down? You could take the train to Liverpool Street from there."

I accepted with relief, much though I would like to have seen more of Emilia.

Philip and I argued, for the first time ever. He wished to stay, to visit Dunwich again and spend time by the sea. When I asked him why, he reddened.

"The girl needs me."

I found that I had clenched my fists, unknowing.

"The girl. Philip, if there is a girl here, she's a fisherman's daughter making sport of you. I know that you've been disappointed—"

"Abandoned! Like her."

The air in his room seemed cool and damp around us, as if an unseen sea-mist had gathered there, brushing against our skin.

"Is that what she says?"

He mumbled something, but would not speak out plainly. I caught only a name. Eva.

"Bring this Eva to me, then." I tried not to glare at him. "Let her show herself, and make clear her intentions."

"I . . ." He stared around, seemingly at everything but me. "I cannot. She will not come with others present."

"She has been here, in this house?"

He wiped one hand across his brow.

"No. I mean, I don't know. In the night, maybe. Perhaps I was dreaming."

"Enough." I tried to soften my tone. "Philip, dear, you know that I care for you. Your mother's ill, and I have no choice but to take some charge here."

He nodded, still looking away.

"Then trust me. You have had a shock, a great upset to your life, and now you seek something to balance that unhappy event. But it is not here, in Suffolk. These lonely shores are not for you, and local superstitions help even less."

"But—"

"You need company, and purpose, which we'll find again in London."

There were other words, but I was still formidable enough to prevail. Somewhat sulkily, he agreed to pack that night.

"You ought to leave that . . . carving for Mrs. Rawkins to examine further," I said. "She might find out more about it on her travels."

"I shall keep it," was his only defiance. "It was meant for me."

I was not fond of automobiles, but was persuaded by Isaiah's bluff, matter-of-fact approach. He stuffed Philip and the cases in the back. I was given goggles, one of Emilia's scarves and placed firmly next to Isaiah in the front. The noise of the engine was uncomfortable at first, but as we sped down narrow lanes I became more at ease. We were heading away from the vicinity of Dunwich, and that was a start.

It was a straightforward journey, a route Isaiah apparently knew well, and we swung down through Suffolk without incident. Philip sat silent in the back seat. I glanced at him once or twice, but he was gazing east over the fields, expressionless. North-east, in fact, towards that low coast where we had sought shells and urchins but found . . . what? The idle carving of a long-dead sailor, probably worth a shilling on a bric-a-brac stall in Covent Garden. That was all.

We made good time. I had booked tickets on the 3:45 London train, but we arrived in Ipswich before noon. Having said our goodbyes to Isaiah, I tipped a porter to secure our cases ready for the train, and encouraged Philip to see something of Ipswich with me.

We must have been some fifteen miles from Felixstowe and the sea, in a place which the girl Eva, real or phantasmal, would hardly know. The weather had cleared, leaving a sunny day. There were cafés and a fine museum. We wandered through the town and admired the scale, if not the delicacy, of the Cliffe brewery with which Isaiah had occasional business.

I did not see a slender figure with long wet hair, standing at the opening of an alleyway near the brewery. I am sure that I did not.

"We should move on," I said, and hurried a puzzled Philip away.

There was a small regatta on the River Orwell, and we decided to spend our last hour in Ipswich watching the boats.

"A fine sight, eh?"

I smiled at him, and he managed a dutiful nod.

I thought him paler again, which worried me. We had sandwiches and lemonade by the river, surrounded by a mixed crowd of boating enthusiasts and idle onlookers. When he went to relieve himself in the nearest public house, I noticed that the right-hand side of his jacket bulged oddly. The carved heart, which I had thought safely stowed in his luggage, must be in his pocket.

Why in God's name had I not forced him to leave it behind us with Emilia?

After five or six minutes had passed and Philip had not returned, I began to worry. I scattered change for the attendant, and went into the tavern. It was almost empty, the crowds being by the river.

"A young man in a cream jacket, clean-shaven, came in here a few minutes ago," I said to the thickset barman. "Have you seen him since?"

"Went out the side-door, lady," he said, tipping his head to an exit I hadn't noticed. "Asked him if he wanted a drink, but he said he had to meet a girl."

The cold I felt then was not of any unnatural nature. It was fear.

I strode out of that side-door, scanning the narrow street. To the right it led into Ipswich, but to the left it went down to the river. Almost running, I pushed past idlers and locals alike. The chair where we had been sitting was empty, but I could see the back of his linen jacket as he slipped between the people on the riverbank.

"Philip!" I cried out, trying to make my way towards him. He was down at the water's edge by then, and I had a presentiment of some dreadful act to come. All I could think of was that damnable carving, and a phrase from Ecclesiastes.

All the rivers run into the sea . . .

"Oh God. Stop him, someone!" Before anyone could grasp who I meant, Philip was in the water. It might have gone differently, but the small boats of the regatta were passing our vantage point, and I was too late. I saw his hat, then his head bobbing in the water—no, surely two heads, one a tangle of long dark hair—and then the boats were on them, oars coming down blindly into the grey-brown river, driving the regatta past us . . .

They pulled my nephew's body from the Orwell a half-hour later. No one else had seen a second person in the water, and no other body could be found. People were very kind, plying me with blankets, tea, anything to hand that might be of comfort. I took a tall man's flask, guessing its contents, and poured brandy down my throat until it burned.

The police asked me to view Philip in the mortuary an hour later and complete the formalities. The police doctor was nervous, but I reached to draw the sheet away myself, to see my nephew's face for the last time.

"He drowned, I suppose," I said, my voice dull. "Or was struck by a boat."

The doctor shook his head.

"I fear... I believe that the young man had a seizure, or some form of cardiac attack."

The sheet fell away from his upper body. Philip's left hand was by his chest, empty but clawed as if clutching at something, and his expression was one of terrible, terrible loss.

I searched his sodden jacket.

The heart had gone.

My sister, always frail, was invalided by the shock, and it was decided that Edward, Philip's elder brother, and I would make all necessary arrangements. I told Edward everything, even down to the most minor events of our stay in Suffolk. He listened without comment, squeezed my hand and said he would need to contact a more experienced friend.

I received two communications of note at my London address that week. The first was from the friend of Edward's, one Henry Dodgson, of whom I knew nothing. He had enclosed a small, yellowing pamphlet, along with a note to express his deepest sympathy. I found his mark upon the second page.

> In the year of Our Lord 1746, it is told, Eva van der Druysen, daughter of a Dutch merchant resident in Dulwich, Suffolk, took her own life. This was done in the most dreadful manner by her tearing into her own breast. The tragedy took place after she was abandoned by one of van der Druysen's captains, not long before their proposed

marriage—and after he had had his way with her. Reliable authorities state that her spirit walks the strand still, intent on bringing destruction to any who find her ruined heart.

The pamphlet was stamped as privately published, but the details of the author were unreadable. Edward would speculate no further on the circumstances or background to his brother's death. Mr. Dodgson, however, appended certain suggestions as to protecting oneself from such malign influences. His ideas would have seemed nonsense to me once, even un-Christian, but after Philip's death, I was no longer so sure of myself.

"He knows of such things, Aunt Beatrice," said Edward, as if that settled it.

A second letter was addressed in Emilia's distinctive handwriting. It held a single newspaper clipping, cut from the *Southwold Examiner* of two days before.

A most curious recent find on the shore at Dunwich has today been handed to the Southwold museum, being a carved wooden heart of some age. The curator plans to place it . . .

I could not read on.

My case is packed. I have my late husband's revolver and money to buy sufficient petroleum products for the task ahead. My nephew's funeral is the day after tomorrow.

Before I see him lowered into the ground, I shall visit the Southwold museum, and I shall not be turned away. I shall see the dark heart of Eva van der Druysen burn until it is no more than ashes, and those ashes buried deep in consecrated ground.

RICHARD GAVIN

BANISHMENTS

RICHARD GAVIN is the author of five books of numinous horror fiction, including *Sylvan Dread* and *At Fear's Altar*. He is presently finalising a sixth collection. Several of his tales have been chosen for previous volumes of *Best New Horror* and his story 'The Hag Stone' was adapted into a short film in 2017.

The author has also published numerous works of esotericism, as well as meditations on the macabre. He lives in Ontario, Canada.

"'Banishments' is one of the rare stories whose genesis I can acutely pinpoint," explains Gavin. "Back in 2014, the neighbourhood where I'd grown up suffered a massive flood when a creek swelled and breached its banks. Watching news footage of the footpaths and creekbanks where I'd spent countless hours exploring, reading books and daydreaming being interred in roaring waters stirred deep feelings in me. It felt as though a piece of my past was being washed away or buried at sea.

"Some months later these impressions and images gained a new and chilling context when the image of a dwarfish iron casket floating down a swollen creek slithered up from my subconscious . . ."

THE STORM HAD swollen the creek and infused it with sludge. The brothers had come to the bank to take in some of the elements' power, perhaps even to feel rinsed and purged by these forces. But the sight of the muddied current gushing past caused Will to think that this brackish water was in truth thicker than the blood that supposedly bonded him to the man standing beside him.

Mutely they watched the parade of bobbing wreckage— a porch rocker, a bicycle tyre, the shorn remnants of a tarp. These and more seemed to be flaunted by the roaring current, like a victor flaunting the spoils of battle; trophies from the homes that the hurricane had pummelled.

Dylan sighed melodramatically; a wordless urging for them to be moving on. The pair stood under a sky that glimmered dully, like a vast slab of irradiant granite. Will was secretly counting the seconds until this ritual of contrived grief could be tastefully concluded. He opened his mouth to speak, to remind Dylan that his house had been scarcely grazed by the storm, when they witnessed Death encroaching.

It came shimmying along the bends, using the current as its pallbearer. Under a sky whose grey conveyed a celestial exhaustion, death swam swiftly. It came in the form of an oblong box of tarnished iron. A fat padlock sculpted in the shape of a spade bounced on its latch, clunking against the angled side; a lone drumbeat to provide the scene a dirge. The coffin bobbed, spun in an eddy, then jutted towards the bank behind Dylan's home. Its motion was so forthright that Will believed it was meant to reach them. It grew entangled in the low-looming branches and thickets that bearded the mud.

Will watched as his brother charged down the embankment and entered the creek until its rushing waters rimmed his waist. Dylan managed to grip the end of the case just before it drifted out of reach. Dragging it towards him, he nearly lost his footing, the sight of which inspired Will to leap to the water's edge.

Both of Dylan's hands were now clutching the oblong box. His movements were unnervingly jerky.

"Heavy!" he shouted.

Will reached out to keep his brother righted.

The case struck the bank with a thump, followed by a faint sucking sound as the clay began to inter it. Will concluded that it must have been a struggle for the creek to keep this weighty thing afloat.

Dylan stood shivering. His pants hung heavy upon his legs and his boots were weighted with frigid water. The brothers took a moment to study their treasure, which was, they discovered, more akin to a basket than a box. It was composed of iron bands, each approximately ten centimetres wide. The bands were woven together as one might do with wicker. The knit was airtight. Not a speck of the interior was visible. Will used the heel of his hand to wipe away some of the droplets from the lid. Two of the bands—one vertical, the other horizontal—felt rougher than the rest. Kneeling, squinting, Will surveyed the engravings.

If words they were, they were in a language of which Will knew nothing. If symbols, Will had neither faith nor imagination enough to understand them. The markings were crude. Their asymmetry and jagged texture suggested that the engraver was rushed, or possibly enraged. The wedges, gashes and curlicues formed a decorated cross that stood out from the rest of the iron weave.

Will was suddenly seized by a divergent memory: he hearkened back to Dylan's and his parochial education. He envisioned the two of them now as being Pharaoh's daughters, rescuing a floating ark from its reedy doom.

"Let's get it inside," Dylan said, breaking his brother's reverie. "I'm freezing to death."

Past draped windows and still backyards the brothers carted their strange and grim treasure.

They returned to the house. Will entered first, snapping on the chandelier as a defence against the gloom. The light made the dining room inappropriately cosy. It also illuminated Julie's letter, which had been left on the walnut table—two tiny islands of white upon a sea of black wood. When Will had first arrived, he'd found his younger sibling locked in a toxic fixation with this missive. Dylan had not merely studied it to the point of being able to recite both pages from memory, but had begun to autopsy its script in search of hidden truths. Like a cryptographer, he was compiling lists that twisted the "Dear John" note into anagrams, into weird insect-looking hybrids of letters, not unlike the iron basket's engravings.

Will hurried to the table and swept away the hand-written leaves and the handsome envelope that had held them.

Dylan approached the table.

The foul run-off from the iron case made a brown stippling pattern on the carpet. Dylan grunted as he set down the box.

Will held out his hands dramatically. "What now?"

Dylan, breathing heavily, tapped the heart-shaped padlock and then exited the room. For Will the wait seemed vast. When his brother returned, he came bearing a small tool chest. Mute with focus, Dylan went about unlocking the oblong box.

A squeeze of bolt-cutters made short work of the heart-shaped lock, which fell uselessly to the floor. Will studied this heart, which, despite being made of iron, could evidently be broken as readily as any other.

"Ready?" asked Dylan. Will shrugged. He truly was unsure.

The clasps that held the lid in place made a shrill peeping noise as Dylan peeled them back. He asked for his brother's assistance in lifting off the lid.

One glimpse of what the box contained caused Will to lose his grip. The lid crashed against the dining table, knocking over one of the high-backed chairs in its descent. Dylan brought a hand to his mouth.

The infant corpse was hideously well preserved. Its flesh, which looked as though it had been doused in powdered azure, still sat plump upon the bones. Its eyes were shut but its mouth was mangled wide, its final mewl trapped silently in time. Naked as the day it was born—if born it was—the babe's body glistened under the electric chandelier's clinical light. Will, who was unable to bring himself to study the thing closely, assumed this sheen was creek water, but he made no effort to confirm this.

The creature's head was horrible. Will was unsure whether it was supposed to be a canine or a swine. Either way it was misshapen, like a hammer-forged sculpture by an unskilled artist. It also looked like it had been skinned. Its anatomy was hideously apparent.

"Look," urged Dylan, "come see. It's a wax figure. It's just so…"

"Gruesome?" offered Will.

"…so real…"

He was touching it now, his fingers passing in a reverential pattern over arms, belly and tortured face. "Feels like it's made of wax."

This process ended with a hiss. Will looked at his brother, whose fingers were welling up with blood.

"Its eyes are filled with pins."

Will's brow furrowed. He leaned into the coffin. His brother's blood sat like minuscule gems upon the infant's livid brow, shining fresh like the beads of a sanguine rosary. Dylan was correct. What had been inlaid into the waxen eyelids were not lashes but rows of keen pins. The tongue appeared to be some form of curved blade. Will was also able to see the strange studded rows that lined the baby's wrists, shoulders, waist. They were nails—rugged and angular, the kind an old-world blacksmith might have wrought with hammer and flame. Some of the nails had been welded to the coffin itself. These held the figure in place, bound it. (Though he hadn't wanted to, Will accidentally noted that the infant was sexless.)

"There's salt in its mouth," Will added.

Radiating from the casket's interior was the stench of musty vegetation, the decay one smells just before winter buries autumn's rot. Shielding his nose, Will stared down at the collection of waterlogged roots, leaves and petals that clung to the bottom of the box. This strange potpourri had formed a bed for the eidolon of crib death. The underside of several iron bands also bore the same mad engravings as the cross on the lid.

"We should call someone," suggested Will.

"Like who, the police? There's been no crime here."

"Maybe not, but this isn't right."

Dylan replaced the iron lid. "We don't even know what this is. It could be valuable. A work of art, maybe even some kind of relic.

I'll do some online research later." Dylan lifted the casket with a grunt.

"Where are you taking it?"

"Downstairs. I'm going to towel it off so I can get some clear pictures of those engravings. Somebody has to know what they mean."

Will stood listening to the clunks and puttering coming from the basement. His brother began to whistle some cheery, improvised tune.

For supper Will prepared them pork chops and steamed greens. They ate at the tiny kitchen table, for Will was unable to bear dining where the casket had been.

The only soundtrack to their meal was the sound of their own chewing. Dylan scarcely lifted his gaze from his phone, which sat next to his plate. He scrolled through photo after photo of the infant effigy, of each incised character upon the iron coffin.

"How many pictures of that thing did you take?" Will finally asked, uncapping a fresh beer. He did not take his eyes off his brother as he drank.

Dylan merely shrugged.

"Why don't you put that thing away so we can talk about what's really going on?"

The wooden chair creaked as Dylan leaned back. "What's there to say? Julie left. End of story."

"There's a whole lot to say," replied Will. "Why don't you tell me how it reached this point? As far as I knew, you and Julie had the perfect marriage. Not to mention a free house with no mortgage to carry." Will could hear the edge creeping into his voice but didn't care. "No kids to take your money or your time, free lodgings. And then two days ago I read this panicky social media post from you, telling all your friends that she's gone. When I phoned, you sounded like a shattered man. You were barely coherent. I tell you I'm coming home to see you, and now you expect me to believe that after just one day you're fine?"

"I'm getting there."

"Well that's something, I suppose." Will rubbed his chin, sighed.

"Can you tell me what happened at least? I mean, not every detail, but just what led to Julie walking out?"

Dylan shrugged. "Two days ago she left me that letter telling me that we've drifted apart. She said she doesn't love me anymore. I told her to stay away for good. She said she would." Coolly, he then took up his phone. "So it looks like those engravings are a mix of all sorts of different languages; Coptic, Germanic Runes, ancient Greek."

Though he didn't fancy talking about their grotesque find, Will resigned himself to the fact that the topic of conversation had irretrievably shifted. "Did you find out what any of them mean?"

Will was given a simple "yes" as an answer but received no elaboration. After a few frustrating moments had passed he rose and hastily collected the plates.

Later he went down to their father's old workroom, where the casket sat upon the antiquated workbench. Dylan had already settled onto a wooden stool and had resumed his study of the etchings, referencing them against various websites on his phone.

"Where do you suppose it came from?" Dylan's tone was so wistful it rendered his question rhetorical. "Upstream obviously, but from where?"

"What, are you planning on returning it somehow?"

"I want to see if there's more. I want to know."

"Know *what*? Dylan, you'd better start giving me some straight answers. I came all the way back here to help you, so the least you can do is be honest with me."

Unable to bear being ignored, Will retreated upstairs in a manner both childish and melodramatic. Storming off to the bedroom he'd occupied until he left home at sixteen felt surreal, but surreal in an ugly, off-putting way, like he was willingly stepping back into the very cell from which he'd managed to escape years earlier. The original wardens might have perished, but the prison was being maintained by the heir apparent.

He stood listening to a house that had grown too still. Stepping into the hall, he found it vacant and dim. Descending the stairs, Will's nose was affronted by the scent of smoke.

"Dylan?" he called. When no reply came, Will hurried to the

basement, where the smoke was thickest and its fragrance was chokingly strong. His eyes stinging, he made his way to the workbench, where faint embers spat upwards like tiny fireflies.

The floor suddenly went unstable beneath him. Will was hurled forwards. Peering through the smoke, he could just discern the dozens of woodscrews that carpeted the concrete and had tripped him up. Turning his gaze to the workbench, he saw the last of the embers fluttering down in grey husks to the open Mason jar that sat half-filled with the black remnants of burned paper. The jar was one of dozens their late father had used to store screws, nuts, bolts. This one had been set atop the casket.

Amongst the jar's blackened leavings was a scrap of paper that had not succumbed to the flames. Will recognised Julie's handwriting. He called his brother's name. The only sound was the patter of rain beginning to strike the windows.

He hadn't intended on falling asleep. He'd only retired to the living room sofa because there seemed little else he *could* do. He'd tried to watch television, but the storm had knocked out the satellite signal. The newspaper was a jumble of meaningless words. There had been no sign of Dylan.

He'd closed his eyes and felt a soothing numbness passing through him. He'd watched distorted memories of his own boyhood in this very house pass across his mind's eye.

Had he always felt this way about his brother, he wondered? Always brimming with such jealousy over the ease and comfort with which Dylan's life seemed to have been blessed? Had it not been his own decision to leave home at sixteen and allow himself to grow estranged from his kin? Not even the successive deaths of both his parents was enough to lure Will back. It took discovering that Dylan had inherited the house and was now enjoying a happy marriage.

Will had learned of this through obsessive, covert searches on social media. He was grateful for the technology that allowed him to keep tabs on his brother's life cheaply and easily. It was this same medium that had allowed Will to watch his brother's life dissolving. Ever a sponge sopping up attention, Dylan posted regular updates about his crumbling marriage, which gave Will the privilege of watching his brother's life crumble in real time. Only after a particularly fatalistic-sounding post about how Julie had left for good did Will finally attempt to reach out. Dylan had positively gushed over his brother's first communication in two decades. He'd immediately invited him back to the old house. Little did he suspect that what was driving Will's actions was not empathy but *schadenfreude.*

His sadistic pleasure was short-lived. Within hours of arriving home, Will found his brother's state of mind . . . disquieting. Whatever heart-sickness Dylan had been detailing for his online friends seemed to have been replaced by a kind of mania. Will had even wondered if the whole drama had been nothing more than a ploy to bait him back to this suburban trap. But to what end?

Will's reverie was violently disrupted by a phone ringing. Blindly he fished out his cell from his shirt pocket. It was turned off.

Across the room, Dylan's cell phone rattled upon the dining room table. Will rose and shuffled towards it.

The caller ID consisted of a smiling selfie of Julie, along with her name and a tiny heart icon glowing beside it. Will took up the phone and wrestled with the idea of answering it. It went still and silent before he could decide.

He turned and began to search the house for his brother, but his efforts were in vain. Only after he'd stepped outside to check the backyard did he spot Dylan. He was stepping through the gate at the far end of the yard. From the vantage of the back deck, Will could see beyond the wooden fence to the elegiac creek that rushed ahead in order to eventually merge with Baintree Lake.

Dylan crossed the yard. He was soaked to the skin. His shoes were slathered with mud. As his brother climbed the deck stairs, Will was able to see that Dylan's eyes were glassy, were fey.

"Where were you?" he asked. Dylan pressed past him. His passage through the house left earthen footprints on the carpet. Stopping in the living room, Dylan began to peel away his dripping clothes. They plopped onto the floor. Stripped, Dylan shuffled down the hall towards the bathroom. Will heard the door click shut, then the telltale sound of running water.

He waited until after Dylan finished showering and had returned to the living room, dressed in socks and a terrycloth robe. He towelled his hair absentmindedly, staring at the wet stains on the carpet.

"I hung your clothes on the rack downstairs," Will explained "and I tried to wash off the footprints as best I could. Mind telling me where you were all night?"

Dylan's mouth hitched into an unsettling half-smile. "What, you taking over for Mom now that you're back?"

"I'm *not* back. And I'm not resurrecting Mom. I'm just worried about you."

"There's nothing to worry about, truly *nothing*." Dylan chortled weirdly.

"Julie called your cell just before you came in."

These words choked off Dylan's meandering laughter. They also drained the blood from his face.

"*What?*"

Nonplussed, Will reached for Dylan's cell phone and displayed it, like the bearer of proof in some grand epistemology. "Looks like she left you a voicemail."

With a quaking hand Dylan slid the phone free. He had noticeable difficulty manipulating the keypad, but eventually he held the phone to his ear.

From where he stood, Will could just discern the mousy rasps of a voice.

Dylan's arm dropped. His phone clunked against the floor.

"What is it?" asked Will frantically, "what'd she say?" He scooped up Dylan's dropped phone and slid it into the pocket of his trousers.

Wordlessly, Dylan advanced to the master bedroom. Will followed, spitting out a string of brief and frantic questions, none of which were answered.

Now dressed, Dylan stepped back into the hall. He was breathing heavily. "We have to return it," was all he said before charging down-stairs.

He resurfaced bearing the iron casket. Will wrested on his shoes and tried to keep pace with his brother, who was already unlatching the gate at the rear of the yard. The creek was positively roaring as

Will struggled to stay at Dylan's heels. The rain was intensifying, portending another storm.

"Where are we going?" he asked.

"Not far," Dylan replied. "I'll put it back. I'll make it right."

Together they traipsed the back of Baintree Common. In boyhood Will had played endlessly along these leafy banks, both with friends and with his brother. Though the housing complex had not appreciably changed over the years, its present aura felt threatening.

"Here it is!" declared Dylan. "Help me with the fence."

"Whose house is this?" Will rasped as he gripped one of the fence boards. He watched his brother reverentially slip the woven coffin through the gap and then painfully wriggle himself through. He followed. It was obvious that quizzing Dylan was futile.

The backyard of this home was far better maintained than that of his boyhood home. Will halted when he saw Dylan approach the sliding glass door. He waited to see who would answer his brother's rapping.

But Dylan did not knock; instead he set the casket down on the lawn and yanked at the door, throwing his weight into the task until the lock gave.

Aghast, Will began to feel as though he was watching a movie rather than living the experience. He saw his brother calmly take up the casket and slip past the ruined door. Panicked that he might be spotted, Will found himself following.

The strange house was immaculate in both upkeep and solitude. Standing in the kitchen, staring at the stainless steel appliances and the polished floor, caused Will to ache for his mother.

Dylan was noisily moving through the lower chambers. Will rushed to the descending stairwell. Once there he made note of a trio of framed photographs that hung on the main landing. Wedding photos, enlarged and richly coloured. The groom was a stout man with a crew-cut hairstyle and slender glasses balanced on a slightly bent nose. The bride was blonde and rather pretty.

Will's hand felt for the stair's railing. He gripped it and forced himself to breathe.

The bride in the photographs was Julie.

Will hissed his brother's name, for his throat allowed for nothing louder.

"I think it came from here," Dylan called back. "Come see."

Will's every step was reticent. His heart was thudding loudly. His saliva tasted of metal.

The chamber in which Dylan stood was scarcely broader than a storage closet. An old-fashioned laundry tub stood against a wall of cinderblocks with yellowing mortar. A cold draft lifted tufts of cobwebs from the grey brickwork. They lapped at the air like spectral tongues. The tiny room was uncharacte-istically neglected and decayed compared to the rest of the house.

"Look!" cried Dylan. He pressed the chisel forwards so that his brother might inspect it. The chisel's blade was caked with bluish wax. "This is what they used to sculpt it! And look down there!" Dylan pointed to the concrete floor, which had been stained barn-red. The paint was bubbled and peeling. Moving nearer, Will smelled flowers and something like old potatoes. There was a drain grille set into the floor. "I'll bet you they just lifted this grate and sent that thing downstream towards our house. Listen! You can hear the current through the grate. I watched this house all night from the banks, just waiting for them to leave for work. I knew it must have come from them. I *knew* it!"

"From *who*?" Will managed. "Dylan, whose house is this?" He lifted his hand. "Up there. Up there I saw..." He swallowed. "What happened to Julie?"

Dylan was already crouching down to pry the grill from its nest. He looked up at his brother. His expression was one of shock. "There is no Julie," he said, as though it was the dullest of facts. "I made her up."

"But her pictures...upstairs there are..."

"I know. I copied all her photos from her social media account. Her real name is Chantal. She and her husband have lived in Baintree for a few years now. I've never met her, I just like the way she looks, so I made her my wife."

Will shook his head. "But there are all those photos of the two of you on your profile," he protested. "And with other people as well."

"Photoshop. None of those people exist. The names of all my friends on social media? They're all fake accounts that I created. In fact, you're the only real person out of any of my online friends. The others are just stolen pictures and fake names."

Will bent over. It was as if his brother's revelation had struck him in the solar plexus. "Why?" he whispered. "Why, Dylan?"

"It wasn't supposed to go this far. I never thought you'd actually come, even if I did post news about my wife leaving me. You probably shouldn't be here."

"Neither of us should be *here*! Not in this house! Now let's go. This is crazy. Let's go home. We'll talk about it there, not here."

"Not until I see if this is how they sent it down river. Help me lift this grate up."

Will was stock-still. A revelation had caused him to seize up. It took a great deal of willpower just to bring his hand to his pocket and free his brother's cell phone.

"What is it?" Dylan spat.

"She called you . . . Julie called you. You heard her voice. Let me hear her message. Dylan? I want to hear that message."

When his brother refused to yield from jimmying the grate in the floor, Will began frantically thumbing and scrolling about Dylan's phone.

"What are you doing?" Dylan shouted. He stood and lunged for the phone. The grate slipped from his fingers and clanged down viciously upon its frame. Before Dylan was able to yank the phone away Will had managed to bring up "Julie's" number from the call history. He pressed the DIAL icon. A purling noise leaked through the phone's speaker.

A beat later this noise was usurped by a hideous buzzing that seemed to be emanating from inside the iron coffin.

The brothers were paralysed. They stared into one another's fear-widened eyes. Neither of them could bring themselves to face the buzzing casket. Again and again the phone rang. Even after Will dashed his brother's device against that decaying red floor and saw it splinter, the casket continued to hum.

Dylan advanced to the casket. Its lid hit the floor noisily.

The bluish thing was wriggling. Dylan took up the homeowner's chisel and began to tear the thing to pieces.

"No!" screamed Will, though he was unsure exactly why. Rushing up alongside his brother, he peered over the rim, with its arcane etchings, and looked at the pristine mutilation. The livid wax curled back in ugly whitish rinds and rained down in clumps as Dylan continued to slash and twist and gouge. Though merely an effigy, its autopsy made Will's stomach flip. He watched the torso part and smear as his brother fished out the vibrating phone, which went still and silent the instant it was freed from its host.

Now it was Will who was wrestling free the floor grate. Dylan simply shuffled past him. Though he averted his eyes from the carnage, Will dutifully collected phone, carcass and casket, dropping each in turn into the pipe. He heard them splash when they struck the watery base that churned somewhere below.

He then ran as he had never run before. Outside the rain flailed and swept like great shapeless wings. Will wended the length of the raging creek, his feet puncturing the sucking clay that seemed to be slipping into the creek moment by moment.

His relief at spotting Dylan up ahead was immense. He shouted his brother's name. The maelstrom swirled his voice into its cacophony, muzzling it. Dylan was leisurely sauntering along the bank, whereas he was running full measure. He could not close the gap between them. Time and again he cried out for Dylan but received not even a backwards glance.

His frustration and fear ascending, Will took up a rock and hurled it at his brother's back. But before the stone could strike him, Dylan veered dramatically to his left.

The gate to their backyard was still hanging open by the time Will reached it. He passed through and made his way towards the back deck.

He was stunned by the sight of figures, just barely visible through the glass doors, milling about the dining room. A peek into the kitchen window, which was veiled by Mother's handmade curtains, revealed similarly obscure shapes shifting, gesturing, talking. Some of the figures were familiar to Will, having seen their likenesses on

Dylan's social media page. Though the pattern of the lace curtains seemed to pixelate their faces.

The din of this unbidden gathering was audible even through the storm. The wan afternoon reduced the house's interior to a cave, but Will guessed that Dylan's guests numbered in the dozens. He scaled the steps of the deck. He wanted very much to see his brother.

Moving to the glass door, Will suddenly stumbled. He looked down to see Dylan's shoes sitting tidily side-by-side. The downpour had already rinsed away much of the river mud. Will reached down to collect the shoes but discovered that they had been nailed to the wooden deck. The spikes that pinioned them were chunky and black, akin to the ones that pinioned the effigy to its casket.

The glass door slid back and the susurrus instantly quieted.

Something mewled from the recesses of the house, something that sounded pained.

One of the figures stepped into the half-light and reached a flickering, blurry hand through the open doorway.

Will attempted to flee but found that he, too, had been rooted.

SIMON STRANTZAS

THE FLOWER UNFOLDS

SIMON STRANTZAS is the author of the collections *Nothing is Everything, Burnt Black Suns, Nightingale Songs, Cold to the Touch* and *Beneath the Surface*, as well as the editor of the anthology *Aickman's Heirs*, a finalist for both the World Fantasy and British Fantasy Awards, and the winner of the Shirley Jackson Award. He has also edited *Shadows Edge* and was the guest editor of the third volume of *The Year's Best Weird Fiction*.

His writing has been reprinted in *Best Horror of the Year, Year's Best Weird Fiction* and *Year's Best Dark Fantasy & Horror*, and appeared in publications such as *Cemetery Dance, PostScripts* and *Nightmare*. His short story, 'Pinholes in Black Muslin', was a finalist for the British Fantasy Award, and his collection, *Burnt Black Suns*, a finalist for the Shirley Jackson Award. He lives with his wife in Toronto, Canada.

This is his seventh appearance in the *Best New Horror* series.

"I wrote this story in an attempt to return to the 'strange stories' I'd written more often earlier in my career, back before I found myself side-tracked by the growing 'weird' movement and its more overt Lovecraftian influences.

"This story takes its inspiration from the experiences my mother shared with me about her days working deep in the city, combined with my own experiences doing much the same in an albeit different sort of job. Woven through this is a touch of Robert Aickman's sense of mystery and sensuality, and the end result I think is a story that touches on a lot of the anxieties we feel as we find ourselves increasingly distanced from nature and from those primal urges that drive us."

CANDICE KNEW TWO unassailable facts. The first was she looked every day of her forty-five years; the second was she was stuck at her job forever. Some days were bearable, when the rest of the office staff, all fresh from college and eager, forgot she existed in her tiny cubicle near the rear exit, and she was able to fall into her head while her hands automatically did their work. But the rest of her time was a struggle to avoid dealing with any of them. Each had the same look when they saw her—pity, irritation, a hint of disgust. They did not want her around, and though they did nothing about it, the message was quite clear: she was not like them; she was not one of them; she would never be welcomed by them. If there was any salve at all, it was that few would last beyond the first four weeks, and fewer still beyond the first twelve. By the end of the year, they would be replaced by an entirely new group while she remained a permanent fixture at the back of the office.

At least the elevator was close to her. Sometimes she heard its drone as it crawled up and down Simpson Tower, delivering loads of people to and from their offices. From her desk she heard every gear jump and cable slip. The elevator sometimes ground, sometimes squeaked, and always shuddered and hummed, but it was a reminder that everything moved, everyone went places, and she could too. It was as easy as pressing a button. Sometimes imagining going made it easier to stay.

When her telephone rang, Candice jumped, unprepared for the sound. The small LED on its face reflected a series of zeroes in an aborted effort to display the caller's number. Instead, all Candice knew was it came from inside the network.

"Candice Lourdes. May I help you?"

"I need you in my office," said Ms. Flask.

Candice's knees wobbled as she stood. They had started complaining only a few months before, but it had taken her some time to realise it was not because they were injured, but because they were no longer young. It caused her to shuffle slightly down the corridor, and though the effect would subside in fewer than two minutes, it was long enough that the front office staff had a chance to watch her pass. Most simply ignored her, treated her as invisible, and as difficult as that was to bear, it was better than the alternative, which was a series of scowls. She felt her appearance wordlessly judged: her hair was too flat, they'd whisper, too oily; she didn't wear enough make-up, or fashionable clothes; her nose was too crooked, her jaw too square... She had never been more than average, but she had once been able to coast on her youth. Those days had regrettably passed her by, and the woman that remained felt defeated and disappointed whenever the subject of someone else's glare. She did her best to skirt the bank of cubicles and remain invisible, but it was hopeless.

She knocked on Ms. Flask's door and entered. Her manager sat behind a large oak desk, the only piece of permanent furniture in the office. Her ear was to her telephone's receiver, and she motioned for Candice to sit. Flask's face was red and alive with complicated political manoeuvring.

Candice waited patiently. Flask's desk was covered in baubles and photos of her and her overweight husband, their overweight children. Candice could not stop herself from staring. The family was on a trip somewhere warm, though each was dressed in long sleeves and a hat. Sand was trapped between the folds of her youngest's arms. When Flask addressed her, hand cupping the end of the telephone receiver, Candice tried to react as though she'd seen nothing, as though there weren't any photographs at all.

"I need you to bring these forms up to seventeen. Silvia needs them for payroll." Flask uncovered the receiver and spoke angrily into it. "You tell him he better unless he's looking for a big change." It took too long for Candice to intuit she'd been dismissed. She stood and picked up the stack of pages. Flask scribbled furiously on her legal pad, then paused before unleashing a tirade of profanity upon whomever was unlucky enough to be at the other end of the line.

Candice slunk through the glass doors at the front of the office. The receptionist didn't bother lifting her head as she passed. Candice did her best to put it out of her mind as she walked across to the elevator and pressed the call button, pleased to be the only one waiting. The glass between her and the office acted as an impenetrable barrier, and having passed its threshold she felt somewhat better. Any break from the deadening office atmosphere, if only for the time it took to deliver files to another floor, was heartening and helped replenish her reserves.

There was the normal hum and clanking of metal as she waited, and when the elevator arrived and the doors parted Candice's heart skipped. The car was empty. She exhaled the breath she'd been holding and stepped inside.

No sooner had she done so than there was a shout from down the corridor instructing her to hold the doors. She did nothing, but a giant, suited man appeared before her just the same. Well over six foot tall and smelling faintly of rosewater, he slipped into the car and smiled through the curls of his beard before pressing the button for the top floor. Candice ceded the car's space, pushing herself into the rear mirrored corner in hopes she might vanish, all the while keeping her eyes trained on a small circular stain on the carpeted floor. The large man spoke, but she could not hear him. In the trap, all sound was muted and distant. She closed her eyes and willed herself to calm down. She could ride the elevator two floors. Two floors, and then she would have arrived and could escape. Only two floors to freedom.

But the trip was endless. She waited an interminable age, hugging the files to her chest, her lungs throbbing beneath, desperate for air, and when she finally heard the gentle chime she worried it was her ears playing tricks. The car slowed, then shuddered to a stop, and the opening doors flooded the car with brightness and the odour of soil and flowers instead of the expected stale air of floor seventeen. Candice opened her eyes a crack as her giant companion disembarked, and realised she had travelled to the top floor. Had she forgotten to press the button for the seventeenth? The question lingered only until she opened her eyes wider and saw her destination.

The Botanical Garden spanned the entire top floor of Simpson Tower. Stepping into the faceted glass enclosure was as stepping into paradise. The rooftop garden was divided into rows of plants and flowers, a cascade of colours and scents that overwhelmed Candice, wrapped her in warmth. With uncharacteristic abandon she walked the aisles, past small benches set out to rest upon, ignoring the handful of other people that milled about the greenery, and looked at a variety of plants in turn while a gentle breeze brushed her face, tickling the small hairs on her forehead.

The sun caressed her skin through the many windows, and she turned towards it and closed her eyes. Dots appeared behind her lids, a flutter of coloured lights dancing in strange patterns. When she finally turned away and opened her eyes she wondered for a moment where she had been transported. Everything appeared unreal, hyper-coloured, all except one section of the garden that lay beyond. It was trapped in the shadow of a neighbouring building, and at the end of the aisle an archway stood, wrapped in clinging vines.

"It's beautiful up here, isn't it?"

Candice shook. Beside her stood the large man from the elevator, his chequered blazer reflected in the wicker baskets hanging above. Sunlight haloed his soft creamed hair, his beard hinted with grey. She collapsed in on herself, shrank from his scrutiny, pulled the files close to act as a barrier. But he would not be so easily dissuaded.

"I've been coming up here for months. Usually, I have my lunch just over there." He pointed lazily across the rooftop. "Why would anyone want to be any place but here? It's a mystery."

Candice would not look at him. She wanted to flee, but was too terrified and self-conscious to do anything but remain perfectly still. Only her heart moved, and it pounded.

"I don't think I've seen you up here before. I'm Ben Stanley."

Candice stared at the ground.

"Lourdes," she whispered.

He leaned his enormous bearded face towards her.

"Come again?"

"Candice Lourdes."

"Well, it's nice meeting you, Lourdes, Candice Lourdes. There are some lovely orange lilies over on the south side of the garden you should smell before you go. They've really opened up in this air."

He placed his hand on her shoulder gently, briefly, before walking away. As he did she marvelled she'd let him touch her at all. Her body did not rebel. Nevertheless, once she was certain he had gone, Candice moved as quickly as she could to the elevator to escape the garden and deliver the wrinkled files she had crushed like petals between her fingers.

By the next day, Candice had promised herself two things: the first was to never return to the top of Simpson Tower; the second was to stop thinking about Ben Stanley's warm hand on her shoulder. Yet neither was as easy as she'd hoped. In the morning haze that accompanied her sleepless night, she had unthinkingly selected her nicest skirt to wear despite it being tight across the hips, and tried to wrestle her hair into a style that did not appear damp. Her mind idled on the subway, taking the elevator up to the top floor to meet Ben Stanley amongst the flowers, and the smile it brought to her face evoked strange glances. Yet when she arrived at the office the only comment made was by a young temp who asked, aghast, "What are you *wearing*?" Candice did not speak. As soon as she was able she sneaked off to the washroom and wiped off her make-up. She then retreated to her office and put on an old sweater that covered her bare arms.

When Candice's lunch hour was at hand, she found herself defeated before the elevator doors, finger hovering over the buttons, unable to decide which direction she should travel. She felt the gentle draw of the flowers and plants on the rooftop, yet knew also the danger the visit posed. Taking the elevator down was safer—she knew what to expect. Her heart raced as she watched her finger drift towards the familiar and practised route. The safer route. But she found she could not press the button. Her body was betraying her. Instead it drove her finger into the other button, the UP button, summoning the shuddering box from the depths of the tower so it might propel her skyward.

When the doors opened, she felt an uncomfortable relief and unbearable disappointment. The car was empty. Completely and utterly empty.

She closed her eyes and inhaled. Perhaps it came from the elevator shaft, perhaps from the building's ventilation, perhaps it was mere imagination, but Candice smelled the summer flowers, felt the warm breeze, tasted happiness as it wafted past. It lasted forever. She opened her eyes and stepped into the empty elevator. It quietly hummed as it ascended.

The rooftop garden was busier than Candice remembered. Men in pressed suits spoke with women in blazers and pencil skirts, walking, sitting and laughing, while elderly ladies in neon colours inspected the plant-life, small white purses hanging from their scooped shoulders, faces unfathomably loose. Candice stood on her toes and scanned the crowd but saw no one of unreasonable size, no one with a beard so thick it was like a bush. The sweat at the base of her spine was cold, and a hinted dizziness unmoored her—both multiplied by the mixture of floral scents.

As she explored the rooftop garden she realised every sound was distorted. The giant windows overhead reflected noise in odd directions, bouncing it off the floor or the metal struts, causing some corners to be so quiet they might be miles away, and others so loud it was as though people were yelling directly into her ears. The echoes stretched and bent around the aisles of flowers and greenery, intersecting with the potted autumn clematis and the reed grass that gathered around their warted stems. But Candice didn't mind any of it. In that space, she was free in a way she was not when inside the office, or on the street awaiting her relay of buses. Or even at home, alone in her cramped one-bedroom apartment. Every moment of every day was planned out for her, controlled. But there in the garden, she felt unburdened. And after a few minutes, she couldn't remember having ever felt different.

"I see you're back," said the amused voice behind her. Ben Stanley stood there, barrel chest near her face, dark beard hugging his chin. Perhaps she imagined some shadow dancing there.

"I—I just wanted—I mean I only came—"

He waved his hand to silence her.

"There's nothing to be ashamed of. We are all up here for the same reason. We all deserve to explore ourselves whenever we'd like."

Candice nodded, though she didn't understand what he meant.

"Would you like to join me?" he asked, and pointed to the bench on which he'd been sitting, a bench she had somehow overlooked. Along the seat was an unfolded blanket and a plate of green olives and cubes of yellow cheese. "I have more than enough for two."

Candice didn't speak, and Ben Stanley did not wait for her. He swooped his hand to indicate she should follow, then took a seat. His tiny glazed eyes poked out over round cheeks as he looked up at her, and all she could smell were the lilacs from two aisles away.

She fought her urge to flee. His smile curled around his temples.

"Fruit?" he asked, opening a small cooler hidden behind the bench. A pair of ladies in their seventies strolled by, sagging heads pushing out of their chests, and Candice waited until they were gone before taking some grapes with a polite smile. She held them over her trembling hand and ate them one at a time. She blinked slowly, then swallowed, and immediately regretted it. They tasted gritty and bitter, and she felt ill.

"So, Candice Lourdes, tell me: do you work in the building?"

She squeaked, her throat constricted from terror. She coughed to clear it, but only managed to loosen the muscles enough for sound to squeeze through.

"Yes," she said, her voice tiny, her eyes trained on the shadows.

"Well, don't make me guess. I imagine it's on the fifteenth floor? Where we first met in the elevator?"

Her face flushed with fire and she had to turn away in case she wept. She saw aisles of flowers all bent towards her.

"I've always thought of the fifteenth floor as 'our' floor—we've had such good times there."

She looked at him, forgetting her fears in her immediate confusion, and he bellowed a laugh. All the glass above rattled.

"You're a joy, Candice. A joy. Here, have some cheese."

He held up the plate for her, but she didn't feel like eating anything more. It smelled as though it had gone off. She felt overwhelmed by the heat, by the muted sounds, by the stream of passing people, by the omnipresent floral smell, and by the sheer mass of Ben Stanley, who impossibly grew larger the longer she stayed.

"I—I have to go." She attempted to stand but her legs buckled, and before she knew what happened Ben Stanley had her in his arms. She wondered idly if she might also fit in his palm.

"Are you okay? Do you need some water?"

"No, no," she protested, wondering if her voice was as slurred as it sounded. "I just need to get back. My break is over."

"Let me walk you to the elevator," he said, and did not let her protests deter him.

The doors opened as soon as they arrived, and Candice wondered if she'd missed when he pushed the button, or when the other passengers had walked out. Ben made sure she was safely deposited inside the box, then pressed the fifteenth-floor button for her.

"You be careful," he smiled. "I hope I see you soon."

She nodded impatiently, jabbing at the CLOSE button until the metal doors slid shut. Trapped suddenly and unexpectedly in so small a space, Candice's stomach convulsed, and she could not keep it from reversing. It pushed its contents up her throat in a rush and she vomited in the corner, blanketing the stain she had studied for so many years. She wiped her mouth, humiliated, and stuck her jittering hands in her pockets to quell them. She did not look at the chewed green grapes floating in her sick.

The succeeding week followed the same routine. Candice refused to go in the elevator, instead making the gruelling climb up the stairs to the office. She couldn't afford to be in that small box again. Her shame over what had happened neutered any inclination to explore the garden, to encounter the strange Ben Stanley again. He was simply too much for her in every way—too present, too intrusive—and she found it suffocating to even think of him. It was much safer to eat only at her desk, hiding in the back office, nibbling her homemade sandwiches while in the break room the younger staff made a ruckus. When her telephone rang with an internal number, she avoided answering it, and no one bothered to find out why. Ms. Flask likely found someone else to torment into running errands, leaving Candice to drown herself in work until night came, at which point she descended the echoing stairwell as quickly as she could. No matter how she tried to mask it, though, the scent of the botanical garden flowers lingered—first in her clothes, then on her skin, and soon enough her every thought was corrupted by a wide field of flowers, the scents of lavender and ground roses in the breeze. She left stacks of work on the edges of her desk and huddled with her dry sandwiches and water, fluorescent bulb above humming erratically. She watched the elevators and waited, but when those doors slid open no one ever emerged looking for her.

Sometimes, it felt like aeons since she'd last spoken. Her days were a series of stairs and hidden cubicles, flickering fluorescents and vacant-eyed commuters adrift in underground tunnels. She woke, worked, dined, slept; over and over again. At times she was curious if she still had a voice, but could not gather the nerve to test it. Instead, she closed her mouth and felt the pressure of her depression dig in its weighted talons. Soon enough, even sleep was denied her.

Having woken without anything to occupy her frazzled mind, Candice left for work a half-hour early, her trip unusually silent. The subway car she travelled in was devoid of other passengers, and when she arrived at her destination platform it too was unpopulated. It would not be long before the sun rose and rush hour arrived, flooding the tunnels and streets with drab business men and women sprinting to nowhere.

The windows of Simpson Tower were frozen when she arrived, frost turning them opaque and milky. The hydraulic doors still functioned, however, and inside the lobby was warm and newly lit. The entrance to the stairs, however, had yet to be unlocked. She tried the handle with as much force as she could muster, a tiny panic growing as she did, but there was no movement at all, and no indication in the empty lobby of anyone coming to unlock it. Even the security desk was vacant. She wondered if she should leave and return later, but there was nowhere to go. She swallowed and looked at the elevator doors, then around in vain for another option. Any option at all. But there was only one.

Her stomach rolled in protest, her mouth dried. Her hands

trembled as she pressed the button to summon the elevator towards her. The car shuddered and ground, moving slowly from floor to floor, the pale display's lit orange number decreasing incrementally. When the car reached the lobby, she felt its gears slip before the doors staggered and wrenched apart. The mirrored walls inside were murky with grime, and it was not until she bravely stepped in with held breath and turned to press the fifteenth-floor button that she noticed the familiar stain on the carpet was gone. She stared at the void the entire way up.

The office was vacant and locked. She inserted her key, the heavy bolt sliding back with a satisfying snap, and merged with the dark. No one else would be there so early, and the air in the dark was queerly muted, the carpet muffling her footsteps. Candice visited each area in turn, flipping light switches in succession, ignoring the flicker and buzz of the fluorescents gradually warming. Soon the sound was joined by a random chirping, so faint she was not certain where it emanated from, nor what she'd done to initiate it. Perhaps that insectan drone had always been there, masked by the noise of office bustle, but in the quiet of morning the sounds were deafening, and she put her hands over her ears to silence them. It made no difference; they would not diminish.

Candice frowned, then shuffled to her desk and slipped into her worn leather chair behind it. Her computer rattled to life, vibrating as the drive spun, the fans revolving. A pale green cursor faded into view, blinking slowing as though taking breath, before the computer screen displayed line after line of unreadable code, paging rapidly. Candice mashed the keys, hoping to stop the flood, and though she saw those letters she typed appear in the intervals she typed them, none slowed the cascade or remained on screen for more than a few seconds before the wave of garbage data swept them away.

She pounded the keyboard but it made no difference. Coming in early and immersing herself in work was supposed to distract her from thoughts of Ben and the garden, but without access to the computer network she was helpless to prevent their invasion at every unoccupied moment. She tried to focus on anything else, tried to ground herself in the present to break the spell. She touched things around her, one at a time, calling out their names to fix them in reality, and she alongside. "Desk. Chair. Computer," she said. "Wall. Stapler. Telephone."

It was no use. Details about Ben Stanley filled the quiet seconds in her mind, flashes of him sliced between thoughts; his towering figure, his floral scent from the garden, that deep laugh, the warmth of his touch. His eyes, though small and recessed over protruding cheeks were mesmerising, and she found herself remembering those black stones more than anything else. How they glinted in the daylight. Her fear was immense, but for the first time it was a terror that invigorated her. It was like nothing she had experienced—not like her father, overbearing and reeking of sweat; not her mother, timid and perfumed. Not like the sweating students she had been so removed from, or the worn leather adults that took their place. All these people stood too close to her, tried to grab her and push her. From all their flesh her skin recoiled. But from Ben Stanley's, it heated. She could feel it in her face. She could feel it between her legs. Her mouth lined with cotton.

A chime drew her from her reverie, so familiar she did not realise at first it had sounded, and when she did she wasn't certain she hadn't imagined it. The humming drone returned, amplified somehow, a double sine wave that rattled the small bones in her skull. She padded out of her office towards reception, wondering if Ms. Flask or an eager staff member had arrived, despite it being impossible without her hearing. But when Candice reached reception she saw the elevator doors standing open beyond the office glass, dim light spreading outwards.

Candice tested the lock, yet could not shake the feeling someone had managed to sneak into the office. Why else would the elevator car be there, its doors open? She hadn't summoned it. The car waited, beckoned, drew her towards it, and Candice hesitated, then turned the office lock. The bolt fell heavily, and when she opened the door the smell of flowers overwhelmed her. The world swayed and her mouth once again dried. She staggered forwards with closed eyes.

It seemed to span no longer than a blink, but when Candice was once more aware of herself she discovered she was seated against the mirrored wall of the elevator car, skirt pulled up across her doughy thighs, a foot-long run in her hosiery. She shook her head and rolled onto her scuffed knees, fearful someone might summon the elevator and see her there, dishevelled. She trembled as she reached up and took hold of the railing.

Had she pressed the button for the top floor in her stupor? She must have, as it was lit dull orange, but she had no memory of doing so. Something wrong was happening, something that brought her to the edge of hysteria, but she managed to tamp it down, convinced herself there was an explanation, if only she had time to work it out. Breathing slowly helped, and when she felt calm enough to function again, the first thing she tried to do was step off the elevator. But the closing doors prevented that, and with a short buzz the car lurched into ascent; it would not be stopped no matter how many times she hit other buttons. It headed towards the top floor where the botanical garden waited.

The doors opened on the unoccupied garden. The lights were turned to a dim low, the giant thermal windows making up the polygonal dome brushed with a layer of frosted ice, refracting the rising sun's light. Each window became a haloed fractal, and the odd angles sent curious shadows down the aisles of closed flowers, petals folded gently inside, pistils turned downwards. The potted vegetation edged towards her impossibly, though it might have simply been those shadows cast by the overhead sun against towering skyscrapers. The atmosphere was filled with restrained potential—every inch of the garden asleep, its dream seeping outwards in a hazed umbra. Candice worried she might be asleep as well, her limbs slowed by the weight of the fragrant air as she lifted them to stab at the fifteenth-floor button. But it did not light up. She was trapped in the too-sweet miasma of the waking garden. It would not be denied.

She stepped out and was immediately confronted with the cloying odour; she closed her eyes, inhaled deeply, a rush of nostalgia flooding her senses. Instantly, she was transported to her childhood in the park, lying by the small creek, listening to wind blow through the grass. She could still taste the tang of it. But the resurrected memory was not as peaceful as before. The leaves were skeletal from insectan mandibles, the creek bubbled viscous foam, the wind carried with it something rotten. She felt a presence there in her waking dream, something that loomed over her, a shadow heavy enough to pin her. She shook her head but it took all her strength to do so, the waves of dislocation like stagnant water. She shook and shook and shook, flailing to be free, and when she finally managed to wake herself she did so with a gasp, sucking in air to refill her suffocated lungs. Yet as she remained bent, struggling for breath, the sensation of a looming presence intensified. Candice cleared her throat, fearful of what she had to do. "Hello? Is there someone here?" Her wavering voice echoed on the buzzing glass, and the sound discomforted her. Something strange was occurring. She withdrew into the dim aisles. "Please say something."

But no one spoke. Another rustle. Like a bird amongst branches. Candice spun but saw only plants. Honeysuckle. Cotoneaster. Dark Beauty toad lilies. The plants lining the aisle all were absolutely still, and yet Candice felt cold, as though they were deliberately still. The flowers... there was no other way to explain it: They were *watching* her. Coaxing her. Whispering to her. She pulled her blouse closer to her chest and retreated another step.

She travelled the aisles one by one as though confined to her daydream. Movements dragged, reactions delayed, and when she struggled to cohere her muddled thoughts and make sense of the puzzle, it proved impossible. There was something about the garden that she could resist when seated a few floors beneath, but in its presence cast too strong a spell.

Part of her hoped she wasn't alone. She kept looking around, searching for Ben Stanley amongst the empty benches and closed flowers. But why should he be there? Other than the fact that he simply *belonged* there, belonged in a way Candice did not. His beard, his height—he seemed a part of the landscape, another tree in the forest, the swirls in his hair and beard repeated in the swirls of garden branches and vines. It was Candice that was the interloper, stumbling over roots she could not see, scratched by wisp-thin branches. But in her haze she felt unquestionably welcomed; the garden's arms were open, ready to embrace her.

Under the arch strange shadows moved, and though it could easily have been a reflection on the glass beyond, Candice wondered. It seemed so alien, so different from any world she had ever known, ever imagined. She took a step closer and the images moved, unfolded, opened to reveal more of themselves. She felt light-headed but continued down the aisle, breathing heavier as she got closer. The heat of the garden had risen with the sun, and beads of sweat formed on her forehead. Candice's body vibrated gently with every step she took towards the archway shaded from the morning sun. It was a tickle at the base of her neck which became a warm river flowing downwards along the channel of her spine. The slow hazy world took on a different appearance, one where her eyesight was heightened, showing her each pattern of budding petal, each dew-covered thorn on those plants surrounding her. And the vibrations continued as she entered that dark aisle. They washed over her neck; numbed her arms, her chest; sped her heart. They flowed downwards until they met the warmth from her back, a spiralling eddy between her legs. She bit down on her lip, bent over and gasped. Her mind flooded with images of Ben Stanley, now twenty feet tall, reaching out and enveloping her in his massive arms, his face the landscape of the desert, his eyes the expanse of the sea. He reached down and plucked her from where she stood and she screamed as the sky turned vibrant and everything exploded outwards in streaks of crimson flame. Stars and suns lit her vision, colours streaming over her eyes, an eternal cascade bathing her, invading her, transforming her. It continued for aeons, and yet ended too quickly, abandoning Candice to the dull realities of the physical world. The botanical garden faded back into view, one unfurled flower at a time, and she stumbled upon entering it once more. The archway before her filtered the light from the rising sun, burned clean of any shadows that had once gathered there. Nothing seemed amiss about it any longer. She heard behind her distant voices shouting something, but whatever words they spoke were transient in her decaying memory.

Ms. Flask was unimpressed. The financial reports due on her desk before her weekly teleconference had not appeared, and for the first time since assuming her position she was forced to make excuses to the board. It made her appear weak, incapable of running her team, and that she could not abide. It was enough that they snickered about her weight, called her names, but until that moment they could never have claimed her incompetent. It would not do. Not at all.

Candice had been missing for three days, and in that time no one knew where she had gone. True, she was hardly irreplaceable—Ms. Flask would have done so immediately if possible. But Candice had been there long enough that only she understood how to extract the numbers Ms. Flask needed. The reporting of those quotas was perhaps more important than those quotas themselves, and ever-dependable Candice was key. Except she was not quite so "ever-dependable" any longer, and that was a problem too large to solve over the telephone. She had to be made an example of.

Ms. Flask stormed through the office towards Candice's cubicle, quietly enjoying the terror that spun around her as she cut a swath through the office. The newest employees rattled in their seats, the rest kept their heads down and feigned work, too afraid to look at her. When she faced down Candice, it would be with the power collected from their aggregate fear.

But Candice was not as Ms. Flask expected. The woman sat at her desk on the telephone, and offered no more than a half-smile in her manager's direction. Ms. Flask was impotent with rage as she watched Candice's brightly painted nails clicking on the desk, but all she could do was wordlessly broadcast her irritation. Yet Candice's smile never faltered. When she finally hung up, Ms. Flask's power felt strangely flattened. It was a foreign sensation and one she did not care for.

"Ms. Lourdes, where have you been?"

"I took some personal days. All the forms have been sent to HR."

Ms. Flask made a mental note to verify that when she returned to her desk, and to ensure no errors were committed filling out those forms. "That may be, but you had reports due this morning that never arrived."

"That's weird," Candice said, her brow furrowed unconvincingly. She checked her watch, then pushed her loose hair behind her ear. "I came in early today to catch up on everything."

"Well, I received nothing."

Candice shrugged. "Would you like me to send them again?"

"Yes, of course."

Ms. Flask remained in the doorway, staring as the unperturbed Candice lazily checked her watch. Everything about the woman was wrong, and it was far more disconcerting than the missing reports. Ms. Flask could not put her finger on why, but it made her uncomfortable.

"Do you have somewhere else you have to be, Ms. Lourdes?"

Candice laughed incredulously at Ms. Flask. She laughed like sparking steel, then crossed her smooth bare legs.

"Not yet," Candice said, and touched her tongue to her lips.

ALISON MOORE

THE VOICE OF THE PEOPLE

A LISON MOORE's short fiction has been included in *Best British Short Stories* and *Best British Horror*, broadcast on BBC Radio, and collected in *The Pre-War House and Other Stories*.

Her first novel, *The Lighthouse*, was short-listed for the Man Booker Prize and the National Book Awards, winning the McKitterick Prize. Both *The Lighthouse* and her second novel, *He Wants*, were "*Observer* Books of the Year". Reviews of her third novel, *Death and the Seaside*, referred to her as the "Talented creator of a new English grotesque" (Isabel Berwick, *The Financial Times*) and as "One of the most gifted and interesting writers of weird fiction in Britain today" (Nina Allan, *The Spider's House*). Her fourth novel, *Missing*, was published in 2018, along with her first book for children, *Sunny and the Ghosts*, to be followed by *Sunny and the Hotel Splendid*.

She lives in a village on the Leicestershire-Nottinghamshire border with her husband and son, and is an honorary lecturer in the School of English at the University of Nottingham.

"I am indebted to a series of sluggish pigeons seen on the road between my house and the local B&Q hardware store," reveals the author. "When I got to the B&Q car park I made some notes, and on the way home I stopped to write a bit more. I got back with the whole story sketched out, and some sealant."

O N THE DAY of the protest, Glenda decided to drive out to the retail park to buy weedkiller. She was just setting out, getting into third gear, when a pigeon dawdling in the road caused her to brake hard. The pigeon seemed oblivious, even when Glenda's two-tonne car was virtually on top of it. Perhaps the car actually was on top of it, because having stopped dead, Glenda could not see the pigeon anywhere. She was just about to get out to look beneath her wheels when she saw the pigeon wandering to the side of the road. She watched its strangely sluggish progress, and then drove on, towards the edge of the village.

The garden was really Dougie's responsibility, but work was taking it out of him these days. On his day off, he just lay on the sofa, with the cat asleep on top of him, or sometimes the cat fell asleep on the carpet or in the lengthening grass, wherever it happened to be. Dougie himself did not really sleep, he just lay there, with no energy for Glenda, or for his projects: at the far end of the overgrown garden, a half-dug pond had been abandoned; and the second-hand furniture that he had bought to spruce up was gathering dust in the spare room. The last piece he had done was the little table on which their telephone stood: he had spent weeks sanding and then staining and varnishing it, although Glenda hated it, the darkness of its wood, and its rickety, skeletal legs.

She had just got onto a faster stretch of road leading out of the village when another pigeon staggered out in front of her car, not even flinching away from the vehicle as she skimmed past. She wondered what was wrong with these pigeons; they were like zombies.

It was not just Dougie; it seemed to be everyone who worked at that factory. They had all lost their pep. No one in the village liked the factory, although the men needed the jobs; it employed hundreds of them. It was an ugly, stony-faced building, ruining what had been a nice stretch of riverside, at a spot where the locals used to swim—

some still did, but not many. The women had been worrying about the factory's emissions, about what exactly was going into the air. Sometimes the smoke that went into the clouds looked yellow. And was anything going into the river, anything that should not be? Dougie used to fish there, but he did not do that anymore. And there was that terrible smell, which had to be coming from the factory.

At the bend, where the road turned away from the river, there was a pigeon, flattened against the tarmac. Its grey wings were splayed around its crushed body. Its underbelly was turned up to face the sky, to face the wheels of the oncoming traffic. These pigeons reminded Glenda of the summer outbreak of flying ants, which did not fly off at the flap of a hand as houseflies did; or they reminded her of the houseflies themselves, the listlessness that came over them at the end of the summer, leaving them too slow to avoid the swatter. But she had never before noticed the phenomenon in birds or other creatures.

Glenda had written the council a letter, which the other women had signed. The letter asked questions about those emissions; it suggested that the factory might be affecting the health of the workers; it requested a thorough investigation and the suspension of operations pending the results. The men had not signed the letter. The letter had been forwarded to a secretary who would liaise with the relevant committee; it was then, after somebody's holiday, to be discussed at a forthcoming meeting. Not having heard anything for a while, Glenda had left messages on a council answerphone. In the meantime, the women were going to go on a protest march. "We never used to take things lying down," Glenda had said to the women. "When we were students, we used to march." They used to go down to London, on coaches; they had marched through the capital in their thousands, to force things to change. "We *should*," the women had said in response. "We *should* do that." Since then, they had been meeting every Wednesday morning at Fiona's house. Fiona had provided refreshments while they made placards, nailing boards to wooden sticks and painting slogans on them—WE WANT ANSWERS!—slogans that they would shout as they marched. They had photocopied flyers to put through people's letterboxes. They had notified the local paper.

Glenda glanced at the dashboard clock. It was almost noon; they were due to meet to start the protest at one o'clock. They would march down Union Street to the river, right down to the factory. They would stand outside that grim building and stamp their feet and shout, make some noise. Someone would have to respond; something would have to be done.

She pulled into the car park of the Do-It-Yourself store, disturbing a couple of birds, which flapped up into the air and flew away. She parked near the entrance and went inside the store. As she entered the gardening section, she recognised a neighbour who was standing looking at the lawnmowers. Glenda said hello. She could not think of her neighbour's name. The woman continued to stare at a lawnmower, and Glenda thought that she had not heard her, but then the woman said, "I've been here for hours. I just can't decide."

"Are you coming on the protest?" asked Glenda.

"I just can't decide," said the woman.

Glenda turned away and picked up a spray-gun bottle of ready-to-use weedkiller. She took it over to the till, where the cashier was sharing a joke with a man who had bought paint in a shade called "Nursery". The colour looked putrid to Glenda. The man turned away and the cashier looked at Glenda and said, "Are you all right?"

"I'm fine," said Glenda, lifting her free hand and touching her face. "It's just a rash." She handed over the weedkiller and the cashier scanned it. Glenda looked at the silver and copper in her purse. She could not be bothered to count out the coins. She handed over a note and waited for her change, and then stood struggling with the zip of her purse. She took her weedkiller and moved towards the exit, aware of the cashier watching her as she walked away.

She strapped the weedkiller into the passenger seat, as if it were a child. She did not want it sliding around, busting open, weedkiller going everywhere. She drove home slowly, carefully.

It was after one o'clock when she returned to the outskirts of the village, where she found Fiona sitting on the kerb, with a placard on the pavement beside her. Glenda came to a stop and wound down her window. She said to Fiona, "Have they gone already?"

Fiona raised her eyes. "Who?"

"The other women," said Glenda. "Have they started the march?"

"No one else has turned up," said Fiona.

"Oh," said Glenda. "Well, I have to take the car home, then I'm going to walk back down here and join you. Even if it's just the two of us, we can still march down to the factory. We can still make some noise." She drove home, passing a car that was so badly parked it looked as if it had just been abandoned mid-manoeuvre, and stopping to move a child's bike that had been left lying across the road. She backed her car into a kerbside space and took the weedkiller inside. She put on some sunscreen and checked her appearance in the mirror. She was wearing the olive-green eyeliner that Dougie had once said brought alive her copper-coloured eyes, but now she wondered if it was just making her look a bit ill. She put down some food for the cat. By the time she got back down to the corner with her placard, Fiona was no longer there. Glenda thought about going to the factory anyway, on her own, but she did not really think she had the energy.

When Glenda got home again, she filled a glass with water from the tap, and drank it standing at the sink. It was past lunchtime, but she was not hungry, and there was still food in the cat's bowl from before. She went through to the lounge and sat down in an armchair, next to the second-hand table with the phone on it. She had disliked that table, she thought, but now she could not really see what was wrong with it; she did not have any strong feelings about it either way. Next to the phone were her phone numbers. There was the number for the council—she would have to call them again at some point, about that letter she had sent to them. And there was Fiona's number—she ought to call her; she ought to call everyone. The protest would have to be rescheduled. The numbers seemed to blur; she must be tired. She switched on the TV and watched the afternoon programmes. She was still sitting there when Dougie came in from the factory. He lay down on the sofa.

"Have you seen the cat?" asked Glenda.

"Uh-uh," said Dougie.

In between TV programmes, Glenda said, "I'm going to go up to bed," but she did not actually move for a while.

234 ⁖ ALISON MOORE

Eventually, she got to the bathroom and picked up her toothbrush. She looked at herself in the mirror. It felt like being stared at by a stranger. Her eyes were the colour of dull pennies. She left the bathroom and got into bed. She looked at her book but she felt that she just wanted to sleep. She realised that she had somehow not cleaned her teeth after all. She thought about her unbrushed teeth rotting in the night, but she did not get up again; she just left them.

A week and a half later, Glenda found the cat beneath the back wheel of her car, against the kerb. It must not have moved out of the way when Glenda was parking. She had not been anywhere since the previous weekend, when she went to fetch that weedkiller.

She stood at the kerb, trying to remember what she had come outside for. There was no point driving over to Fiona's house: the group had dissolved.

Glenda's placard was still propped against the front wall. She picked it up, looking at the faded lettering: WE WANT ANSWERS! Had she written that? It did not sound like her, like something she would say. Perhaps she had got somebody else's placard by mistake. She stood on the pavement, near the kerb. She could see the factory chimney in the distance, down by the river, belching its mustard smoke into the sky. Dougie would be taking his lunch break soon. She could walk down there and try to see him, see if he was feeling any better. If she found, on the way, that she did not want to keep carrying the placard, which may or may not have been hers, she could just leave it somewhere.

She stepped into the road, with the sign hanging down, the message (WE WANT ANSWERS!) dangling in the gutter. She moved out into the road, slowly, as if she were stepping through the mud at the edge of the river, mud in which Dougie had seen fish lying belly up.

She did have a sense of the size and weight of the vehicle that was coming towards her. She was not oblivious to the juggernaut that was bearing down on her. But it felt more peripheral, more distant, than it was. She was moving forward, looking towards the far side of the road, but with no great sense of urgency.

WILLIAM F. NOLAN

CARNIVOROUS

WILLIAM F. NOLAN writes mostly in the science fiction, fantasy and horror genres. Though best known for co-authoring the classic science fiction novel *Logan's Run* with George Clayton Johnson, Nolan is the author of more than 2,000 pieces (fiction, non-fiction, articles and books), and has edited twenty-six anthologies in his sixty-plus year career.

Adept at poetry and screenwriting as well as fiction (with more than twenty produced scripts to his credit), he was co-writer (with Dan Curtis) of the screenplay for the 1976 horror movie *Burnt Offerings*, and co-wrote the TV movie *Trilogy of Terror* with Richard Matheson.

An artist, Nolan worked at Hallmark Cards and in comic books before becoming an author. During the 1950s, he was an integral part of the writing ensemble known as "The Group" (also called "The Southern California Writing School" by former *Los Angeles Times* critic Robert Kirsch), which included numerous veteran and soon-to-be well-known genre writers, such as Matheson and Johnson, Ray Bradbury, Charles Beaumont and John Tomerlin, many of whom wrote for Rod Serling's *The Twilight Zone* series. Nolan is also considered a leading expert on Dashiell Hammett, and pulps such as *Black Mask* and *Western Story*, and is the world authority on the works of prolific scribe Max Brand.

Of his numerous awards, there are several of which he is most proud: being voted a Living Legend in Dark Fantasy by the International Horror Guild in 2002; twice winning the Edgar Allan Poe Award from the Mystery Writers of America; being awarded the honorary title of Author Emeritus by the Science Fiction and Fantasy Writers of America in 2006; receiving the Lifetime Achievement Award from the Horror Writers Association in 2010; and as recipient of the 2013 World Fantasy Convention Award, along with Brian W. Aldiss. He was also named a World Horror Society Grand Master in 2015.

"I have long had an interest in carnivorous plants," explains the vegetarian author. "They are fascinating to me because they turn the tables—instead of animals eating *them*, they have the capability of eating animals! How terrifying to think that something we normally think of as no threat at all can do us injury. It's one thing that made John Wyndham's *The Day of the Triffids* such a shock. During my research for this story, I came across many more species than I even realised existed!

"Some of the dynamic of the couple is based on my real life. My marriage wasn't as great as I would have liked. As a result, I poured some of my irritation into this tale, which I think turned out pretty well. I hope the readers agree . . . and watch out for those plants!"

"I WILL NOT SPEND another winter in this city!" declared Martha Burns. She paced the living room of their small apartment, stared out the window at the yard littered with wind-snapped branches. A fresh gust rattled the pane. To Martha, these constant, battering gusts seemed truly demonic, with the worst yet to come. Winter, in Chicago, had barely begun, and the cold spring months ahead were only a minor improvement. The cold was dreadful, penetrating, exhausting—a gradual erosion of the soul.

She faced her husband, desperation in her eyes. "This awful wind . . . the snow . . . the ice . . . The weather is killing me, Dave! I need to see some greenery—trees, flowers, plants. I'm tired of this grey world of concrete and steel. It was so freezing cold shopping the Loop this afternoon that the little hairs in my nose froze up. No more of these damn winters!"

Dave Burns agreed. As a boy in Missouri—young, eager, full of energy—he had looked forward to each winter...sledding down the hill on 34th with Tommy Griffith who lived at the end of the block...helping Dad build a six-foot snowman in the back yard...a time for tossing iced snowballs at Jimmy Farmer, his worst enemy...a time for Mom's hot apple cider...skating Troost Lake...and watching a zillion fast-falling white flakes cover the streets and sidewalks, turning Kansas City into a crystal wonderland.

But he was no longer that snow-loving boy. He was a balding, overweight, forty-year-old manager of a barely profitable music store in downtown Chicago—who hated winter.

"Okay," he told Martha, "I'll get Sid Collins to fill in at the store and we'll head for California. Sid lived there in the 1970s. Says it never gets really cold in Los Angeles. Sunshine all year round. I'll post an online ad and see what turns up. Gotta admit this bloody cold is killing us both."

The ad was brief and to the point:

WANTED: Chicago couple seek rental of modest house in L.A. area for winter/spring months. Must be reasonably priced. Contact information provided once terms are met.

The ad was answered by a woman who said she would call soon.

A few days later, a woman who identified herself as Viola P. Fanning called. If a suitable agreement could be reached, she was prepared to offer them her home in the Santa Monica suburb of Greater Los Angeles for the desired period, all utilities paid. The house, she explained, was quite old. "But I have faithfully maintained it. And there is an upstairs view of the ocean."

"Sounds wonderful!" exclaimed Martha. "I can't *wait* to sunbathe on the beach!"

"We should complete this discussion via Skype," declared the woman. "It is important, at this point, that we establish visual contact."

"Of course," said Martha. "I understand . . . about visual contact."

Dave expressed doubt to his wife after the call had ended. "Let's not rush into this—take it one step at a time. We can't handle anything fancy. Rent in California is sky-high. We don't know *what* she'll charge."

"But our ad said 'reasonable'. I'm sure we'll be able to afford it." She shivered. "Oh, Dave, we've just *got* to get out of this miserable cold!"

Dave Burns nodded. "That's what we both want."

The Skype call came through the next day. The screen image of Viola Fanning was that of a stark-faced woman in her late sixties, attired in black, with a flow of Victorian lace at her throat. Her grey hair was pulled back into a tight bun, her eyes cold and night-haunted.

"I am an avid collector," the woman on the screen told them. "I am particularly fond of fungoid plants. In Europe, if I am fortunate, I shall unearth several rare species. I expect to remain overseas into fall, and—if I am satisfied that you meet *my* requirements—you may have the house here in California for a period of five months."

Dave was suddenly sceptical. "And just what *are* your requirements, Ms. Fanning?"

"You must not be accompanied by pets or children. I dislike cats and dogs—and children are messy. I will not tolerate them."

"There's just the two of us," said Martha.

"My primary concern is the proper care of my darlings." Her dark eyes bore into them. "Do either of you know anything about plants?"

"I was good in botany in college," said Martha, "but I'm no expert."

"Are you diligent about following instructions? My dearly departed husband wasn't too careful about that."

"I would say so."

"My darlings require special care. They are, each of them, very close to my heart. They're the only link to my family that I have left."

"Me," Dave declared, "I'm into flowers. Like roses. All kinds of roses."

Her dark eyes flashed. "My darlings are much more than *roses*."

She made the word sound obscene. "They are sensitive and intelligent."

"I've never thought of plants that way," he admitted, adjusting his chair to face the screen. "Before we discuss this any further we have to know what the rent will be. We can't afford a—"

She waved the problem aside. "You need have no concern in that regard. The house is yours, rent free, if you follow my instructions."

Martha was nudging him, nodding vigorously. Her whisper was strident: "Tell her *yes!*"

"Your offer is most generous, Ms. Fanning. I'm sure we can take good care of your plants if that's all you want."

"Nothing more," said the dark woman. "You will find some bottles in the greenhouse containing the food for my darlings. So...do we have a deal?" And she smiled, but her eyes remained cold.

"Yeah," said Dave. "We have a deal."

A large manila envelope later arrived at their Chicago apartment, a contract enclosed along with a hand-written note:

> In accepting this contract, you agree, totally and completely, to comply with the terms contained herein. Any alteration shall result in the immediate termination of the agreement.
>
> WARNING: You are not to enter the laboratory behind the greenhouse. Entry is forbidden. The work done there must remain private.

The note was signed V.P.F. Dave began scanning the pages. Two paragraphs in the contract were underlined in red:

> My plants must be fed twice during each 24-hour period: at noon and again at midnight. Their feed must consist only of the bottled food from the greenhouse.
>
> Additionally, Mrs. Burns must sing to my plants after each nightly feeding. They adore romantic songs. Their particular favourites are 'In the Good Old Summertime', 'I Dream of

Jeannie with the Light Brown Hair', and 'In the Sweet Bye and Bye'. No other songs may be substituted. Lyrics are provided.

"Well, that cuts it!" Dave tossed aside the contract with a snarl of disgust. "The old bat is a fruitcake. Totally out of her freaking mind. She can't expect us to—"

"But we have no other options," declared Martha. "Our personal stuff is already on the way to California. And we're getting the place for *free!* We can't back out now."

Dave shook his head. "This whole set-up is crazy. We haven't even seen the house yet. Could be a shack."

"In Santa Monica? C'mon, hon, get real. There are no 'shacks' in Santa Monica."

"I still say the whole thing is crazy. But..." His voice softened. "Guess you're right. We have no other options."

The Fanning house was far from a shack, eliciting a burst of joy from Martha.

The screen-porched two-storey structure, freshly painted in dandelion yellow, was located at the end of a quiet cul-de-sac. It nested in a mass of neat green shrubbery, fenced by opposing box hedges. A flagstone path, through the well-trimmed yard, led to brightly-coloured wooden steps fronting an oak door.

Inside, the house was decorated in ornate Victorian style. Heavy velvet drapes, dark, artfully carved furniture. Lace curtains. Leaded windows, flashing a variety of rainbow colours. The master bedroom was, in Dave's words, "super cool," and the kitchen, to Martha's delight, was three times the size of theirs in Chicago.

Of course, the weather was perfect.

Martha cupped her hands, eyes shining. "Oh, Dave, isn't it just— just *grand?*"

Dave was grinning. "Pretty neat, I'd say. Even has a good-sized library. And there's a gazebo out back next to the greenhouse. Yep, the old gal sure has kept the place up, I'll give her that."

"We're so lucky to be here."

"Yeah," Dave nodded. "Lucky."

"It's getting towards noon," Martha reported to Dave. He was in porch shade, seated in the chain swing, reading a book. "Feeding time for the plants."

He looked annoyed. "Let 'em wait. I want to check out the rest of Fanning's library. Some great books there. Classics!" He held up the thick volume he'd been reading. "*Moby-Dick*. First edition!"

She frowned. "I'm ashamed of you! We promised to take proper care of her plants. If you won't go with me, I'll go alone."

"Suit yourself," he said, returning to his book.

After she'd left the porch, Dave relented. "Aw, hell!" he muttered—and caught up with her at the greenhouse door. "You laid a guilt trip on me," he mock-complained.

She smiled at his words. "C'mon, let's meet the gang."

Sliding open the glass door, they entered the greenhouse. The odour was not pleasant.

"I thought plants were supposed to smell sweet," said Dave.

"Different plants give off different odours," she said, scanning the area. "The one that's *really* foul isn't here. Native to Indonesia. Called the 'corpse plant' because it smells like a rotting body. Eats the dead flesh of its prey—dung beetles and other insects."

"Jeez!" Dave grunted. "That one sounds really gross."

"It's also quite large. Can grow up to ten feet. It's purple, with a long yellow tubular stalk thrusting up from the centre, like—"

"Like it's giving you the finger."

She laughed. "Exactly! They say its stench attracts prey."

"How do you know all this stuff?"

"Botany, remember? I've told you before that I majored in science at college. Botany was big for me."

"You haven't talked much about your college days."

"Why talk about the past? It's over and done with." Impish chuckle. "I've noticed you don't talk much about your life with all those bosomy Missouri chicks."

"Touché."

They both smiled.

∾

The greenhouse was wide and deep, with columned shafts of sunlight spearing down from the beamed glass roof. Boxed plants were on tables everywhere, and the whole place was lined with a fuzzy moss exuding a faint orangish glow.

"What about roses?" asked Dave. "Where are they? Thought I'd see a lot of roses."

"Obviously Ms. Fanning prefers exotic plants." Spotting a shelf to their left, she nodded. "Ah . . . the food for her darlings." She removed an odd-shaped bottle of luminescent, orange-pink liquid from several others on the shelf. "Ought to be enough here to last a while."

"The old gal is certainly freaked out on plants," he declared.

The tables created a series of aisles with various plants on top of them. Most were unlabelled and looked as though they were dying from lack of care. Except, of course, the tables in the area closest to the back. The moss was especially thick on these tables, beginning to climb the walls in verdant cascades.

"All these here are carnivorous—not indigenous to California. This moss is unusual: it appears to be exhibiting a form of biolumin-escence. How curious!"

"Bio-whatsit?"

"Bioluminescence—a phenomenon where certain plants and animals can produce their own light. They can glow, in other words."

Dave shook his head in bewilderment as they moved along the aisle.

"Okay, Professor, give me a rundown on 'carnivorous'. Educate me."

"Well, there are over seven hundred types of carnivorous plants," she explained. "They're predators, trapping small creatures like flies and digesting them. Some use mechanical means to kill prey, à la the Venus Flytrap, or pitcher plants. Still others, such as the Sundew, exude a sticky kind of mucus, similar to tree sap, and the insects can't get away."

"That's sickening," said Dave. He leaned forwards to examine a boxed specimen at closer range. "Ugly critter!"

"Not everyone would agree. Beauty is in the eye of the beholder."

"Not *this* beholder," he said firmly. "They're all ugly as hell." He pointed at another nearby plant, a Flytrap. "Just like that sucker."

"Oh, lighten up, dear!" said Martha. "Hollywood even makes movies based on these types of plants. Remember *The Little Shop of Horrors* or *Day of the Triffids*?"

The plant's blood-red centre featured a large open mouth ringed, top to bottom, with sharp, flexible teeth. It quivered slightly under a mild breeze from an overhead roof vent, creating the appearance of conscious life.

"Damn thing's moving," declared Dave. "It's alive!"

"It *is* alive in one sense," said Martha, "but not in the sense that animals are."

Dave took a nervous step back from the plants. "Are they... *dangerous?*"

"Only to the prey they trap and devour."

"Well, that's comforting to know. But still..." His voice trailed off.

"There are others here that also qualify as major predators," Martha stated. "If you're a fly or cricket, that is." She moved along the line of boxes. "This one"—nodding toward a spiny red-and-yellow specimen with sinuous, tentacle-like shoots—"he's a nasty little baby."

A slow surge of glistening sap oozed from its centre stem, which was covered with a hard-shelled, bark-like substance.

"*Very* nasty," said Dave.

"Next we have the 'Tiger Lily'. Called that for the shape of its head."

Bulbous, swollen, fanged, its snake-like head was speckled in bilious green. It drew a grunt of revulsion from Dave.

The adjoining box contained a plant whose fungoid leaves formed a hooded funnel.

"It's very effective," said Martha. "Insects are weakened by its narcotic nectar. They fall into the funnel and are consumed."

"How charming," said Dave.

She kept moving along the line. "Then we have this little rascal. Imported from China, and quite an efficient predator."

It brandished sword-sharp leaves with lithe tendrils protruding from its central stem, and was notably larger than the other plants. Dave found it grotesque.

"I must admit this one's a little creepy," said Martha. "It can paralyse and swallow animals as large as a baby rat."

"Ugh!" Dave shook his head. "You sure seem to be up on all this... *plant* stuff."

"Botany, babe, botany! It was one of my best subjects."

"Uh-huh," said Dave. "Well, it sure ain't mine!"

Martha glanced down at the silver watch on her left wrist. "Oops! Feeding time for the gang." She took one of the odd-shaped bottles from her purse, handing it to Dave. "You do the honours." Impish grin. "You need to bond with our leafy friends."

Dave held the bottle of orange-pink fluid up to the light. "Christ! There are all kinds of bugs floating in this thing!"

"Perfectly normal," said Martha. "It's what they eat."

"I'll tell you what it perfectly is—it's perfectly disgusting." He handed the bottle back to her. "*You* feed 'em. I'm outta here."

Stepping swiftly away, he exited the greenhouse.

Just after midnight. Dave was deep into a first edition of *Oliver Twist* when Martha entered the library. She kissed him on his cheek.

"Time for my début," she said. "My leafy audience awaits."

Dave scowled at her. "You don't actually mean to *sing* to a bunch of plants?"

"It's in our contract," she reminded him. "Three songs after the midnight feeding. We agreed to it."

"I can't believe you're doing this!"

"*Believe* it." She smiled. "I have a rather good voice. Sang in the school choir. It'll be fun."

"You have a weird idea of fun."

"Care to join me for my audition?"

"No thanks, I'll pass. I'll stick with Dickens."

"Your choice," she said, kissed him on the cheek again, and left.

As the night deepened, Dave heard his wife's lilting contralto drifting to him from the dimly lit greenhouse. The song was 'In the Sweet Bye and Bye'.

He put his book down and moved to the window where he could see the greenhouse, enjoying his wife's singing.

"She's not half-bad—gotta give it to her."

With each rise and warble of her voice, he noticed that the orange-pink glow under the doorframe of the greenhouse intensified; when she stopped to take a breath, the glow lessened considerably. He observed that the seam around the door to the lab did the same, as though there were more moss inside it.

"Well, I'll be. That's plain *weird*. Gives me the damn creeps!"

Four months later, the phone rang.

Martha answered. "Oh, Ms. Fanning...what a nice surprise to hear from you... Yes, yes, all the plants are fine... I assure you we're been taking excellent care of them... They certainly are *hungry* little fellows..." A pause. "Of *course* we'll be ready to leave...all right then..."

Martha put down the phone. "That was—"

"I heard," nodded Dave. "She still in Europe?"

"So far as I know. Says she'll be out of touch until her return. She's in the woods somewhere hunting fungus."

"What a nutty old dame."

Martha sighed. "Been so lovely being here, the wonderful weather and all. I'll miss it." Another sigh. "I *hate* going home!"

"Sid called from the store. Things are looking up. Seems we made a smart move investing in vinyl. It's making a big comeback. Hot with the younger set."

"That's nice," said Martha. Her tone was strained.

"What's wrong?" Dave asked. "You look worried."

"That's because I *am*," she confessed. "The plant food's getting low. We're almost out of bottles and now I've realised I can't reach Ms. Fanning again."

"Gonna be all right," he told her. "We've probably got enough until she gets back."

"I hope so," said Martha. "I really hope so."

The following weekend found Martha coughing violently, breaking loose chunks of orange, glowing phlegm; the accompanying stabbing headaches sent her reeling to bed.

Dave called a local doctor, a sallow-faced man named Sutter, radiating authority, who agreed to examine Martha at the house.

"Your wife is suffering from a severe bronchial infection of some sort," Sutter declared. "Running a high fever. She needs to be hospitalised."

"It's that serious?"

"Yes, Mister Burns, it's *that* serious."

After Sutter left, Dave stood at the living-room window, staring numbly into the darkness. The soft glow of the moss coming from the greenhouse and lab put him on edge. His fists were clenched, his heart racing. *What the hell's wrong with her? Is that damn plant food radioactive or something? My God, what if something happens to Martha?* It would be the end of his world.

The ambulance arrived for Martha Burns that same night. Dave gently stroked her fevered cheek as she was placed inside. "You'll be just fine," he told her. "I'm right here with you, and everything's gonna be fine."

Later, Dr. Sutter told Dave that, thanks to antibiotics and an antifungal to treat her infection, his wife was much improved but needed to remain in the hospital for another seven to ten days.

Dave was greatly relieved and made frequent visits. Each time she asked him about the plants. Are they okay? Is he feeding them on schedule? "Yeah, and it's a bummer. Stinks in there. Hate feeding those damn things. And I sure don't sing to them!"

"What about their bottled food? Is it holding up?"

"Not really. Been stretching it by feeding 'em smaller amounts, but we're running out fast."

She frowned, eyes clouded with concern. "There must be more food! Try the lab. She might be keeping some extra bottles there."

"But she warned us not to—"

"I know, hon, but this is an emergency."

"Okay then, I'll pick the lock and have a look inside."

"Can you do that?"

"No sweat. Used to practise magic when I was a kid. Locks are a cinch."

Martha relaxed back into her pillow.

"Can I get you anything? Do you need anything?"

"Thanks, hon, but right now all I need is sleep."

Her eyes closed.

It was the last time they were together.

At the lab, Dave had no trouble picking the ancient lock.

It was late afternoon, and the sun had dropped below the horizon. Dave's long shadow preceded him as he scanned the area. The interior was jammed with filing cabinets, glass beakers and the usual laboratory equipment. It was overrun with thick moss—but no bottled plant food.

A circular metal ring in the middle of the lab floor caught Dave's attention. When he pulled back a trapdoor laced with cobwebs, a gust of extremely cold air billowed up from the darkness below. Was this a storage area? Maybe the bottles were kept there.

Damp concrete steps led downward to a brick-walled, night-black cellar. Dave descended into the chilled darkness, using a small pocket flash he'd taken from the house to illumine the moss-covered walls. It cast a thin beam of light ahead of him. No food bottles; all the shelves were empty.

Then he saw it—an orange glowing mass of choking moss huddled in a far corner. Dave centred the flash beam on the shape. To his horror, it appeared to be a man covered in rotted vines and thick, viscid leaves. Not entirely a man, but something that had once *been* a man—something that was no longer human.

Dave drew in a tight breath. So this was Viola Fanning's infernal manifestation—the deformed end product of a twisted mind. *Was this her dead husband? Some insane science project gone awry, now locked away in the lab?* Dave found a wall switch by the stairs and snapped on the overheads. The dark figure stirred into life, awakened from its hibernation by the sudden burst of light. A long, furry tongue unfurled like a fiddlehead from a hole in what seemed to be a ruined face. Leafy creepers looped its body, and barbed, razored thorns thrust out from the torso, which appeared to be comprised of woody vines and bone that had fused together under a tight skin of smooth bark. A mass of throbbing feelers knit together to form the misshapen head; a reeking growth of grey fungus obscured half of its bulk.

The thing's gelatinous eyes, seeping sticky resin, fastened on Dave Burns; its voice was hollow and rasping: "Need...feed friends... hungry...you *not* feed enough!"

This creature sensed the plants' unabated hunger—perhaps linked to them by some unifying psychic force—plant to plant-thing.

The angry creature advanced, gnarled hands outstretched.

Dave knew he had to act. Scooping up a three-legged metal stool, he smashed it across the creature's head. Pus-coloured fluid spurted from the wound, as the thing surged forwards to encircle Dave's body in its spiny arms. As moss encircled his legs, trapping him, Dave's ribs cracked audibly—and he cried out in sharp agony as his backbone snapped. Pain, like blazed lightning, engulfed him. Then it was over.

Dave Burns would never feel pain again.

A hedge trimmer had been placed, along with other garden tools, on a high shelf in the lab. Viola Fanning had used it to trim the box hedge. The creature grasped the metal saw awkwardly and switched it on, hovering over the broken body now glowing and oozing at its feet; Dave was already being ingested by the moss enveloping the lab, causing the weak orange glow to intensify as the plants fed on his body. It did not take long to reduce Dave Burns to small pieces with the trimmer. *Very* small pieces. His remains filled a canvas sack that the creature dragged into the greenhouse.

Time to feed itself—and its hungry friends.

Martha had phoned Dave to pick her up at the hospital, but had been unable to reach him. After Dr. Sutter had signed her medical discharge, she took a taxi back to the Fanning house.

Martha keyed open the front door, calling out to Dave: "Hon, I'm home!"

No reply. Silence.

Maybe he was out in the yard, she told herself. *Hadn't heard the phone ringing. Ought to be back inside by now. Maybe he's in the library, deep into some first edition.* She checked there. Empty. No Dave. The gazebo then? Maybe taking a morning nap in the shade. *No, not there either.* Puzzled, she tried the greenhouse. Why would he be here considering his marked distaste for plants?

Martha never found her husband.

What she did find stunned and revolted her: pieces of a human-like creature straight out of her worst nightmares. Gummy plant nectar covered what remained of the slimed body parts, glistening wetly from a canvas sack in the shafted sunlight. The plants had also overgrown their containers, spilling out onto the sides of the table, commingling with the abundant overgrowth of glowing moss, which was now spreading away from the greenhouse so much that she could actually *see* the tendrils and vines slithering away from the building, through the yard, and up the trees at the neighbour's place in a thick, ropy display.

Martha screamed.

"Thought I'd heard everything, but I just can't figure this," declared Sheriff Nelson Brock, taking her statement at the police station. He was a tall man, big in girth, eyes hidden behind mirrored glasses. "Don't make no sense. Never heard nothing like it. Oh, I can figure your mister plain taking off somewhere on his own, for God knows what reason, but *this* . . . "

Martha Burns, still badly shaken, her eyes swollen from lack of sleep, stared at the big man.

"The *plants*," she whispered. "They're taking over—please do something before it's too late!"

Outside, a hard rain began.

ANGELA SLATTER

A Song of Dust

A NGELA SLATTER's debut novel, *Vigil*, was published by Jo Fletcher Books in 2016, with the sequels, *Corpselight* and *Restoration*, following in 2017 and 2018, respectively. She is the author of nine short story collections, including *The Girl with No Hands and Other Tales, Sourdough and Other Stories, The Bitterwood Bible and Other Recountings, Black-Winged Angels, Winter Children and Other Chilling Tales* and *A Feast of Sorrows: Stories*.

Her work has been adapted for the screen, and translated into French, Chinese, Spanish, Japanese, Russian and Bulgarian. The author has won a World Fantasy Award, a British Fantasy Award, a Ditmar Award, an Australian Shadows Award and six Aurealis Awards.

"Editor Mark Morris had asked for a story for the first volume of *New Fears*," she recalls, "and I'd been reading a book about jewelled saints, *Heavenly Bodies: Cult Treasures & Spectacular Saints from the Catacombs* by Paul Koudounaris.

"I'd used the idea before in a story set in the 'Sourdough' universe, but I wanted to add something more to it—hence the idea of the bewitched death jewellery to help keep the dead beneath. I wanted to have an early St. Dymphma's poison girl as my main character, and to revisit the Misses Meyrick and Hepsibah Ballantine. And I also wanted to plant an ancestress for Cordelia and Bethany

251

Lawrence, who feature in the third 'Sourdough' cycle mosaic, *The Tallow-Wife and Other Tales*."

I SOBEL HESITATES OUTSIDE the grand door to the chamber she'd thought to share with Adolphus. It's a work of art, with carven figures of Adam and Lilith standing in front of a tree, a cat at the base, a piece of fruit in transit between First Man and First Woman so one cannot tell if she offers to he, or otherwise.

Her recent exertions have drained what little strength she had, and the food she'd found in the main kitchen (all servants asleep, the odour of stale mead rising from them like swamp gas) sits heavily in a stomach shrunk so very small by a denial not hers. The polished wooden floorboards of the gallery are cold beneath her thin feet—so thin! Never so slender all her life. A little starvation will do wonders, she thinks. As she moved through the house, she'd caught sight of herself in more than one filigreed mirror and seen all the changes etched upon her: silver traceries in the dishevelled dark hair, face terribly narrow—who'd have known those fine cheekbones had lain beneath all that fat?—mouth still a cupid's-bow pout and nose pert, but the eyes are sunken deep and, she'd almost swear to it, their colour changed from light green to deepest black as if night resides in them. The dress balloons around her new form, so much wasted fabric one might make a ship's sail from the excess.

How long before the plumpness returns? Before her cheeks have apples, the lines in her face are smoothed out? She can smell again, now, but all she can discern is the scent of her own body, unwashed for so long. A bath, she thinks longingly, then draws her attention back to where it needs to be: the door.

Or, rather, what lies behind it.

She reaches out, looks at the twiggish fingers, the black half-moons of dirt beneath the nails, how weirdly white her hand appears on the doorknob shaped like a wolf's head, so bulbous she can barely grasp it properly. She takes a deep, deep breath, and turns the handle.

Isobel woke with a weight on her eyes, cold and dead.

Her mouth, too, was similarly burdened: lips pressed down and thin metallic tendrils crept between them. Her forehead was banded by something chill and hard, a line running the length of her nose, her cheeks and chin encased; as if she wore a helmet she had no memory of applying before bed. She had no memory either of going to sleep. Her throat and arms were mercifully free, but chest, abdomen and hands were encumbered. Not a cage, then.

Remain calm, she told herself, *slow your breathing*. She'd been taught at St. Dymphna's to assess situations carefully; easier said than done when you couldn't open your eyes.

Rings, she thought. *Rings on my fingers and bells on my toes.* She tried to wiggle her feet, found them unwilling to respond, still quite numb; pins and needles were beginning, however, so some sign of hope. Wrists encircled, entrapped by... bracelets and bangles. She twitched her digits; only one finger bore a reasonable burden, a thin metal ribbon. Her husband's family, no matter their wealth, always insisted on a wedding band as plain as day. For love, they believed, must be unadorned.

My husband, she thought, and wondered where he was.

Adolphus Wollstonecraft.

Surely he'd not have deserted her? Not so soon at any rate. Then she recalled they'd only just been married. That this morning she was preparing for her marriage, surrounded by Adolphus' girl cousins, so numerous that she'd had to pause before addressing each one so as not to get a name wrong and thereby cause offence (excepting Cousins Enyd and Delwyn, of course, they'd become so close!). All of them dressed as bridesmaids for she had neither sisters, nor cousins, nor aunts, nor friends who might stand her this service; all of them a whirl of pastel colours and soft fabrics, the light from the candelabra picking out the rich necklaces and earrings, brooches and hair ornaments, finer than any queen might own. Yet none as lovely as those Isobel brought with her, inheritances from mother and grandmothers, aunts and great-aunts, the items that came to Isobel because she was the last of her line, the single point where all things might end or begin again depending on the whims of her womb.

She ran her tongue over her teeth, prodded at the wires and was able to dislodge them with a dull, wet clink against the bone of her teeth. But there was something else: her canines were larger, augmented, and polished, a series of cool smoothnesses and sharp edges. She caught the tip of her tongue on one of those edges and tasted a burst of iron tang, imagined the bleed as a red blossoming.

She opened her mouth wider, felt the weight on her lips half-fall into the cavity; she turned her head, spat, and the mouthpiece fell away; the wires, reluctantly giving up their grip on her dentition, hit the softness she was lying on with a slithering *plink*. Whatever had been attached to her canines remained, however, so firmly affixed she was wary of interfering with them after that first cut. They would wait.

The weights over her eyes and face had also loosened with the movement of her head. She shook harder and with a tinkle and a chink they were gone, landing wherever the other things had. Whatever she reclined upon was soft but compacted by the weight of her body. How long had she been there?

Where was she?

Isobel opened her lids, though the lashes felt glued with sleep, with the sandman's dust. She blinked vigorously, but there was only blackness even when she widened her eyes. She closed them again, breathed slowly to calm herself, then shallowly when she realised the air was stale with a hint of old decay.

I am asleep, she thought. *I am asleep and dreaming in my marital bed.* But she still could not summon the details of her wedding eve, of neither feast nor fornication, and surely she should? Surely good or bad, she would remember that? The touches, the sighs, the delight? The pain, the weight, the imposition? Surely she'd recall at least one of the things the other girls at St. Dymphna's had whispered of at night in their dormer attic when they should have been resting?

"I am asleep," she said out loud. "I am asleep and in my bridal bed."

"Oh no, you're not," came a voice from the darkness, brittle and raw, with a hint of amusement. Not Adolphus, no. A woman. A woman who'd not spoken in a very long time by the sound of it.

Isobel startled, jerked; things that weighed on her chest slipped and slid off with a jingle. She sat up, but her head connected with a rough low rock shelf; the skin parted at her hairline and she felt a slow welling of blood on her forehead. It took a while before she could speak.

"Who are you? Where am I?" The Misses Meyrick had always instructed their pupils to ask questions whenever they could: *You never know what skerrick of information might help you survive.*

"I am you," answered the woman, and Isobel wondered if she'd gone mad, prayed to wake from the dream. "Well, you *before* you, I suppose. And you are me, after me."

"Don't speak in riddles! Tell me how to wake! I bid you, spirit, release me from this delusion!"

"Oh, you think yourself ridden by the mare of night?" The pitch lightened with surprise, then fragmented into giggles, each as sharp as a pin. There was an echo, too, wherever they were. Then the tone steadied, though mirth remained in evidence. "Oh, no. Oh no, poor Isobel. You are sadly awake. Alert at long last."

"Who are you? Why am I here? Where is my husband? I was at my wedding banquet . . ." she trailed off, not truly able to remember if there was any trace of the feast in her mind. She thought she remembered someone—Adolphus' mother?—tugging the veil down over her face, readying her for the procession through the castle. Or was it Cousin Enyd? Or Cousin Delwyn? Or? Or? Or?

Someone had lifted the veil, certainly, for it was bunched behind her head, pillowing her neck. Surely later, after *volo* had been said, the echoes of the vows running along the walls and floor and vaulted ceiling of the small chapel, barely big enough to hold that fine family. So small a chapel, in fact, that only relatives had been bid to attend at the Wollstonecrafts' isolated estate.

And the Misses Meyrick. She cannot forget *them.*

Isobel's erstwhile school marms, not invited, had come anyway to watch, to witness the choice she'd made, all their good training, her mother's good money, gone to waste. They did not speak to her, neither Orla nor Fidelma, not a word of congratulation nor censure. Naught but disappointed looks as she and Adolphus walked down the aisle as man and wife.

There!

A memory, solid and stable. Pacing beside her handsome new husband, and the Misses Meyrick so far from their school for poison girls and looking at her as if she'd left their house to burn; left them to shame. So, not a happy memory but a memory nonetheless. A real one. A true one. Something to hold on to.

And another memory: the Misses Meyrick once again at the wedding feast, waiting by the doors while the happy couple were greeted and congratulated by their guests. Isobel thinking *I must speak to them for they loved me in their own fashion!* so she'd picked her way through the crowd until she stood before her old instructors in their gowns magnificent, their eyes bright, Orla's left blue, her right yellow; in Fidelma the colours were reversed. Long moments passed before Fidelma spoke.

"Your mother," she said, "would be ashamed."

Orla stepped behind her and Isobel felt terror like she never had before; but the woman merely said, "Pish!" and showed her a hairpin with a long silver shaft and a jewelled head shaped like a daisy; the outer petals were of diamonds, and the floret, divided distinctly into two halves, of yellow topazes. Then she slid it into Isobel's finely constructed hairstyle, beneath the long veil so no one might see the ornament and note how exquisite it was. "This," said Orla, "is the last thing we can do for you."

Before she could reply, the Misses Meyrick seemed to fade from the room, although she knows she saw them move, saw them walk away with elegant contempt, yet somehow it seemed that it was not a mere exit they committed, but a Departure.

Then the other voice repeated, "Wedding feast?" and Isobel was brought back to the stygian confines of . . . wherever she was.

"Wedding feast, I remember my own. All those fine families, all those relations of blood, all of Adolphus' cousins and aunts and uncles. I had no one, myself, being an orphan of very rich parentage, but he said to me, 'Kitten'—'Kitty', actually, for he called me by that endearment—'Kitty, my sweet, they all adore you! It's like you're one of our very own, a true Wollstonecraft. Cousins Enyd and Delwyn say the same.' And those very cousins sat beside me at the wedding feast, making sure I drank from my goblet the wine my husband poured for me and they considerately topped up." The woman in the darkness cackled. "Does this sound familiar?"

"Where am I?' asked Isobel in a very small voice. She did not say that it all sounded very familiar indeed. She carefully raised her hands until the fingertips touched the rough stone of the low ceiling. She inched them along, felt the scrape of rock, found a place where roof joined wall; but there was only the hint of a line, a thin parsimonious suggestion on her skin, not a chink, not a gap where air or light might creep in.

How many feet between where she lay and the ceiling? Two? Three? Ceiling? *Lid?* That last thought made her shudder and she shook it away.

"You're where you've been these past twelve months, sleeping like the dead." The voice dropped low, secretive. "But I knew you yet lived. I could hear the slow, slow beat of your heart, the slug-slug of your blood, the base breath that made your chest only just rise and fall."

"Twelve months? Don't be a fool. I'd have died!"

"And you were meant to! But when you're so very nearly dead, everything becomes *unhurried*, blood, breath, appetite. You'll be ravenous soon, now that I've mentioned it."

As if in response Isobel's stomach growled and cramped. She put a hand to it, discovered a kind of armour there, a lumpen embossed corset that might well turn aside a knife blade. At its sides she located small latches, which opened easily; presumably no one expected the deceased to undress themselves.

"The poison they used," mused her companion, "is a strange mix: too little and it will render you ill, too much it will send you into a sleep undiscernible from true death, but if the amount is *juuust* right, then and only then you'll die. And it was new when used on me, so I died. It was old when used on you and Adolphus panicked and used too much, so you but slept."

"You're lying. You're mad."

"Oh, ho! Mad am I? That's possible, I suppose, I've been here a long while with only my thoughts, waiting for you to wake, and before that no one but myself to talk to. Who wouldn't go a little mad?' A sigh shifted the blackness, Isobel was almost certain she could see it. "Shall I show you? Where we are? Then we can discuss my mendacity or otherwise. Well?"

"Yes," said Isobel faintly.

For a second there was nothing, no sound, no movement, and then: a light. A tiny pinprick of luminous green, a point that pulsed and grew, strengthened and increased its ambit. The glow lit upon the things that had fallen from Isobel when she sat so precipitously; it caught at their lovely edges, lodged in facets, made it appear as if a hundred small fires had kindled on the musty purple silk.

She was distracted by a king's ransom in jewellery, but not of a common sort. Rich and rare, the cut and settings were of ancient design, almost foreign it was so antique, and Isobel could not think of where she'd seen its like before. None of it was hers, not one piece of the Lawrence family jewels to be seen, not a *single* thing she recognised. She put a hand to the back of her head, beneath the veil which had become odd in its texture, and found the one gem no one knew she had—no one but the Meyricks—the hairpin, its cool hard daisy arrangement reassuring.

Then she gazed around the space, found it to be a box, six feet by six feet by two and half, a flattened mattress beneath her. Such a small room! A bed-closet perhaps, but no sign of a door, of any egress. And that mattress . . . not like any she'd ever seen, without either ticking or calico, neither down nor rushes to make it plump, but there was the smell of old lavender . . . no, more like . . . the lining for a death bed.

She sought her companion. Saw . . .

Saw . . .

Saw nothing but a skeleton in a jaundiced wedding dress, blue and gold boots with silver buttons up the side, a manically grinning skull from which red hair and a lopsided veil hung. The body was adorned with strange *bijoux* akin to those Isobel herself had worn.

And the body was glowing; glowing with the same green luminescence that had shown Isobel her location.

Isobel remembered at last that she'd seen such exquisite corpses before, in places where the wealthy venerated their dead and turned them into glittering saints. Old families and High Church. The Wollstonecrafts carried both in their bloodline.

And Isobel, comprehending at last where she was, began to scream.

The room, the Master's Chamber, is redolent of stale alcohol, spent seed and strong tobacco or perhaps incense. Some kind of drug? Isobel notices a kind of pipe in one corner, perhaps three feet high, made of blown glass in colours that have the same sheen as oil on water. There are silken tassels and a mouthpiece and tubing. She'd heard of such things at St. Dymphna's: Hepsibah Ballantyne had averred it a fine way to poison someone. Mistress Ballantyne had always said that to best murder another, one should discover their habits and run parallel to them, insert your lethal blow into the usual flow of their life, so that way the difference you made would most like not be noticed.

Isobel looks to the bed which is located beneath a bank of diamond-paned glass. In said bed, so enormous that it might fit six, she sees three figures. The covers are thrown back, as are the window shutters, for the eve is balmy, moonlit; one of her nannies always said that sleeping in moonlight let madness in. How many Wollstonecrafts have slept thus?

Summer, she thinks, as it was when I married. A summer bride, lying winter-cold for so very long. No mourning for Adolphus, she notes, and no sleeping alone.

Her husband lies between the recumbent figures of Cousins Enyd and Delwyn, their dark Wollstonecraft locks spread tousled across crisp white pillowcases, their naked forms on crumpled sheets. Two girls Isobel had thought friends or like to become so. Their slumber is that of the well-used. There can be no mistaking it; the dead bride did not lie. She did not need to when she'd said *The Wollstonecrafts breed only amongst themselves and they are* prolific, *hiding those whose parents are too closely related to each other in attics and cellars, hiding those who show too much the double, triple, quadruple blossoming of blood.*

Isobel thinks, memories flooding now, of all those Wollstonecrafts at the wedding feast, watching her so avidly. She wonders how she ever thought their eyes gleamed with love and happiness, their lips curved in welcome, not avarice. Perhaps she could not see their greed because her own was so intense as she gulped from the bridal cup held by Adolphus, offered so generously to her first—against tradition!—a sign of his devotion, his love for his young wife. She has, even now, no recollection of falling asleep at the table, of drifting into what her new family thought was death. There is only the memory of the cup, the dark liquid within, her husband's tender smile.

Nor does she even now recollect crossing the wide room, yet somehow she is standing beside the great bed, staring down at Cousin Enyd whose tiny waist she's always admired; on Enyd's left wrist is a diamond bracelet that had belonged to Isobel's mother. Isobel's hand goes to the back of her own head, fidgets beneath the friable veil and finds the hair pin that was the final gift of Orla and Fidelma Meyrick. The gems and metal are cool against her fingers and the pin comes out with no complaint. Isobel looks at it carefully, remembers the instructions from one of the weaponry classes, then gives a nod of satisfaction. These three have been drinking, smoking, heavily; all of them snore. They'll not wake easily.

She leans over Cousin Enyd, lowers the hairpin point-first to the cockleshell of the ear facing her, then depresses the left side of the daisy's centre. A single tiny drop of paralytic poison, so powerful she fears to get it on her own skin, oozes from the tip of the pin and drips into the shadowy coil of Enyd's ear. Isobel waits for a count of five, then swiftly plunges the shaft into the narrow canal; her fingers push the right side of the daisy design and the length of the pin splits into four very fine, very sharp, very tough lengths which tear into the brain. Cousin Enyd hardly moves, giving just the tiniest of shudders as she voids her bladder and bowels, but the stink of it barely registers above the other rich scents in the room.

Isobel creeps softly around the other side of the bed and repeats the process on Cousin Delwyn, whose rich thick curls she'd often envied; around this one's swan-like neck is the emerald and pearl locket that had belonged to Isobel's grandmother. Delwyn dies no more noisily than did Enyd, though she is fleshier, larger, there is less poison and the paralysis is not so entire; she twitches, kicks too close to Adolphus and Isobel must swiftly grab at the limb, hold it in place until the tremors still. Isobel feels a twinge of pride; the time at St. Dymphna's was neither wasted nor its lessons lost. Orla Meyrick herself couldn't have executed these deaths any more tidily.

Adolphus still has not stirred.

Isobel slips her stolen jewellery into the hidden pocket of her dress, then steps away, takes up position between the bed and the door. Her breathing remains steady—it did not change even as she slaughtered those false cousins—and what she feels moving through her is a cold thing, a passionless fury, a determination to one end. She takes a breath and begins to sing.

"Are you quite finished?" came the voice when Isobel at last ran out of breath and fear. "Pride of St. Dymphna's you are."

"How do you know—?"

"I've had twelve months to wander around in your sleeping mind—no point looking like that. I'm bored and have been for a very long time. A saint couldn't have stopped herself. I can't do anything else, can't move from here. I've only got a little energy and I'm saving that for something rather more special than comforting you or a mere haunting."

"How did I get here? How did *you* get here?" wept Isobel, stung by the corpse's callousness.

"Our husband, you little fool! Adolphus Trajan Wollstonecraft. We're not the first brides he's disposed of for the sake of their fortunes, but *you* were the first one who was supposed to kill him. And failed to do so quite spectacularly. Imagine all the trouble you could have saved. No doubt, there'll be more betrotheds after us when his goodly period of mourning is done, and all your wealth run through!"

"How many?" asked Isobel, shocked out of her sobs.

"Four. Buried on the other side of the altar. I'm sure they've got fresh new maidens picked out to take up residence beside us in the fullness of time."

"But you can talk, make this light . . . "

"And small, bitter consolation that it is. As I said, I can't haunt anyone. Hepsibah Ballantyne knows her business too well for that."

Isobel startled at the name, thinking about the poisons mistress who came to St. Dymphna's and taught the girls to brew dark potions. There were whispers that the woman was a coffin-maker, too, and indeed that was where her renown lay; the facility with poison was a happy coincidence and a secret for St. Dymphna's headmistresses and students. A lucrative habit borne of her more-than-passing interest in death.

"My, what interesting things you keep hidden in your heart and head. I only knew her name from conversations I'd heard Adolphus and his mother have as they crossed the floor above my tomb—they've a fondness for plotting in the chapel, perhaps it makes them feel justified and holy." The corpse sounded sad.

"Poison," said Isobel.

"And there are these jewels, of course. Not contented with paying a premium for death-beds to keep us beneath, they laid these cursed gems over us."

Isobel prodded at the attachments to her canines, and the dead bride said, "Those are to stop us from becoming vampires or some other such blood ghosts. They made us saints against our will, the ecstatic dead to cover their crimes, to keep us from haunting them, from ever getting vengeance."

"But I'm not dead," said Isobel softly.

"No, indeed you are not!" Gleeful now. "None of the chains the living have placed upon you have taken, sweet Isobel, and you are fit for my purpose!"

Isobel listened, watched the still form; there was only the sickly pulsing green light to tell her she wasn't truly alone, that the voice wasn't simply in her head. But what if it *was*? What if the light was an hallucination too? Perhaps this was her punishment.

Punishment for what?

For leaving St. Dymphna's the moment her mother died?

For denying her duty?

For falling in love with the man she was meant to murder?

For being so foolish as to trust?

"Why did you do it? Trust him? You were better off than any of us. You were trained. You had a goal, a duty."

"Get out of my head! I'm conscious now and I don't appreciate you using it as your playground!" Isobel shouted so loudly that her ears hurt in the confined space.

"I'm sorry," said the dead bride. "There's little call for etiquette down here so I forget."

"For him. He was older by a little, funny, sweet and smart. He didn't care that I was fat. He was...kind. I met him before I was sent to St. Dymphna's. I knew almost from the cradle what I was meant to do, that the very point of my life was to destroy another's—to avenge an ancient and dusty death, an ancestress of mine murdered at the hands of his forefathers." Isobel paused. "But I met him and I loved him from the first even though I knew I shouldn't. I thought...I thought I might draw it out, put off taking his life until after my mother died, until there was no one left to care. Then he and I could be happy, the past forgotten, dead and buried.

"Then my mother did die, sooner rather than later, before I'd even finished my schooling. I left St. Dymphna's the very day after the news arrived. I went to him, went to his home, we planned our life together."

"They're not as fabulously prosperous as they appear, you know. There's much tat and shine for show, but the vaults are empty, more often than not with but a few pieces of gold, candlesticks and crested salvers. The family silver has been pawned and redeemed time and again—the silversmiths of Caulder know the Wollstonecrafts of old."

"But—"

"Rich brides are this family's business. We're lambs to them, meat on the table, money in the bank, brides in caskets. Did you not wonder that there were no friends invited to your nuptials? None there but Wollstonecrafts? That they live so far from anything despite their supposed wealth? It's hard to keep secrets in cities where everyone's watching to see what move you make, where the well-to-do keep better track of their daughters." A long sigh. "You signed over everything, didn't you? All the riches your mother gathered, the businesses she built, all the prosperity and majesty that clever merchant queen reaped from her investments over the years, and you signed it away for a piece of cock." A giggle, rueful. "Don't feel too great a fool, I did the same, and brides before me and thee who were otherwise reckoned clever. I . . . I was ugly, yet he convinced me he loved me, that he cared not a jot for beauty."

"But Adolphus *loved* me. He didn't know what I gave up for him, that I put his life first." But she thought of the tiny moments, the signs she'd ignored: all the occasions when plans for what came after the wedding were put off, discussions avoided. *Don't you worry about that, my dear, we've plenty of time for that later.* Yet how quickly he'd begged she sign documents that transferred her ownerships to him in case of a dreadful tragedy, which would of course never happen.

"You think not? The poison he used came from Ballantyne, who knew you at the school, who outfitted this very coffin-tomb, this death-bed just as she did the others—she's not so skilled with stone as wood, but she did a good enough job to trap me. You let him live Isobel, but no good deed ever goes unpunished." The skeleton gave a rueful chuckle. "And I doubt you're the first poison girl to flee that venerable institution, to choose love over duty."

"I was, you know. The Misses told me with great relish and umbrage," confessed Isobel.

"Ah. My tale is your tale, or at least so close that the differing details barely matter. But at last something can be done." The voice rose like a victory hymn.

"You're dead," said Isobel, toneless, lifeless. "You're dead and I'm trapped. Even if he's betrayed me"— *if?*— "nothing can be done."

"Do you have the engagement ring he gave you? An enormous sapphire, if memory serves correct, blue as a hot afternoon sky?"

Isobel examined her fingers, looked to where the item in question should be, but there were only the ornate rings joined to each other by golden chains, the things meant to hold her in place. She pulled them off, added them to the glittering pile beside her.

"No. Just the wedding band," mused the dead bride. "The same for all of us. No point in wasting an engagement ring when you can re-use it, like a dog collar. They don't want to trouble themselves with a costly replacement, and they can't use *these*"—Isobel knew she meant the cursed things—"Gods forbid anything should happen to the *lamb* before the wedding, before the Wollstonecrafts get the fortune for which they've worked so hard!"

Isobel looked at the other's skeletal hands, wrapped around a posy of dead yet somehow intact roses. A strong breeze would interrupt their carefully held structure. On one finger she could make out the dull gleam of a ring identical to hers.

"I'll die here," she said. "I'll starve as a trusting fool deserves to. I'll suffocate." Suddenly the air felt thinner, staler, her lungs more demanding. "But I'll go mad first."

"And what a delightful change that will be," sniggered the dead bride. "You'll not likely starve any time soon, although you're looking thin, yet not so thin as I. There's plenty of air, you silly bint. As for madness, sometimes by taking refuge in it for a time is the only way to maintain a modicum of sanity."

Isobel realised then that her own dress—with all the ribbons and frills and bows meant to make her beautiful, but which just made her look even more enormous—was terribly, terribly large on her. That none of the weight she'd carried around all her life, that drove her mother and nannies to despair, remained.

Reading her thoughts again, the dead one said, "Bet you never expected you'd be grateful for that fat! What do you think kept you alive all these months?"

"I don't want to live," wailed Isobel, knowing it was stupid as soon as the words were out.

"Ye gods, the stock at St. Dymphna's is poor. A man betrayed you and you want to die?"

"No. I...I betrayed my mother, my teachers, by trusting him, by choosing him." Isobel thought of the Misses Meyrick and their steely countenances.

"And you think dying is the choice they'd want you to make? You, upon whom so much effort was expended to make you more *active*?" The dead bride tut-tutted. "It would be easier, certainly, to expire, but St. Dymphna's girls, as I understand it, aren't made for easy paths.

You weren't descended from milksops or weeping maidens; the women before you carried sword and shield, they fought in the open, their blood was red and rich and violent! It's in your veins, Isobel, so pull yourself together!"

"But I can't get out—"

"Of course you can, there's a way, a way for the living."

Isobel sat up at straight as she could, stared at the unmoving form. "How?"

"Ah, now that's information for which you must bargain, Isobel girl."

"Tell me now or I swear I'll scatter your bones, I'll grind them to dust even if it makes my fingers bleed!"

"That's the spirit! Now calm down. In return for my very useful knowledge, you will make me a promise, a promise by which you'll set more store than any ever before or so help me—"

Isobel did not pause. "I will promise you anything, just get me out of this tomb!"

The song is one the dead bride advised, tried to teach until Isobel comprehended that she already knew it from her old life, a tune sung by this nanny or that governess. Her husband does not stir, so she sings louder still for there's no one to wake but Adolphus. She wonders how he's spent his days since her death, then decides she can probably guess. Sings more loudly, more sweetly, until her patience runs out and she fair shouts, "Adolphus!"

He sits up, stunned, blinking in that strange mix of darkness and moonlight and receding sleep that render him blind for long moments. He does not notice the still bodies of his cousins on either side of him, does not spare them a glance. He sees only Isobel.

She imagines she must look close to the spectre he tried so hard to make her. She smiles and follows the script. "Adolphus, my love, fear not. You're simply dreaming."

She can see him struggling to recognise her and she remembers how changed she is from the lumbering lumpy girl he said he loved above all others. That all those places he caressed and fondled and fingered are so much easier to find now.

"It's Isobel, my love. See you dream me how I truly was, how I truly wished to be. Still you know my heart!"

"But you're dead, my Isobel." Fear silvers his tone.

"Oh yes! So very dead and you do but dream me, but there is something I must tell you, something that threatens your very house and future. My love has drawn me back. Will you follow and see?"

"But of course! That you should still care for me beyond death! It warms my heart," he says and creeps to the end of the bed so as not to disturb his cousins' rest. He reaches for her and Isobel holds up a warning hand.

"The living cannot touch the dead, my love! Lest you be drawn down to lie beside me." Adolphus nods. Isobel smiles. "Then come and allow me to render you this last service."

The moment she turns her back she knows it for a mistake, but she was brimming with confidence that her deception had worked, that she'd *won*. She can almost feel Orla and Fidelma's disapproving stares just as she can feel the steel of her husband's fingers closing around her left wrist.

"Little fool, little bitch! Do you think I've not created enough ghosts to know one? That I cannot tell the smell of warm blood from cold? 'My love has drawn me back.' Gods, what a lackwit you must think me, as much of a one as yourself."

Isobel struggles, but her strength is so depleted from her long slumber that she cannot make any headway.

"Fear not, sweet Isobel, I'll put you back where you belong."

Isobel kicks him in the groin, watches with not inconsiderable delight as he doubles over, then she remembers to flee. She flings the door closed behind her, starts towards the grand staircase. She is halfway down when she hears the crash of wood against wall that says her husband is in pursuit. Her strength is fading, her speed bleeding to nothing. At the bottom of the stairs she must cross the marble floor, pass through the darkened arched doorway, and down the few worn steps into the chapel, and thence to the altar.

What if he catches her first?

What if he takes it in his head to strangle her then and there for there's no one who might look for her, no one to suspect she lives, there are no appearances to be maintained. Even if some family member of his might wander by, they've no cause to save her. From behind comes a growl, a roar of such surpassing anger and viciousness that she finds her feet have wings. An extra burst of speed gets her to the entrance hall, almost skidding on marble tiles as she goes. When she passes through the doorway she does not touch the steps, but rather flies several yards into the chapel, landing at the third row of pews, the impact jarring every bone in her body, so much so that she's sure she must rattle. She stumbles her way towards the altar with its shimmer of precious plate, and splashes of colour on the bright white cloth covering where moonlight pierces the stained glass window.

Adolphus is enraged, he'll not see the open tombs, the floor slid back by dint of the secret switches the dead bride told her about, a handy bit of knowledge plucked from one of the passing ghosts of the Wollstonecrafts' castle, a stonemason who'd built the secret passages and the tombs at the request of a great-great-great Wollstonecraft grandfather whose terror was to be buried alive. But such escapes are no use to the dead, and the grandparent was indeed thoroughly deceased when put into the tomb—although his bones and those of other departed were shifted and shuffled when the present generation began their business of burying brides. The stone mason himself, another trusting fool, had been put to death as soon as the work was completed.

This plan, fumes Isobel, was not best thought-out and she resents the dead bride for not having formulated a better strategy in all her time lying in the crypt. Then again, perhaps she never was very practical in life. Isobel, St. Dymphna's drop-out though she might be, is quite certain she'd have come up with something—*anything*—better.

Adolphus does not see the four figures slumped in the front pews, and Isobel runs past them, skidding to a halt before the altar. Her husband comes to a stop a foot from her, cursing and spitting and telling her precisely what he thought of her in life and death; if she had any lingering doubts about his role in her demise they are dispelled once and for all.

"I will put you back in the ground, sweet Isobel. Although these months beneath have done you good, who'd have thought under all that fat you were so terribly lovely?"

"Would it have stopped you from murdering me?" she asks out of sheer curiosity.

He shakes his head, his grin a wolf's. "No. But I might have taken a little more fun with you. I might do so now. I have, after all, a husband's rights."

"Will you exercise them on all of us?" Isobel says so quietly, so calmly that he is thrown off by her lack of fear, her lack of panic.

"Us?" He tilts his head. "Madness, I suppose, from the darkness."

"Madness no doubt, but one you will share, my love. Come, greet your maidens. They wait at your back like good wives."

Adolphus, seemingly unwilling to take his eyes from her, turns his head only a little, but it is enough for him to see what waits in the periphery. Four of his spouses, skeletons all, released from their beds and gilded cages by Isobel, stand with effort, bones a'clacking and a'creaking, hair falling from heads to shoulders, and thence into empty rib cages. Their frocks have entirely decayed, leaving only threads and rags caught here in a joint, there on a bone, as if they might show their husband their nakedness entire, in mimicry of the wedding night he denied them. There is, however, no sign of cartilage or tendons or muscles to show how they might be held together. Sheer will and malice, imagines Isobel, and not a little magic resulting from both.

She takes in the skulls with their hairline fractures, the stains decay has left, the wisps of hair that was once so glorious. At least one has a limp, another lacks an arm; a brigade of the halt and the lame, the obese and the damned ugly, all especially susceptible to any scrap of kindness, and unwary that their value to their husband was no greater than monetary. She wonders if the dead bride—her companion and guide—was a witch in life, undiscovered, for her powers to remain so long after death. Or perhaps she was simply a girl with hopes and dreams that curdled dark and sour and kept the strongest part of her, the bravest part, the worst part, alive.

Adolphus has gone astonishingly pale, as if his blood has turned coward and fled. His lips move, producing only, "Whuh, whuh, whuh."

"'Whuh?' What are you trying to say, my love? What is this sorcery? None but what you created yourself by murder and deceit."

The brides shuffle forward, closing in on Adolphus who backs away, hands raised as if that will stop their awful progress with its accompanying symphony of clacking and rattling.

"What I want you to know, my love, is this: tonight your house will fall. I will put every Wollstonecraft here to the sword. Then I will make it my business to hunt down every bastard, bitch and by-blow who fell from your family tree and destroy them too. Your bloodline will be wiped from the face of the earth, and I swear before you and your wives that I shall make this my life's work."

The corpse brides reach towards their husband, thin fingers, bony arms, ravaged joints, and with a cry Adolphus steps backwards. He does not see the open maw behind him, so he falls, arms windmilling, then there is a silence as he drops, then the *whump!* and *crack!* as he lands, dust flying into the air.

Isobel and her sister-spouses peer over the edge.

Adolphus lies in the tomb Isobel so recently occupied, recumbent upon the form of the dead bride, her own cursed jewellery removed. Isobel is sure she can see some broken bones on the skeletal girl where the impact has been too much, but while Adolphus remains stunned the dead bride's arms begin to move. They curve up and over, around her husband before he realises what's going on. The fingers of her right hand clench together into a spear and this she plunges into Adolphus' chest, the flesh of which parts as if it is no more than warm butter. There is the breaking of ribs prised apart and the wet sucking sound of red muscle meat being found and enclosed by a bony cage of palm and fingers.

"Your heart, my love," says the dead bride, "shall ever be mine."

And with that there is a great sigh as from many mouths. Adolphus ceases to move, his eyes glaze over. The girl in the tomb does not answer when Isobel calls, and she can no longer sense any presence other than her own. The chorus of brides falls to the flagstones, become dust even as Isobel watches. She is meticulous, though, ensuring they will have somewhere to rest, and brushes their final remains into the crypt. It falls on Adolphus and his final bride like confetti for the dead. Isobel, feeling bereft that she cannot say goodbye to her sisters, whispers farewell and hopes they will hear it somewhere, then locates the switch to close the lid of the tomb, and then the second one that puts the floor back in place. When she is done it looks as if nothing ever happened here.

Isobel rises. There are weapons to be had in the house, sabres and stilettos that hang on walls for display, but will be just as fine used for their true purpose. She will spill all the blood to be found, she will put them to the sword and then set fire to the hangings in the bedrooms, the parlours, the grand hall. She will burn the place utterly to the ground.

No full graduate of St. Dymphna's could do better, she is certain. She'll not return to the Misses Meyrick, though she might write to them from time to time as she crosses another Wollstonecraft off her list. Isobel will not hunt Hepsibah Ballantyne, for she was merely doing her job, and the poison used on Isobel was not *intended* for her. Oh, she'll find the coffin-maker, employ her for her own ends— it's a fool who wastes a good poisons woman—but first of all she'll put a good scare into Hepsibah Ballantyne just for fun. She might even keep the gems on her canines long enough to give Ballantyne a glittering, terrifying smile.

Isobel takes one last look at the chapel, finds she cannot distinguish the joins where the floor might open up again if she were to press the right parts of the frieze carved into the altar. And she understands, then, the only thing that will truly haunt her as she goes upon her way: that she did not ask the dead bride, the one who came before her, for her name.

DANNY RHODES

BORDER COUNTRY

DANNY RHODES' short stories have appeared in publications on both sides of the Atlantic, including *Black Static* magazine in the UK and *Cemetery Dance* magazine in America. He says that seeing his work in these publications and now, at last, in *Best New Horror*, signals the fulfilment of an ambition stretching across almost two decades.

Rhodes is the author of three contemporary novels—*Asboville* (2006), *Soldier Boy* (2009) and *FAN* (2014)—and he is currently working on a collection of horror tales and a horror novel. He is a member of the Horror Writers Association, and a mentor on the HWA's Mentor Program.

"'Border Country' was inspired by a camping trip to Wenlock Edge in Shropshire," explains the author. "If you have children, you'll know how it feels when, at any given moment, a child does something that makes you realise they are growing up.

"One night on the trip my son, who still likes to have the landing light on at home when he goes to bed, roused himself from sleep and set off for the campsite toilet alone. He simply picked up the torch and off he went. I lay there for a few seconds, contemplating this event, then jumped from the bed and followed him. But I didn't want to break the spell. I kept my distance and waited halfway down the slope for him to return, which he duly did. The story, of course, relays a different turn of events.

"Some of my short horror fiction barely contains any horror at all. With 'Border Country' I set myself a challenge to write something genuinely frightening. As with all of my short work, however, I wanted to retain ambiguity. M.R. James states it best in his essay 'Some Remarks on Ghost Stories': 'Reticence conduces to effect, blatancy ruins.'"

THE ROAD TO the campsite was steep and dark. Rob dabbed his foot on the brake pedal. With good reason. Halfway down the hill he passed a gouged trunk, crushed vegetation, a wilted garland of flowers. Amongst all of this was a fading photograph in a plastic wallet.

A shrine to a crash victim.

Rob glanced at the mirror. Max was sleeping. That was good. The shrine wasn't something he wanted his son to see. He'd ask questions. Rob would be forced to supply answers. The thought of it turned his skin cold.

Rob spotted the crudely daubed sign for the campsite further down the hill. He turned the car on to a rutted farm track and nodded to himself. He was looking for an old-fashioned site where he could spend some quality time with his boy. Ridge Farm would do fine. It was situated on the edge of an escarpment, a thick blanket of trees above it, a rural patchwork of woodland, field and furrow below. Beyond everything were the bleak and wild mountains of the border country.

The farmhouse was tucked away at the bottom of the track. Rob stopped the car in front of a metal gate. He climbed out and stood for a moment, looking over the gate at the working innards of the place, at a dilapidated barn, a rusting grain silo, a battered tractor. Pieces of old farm machinery were scattered amongst weeds that had pushed their way through cracks in the concrete. An ageing dog padded across the yard, stopped to sniff in his direction, dropped its head and then moved unsteadily away.

Rob pushed open a rickety wooden side gate and followed the path behind the small wash-house. The pamphlet laden with spelling errors he'd received in the post suggested the wash-house contained two showers and two toilets. There was an outdoor sink next to it for washing dishes. That was all. Rob didn't care. He wasn't into the big sites with their abundance of facilities and distractions. Sarah would have disagreed, wanted somewhere more suited to Max, but Sarah wasn't here.

There was a door at the back of the farmhouse. Rob pressed the button for the doorbell. A muted buzz sounded beyond the door. He thought he heard a drawn-out sigh, certainly heard a chair being scraped back, footsteps on linoleum. The door half-opened and a weary looking woman appeared.

"Hello," he said. "I'm booked in for the weekend."

"Taylor," said the woman. It wasn't a question.

"Yes," said Rob.

"You're the last," she said. "We're very quiet. Choose any pitch. There's cooked breakfast if you want it. Five pounds each. If you want to fish that's five pounds too."

Rob handed over his cash. The woman took it without ceremony.

"Thanks then," said Rob. "The weather looks . . . "

But the woman was already forcing the door closed.

Rob smiled wryly to himself and turned around. A malnourished cat hopped onto the wall in front of him. It had something in its mouth. A vole perhaps. Rob saw the limp tail, the dangling head, the vacant stare of death. He peered beyond the cat in the direction of the camping field where the escarpment had been sculpted into a series of flat steps. On each of these steps was a pitch for a tent. Only one of the pitches was occupied. He shrugged. It didn't matter. He wasn't here to socialise with strangers. Just his boy.

When he got back to the car, Max was peering out of the window. He looked confused. Rob smiled at him and Max smiled back. For the briefest second Rob saw the teenager his son would become and once again he wondered where the eight years had gone, what had happened to his marriage. He thought about how his life had changed since the day his son first came into the world, the things he'd learned about himself, the things he and Sarah had learned about each other.

Harsh truths.

Later, after the two of them had eaten, Rob left Max in the tent and wandered down to the wash-house. He went to the toilet, stood at the outside sink looking up towards the campsite and the darkening wood beyond. In the purple twilight the trees seemed closer to the site than before, as if they were encroaching down the hill, shoot by shoot, stem by stem.

The bellow of a cow snatched Rob's thoughts away. He turned, skirted the farmhouse, located the open-sided cattle barn. The woman was in amongst the cattle, ankle-deep in straw, trying to separate an individual cow from the rest. She was struggling. As Rob watched, the cow buffeted her. She fell, yelped, clambered back to her feet and started scolding the cow as though it were a child.

"How dare you? How dare you?"

She shouted the same question over and over, kicking the cow in anger, beating at its body with a plastic bucket. It might have been comical but it wasn't.

"Stupid bitch," the woman shouted. "You stupid, stupid bitch."

Rob drew back out of sight, embarrassed. He felt his shoulders knot as he ducked into the shower block and flicked on the light. A moth flitted around the exposed bulb and a large black spider withdrew into a funnel-shaped web. The shower basin was covered in grime. When he turned the shower on, a sad trickle of water ran from the nozzle. He turned the shower off again, washed himself from the sink instead. The woods, he noticed, were just a shapeless black mass now, with no defined edge at all.

Max was playing a game on his phone when Rob got back to the tent.

"Did your mum pack you a book?" asked Rob.

"I think so," said Max.

"Ten minutes reading before lights out," said Rob.

Max switched off his phone and took out his reading book. Rob watched him. He was a good boy. He'd handled all of the stuff Rob and Sarah had thrown at him and come out all right, a role model for both of them.

"What are you reading?" asked Rob.

"*The Iron Man*," said Max.

Rob smiled.

"I read that when I was a boy," he said. "It's a great book."

"It's okay," said Max. "I hope he finds his ear."

Night fell. Rob sat at the entrance to the tent. Oddly, he thought about Sarah more when he was with Max, about what might have been. But it was too late for all of that. When he looked back at his boy he saw he was already sleeping. He moved to sit by the fire pit, took out a beer and sat looking up at the canopy of stars, occasionally hearing the murmur of conversation from the other tent, the rustle of a sleeping bag, the whisper of a turning page. When the light in the tent was extinguished and the sounds along with it, Rob stared out towards the blinking lights of the border country, the remote cottages and the red pinprick signal of a phone mast at the top of a distant hill.

Now and then, a sheep bleated in the darkness.

The sun was bright the next morning. Rob carried their gear down to the nearest fishing pond, located a promising swim and set up the rods. He was surprised at Max's patience. He'd expected him to be reeling in and casting out every thirty seconds, the way little boys were somehow modelled, but Max seemed more than happy to wait things out. He sat upright and still, his eyes focussed on his float.

"You're quiet," said Rob.

Max shrugged.

He wondered if Max was missing his mum. He decided not to enquire. He wanted to hug his son, but he couldn't bring himself to do it. The same reticence had hampered his relationship with Sarah, before all of the other stuff. It didn't matter. He told himself to concentrate on the moment, live in the present, focus on the day ahead, and the fish in the pond.

But there were no fish.

After two hours of inaction, Rob led Max through the farmyard in the direction of the farther ponds. As they passed the farmhouse he thought he saw the woman in the front window, a furtive movement behind the yellowing net curtains, but she didn't appear.

The old dog shifted in its kennel and exhaled.

"The dog looks sick," said Max.

Rob nodded.

"Keep away from it," he said, taking Max's hand. "Dogs that are suffering can be unpredictable."

The ponds at the lowest end of the farm were choked with algae, unmanaged, desperate for attention. The fishing swims were clogged with weed. When Rob stepped on to one of the wooden platforms it almost collapsed beneath him.

"Let's give up with the fishing," said Rob. "We'll do something else instead."

Wandering up the hill towards the tent, Rob thought about the woman and the incident with the cow. He thought about the old dog too, barely clinging to life. He pictured a world in which he owned the farm, imagined healthily stocked ponds, a bustling campsite, a shop selling organic produce. He pictured Sarah's scornful face. Would he make a better job of it than this? Would he truly?

Back at the tent he took out the model glider he'd bought for the trip. For a while Max seemed to be into it, but then he returned to his phone. Rob felt a tinge of disappointment, recalling flying gliders with his own father, but conceivably the time they'd spent was no different, fleeting minutes elongated and rose-tinted by the passing years. His father had been absent a lot, much like he was absent from Max's life, though the circumstances were different and his parents had somehow stayed together.

Everything repeated itself. Wasn't that what they said? Sons became their fathers? He hoped for Max's sake it wasn't the case.

A girl strode up the steep slope. She was dressed for the outdoors in a fleece and walking boots. Rob noticed her lean calf muscles, the control and grace of her movement. He nodded hello. To his surprise, she wandered over to him.

"Hi," she said. "I'm Claire."

"Rob," he said. "Rob and Max." He gestured towards the set of feet sticking out of the tent flap.

"Father and son time?" she asked.

"Something like that," he said.

"How is it?" she asked. She gestured towards the surrounding farm.

"It's okay," he said. "It's all I was looking for."

Did she glance towards his left hand? Check to see if he was wearing a ring? He casually turned his hand in her direction, just to make it obvious he wasn't.

"We use this site quite a bit," said the girl. "Though we're thinking this might be the last time."

We.

"It's going to ruin," she whispered. "The son died a year ago. Fell into the slurry pit. It was just the two of them, so she's on her own now. I don't think she's coping. I think she's unwell."

"I noticed the showers," he said.

The girl nodded. "It feels different now," she said. "Like we're a burden."

He thought about the previous evening, the door closing in his face. A bearded man emerged from the tent further up the slope. The girl looked in his direction.

"This is Rob and Max," she shouted.

Rob raised a hand in greeting but the bearded man remained at a distance.

"That's Kristian," she said. "My fiancé. We're hiking the border in sections. He wants to get going."

"Right," said Rob. "We're off out too." He waved a leaflet at her. *The Witch Cave.*

"Ah, the local legend," she said. "It's good fun. You'll enjoy it."

He shrugged. "More for the boy," he said.

The girl wandered up the slope and disappeared into her tent. Rob heard the sound of agitated voices, felt the familiar anxiety. He thought about Sarah. Things were better how they were. Better like this. For all three of them.

He looked down at the leaflet. The artist had done a good job of portraying the witch, an old crone, necessarily ugly. He remembered the witch in *Snow White*, his mother having to take him out of the cinema because he was scared. He folded the leaflet into his pocket.

He called out to Max.

"I'm going to order breakfast for tomorrow. Then we're off to the cave."

He was thinking about the witch as he knocked on the farmhouse door. And *Hansel and Gretel*. He was thinking about that story too. Old crones. Lonely souls ripe for persecution.

The woman appeared.

"I'd like to order two breakfasts for the morning if possible. One for me and one for my son."

Did the woman recoil a touch when he said the word 'son'? As if it were a forbidden word?

She wrote his order down on a post-it note all the same, wrote 'beans' as 'beens'. He wondered if she'd ever gone to school.

She could obviously read though. There was a newspaper on the table behind her. The headline read: TRIBUTES FOR 19-YEAR-OLD KILLED IN ACCIDENT.

"I saw the shrine," he said. "At the top of the hill."

The woman shook her head. "This was just two days ago," she said, gesturing towards the paper. "Teenagers. They drive too fast. Accidents happen. People die."

He nodded. He realised she was closing the door on him again. It scraped on the linoleum as he stepped out of the way.

"We're off to the witch cave," he said, but she didn't seem to hear him.

Rob drove out of the campsite. He passed the couple. They were on foot, the guy ten yards ahead of the girl. The girl waved at Rob and he waved back.

In another life... he thought.

He followed the lane down the hill to the bend at the bottom. Sure enough, there was a second shrine amongst the scarred tree trunks. The flowers were fresh, the hand-written tributes still decipherable if a person wanted to read them.

Though there had not been any rain since they arrived, the lane was damp. He wondered if it was perpetually dismal under the trees, one of those places that never saw sunlight. There was moss growing on the boulders. He spotted some red and white toadstools in the dead wood of a fallen tree. He thought about the local legend. If ever there was a place for one to propagate, this was it. He felt for the leaflet in his back pocket, then grabbed the steering wheel again with his free hand. For a moment he'd felt the car getting away from him.

Something shifted in the trees off to his right.

Was it a deer?

"Did you see that, Dad?" asked Max.

"I think so," he said.

"She was just standing there."

Rob wondered how Max knew the deer was female.

He drove out of the trees into the sunlight, experiencing a peculiar feeling of relief. At the next junction he spotted the garish sign for a fried chicken drive-thru.

That's why they come this way, he thought. *That's the lure.*

He crossed the main road and continued up a narrow lane to the car park for the witch cave.

"Are we there?" asked his son.

"Yep," he said. "It's meant to be great."

He took out the leaflet and looked at the picture of the witch, then folded it back into his palm. Some artists were just too good at their job.

"Why did they think she was a witch?" asked Max.

They were sitting in the car at the drive-thru, Max munching on chips, Rob sipping a scalding coffee.

"Because she looked strange," said Rob. "And because she acted strangely. That's why she lived in the cave. To get away from people. It was a different time. People believed all sorts of things. Especially out here."

"She didn't like people."

"I think it was more that people didn't like her," Rob said.

"She killed the children," said Max.

Rob shook his head. "The children died but I don't think she killed them. She just got the blame because the villagers didn't like her."

"It said she gave them the sacks to bury the children in, and that the next day the children died."

"It also said the sacks might have contained remedies," said Max. "Things to make the children better. But the children were too sick."

"So she might have been trying to help the children?" asked Max. He scratched the back of his head, a physical gesture that once again made him look momentarily older than his years. "I'd have been kind to her," he said.

"I know you would," said Rob. "Your mum's doing a good job."

He looked at his son, at his hands, his face, his bright eyes. He felt a surge of love for his boy, almost overwhelming.

"Dave's kind to Mum," said Max.

The stab pierced his heart. But his son was grinning, innocent of the blow he'd delivered. It wasn't his fault.

"Your mum's not a witch though," said Rob. "Or maybe she is." He made a face.

Max laughed.

Rob managed to laugh too, but it was different driving back along the lane towards the campsite. His mood had darkened. He kept thinking about Sarah and Dave, about the relationship Dave had with Max, about the future. There was no clarity to any of it, just a variegated succession of images. Sarah and Dave on a sofa with Max wedged in between, the three of them laughing at a family film. Max in his brand new uniform on the first day of secondary school, Dave with his hands on Max's shoulders. Max asleep in his room. The fishing posters on the wall. Dave checking on Max before bedtime. Sarah stepping out of the shower, naked. Dave following her into their bedroom. Their bedroom door closing...

He forced the thoughts away.

The shadows in the woods were thicker now, the surface of the lane slick with moisture. It wouldn't take much, a lack of concentration, a little too much pressure on the accelerator, a little too much keenness on the brakes. The sort of things inexperienced teenage drivers were susceptible to. He felt the numbing impact, the unbearable pain, the cold terror of impending death. He felt the dark abnormal silence of the lane.

And something else. A feeling in the pit of his stomach. That it wasn't just the damp surface of the lane, the awkward bends, the reckless nature of youth.

The gouged trunk. The slurry pit. The stagnant water.

All wasn't well in this place.

For the briefest moment he thought he saw something in the trees again, a shifting form.

But it was nothing.

He reached the bend. He slowed the car to a crawl. He passed the shrine. A fresh set of flowers had been placed amongst the others and a wreath spelling out the word SON.

To lose a child.

Rob gripped the steering wheel tighter, focussed on the lane and tried to block the image from his mind. He couldn't cope, he realised. Such a thing would crush him, render him incapable of living.

Evening came. Rob braved the pathetic showers then wandered back up the slope to find Max sitting contentedly in the entrance to the tent. Beside him was a sack full of firewood.

"The lady was here," said Max.

"We have enough wood," said Rob.

"She said I was precious," said Max.

"You are," said Rob. "You know you are."

"She had cold hands."

Rob looked at his son, then down the hill towards the farmhouse. He didn't take the wood back. He used it instead, to build a roaring fire. They cooked sausages on it. They cooked marshmallows. When Max returned to his phone, Rob settled by the fire with a beer. He stared out across the fields below, at the stretching shadows, at the vast, featureless slopes of the border country in the distance. There was something about the timeless nature of the landscape that lent itself to legends and curiosities, to witches and witchcraft, curses and dark magic. And an overpowering sense of futility too, a wilderness in which man and all his undertakings were largely irrelevant.

He spotted the woman delivering sacks of feed to the sheep. He watched her return the tractor to the yard, watched her climb down from the machine in her thick jacket, watched her make her way across the yard to the house. The old dog lifted its head, rose to its feet, stretched, considered moving towards her, and then sank back down again. He thought he could hear it whining.

The woman stopped in the middle of the yard and looked long and hard at the dog, and Rob knew she was thinking what he was thinking, that sooner or later a creature is no good to itself, that sooner or later…

She carried a single cloth sack in her hands.

The shadow of the escarpment spread effortlessly across the campsite, the farmyard, the distant fields. Rob put some more wood on the fire.

When Max was asleep, he pulled the sleeping bag up to his son's chin and pushed the hair from his face. He loved his son the most when he was sleeping, loved the little quiet moments before his own bedtime when he stood watch like this, staring down at Max's contented face, his perfect skin, like a doll, like a cherub. He missed these moments. He missed them more and more even as they passed.

Rob drank a beer in the dark. He stared at the fire pit and the white-hot centre of the flames. They'd burned their witch in the end, celebrated her demise as she cursed them and all their offspring, though thankfully he'd managed to steer Max away from that information. Perhaps it wasn't true anyway. Perhaps it was just a story.

He heard the woman going about her business, the sound of her dragging something across the yard. And he heard voices coming from the other tent, voices filled with forced restraint. The bearded guy appeared and marched down the hill. Rob gestured to him, but once again he barely registered Rob's presence. Rob watched him get into his car, flick on the lights, and drive along the track towards the farm exit.

Too fast. Way too fast.

Rob finished his beer and opened another.

The girl walked down the slope to where he was seated.

"Hi," she said. "How was today?"

She perched herself on the edge of the wooden table. She looked pretty in the orange glow from the fire.

"Good," he said. "Interesting. A bit unsettling too, if I'm honest."

"I expect it's worse for a parent," she said. "Was your son scared?"

Rob shook his head. "Far from it," he said. "He felt sorry for her. He wanted to look after her. He's like that."

"Must be strong nurturing," she said. She touched her wrist with the thumb of her other hand.

Rob shrugged.

"Is his mum at work or something?" the girl asked.

"No," said Rob. "His mum . . . we're not together anymore."

"Oh," she said. "Sorry."

"It was a long time ago," said Rob. Except it wasn't. Not really.

"I'd like children," said the girl. "But Kristian doesn't want any."

She touched her wrist again and stared along the track towards the farm entrance.

"Are you okay?" asked Rob.

"I twisted my wrist," she said. "I'm fine." She stared into the darkness.

A light popped on in an upstairs window of the farmhouse. A shadow moved beyond the set of floral curtains. The two of them gazed through the stillness at the farmhouse, towards the thin wash of yellow light.

"It must be hard on her," Rob said. "Losing her son like that."

He realised the girl was looking straight at him.

"We found another campsite. A few miles up the road. We're going to move our stuff there. Are you here all week?"

"No," said Rob. "Just tonight. Max has school on Monday. I have to give him back."

"That must be hard," she said.

"It is what it is," he said.

There was nothing else he could say. He thought about asking for the girl's number, or offering his own. He thought about those things. Before he could decide how, a set of car headlights entered the farm track. The girl stiffened.

"I have to get packing," she said.

She moved away from him, up the slope in the direction of her tent. He watched her go. He'd always been attracted to vulnerable women and never been able to live up to the job of staying with one. The car pulled up and the girl's fiancé got out. He pounded up the slope. This time he offered Rob a perfunctory nod.

Wanker, thought Rob.

He spent much of the next hour thinking about being replaced as a father, about the mistakes he'd made, the irreparable damage, the shouting, the crying, the empty void of nothingness that his relationship with his son's mother had become. At one time, they'd created a life.

He listened to the muffled conversation coming from the tent above. When he heard the girl laugh, he grimaced.

He watched the twinkling lights dotted in the darkness.

He witnessed the feeble light in the farmhouse bedroom go off.

He followed the lights of a car as it negotiated the dark lanes far below and heard the distant hammering bass of a car stereo. He imagined the car careering off the road, rolling and smashing into a tree. He thought of shattered lives, distraught parents, grandparents, siblings, friends.

He thought about a lonely old woman residing in a remote farmhouse and another living out her days in a secluded cave. He turned to look at the tree-line. It was just a smudge in the darkness and it hadn't moved in the time he'd been at the campsite. It was just a foolish notion he'd had.

He put out the fire, scrambled around to the back of the tent and pissed into the foliage, then he crawled into the tent and into his sleeping bag. Beside him, Max slept as eight-year-old boys should sleep, without burden, without care.

It was later.

Rob woke to hear Max's soft voice.

"Dad," whispered Max. "Dad."

"What?" asked Rob. "What is it?"

"I need the toilet."

"Okay," said Rob, struggling to rise from the fog. "Okay."

His head was heavy. He could barely open his eyes.

He heard Max unzip the tent and push his way through the flap.

"Max," said Rob.

"I'll be okay, Dad," said Max. "I've got the torch. And the old lady will look after me."

"She'll be in bed," Rob said.

But Max was already outside.

Rob forced himself awake. He rubbed his eyes. He realised where he was, what was happening. His son was heading to the toilet alone. He felt a surge of apprehension. Cocooned in his sleeping bag, he crawled to the tent entrance. He watched the torchlight dancing down the slope towards the toilet block.

It was okay. It was part of growing up. It was okay.

The torchlight disappeared beyond the shrubbery. Rob heard the toilet door swing open and closed and the click of the light switch. He felt a swell of pride to think his eight-year-old boy could do such a thing as visit a toilet block alone in the middle of the night like this, in a strange place like this, without fear, without protest, without histrionics. And he felt the familiar nagging, the bitter taste of self-disgust. Couldn't he have dragged himself awake a little quicker? Couldn't he have gone with his son? He was a terrible excuse for a father. Sarah was right. He always had been.

Rob waited.

He extracted himself from his sleeping bag and stood at the tent entrance, staring at the black void beneath him, above him, all around him. He looked across the valley, trying to discern horizon from sky, but the border country was one and the same—earth and air, real and imaginary. There was no other place like it.

He thought about the bend in the road.

He thought about the witch from *Snow White*.

He heard a rustling in the undergrowth and turned in its direction. As soon as he did, the rustling ceased. He waited, trying not to make a sound. The rustling started again. Some nocturnal animal foraging for food. A badger perhaps. Or something else. Something that had come down from the hills.

288

Something ageless.

Something wild.

Rob shook himself loose of his imaginings. The farmhouse beneath him was a grey silhouette.

All was silent.

All was still.

He promised himself he'd be better from now on, less frustrated, less angry, less occupied. The weekend had been a start, but even on this trip he'd been more engaged with cooking, carrying, organising—occupied with being a father, but not a dad. There was a difference. He thought about his son, alone in the dark. He thought about Sarah's hesitancy in letting him take Max away in the first place, her concerns about his ability to look after a boy of eight even if it was their boy.

His boy. Max was *his* boy.

Rob contemplated the time that had passed since he'd let Max venture to the toilet alone. Anxiety gripped him. How long *had* it been? He ducked back inside the tent, searching for his phone. It had a torch, but the battery was low. No matter. He turned on the torch and pointed it into the night.

He thought he could hear voices. He thought he could hear Max's voice and the hushed, barely perceptible voice of another. Who was Max talking to?

Rob started making his way down the slope.

He heard the toilet door slam shut, the sound of stones clicking against stones.

"Max," he whispered, as loudly as the night allowed.

There was no reply.

He thought he heard the sound of a woman's voice but it was barely perceptible, hardly a sound at all.

Rob ran down the slope.

"Max," he said. Louder now. With urgency.

He reached the rickety gate, pushed it open, skirted the outhouse. The toilet block was empty. The funnel-like web trembled. He felt something growing inside of him, a bone-gnawing fear. He ducked around the back of the farmhouse. There were no lights on, no signs of life. He hammered on the door. Nobody came to answer it. There was no movement at all. He circled the house until he reached the farmyard, pointed the torch in the direction of the dog kennel. The dog kennel was empty, the old dog nowhere to be seen.

He clambered over the farmyard gate, shivering now, unable to control his nervous energy. He spotted the flash of a torch light, far away in the next field.

"Max," he shouted. "Max!"

Rob ran across the field in the direction of the torchlight. The light skipped away from him. He tried to shout, but running and shouting were hard. He was dizzy from the sudden exertion, from a lack of oxygen, from the alcohol in his bloodstream. But he was gaining. He felt a surge of hope. He'd reach Max. He'd pull his boy into his arms, take him away from this place, repair the damage with Sarah, wrestle her free from Dave, learn from his mistakes.

All would be well.

His phone lost its power and the darkness swallowed him.

The torchlight in the field winked.

It seemed to be further away.

How could it be further away?

Something screamed in the night, something shrill and severe. An owl? A fox? A child?

"Max," he screamed. "Max!"

The torchlight in the field went out.

Rob tried to run across the field, but there was nothing to see now, nothing to orientate himself against. The darkness became a physical entity. Like water. Like oil. It resisted his movements. He had to force his way through it, blindly and impossibly.

He fought for breath as he waded into an ever-deepening sea of darkness. It was possible to drown in darkness, he realised, to sink into its depths and never return.

He stumbled blindly onwards until his right shinbone struck an object. He was sent sprawling. For a moment he lay in the field, his nose buried in the damp grass, then he pulled himself up, turned to look at the thing he'd fallen over. He couldn't see very much, just an unnatural contour in the gloom.

He squinted into the blackness.

It was a cloth sack. As he crawled towards it he thought he saw something move in the periphery of his vision, something slipping away into the folds of night, something in a thick coat, or a heavy shawl, something.

Someone.

Something.

Rob knelt in the grass, pressed his palms against the cloth sack. He felt its coarse texture, reached inside it, registered the warm, organic bulk of its contents.

He screamed in the catastrophic darkness.

TIM LEBBON

In Stone

TIM LEBBON is a *New York Times* best-selling writer from South Wales. He's had over forty novels published to date, as well as hundreds of novellas and short stories. Recent novels include thrillers *The Hunt* and *The Family Man*, as well as *The Silence, Relics, The Folded Land* and the "Rage War" trilogy of *Alien/Predator* novels.

The movie of his story 'Pay the Ghost', starring Nicolas Cage, was released Halloween 2015. *The Silence*, starring Stanley Tucci and Kiernan Shipka, is due for release early 2019, and screenplays *Playtime* (with Stephen Volk) and *My Haunted House* are currently in development.

Lebbon has won four British Fantasy Awards, a Bram Stoker Award and a Scribe Award, and has been a finalist for World Fantasy, International Horror Guild and Shirley Jackson Awards. His work has appeared in numerous "Year's Best" anthologies.

"This story was probably seeded years ago," says the author, "when I used to live, and go out drinking with friends, in Newport. I'd often end up walking home alone, and even when I was in my late teens my imagination often went into overdrive.

"It wasn't the safest town late at night, with dozens of pubs and clubs kicking out at the same time, and I think that heightened state of alert probably meant that the alleys and short-cuts I took on the way home held an even heavier sense of dread and, sometimes, *wrongness*.

"There were also a few familiar 'characters' who became known to us—people who we did our best to avoid, especially when it was dark and late, the streets were quieter and more mysterious, and their true natures were difficult to perceive."

SEVERAL WEEKS FOLLOWING the death of a close friend, I started walking alone at night. I was having trouble sleeping, and I think it was a way of trying to reclaim that time for myself. Instead of lying in the darkness remembering Nigel, feeling regret that we'd let the time between meetings stretch further each year, I took to the streets. There was nothing worse than staring at the ceiling and seeing all the bad parts of my life mapped there in cracks, spider-webs and the trails of a paint brush. I thought perhaps walking in the dark might help me really think.

On the fifth night of wandering the streets, I saw the woman.

I was close to the centre of town. It was raining, and the few working streetlights cast speckled, splashed patterns across the pavement, giving the impression that nothing was still in the silent night. Over the past hour I'd seen several people. One was a night worker—a nurse or fireman, perhaps—hurrying along the street wearing a backpack and with a definite destination in mind. A couple were youths, so drunk that they could barely walk or talk. One was a homeless woman I'd seen before. Two dogs accompanied her like shadows, and she muttered to herself too quietly for me to hear.

They all saw me. The worker veered around me slightly, the youths muttered and giggled, and the homeless woman's dogs paused and sniffed in my direction.

But the new woman didn't look or act like everyone else. At three or four in the morning, anyone left out in the streets wanted to be alone. Closeness was avoided, and other than perhaps a curt nod, no contact was made. It was as if darkness brought out mysteries and hidden stories in people and made them solid, and that suited me just fine. I wasn't out there to speak to anyone else; I was attempting to talk to myself.

There was something about her that immediately caught my attention. Walking in a world of her own, she followed no obvious route through the heavy rain, moving back and forth across the silent main street, sometimes walking on the sidewalk and sometimes the road. The weather did not appear to concern her. Even though it was summer, the rain was cool and the night cooler, but she walked without a coat or jacket of any kind. She wore loose trousers and a vest top, and I really shouldn't have followed her.

But Nigel told me to. It was his voice I heard in my head saying, *Wonder what she's up to?* He had always been curious and interested in other people, the one most likely to get chatting to strangers if we went for a drink. Last time I'd seen him he'd been more garrulous than ever, and I wondered if that was a way of hiding his deeper problems and fears. He could say so much, but still didn't know how to ask for help.

The woman drifted from the main street to a narrower road between shops, and I followed. I held back a little—I had no wish to frighten or trouble her—but tried to make sure I kept her in sight. The rain was falling heavier now, and I had to throw up my hood to shield my eyes and face. The side street was not lit. Rain blanketed the night, making everything even darker and giving a constant shimmer to reality. Her movements were nebulous and fluid, slipping in and out of the darkness like a porpoise dancing through waves.

To my left and right, large spaces opened up. These were the service yards of big shops, covered delivery and storage areas that I barely noticed if walking these streets during the day. Now, they were pitch-black burrows where anything might exist, and I was pleased when the woman passed them by.

As she neared a smaller street, she paused. I also stopped, tucking in close to a wall. I suddenly felt uncomfortable following her. I was no threat, but no one else would believe that. If people saw me stalking the woman, they might think the worst. If she saw me, I might frighten her.

I was about to turn and walk back the way I'd come when something gave me pause.

The street ahead was a place I knew well, home to a series of smaller, independent shops, a couple of nice pubs, and a few restaurants. Nigel and I had eaten and drunk there, and I'd walked that way more times than I could recall. In the stormy night, it glowed with reflected neon from shop windows. A rush of memories washed over me, and I gasped.

The woman seemed to hear. She tilted her head slightly, then walked out into this narrower road. I followed. I had the sudden sense that I was witnessing something secret. I felt like an intruder, emerging from my safe, warm home to stroll dark streets I knew nothing about.

During the day, this place was a bustling centre of commerce and fun. Now it was a whole new world.

By the time I moved out onto the street, the woman had paused beside a series of bronze sculptures on plinths. They'd been placed fifteen years before as part of the millennium celebrations, and I hardly ever noticed them. Seeing them at night, flowing with water that shimmered and reflected weak light, gave them a strange form of life.

The woman was staring past the sculptures and into the mouth of a narrow alley. I knew the place. It was a dead-end passageway between a fast-food joint and a newsagents. I'd stumbled down there once years ago, drunk, a young woman holding onto my arm as if I could be more stable than her. I had vague memories of what we'd done. Shambolic, clumsy sex amongst split bags of refuse and broken bottles did not make me particularly proud, and I'd only ever spoken of that moment with Nigel.

As I wondered what her interest might be in that grubby place, and just what it was about her that troubled me, she began to take off her clothes.

I caught my breath and pulled back around the corner. I felt unaccountably guilty witnessing the woman's shedding of clothing, even though she was doing it in the middle of the street. Her shoes came off first, then her vest and trousers. Naked, she stretched her arms to the air and let the rain run across her body. She might have been beautiful.

Rain flowed into my eyes. I wiped them and looked again. There was something wrong.

The woman was moving past the bronze statues and heading towards the entrance to the alley. Her motion seemed strange. She drifted rather than walked, limbs swinging slightly out of time, her movements not quite human. Her pale skin grew darker. Her hair became a more solid cap around her head. She slowed before the alley—hesitant, or relishing the moment—then stepped into its shadows.

As she passed out of sight, I had the very real sense that she was no longer there.

I ran into the night.

"And you ran all the way home?"

"Yeah."

"Dude. You. Running."

I laughed. "Who'd have thunk it?"

Ashley licked her finger and used it to pick up cake crumbs from her plate. Finger still in her mouth, she caught my attention and raised an eyebrow. I rolled my eyes. Ash had been my best friend since we were both babies, and although I couldn't help but acknowledge her beauty, I'd never been drawn to her in that way.

"Still not sleeping?" she asked.

"No. Not well at all."

"Hence the walking at night."

I nodded.

"You're very, very weird."

We both sipped at our coffees, comfortable in our silence. The café around was filled with conversation and soft music, merging into a background noise that kept our own chat private.

"Maybe she was a prostitute."

"No."

"You're sure?"

I nodded.

"So you'd recognise one?" She had that cheeky glint in her eyes, and I couldn't help but smile. Ashley called herself shallow, but I knew that wasn't true at all. She was simply someone who knew how to regulate her depths. She'd been a levelling force in my life forever, and never more than since Nigel stepped from that ledge.

"It's only around the corner," I said. "Will you come with me?"

"And search for the mysterious vanishing woman? You bet!"

We left the café. It had stopped raining and the town was alive with lunchtime buzz. Ash and I met for lunch at least once each week, working within ten minutes of each other making it easy. I dreaded her leaving to work elsewhere. She'd mentioned it once or twice, and I knew that she'd had a couple of interviews. It was only a matter of time. Ash was not someone that life held back, and the world was calling.

"It will get easier," she said, hooking her arm through mine as we walked.

"Yeah, I know."

"Wish I'd known him better."

I nodded. Felt a lump in my throat and swallowed it down. "Me too."

As we approached the place where I'd seen the woman earlier that morning, I heard the cheerful shouts and laughter of a group of school kids. They were maybe nine or ten, posing around the bronze statues as teachers took photos. They probably shouldn't have been up on the plinths, but no one would tell them to get down. Who would intrude on such excitement and joy?

I headed past the statues and children, aiming for the alley between newsagents and the fast-food joint, which was doing a busy trade. People queued out the door. A young woman emerged from the alley, wearing an apron with the takeaway's name emblazoned across the front. She offered us a quick smile, then pushed past the queue and back into the shop. I felt a release of tension from my shoulders, a relaxing in my gut. Ash must have felt it too.

"See?" she said. "No gruesome murders."

I turned to her and nodded, and then something caught my eye. A litter-bin stood beside a bench close to the statues, and splayed across its lip was a dirtied white vest.

"Oh," I said. I blinked, remembering the woman lifting the vest up over her head.

"What?" Ash asked.

I pointed at the vest. "Why wouldn't she dress again afterwards?" After what, I did not say, or even wish to consider. She must have walked home naked. If she had walked home at all.

I headed for the alley, and Ash came with me. It smelled of piss. No surprise there. But it also smelled of rain, fresh and sharp, even though it had stopped raining even before I'd finished running home eight hours before.

"Delightful," Ash said. She stepped over a pool of vomit on the ground.

It was unremarkable, a narrow alley with a dead end thirty feet in, dirty rendered wall on one side, old bare brick on the other. A couple of metal doorways were set into the walls, without handles and looking as if they'd been locked for decades. There were a few black bin bags, one of them split and gnawed at by night creatures—cats, rats, foxes. A pile of dog crap held a smeared shoe print. A dead rat festered against the blank end wall.

"She didn't come out again," I said.

"Not while you were watching."

"But her clothes."

Ash shrugged.

I walked the length of the alley, fearing what I might see, eager to make sure there was nothing there. I shifted a couple of rubbish bags with my foot, releasing a foul stink that made me gag.

"Jesus, what a wonderful smell you've found!" Ash said.

I covered my mouth with the collar of my coat and went in deeper, shoving bags aside with my feet. Old wrappers spilled, slick with rotting food. Things crawled in there, dark and wet, reminding me of the nude woman flowing with rainwater, silvery, flexing and shifting like something inhuman. I bent down to look closer and saw a nest of slugs, leaving trails like slow echoes and pulsing like something's insides.

"Weird," Ash said. She was looking at a spread of brickwork close to the ground, a few feet from the end of the alley. I went to her and stood close, our coats brushing. She grabbed my hand.

"What?"

"Don't know," she said. She shivered. "Let's go."

"Hang on." I crouched, leaning in closer, trying not to block out precious light so that I could see what she'd seen.

"Come on. Let's go."

"What is that?" I asked. But neither of us could answer.

The bricks were old and crumbling, covered with black moss, joints clotted with decades of filth. This wall had never seen sunlight, and perpetual shadow had driven darkness into the brick faces and the mortar in between. Across a spread of brickwork, something protruded. It looked like a swathe of dark pink pustules, solid-looking rather than soft, dry and dusty even though the brickwork around them was damp. I reached out to touch, but Ash grabbed my arm.

"What if it's poisonous?" she asked.

"It's just the bricks," I said. "Frost-blown, maybe. They've deformed over time." I reached out again, but didn't quite touch. Something held me back. Something about the shape of the feature, the way it swept up from the ground and spanned several courses of bricks.

It looked like an arm reaching from the ground, embedded in the wall and only just protruding. At its end, a clenched fist of brickwork protruded more than elsewhere, cracked and threatening to disintegrate at any moment.

I wondered what that fist might hold.

Ash grabbed my coat and pulled me upright, shoving me before her along the alley and back into the street. "It should be cleaned," she said. But she didn't enter the fast-food shop or the newsagents to share this opinion with them. Instead, she headed back to work.

I stood there for a while looking at the discarded clothing in the litter-bin. It was slowly being buried beneath lunchtime refuse—coffee cups, crisp bags, sandwich wrappers. Soon it would be completely out of sight. Forgotten.

I wondered where the woman had gone.

"I'm sorry," Ash said. She'd called me after work, on the way to her boyfriend's place.

"For what?" I was in the park, beyond which lay the old terraced house where I lived. It was raining again, and a few umbrellas and coats hid anonymous people as they took various paths home.

"I just . . . that place at lunchtime felt a bit odd. Didn't it?"

"Yeah." But I couldn't quite verbalise how the alley had felt strange. *Like somewhere else*, I might have said. The idea crossed my mind that I'd seen a ghost, but I had never believed in them. I was a rationalist, an atheist, and until Nigel's death I'd been happy and comfortable with that. Since he'd taken his own life, I had been struggling. Not for him, because he was gone now, flickering out from a wonderful, expansive consciousness to nothing in the space of a pavement impact. But for me. All that was left of Nigel was in my mind, and the minds of those who loved him. That didn't seem much to leave behind.

I thought of those weird shapes across the rotting brickwork, blown clay in the shape of a rising, clasping arm and hand.

"Max says hi."

"Hi, Max."

"See you soon. And don't go wandering tonight. Weather forecast is awful, and you need sleep."

"Damn right. Bottle of wine, then bed, like a good boy."

"Good boy." Ash hung up, leaving me alone in the park with the rain, and the puddles, and the memory of a time me, Nigel and a few others came here to play football when we were kids. I thought I heard his laugh. But it was someone else, and I started walking again before whoever was laughing caught up with me.

Wind roared around my house and made the roof creak, rain hammered against the closed windows, and next door's dog barked, waiting for them to come home.

I tried to sleep for a while, but failed miserably. The brief buzz I'd had from the bottle of wine was gone, melted away into the darkness of my bedroom. I lay awake for a while staring into the shadows.

Then I got up, dressed, slipped on my raincoat that was still wet from walking home from work, and went out into the night.

It was almost two in the morning.

I walked into the city. I lived in a suburb, but it was only fifteen minutes through the park, past the hospital and into town. All that time I saw no other pedestrians, and only a few cars. Some of them were police vehicles, and one slowed when it passed me, a pale face peering from the window obscured and made fluid by rain impacting the glass. I stared back, hiding nothing. The car moved on.

I was heading along the main street, intending to visit that alley again. There had been something strange about the woman, but I found that I was not afraid. I had no idea why. Maybe it had been Ash's strange, repulsed reaction to that feature on the wall, and my realisation that I was less troubled than her.

The weather was atrocious. Wind howled along the town's main thoroughfares like a beast unleashed, revelling in the fact that there was no one there to view its night-time cavortings. It whistled through the slats of fixed benches, rattled shutters on jewellers' shops, and flung litter into piles in doorways and against wet walls. Rain lashed almost horizontally, spiking into my face and against my front, the coat hardly any barrier at all.

I leaned into the wind and rain, working my way through the town, and the night was alive around me.

I saw a few people. It was earlier than I usually chose to walk, and a couple of the later clubs had only kicked out an hour or so before. A few drunks huddled against the weather and tried to remember where they lived. Some were in pairs, more alone. I also saw the homeless woman with the dogs. The hounds looked my way, but I don't think they growled, or if they did the wind carried the sound away. Maybe they were growing used to me.

There's a part of town where five roads converge. People call it a square, though it isn't really. It's disordered and accidental, the same as most people who pass through from midnight onwards. That night it was a wilder place, and as I approached along the main street I had to stop and stare. The square seemed primeval. Great cliffs of brick, stone and glass rose up on all sides, channelling torrents of wind and rain that met in the middle as if in battle. A tornado of litter and rain twisted back and forth, throwing off its contents and sucking more in. The sound was staggering, the effect intimidating. I could see shop windows flexing beneath the onslaught, as if the buildings themselves were breathing great, slow, considered breaths.

I stood there for a while just watching, and then as if carried like shreds of refuse on the storm, memories of Nigel came in.

We cross the square, arms around each other's shoulders. It's a Saturday afternoon and we've been in the pub all day, ostensibly to watch a big rugby match, though neither of us is really into sport. The atmosphere was electric, the pub a sea of shirts of two colours, good-natured banter fuelled by beer turning into hearty singing, and much friendly mockery of the losing team. It's been refreshing and upbeat, and Nigel has said that tribal warfare has never been so much fun. We're going to buy food. We head down one of the narrower streets—

—and Nigel reels from the blow, staggering back into a doorway as the big, thick thug storms after him. I've never been so afraid in my life. But that's Nigel getting picked on for no reason. We simply walked the wrong way and met the wrong nutter. He's drunk, that's obvious, and though I'm not one to judge by first appearances, he looks like he likes a fight.

He launches another punch at Nigel, then I'm piling into the bastard from behind, shoving him forwards as hard as I can into the shop window. Glass cracks. He half-turns to glare at me, murder in his eyes and blood running from a cut in his forehead. Nigel lands a punch on his nose, a pile-driving crunch that we'll talk about for years to come—

—we're following two girls who have been smiling at us all afternoon. We're too old to stay at home, too young to hit the pubs, so town is our afternoon playground, and today feels special. Nigel is the good-looking one, and both girls have been eyeing him. I'll become used to playing second fiddle to my friend.

I sighed, and my breath was lost to the storm like so many

memories. His death still hit me like this, and I wasn't sure I'd ever grow used to it.

Buffeted by high winds, soaked to the skin, I decided to make my way home.

The shape started across the square just as I took my first step. It was a man, perhaps late fifties, long grey hair swirling around his head and coat flapping in the wind. Yet none of his movements seemed quite right. His hair moved a little too slowly, like flexing wire on a stop-motion mannequin instead of real hair. His coat seemed to shift and wave in slow motion. He paced across the square with a definite destination in mind.

He looked just like the woman I'd seen the night before. Out of place, removed from his turbulent surroundings, walking his own path through a city that seemed unable to contain him.

I followed.

Walking across the square, emerging from the shelter of the buildings, I submitted myself to the full force of the storm. It was as if with every step I took, the storm focussed all of its attention on me, driving along streets and roads and smashing together at that violent junction. I staggered left and right, arms spread for balance, the hood of my coat alternately filling with wind and acting like a sail, then flattening against my scalp like a second skin. I forged on, head down, thinking of arctic explorers fighting against harsh gales to reach their goal. Rain stung my face. I could hardly see anything, squinting at the ground just ahead of me to see where I was going. I crossed the paved area, then a road, and then finally I felt the storm lessen as I neared another building. Hugging myself to its shelter, I looked ahead and saw the man. He was barely visible, a hundred metres ahead and already passing into the night. Winds whipped around him. Rain hammered down, dancing sworls in weak streetlights.

Between one blink and the next, the man was gone.

I strode ahead, moving fast to try and catch up. The storm screamed at me, threatening or warning. I paid no heed. I needed to see the man again, follow him, try to talk with him. I walked back and forth along the street, passing closed shops and cafés, and saw nothing. I ventured into doorways in case he had fallen and was hidden beneath piles of wind-blown litter. When I faced a narrow arcade, I pressed against the metal grille securing its entrance and tried to see deeper.

The night seemed even darker in there, and more still. The shadows were heavy. Watching, I also felt watched.

I took a couple of steps back. My breath was stolen by the wind. Glass smashed in the distance. A car alarm erupted somewhere out of sight, and part of a large advertising hoarding bounced along the road towards the square, shedding parts of itself as it went.

Even if the arcade was not locked up, I would not have wanted to go that way.

I hurried back through the square and started towards home. I saw a couple of other people, and they avoided me as surely as I avoided them.

I slept for three hours that night, naked and cold in my bed with wet clothes piled beside me. Dawn woke me. The man haunted my dreams even as I lay in bed awake, still walking, grey hair and coat shifting to some force other than the storm.

Morning brought relative calm. As I ate breakfast I watched the news, and saw that the storm had wreaked havoc across the country. Damage was in the millions. Miraculously, no one had died.

I chewed cereal that tasted like cardboard and thought about that. No one had died.

It was a Saturday, and as I followed my previous night's route into town, the streets soon started to bustle with cheerful shoppers, gangs of kids laughing and joking, and people all with somewhere to go.

I had somewhere to go as well. The square was a very different place from just a few hours before, full of people and life, none of them aware of the shattering storm that had existed there so recently. The storm was a dangerous animal, come and gone again, and it had visited with almost no one knowing.

Across the square and along the street where the man had disappeared, I expected to see his discarded coat slowly being buried in a litter bin or draped over the back of a bench. There was nothing.

The arcade was open. Home to a café, a clothes shop, a candle shop and a second-hand bookseller, it wasn't somewhere I ventured frequently. In daylight, it looked less threatening. I stepped inside. A waft of perfumed air hit me from the candle shop, followed by the scent of frying bacon. It felt safe and warm.

I tripped, stumbled, almost fell, and a youth reached out and grabbed my arm to stop me hitting the ground.

"You all right, mate?"

"Yes," I said, startled. "Thanks."

"No worries. They should fix that." He nodded vaguely at my feet then went on his way, headphones in and thumb stroking his phone.

I looked down. The mosaic floor covering was humped as if pushed up by something from below. Yellow paint had been sprayed across the area some time ago, either a warning to beware or an indication of somewhere that needed to be fixed. No one had fixed it. The paint was faded and chipped, worn away by thousands of feet.

"Hey!" I called after the kid. "You know what happened here?" But he had his headphones in and was already leaving the arcade.

I frowned and moved sideways, shifting my perspective of the raised area. The mosaic tiles weren't only pushed up a little from below, forming the dangerous swelling that I'd tripped on. There was something in their clay shapes.

It looked like a face.

I gasped, closed my eyes, turned away and leaned against a wall. When I opened my eyes again I was looking through a window at an old man sitting inside the café, nursing a mug of tea. He stared at me, and past me, then looked down at his phone.

I glanced down at the ground again.

It *might* have been a face. The curve of one cheek, forehead, the hollow of an eye-socket, and splayed out behind it was a flow of irregularities in the old tiles that resembled long, grey hair.

"Oh, God," I said. I wanted to grab someone and ask them if they saw what I saw. But if they didn't, what then? What could I say, ask, believe?

I took a photo of the raised area then hurried away, because there was someone I could ask. Ash was my leveller. She would hear me out.

As it turned out, Ash had already phoned that morning and left a message on my landline.

"Hey. Give me a call. Got some news."

I made some coffee first. Every step towards home had calmed my panic, and I was feeling more and more foolish over what I thought I'd seen. As I waited for the coffee to brew, every second that passed seemed to bring me closer to normality once more. Looking at my phone helped. The photo I'd taken showed nothing amiss, other than a slightly misshapen area in the arcade floor. However I viewed it, whether I zoomed in or not, there was no face.

But that's right, I thought. *Because it's daytime. They only come out at night.*

The idea came from nowhere, and was chilling.

The phone rang as I was pouring coffee. I jumped and spilled some, cursed, snapped up the phone.

"Hey, it's me," Ash said. "Fancy a coffee?"

"I just made one."

"Right. Can I come over?"

"Er … why?" It wasn't often that Ash and I saw each other on the weekends. She was usually doing stuff with Max, and I was busy with the football club, or meeting friends, or travelling down to Devon to visit my family. Dad would grumble and talk about politics. Mum would ask if I'd met a nice girl yet.

"Max and I are moving away. I got that job in Wales. I heard yesterday."

"Oh. Wow."

"You okay?"

"Yeah, sure. Of course. Delighted for you!"

Ash was silent for a while. "You go walking last night?"

"No." Once uttered, I couldn't take back the lie. I wasn't sure why. Maybe because Ash had already started to move away, and to include her in my troubles would be selfish. She'd wanted this for a long time. That didn't mean I had to be happy, but I could still be pleased for her.

"So I can come over, tell you all about it?"

"Come on over."

"I'll bring cake."

"You know me so well."

"The city eats people," she said. She took a bite of cake as if to illustrate the fact. "We're communal animals, but we're not meant to be somewhere with so many other people. Why do you think places like London feel so impersonal? Live in a small village, a hamlet, know almost everyone there, that's when you're happiest. Here . . . it's like we've created a monster and we're feeding it every day."

Her comments hit me hard. They sounded like her trying to defend her decision to leave for somewhere more rural, and that wasn't like Ash—she was always headstrong and positive. Maybe she was worried about me.

"You think that's why Nigel did what he did?"

Ash raised her eyebrows, as if she'd never even considered it.

"I think Nigel was a sensitive soul. Life was too much for him, and living in the city didn't help at all. But no, he had his own real problems, only aggravated by being here. What I mean is . . . people disappear. One day they're here, the next they're gone, and it's as if they've vanished into nothing. Know what I mean? The city eats them, spits nothing out, and eventually they're just forgotten."

"That's pretty depressing."

"I don't want to disappear," she said.

"You never could. You're too . . . wonderful." I grinned, bashful at the compliment. But she saw how serious I was, because she didn't take the piss.

"You should leave too." She tapped her engagement ring against her mug.

"I'm . . . not sure I could."

"Really? You love this place so much?"

I shook my head. No, I didn't love the city at all. I just couldn't imagine anywhere else feeling like home.

We chatted some more, then talked about her leaving party which she'd be throwing in a couple of week's time. She wanted me to DJ there. I said I was honoured, and I'd only do it if I could throw in some AC/DC. She hated them, but relented.

As she finished her cake I thought of the city eating people, and the outline of a face in broken tiles, and the bubbled surface of blown bricks in the shape of an arm with clenched fist.

Now that I had an idea of what to look for, I saw the city in a whole new light.

That Sunday afternoon I walked. There were plenty of people around because many of the shops remained open, and the place felt relatively safe. But as time passed by, and I saw more, that sense of safety began to evaporate.

By the end of the afternoon I felt like a meal in the jaws of a beast.

I saw distortion in an old swimming pool's caged-over window, and if I looked at just the right angle I could make out the shadow of a naked torso in the imperfect glass.

At the base of an old hotel's side-wall, where access chutes into the basement had been concreted over, two knotted protuberances might have been hands with fingers broken off. Clasping for air forever, the stumpy remains of digits pointing accusingly at everyone left alive.

The stepped marble plinth of a war memorial had been damaged by vehicle impacts and the effects of frost, but there was another imperfection in its structure that became obvious to me now. The curve of a back, ribs plain to those who could see, one shoulder blade arched as if the buried subject were swimming against its solid surroundings.

Finally I decided to go to the place where Nigel had died. I had only been there once since his death, and facing the reality of the scene had been too disturbing. Now, there was more I had to see.

I would go at night. I dreaded what I might find.

It was three in the morning, and the homeless woman was there with her dogs once more. The creatures glanced at me, then as I started to approach they pulled on their leashes, one whining, the other snarling.

"I haven't got anything!" the woman said. The fear in her voice was awful.

"I'm no harm," I said. "I just want to—"

"What are you doing here at three in the morning, then?" she snapped.

"What are you?"

She didn't answer this. Instead, she tugged on the leads and settled her dogs. We were outside a pub, long-since closed for the night, and she leaned against some hand-railing that delineated its outdoor smoking area.

"I'm walking because someone I know died," I said. "A friend. And I want to know . . ." *Whether the city took him*, I wanted to say, but I wasn't sure how that might sound. "I'm going to see . . ."

"Plenty wrong with the city at night," the woman said. "During the day, people keep it alive. Probably best you go home."

"But I've seen you before. You're always walking."

"I know where not to go."

"How?"

"Experience." She muttered something under her breath. I couldn't see her face properly, and I didn't want to go any closer in case that looked threatening. Perhaps she was talking to her dogs.

"I'm going to the old station building," I said. I hoped that might encourage some comment, positive or negative.

"Hmm."

"Should I?" I asked.

I saw her silhouette shrug. "You should just go home." She started walking away and the dogs followed. When I tried to trail after her the animals turned and growled, both of them this time. I slowed, then stopped.

"Why?" I asked, expecting no reply.

"Make a habit of this and the city will notice you." Then she was gone, keeping to the middle of the street and avoiding the deep shadows beside buildings.

The night was quiet and still, no storms, no rain, and on the way through town I saw several other walkers. I wasn't sure who or what they were. I did not follow them. I was also careful to keep my distance, partly because they scared me, but also because they deserved their privacy and peace.

I carried on towards the old station building. It was six storeys high, converted into an office block a decade before, and Nigel had worked in an advertising agency on the second floor. That morning he'd taken the stairs, walked past the door exiting the staircase into his studio, and continued to the top. The maintenance door into the plant room on the roof should have been locked, but he'd planned his morning enough to make sure he had a key.

Once out on the roof, no one knew what he had seen, said or done. There was no note. Three people in the street below had seen him step up onto the parapet. Without hesitation he had walked out into nothing.

Where he'd hit the ground there was a raised planting bed at the refurbished building's entrance. He'd struck its wall, breaking his back. I went there now, a torch in my hand, dread in my heart.

At every moment I expected to see Nigel walking somewhere ahead of me. The echo of a man taken by the city and clasped to its dark, concrete heart, out of place and no longer of this world. But I was alone.

I searched for half an hour—the brick paved area around the entrance, the planter wall, the soil and shrubs of the planter itself. But I found no sign of Nigel. As every minute passed by my sense of apprehension lifted some more.

He's not here. The city didn't get him. It didn't eat him.

People had seen him jump, and perhaps that made a difference. He hadn't died alone with only the cold concrete for company. His body hadn't lain there for hours or days afterwards, night crawling across him, darkness coalescing around him. Even dead, Nigel had remained in the human world, because his suicide was born of it.

Though still sad at his death, I felt relieved that he had escaped something worse.

My mood buoyed, I started for home as dawn peered across the built-up skyline. Yet something was different. The skyline I saw looked slightly out of skew, as if new buildings had risen during the night and others had been taken down. The silence remained, broken only by cautious footsteps echoing from unknown walls. Occasional strangers avoided each other's glances. But there was now something else that I had never noticed before. In the silence that hung over the city, a terrible intelligence held its breath.

As I reached home, I feared that the city had noticed me at last.

RAMSEY CAMPBELL

SPEAKING STILL

RAMSEY CAMPBELL is described by *The Oxford Companion to English Literature* as "Britain's most respected living horror writer". He has been given more awards than any other writer in the field, including the Grand Master Award of the World Horror Convention, the Lifetime Achievement Award of the Horror Writers Association, the Living Legend Award of the International Horror Guild, and the World Fantasy Lifetime Achievement Award. In 2015 he was made an Honorary Fellow of Liverpool John Moores University for outstanding services to literature.

Among his novels are *The Face That Must Die, Incarnate, Midnight Sun, The Count of Eleven, Silent Children, The Darkest Part of the Woods, The Overnight, Secret Story, The Grin of the Dark, Thieving Fear, Creatures of the Pool, The Seven Days of Cain, Ghosts Know, The Kind Folk, Think Yourself Lucky* and *Thirteen Days by Sunset Beach*. PS Publishing recently brought out his "Brichester Mythos" trilogy, consisting of *The Searching Dead, Born to the Dark* and *The Way of the Worm*.

Needing Ghosts, The Last Revelation of Gla'aki, The Pretence and *The Booking* are novellas, and his collections include *Waking Nightmares, Alone with the Horrors, Ghosts and Grisly Things, Told by the Dead, Just Behind You, Holes for Faces, Fearful Implications* and *By the Light of My Skull*. The author's non-fiction is collected as

Ramsey Campbell, Probably, while *Limericks of the Alarming and Phantasmal* is a history of horror fiction in the form of fifty limericks.

Campbell's novels *The Nameless* and *Pact of the Fathers* have been filmed in Spain, where a film of *The Influence* is in production. He is the President of the Society of Fantastic Films and lives on Merseyside with his wife Jenny. His pleasures include classical music, good food and wine, and whatever's in that pipe.

"This tale arose from thoughts I had about recording calls on my iPhone," says the author, "specifically the games I play with scammers. Sometimes I speak to them in an invented language, although our friends the Proberts witnessed one where I responded with maniacal laughter. It turns out that you need to download a recording app, which I've yet to do.

"I think the embryo from which the tale developed was actually older, related to the answering machine on our landline, which preserved a call from an old friend after he'd died. What if such a call changed over time or somehow led to others? Fear of loss shaped this story too."

A S SOON AS I opened the door of the Hole Full of Toad I saw Daniel. I'd meant to be first at the pub and have a drink waiting for him, but he was seated near the bar with his back to me and talking on his phone. I was crossing the discoloured carpet between the stout old tables scarred by cigarettes at least a decade old when he noticed me. "Goodbye for now, my love," he murmured and stood up, pocketing his phone. "You look ready for a drink."

It was our regular greeting, but I could tell he hoped I hadn't overheard his other words. Embarrassment made me facetious. "What's tonight's tipple?"

"Mummy's Medicine," he said and pointed at his tankard. "Not as urinary as it might appear."

"It's what the doctor ordered, is it?"

"It's what this one prescribes."

Though we'd performed this routine in the past, it felt too deliberate now. "I'll be the second opinion," I said to bring it to an end.

When he brought me a yeasty pint I found it palatable enough. We always tried the guest ale and then usually reverted to our favourite. Daniel took a manful gulp and wiped foam from his stubbly upper lip. He'd grown less plump over the last few months, but his skin was lagging behind, so that his roundish face reminded me of a balloon left over from a party, wrinkled but maintaining an unalterable wide-eyed smile that might have contained a mute plea. He kept up the smile as he said "Ask me the question, Bill."

"How have you been?"

"I'd prefer to forget most of that if you don't mind. I've seen colleagues lose patients, but that's nothing like the same." Daniel opened his eyes wider still, which looked like a bid to take more of a hold on the moment if not to drive back any moisture. "The job's helping now," he said, "but that wasn't the question I thought you'd have."

"I'd better let you tell me what it ought to be."

"Weren't you wondering who I was talking to when you came in?"

"Honestly, Daniel, that's none of my business. If you've found someone—"

"You think I'd be involved with someone else so soon. Or do you think I already was?"

"I'm sorry for presuming. I must have misheard."

"I don't think so. Perhaps you missed the obvious." As if taking pity on me Daniel said "I was talking to Dorothy, Bill."

I thought this was quite a distance from the obvious, but stopped my mouth with a drink. "No need to be confused," Daniel said. "She's still there. Would you like to hear?"

"Please," I said, though it didn't feel much like an invitation.

He took out his phone and opened an album to show me a photograph. "That's the last I have of her. She wanted me to take it, so I did."

It had the skewed look of a hasty shot. His wife was sitting up in a hospital bed. She'd lost far more weight than Daniel and was virtually bald, but was matching if not besting the smile I imagined he'd given her. "I wasn't talking to her there tonight, though," Daniel said. "Bend your ear to this."

He brought up a list of calls received, and I leaned towards the phone as he retrieved one. "Don't bother visiting me this afternoon," Dorothy said. "They'll be having a look. I expect I'll be out of it this evening, so I may not be worth your journey then either."

I found I'd grown shy of meeting Daniel's eyes, especially when he said "That's the last I ever heard from her. I went in, and I didn't leave her after that till the end."

"You did say."

"That isn't all I've kept. I'm only glad I haven't erased anything since last year."

The calls skimmed up the screen until he touched a listing with a moist forefinger. This time his wife was telling him which super-market aisle she was in and which items he should find elsewhere in the store. "She sounds more like she used to, doesn't she?" Daniel said.

Her voice was far stronger and brisker than it had been in the call from the hospital. As I tried not to feel too saddened by his need to preserve every trace of her Daniel said "But that isn't really her either."

It seemed unsafe to say more than "How is that, Daniel?"

"She built herself up around the self she never quite got rid of. Sometimes I think the children we all used to be are lying in wait inside us, maybe hoping we won't rouse them." As he returned the phone to his pocket he said "Thank God she's free of her mother at last."

"I thought her mother died years ago."

"Not in Dorothy's mind," Daniel said and shut his eyes so hard that he might have been trying to crush a memory. "Tell me an exciting tale of accountancy, Bill."

This was another of our old jokes that I hadn't heard for weeks. I did my best to generate suspense from a call I'd made on a client's behalf to the tax collector, and then I was glad to hear news from the medical world. When the pub shut we went in opposite directions, having established that we'd meet next week. I glanced back to see that Daniel had stopped beneath a streetlamp and taken out his phone, but I couldn't tell whether he was speaking.

My wife Jane was in bed and on the way to sleep. "How was your friend?" she said most of.

"Missing Dorothy."

"Well, I should expect so. I hope you'll miss me too."

I rather wished her sleepiness hadn't let that slip out, though of course she only meant if she was first to go when the inevitable came, surely quite a few years hence. I'd managed to put all this out of my head by the time I joined her, and Daniel's situation had gone too. I can't say I thought about him much in the ensuing week, but when Monday came around I looked forward to catching up with him. Given his concern for all his patients, I was hoping a week's work might have helped him.

The pub was in sight when I saw him outside. Since he was talking on his phone, I wasn't sure whether to hang back, especially since I couldn't see his face. I compromised by making for the entrance, which he wasn't far from, and heard him say "You'll be all right, Dorothy. You've still got the right kind of strength."

As I tried to steal into the pub the door creaked. Daniel turned, belatedly hitching up his smile, and shoved the phone into his pocket. "Yes, I'm ready for a drink."

He dodged into the pub at once, so that I wondered if he meant to restrict the conversation we might have had. When I brought two pints of Hound's Howl to the table, however, he was ready to talk. "Some of the doctors who are coming up," he said, "you'd wonder if they need a doctor. There's a call to reclassify schizophrenia as a spectrum instead of a disease."

"That isn't your area, though."

"I know more than I'd like to about it." He downed a cloudy mouthful as though to douse his fierceness. "I'm just glad they weren't taking that approach," he said, "when they diagnosed Dorothy's mother."

"I didn't know she had that problem, Daniel."

"Dorothy never wanted it discussed, even with friends. Her mother brought her up never to talk about her. Even I didn't realise what was wrong till her mother couldn't hide it any more."

"How recently was that?"

"Too recently. For most of our marriage I didn't know about Dorothy's childhood."

So we hadn't strayed so far from his preoccupation after all. "What was it like?" I said.

"I'll tell you just one thing I won't forget. When Dorothy was little, before she was even at school..." This time his gulp of ale seemed intended to fortify him. "If she did anything her mother thought was bad, and there was no predicting what that might be next," he said, "she'd be locked in her room with no light, and she'd be told that something worse than she could possibly imagine would come for her if she dared to put the light on."

I felt bound to ask "Did she?"

"Not till years later, and do you know what the old, do you know what her mother did then? Took the bulb out of the socket and wouldn't let her have one in her room."

I was running out of questions I wanted to ask. "How did all that affect Dorothy, do you think?"

"She told me not at all by then. She said she challenged whatever she was meant to be scared of to show itself, and of course nothing did. She assured me that toughened her up and she was never afraid of anything her mother imagined again."

"More power to her."

"If it was true. I'm just afraid she kept it hidden deep down in herself."

"Daniel, please don't take this the wrong way, but at least you needn't worry any more."

I thought he'd opened his mouth to speak, but he gave himself a drink instead. His throat worked before he muttered "You didn't meet her mother."

"And if I had..."

"Call me fanciful, but whenever she came into a room you'd feel as if she'd turned it dark."

"I suppose you might when you knew what she'd done to your wife."

"I felt like that before I knew." Daniel reinforced this with a stare that looked trapped by the memory. "And I think having her committed brought everything back," he said, "even if Dorothy tried not to show it did."

"Surely she'd have been relieved that her mother was being taken care of."

"You'd hope so." With more conviction than I thought was warranted he said "She kept telling Dorothy that if we had her shut away she'd make sure Dorothy was with her."

"But she wasn't, so I should think—"

"It was all she talked about when she was dying. She said she'd wait for Dorothy in the dark, and she'd be made of worms."

"That's second childhood stuff, wouldn't you agree? I hope your wife thought so."

Daniel's tankard stopped short of his mouth. "Whose childhood, Bill?"

"You know I meant her mother's. I never knew Dorothy to be anything but strong."

As he took a drink I saw him ponder how to go on. "You caught what I was saying earlier."

"I didn't mean to eavesdrop."

"I might have myself." Even more like an apology he said "I wouldn't ask this of anyone except a good friend."

With no idea where this was leading I could only say "Then you can ask me."

"Do you think Dorothy could hear me?"

"When do you mean?"

I was bracing myself to be told that he had her last moments in mind, and was nowhere near ready to hear him say "Now."

"We can't know, can we?" In a bid to raise his spirits I said "In a way we're keeping her alive by talking about her."

"I wasn't thinking of you." Though his smile winced in case he'd sounded rude, he carried on. "I mean when I'm speaking to her on the phone," he said.

I took all the care I could over answering. "You'd like to think so."

"Yes, but I'm asking what you think."

"I won't say you're wrong, Daniel."

"All right, Bill, you're discharged. The ordeal's over." Humour deserted him as he said "I wonder what your wife would say. She's the computer expert, after all."

I'd begun to wonder how potent our drinks were. "How did we get on to computers?"

"They've been on my mind a good deal recently. I'm starting to believe they may have made a kind of afterlife."

"All the photos of Dorothy you'll have, you mean." When he didn't respond I said "Her voice."

"That's what I've kept, my wife in electronic form."

"And you still have all your memories of her."

"I don't want you to think I'm being maudlin." As I made to deny it he said "I just wonder how much of her that is."

"I'm afraid I'm not following."

"All of us are electronic where it counts, aren't we? What they used to call the soul, that's a mass of electronic impulses in the brain. Even if they didn't have a place to go before, perhaps they have one now."

Though I might have liked to take a drink rather than speak I said "We're still talking about computers."

"Yes, the Internet. That's where everything we know is turned into electronic form. Perhaps I haven't got it right, though," Daniel said, and I was hoping rationality had overtaken him until he added "Perhaps it gives us access to a place that was already there."

I no longer knew how to respond. I was lingering over a mouthful of ale when Daniel said "I realise you aren't going to accept it without proof."

"That would be a help."

He took out his phone at once. "There's another message," he said.

He left a moist print on an entry in the list before turning the phone towards me. His wife's voice sounded weaker or more distant than it previously had. "Are you there? You're not there, are you? Don't be—"

I assumed she'd cut herself off by mistake, since I'd heard a trace of nervousness. "Was she asking you not to be long?"

"I hope that's it, but that isn't the point. That's her most recent message, Bill."

"I thought you told me the one you played last week was."

"It was then," Daniel said and showed me the phone. "As you see, now this is top of the list."

"But it hasn't got a date."

"And don't you wonder how that could happen?"

When I had no explanation, though I might have pointed out that the caller was unnamed as well, he said "Would you mind asking your wife?"

"I'll call you when I have, shall I?"

"No need for me to trouble you so much. Next time we meet will be fine."

I thought he was doing his best to put the issue out of his mind, despite forgetting to make his accountancy joke. Instead he told me at considerable length how medicine and surgery would soon be able to prolong life, though I couldn't tell whether he regretted that the developments came too late for his wife or was glad that they hadn't been there for her mother. I felt as though his monologue was postponing what he was anxious to say, and then I grasped that I mightn't be the person he was desperate to address.

We'd hardly parted outside the pub when I heard him on his phone. Either he wanted me to hear or no longer cared whether I did. "Dorothy, I'm sorry I missed your call. I don't know when it was, because I didn't hear it ring. I'll keep an eye on the phone whenever I can, just in case. I know we'll be together again soon, and then we'll have all the time there is."

He sounded like someone I hardly knew—as unlike the self he presented to the world as he'd said his wife differed from hers. As I headed for home the call I'd heard made the autumn night feel as cold as black ice. Jane was asleep, having driven fifty miles to revive all the computers in a large office. When I caught up with her at breakfast I found I was anxious to learn "Do you know if there's a reason why a missed call wouldn't show a date?"

"You can't withhold those, only the number."

"I thought so, but Daniel has one with no date."

"He'd have had to delete the information himself, though I don't know how." Jane abandoned the delicate frown that had narrowed her keen eyes and said "How was he this week?"

"I'm not sure he's coping that well. He's kept all the messages his wife left on the phone, but he seems to be convincing himself he can still hear from her."

"Maybe that's how he's coping. I don't see the harm if it doesn't put his patients at risk."

I couldn't believe Daniel would let that happen. If he thought he was growing incompetent, surely he would take leave rather than risk botching an operation. Perhaps Jane was right, and his preoccupation was no worse than a comfort to him. However irrational it was, I came to accept it on his behalf as the week went on, until Samira stopped me as I returned from convincing a client to keep receipts for six years, not just one. "A Doctor Hargreaves was asking for you, Bill," she said. "You aren't sick, are you?"

"No, he's a friend."

"It was only that it sounded urgent. He says don't call unless you have to, otherwise he'll see you tonight as usual."

Friday was by no means usual, and if Jane hadn't gone away overnight to deal with an office-wide computer crash I would have felt unreasonable for leaving her alone two nights in a week. I reached the pub earlier than normal, only to find Daniel already at a table. He'd been drinking fast or for a while, since his tankard was less than half full, and when he brought me a pint of Mohammed's Prohibition he treated himself to its twin. "There's another message," he said.

His smile looked determined not to yield but close to meaningless. When he brought out the phone I saw that the new message was undated and unidentified. "Jane doesn't know how there can't be a date," I said and risked adding "Don't you think that means it needn't be new?"

"It wasn't there before. I'd have listened if it was."

"I'm saying it could have been delayed. Maybe there's a glitch that left out the date as well."

His only response was to set the message off and turn the phone towards my ear, waving my hand away when I made to take the mobile. Even when I ducked towards it I could scarcely hear for the mass of unchecked conver-sations in the pub. The voice was feebler than before, barely recognisable as Dorothy's. "I don't like this. I don't know where I am." I could have thought it was as small as a child's. "It's dark and wet," Dorothy protested. "I think it's wriggling, or I am. Can't you hear?"

A hiss of static followed, which sounded as if some kind of collapse had overwhelmed the call. Once he'd pocketed the phone Daniel gazed expectantly if not beseechingly at me, but I was loath to share my first thought—that Dorothy had inherited her mother's mental problem, which had overtaken her at her lowest ebb. I compromised by saying "Do you think that's how she felt when she was waiting for you at the hospital? She wasn't like that once you got there, was she?"

"She was barely conscious. She hardly seemed to know I was there."

"I'm sure you must have made the feelings go away, so she couldn't have had them at the end."

His smile had begun to look less studied. "You're suggesting she made this call from the hospital."

"I'm sure that has to be it. I've had calls that got lost in the ether for days. I'll ask Jane what's the longest delay she knows about if you like."

"I've already spoken to the hospital. They say she wasn't capable of phoning once they'd run the tests."

"That proves they're wrong about this call then, doesn't it? She'd already made the one asking you not to be late."

"I don't believe she did say that, or from the hospital." His smile was making itself plain now—amusement so wry it was more like regret. "I don't think she was cut off," he said. "She was saying someone wasn't there, if you remember. I think she was telling them not to be."

"Come on, Daniel," I said, perhaps too heartily. "Who could she have been talking to on your phone except you? And you're the last person she would have wanted to put off."

Either this persuaded him to some extent or he preferred not to answer. Soon he was expounding on the merits of euthanasia and assisted suicide. I suspect that he sensed I was glad to be spared more of his obsession, because when we left the pub he said "I should think you've had enough of me for a week."

"I'd be less of a friend if I had. Let's make it Monday as ever," I said and was relieved not to see him take out his phone as he vanished into the dark.

Jane's task was more complex than she'd anticipated, and she wasn't home on Saturday until I'd gone to bed. On Monday morning I was ashamed to realise I'd forgotten to quiz her on Daniel's behalf. "How long do you think a call to a mobile could be held up?" I said.

"Quite some time," Jane said and poured herself a coffee even blacker than the one she'd just had. "A client of mine had a call turn up months late."

"I knew it," I said and thought of phoning Daniel at once. "Daniel keeps getting calls from his wife that he thinks are new. You'd say they're delayed, wouldn't you? I'll tell him."

"I don't know if you should do that." Jane took a sip so black that sensing its harshness made me wince. "I've never heard of staggered delays, if that's what you're describing," she said. "I wouldn't think it's possible."

I decided against phoning Daniel. By the time I saw him that night I might have worked out what to say. I hadn't when I reached the office, and meetings with clients left me no chance. I was at my desk and working on an e-mail in which words were shorter and less abundant than numbers when the receptionist rang me. "There's a gentleman to see you, Bill."

"Could you ask him what he'd like to drink? He isn't due for half an hour."

"He isn't your appointment. He says you're a friend." With a hint of doubt Jody said "Doctor Hargreaves."

For a moment I was tempted to declare myself unavailable, and then I felt worse than remorseful. I hurried into the lobby to find Daniel crouched on a chair. He was consulting his phone or guarding it, and his stance looked close to foetal. When he glanced up I thought he was struggling to remember how to smile. "Can we talk somewhere private?" he said almost too low to be heard.

Six straight chairs faced six more across a bare table in the nearest conference room. Daniel slumped onto a chair while I shut the door, and as I sat opposite him he said "She's there again, Bill."

"Jane says calls can be delayed for months."

"I don't think they were calls in the first place." He laid his phone between us on the table and rested his distressed gaze on the dormant screen. "I'm sure this one isn't," he said.

"What else could it be?"

"I believe I've made some kind of connection." He planted his hands on either side of the phone, and moisture swelled under his fingers. "Maybe keeping her on the phone helped, and I'm sure trying to speak to her did," he said. "I think we're hearing her as she is now."

I might have preferred not to listen to the evidence, but I was determined to help if I could. "Let me hear then, Daniel."

The marks of his hands were still fading from the table when he brought up the latest entry on the list. This one was bereft of details too. Even though he'd switched the speaker on, the voice was almost inaudibly faint. "It's dark because I've got no eyes. That's why the dark is so big. Or it's eating its way in because it's made of worms. They're all I'm going to be …"

Daniel dabbed at the phone with a moist fingertip once the thin diminished voice fell silent. Though I was appalled by the way Dorothy's terrors had reduced her to the state of a fearful child, I tried my best to reassure him. "It has to be an old call, Daniel. It's sad, but it's only more of the thoughts you cured her of by being with her at the end."

"You haven't heard it all yet." He raised a finger, and a qualm plucked at my guts as I realised he had only paused the message. "Tell me what you hear," he said like some kind of plea.

"That's me. It's only me, or it's the dark. I can't really feel it, it's only dark. Like being asleep and dreaming. Just dark and my imagination." The voice might have been drifting into a reminiscent stupor, but then it grew louder. "Who is that?" it cried, and a rush of static unpleasantly suggestive of moisture seemed to end by forming an answer. "Me."

Daniel clasped the phone protectively, to no effect I could imagine. "You heard, didn't you? You heard the other voice."

"I heard Dorothy, Daniel." However sharp and shrill the final word had been, surely that signified no more than impatience. "She was saying what she said before," I insisted. "Don't let it upset you, but she meant she was by herself. And then you came and stayed with her till the end."

"I wish I could believe that." Although he was staring at me, he appeared to see a sight considerably less welcome than I hoped I was. "I'm afraid I didn't just bring her by calling," he said. "I think I attracted something else."

I could have argued but confined myself to saying "Do you mind if we discuss it tonight? I need to get ready for a meeting soon."

"I'll give tonight a miss if you don't mind. I have to be prepared as well."

I imagined him sitting alone at home with the phone in his hand while he waited for yet another tardy message. Should I have insisted he came out for a drink? All I said was "Next Monday, then."

"Monday," Daniel said as though the prospect was irrelevant if not unimaginably remote.

He scarcely seemed to hear me wish him well as I saw him out of the building. Interviews and official phone calls took up my afternoon, and a job kept Jane away overnight. Our empty house felt like an omen of a future in which one of us would be on our own, and I was more than glad when she called me at breakfast to say she was starting for home. "And here's something to tell Daniel if you think you should," she said. "I've found a case where somebody made several calls in an hour but the person they were calling kept receiving them for most of a week."

I thought this was worth passing on to Daniel, and as soon as I'd said goodbye to Jane I rang him. His phone was unresponsive, refusing even to accept messages. I blamed his interpretation of his wife's calls for making the utter silence feel like darkness so complete it could engulf all sound. I phoned the hospital where he worked, only to learn that he'd cancelled all his operations. They had no idea how long he would be on leave, and wished they knew.

My first meeting of the day was after lunch. As I drove to the suburb next to mine I tried to think what to say to Daniel. I was hoping to persuade him that he needed someone else's help. His broad house—one of a conjoined pair—was emptily pregnant with a bay window and shaded by a sycamore that had strewn the front lawn with seeds. Sunlight muffled by unbroken cloud made the front room look dusty if not abandoned. I was ringing the bell a third time when Daniel's neighbour emerged from her house, pointing a key at her car to wake it up. "He went out earlier," she said. "He'll be at work."

At once I knew where he might be. In five minutes I was at the graveyard where I'd attended Dorothy's funeral. Her plot was in the newest section, where the turf wouldn't have looked out of place in a garden centre and the headstones were so clean they could have advertised the stonemason's shop. Once I'd parked the car a wind followed me across the grass, and I heard the discreet whispering of cypresses. My footfalls weren't much louder. I was trying to be unobtrusive, having seen Daniel.

He was kneeling on Dorothy's grave with his back to me. He hadn't reacted when I shut the car door, admittedly as quietly as I could. While I was reluctant to disturb him, I wanted to know what state he was in. I strained my ears but heard only the reticently restless trees. At least I wouldn't interrupt Daniel at prayer or in attempted conversation, and as I approached he stirred as though he was about to greet me. No, a shadow was patting his shoulder, a faint ineffectual gesture on the part of a cypress. In fact he was so immobile that I couldn't help clearing my throat to rouse him. This brought no visible response, and I'd grown nervous by the time I came close enough to see his face.

He wasn't merely kneeling. His chest rested against the headstone, and his chin was propped on the sharp edge. However uncomfortable that might have been, he showed no sign of pain. His fixed smile looked fiercely determined, and his eyes were stretched so wide that I could only wonder what he'd been striving to see. They saw nothing now, because nobody was using them. When I closed the lids I imagined shutting in the dark.

His phone had fallen from one dangling hand and lay beside the headstone. I retrieved it, finding it chilly with dew, and wiped it on my sleeve. For a moment I was pitifully relieved that I wouldn't be able to look for any messages, since the phone was activated by a passcode, and then I recalled seeing Daniel type his birthdate. Before I could panic I keyed in the digits and brought up the list of messages. All the latest ones were unnamed and dateless, and there were two more than I'd previously seen.

I opened the first one and held my breath. The pleading voice wasn't much louder than the cypresses, and I fancied that it sounded afraid to be heard or else acknowledged. "Leave me alone. You're just the dark and worms. You're just a dream and I want a different one." At first I thought the noise that followed was just a loose mass of static, and then it began to form words. "Mother's here now," it said. "She's what she promised she would be. There's nobody for you to tell and nobody to see. She'll be with you always like a mother should."

I struggled to believe the explanation I would have given Daniel— that it was yet another deferred call from Dorothy, which was why she was referring to her mother in the third person—but not only the usage made the voice seem inhuman. It no longer resembled static so much as the writhing of numerous worms, an image I tried to drive out of my head as I played the last message. I almost wish I'd left it unheard. An onslaught of slithering swelled out of the speaker in wordless triumph, and in its midst I seemed to hear a plea crushed almost beyond audibility but fighting to shape words. I couldn't bear much of this, and I was reaching to turn it off when another voice went some way towards blotting out the relentless clamour. "I'm here as well."

It was unmistakably Daniel's, though it sounded in need of regaining strength. In less than a second the message came to an end. I closed my fist around the phone and tried to tell myself that Daniel could have recorded his voice over the last part of an existing message. The idea he'd left in my mind days ago was stronger: that the phone, or the way he'd sought not just to preserve all its recordings of his wife but to contact her, had somehow caused the situation. Perhaps I was mistaken, but by the time I doubted my decision it was too late. I found the edit button for the messages and let out a protracted shaky breath as I hit ERASE ALL.

I used Daniel's phone to call the police. Weeks later the inquest confirmed that he'd poisoned himself. When the police finished questioning me I drove from the graveyard to work. Though I yearned to be home, I managed to deal with several clients. At last I was at our front door, and when Jane opened it she gasped as if my embrace had driven out all her breath. "No need to hang on so tight. I'm not going anywhere," she said, and I wondered how I could even begin to explain.

MICHAEL BAILEY

UNDERWATER FERRIS WHEEL

MICHAEL BAILEY is a freelance writer, editor and book designer, and the recipient of more than two dozen literary awards, including the Bram Stoker Award, Benjamin Franklin Award, Eric Hoffer Book Award, the Independent Publisher Book Award, International Book Award, and others.

His novels include *Palindrome Hannah, Phoenix Rose* and the forthcoming *Psychotropic Dragon*, and he has published two short story and poetry collections, *Scales and Petals* and *Inkblots and Blood Spots*. Bailey has also edited such anthologies as *Pellucid Lunacy, Qualia Nous, The Library of the Dead, You Human, Adam's Ladder, Prisms* and four volumes of *Chiral Mad* (the latest composed entirely of collaborations). He is currently working on a science fiction thriller entitled *Seen in Distant Stars*, as well as *Seven Minutes*, a memoir on surviving the forever-burning wildfires of California.

"This was one of the late Jack Ketchum's favourite short stories of mine," recalls Bailey. "It was originally an experiment in blending second- and third-person narratives."

THE LANKY GENTLEMAN in the pinstripe suit and moth-eaten neck ruffle staggers forwards. He holds a card for you to take:

COME RIDE THE UNDERWATER FERRIS WHEEL

There is a mixed scent of caramel corn, candied apples, corn dogs and spilled beer as Cate waits her turn in line with her son. The trailer has a sign lit with small yellowing bulbs, which works cordially with the other food trailers to light up the otherwise dark path of sweets, meats and deep-fried foods on sticks.

She lets go of Ian long enough to dig in her purse for money.

"Large cotton candy," she says to the man leaning over the counter.

"Stick or bagged?" he says, pointing to the pre-filled plastic bags of rainbow clouds lining the inside of the trailer.

In back, a man wearing a hairnet spins pink silk onto a conical cone of white paper.

She takes in the smells of hot sugar and oil.

"Stick," Cate says, and then adds a couple of corn dogs to the order.

She turns to her son to see if he wants ketchup or mustard or both, but he's gone. The couple standing in his place looks past her to the menu.

"Ian?"

She expects him at the ticket counter because he wanted more rides, not food, and he isn't there, nor is he wandering around the carny games across the promenade.

The others in line don't seem bothered that he's disappeared.

Cate holds a twenty-dollar bill instead of her son and no longer is she hungry, the appetite for junk food replaced with a gut-wrenching feeling of losing him. The man leaning through the window balances a pair of hefty golden corn dogs in one hand, the other expecting money. She hands him the bill, not remembering having taken the cotton candy.

"Ma'am?"

He holds her food, calling for her as she calls for Ian.

"Did you see a boy," Cate says to the couple, her hand waist-high to estimate height, "blond hair, red and white striped shirt?"

Ian had chosen his outfit to match the tents he'd seen from the road when they were first setting up the carnival, she knew, because he had pestered her the entire week to go.

Shaking their heads, they take her place as she steps out of line. Hundreds fill the food court and labyrinth of walking paths.

"Ma'am?" the man calls again.

She no longer cares about the food or the money. She holds onto the cotton candy like a beacon, hoping Ian will see the pink light and come running from out of the darkness.

"One more ride, after we eat something," Mom says.

She drags him through the crowd, making her own path. Behind them, Ian's wake is swallowed by kids able to ride the bigger rides (by themselves), drunken men stumbling around and yelling, hanging off each other, beers sloshing over plastic cups (even though Ian knew there's this place called the beer tree where they're supposed to drink), and other kids—Ian's age—dragged around by their parents.

Heavy metal music blasts from speakers hidden around the rides, and then pop music, and then what the older kids at school call dub step, and then country. The music changes as rapidly as the scenery, fading in and out as they make their way from the rides to the food court.

He has enough tickets clenched in his fist for two rides, but his mom wants to go with him on the Ferris wheel after they eat and that will eat all ten that are left.

"One last ride," she had said, meaning either the marvel of their day would soon end, or they'd be going to the stupid adult stuff, like seeing the animals, or going to the building with all the paintings and quilts, or to the place with the judged fruits and vegetables and jarred stuff, which they could see any other day by going to the grocery store.

And they still hadn't played any games.

"Step up, son," says a man who isn't his father. He holds a softball that's supposed to be tossed into a tilted basket without bouncing out. "It's easy," he says, tossing the ball underhand, and it *is* easy because it stays in the basket, and he wasn't even looking at it.

"You can win one of these to take home."

Stuffed animals bigger than real animals hang from their necks.

"Can we play games?"

"After we eat, maybe."

Maybe means no most times.

The man with unkempt hair and brownish teeth leans out of the booth. Three baskets are lined behind him, no one else playing his game.

"Free game for the boy," he says.

"Mom!"

"There are no free games," she says, pulling him along.

The man puts his hand to his heart.

"Honest. One free toss."

"Please, Mom?"

"A gift from me to you," the man says. "No money involved, I promise. Let the boy win something to take home. One free throw."

They stop.

A bright disc of moon shines onto them.

Ian already knows he wants the dragon. It's red and about two feet long and has a forked tongue hanging out of its mouth.

The man wanting him to win the stuffed animal is within what his mom had warned as "grabbing distance", holding out a yellow dimpled softball like they have in the batting cages. He tosses another behind his back, which spins in mid-air and lands in the basket.

"One," says his mom.

"There we go! Step up to the counter here, but don't lean over, and simply toss it in."

He throws another spinning ball and makes it in, and Ian thinks he might have it down. It just takes some backspin and needs to brush the upper, back portion of the basket.

Ian takes the ball, tries to copy the technique. The throw looks similar, but the ball hits the bottom of the basket and comes shooting out.

"Good try! I think you almost have it down." He holds out another yellow ball. "One more go at it."

"That's how they work," his mom whispers to him. "See?"

"One more for the boy."

"No thank you," she says.

The man in the booth sets the ball on the counter. "Try it again. No gimmicks. I want to see the boy get one in. You can try it, too," he says, placing a ball in front of her as well.

This time his mom's the one smiling, but her teeth are much whiter. She hesitates and drops Ian's hand.

"One more," she says.

She picks up the ball and throws it underhand, but doesn't put any spin on it so it bounces back at her and she has to pick it off the ground.

"The boy's going to do it," the man says. "I have a good feeling about this one."

Ian takes his turn and again concentrates. He needs to throw it like last time, but not as high. Softly, he lets it roll off the tips of his fingers and there's plenty of backspin. It hits the basket in the right spot, nearly rolls out, but remains inside.

"He's a natural," the man in the booth says, crouching behind the counter.

Ian points to the dragon, but the man stands upright with a goofy smile. His prize is a cheap metallic-looking pinwheel tacked to the end of a straw that matches his shirt.

"Ah, you want the dragon," he says. "You gotta work your way up to that one by trading up from the smaller prizes."

He hadn't noticed the various price levels until now.

"That's how they work," his mom says.

You flip the card in your hand to find the other side black. The white side, with the message about the underwater Ferris wheel, contains only the invitation to ride it and nothing more. The lanky man in the pinstripe suit is gone. You took the card and read the words and sometime in between, the man resembling a make-up-less clown vanished into the crowd, his pinstripe coattails consumed by kids holding balloon animals.

Cate wanders, but not far. She doesn't want to stray from the food court because Ian can't be far and he's not prone to exploring on his own. She nearly steps onto a lone ticket, remembering Ian's longing for one final ride, and retrieves it from the ground.

⁊

Like money in his wallet, Ian counts the red tear-off tickets to make sure there are still ten. He lets them accordion out, the last ticket lapping a puddle of a spilled soda. He holds his mom's hand as she drags him around. It would be much easier to count them if he had his other hand. He tugs and his mom tugs back to let him know she's in control and that counting won't be very easy.

He's not even hungry, but they pass through ever-changing music and laughing and cheering and the shrill of those flipping cages on the *Zipper*, kids screaming through the fast loop of the *Ring of Fire*—yellow and red bulbs flashing in circular patterns as the coaster cycles, first clockwise, then counter-clockwise—and the mesmerising vertical array of green, white and blue bars of light on the *Graviton* as it spins like a flying saucer *dreidel*.

A tongue of tickets trails behind as he counts. He folds them, one onto the next, with the flip of his index finger and thumb. He gets to five when a Goth girl he recognises from school bumps into his shoulder and jars them loose.

They stop at a path of pavement to let a medic golf cart pass, and that's when Ian notices what he thinks is a clown. He doesn't resemble the colourful clowns with the big feet and honking noses and painted faces, and he's not one of those clowns seen around the park squeak-tying balloons into poodles and pirate swords. This one's unremarkable, except for the scrunched doily thing around his neck. He looks like someone from an old black-and-white photograph, like the ones hanging on his grandma's wall: pictures of his grandparents' parents. He thinks of this because the man is not smiling—lips pressed in a flat line—like old people in old photographs, dressed in what he thinks is an old black suit and jacket.

And he stares, eyes not moving away.

The cart is suddenly gone, the world no longer paused. A soft tug on his hand tells him they're moving again and Ian looks at his feet for only a moment because someone's stepped on his laces and he nearly stumbles. Looking back, the man is gone, the crowd alive in his place.

"You've never had cotton candy before, have you," his mom says.

Ian shakes his head no, although she doesn't see him do it.

"When I was your age, I loved cotton candy," she says over the noise. "Me and your father used to go to the Brendan Carnival every year when it was still around."

When Dad was still around.

She always started conversations this way, always talking about what they did as a couple before Dad died, before a non-drunk driver clipped his car and drove him off the cliffs and into the ocean where he drowned.

"Your father always liked the candied apples. He had a sweet tooth. Sometimes we'd share the . . . I'm not sure what it was called, but it was multicoloured popcorn in these little rectangular shapes wrapped in plastic; each clustered section of colour was a different flavour, like orange or cherry or grape, kind of like caramel corn but different. I haven't had that in years."

The symphony of carnival noise dulls the closer they get to the food court, the lights brighter, and the stench of puke, beer and cigarette smoke lingering, yet overpowered by Chinese food, barbeque and deep-fried everything.

"Wait until you try the corn dogs. Your father used to love those, too."

Nine tickets. There are only nine.

"Mom, we need to get another ticket to ride the—"

"No rides until after we eat. Here, this one looks good."

They stop in front of a trailer lit up in yellow bulbs and the entire thing glows. One of the smaller bulbs in the word SNACKS is missing, like his tenth ticket.

You attempt to follow him, but he weaves in and out of the multitude of people as if gliding over ice: a glimpse of a coattail, a pinstripe leg, night-black hair. He is quickly absorbed into crowds of parents and children and ages in-between. The wind picks up and you drop the card, which flaps along the ground like a dead butterfly. It flips over and along the ground as easily as it flipped in your hand, and you can read the words in a strobe-like flutter of black and white—the invitation for the ride.

Cate turns a boy around, but it's not Ian.

She calls his name again and then sees him standing in front of a game booth fifty feet away. Warmth flushes through her body as she remembers to breathe, the thought of losing Ian more than she can handle. Losing a husband is one thing, but losing their only son who resembles him so undeniably...

"Ian!" she says, willing her voice to reach him.

He turns just then, but not in her direction, and her heart drops.

Running to him, she continues to call his name, jouncing shoulders against those in her path and nearly trampling people over entirely. A baby stroller built for two trips her and she falls and scrapes her knee, rises, and keeps going, somehow never losing grasp of the lone red ticket and the cotton candy she points to the sky. Ian passes in and out of view, as if projected against the throng of fairgoers from a spinning shadow lamp.

"Ian!"

One moment he's there, another he's not.

A flash of silver and the pinwheel he no longer wants falls to the ground. A gangly man leans over to pick it up—one of the carnival folk, perhaps. He's the only immobile person in the multitude and wears a black pinstripe suit, as out of place in the crowd as would be a dandelion disguised in a bouquet of yellow roses. An aged neck-ruffle strangles his throat and he smiles as she approaches.

He offers the pinwheel, but she doesn't want it. She wants her son.

Cate looks around him frantically.

"Did you see the boy who dropped that?"

The silence tells her he's mute. He stares at her, expressionless, his face drained of both colour and emotion.

"I'm looking for my son, Ian. He dropped this," she says, taking it from him, "and you just picked it up. Did you see where he was going?"

He doesn't point, nor does he say anything. He simply takes his finger and spins the cheap toy on the stick and magically reveals a card from one of his shirtsleeves. The man stands there a moment before facing the ocean pier.

He tugs on his mom's hand, but she doesn't tug back to let him know she's still in control. Glancing up, Ian finds that he's not holding his mother's hand at all, but the hand of a tall man with long arms that dangle well past his knees. He can't remember ever letting go, but he must have, and somehow grabbed this man instead. Clammy fingers curl around his own. It's the man who isn't a clown, the old photograph man he saw before.

Ian jump-startles and the man lets go.

He isn't scary because he doesn't wear a fake face like regular clowns who pretend to be happy or sad or sometimes mad. He has a normal face.

He hands Ian a card.

"Are you supposed to be a mime?"

He doesn't say anything.

"I read a story once about a mime and he never said anything, either. He would pretend to be stuck in invisible boxes and climb ropes that weren't really there. But he wore make-up and had a white face and black lips like Charlie Chaplin. I don't know who that is, but my mom says he looked like Charlie Chaplin."

He shows Ian the rest of the cards, which are bound together with a rubber band. His dad used to do card tricks, so Ian knows what to do. He's supposed to take a card and look at it without showing and hand it back. Ian's card is a stained joker with worn edges and a crease down the middle. The joker wears a jester hat and rides a unicycle and looks drawn in scribbles of pen.

Before handing it back, the cards are splayed before him, at least two dozen. They are all different. About half are standard playing cards of different makes, some old, some new; mixed within are handmade cards like the joker, along with some baseball cards, a library card, credit cards and a few driver's licenses from different states.

Ian hands the card to him face-down and watches as it's shuffled into the deck over and over again, and in lots of different ways. The unsmiling *carny*—his mom would call him—bends the cards and bends them back like his dad used to, and shuffles them flat in the air with his thumbs and then reverses the cards in an arc to slide them into place—what his dad deemed "the bridge".

He hands the deck to Ian.

"I pick one?"

The man doesn't say anything.

Expecting his card to be on top because the back looks similar, Ian lifts a three of diamonds, which looks as though someone with shaky fingers drew the number with black crayon and then smudged three red diamonds on the card with lipstick. The one after it isn't his card either, but a jack of clubs. He flips over the next card with stats printed on the back and it's a rookie card for someone who used to play on a team called the Royals; over the player's face is a smiley face sticker with the eyes scratched out. The next card is a VISA. The next is a king of hearts from a standard Bicycle deck, followed by a ripped-in-half five dollar bill with a spade drawn in Sharpie over the president's face, and then a seven of clubs, and then another hand-drawn card.

Confused, Ian hands the deck back to him.

The man wraps a rubber band around them and slides them into his suit pocket.

"What's the trick?"

The man holds out his hand, as if peddling for money.

That's how they work, his mom would say.

Three of the fingers curl until he's pointing at Ian's pinwheel.

As if on cue, a cool breeze spins the cheap metallic flower around, which Ian didn't want anyway; he had wanted the dragon but they didn't have enough money to pay for more games, even though he would have given up food to pay for a few more tosses into the basket so he could win the bigger prize. Dad would have let them play. If he hadn't died, they'd have enough money to play more games and ride more rides and really have fun.

Ian gladly gives it to him. In the process, the man who looks sort of like a clown clumsily drops it as part of a gag and they both fetch for it on the ground. Lying next to the cheap toy is Ian's joker card, which the trickster silently places into his pocket with the others.

He pulls out another card, but this time it's not one of the strange playing cards; it's a business card with a black side that reflects the moon and a white side that absorbs its light. A trade for the pinwheel, it seems. Printed on the white side is an invitation.

You hand the carnival worker five red tickets and he lets you past the chain and through the gate. A set of aluminium steps leads to a grated path to the ten-storey wheel. Every angle of metal is lit by long neon lights and flashing bulbs that cycle in hypnotic patterns. The cart awaits—the slightly rocking yellow one with the number eight on the side. You are alone for the ride as you were in line, the carnival empty. A mechanical click and the wheel moves. The world drops with the wind at your back. You elevate in a reverse motion with the giant silver axle as you rotate around. Rods and lights and the other carts fall as you rise. At the peak, black water rises from the pier, and for a moment you float above it all, nothing but sky and water and the thin line between. The entire lit wheel is cast against the water, appearing as though there are riders beneath the placid surface revolving horizontally, perhaps looking up to you in the stars. You see your reflection on the water, and then you free-fall fly, arms stretched outwards, the wind at your face. The water rising.

COME SEE THE UNDERWATER FERRIS WHEEL

Cate reads the card a second time and when she looks up from it, the man in the pinstripe suit is gone, like her son.

"Ian!" she calls.

She parts through people on her way to the water's edge, which seems so far away. Why would he go to the pier? Somehow she knew he'd be there, and somehow the man with the moth-eaten neck ruffle knew. He was leading her to the...

Your father and I would always ride the Ferris wheel, she had told Ian in the car. That's where she'd find him. She couldn't stop talking about it on their way to the carnival. *It was always the last thing we did before going home*, she had said.

Running takes the air from her lungs and pierces her side, but she spots him at the base of the ride, gazing up in wonder. She spins him around to find his eyes glossy and terrified.

"There's no underwater Ferris wheel," Ian tells the water.

There's only the reflection of the *real* Ferris wheel.

"The card's a lie."

He walks along the planks, peering over the side to the black water. If there *was* an underwater ride, he'd at least see some kind of glowing light from below.

One last ride, his mom said.

Suddenly, his stomach aches empty and craves a corn dog now. He doesn't remember ever letting go of her hand while in line, but he must've let go at some point and grabbed the hand of the clown who wasn't really a clown—the man with the bad card trick who gave him the stupid invitation to see something that wasn't even there.

Mom had warned him to stay close and not to wander.

Ian knew the park and could find his way around easily enough, but finding his mom would be like finding his dad's body, which the people looking for him couldn't do after he went over the cliff. Even if he found his mom, she'd be mad and they'd leave early. They wouldn't ride the Ferris wheel as their last ride like she remembered doing with Dad. Ian only had nine tickets anyway because he dropped one. He holds them to the light, counting again to make sure.

The placid water breaks, enveloping you as you ride the yellow cart beneath the surface. Round you go as the un-reflection of the Ferris wheel above glows through a watery blur. As you come round, you see them gathered on the pier. A woman and boy embrace and it feels like home.

MARK SAMUELS

IN THE COMPLEX

MARK SAMUELS lives in Kings Langley, England. He is the author of six short story collections (*The White Hands and Other Weird Tales, Black Altars, Glyphotech & Other Macabre Processes, The Man Who Collected Machen, Written in Darkness* and *The Prozess Manifestations*) and two novels (*The Face of Twilight* and *A Pilgrim Strange*r).

His latest volume is a collection of essays from Ulymas Press on authors of weird fiction, entitled *Prophecies and Dooms*, while Hippocampus Press is scheduled to release a "Best of Mark Samuels" volume, *The Age of Decayed Futurity* edited by S.T. Joshi, in late 2019.

About 'In the Complex' Samuels explains: "This story is partially inspired by two misfortunes that occurred to me in 2017—sudden homelessness and subsequent hospitalisation. The third inspiration was not misfortune, but rather a new locale initially coloured by the ongoing mental after-shocks of the then-recent traumatic experiences."

THE TRAINS ARE more frequent than ever. Their rumbling approach makes the room shake and causes the single, bare light bulb overhead to chart a tiny circle on its short cable. I make a small line on the wall in pencil as each train passes. I have not recorded fewer than five hundred a day. Each time the orderly enters the room with my daily ration of food he scrubs away the marks I have previously made. Whether he allows me to keep possession of the pencil through indifference or via an official order I cannot say. He refuses to speak a single word. For a long time I wished for a window to see outside, even one that was barred, tiny and high, as in a prisoner's cell. But no longer. I am not, after all, entitled to the rights of a prisoner. Dr. Prozess has finally explained the facts to me; I am a symptom of a disease. He is the antidote to it.

When they brought me here, by ambulance, in the dead of night, I first insisted I felt perfectly well and saw no need. But the orderlies calmly showed me the documents that confirmed my health was potentially in serious danger, explained sagely that an attack could occur at any moment, and ended by insisting that the peril was confined not only to myself but could affect others around me. I had a responsibility to be reasonable in the matter. If my condition worsened, as it was likely to do, then they would be obliged to confine me involuntarily anyway. To demonstrate compliance at this stage would be the first step on my road to recovery.

Lying in the back of the ambulance, they strapped me down and administered a sedative by injection, and I slipped in and out of full awareness as the vehicle raced through the streets. I could not doubt, due to the length of the journey, that I had been taken out of the brightly-lit metropolitan area altogether and into the depths of the utterly dark countryside. When the ambulance reached its destination I was still groggy and they carried me across a driveway. The sound of shoes crunching gravel underfoot was accompanied by the rumbling of the trains nearby as the engine-cars hauled carriages over the tracks. I tried to gain some idea of my surroundings, but thick cloud covered the night sky. No outside light emanated from the building into which I was delivered. Only when we had passed through a set of huge metal doors was it possible to see again; and my eyes smarted at the sudden, brilliant white-blue glare caused by endless overhead strip lighting.

When my vision adjusted I saw that the shadows were all wrong, like those of vast insects. They were cast upon the tiled walls, not the floors. They were the type of grotesque, distorted shapes that are thrown up by searchlights. I called out to be unstrapped from the stretcher but was told, with a hiss, to be quiet.

On and on they carried me, deep into the labyrinth of what appeared to be a vast, level complex. As I turned my head from side to side I saw no sign of any other persons roaming inside the structure.

I could, however, still detect the sounds of the trains passing in the distance.

At last the orderlies carried me into a room with a single overhead bulb, gave me a different injection, and left me there as I sank into unconsciousness.

Pain accompanied my awakening. My upper front teeth were broken. My lips were swollen and encrusted with blood. I could not see clearly through my right eye, which had half closed-up. I tried to call out but could make only a gurgling noise in the back of my throat. I was strapped to the bed in an unfamiliar grey smock. My possessions had been taken away, including my phone and watch, so I could not determine how much time had passed.

Was it morning?

The trains were still running. I could hear them. Perhaps they were freight trains—which often run through the whole night.

Hours later the orderly made his first appearance. It was very brief. I think he simply wanted to make sure I was still alive. He would not reply to any of my questions but when he returned for a second visit, again, hours later, he tossed a crumpled note onto my bed upon which were a few words scrawled in pencil:

You did this to yourself.

When he departed, I heard the sound of bubbling laughter piped into my cell via what I presumed were hidden speakers. The sound must have been looped—a recording—because its intensity did not vary, and it went on and on and on until I actually began screaming to try and block it out. Gradually, almost imperceptibly, the volume faded to zero and I became aware once more of that omnipresent, dim rumble of trains in the background.

I think I passed days in this fashion. The orderly, though, must have entered the room on the few occasions I slept, for the jug of brackish water was replenished and two dollops of congealed muck, mostly rice, were left for me to eat from a round plastic plate. The bedpan was much less frequently replaced and its stench permeated the interior of the cell.

They had removed the bonds that had kept me immobile, but I scarcely had the strength even to make a circuit of the room in search of its hidden speakers. When the noise of laughter returned it seemed to emanate from all directions at once, as if mocking my attempts to isolate the source.

It was, however, during one of these circuits, that I discovered the stub of pencil left behind by the orderly. The thing must have fallen from his pocket and rolled out of sight, concealed underneath the bed. Then again, perhaps it had been placed there deliberately, as part of some test—or experiment—which I could not fathom. I knew that it formed some sort of link with the reason for my being confined in the first instance, and that the use I made of it would be of significant import. Whether or not they anticipated my first impulse I cannot say; but it was to drive the point into the artery below my left ear, push deep, and put an end to everything.

Instead, I began marking on the wall the passage of each train as it passed by. Quite why I began to do so it is difficult to explain; but to keep a strictly accurate record became an obsession with me. I felt, in some profound yet irrational way, that the rhythm of my own existence was intimately connected with their continued, regular motion. Some long delay between one and the next wrought panic in me, like that overwhelming sense of doom that prefigures impending heart failure.

And so further days passed.

Although the marks on the wall were regularly erased, I was allowed to keep the pencil. Perhaps I had done something that was expected of me, and regarded as the correct behaviour, for the orderly handed me another note, one which this time read:

You are to be taken on a visit tomorrow.

I had no idea exactly what this meant. Was I to be taken around the confines of the building or permitted to leave it (presumably accompanied by my captors)? I found it hard to believe that the latter could be the case. They surely would anticipate that the first thought to spring into my mind—as indeed it had done—was to consider an attempt to get away from their clutches altogether.

I turned the question over and over again in my head during the waiting period. Moreover, as I did so, I gradually realised that a new consideration bubbled up therein. I became increasingly anxious that, due to this turn of events, trains would pass without my being able to keep up-to-date my record of their existence. I seriously considered making a protest about being taken on this "visit", but then considered that the manner in which the note was phrased was more in the nature of an instruction, or an order, than a request. To make any objection might well mean the privileges I had gained since my arrival might be revoked. As a consequence, I might even damage myself, as I had been assured I had done previously, and I had no desire to re-open wounds that had only just begun to heal properly.

But I need not have concerned myself.

Before being taken on the visit, while being tied into a wheelchair for that purpose, the kindly orderly sat on the edge of my bed and continued to detail the passage of the trains on my behalf with the stub of pencil, since I could not do so.

I was ferried about the structure by another orderly I had not previously seen, an individual as silent and inscrutable as his fellow employee.

We passed down narrow corridors illuminated by the overhead strip-lighting I recalled from my last trip, and I saw again, too, the crazily distorted shadows on the tiled walls. They disturbed me more than ever. I had thought them to be drug-hallucinations or faulty memories on my part. Now there could be no doubt that they were as real as all the other objects I saw here in the complex. My mind, you see, was remarkably clear and focused; without any of the mental turmoil that had dogged my arrival.

At last the journey terminated at the entrance to another cell. The orderly slid open the metal cover of a spy-hole, glanced within, turned on the light, unlocked the steel door and wheeled me into deepest darkness.

He then walked out and re-locked the door behind him, with me still tied to the wheelchair.

I could see nothing. The blind void inside that cell almost seemed tangible, as if I had been plunged bodily into a huge tank of thick black ink. I even struggled for breath, such was the shock of the transition. And then my hearing and smell began to gain in alertness; in reaction to the sudden sensory cessation from my eyesight. I detected a low moaning whisper, gradually getting closer and closer, accompanied by the rank smell of a long-unwashed body. Something flopped towards me awkwardly in the darkness, half-crawling and half-dragging itself across the short distance between us. The stench increased.

I struggled in the wheelchair, but my binds prevented any movement away from the approaching entity, which sniffed the air around me greedily.

It got hold of my legs, pulling itself up onto me. I turned my head away, but my chin was gripped by a claw-like hand, more bone than flesh. The stench now made me gag and a wet, curiously hollow mouth closed over my own and then slithered a wet path across my cheeks and neck. An inanity punctuated the assault, words in a language from the back of its throat. Words I seemed to know but could not understand, and definitely not foreign—"ereh fo tuo em teg"—something grossly reversed in its form.

I struggled as best I could in the total darkness, resisting the clamour of the creature, shouting out for the orderly; nauseous with terror and repulsion.

The door was unlocked.

The thing that had latched onto me slipped away, crawling back to the corner whence it came.

A shaft of vivid blue-light invaded the room as the door was thrust open.

My eyes smarted at the flash, powerful as a lightning burst. The scene was doubtless rendered stark and clear to the orderly; he must have seen a tableau wrought from nightmare-made-life.

But I was stunned by the intensity of the illumination and, before my pupils could make the adjustment, was turned around and wheeled out of the cell, back towards my own.

When I had the opportunity to examine it again, shortly after the visit I have described, I had the distinct impression that the orderly had not kept up my accurate record of the passing of the trains. Some of his pencil marks were scarcely visible, as if he were unsure whether a train had really passed by or not. His attempt to substitute for me was slovenly, even if kindly in intent. Also, the number he set down in my absence appeared insufficient for the time that had passed. The trains kept to a regular schedule, of this I was certain; even though I could not confirm the fact by reference to the likes of a clock or stopwatch. (I would have given anything to obtain such a device.) It seemed to me that I had to try and impress upon the power running the complex that to cause my absence from my work was neither in their best interests or mine.

During a lull in the passage of the trains back and forth, I found time to write a single sentence of complaint amidst the myriad of the day's small straight lines.

"I request not to be taken again from my cell," I wrote.

The following morning when I awoke the message was gone, with all of my lines (which was usual). They had obviously reacted badly to my impetuous request, however, since my feet had been crudely amputated at the ankles during the night. The stumps were wrapped in blood-caked bandages. Written multiple times on the bandages, although somewhat obscured by deep red stains, was the reply:

You brought this upon yourself.

The speakers were on full blast for the whole day.

Thoughtfully, though, they still allowed me use of the pencil.

I refrained (as I am sure you will appreciate) from making any other requests during the weeks that followed, and duly suffered no further, self-responsible, mutilation. I had the business of the trains to occupy me, after all, and did not care for any distraction from that all-important task. Although I had been corrected, I had also been left to concentrate on my work and had not been taken away again from my cell, which was quite in accordance with the request I had written down. The loss of my feet proved less of a punishment than I first imagined. For I had nowhere to go in any case, and no desire to be elsewhere. In fact, I even felt gratitude that they had been so considerate in their chastisement. I don't doubt that the power behind the complex knew that the removal of my hands instead of my feet would have been for me truly intolerable.

The wheelchair now stood as a fixture in the corner of my cell and I would periodically sit in it and navigate around the room for my own amusement, especially when the speakers were on full blast. Of course I kept a mental account of trains passing whilst occupied in this diversion and then added them to the daily record on the wall once I had completed my circular navigations.

You may wonder whether I ever thought of the outside world or of my past life, but I can honestly state that it is of little importance to me and a subject upon which I did not much dwell—except in one regard. After all, it was my actions therein that had led to my present state of affairs, and to this making amends for it, an extraction as much for my own benefit as for society's benefit. My disease would infect others and my quarantine was only right. Communicable disease of my type is a form of violence when those afflicted by it refuse treatment. It is even more dangerous because it manifests itself unseen, with no physical symptoms.

One afternoon I found my cell unlocked. The door was left ever so slightly ajar. I thought at first that the crack between the jamb and frame was an illusion. Wheeling myself over to it however, I discovered my eyes were not deceiving me.

This, of course, presented me with a dilemma.

Had it been purposefully left unlocked or not? Was it a test of some kind?

I could scarcely neglect my work of recording the trains passing by and satisfy my curiosity on some unauthorised jaunt along the outside corridors. In any case, I had already advised them I did not wish to leave the cell. But what if I were meant to leave the cell?

Removal of my feet had been a consequence of my expressing that desire to remain inside. And I was not leaving the confines of the whole complex itself after all, just venturing beyond this tiny sub-section of it.

Perhaps there was a solution.

I wheeled myself back to the wall and rapidly filled in enough pencil marks in advance to cover the period of my absence. Provided I returned to my cell within an hour or so it was impossible for me to have fallen behind in the tally. Recall, too, that I was very likely to encounter no one else wandering the corridors at this time. The orderlies made their rounds only in the morning.

Having satisfied myself that the amount of marks I had made were sufficient, I returned to the door, and slowly opened it wider, ensuring that I made as little noise as possible.

The corridor was deserted and stretched out ahead of me in both directions. I decided to turn right, though I had no idea whether this would lead me deeper into the complex or out towards its edge. There were no crazily angled shadows on the walls, an absence which seemed to me to be significant, though I could not say why.

I wheeled myself along for several minutes, passing locked cells. No sounds came from within them, so I imagined they were either empty or else occupied by the silent. If the force running the complex felt it necessary to remove limbs then it was entirely possible that tongues, too, might be extracted.

The unaccustomed exertion took its toll on my body and I had to pause in order to recuperate. My arms ached and my breathing was laboured. While I sat there, marooned in the labyrinth, I caught the noise of the trains passing—their dim rumble muffled; and thus reaching me from further off in the distance than from my own cell. I therefore deduced I had travelled deeper into the complex.

And then I detected another sound, not mechanical but, rather, insect-like. Long, drawn-out and chitinous in nature. It went on and on, rising and falling in tone. I continued to sit there. Should I seek out the source or avoid it altogether? There was no guarantee that I would not be putting myself in danger by satisfying my curiosity.

However, while I was debating the point in my own mind, I felt someone take hold of the back of my wheelchair and shove me forwards. An orderly had crept up behind me unawares, probably just exiting from one of the cells I had passed. I had not heard his footfalls and turned back and down to see he was wearing rubber-soled, white canvas shoes. My head still twisted back, I glanced up at his face. It was a mask of benign indifference.

He ignored all of my attempts to impede our progress towards the source of the disturbance; my cries of protests, reasoning, apologies and even put me in a headlock when I tried physically to resist by clambering out of the wheelchair.

Had I, then, been observed all along? Had my cell door been left ajar not through oversight but on purpose? I could reach no other conclusion. It seemed important to them to impress upon me the fact that each punishment they inflicted upon me was a direct consequence of exercising my own free will. They were not, in and of themselves, directly to blame.

The noise like insects massing grew even louder and the orderly wheeled me through a series of double doors, straight into the heart of the commotion.

I was in a former library of vast proportions. It was circular in design, the interior architecture baroque, and built across four open-plan floors. The place was in total chaos. Columns of high, carved wooden shelves and antique bookcases had either been denuded of their contents or else overturned and left in a state of wreckage. Most of the books had been stripped of their essence; innumerable torn pages littered the floors and the remains had been tossed down into the central well at the core of the structure. Scattered amidst the library were hordes of mutilated inmates each dressed, as I was, in a grey smock. They were the source of the chitinous noise. It rose and fell in unison as they worked, pulling volumes from the shelves and tearing them to pieces. Some lacked hands for the task and used their teeth.

All of them had been blinded—eyes extracted at the root with the surrounding skin sewn back.

Black holes gaped sightlessly—abominable flowers in the stark blue-white electric glare.

The orderly bent down to my right ear and whispered into it, ever so softly, some lines of doggerel.

the fear of masks removed
as black lightning illumines
new quests for nothing
the amnesiac thoughts
of dying brains
repeated but forgotten

I thought, then, he might reach for my eyes in order to pluck them out with his long bony fingers, but instead he turned me around and wheeled me along the winding length of corridors back to my cell.

I noticed that the shadows had returned.

On the bed was another note for me. It read:

You left too many marks.

The next time I awoke I found they had severed my left hand.

Throughout the same day the familiar orderly began ferrying piles of books into my cell. He brought them in cardboard boxes, dumped the contents on the floor and then returned with more. This went on for the several hours. While he was absent I arranged them into free-standing columns as best I could whilst sat amongst them and with only one hand now remaining to me. I did not take much note of their actual contents or titles although I was aware that they were a mixture of old and new volumes, paperbacks and hardbacks, and all rather battered (although not torn apart). I did note, however, since the fact was so remarkable, they were all written under the same byline: Dr. Prozess.

I also neglected to keep up with my record of the trains passing while I was engaged in this new activity. I was immediately tormented by the question of what exactly constituted the appropriate response to this fresh development concerning the arrival of all these books.

Was I meant to read them or destroy them?

Even doing neither might be interpreted as an act of sedition.

I opened one at random. The first words I encountered were:

You are not to read this book.

I closed it and picked up another. This time the first words were:

Forget about this book.

I decided to open just one more and no others. The words my gaze fell upon were:

You are the book.

Then they turned on the speakers again and I couldn't hear the trains at all.

The next thing I was aware of was being wheeled along the corridors. I knew I had greatly offended the rules of the complex this time and that I was at last going to meet Dr. Prozess face-to-face. What revelations he had in store for me would be more interesting than the mediocre threat of removing my right hand or my eyes. Perhaps it would be necessary to slice into my brain, so that only the parts that registered the appropriately infinite degree of pain and terror would be left intact. The drooling sutures criss-crossing my shaven skull told me that they had probably already monkeyed around with my memory.

They were taking me outside of the complex. We passed several signs with arrows pointing the way to the exit. I tried to ignore the gleefully dancing insectoid shadows upon the walls.

At last there was a familiar set of titanic metal doors up ahead. On their inside was scrawled the legend:

Exit and Prozess

Then I saw the outside world for myself.

A television-sky receiving a broadcast of a close-up of the deaths-head moon. Brilliant, dazzling blacks and whites, combining and recombining; maddening in its intensity; a heaven of unendurably nightmarish static. Sublunary shadows stretched in all directions over a landscape of hills and vales, criss-crossed by motorway flyovers and surface level railway lines. Endless automated freight trains, all riven by rust and corrosion, rumbled along the tracks, back and forth, while huge self-driving lorries, caked in soot, their combustion engines groaning, rolled arduously above them. And in between the railway lines and the roads, there was a dull grey carpet of motion, a countryside of refuse and ashes teeming with a sea of deformed locusts pock-mocked by the reductionism of lunar fever, things that might once—before the strange revelations of Dr. Prozess that is— have been human beings.

I covered my eyes, but my skin tingled and then began to peel as the seeping corrosion of inevitable futurity worked its backward effect upon me.

After being taken back to my cell, the overhead light had been turned off for good and I was left to stew forever in total darkness. The speakers were left on continuously, at full volume, and I slipped in and out of consciousness; unable to think coherently due to chronic sleep deprivation. My existence became an indistinguishable monotony of exhaustion and of horror.

Other parts of my body were removed on a weekly basis; even certain internal organs.

Eventually, I ceased to notice the noise from the speakers. I tried to detect the noise of the trains but the depthless silence was as absolute as the darkness.

Then, one time, an incalculable period later, I dreamt I had a visitor.

The door to my cell was unlocked. Another inmate from elsewhere in the complex was wheeled inside but I could not hear what he said, having no ears.

Instead I sniffed the air, located a strangely familiar scent and hauled my rotten, mutilated carcass towards its source, trying desperately to communi-cate my misery.

I could see nothing through the hollow craters where my eyes should have been.

I found the footless legs of my visitor, clambered up onto its lap and held it in an embrace, desperate for any human contact, and managed to gargle out the words "ereh fo tuo em teg" from the back of my throat.

But they swiftly took my visitor away.

Now they have finally loaded me onto one of the trains whose destination is nowhere, along with all the others of my ilk from the complex—we who had brought this fate upon ourselves.

And thus, of necessity, to be utterly forgotten, as futurity must redact the past.

FELICE PICANO

AFTER SUNSET IN THE SECOND DRAWING ROOM

F ELICE PICANO's stories have appeared in scores of magazines
and anthologies, including the horror anthologies *New Terrors*
#1 edited by Ramsey Campbell and *Scare Care* edited by Graham
Masterton.

A much-translated novelist, he recently published several award-
winning memoirs such as *True Stories* and *Nights at Rizzoli*. Newer
collections of his stories include *Tales from a Distant Planet* and
Twelve O'Clock Tales. His tell-all Hollywood novel, *Justify My Sins*,
and the collection *Three Strange Stories* will both be published in
2019.

"I've lived at the West Hollywood/Beverly Hills city lines near the
Sunset Strip for over a decade," says Picano, "and bicycled and
walked the surrounding streets for years, alone and with friends.

"We always remarked upon a particular house that appeared to be
all but closed. So, we were surprised when we discovered it had been
inhabited by a woman who'd lived in it for nine decades, since it was
built.

"The sale of the place was newsworthy. But we wondered about
how she'd lived there. And with whom."

W E'D KNOWN THE house for years, naturally, as both of us lived nearby just on the other side of the Doheny Drive city-line. As a kid, who'd grown up in the Norma Triangle, I had pals who lived on the opposite side of its long, straight, tree-shaded street and I'd bicycled past it too many times to recall. Once we'd settled into our first condo, as adults, we'd stroll past it many a weekend afternoon, or take a long way home on purpose, to detour past it, after a particularly pleasant Sunday brunch a few blocks away that we didn't wish to end quite yet.

There was nothing extraordinary about the good-sized, two-storey Mediterranean-style house built when that eastern part of Beverly Hills was still new. Nothing, of course, for the single, quite extraordinary thing: it had never been up for sale. The house remained in the hands of the Bellamys, who'd commissioned it and erected it way back in 1922 and had lived in it ever since.

That was a rarity, and the news about it being sold was extra-ordinary enough that it was written up in the *L.A. Times* as well as in our three local papers—we're a very *civic* community here. That was when the world learned the story of Frances Lodge Bellamy. She'd lived there—alone save for servants—until the age of ninety-seven, having moved into the house at the age of nine, along with her parents and two older sisters, when the family relocated from Milwaukee to what was still the "Golden West" of California. Frances slept in her childhood bedroom in the house, up a flight of stairs on the second floor, until a few years ago, when she'd weakened; so a bedroom was set up for her downstairs, in what was known as the second drawing room.

That bed was still in the house when we managed to get in to look. We'd seen the FOR SALE sign while passing by that Sunday after brunch at our usual place, and we knew we had to act immediately. So, we'd stood in front and phoned the number on the sign. A half-hour later we were inside.

"I'd just put up the sign," the realtor, said, when we called. "Not ten minutes before you called. I was on my way back home, to Trousdale Estates."

"We live nearby and know the house since we were children," Ashleigh said. "Please, please, please, come back and let us have a look. I don't know what I'll do if I can't at least look at it. I've been dying to for so many years."

"Young as we are, we can afford it," I then added. "I'm contracted to write a minimum of twelve one-hour shows for a new TCM series in the coming six months. It's so locked-in that I will be paid whether they air the episodes or not."

Jazmina agreed to return, so we were under the front porch trellis hung with "Anima Mea" bougainvillea and huge grape-like pouches of lilac. In fact, we were spread out on the built-in concrete bench, with Ash's legs up on my lap, so that we felt almost at home by the time Jazmina arrived.

"Oh, my god, you're huge!" the realtor said to Ashleigh. "When are you due?"

"Yesterday! That's why we need a big house. We're in a one-and-den flat. I'm having twins."

"This place has two masters, two other bedrooms upstairs and a servant's room downstairs. Plus the temporary bedroom that was set up for the owner on the first floor," Jazmina added, unlocking the front door for us. "Although most people would probably want to use that as an office, since it's right off the breakfast room and it has its own private garden. The old construction plans I looked at call it the second drawing room." She made a sweet face at us, and we all smiled at the old-timiness.

Jazmina told us the house was not quite emptied out because the only heir, some child of a nephew, told her to leave it for the new owners. Jazmina said that what had gone unspoken during that call was the fact that the relative was sure she'd do well enough just with the house sale.

The cute entry's double doors led to a good-sized foyer and sweeping staircase up, along with a discreet elevator to the second floor that Ash would find handy. The surprise was the second drawing room at the rear of the house with its own separate garden. It had the smallest of the four fireplaces on the first floor (there were two more upstairs) and the only inside-to-outside French doors, which Jazmina needed my help opening. Not because they were stuck, but because once the frilly curtains and heavy curtains also were drawn aside and the glass doors unlocked, there was another set of security all-wooden doors over those: kind of like hurricane windows at the shore.

Once all of that was open, the deep spring, intense odour of jasmine, verbena and pseudo-orange blossom filled the room. From where Ashleigh plunked herself down in an overstuffed-looking little chair, she pointed out a dozen rose bushes, three colours of hibiscus, gardenias, tall ginger, bird of paradise and even frilly white- and red-hybrid canna lilies.

"Her cousin told me this was Frances' favourite room in the house," Jazmina said. "He said that it held special memories for her and that Frances told her the room was almost alive."

"I'll collapse and die and never give birth to twins," Ash said, "unless I can live in this house and stay in this room."

Yes, pregnancy made her over-dramatise. And no, I'd still not gotten used to it. But Jazmina smiled. "Like I said, it just came on the market. I told one other person about it. But I think they'll find it too big. So," she said, looking at me, "Noah? Ashleigh, why don't we go into the kitchen and why don't see if we can't come up with some figures we can live with?"

A month-and-a-half later, the second bedroom was a nursery and the one adjoining that was an *au pair*'s room. I liked the library, but it was just a little too formal for a home office for me, so I took the upstairs second master's suite, which had a good-sized dressing room that I could use for all my CDs, and my files, and what Ash called "all your other stuff that you absolutely refuse to give up." She kept the second drawing room on the first floor for her own, a den-slash-home office.

Which meant, essentially, that she moved a lovely Queen Anne period knockoff desk in there, along with a matching chair.

Whenever she was free, she'd read and write in there. Ash and I had met at a film script "summer boot camp"—a four week jag with twenty-five other twenty-somethings in the fire-prone hills above Montecito. She had worked with me on the stories of the TCM series, and so she was on the payroll too. Luckily, she gave birth at the beginning of the TV actor's hiatus, before production of the second six programmes could begin shooting. Ash was as invested in the series as much I was and she was totally ready—at least at home-ready with an infant nearby—when we began shooting again.

That hiatus had allowed us to settle into the house and figure out where to put our furniture, what of Frances Bellamy's to keep, and what could go on consignment-sale in L.A. or down in Palm Springs (where they loved '30s to '50s stuff even more than in Silver Lake).

By the next hiatus we had modernised a great deal. My brother Ty and his husband Carl own and operate Up to U, with a fifty-foot long showroom on Beverly Blvd. where CAA used to have offices. Together they redid our new downstairs, room by room, keeping it "eclectic but somehow new", painting the brick fireplaces "cantaloupe and cream, fawn and okapi." Ash and I referred to the rooms as the "Soda Shop Parlour" and the "Zoological Dining Room". Upstairs they re-did my office too, in colours they called "masculine—you know". Ty told me—"concrete, putty, sienna and spruce," which I told him sounded like '90s blue-collar folkies.

Only the second drawing room remained untouched—except for Ty's clever desk and chair addition—because, as Carl said for all of us, "It's just perfect, exactly the way it is."

Since I was never in there, I didn't care. It was Ash's hideaway just as "Concrete and Spruce" was my own—although mine was located at the top of the stairs, opposite the elevator, and so a much more public room. The difference reflected our two personalities, really. Ash always looked pretty and mysterious in the background at our business meetings. She really only came in at the end, "for the kill," as she put it, after I'd done most of the talking.

Which might explain why it took a good eight months for me to realise...well, to realise that anything at all was going on with the room—and the little garden. Maybe even more so with the garden.

Four of our producers were also married: Laisa and Gideon Steinkerque, even if we preferred the other couple of our producers, Jimmie Bruri and Scott Grizzi. It was Laisa who cottoned onto the second drawing room. They were all in the house for a celebratory dinner, the day after the first season's "wrap" party, and Laisa disappeared into the powder-room, until it was noticeable and Gideon went to get her. Ash made "get 'em" eyes at me and so I went too. At night, the big house with lots of halls and doors could be a little confusing to navigate.

We found her inside the second drawing room. "Laisa, we're over there!" Gideon pointed in the opposite direction.

"Oh, I know. I was headed back, but I thought I heard people this way. I thought some of you had moved in here."

"We didn't. We're still in the dining room," I said.

"The dining room—over there!" Gideon, who was a little *stunada* repeated and pointed.

I pointed him in the direction of his own hand, ordering: "Go!"

I took Laisa by the elbow and said, "Madam!"

"It's a perfectly lovely little room," she said, apologetically. "You guys are so lucky. Our house doesn't have anything close to this."

"I heard that!" Gideon said.

"Well, does it?" she asked.

She explained again at the dinner table, and I would have forgotten it except that when Laisa was in the kitchen with the *au pair* later on that night, I heard the latter ask in her distinctive Caribbean accent, "What kind of voices, Miz Steinkerque?" And Laisa asked back, "Why? Have you heard anything there?" To which the *au pair* replied hastily, "Oh, I never go in that room at all. Be *duppies* in there."

Skip a few months and I'm on the phone in a conference-call with the Bahamas, where we're thinking of shooting an entire three sequences, discussing locations with a woman named Esmeralda Sligh, who has the same accent as the *au pair*—whom we'd replaced by the way. So, I asked her what the word *duppy* meant.

"*Haints.* Them that cannot rest in this life or the next."

"Spirits?"

"You might say. *Haints.*"

Esmeralda said she had just the place for us to use—it was big, it was new-ish, it was barely ten minutes outside of Georgetown.

I went to my trusty OED and found the word "*Haints*" equals "Haunts". To which I said aloud, "That's crazy!"

It was Laisa who convinced Ashleigh into using the second drawing room as a cocktail party area

The night before, Ash was upset over the preparations for the dinner party the next day and I couldn't figure out why.

"You can do this kind of gathering sleep-walking Ash! You know that as well as I do. What's going on?"

"I don't know. Maybe it's the second drawing room."

"It's your private room. I get it. You don't want it invaded. So why can't we have cocktails outside in the garden? Move all the chairs and even, I don't know, the bed halfway out there with lots of throw pillows?"

"That won't help," she said. "It's even worse out there."

I stared at her. Worse? Why worse? "Ash! Tell me, what's worse?"

"You're going to say it's stupid."

"We've suddenly got secrets from each other? What did our marriage vows say? Remember? No secrets ever."

She sighed and said, "No secrets ever. Here goes. Laisa's not the only one who has heard voices."

"The *duppies*?"

"Well, I don't know what they are. They're just kind of whispers. Of course the twins noticed right away. Their hearing must be super-sharp at that age, so I never bring them in there anymore."

This was a secret indeed. "Go on! Tell me about the whispers?"

"Well, there are two of them: a man and a woman. They're both very cultivated. East Coast, old-time cultivated, if you know what I mean."

"Like in black and white movies cultivated?"

"Exactly. With that kind of . . . " she raised her nose high in the air, "*accent*. And they're . . . I don't know how to put it. They're . . . gossiping about other people. There's a François, and a Nila, and a Gottfried that they talk about."

My lips started forming a smile. So I covered them up.

"Also some American or British names. Anthony. Everson. Damita, Bell something or other."

"Bellamy?" I tried. "Wasn't that the old gal's name? A relative?"

That startled Ashleigh. "You may be right. Bell as in Bellamy! As a rule I don't hear them except, you know, if I come in here later on. I never hear them during the day at all. They don't *ever* bother me when I'm working." She suddenly changed subject. "Jimmie and Gideon liked the changes to the new arc, right?"

"Yes, I already told you. I like them. Gid and Jimmie and Laissa and Scott all like them. Even the leads are going to like them. In short, everyone likes the new changes. You're brilliant, as usual."

"Well, I'm not there, part of the day like you are," she said. "So, I'm never sure what people say."

"People love the changes. People love you. I heard a rumour that there's even a groundswell afloat to have you canonised."

She hit me with that and I hit her back, and we ended up on the floor.

"After dinner, out of nowhere she brought it up again: "You know that wonderful Guatemalan guy your brother uses in his shop? What is he? A carpenter? A wood-finisher? Looks like an Aztec statue come to life?"

"Andres?"

"Andres! When he and Carl came in, and were setting-up my desk, it was like, the sun was setting, which was partly visible from in here, and it was so lovely and the air was soft, and I remember that Andres looked around and I'm sure he too heard the whispers, while Carl didn't. Maybe even more clearly even than I did, and he stuck around fussing until Carl left. I know that because he said, "It's okay, Missus. They are *activos* but not, I don't think, *malo*.""

"He meant 'active but not bad'?" I tried with my high-school Spanish.

"That's what I guessed too."

"Okay. That's the secret, and now it's out. See. Was that so terrible?'

Of course, I could say that because I was already prepped about the *duppies*.

"So here's my idea: it's your office. Your garden. It's totally your call whether we have the cocktail party in here or not. Totally!"

"No. It's stupid. It's our house. We pay the mortgage. We should be able to use every inch of space here any time we wish. I will not be denied," she declared with a rising fist.

I bent down and worshipped at her feet until she knocked me over and we fell onto the floor, laughing.

So, right from the beginning I was a believer. That was never the issue. The problem was that I thought, *well, it's an old place, almost expected to have them . . . duppies. Ashleigh is the only one in the room. She'd even kept the children out. So what harm can the* duppies *do*?

The cocktail party in the second drawing room garden was a complete success. A *suces fou* as the French say. There were maybe eighteen of us altogether, mostly from the series; a few friendly network people, and even an inside/outside wife/critic/promoter of one of them who oddly enough got along with all of us, even though she was twice our age. The women all liked the décor of the room, and the garden. The men appreciated the wet-bar, and even more the bed half-in, half-out of doors, where they could flop, and according to the catering folk, the room and the garden too were in use throughout the night by people.

For the next two weeks everyone who'd been there had something good to say about the party, and so I felt I had to tell Ashleigh that that it was all awesome and her fears were totally unjustified.

She was pleased—what home-maker, party-giver wouldn't be. Then she said something I'll never forget: "The only thing is that Jimmie and Scott are separating."

Dealing with them almost daily, a lot more than she was, and I'd heard absolutely zilch. So I asked, "How do you know this? Did Jimmie tell you?"

She shook her head. "They were alone in the garden and had words. Apparently, it had been building. This wasn't the first time they'd fought over her former husband and kid. Scott put his foot down, and she said absolutely no."

"What about them?"

"It's complicated, but not that important, Noah. What is important is that if they split they endanger the show."

"They're not going to split, and if they do they're professional enough not to back out of the show."

"She didn't want to do it in the first place. And she's got the money, Noah. You know that. It was her dad who was the producer of those hit shows in the '70s and '80s. Not his."

I thought she heard about it from friends. From the caterers. From the girl who cut her hair, and the women in her Pilates class: the usual unimpeachable sources. That's how sure she was. So when she brought it up again the next night, she added, "I've been thinking, Noah. You know our other series?"

She meant our dream series. "Yeah. What about it?"

"Why don't we shop it to Jimmie and her dad?"

"Cutting out Scott and Gideon and Laissa?"

"We can bring in the Steinkerques later. Scott won't want to have anything to do with it once they're apart. You know how he gets—all black and white. No greys!"

We'd worked that to our advantage in the past.

I said I'd think about it. Four days later, Ash arranged for us to take the kids and hang out at Jimmie's dad's beach place in Malibu for the day. This was a delicious treat, and she knew I loved going there in the past, since I'd known Jimmie and Scott a lot longer. It was August, and hot and perfect for the beach, and so of course I said yes.

Towards the end of that day, with the twins snoring away, and Jimmie and her sister Reena and Ash all making dinner and drinking too much Pinot inside, Hamilton Bruri came out to the deck with what he called "a refill".

"This is a Noir I picked up the last night it was open one season at the Crater Lake Hotel," he began. I'd known Ham since I was eighteen, and above all things about him I loved his stories. I mean, he'd made a billion with his stories on series, right? So I laughed as he poured this almost black wine for me.

"I'm needed the next day at a promotional in Portland and then in Seattle the day after, before shooting in Vancouver," he says. "So I drove down to Medford, where I did my first directing at the

Shakespeare Festival. Hung out with a few folks, for old times' sake. Then drove up the mountain to the lake. It's like early October. It was eighty-five degrees in Medford. When I reach the hotel it's thirty-one and snow and ice are on the ground.

"I'm the last guest to check in for the season. Everyone is leaving by 2:00 p.m. the next day, and it's closing down for the winter, like the place in that Kubrick movie. I enter this pine lodge-pole wonderment from the 1920s—a dining room two stories tall, fireplace yeah big, and I'm the last diner of the season. They put me at a table for one, aside a little, and I'm sure every damn person there asked who I was. I order a half-bottle of this highly recommended Pinot and salmon and whatever that's easy, and when I go to pay, the waiter hands me the bottle and says take it: they're closing for the winter. I like it so much, I buy six bottles the next day down in the Willamette Valley, right at the winery. This is the last one of those.

"By the way, the lake was black, the night clear, and as it's 7,800 feet up, there were a million stars reflected in the water. I stayed on the room's balcony looking at it and polishing off the bottle, and I fell asleep out there with fur blankets."

"It's a wonderful story—and wine." I tasted and declared, "Black cherries and blackberries! Which I guess all grow in the Willamette Valley."

"Now you tell me a story," Ham said

"Sure. What story?"

"You know what story, Noah. Yours and Ash's new series story!"

That story was *Oratorio in Black* and well, its history now, isn't it?

Scott pulled out of season three of the other series, once he and Jimmie separated, as Ashleigh had predicted. They entered a long, messy, vituperative divorce. He was unhappy to hear about our new series. With Ham on board, we took it to HBO and got premium treatment there—as it deserved. When we later pulled in Gideon and Laisa for their expertise and connections, they of course approached Scott with our blessing, but he blew up in their faces: why hadn't I come to him first?

Ash asked what the outcome of that was. "You mean the outcome of breaking-off totally with my friend from the eighth grade who I'd shared all my dreams with?" She never asked again.

What I didn't tell her was what happened in the men's room at the Emmys two years later, once season one of *Oratorio* had aired and had gotten a skillion nominations, including a writing one for us, and then the award. I was off stage and had to urinate, and I was washing my hands when Scott came out of a stall and our eyes locked in the mirror above me. We'd not seen each other in maybe two years, and I didn't know what to say. He was pretty drunk, of course, which partly explained why he suddenly undid his pants, turned around, bent over and mooned me. I thought it was funny and pure Scott from middle school, but as more people were coming in, I got embarrassed. "Very nice. Even better muscled than when you were on the gym team. Now put your pants back on."

He didn't though, and so they were treated to the sight of him, bare-assed, bumping into my front and drunkenly saying, "Why, Noah? Why hide it? Since everyone already knows that you screwed me royally once, and I'm guessing you're raring' to do it again!"

I fled, and so did they. A few minutes later, someone came over to our table and whispered to Gideon, who left to help Scott out of the men's room and into a limo.

There we were, with two series going great, and Ash decided she wanted a sister for the boys. So she didn't come back into production with me part of a day, but instead stayed home working on her own projects. Which, later on, I could understand was because while I wanted to be where the action was, she wanted to be more in the know. And evidently daughter number one and daughter number two didn't have as sharp hearing as their brothers, and so she could keep them with her in her office during the day.

Explaining the next piece of information that came my way following another one of our cocktail parties and buffets, this time for the staff and cast of *Oratorio*, and so the place was full, every downstairs room in use. It was a big, joyous, noisy event. And the HBO exec was friendly as hell and said, "C'mon now, Noah. Don't be coy. What else do you guys have up your sleeves?"

It was totally true that we were working on another series, and I was ready to bring it to Ham and Jimmie, but Ash had twice said it wasn't ready. So I played coy and promised he'd have something in a few weeks.

I didn't spend a lot of time with either of the Bruris that night, but evidently Ashleigh did because the next day at dinner she said, "Let's call a meeting with that HBO exec? What's his name, Alton something?"

"Shouldn't we have a meet with Ham first?" I asked. I mean, it was a given at this point: Ham. Jimmie. Then the Steinkerques. Then the exec.

Ashleigh said, "Ham won't live to see it into production."

The classic wine-all-over-the-dinner was my response.

She turned icy. "If he's got six months, it's a lot. It's a poly. It's already metastasised into his lungs and brain."

"What are you talking about, Ashleigh?"

"Cancer, Noah. The big C. Ham's big C."

"We're having the meeting with him, Ash. I mean, even if you are right, we have to do it! Out of respect."

We did, at the beach house in Malibu a week later. Hamilton was obviously sick, which I'd never seen at the party or before, and where Jimmie was nowhere in sight. Ash helped the full-time nurse with the dinner preparation, and it was wonderful, and when it was done, they were cleaning up and we were out on the deck. I told the series story to Ham, and he reacted wonderfully: "Pure gold!"

"We knew you'd love it."

"I love it, Noah. But it's too rich for me. The only gold I need now is what they're shooting into the back of my neck every week to stabilise the radiation."

"What about Jim—?"

"Don't bother her with it, either. She's going through her own things. You know Scott showed up again, and they're on and off. And she's having a hell of a hard time with me, being a Daddy's girl and all. I'll tell her you wanted to include her. I'm sure she'll take a pass. But it's pure gold, kid . . . " He paused. "You know, I always thought they would be my heirs in the Biz: Scott and Jimmie. But they're not. They're too easily distracted. It's you guys. You're the rock-solid ones."

Ash came out onto the deck.

"Just in time," Ham said. "I want you to hear this too, hon. The girls will get plenty from me. Houses all over the west, vacation condos from here to Bora Bora, a loft in Manhattan. Why don't I let you two have this place? I know how much you love it since you were a teenager."

We said, no, no, no. Ham died three months later. And a few months after that I received the title to the beach house in his will.

To my surprise, the HBO exec hadn't expected nor, for that matter, even needed the Bruris in our meeting about the new series. "You four have legs enough."

He liked the story and our casting ideas, and we went for a celebratory dinner right afterwards, Ash and me and the Steinkerques.

I was gazing out my office window when this *ginormous* Rolls-Royce pulled up along the front of our house; I mean, so big it took up one and three-quarter parking spaces, and was one of the subtle battleship-grey and slate-blue two-tone "saloons", with white wall tyres four-feet high.

This driver with—I swear—a cap and uniform, exits, comes around and opens the back door, and helps out this tall, elderly woman: the kind of woman you would expect to see come out of such a wagon, and she begins walking up to our door.

The twins are at pre-school, and Ash is out somewhere doing something, but the *au pair* and the infant girls are napping. I don't want them to wake for at least another hour, or I'll get no work done at all. I shut their door, rush downstairs, and catch the front door, just as she's about to ring the bell.

She's surprised, but asks if I'm Noah, and then says she's someone or other and has something to tell me, can she come in?

She comes into the big foyer and looks around.

"Little girls upstairs napping," I stage whisper, pointing upstairs.

"How about the library then," she says, and walks right in like she owns the place. I follow and close the library door, and she looks around and sits herself down in one of the two wing-tip chairs we left there.

"Um? Coffee? Tea? Ice-water?"

"My generation drinks, dear. Why don't you get me a sherry."

She nods in the direction of the half-bar hidden as a book cabinet, and I go get it for her, and a tonic water for me. I perch, and she sips, and then puts it down and says: "I spoke to your wife by phone, but it did no good."

All I could think was—*what a great opening line for an episode!*

"Again my name is," she adds, and it turns out to be Alexandra Laws Pfaff, said as though I should know it.

"I found you and your wife through several other people. I happened to be with an old friend from back east in _____", naming the best consignment house in Rancho Mirage, "and saw the big aspen wood console for sale. A mark on the side confirmed that it was from this house, from the front parlour in particular."

"Yes, we re-did most of the rooms down here."

"But not the second drawing room with the garden."

"No. Not much work in there." Now I was intrigued.

"Seeing the console for sale, I knew that Fran was gone and the house was sold. I used a bit of leverage with the middle-men and I obtained your names."

"Fair enough."

"As I said, I spoke to Ashleigh—that's her name, isn't it?—a few days ago, and she paid no attention to me. So, I'm trying again, with you."

"What about?"

"About the second drawing room and garden."

She let that hang there a half-minute.

"You mean about the *duppies*. Uh, the whispers?"

"Well, you at least admit it. She wouldn't."

"I admit it. But what about them?"

She looked startled at that. "What about them? They're dangerous, young man. That room should be locked up and the door sealed."

"Because...?"

"Because it ruined a great many lives once, and will do so again."

Now she had my complete interest.

"You know who the whispers come from, don't you?" she asked.

"I'm guessing Frances whatever-her-name and someone else."

That surprised her. "Oh! There are two now!"

"Before there was only one?" I asked.

"Yes. Always just the one. But one was bad enough."

"And that one was?"

"Ben Allingham. Benedict Allingham. Fran's closest friend. In life and in death. He came out here in '38, I believe, to be in the movies, and did several in supporting roles over a period, but somehow that didn't work out. I think it's because film doesn't lie, and it picked up the real Ben Allingham, and no one wanted to see that. Especially not as a leading man."

I settled back in my chair and gestured for her to continue.

"He got involved in promotion for pictures. It was the absolute heyday of the movie studios and he made a great front man, did that awfully well. So well, that when the war came, they managed to keep him out of it for two years, and when he went in it was with a film-crew to the Pacific. He saw no action closer than a mile away, and that through a lens. He returned here in '46 and took up his old position. But he had disappointments. A woman of means he'd assiduously courted married someone else. Another potential wife had gone east, and then Fran—who was well into being of marriageable age by then—decided not to marry at all, but to be 'Aunt Fran' to her many nephews and nieces. Ben's work changed as the studios did, and then as they lost ground to television. He wasn't really needed . . . No one knew if the auto accident he died in was intentional or not. A large truck was involved, and its driver escaped with minor injuries. So it was only Fran."

"By then I was already on the scene here. I'm younger than Fran by a decade, and I came here with friends for a party. She and I got along wonderfully well, and of course I comforted her when the news about Ben came. She was devastated. She retreated and totally closed down. This house used to be so filled with people, with parties, with events of all kinds—some studio-related, some not—but every room downstairs here would be filled with people. I don't know how to describe how marvellous that was."

"We're in the Business and have parties here too. We know how great the house is for entertaining."

"I've heard. That's exactly why it's especially dangerous for the both of you. Had Persian jewellers bought the place, I mightn't be here."

"But it's just gossip, my wife told me."

"It was always 'just gossip'!"

"I don't understand."

"How do I say this? A year or so after Ben died, Fran was suddenly radiant. I thought, *Oh good, she has a new friend.* It wasn't true. What was true was that Ben had returned here, to the second drawing room, where they always used to be, before and after the parties they used to throw. She admitted it to me over time, and then let me witness it. It was Ben, all right. And he wasn't one of those—I don't know what they call them—repetitive spirits, those who repeat an action over and over, unaware of their surroundings. No, he was still, somehow, gossiping."

"He's an *activo*," I said, and explained. "That's what a Latin gentlemen told Ash."

"Very active. As you've noticed, haven't you?"

"Only second-hand. Ash notices. We use the room and garden for cocktail parties for our TV series. Afterwards, Ash knows things about people she shouldn't know."

"Bad things?"

"This couple is breaking up. That man is dying of cancer."

"And like Ben and Fran, you somehow profit from this knowledge."

I should have kicked Alexandra Laws Pfaff out then. If I had faked outrage and gotten her out, none of the rest would have happened. Or so I sometimes tell myself. Instead I replied, "Have we profited by the gossip she heard? I'll say we have!"

"That's why it's so dangerous, young man."

"But Frances lived to ninety-seven. It didn't harm her."

"Didn't it? I was her very last friend, and I stepped away for good twenty-five years ago. She remained alone here with servants she didn't like or trust, who'd turn over almost annually. She stayed with no friends but ... " Alexandra Laws Pfaff nodded in the direction of the second drawing room, ". . . that monstrosity."

"But ... I don't get it. How ... "

"He developed a sort of tic, Ben did. I think I was the first one to notice it. He'd be going along all witty and urbane, and just as he was about to say something really cruel or devious about someone, something that would cause them great harm, his upper lip curled slightly. It happened time after time. Maybe that was what the camera picked up, that kept him out of films—that tiny sneer, that sign of his sense of entitlement and of his superiority, and especially of his contempt."

"Within a year or so after his whispering began, Fran developed that same tic. The first time I noticed it, I wasn't sure. So I asked the man I was dating, whom I married, if he'd be a dear and watch her closely when I brought up a certain person's name. I did. He did. That confirmed it."

"A tic?"

"Like this ... " Her upper lip curled a bit above her eyetooth. It was a tiny thing, and I could see why she'd need it confirmed. But it was awful.

"Yes. I see it now."

"Good!" She finished her sherry in another long sip, and sighed and put on her lace gloves. "Well, I've said what I had to. You've been courteous and listened. There's no more I can do."

She stood up and left. In the foyer, she hesitated and turned. Unbidden, I asked, "Do you want to see it? The second drawing room?"

For the first time since I'd met her, a look of unease came onto the old lady's face and her pale blue eyes darted.

"C'mon," I said. "A peek can't harm you."

I drew her through the corridor. The door was ajar as it usually was during the day. She stood on the lintel and peered in, then quickly turned.

"It looks the same," she said, relieved or scared, I couldn't tell which.

"Except for my wife's new desk and chair."

"Yes. But even those are in the style of ... the room. He'd approve. I'm sure they both approve."

Alexandra Laws Pfaff marched out of the house and into the huge Rolls. But not out of my mind.

I wouldn't have said a word about Alexandra's visit, but it was such a *weird* visit, and the back-story so damn interesting and Old-Hollywood-ish, that I simply had to tell someone. Who better than my best friend, who happened to be my wife? After dinner. That night.

Terrible idea. Her response was ice cold: "So she got to you?"

"What do you mean 'got to me'?"

"She tried to get to me, and when it didn't work she got to you."

I let my first reaction pass, drew down a big gulp of Chardonnay and then asked, "So you don't think it's an interesting story?"

"If it's true!"

"If it's not, why do you think she even bothered to get to either of us?"

"She's an old dame. All her friends are probably dead. She wants to be important for a few moments. She's just like those old ladies you see at the CVS check-out line, doing anything they can to keep the cashier or anyone at all taking to them, since they have no one else to talk to at home, while we wait and wait for them to finish."

That was a pretty cold thing to say, and not like Ash at all. I didn't think Alexandra Laws Pfaff was a bit like those old ladies at CVS. After all, she had her chauffeur and probably other staff to keep her company. The rich usually do. What did Robert Frost call it? *Boughten friendship at her side.*

I let it drop.

Five minutes later we're in some other conversation altogether, and the oddest thing happened: we'd been talking about a new intern in Laisa Steinkerques' office, a new production assistant. He was young, and good-looking, and obviously went to the gym, and Ashleigh said, "What she likes about him is how tight he wears those black denims of his. I mean, the other day I met her for lunch at her office, and he was sitting on the edge of the desk talking to her, and she was sitting in her office chair and his junk was right there, in her face."

I tried saying, "I'm told some women like guys who display."

"Put Mrs. Steinkerque number one on that list. But then he certainly wouldn't be the first of her personal assistants to display." And then just before she smiled, Ashleigh's upper lip curled into a tiny sneer. She laughed and changed the subject.

Admittedly we'd almost had a full bottle of oak cask-fermented thirty-dollar wine between us, so I wasn't totally sober, but I sobered up instantly because I swear, the hair went up on the back of my neck.

"Poor Gideon. He doesn't suspect a thing," Ash added.

I got myself out of there somehow and up to my desk, and that's when I wrote down all these notes and what we said during Alexandra's visit.

After that, something almost had to happen.

It did. Right after that season's wrap party at our place, naturally, for season two of *Oratorio in Black*.

It was in the SUV with the twins all muddy and fatigued and sleepy after some pre-organised and, thankfully, disorganised after pre-school soccer game. Ash had been there with another mother an hour and I'd arrived later, but the boys were delighted anyway. Their tiny tots "team" more-or-less won, and so I said I'd take them out and treat all of us to Wienerschnitzel, ten miles away, which they'd seen advertised on TV and which they were just old enough to love saying a hundred and twenty times in different ways and with different accents—well, their five-year old ideas of accents. It was one of those moments when I was just utterly happy with them, with us, with Ash and with my entire life.

Coming back, somewhere on Sunset Blvd., Ashleigh said out of nowhere, "You know, we're going to have to think about re-casting for Jed soon. I mean seriously, Noah."

"Jed" being the second lead of *Oratorio*.

Everything in my body went on full red-alert at that, since this was how these conversations based on the whispers always began. But I decided to keep it cool, and I said, "Why's that, Ash?"

"Well, I'm hearing Tony's involved with that Romanian model. What's her name? Rudii? And that she wants him in London. He's so whipped, he'll do whatever she asks."

"I'll talk to him, tomorrow."

"God! Don't do *that*!"

"How else will we know for sure?"

"We already know for sure."

She said it with the same certainty that she'd told me of Ham Bruri's cancer and Scott and Jimmie's break-up, and I said, "Tell you what, I'll be friendly and diplomatic and completely sympathetic with him. And I'll ask."

"We can grab Nick _____" and she named a real comer from another series who we both knew, and knew from early scripts would be written out of it in a few episodes. "We'll kill off Jed," Ashleigh continued, "and write-in someone new for Nick. Say a younger brother, bent on revenge."

I said nothing further, and she didn't push it. We carried the still-sleeping boys up to bed, undressed them, and checked in on the girls and the *au pair*, all snoring away; and after that, I went into my office and closed the door.

The following day I made a point of going onto the set and chatting-up Tony to ask what he thought "Jed" should take on next season. He was full of ideas and totally enthusiastic. So, I asked, "Well, what about your squeeze? She's in London, no?"

"Yeah, but she can get work here. I'm not going anywhere Noah, if you're expanding my part." We talked a bit more, and he confirmed what he'd first said two more times.

That came up with Ashleigh and Laisa at our next production meeting—with the body-builder taking up a lot of room at the conference table while taking notes—and of course Gideon too busy looking at his iPhone.

As we summed up our final two shoots, I said as off-handedly as possible, "So me and Tony had this impromptu long talk. He wants a contract up-front for next season, and he wants his arc expanded from four to seven episodes. I told him we'd discuss it."

Gideon said, "Did you see his reviews on _____'s site?", mentioning a strangely powerful Twitter critic. "You guys should write Tony an arc for a dozen episodes." Laisa agreed. Only Ash said nothing…

. . . until we left for dinner out with the Steinkerques afterwards, then she said: "Why did you cut me off at the knees, Noah? I had Nick _____ sewed up."

"Your information was wrong, Ash. Tony was going nowhere near London. I asked, and he said: 'Rudii can move here, if she wants to. If not, tough-titty. Plenty of models in the sea.'" To placate Ashleigh, I added, "And since you have Nick sewed up, let's write a role for him and have them both in the series. It's big enough to handle two young machos."

But I'd crossed her, and she fumed. I mean, the heat radiated off her head—like a convertible's hood on an August day on a two-lane road in West Texas. But she said nothing.

Not then. Even so, right after that, the subtle changes occurred between us, and those soon became unmistakable.

Since it seems to be my destiny to lose just when I am winning something—*viz* Ham and Scott, not to mention others—the night we received the Best Series Emmy for *Oratorio* season two was the night Ash and I had our first and last real argument.

She moved downstairs, I remained upstairs, and we only spoke through lawyers.

Cut to two years later. I was at one of those West Hollywood places that change like clockwork every three years that people in the business flock to for lunches, this one with an indoor-outdoor central area.

My guest had left, and I'm paying when I notice Ashleigh at a centre-table. Of course, we'd spoken and seen each other as we exchanged kids from what was now her house to my Malibu place. It was polite. Unlike Jimmie and Scott, our divorce was easy, respectful, unemotional, forever.

The light was soft, falling angled through a skylight onto her. At first glance she looks wonderful and my heart broke a little all over again, just as it had almost every day of our separation, breaking anew over all that we'd built and then lost.

She's having a one-on-one with a younger man who has "writer" written all over him. Probably from back East. I knew for a fact she was involved producing shows, although not with me, nor with any of our former collaborators.

The writer excused himself and got up, and I was tempted to go over and say how beautiful she looked. I was up and moving when she got a phone call and answered it, and she ... *changed*. I don't know how else to put it. Her face in profile seemed to set and harden, her eyelids dropped to half-mast, her fingers on the damask tablecloth became like claws. She listened and began to talk into the phone in single words, one after another: rat-a-tat-tat. Then her upper lip curled, and the hair stood up on the back of my neck, and I all but fell down. I had to sit a minute to regroup.

A few minutes later, I bumped into her guest.

"You're _____." I suddenly remembered his name. He was a successful playwright for the stage. "And you're working with Ashleigh now?"

"Not yet. Probably. Why?"

"We used to work together. Just be a little ... cautious with her."

"She seems nice enough. I mean you never really know but ... wait a minute, I've seen you," he said. "You're her ex? Right?"

I grabbed him by his Gap corduroy collar and said, "Forget who I am. You've been warned."

I left him annoyed and flustered. I could see him returning to her table while Alfonso was taking forever to bring me the Tesla, but Ash calmed him. She was always good at calming me down too.

I told myself, *Forget about it Jake. It's Chinatown*, and drove off.

So, both he and I had been warned, hadn't we?

Big slash-cut now to seven months later. I was driving the kids and their nanny home from a five-day weekend in Santa Barbara with my folks. We'd just arrived on the street of our old house.

This was a quiet neighbourhood. Not that day. It was filled with cop-cars and policemen, one of whom was putting up yellow tape.

I got out, and a plainclothes cop challenged me, pad in hand. "You are?"

"What happened?"

"Again! You are?"

"I'm Ashleigh's ex-husband. I've had the children for a week out of town, and it's her week, so I'm returning them."

Heard our neighbour, Mrs. Neidich, talking with the nanny and kids at the SUV back window.

"You'll have to keep the kids a while longer."

"What? Why? Oh my God. Is she okay? Ashleigh!" I yelled, while trying to get inside. "Ash!"

Two uniformed guys stopped me and pulled me over to the side of the house.

The plainclothes cop joined us, pad in hand.

"As a rule, did your ex-wife keep the French doors onto the back open at night?"

"Not when I lived here, I don't think. Why? Was she burgled? Please tell me she's okay."

One of my twins was saying he had to go to the bathroom.

The cop shook his head and then said, "We think that's how the perpetrator entered—through the open French doors. And she was right there."

Ice shot up my spine.

"Daddy, I have to go *now*!" Scottie cried.

I'll bring them into my house," Mrs. Neidich offered.

"You do that," the detective said. "Could you bring them *all* inside?"

She enticed them, saying, "You can all use the bathroom, and I'll make us cookies. Okay?"

My hand had covered my mouth, as if afraid of what it would say next. I unclasped it long enough to utter, "Where is she?"

"A back office that's also a bedroom. With a separate garden. You can't go in. But you'll need to come down to the station and to the coroner's office too, later on."

That's when I knew for sure.

"Was this a bad divorce?" he asked.

"No," I mumbled, half-sobbing, "It was mutual . . . We remained on good terms. Mostly for the children."

I couldn't believe it was happening.

I must have been a real mess, because a nice policewoman came over to me, took me aside, and blocked me from onlookers while I proceeded to break down.

When I finally got my bearings again, I asked, "Is it okay if I get the kids settled back in my place before I come to . . . where? The Beverly Hills police station? And can the nanny get in to retrieve the kids' stuff they'll need?"

"Of course. But she will have to be escorted."

"It'll all be upstairs. It's nowhere near that . . . room."

According to my dozens of friends and associates who called, texted, and e-mailed, and were all so happy I hadn't been anywhere near the place, Ashleigh's death occurred after midnight in the downstairs second drawing room, which apparently had become her bedroom. I'd not followed her career arc closely, so I was shocked when they more or less agreed that she'd screwed over so many people that they were not surprised by her awful end.

Luckily, all four kids and the *au pair* were with me that entire week at the beach house, but even so it had to be traumatic for them.

Sometime after that, while re-reading my notes from Alexandra Laws Pfaff, I remember thinking, *Maybe* someone else *was there that night, besides Ben Alligham and that truck driver? Maybe someone actually* forced *his car into the front of that twelve-wheeler*?

Our friends fondly recall our parties, and ask what I'll do with the big house.

I don't really know and so far, I can afford to be indecisive. It is historic, and soon enough the City of Beverly Hills might decide to designate the house as such, and then I would not be able to tear it down at all. But the place is closed-up for now, with one room in particular sealed off from both ends

I send Alexandra a gift on the anniversary of her visit. She calls me, and we chat each time for a few minutes.

I think she's getting a little dotty, and I know she's confined to a wheelchair. The last time we spoke, she said, "I've been quite resourceful, Noah, for one so limited in motion. I was able to locate a person who will do almost anything for a certain sum of money."

It didn't strike me at the time to ask what she meant. She didn't mention it during the next call, and not long after she died, leaving a trust fund for my childrens' college tuition. She didn't trust that my luck in television will last.

I'm socking away money too. The twins and the girls are growing nicely, and some day they may even have a stepmother, since I'm dating again. They know her and like her.

No, I'm more afraid that one of the kids will eventually get into that house, while I'm away or after I'm gone.

That's why I'm writing this, for them, in case anything happens to me.

Because I know they're still in there: Frances Lodge Bellamy, and Ben Allingham and, who knows, probably Ashleigh too. And once sunset arrives, there they sit or stand with highball glasses or Bordeaux glasses in hand, in the second drawing room garden. They gossip, just gossip, because that's all it takes, really.

They gossip a mile a minute.

NICHOLAS ROYLE

DISPOSSESSION

NICHOLAS ROYLE is the author of three short story collections—*Mortality, Ornithology* and *The Dummy and Other Uncanny Stories*—and seven novels, including *Counterparts, Regicide* and *First Novel*. He has edited more than twenty anthologies and is series editor of *Best British Short Stories*.

Reader in Creative Writing at the Manchester Writing School at Manchester Metropolitan University, he is head judge of the Manchester Fiction Prize. Nightjar Press, which he founded to publish signed, limited-edition short stories in chapbook format, celebrates its tenth birthday in 2019.

"I wrote 'Dispossession' for a planned Joel Lane tribute anthology, *The Dispossessed and Other Weird Tales*, but the project hit a rocky patch and looked unlikely to happen, and I needed a story to send to Michael Kelly for *Shadows & Tall Trees*.

"I thought if Joel was looking down from above he wouldn't mind, and so I pulled the story. My title had been partly inspired by the title of the anthology and partly by fears I was exploring in other stories at the time."

THREE MONTHS AGO I moved to a new place and, while my new flat more than meets my needs, I'm finding that the old one is increasingly on my mind. I can't dismiss this as nostalgia, because I really wasn't ever happy there, but I can't stop thinking about the old place. The other night I even dreamed about it.

For a number of reasons, I was glad to move. I was moving from a rented studio, which was too small for me to have my children to stay, into a three-bedroom flat that I was buying. My children, who had never used the keys I had had cut for them for the old place, would get a bedroom each, which they would use two nights a week and alternate weekends, according to the agree-ment with my ex, and I would be able to get the rest of my stuff out of storage.

The flat is on the top floor of a three-storey development dating from the 1950s. There are a number of blocks, each comprising six or ten or a dozen flats, separated by communal gardens. I've filled the flat with cheap units and shelved my books according to size, doubling up where possible. I don't need to know how to find particular titles. I haven't read a book in two years. Yet I can't bring myself to give them away. I've bought new clothes for the children and these are stored in drawers in their respective bedrooms.

My son's bedroom is situated at the back of the flat, his windows offering a view across a courtyard to the rear of another block. You get the same view from the bathroom, if you open the frosted windows, and the kitchen, which is where I keep my binoculars, in an eye-level cupboard to the right of the sink. The flat opposite mine has been empty for a week, the soft outlines of shampoo bottles removed from the bathroom window ledge. Two days ago I watched a man painting woodwork in the kitchen. Since then, nothing.

After I moved, I would occasionally walk past my old place on the way to the shops, but, at first, I barely gave it a second glance. Then one day the letting agents rang me to say that the new tenant was having difficulties with the phone company and would I be kind enough to give them my old number, so they could give it to her and she could tell the phone company what it was. It seemed a funny way around to do things, but I looked it up. A couple of days later they called again, wanting to know if I had had broadband installed in the old flat without encountering any major difficulties. I said that I had and I named the provider.

The thing about the letting agents was that we had parted on bad terms. They had complained about the state of the flat when I moved out and surrendered my keys. Citing patches of peeling paint on the walls, soot on the ceiling and stubborn stains on the carpet, they had refused to return my deposit in its entirety and had informed me of their intention to deduct certain amounts, which were itemised on a memo that came attached to a tetchy e-mail. I challenged their proposal, pointing out that the paint had peeled from the walls only where it had been behind furniture, which suggested to me that either damp or poor decorating was to blame. Also, although I had not told them this, when I had emptied the flat, I had gone round covering up the nail holes in the walls with Tipp-Ex. I hadn't anticipated any problems with the refunding of the deposit.

After an exchange of unfriendly e-mails, they agreed to halve the amount they intended to charge for cleaning and redecorating. I felt by that point that I had no choice but to give in.

So, when the agents started phoning me with regard to the difficulties the new tenant was experiencing, I didn't particularly welcome the contact. I felt like offering to be put directly in touch with her.

But it got me thinking and it reminded me of how I'd felt when I had just moved in, two years earlier. The flat had been unfurnished, superficially clean, but I had found myself wanting there to be some kind of trace left by the previous tenant, some clue to his or her identity. I didn't feel that he or she could be held accountable for the curtain rail that became detached from its fittings if you opened the curtain too far on one side, or for the lumpy lino in the kitchen. I found the trace I was looking for in the wardrobe cupboard in the hall. In it I found a number of empty hangers from mid-range high street fashion stores, some marked 14, others 16. I imagined a young woman, her weight fluctuating over the months or years that she lived there. I wondered what she might have looked like. I wondered where she might have gone to. I wondered if she ever gave a thought to the place she had left behind.

I was grateful for her clothes hangers, having brought few with me from the house I had shared with my ex. I remember the estate agent who showed me around. It takes special skill to show someone around a studio flat. But this studio was the best of a fairly bad bunch that I had viewed over the previous week. I remember looking at him when he had shown me a smaller one, where the kitchen was so small the position of the cooker prevented two of the cupboard doors from being opened.

The landlord will remove the cooker if you don't want it, the estate agent said.

I said nothing in response to this.

It will get harder to find a good place in the new year, he said.

Why's that, I asked?

Because couples struggle through Christmas together, he explained, and realise they can't do it any more. Come January the men are out looking for flats.

I studied the expression on his face—scorn? Despair?—and tried to work out if he, too, was living in a rented studio. He hadn't once looked me in the eye.

I took the next flat he showed me—the studio with the clothes hangers whose previous owner had, I imagined, jumped from size 14 to size 16 as she had become unhappier, alone in the flat and perhaps alone in the world, and then back to 14 once she had made up her mind to move out.

I put up a picture in my daughter's room. A framed collage of images of butterflies cut out of magazines that she made in Year 9. I also have a go at fixing the window blind, which has been catching on one side. I open the top drawer of her chest of drawers and look through her tights and socks and underwear. I take out a pair of tights and hold them to my nose—they smell only of fabric softener—then drop them on the floor.

In my son's room, I go through his football shirts. I take one out and unfold it on his bed.

The intercom buzzes and I go to the door to pick up.

Post, says a voice.

I press the button and hear the door open down below in the communal hallway. I wait until I hear it shut again and then open my door and go down to see if there's anything for me or if, as is usually the case, I was simply the only one at home to let in the postman. In my pigeonhole I find a padded envelope.

In the kitchen I put the package down on the table while I get out bread, chopping board and bread knife, and cheese from the fridge, and make myself a sandwich. While I eat this, I open the padded envelope to reveal a proof copy of a forthcoming novel. I take the book into the living room and find room for it on a shelf full of similar-sized books. My eye briefly lingers on the spines of the books. Novels, short story collections, a non-fiction book about the night, an anthology of sea stories. An academic study of a certain school of French literature. A book about underground films. All they have in common is size.

In the old flat, there had been room for no more than two bookcases. I had taken books relating to what I was working on at the time, plus a couple of series for teenagers that I was in the process of collecting. I had bought one or two of those titles originally, secondhand, for my son, as I had enjoyed them at his age, but he had lost interest in reading, so I had carried on buying them, from charity shops and second-hand bookshops, partly out of nostalgia and partly out of a dimly understood need to collect them on my son's behalf, even though he had no interest in them.

Sometimes I would hear voices in the old flat. The first time I heard them, I couldn't figure out where they were coming from. My first thought was from beyond the wall behind my bed, but when I worked out that that was outside—and my flat was at the top of the converted house—I ruled that out. Then I thought I could hear them better if I approached the wall where my desk was, but I pretty soon ruled that out, too. I only figured it out by accident. I opened the door to the boiler cupboard to get the vacuum cleaner out and there I heard voices. I realised they were the same voices, still quite muffled, but I could hear them better in the boiler cupboard than anywhere else in the flat. So, from that point on, I kept the vacuum cleaner under my desk, leaving enough room in the boiler cupboard for me to stand in there and close the door behind me.

One of my then neighbours—either the woman in her forties from the floor below or the younger woman from the flat just down the half-landing from mine—was talking to a man. They sounded like a couple. The conversations were banal, but I found the cadences of their speech, the rhythms of their dialogue, soothing, lulling. I could spend up to an hour in there at a time, sometimes longer.

I'm in the kitchen bending down in front of the washing machine, loading it with my few items of laundry. I shake powder into the tray, then add conditioner, and close everything up. I pause a moment before pressing the start button. My knees pop as I stand up. I go to my bedroom and have a quick look around, but it doesn't appear as if I have missed anything. In my daughter's room I pick up a pair of tights from the floor and there's a football shirt on my son's bed that could do with a wash. Back in the kitchen I open the machine, add these items, slam the door and set it going.

I stand up again and look out of the window. The windows opposite are bathed in wintry sunlight. In the ground-floor flat directly across from mine—two below the empty flat—a young man and a woman are standing in the kitchen facing each other. His upper body is leaning forward, while she backs off slightly. He points, jabbing at the air between them, his shirt buttoned at the cuff. But he is the one who leaves the room. She remains where she is, rocking slightly to and fro, then turns on her heel towards the sink and the window. She rests her hands on the edge of the sink. I lower the binoculars for a moment to check that my kitchen light isn't switched on and when I lift them back up again she is pouring herself a glass of water from the tap.

In the kitchen of our family house, the four of us had sat down at the kitchen table. My wife and I—was she already my ex? Effectively, yes. I had told her. We had talked. It had been a few weeks—my ex and our two children.

I heard myself saying banal and unspeakable things.

Everything else will stay the same, I finished.

I stressed this point. We both did, my ex backing me up for the sake of the children.

My daughter looked faintly embarrassed, while my son's expression darkened quickly. I had never seen such a swift and dramatic transformation in a person's face. Something fluttered inside my chest. Desperate hopes revealed as vain. The worst that could happen, now happening. I was destroying my life and possibly theirs. My son got up and walked out of the room.

The washing machine signals the end of its cycle with a high-pitched beep. I open the door and pull the wet clothes out and drop them into the basket. I drape shirts, T-shirts and my son's football top on hangers and hang these on door handles around the flat, a 14 here, a 16 there. Smaller items, including my daughter's tights, I fold neatly over the radiators.

Job done, I pull out my phone and look at it. I realise I'm frowning.

I text my ex, reminding her it's a Thursday and I'm wondering where the children are.

She doesn't reply.

I call her.

What do you want?

It's Thursday, I say.

Don't, she says. Just stop it.

She hangs up.

I go into the children's rooms. They are very tidy. Really very tidy.

I find myself back in the kitchen looking at the flats opposite. The top flat is still empty. The middle flat is in darkness. In the kitchen of the ground-floor flat a single glass sits on the worktop.

I look around my own kitchen. The bread left out, going stale. The bread board. The bread knife.

I turn to the kitchen drawers and open the second one down. I rummage around and come up with the keys I'd had cut for the children and hadn't handed in to the letting agents.

I walk over to the old flat, the contents of my bag rattling with each step. I look up at the window, which is dark. Maybe she is out in one of the local bars or restaurants, or at work, or studying in a university library, or away for a spell. I press the buzzer and wait for a response, which doesn't come. I use my key to gain entry. The entrance hall looks the same. I see some junk mail addressed to me lying on the floor beneath the pigeonholes and I leave it there as I head for the stairs. On the half-landings I pass doors that were once familiar to me. A television can be heard behind one of them; cooking smells emanate from another. When I reach the top of the building I stand with my ear to my door. It still feels like my door. The key turns in the lock and I enter.

The flat is warm. She can't be far away. It doesn't look like it did in my dream; the bed is smaller, but it's in the same place. She has a cheap white desk where I used to have my sofa and coffee table. Her TV is where my desk was.

I hear footsteps on the stairs, a key in the lock. I cross the ten feet to the boiler cupboard in the time it takes her to open the door, and while she is closing the door to the flat I close the door to the boiler cupboard behind me.

I hear her moving around, even above the suddenly deafening sound of my heartbeat. I can also hear voices coming from behind the boiler. In my dream there had been a large window in the kitchen allowing access to a grassy slope. I had jumped from tussock to tussock, feeling buoyant and free.

I close my hands around the contents of my bag and try to listen only to the voices.

REGGIE OLIVER

THE ENDLESS CORRIDOR

REGGIE OLIVER is an actor, director, playwright and award-winning author of fiction. Published work includes six plays, three novels, eight volumes of short stories (including *Mrs. Midnight*, winner of Children of the Night Award for best work of supernatural fiction) and the biography of Stella Gibbons, *Out of the Woodshed*.

His stories have appeared in over seventy anthologies and three "selected" editions of his stories have been published: *Dramas from the Depths* (Centipede Press, 2010), *Shadow Plays* (Egeus, 2012) and *The Sea of Blood* (Dark Regions, 2015).

Recent work includes the novel *The Boke of the Divill*, the collections *Holidays from Hell* and *The Ballet of Dr. Caligari and Madder Mysteries*, and *The Hauntings at Tankerton Park and How They Got Rid of Them*—a children's book with over 80 illustrations by the author.

Oliver's story 'Flowers of the Sea' was included in the *Folio Book of Horror Stories* (The Folio Society, 2018) amongst such classic luminaries of the genre as Poe, Lovecraft and M.R. James. He is also an illustrator, and has completed illustrations for a deluxe edition of Susan Hill's classic ghost story *The Woman in Black* from Centipede Press. The author is currently working on the second volume of his epic horror trilogy, "The Dracula Papers".

"Peter Scupham is a fine poet, a dealer in antiquarian books and a delightful man," says Oliver. "He lives, with his books, his cats, and his partner Margaret Steward in an exquisite, small 16th century manor house in Norfolk. It is always a moment of excitement for me when one of his catalogues comes through the post.

"On this occasion, I was particularly thrilled because he had on offer, for a very reasonable sum, a first edition of one of my favourite books: *Recollections of an Excursion to the Monasteries of Alcobaca and Batalha* by William Beckford (Richard Bentley, 1835). Beckford was the author of that superlative early Gothic horror novel, *Vathek*, but this book, despite its clumsy title, is equally brilliant in its way, even though it is only a travelogue. I had given away my previous copy to a friend and couldn't get it back, so I had an excuse for buying it.

"When it arrived, a beautiful leather-bound edition, I re-read it with such pleasure that it proved the starting point and inspiration for this story; that, and other things that were in my mind at the time. But the title and central idea came almost immediately. I wondered why.

"It was only after finishing the story, and on re-reading Beckford's book yet again, that I saw it had come directly from the opening sentence of the sixth chapter: 'I rose early, slipped out of my pompous apartment, strayed about endless corridors—not a soul stirring...'"

B EFORE MY BOOK about him was published you could be excused for never having heard of William Sotheran. God, that sounds arrogant! I apologise—no, I don't! It's a fact.

If you *had* known about him before then, it would almost certainly have been through an eight-line quotation of his verse in a celebrated essay by Thomas de Quincey entitled 'Of Art and Madness' in *The Edinburgh Review* of December 1823:

I roamed the endless corridor of Fame,
To seek a niche, a statue, or a name;

But none could find that might belong to me:
I wondered if I was, or e'er could be.
We have our hour and leave a fleeting trace:
A stone-carved name, a tear upon a face;
Even before our mortal frame's decay
The stone has cracked, the tear is wiped away.

These lines and a few more besides can sometimes be found in old anthologies or books of quotations. They come from a poem of about 1,500 lines entitled 'The Castle of Oblivion' which was published in 1817, the year of its author's death.

That date, 1817, I am almost ashamed to say, was what really started it. If you are, like me, a young academic, at the start of her career, you will be all too aware of the need to publish. You simply cannot climb the greasy pole in the world of scholarship without having at least one "seminal study" to your name. In addition, it has become increasingly necessary for you to have what is called "impact"; in other words you must make a discovery or come up with an idea that is noticed in the world beyond higher education. An article in one of the broadsheet Sunday papers, or better still a radio or television programme, preferably with you as presenter, will do the trick. Then you will become an asset to your university or college; you will be valued; you will be promoted. Fail to make an impact and you become expendable. That is why I embarked on a study of the poet William Sotheran, with the bi-centenary of both his death and the publication of his major work looming.

I lecture in English Literature at Wessex University and I specialise in the Romantics. As you can imagine, the subject has been fairly well covered. You can't move for studies of Byron, Keats, Shelley, Coleridge, Wordsworth and the like. The trick is to break new ground, to find some minor but significant figure who has not been "done" before. So I thought my luck was in when a couple of years ago I stumbled on Sotheran.

Briefly, William Sotheran (1793-1817) was the younger son of a baronet, Sir Selwyn Sotheran. He was well connected, his mother being a Wellesley and a sister of the Duke of Wellington. It was perhaps from her side of the family that he inherited the urge to excel from an early age, which he did. At the age of eighteen he composed a tragedy in verse, 'Belisarius', which showed such promise that it was accepted for performance at Covent Garden with John Philip Kemble in the title role. (It lasted three nights.) At Oxford he continued to write verse, and, after Oxford, took holy orders, the traditional career choice of the aristocratic younger son. But he seems to have been of a restless temperament, and in 1816 he embarked on a tour of the continent, then recovering from the Napoleonic wars. Shortly after his return in January 1817, he began to show signs of mental instability. Then in August of that year while travelling by mail coach from London to Bath to take up a position of curate in the parish of Fonthill, he made an unprovoked attack on a woman with whom he happened to be travelling. Family influence saved him from criminal prosecution, and he was confined to a private asylum where he died a few months later from causes unknown. Syphilitic dementia has been put forward as a possible cause.

Shortly before his death, his best known work, 'The Castle of Oblivion', was published. I won't go into detail; you will have to read it yourself, because I genuinely think it is worth reading. I am not promoting it simply to further my academic career. But if you are going to understand or believe what happened to me I have to say something about it. De Quincey, in his famous essay, while admiring it, obviously believed it to be the product of an unbalanced mind, but I am not so sure. True, the poem was published while Sotheran was in an asylum, but we have no idea exactly when he wrote it, though a rather oblique reference in the poem to Waterloo and Napoleon's final exile fixes the date of composition as no earlier than 1815.

It is in the form of an allegorical epic. The hero, sometimes referred to as "the Poet", but in other parts of the poem speaking in the first person, is in the process of climbing a mountain which in one passage is called Parnassus. It is clear that the actual mountain in Greece of that name is not intended, and that *Parnassus* is used for its mythical association with Apollo and the Muses. The Poet meets with various adventures on his way up and, when he thinks he is very near the summit, he suddenly finds that the whole of the top of the mountain is crowned by a great and ancient fortress, the eponymous *Castle of Oblivion*. The poet enters the castle and there things get very weird indeed. The poem begins to resemble a contemporary Gothic novel of the most lurid kind, and the hero has a succession of horrific and bizarre escapades involving flying skeletons, giant toads dressed as monks, strange shifts in perspective, and, worse still … No! You'll just have to read it for yourself! Eventually the poet makes his escape but the experience has shattered him and he retires to, as Sotheran puts it, "a hermitage obscure", there to live out the rest of his life, the final couplets reading:

> *Down lonely paths in some sequestered glade*
> *Where yew trees cast their melancholy shade*
> *He wanders now, a neighbour of the dead*
> *His deeds dishonoured and his verse unread.*

It is on the basis of the episodes in the castle that De Quincey decided that 'The Castle of Oblivion' must be the work of someone who was already insane. Nowadays our view of what is sane and what is not is more nuanced and, besides, I think I can grasp a kind of meaning behind all that strangeness. Or I thought I could. Maybe. Where was I?

Well, it is almost two years ago now since I began seriously researching Sotheran, and, almost immediately, I had the most extraordinary piece of luck. Luck? Was it luck? Oh, hell, judge for yourselves!

I had gone to London to visit the British Library, which holds the only extant printed copy of Sotheran's tragedy 'Belisarius'. It's pretty hard going, as most verse dramas from the early 19th century are, though it is an astonishingly accomplished piece of work for an eighteen year old. The only sign of real dramatic life comes in the final act, when the great Byzantine general Belisarius is seen blind, forgotten and disgraced, begging at the Pincian Gate in Rome. (This was a popular legend beloved of painters and opera composers: history tells a different story, but never mind.) His last speech ends as follows:

For Time, the only conqueror at last,
Extinguishes the lamp of glorious fame
And with a shrug of his great sable robe
Enfolds the world in universal night. (He expires.)

Even in this early work Sotheran seems to have had an almost pathological obsession with fame and the transience of reputation. We imagine it is only our age that is celebrity obsessed, but we are wrong. I was beginning to think that I had the key to his character and art. I made notes; I jotted down quotations. I experienced the thrill that all academics feel when they believe they have a thesis, an original focus for their studies—a book!

I emerged from the British Library at around five. It was an inky October evening. The sky hung low and threatened rain; in spite of which I was feeling rather exultant. Then, as I was crossing the Concourse with the great bronze statue of Newton in it, a male voice just behind me said:

"Hey, madam! You dropped this!" and a grubby copy of the *Daily Mail* was thrust into my hand.

Madam! I am thirty-two; I am unmarried and I have never been called "madam" in my life before. And I never read the *Daily Mail*! Nobody at Wessex University would allow themselves to be seen dead with the *Daily Mail*: it's *The Guardian* or nothing.

I caught only a brief glimpse of the man who had given me the paper. He looked like some sort of tramp. I had an impression of lank, straggling hair over a long rusty black greatcoat and dark, lugubrious eyes. By the time I had recovered myself sufficiently to repudiate the doubtful gift, he had shuffled off somewhere. I might have thrown the wretched newspaper into a nearby bin, only I had a long train journey back to Wessex ahead of me and I felt in need of some light reading after the adolescent glooms of 'Belisarius'.

As it turned out, what with the crowds on the Underground, a delay in a tunnel, and a consequent rush to catch the 5:30 from Paddington, it was only when I was safely on the train to Morchester that I had the leisure to look at my *Daily Mail*. I began to leaf through it irritably, now thoroughly angry that I had meekly accepted it from a total stranger. To add to my annoyance, I noticed that it wasn't even today's newspaper—it was two days old. I was just about to throw it away when my eye caught a headline.

NONE OF YOUR "FRACKING" BUSINESS SAYS PEER

As it happens, my partner Julia is head of Environmental Studies at Wessex, and so naturally I take an interest in such matters.

Apparently a certain Lord Glimham was allowing a company to prospect for shale gas on his estate and the locals, assisted by various environmental groups, were objecting strongly. Glimham had responded to their protests dismissively by saying that it was "nobody else's ******* business" and this had inflamed the situation still further. A photograph of his Lordship showed an overweight, red-faced, truculent looking person of about fifty in a tweed Norfolk jacket; an easy man to hate, I thought. Then, further down the page a paragraph made my heart jump.

> In the nearby village of Glimham Parva there have been various demonstrations. Lord Glimham's effigy has been burnt on the Green and the inn sign of the local pub, The Sotheran Arms, has been defaced, Sotheran being Lord Glimham's family name.

Could it be . . . ? I got out my tablet and began to Google frantically. Yes, it was the same family. William's elder brother George had been a cabinet minister in Sir Robert Peel's 1841 administration and was consequently raised to the peerage. He took his title from the family estates at Glimham. The present Lord Glimham was the fifth Baron and still lived at the ancient family seat of Glimham Hall, where William Sotheran had been raised. Could there still be papers relating to William Sotheran in the ancestral home?

As soon as I got back to my flat in Morchester I began to compose a letter to Lord Glimham. It was my partner Julia who suggested that I should gently hint that it might improve his Lordship's tarnished image if it were known that he was helping me in my researches. I sent the letter on University of Wessex headed notepaper but I included my own mobile number and e-mail address.

To my amazement, only two days after I had sent the letter, I had a phone call on my mobile.

"Glimham here. What's all this about William Sotheran?"

The voice was loud, braying, assertive—why do posh people have such loud voices?—but I detected a certain hesitancy, a vulnerability even, under the bluster. Arrogance is nearly always a carapace. Within a few minutes I found I was being invited down to Glimham the following Friday. When I told Julia about it, all excitement, she looked at me quizzically.

"You're not going to leave me, are you, for this William Sotheran?"

It was a joke, of course, and we both laughed, but I thought that Julia spoke not entirely in jest.

At the gates of the Glimham estate I encountered a huddle of protesters watched over by a single glum policeman. There was a smattering of young people, but most of them were very middle-class retired types with grey hair. They had Thermos flasks and camp stools with them for rest and refreshment. They shouted "No more fracking!" at me as I passed through the gates and onto the long drive up to the house. I felt vaguely guilty that I had not responded to them in some way.

I drove through a mixture of park and farmland until, in a dip, I found Glimham Hall. It was not an architectural gem: a plain Queen Anne box of red brick, like a doll's house, with a few ill-advised Victorian additions and excrescences. As soon as I was parked on the gravel drive in front of the Victorian limestone portico, Lord Glimham in his green tweed Norfolk jacket emerged to greet me. I had taken the trouble to arrive precisely at the time agreed.

I had not expected to like Glimham, and I didn't, but at least you knew where you were: some way beneath him admittedly. He treated me rather as if I were a high-class plumber come to look at his drains. He ushered me into the drawing room where his wife, a skeletal blonde who might once have been beautiful, offered me a small cup of coffee and then never spoke again.

"To tell the truth," said Glimham who was not one for polite preliminaries. "we don't talk much about William in the family." It was as if William Sotheran were still around, a disgraced uncle perhaps. "But I think we have some papers relating to him. Do you suppose they could be valuable?"

"Very much so," I said. I knew that he was talking of commercial value and I meant value of another kind, but I did not enlighten him.

"Nobody seems to realise how much it costs to keep a place like this going. I'm hanging on by the skin of my teeth. That's what those unspeakably ghastly people at the gate can't understand. I don't want a lot of frackers all over my land, any more than they do, but I'm at the end of my tether. If the fracking chaps don't come up with the goods I'll have to sell up. Glimham has been in the family for over 300 years, you know."

I nodded sympathetically: it was a point of view.

I had barely finished my coffee when he was taking me through to "the library", a long room lined floor to ceiling with bookcases above oak *muniment* cupboards. Apart from a shelf of Dick Francis thrillers and sporting manuals, none of the books looked as if they had been read or even handled for 100 years or so.

Glimham pointed to a desk on which reposed a number of deed boxes.

"Funny thing," he said. "I had a scout around before you came, to see what there was about old William. Thought I'd have a devil of a job finding anything, but my black Lab Stephen began snuffling and pawing at one of those cupboards." He pointed to a row of *muniment* cupboards. "So I unlocked it and these boxes practically fell out. Inside, family papers and stuff about William. Got it in one, thanks to a Labrador! Old Steve's a bloody good gun dog; but I never imagined he was keen on literature. Eh? Eh?" He seemed immensely pleased by his joke and I was happy to join in the laughter. I was very excited by this time. "Well, I'll leave you to it. Yell if you want anything. Serena, the wife, will be around somewhere." And he quitted the library.

The papers were in complete disorder. Wills, bills, deeds, letters, even old newspaper clippings had been crammed into boxes and forgotten. I was as frustrated by the confusion as I was thrilled by the occasional serendipitous discovery.

Details of William Sotheran's life emerged haphazardly. A long account of Sotheran's assault on the woman in the carriage written by a lawyer for the Sotheran family revealed that his frenzied attack seemed to have been triggered by the lady taking out a small hand mirror from her reticule and scrutinising herself in it. A letter from the keeper of the asylum to which he was confined as a result of this incident writes to the family to say that:

> His conduct is generally sober and gentlemanly, unless he finds himself in proximity with a looking glass, upon which he becomes extremely agitated and sometimes violent. On being asked why this harmless domestic item should occasion such alarm, he replied mysteriously that it was not so much what he saw in a mirror that troubled him as what he did *not* see. I have pressed him to explain further, but he will not.

I found also fragments of his writing, early drafts of some of his poems, all in the same hand which I took to be his. But undoubtedly the most interesting and valuable manuscript of his that I found was in prose. It appeared to be an account of his travels abroad in 1816. Some of it consists of jottings of dates and places, along with a few descriptive notes, but there are longer passages in the form of a journal as well. I had the feeling that he had intended to work it up into a publishable work, but circumstances prevented him. At the head of the manuscript, he tries out various titles: 'The Wandering Poet', 'The Bard Abroad' and 'Childe William's Pilgrimage', this last heavily crossed out. Perhaps he felt that the nod towards Lord Byron's recent work (which, notoriously, made him famous overnight) to be too slavish.

Towards the end of this manuscript there is a passage of sustained narrative, parts of which I must quote:

> My uncle Sir Henry Wellesley [British Ambassador to Spain at the time] received me kindly. He told me that thanks to his brother and my Uncle, the Duke of

Wellington, to whom Spain owed a great debt for its liberation from the Corsican Tyrant, I was to be in high favour with the Spanish people, its court and its nobility. I expressed my wish to see the wonders of this great country and, in particular, its monasteries and religious institutions which, as an ordained priest of the church, albeit of England and not Rome, must interest me greatly. That my concern was more romantic than religious, that I had a yearning to behold:

> *The Horrid crags by toppling convent crown'd*
> *The cork-trees hoar that clothe the shaggy steep...*
> [Byron. 'Childe Harold's Pilgrimage' I.19]

I concealed from my noble kinsman.

Within a few days he had assigned me to the most noble Marquis de Santa Cruz and his brother, the Grand Prior of San Isidore, as my conductors and companions. Far from being reluctant to the task, they seemed most eager to oblige. That their court and ecclesiastical duties were so light, or so wearisome, that they had the leisure and the eagerness to conduct a young English gentleman around the monasteries of Spain was a source of great astonishment to me, but my uncle informed me that it had been the wish of His Majesty himself, King Ferdinand VII, that I should be so honoured. The Marquis was a small meagre man, somewhat in awe of his much larger wife from whom he was doubtless happy to escape. His younger brother, the Grand Prior, was built on an altogether grander scale as befitted his rank. As neither gentleman was anxious to forego an atom of the comforts and conveniences habitual to their stations in life, we set off accompanied by a great array of carriages, mule-drivers, grooms and acolytes, together with my servant Marston and my Arabian steed, Salamanca, a present from my esteemed Uncle, the Duke. We formed altogether a caravan

which, camels and dromedaries excepted, would have cut
no unworthy figure on the route to Mecca.

There is much more in the same ironic style, but I want to cut to
an incident a little further on in the journal.

Our reception by the monks of Alcala had exceeded even
the Grand Prior's expectations, and we set out late that
morning for Guadalajara with heavy hearts and even fuller
stomachs. It was a hot day, and I found the interior of the
carriage oppressive, and its close air, perfumed by the
bodily exhalations of my noble companions, offensive.
While they were disposed to sleep or, as my Lord Prior,
expressed it to "silent prayer and meditation", I was for air
and exercise. I therefore asked permission of my
conductors to take my Arabian and ride ahead of the
caravan. They, with some humorous remarks about the
impetuosity of young Englishmen in midday sun, readily
gave permission. Marston saddled Salamanca and I set
off.

My courser, pampered by the rich provender with which
he had been so abundantly supplied by the good monks of
Alacala, set no bounds to his exertions, even though the
morning sun, unclouded, was approaching its zenith. We
followed the road to Guadalajara as it crossed a wide and
empty plain, at full stretch. Like Phaethon I felt myself:

With flying speed outstrip the Eastern wind
And leave the breezes of the morn behind
[Ovid, *The Metamorphoses: Book 2* ll 158-9
trans Samuel Garth]

Like Phaethon, perhaps, I scorched myself in my
reckless career, but never had I felt an atmosphere so
elastic, so full of life and light. I was on fire with the poetry
of motion and longed to translate my sensations into

deathless verse. At last Salamanca began to tire and I was able to curb his velocity. We found ourselves entering a valley with mountains on either side. One of these mountains I saw was crowned with a fine set of buildings, which I took to be a monastery or convent. Some of it was in a state of decay, but the main part of the structure looked sound, with a handsome bell-tower and a platform on which to walk. I stopped altogether and tied Salamanca to a nearby olive tree in order to gaze in astonishment at this edifice, for it seemed too lonely and remote to sustain a thriving community. No other human dwelling could be seen for miles, and the plain across which I had just ridden so precipitously was almost barren of vegetation. I was just wondering if it could possibly be inhabited when I heard the Angelus sound from the bell tower, and presently I saw a hooded figure appear on the platform. He wore the black cowl of the Benedictine order.

He stood alone and, though he was above a quarter of a mile away and the cowl obscured much of his face, I had the overwhelming impression that he was staring at me. I stared back at him and, for near half an hour, we remained thus occupied in mutual contemplation. What my thoughts were during this mysterious exercise I have no recollection. Then the cowled figure turned and began to glide towards what I took to be the monastery church and was lost from sight. I felt a strong urge to make my way up to the monastery and seek entry, but prudence restrained me. Besides, the heat of the day and my exertions had overwhelmed me with profound exhaustion. I sought the meagre shade of the olive tree to which Salamanca was tethered, sat myself down under it and, despite the discomfort of the stony ground, fell into a doze.

I was awakened suddenly by the cries of the muleteers who formed the advance guard of our little caravan. I roused myself and, with a sore and throbbing head, sought out my guardians' carriage which, for all its foetid atmosphere, would provide me with more comfort and shade than my previous resting-place.

The Marquis and the Grand Prior greeted me with expressions of considerable relief. They had been worried in case I had ridden too far and become lost in this wilderness. I thanked them for their concern, and then pointed out to them the monastery on the hill to their right. I saw the Marquis throw a quick glance at his brother, the Grand Prior, who crossed himself. I asked him to tell me something of the place. The Grand Prior told me that it was the Benedictine Priory of St. Simeon, but that it had been long since abandoned as being too remote and inconvenient even for the most ascetic of that order. Not so I replied, for I had seen a black monk of the Benedictine order standing upon that very platform yonder, and I pointed. Again the brothers exchanged agitated glances, and the Grand Prior shook his head and said I must have been mistaken and perhaps the heat had affected my senses. Might we not at least see if the place was indeed deserted, I asked? No, indeed, the Grand Prior replied, for we were expected at Guadalajara before nightfall and must be on our way.

I did not dispute with him further because I was still suffering from the effects of my exhaustion and the heat. In fact, I was beginning to feel somewhat unwell. I climbed into the carriage, sat down, and almost at once fell into a heavy swoon or sleep and knew no more until we were at the very gates of the Monastery of San Pedro at Guadalajara.

There I remained for several days, though I cannot remember much about it. The heat had so affected me that I fell sick of a fever which disordered my brain. A young novice, Fray Antonio, who had been appointed to look after me, told me after my recovery that, during this period when I was not asleep, I was delirious. During my sickness, according to Fray Antonio, I had risen from my bed many times with the avowed intention of climbing a mountain, and it was all he could do to restrain me. I had insisted to him that the mountain was called "Parnassus" which, he informed me in his simplicity, he had never heard of and was certainly not in Spain. On hearing this, I could not forbear to laugh, which seemed to wound him, but I embraced my novice and told him he was an exceedingly good fellow and we were friends again.

My noble and reverend conductors during this time had deserted me in order to inspect a parcel of land which the Marquis wished to buy, so that I was left to my own devices. This suited me well, for it took me some time to recover my spirits and the monastery at Guadalajara, in fact a Franciscan friary, was quiet and airy, a solemn, plain building, but not destitute of wholesome comforts.

I was nonetheless curious about my experiences, and I asked one of the older friars, Fray Juan, about the Priory of St. Simeon. He seemed reluctant to speak, but when I pressed him, he told me that the place had acquired an evil reputation and had been abandoned before the French came. Guerrillas had for a time used it as a refuge during the war with Napoleon, but even they had deserted it. I asked what was the nature of the evil that had inhabited it, but Fray Juan said only that the isolation of the Priory had turned the heads of its inhabitants, who had previously had the reputation of extreme asceticism and holiness. I asked him if he was quite sure that the Priory was now unoccupied. He hesitated a moment and then said, in a most determined manner, that it was.

I wonder if it was that hesitation which decided me; I cannot say, but I became resolved to visit St. Simeon. My guardians, I was informed, were not to return for some days, so I was at liberty to please myself. I summoned my servant Marston who, during my illness, had gainfully employed himself in a liaison with a local innkeeper's daughter, and commanded him to prepare Salamanca for

an early start the following day. He looked at me doubt-
fully, but when I told him he need not accompany me, he
was all smiles.

I set off the following morning before dawn, so as to
avoid if at all possible the mid-day heat. The day was fresh,
and first light was empurpling the Jarmara Hills as I rode
out. I crossed the Henares river, and gave my Arabian its
head. I felt the bliss of youth and the prospect of glory, yet
why I had embarked upon such a doubtful venture I
cannot say.

The sun was approaching the full blaze of noon when I
came to the valley and the mount of St. Simeon. Whether
it was my own light-headedness or the recuperative powers
of the Franciscan Friary, I was feeling no ill effects from
the heat. I crossed a small stream, allowing Salamanca to
drink his fill from the crystal waters, then, leading my
horse by the reins, I began to climb a wide, stony track
towards the monastery of St. Simeon.

Close to, the edifice seemed more vast in extent and
more ruinous than I had previously supposed. I stopped
before a gateway, half-tumbled, and showing the pock-
marks of shot on its two great pillars, doubtless a memento
of its recent incarnation as a guerrilla fortress. I would have
led my steed through this gate into the inner courtyard,
had not Salamanca utterly refused to proceed a step further
into the monastery precincts. Accordingly, I tied my
Arabian to a gnarled bush that sprang from a confusion of
fallen masonry and proceeded inside alone and on foot.

The structures that I encountered within the monastery
wall had once been magnificent, but were now in a state of
melancholy ruination. Weeds erupted from every crack
and crevice of the marble-flagged pavement, which I
crossed to reach the main entrance. This was in the form of
an elaborately carved ogival arch framing double doors of
oak, bound with elaborate iron arabesques. The wood was
scorched and rotted, and one half of the door had fallen

away from its hinges. Beyond these portals, I could see little light and no trace of human occupation. I could hear nothing but the wind and the beating of my own heart.

I stood for some time at the entrance while I seriously considered my position. It was beginning to seem increasingly probable to me that the vision of the black monk on the monastery battlements a few days before was nothing but a delusion, "proceeding from the heat-oppressed brain". St. Simeon was a deserted ruin, and I should leave this scene of horrid desolation forthwith. Yet there is something that craves the strange sensations that such prospects engender in the poetic soul.

> *. . . This is not solitude: 'tis but to hold*
> *Converse with savage Nature, and view her force unrolled*
> ['Childe Harold' II.25—adapted,
> or misremembered by Sotheran?]

I thrust aside the decaying oak doors and entered a great vaulted hall lit by arched windows now cracked and open to the air beyond, but once richly decked with coloured glass, of which only a few fragments remained to bejewel the ruined pavement. My footsteps echoed, but nothing else was there to stain the silence.

I had come to the foot of a great staircase and was just about to mount it, when I heard a noise behind me. It was no more than an exhalation of breath, but it was as sharp as a sting in that immemorial stillness. I turned, and saw standing some ten feet away from me a cowled figure, the same, I was sure, that I had seen on the monastery battlements a few days before. His hood was up and shadowed most of his face, though I could see that it was lean, clean-shaven and bone-white in colour. The eyes dwelt unseen in cavernous sockets under heavy brows.

In my best halting Spanish I greeted him and begged his pardon for my intrusion. The monk spoke not a word. I bowed and he bowed in return, a low but dignified obeisance, then gestured to me to follow him. I did not venture to engage him in further conversation, suspecting that perhaps his order had bound him to silence.

He led me through a succession of halls and passage-ways, each one vaster, gloomier and more ruined than the last, until finally he ushered me into a great corridor lit by a succession of beams of light coming from circular apertures in the groined vaulting of its roof. The corridor appeared to have no end, and I observed that there were figures coming towards me from a distance. Then I realised that the figures approaching were myself and my ghostly conductor. We had entered from a side door and there were mirrors at either end of the corridor to create the illusion of an infinite recession into a dim obscurity of space.

I turned to ask the monk the significance of this astonishing effect, but he merely put his finger to his lips and, with the gentlest push in the small of my back, propelled me towards one of the mirrors which were of the finest Venetian make, curious possessions for a house of prayer and penitence. When I was within five feet of the glass, he indicated that I should stop and observe what was before me.

I saw myself framed by the mirror; behind me another image of myself, behind that another, and so on in an infinite regression, each one dimmer and gloomier than the last, until I faded into a grey-green obscurity. It was, of course, as I saw it first, a purely natural phenomenon, while at the same time being wholly illusory. I was staring not into infinity, but at a piece of glass backed by a mercury and tin amalgam. The contemplation of this spectacle so absorbed me for some moments that I forgot entirely about the monk, until I noticed that his image could not be seen in the glass. I turned around, and saw that he was standing directly behind me, so that I had obscured any reflection of him.

I was about to make some remark, when he put a finger to his lips again and pointed at the mirror. I turned back and once more, this time with strong inner misgivings, gazed at myself multiplied in the mirror.

The sight I beheld was different from my last encounter with it, though at first I could not discern where the difference lay. By slightly shifting my position in relation to the mirror, I could see more clearly the second image of myself behind the first, and it was then that I received a shock. The second image was the difference. Not only was it dimmer, but it seemed older. At first I tried to dismiss it as a passing illusion, but there were lines on the face which were not present in my most immediate reflection. The hair, moreover was more disordered and had the taint of grey in it. I looked at the third image, which seemed older still. Deep grooves of disappointed hopes curved around my lips and darkened my eyes. My hair was not only greyer but had begun to thin. I blinked, passed my hand over my face, but the illusion—if it was an illusion—remained. Down the endless corridor I stared as each succeeding reflection of myself diminished and decayed until, far in the unreal distance, I could see, faint and small, but still discernible, a grinning skull and skeleton to which a few rags of decayed flesh still adhered. I cried out in horror, and the echo shrieked back at me a thousand times. When I turned from the mirror, I saw that the monk was gone. I was alone.

I ran, and found that I was running towards my infinite self in the opposite direction. This filled me with such terror that it confounded my senses for a while, and some time elapsed before I recovered my wits sufficiently to find the exit from the endless corridor. The monastery had become a labyrinth to my wounded mind, and for a long while I blundered through decaying passages and chambers, and through vast ruined halls, until at last I found my way out into the open air where, to my astonishment, the sun was already beginning to decline into a cloudy and ensanguined west.

I untethered and mounted Salamanca, who seemed to welcome my arrival, and we set off at once on the long ride to Guadalajara. I truly believe that it was my faithful horse, rather than I, who found the way back to our Franciscan sanctuary. We arrived before its gates in starlight, and under a moon without whose guiding illumination Salamanca and I would have been utterly lost.

There is more in this journal, but it is mostly fragmentary. Some of it shows evidence of a deeply troubled mind, but I don't need to quote further. I had taken scans of these and other pages. It was evening, and I had not eaten all day. Needless to say, my hosts offered no refreshment. When I took my leave of Lord Glimham and the skeletal blonde whom I took to be Serena, Lady Glimham, they looked at me searchingly, almost in a concerned way. Glimham asked if the Sotheran papers were "worth selling" and I replied, again ambiguously, that they were of great value.

As I drove my car down towards the entrance gates, the evening sun was low and shone almost directly in my face, masked only by a belt of spidery trees. The protesters were still at the gates, sitting on camp-stools and regaling themselves with sandwiches and Thermos tea. I felt a pang of hunger and, in a momentary loss of concentration, swerved towards them, almost hitting an elderly lady who fell off her stool. The rest shook their fists and yelled at me. To them it had been a deliberate attack on their righteous cause. I felt dazed and confused. It was as if someone or something had taken momentary possession of the steering wheel.

Nothing, except a faint but persistent sense of unease, could restrain the feeling of exhilaration I felt over the next few weeks. I wrote some chapters and a synopsis, then approached a publisher who showed enthusiasm for the project. All was going well, or seemed to be. It was Julia who alerted me to the fact that I was working too hard, lecturing and giving tutorials during the day, writing in the evenings, sparing no thought for myself or others.

My work on Sotheran had almost finished before I paid her any attention.

One evening, on returning from a seminar on Byron, I took a bath. I had begun to pay conscious attention to my exhaustion, but still denied it to the world. A bath, I thought, would dissolve anxieties. I am still young enough to believe in simple remedies.

The area of the bath is surrounded on three sides by mirrors, an idea of Julia's. I have never cared much for the sight of myself naked, and I have always had an aversion to the endless reflection that Sotheran writes about in his memoir. Indeed, the image had preyed upon me rather, and this may explain what appeared to happen next.

The bath had done me good. Cares from the day had dissolved. I rose out of the water and, without giving it much thought, cleared the steam from the mirrors that surrounded me. Before taking my towel, I studied myself in the glass. I had lost weight recently, and was preparing to be pleasantly surprised by what had become of my figure.

The heat of the water had made my skin pinker than usual, and I looked with interest at the infinite recessions of my body in the glass. I found it hard to focus my eyes on the grey-green distance. It was my partner Julia who had put the mirrors up. She liked the paradox of the mirror world, which was at once entirely real and completely false. It was, she said, the simplest and most profound of art installations.

I seemed to be looking at a stranger. It was me, of course, the features were recognisable, but I could claim no ownership over my reflection. The eyes were cold and lustreless—their weariness was ancient. And each succeeding image in the infinitely long line was increasingly strange until, at the apex of the endless vista, I saw something shadowy and utterly alien, with two points of darkness for eyes. Then that thing began to advance, and all sense of perspective collapsed. It was not me at all, but a dark man in a rusty black suit, with a white stock around his throat. He was running down the endless corridor towards me, lank hair waving in a mythical breeze, while my own image shuddered in the vaporous heat. His lugubrious eyes were hungry to possess me, while I was beginning to lose all that I was. I could barely see myself; in a moment I might not exist at all.

A hand on my shoulder; arms around me as I collapsed—it was Julia. She was by me as I recovered, slowly, as far as I am able. I still am, but do not know if I will be. I cannot be what I was: that is certain.

Now I have achieved my "impact". My book, *The Endless Corridor: William Sotheran, Doomed Romantic*, has been published by Bloomsbury, and John Carey has reviewed it favourably in the *Sunday Times*. I have presented a Radio 3 documentary about Sotheran, and my lectureship at Wessex University has been renewed. But Julia walked out on me two days ago, giving no reason, though maybe I can guess. I am chained to a madman. I owe Sotheran, and he is not about to forget my obligation to him. He beckons to me from the Endless Corridor where Fame and Oblivion are one.

STEVE RASNIC TEM

WHATEVER YOU WANT

STEVE RASNIC TEM's latest titles include *Figures Unseen: Selected Stories*, from Valancourt Books, and a middle-grade novel about Halloween, *The Mask Shop of Doctor Blaack*, from Hex Publishers. Forthcoming are two new collections: *Everything is Fine Now*, a collection of his young-adult horror from Omnium Gatherum, and *The Night Doctor & Others* from Centipede Press, collecting the best of his recent horror stories.

"Holidays are complicated emotionally for most of us," Tem says, "and Christmas may be the most complicated holiday of them all. It's a season that promises much, while burdened with a lifetime of regrets and disappointments.

"As children we made our wish-lists of the things we wanted most in the world. As we grew older, we discovered that deciding what you really wanted wasn't as easy as it seemed. Even worse are the wants we can't bring ourselves to admit to, but which always seem to leak out just the same."

THE CHRISTMAS SEASON was impossible to escape, gobbling up more of the calendar with each trip of the world around the sun. This year Trish was appalled to find Christmas aisles in the big box stores just days after the last "Trick or Treat!" of Halloween.

Little Bean was all of three now, but thanks to television able to recognise the holiday for the first time. She'd chattered on and on about "Santy Claws," one of the few clear phrases Trish was able to pick out of a stream of moist gibberish as Little B roamed their small apartment in unrepressed delight... and rage, if Trish ever said *no*. Anger or joy, Little Bean always seemed to be screaming.

Every mother Trish knew said, "Mine did the same thing. They grow out of it." Trish made an effort to believe them. "Don't take it personally." She tried to believe that too, even under a barrage of *I hate you!s*.

"Well, you asked for this." That's what her mother told her. Actually, she hadn't asked for this, not the deadening sameness of motherhood, the isolation of the single mom at the playground, the loss of a future she could now only imagine. Little Bean's dad was supposed to be doing this with her, but he'd wised up, skipped town. She wondered what kind of Christmas *he* was having.

It wasn't that Trish *hadn't* wanted a child. The truth was she just didn't know. And then she had one. And that child would cry and cry as if desperately wanting something she wasn't getting, but Trish had no idea what it was. Was it because Trish secretly hated breast-feeding? Found it painful and somewhat disgusting, her child chewing on her like that? Was it because she'd never wanted to do this, at least not by herself?

Trish had a fleeting notion that one day Little Bean would suddenly start speaking, confessing that she could have told her mother what she had wanted at any time. She just hadn't cared to.

Little Bean wasn't the only person Trish had to please. She had her mother and father, grandparents, friends (at least the few that were left—a bunch had bolted once they realised Trish with a kid was far less fun than Trish without). She had sworn she wasn't going to wait until the last minute to shop, but here she was—Christmas Eve—frantically looking for a parking spot with her child screaming in the back seat.

She drove past the big malls. Their parking lots were full, cars prowling the lanes opportunistically, following shoppers walking out of stores with their arms full. She remembered an old mall farther out, scheduled to be torn down, but remaining open until the end of the holiday. Maybe she'd find unusual things there for the people on her list. They'd be impressed, especially with her having a difficult kid to take care of. It was already late afternoon. Another heavy snow waited in the night. The streets were flooded in steel grey fog.

The road out was poorly-lit, with few houses along the way. The last rays of the setting sun made the distant woods appear on fire. An arc of tree limbs protruding from a snowbank resembled a partially buried giant spider.

Once past the worn-out welcome to the mall sign, construction barriers guided her through the main level of the old shopping complex. Orange cones and plastic webbing blocked everything. She descended a curved road to the basement level, parking crookedly between piles of debris, but so had everyone else. She got out and lifted B from her car seat. Her daughter thankfully was sound asleep. Trish remembered a vast amusement hall on this level. Now the windows were empty and greased.

A dark furry shape in the middle of the sidewalk turned out to be the burnt remains of a Christmas tree, a few soot-blackened balls dangling from its skeletal limbs. She was already feeling discouraged about finding anything good here, but she was running out of time. Too late to shop anywhere else, she was on a mission to find and buy.

Beneath broken concrete the ground moaned as if collapse were imminent. Some cracked exterior steps led to the main level. As darkness filled the risers the steps appeared to float in midair. B weighed almost nothing. When she got to the top she checked the blanket to make sure her daughter was still there. The child's face was pale, but her lips moved, as if whispering secrets Trish was not meant to hear.

Only a few weary-looking shoppers stared into the dimly-lit windows. An older man staggered past her, his overloaded bags hanging down and brushing the snowy sidewalk. His red Christmas sweater bore a giant white clown's face—big googly eyes over the nipples and a misshapen red nose, a wide crooked smile like a rip across the belly. He didn't appear to notice she was there.

There was a manger scene in a display window. Someone had replaced the baby Jesus with a dirty doll's head. The other figures were hunched with filth and looked less-than-human, their tiny faces dismayed. Skinny melting candles on either side leaned with dangerous possibility. A pile of rags on the sidewalk nearby stretched forth a hand clutching a can. The mouth splutter that followed might have been "please!" She gave the genderless arm a wide berth, sure it was a scam. She wanted to think the best of people, but she was never up to the task.

A pile of dirty snow was studded with black stones, a water-logged scarf. It might have just been the remains of a good shovelling, but Trish thought she could make out a face. Dark figures hurried past the mall entrance. Some of them actually ran. "In a hurry for disappointment," she'd often heard her father say.

B stirred as they went through the doors. She thrust her blonde head out of the blanket looking startled. She began to cry, then stopped as she looked around.

"Down," she said, and Trish lowered her to the floor. She clutched three fingers of her mother's hand. Trish felt relieved. Maybe the kid would behave—she needed at least one thing to go right today.

"Toys?" B said weakly, as if afraid of the word.

"No toys today, Bean," Trish replied. "Santa will bring you some tomorrow. We can't be selfish every day—today we shop for other people."

"Santy Claws!"

"That's right, Bean," she replied, distracted. From this angle it was difficult to read the names of the stores. She had no choice but to go down each aisle and find some place still in business.

"Santy!" B cried again, and broke away, running straight ahead into shadows and dim light.

Trish stared for a moment, and then shouted, "Bean! Come back here!" She ran into the murkiness after her, furious. She had absolutely no control over the kid.

They were in some kind of central space, poorly lit, and half of it was blocked off where demolition had already begun. Trish was vaguely aware of a few shoppers circling the area, going in and out of shop doors that opened onto this space. Some were blackened silhouettes, like ambulatory fire victims.

Trish didn't even see the line of children until she ran into the tail end of it, and Bean, waiting with the others. She grabbed onto her little girl and started to pull her away.

"No, Santy!" Bean screamed, squirming.

"Can I help?" The voice was nearby and below her. Trish looked around. A very short old woman in an elf's cap much too big for her head stared up at her.

"I—there's not enough time." Trish was flushed, angry. "There are presents I just *have* to get."

"Leave her here and you can shop. We'll take care of her. She'll visit Santa Claus, and you'll get your shopping done unencumbered."

"Santa Claus?" Trish gazed up the line to its beginning. There was the big chair holding an old man swallowed up by a voluminous red suit. He appeared to be asleep as a small child chattered into his face. Santa's beard was long, but not very full. Large patches appeared to be missing, and that child, leaning so close to the old man, was eating them?

"But I can't just *leave* her here. *Can* I?" She looked back up at Santa. The next child in line crawled up into his unpromising lap. The old man startled, straightening up so quickly the child almost fell. The large reindeer nearby suddenly came to life—someone in costume— and jumped forward, but Santa had already steadied the child with his knobby hands.

"Don't you just *hate* Christmas? I know I do," the elf woman said. "People are *terrible*, and the little brats, aren't they just the *worst* this time of year?" The old woman's grin displayed many missing teeth.

"I . . . well, yes, sometimes." Trish looked down at B, whose eyes were fixed on Santa. "There's just never enough time. And it's not like I get to do anything fun, anything *I* want to do. It's really not fair."

"Do you know what your little girl wants for Christmas?" A new voice, another woman's. Trish turned and was appalled by the towering height of the figure. It was the costumed reindeer from Santa's side—how did she get here so fast? The reindeer suit had brown arms and legs and an enormous white bib covering the torso, a large grotesquely friendly reindeer head with wide-set eyes staring at some distant point in space.

"Everything, everything she sees on TV. She jumps up and down and goes crazy over every single toy commercial. She wants it all." Trish hated the way she sounded, but it was the truth.

"Don't we all," the little old woman said.

"That makes it easy," the voice inside the giant reindeer head replied. "I'll just have Santa tell her she'll get whatever she wants."

"Whatever she wants," Trish repeated. "Well, isn't that great. I'd just settle for getting what I deserve."

"Sometimes it's the same thing, don't you think? Go shop. We'll take care of her. Everything will turn out as it should. I promise. On my oath as a reindeer!"

Trish glanced at Bean, still transfixed, shuffling ahead with the other children. No other parents to be seen. She wouldn't even notice her absence. Her daughter was so self-contained—she cared nothing for Trish at all. "I'll hurry," she said, and turned away.

"Wait!" It was the old woman. Trish turned back around. "What do *you* want for Christmas? We'll put in a word for you with the old man. Anything."

But Trish had no time to think. "Just tell him whatever I want, whatever I deserve." She rushed off, relieved to have a few minutes of shopping time by herself. Bean's dad probably wasn't shopping—he probably wasn't even celebrating Christmas. He was probably just sitting in front of his TV, drinking. Maybe that was sad, but Trish envied him.

The first place she went into was an antique shop, apparently, and the items—a messy clutter of metal and wood, paper and cloth—were poorly displayed. Of course they were *all* going out of business, so a handsome display no longer mattered. And it also didn't matter what she got the relatives, did it? Whatever she got them, Trish knew they would just politely nod—what was the point in trying to please them? She should just do all her shopping here.

A grubby artificial Christmas tree stood just inside the door of the shop. It appeared to have been repaired many times, branches taped or wrapped in greying string. A tiny bird's skull hung from one branch. Other items on the tree were so mossy with dust they were impossible to identify. Others were identifiable, but as inappropriate as the bird's skull—a kitchen whisk, dental floss, a comb—mixed with such traditional decorations as a ceramic angel, an antique star, some lovely blue and green globes.

Trish turned and glanced back at the distant Santa line, still moving slowly. She thought she recognised Bean's yellow jumper. With no sales clerk in sight she ventured deeper into the store.

Several collapsing cartons of grubby ornaments filled one table. The hand-lettered sign read SECONDS. She picked through a few, afraid to dig too deeply in case something nasty lay underneath. Each ornament was distorted in some way—imperfect spheres, lopsided egg shapes—irregular and shifting coloration. The softer ones resembled diseased organs.

An assortment of Jesus dolls—folk art—were gathered in a bin. They all looked like bad Jesuses to her. A box labeled FIRE SALE was full of unidentifiable blackened things, all with hooks to hang from a tree.

In the central part of the store stuffed rats hung from a line stretched overhead. Most wore Santa hats.

"I had a bunch left over from Halloween, but it's the red caps what make them festive, don't you think?"

A thin man with a very wide grin peered down at her. His hair was black and slicked back and had rolls of dust—her mother called them woollies—decorating it here and there.

"Very... clever," she replied.

"Can I help you find what you want?" he asked.

"I'm not sure I know."

"Maybe, maybe not," he said. "Most of us actually do—we're just too afraid to say. We'll be closing soon, by the way."

Trish glanced away, uncomfortable. "I just need a few things, and then I have to go retrieve my daughter. She's visiting Santa."

"Are you sure? They haven't had a Santa in years." He moved a little closer. She could smell the oil in his hair. How could he not know? Santa was set up practically right outside his store.

Trish felt she should leave, but stopped herself. She'd be done in just a few minutes, and then she and the B could go home. "Well, they must have changed their minds. I have to hurry along." She went deeper into the shop, away from him and his greasy, dust-laden hair. She picked up a dusty old brooch for her mother—she could clean it, and she'd get one of those defective ornaments for her father. They never liked anything she gave them anyway. And this, this would let them know exactly how she felt about this horrible holiday. Maybe they would stop expecting her to come—what a relief that would be.

But she still needed something for her sister, the cousins, and whoever else she'd probably forgotten. At the back of the store was a stack of Victorian Christmas cards. She began thumbing through them quickly, seeking something that might actually impress.

The first card to catch her eye bore a picture of an unhappy looking man in stocks being tormented by a jester. HAPPY CHRISTMAS TO YOU! it proclaimed. In the next, a seriously wintry scene of ice and snow, a man was being mauled by an angry polar bear. On another there was some sort of bifurcated root thing with a human head wearing a top hat and monocle. A root branch stuck out like an arm, clutching a heart-shaped object with the message A MERRY CHRISTMAS TO YOU. She held on to these—she didn't really understand them, but they still perfectly expressed everything she was feeling.

On one card a snowman had turned sinister and was threatening a little boy. And here were two dead birds, their feet pointing stiffly upwards—MERRY CHRISTMAS AND HAPPY NEW YEAR! Then another, MAY CHRISTMAS BE MERRY, with a frog dancing with a hideous black beetle as a giant fly held aloft a golden ring. They were all suitably unpleasant. What a wonderful, wonderful shop!

On another card a hideous goat creature with long black fur, twisted horns, and a forked tongue threatened a tub full of babies with a giant fork. Was he really planning to skewer them? Maybe this one was too much. She would give it to her father.

"That be Krampus," the skinny clerk croaked at her elbow.

"Wha-at?" He'd scared her so bad she felt dizzy.

"Krampus. He's the opposite of the Santa Claus. He's the other one, the one what punishes the children who misbehaved during the year.

Tortures them, I reckon. I've got loads of Krampus gear, if you're interested."

"No!" she cried. "What a terrible idea! Who'd want to invent such a thing?" Guiltily, she dropped the cards. She glanced at her fingertips—they were filthy. She quickly rubbed them on her sleeve.

"They invented him to protect the kiddies, I reckon. Keep them from getting into trouble. Sometimes you have to scare those little ones, just to make them behave. They can be like little animals, if you don't."

"No, no you don't!" she cried, and started for the door.

"Sometimes the truth is a scary thing."

She turned and stared at him. "What's that?"

"She needs something she's not getting, but the hateful creature won't tell you what it is. You didn't sign up for this, now did you? You didn't ask for this. This is not what you wanted at all." The clerk's face had gone dark, as had most of the shop.

"I have to go," Trish said, crying. "I have to pick her up."

"But it's too late for all that now," the clerk said, invisible, just a rough voice issuing from the dark. "You already made your choice. They're shutting us down. They're tearing down the mall."

"Who are *they-ey*?" Again the quake in her voice, the awful evidence that she was terrified.

"Why the ones what make the holidays. The ones what make the malls and then tears them all down. The ones what know all the rules in the rule books, but refuse to tell you what they are. The ones what takes the kiddies and does what needs to be done."

Trish ran from the store. "B—Bean!" She shouted at the dark. All light was gone except for a thin line of silver overhead illuminating a narrow shaft of bright dust. Or was it snow?

She wandered around in the thickening black calling her daughter's name, running into things, tripping over what might have been loose tiles or ceiling debris. Once she touched what she was sure were antlers, and begged Santa's assistant for help. But there was no answer. Feeling further down she realised it was just a head with nothing inside.

Eventually the dark ahead of her lightened into shadow, and then lightened again into an amber mist. She stumbled forward into a field where the mall used to be—after they tore it all down. The grass and the tall weeds were whitening gradually under a silencing fall of snow. There the distant trees whose edges still showed a glimmer of flame. There the collapsing haystacks and the broken fences. And then among the naked trees the worn and battered chair and the withered old man dressed in faded red hunched over a yellow bundle in his lap. He appeared to be mumbling something. Or was that just Trish, mumbling to herself?

"Please," she said, like that beggar she'd encountered earlier. "Please, there's been a misunderstanding."

He looked up at her, his beard torn apart, the surrounding skin raw and bleeding. He held the yellow bundle up. "No," he said. "You were asked whatever you wanted."

"But I don't *know* what I wanted! I never have!"

She rushed forward and yanked the bundle from his arms, holding it tightly against her chest as she ran.

She didn't look until later, when she had her child back safely in her car. She wept and apologised, and she promised all she would do to make up for her mistake. But the twisted and weathered log inside the bundle remained silent, although Trish could just make out the beginnings of a nose, and the lines of a delicate mouth, if she stared long enough into the cracked wood.

GARTH NIX

THE SEVENTEEN-YEAR ITCH

G ARTH NIX has been a full-time writer since 2001, but has also worked as a literary agent, marketing consultant, book editor, book publicist, book sales representative, bookseller, and as a part-time soldier in the Australian Army Reserve.

His books include the "Old Kingdom" fantasy series (comprising *Sabriel, Lirael, Abhorsen, Clariel* and *Goldenhand*); SF novels (*Shade's Children* and *A Confusion of Princes*), and a Regency romance with magic (*Newt's Emerald*).

Amongst Nix's novels for children are *The Ragwitch*, the six books of "The Seventh Tower" sequence, "The Keys to the Kingdom" series, and others. He has co-written several books with Sean Williams, including the "Troubletwisters" series, *Spirit Animals Book Three: Blood Ties, Have Sword Will Travel* and the forthcoming sequel, *Let Sleeping Dragons Lie*. A contributor to many anthologies and magazines, the author's selected short fiction has been collected in *Across the Wall* and *To Hold the Bridge*.

More than five million copies of his books have been sold around the world, they have appeared on the best-seller lists of *The New York Times, Publishers Weekly* and *USA Today*, and his work has been translated into forty-two languages. His most recent book is *Frogkisser!*, now being developed as a film by Twentieth Century Fox/Blue Sky Animation.

"The genesis of this story was, perhaps unsurprisingly, an unbearable itch," Nix reveals. "I'd been bitten by something on the chest, probably a small spider, that was lurking in a shirt I took off the washing-line.

"As I tried not to scratch and scratch and scratch at the bite on my chest, I thought of a character also suffering an unbearable and, in his case, endless itch, and that in turn led to thoughts of how that might be dealt with and what might be causing it..."

Six Weeks Before Halloween

"**W**HAT IS THIS?"

The new hospital administrator was peering through the peculiarly curved door, into the interior of the twelve-foot diameter sphere of heavy steel that sat in the middle of the otherwise empty room. The curious object looked like a bathyscaphe or diving bell somehow lost far from the sea. Further compounding the mystery, the interior was completely lined with some sort of rubber or foam-like material, heavily impregnated with the stale smell of ancient piss and shit, hosed out but not forgotten.

"It says here 'Special Restraint Sphere: Broward' on the floor plan," replied her assistant, a young man called Robert Kenneth, a failed MD who was hoping to make a new career in hospital administration. He'd only been at the place—an institution for restraining and forgetting the criminally insane—for two months longer than Dr. Orando, the administrator, who'd arrived the previous Friday and was now looking into every nook and cranny of the place, which had been built in three great surges in 1887, 1952 and 1978.

"What does that mean?"

"Uh, I don't know," said Kenneth. "Um, we do have a patient called Broward. I think."

"What can *you* tell me about this?" asked Orando, turning to the third member of their tour of inspection party. Templar McIndoe, senior orderly, was by far the oldest employee in the hospital, almost seventy and working on past retirement age by special permission and his own dire financial need. He knew everything there was to know about the hospital, though he didn't always share this information.

"Stephen Broward," said the old man. "They built this for him, special, back in '49. That's when he came here, after what he did."

"Nineteen forty-nine? How old is this prisoner?"

"Oh, he's old," said MacIndoe. "Older'n me. Must be ninety-five, ninety-seven, something like that. You've seen him, Mister Kenneth. Guards call him Stubbsy."

"Oh, him," said Kenneth, trying and failing to contain a twist of his mouth, a visceral sign of distaste. "The one with no fingers or toes."

"He's got fingers, sort of," said McIndoe stolidly. "He only cut 'em off from the middle knuckle. But you're right about the toes."

"A self-mutilator?" asked Orando, with clinical interest. "Why do we have him? And why has he been held so long?"

"Murder," replied McIndoe laconically. "Multiple murders. Back in '65 he killed near everyone in the place he was at then, an asylum down at Wickshaw. Twenty, thirty people."

"What?" asked Orando. She frowned. "He can't have. I'd know about something like that. My second doctorate was on the psychology of mass murderers. I covered everyone who killed more than a dozen."

"Just what I was told," said McIndoe, with what he hoped came across as an apologetic shrug. He already knew not to argue with this new administrator, and he needed to keep the job. Just for a few more years...

"And this sphere?"

"Somewhere to put him over Halloween," said McIndoe. "That's when he's particularly...upset."

"You put a patient in there?" asked Orando. She had drawn up to her full, impressive height and was looking at McIndoe like he was some sort of vicious animal.

"Nope," said McIndoe. "He puts himself in there. Morning before Halloween, he asks nice as pie to go in his special room and to not be let out till after the following dawn. Every Halloween, though it's the seventeenth he's always particularly wound up about."

"It looks airtight," said Kenneth. "He'd asphyxiate if he was in any longer than overnight. And there's no facilities..."

"Nothing to scratch with, neither," said McIndoe softly.

"What was that?" asked Orando. "And what's this seventeenth Halloween business?"

"He has this terrible itch," explained McIndoe. "It builds up over time, and it's always worse at Halloween, and it gets worse every year. The peak comes every seventeen years. After that, it ebbs away, builds up again slowly. Nothing to scratch himself on, inside that sphere."

"That's why he cut off his fingers and toes?" asked Kenneth, the twist in his mouth coming back, but fascination in his eyes.

"Reckon so," said McIndoe. "Pulled all his teeth out, too. He hands over his false ones before he goes in."

"What a ludicrous waste of space, not to mention the original investment to build this... this sphere," said Orando with decision. "What were my predecessors thinking to pander to a patient's delusion in such a way? Well. He's not going in that sphere any more. A ninety year-old patient in such a restraint? Not in my hospital. We'll sedate him if necessary, but it's still six weeks to Halloween. A course of therapy—under my direction—should ameliorate or even remove the problem. You said something, McIndoe?"

"Yes, ma'am," replied McIndoe. "This Halloween is a seventeenth year. Broward will be real, I mean real bad—"

"I've already mentioned pandering to delusions!" snapped Orando. "I trust I will not have to deal with psychoses from staff members as well as the patients?"

"No, ma'am," said McIndoe. Already he was thinking ahead to be sure he was rostered off over Halloween. Him and the few friends he still had among the staff.

McIndoe had seen Broward in 2001, and seventeen years before that in 1984, and even seventeen years before that, when he'd first started at the hospital. On each of these three past occasions, he had been greatly relieved there *was* a sphere to put him in.

∞

Ten Days Before Halloween

"How ya doing, Mister Broward?" asked McIndoe, stopping by the tall but stooped old man who was slowly refilling his paper cup from the water cooler in the recreation room.

"Bad," said Broward, grimacing. "That new doctor, the boss one, she keeps giving me different tablets, trying out stuff, and she talks to me during rest period. It's called rest period! I want to sleep then, like I'm supposed to."

"How's the... how's the itch?" asked McIndoe carefully.

Broward looked down at his chest and his stubby, shorn hands in their leather gloves began to close on his sternum before he visibly willed them back to his sides.

"It's bad," he said gloomily. "That doctor reckons she's hypnotised me so I don't want to scratch. But I *do*. Ten days to go... this is going to be a terrible one, I can tell. Even for the full seventeen."

"Seventeen years," whispered McIndoe, looking carefully around the room. He didn't want any of the other staff reporting him as insane.

"Yeah," said Broward. "If old Doc Gutierrez hadn't got me that sphere I'd be really worried right now."

His hands moved again, remnant fingers heading for his chest, stumps reaching to scratch whatever lay beneath his blue patient's smock. Broward grimaced, baring his beautifully white false teeth as he forced his arms to his sides, his hands turned inwards like claws.

"So... so all that talking and hypnotising and the new drugs, they aren't working?" asked McIndoe.

"Nope," replied Broward. "It's itching fierce. But I can hold It off, Mac. I can hold It off until Halloween. And in the sphere... nothing to scratch with. It'll be okay. My great-great-granma, she carried It for more than a hundred years, I reckon. I've been okay more 'en fifty years, haven't I?"

His voice was pleading, eyes wet.

"Yeah, yeah," mumbled McIndoe. He gripped Broward's shoulder, offering him support. There wasn't much muscle there, it was all bone. The old man wasn't much more than skin and bone.

"You're a good man," mumbled Broward. "Hell, you're like family to me..."

His voice tapered off as he said that, and he suddenly looked at McIndoe as if seeming him in a new light.

"Family..." he whispered.

"Yeah, we've known each other long enough," said McIndoe. "Hell, I've known you longer than almost anyone."

He tried to smile, but inside McIndoe felt cold, and old, and frightened. He'd already arranged to be rostered off over Halloween. There was nothing he could do. If he helped Broward get in the sphere, Doctor Orando would just let him out and McIndoe would lose his job, and if he lost his job he lost the house, and he was raising three grandchildren, still four years to get the youngest through high school. There was nothing he could do.

"Shit," said McIndoe bitterly.

"What?" asked Broward. He'd rallied, was standing straighter, taking sips of his water. "Don't worry about what I said... I can hold It off. I can. Don't you worry, Mac. I'll get in that sphere, hold It off another seventeen years! I'll beat my great-great-granma yet!"

"Yeah," said McIndoe. He tried to smile at the near-centenarian being impossibly brave, and failed. "Yeah. Keep up the good work."

He walked away, leaving the old man sipping his water. While he waited for the orderly on the other side to open the door, McIndoe glanced back. Broward was holding the cup between the palms of his hands. The stubs of his fingers were twitching, curling and uncurling.

Making scratching motions in the air.

McIndoe fled, heart hammering, all the way back to his special refuge, the cleaning cupboard on level two of the oldest building. He took the Scotch from behind the loose bricks and took four swallows in quick succession, following it up with a gargle of mint-flavoured mouthwash, also from a bottle hidden behind the bricks.

The Day Before Halloween

"Mister Kenneth. I got to talk to you."

"What is it, McIndoe?"

"Broward. He has *got* to go in the sphere tomorrow."

Kenneth slid out from behind his desk and went to the door, looking to make sure Doctor Orando was not in sight. He shut the door and returned to his desk.

"You've got to help him get in the sphere," repeated McIndoe.

Kenneth fumbled with a pencil, picked it up, drew some doodles on his desk blotter.

"The boss made it clear he's not to go in that thing," he said. "Broward is restrained in Ward Three, and heavily sedated."

"He's still trying to scratch though, isn't he?" asked McIndoe. "Should be out deeper than deep, and he's *still* trying to scratch that itch, right?"

"Uh, yes," said Kenneth. He swallowed several times. "Look… look, McIndoe, were you here in 1966?"

"Yep," said McIndoe. "Nineteen years old, invalided out of the army—I took some shrapnel at Ia Drang—and looking for steady work. It was this or the Down's bakery. I should've gone with the bakery."

"Doctor Gutierrez, the old administrator… she left specific instructions for her successor, confirming what you said about Broward going into the sphere. Kind of odd… a personal letter, as well as the file instruction… she underlined a lot of it."

"She was the best person I ever knew," said McIndoe. "She worked out what would help people, made it happen. Not someone you expect to find in charge, well, you know what we got here. No one wants to know what happens to the people who come here. They get written off, whether they're murderers or just plain don't fit in."

"But Broward *is* a murderer," said Kenneth. "Isn't he? His file isn't clear on that point. He was committed for something to do with that place in Wickshaw, but its records went when it burned down in '49. A lot of people died in the fire, and he was implicated in those deaths. Murder by arson. But was he already a murderer?"

"They burned it themselves," said McIndoe. He was staring over Kenneth's shoulder, looking back, seeing something long past. "Broward said they thought he was inside, that's why they did it. But he'd already got out."

"*Who* burned it?" asked Kenneth. He was doodling faster now, strange, grinning faces with lots of teeth, which he hastily drew over, scribbling heavy, thick lines.

"The staff who were left," said McIndoe. "Least, that's what Broward told me. I looked it up too, you know. Back in the day. They blamed him for the fire, but he didn't do that."

"What did he do?"

"He scratched an itch," said McIndoe. "And you can't let him. He has to go in the sphere."

Kenneth drew a straight line on the paper, then underlined it, three times.

"We can't," he said slowly. "Orando will be here. She wants to observe him. But..."

He hesitated, pencil stabbing down in a sharp, black dot.

"But, you know... tonight, maybe. He's an old man. He might die... with a little bit of—"

"No!" exclaimed McIndoe. "No! Don't you think anyone thought of that before? *He's* thought of it before. We can't kill him. He can't kill himself. And I think... I think he can't even die."

"Why... why not?"

McIndoe didn't answer at once. Kenneth stared at the older man, the pencil broken in his hand. He hadn't even noticed his hands clenching, snapping it in two.

"He wants to scratch that itch... he needs to scratch it," said McIndoe. "There's something inside him. Something that grows real slow, irritating the flesh, getting itchier and itchier. And when it gets to seventeen years old, it's just unbearable and he's got to scratch away and on Halloween it's... I don't know... ripe ..."

"What?" asked Kenneth. "What?"

"He has to scratch that itch, he has to scratch all the way through skin and all," whispered McIndoe. "So it can come out."

Kenneth stared, still not understanding.

"But he *must* be able to die, and if we—"

"You don't get it!" snapped McIndoe. "If he dies, where does whatever is inside him go?"

The two men sat in silence for a long, long minute. Finally Kenneth stood up and dropped the broken halves of the pencil in the trash bin by his desk.

"I . . . I can't go against Orando," said Kenneth. "I need this job."

"Yeah, so do I," said McIndoe. "But you're young, you can get another—"

"I didn't just fail my medical degree," interrupted Kenneth. "I was struck off. Stealing drugs. I'm lucky not to be in jail. Orando's a friend of my dad's, she said she'd give me a chance."

"If we don't do anything . . . people will die."

"Yeah, well, not me," said Kenneth. He wiped his eyes. "I'm calling in sick. You do whatever you got to do, old man. I'm not going to be here."

"I'm not working tomorrow," said McIndoe. "None of the old crew are. And I reckon some of the young ones too, they've felt the vibe. Lot of people'll be sick tomorrow."

"What about the ones that come in?"

"Shit, I don't know!" exploded McIndoe. "Some of the staff at Wickshaw survived. Some of them. I mean, they'll have a chance. The inmates in the newer buildings, they might be all right."

"Maybe it's nothing," said Kenneth. "We're just scaring ourselves. Projection. Lot of crazy people here, right?"

"Sure," said McIndoe bitterly. "But I'm not working tomorrow, and I bet you're still calling in sick."

"Yeah," said Kenneth. "I *am* sick. I got to go home *now*."

Halloween

"This is really very interesting," said Dr. Orando. "I've never seen anything like it. There is nothing in his records to indicate how he could be so resistant to anaesthesia."

"No ma'am," replied the nurse, even though Orando had really been talking to herself. "Uh, he broke a strap before, ma'am. That's not supposed to be possible. We've got six tight on him now and he's still moving against them."

"Hysterical strength," said Orando. She tilted the video camera on its tripod down a little, making sure it captured Broward's wriggling movements under the restraints. His arms were rippling like a snake pinned down by a shovel at the head, and the stubs of his fingers were trying to tear at the sides of the bed.

Scratching, Orando realised. Broward was trying to reach his chest. That was the target for his scratching. His own heart.

"Nurse, I'd like you to cut the patient's robe down from the neck to reveal the sternum, please."

"Doctor? Cut his robe?"

"Yes, that's what I said. This psychosomatic scratching is so developed I am wondering if it's capable of producing a physical effect. I saw some signs of a rash yesterday. A reddening of the skin, though it was transient. I want to see if it has developed further."

The nurse nodded, picked up a pair of scissors and approached the bed. As he did so, Broward's struggles intensified. The IV tube in his arm shivered, constant small movements of Broward's arm making it vibrate. The restraining straps creaked and groaned, the clips screeching as they were slid back and forth against the metal frame of the bed.

The nurse got the scissors in position and started to cut, but he'd hardly slit a few inches when the fire alarm went off, a siren out in the corridor echoed by many others throughout the three buildings. A quick, strobing *whoop-whoop-whoop.*

All the lights went out. When the red-framed emergency lighting came flickering back, the nurse was by the door. He'd dropped the scissors in his hasty retreat.

"Go to your fire station in the main ward," snapped Orando. She snatched up the phone by the bed and dialled the hospital control centre. No one answered, after six rings she hung up and redialled, stabbing the buttons with her penlight. This time her call was answered by a breathy, clearly discomforted guard. There should have been two on duty but a lot of the staff had called in sick that day, something Orando was going to investigate. Probably people wanting time off to be with their kids for Halloween, but they were going to have to pay for it out of their regular holiday entitlements when they got back tomorrow.

"This is Orando. What's going on?"

"Uh, two heat detector trips in Building Three and the mains power and CCTV is out across the complex, which is weird because they should be independent...I can't see what's going on," gasped the guard. "The board says all the inter-building automatic fire doors are closed and City Fire and the police have been automatically notified. I was just...uh...now there's another detector trip, also in Building Three—"

"Make an announcement, Building Three is to be evacuated according to the plan, all other buildings to lockdown, staff to their fire emergency positions," said Orando. "Get the closest orderly in to help you go through the checklist and then get them to call in all the off-duty staff. Patients are to be corralled on the south lawn as per the contingency. I'm on my way over."

She put the phone down and looked back at Broward, eyes running over the monitors to make sure he was still stable. He continued to writhe against the restraints, the clanging of the buckles a counterpoint to the *whoop-whoop* of the fire siren. For a moment, Orando considered whether she should order this building evacuated too, but with the automatic fire doors closed and the relatively new sprinkler system in Building Three she considered there would be time enough to evaluate whether that was necessary, and it would be far better to keep everyone inside if they were not actually at risk from fire or smoke.

Certainly, she considered that Broward should not be moved while he was still being infused with anaesthetics and, though he seemed stable enough, intervention might be required which could not be done on the lawn.

"I will be back shortly, Mister Broward," she said. Orando often spoke to patients, even ones apparently far more deeply sedated than the old man jerking and struggling on the hospital bed in front of her. "Remember. You are not itchy. You do not need to scratch. Relax. Let yourself fall into a deep, healing sleep. All is—"

At that moment one of the straps broke, just broke, with a sound like a gunshot. Orando flinched, but calmed herself. She approached the bed, glancing over at the video camera to be sure it was recording what was happening. Broward had got one arm free and his mangled hand had gone instantly to his chest, stubby remnant fingers digging deep into his flesh.

Orando blinked. There was an odd, fuzzy glint of red under those desperately scratching fingers. A reflection from the emergency lighting, no doubt.

She came closer, careful to keep to the end of the bed, out of reach of that scratching, scrabbling hand. Orando had worked with the dangerously insane for many years and would not risk getting too close. But she had never had such a fascinating patient, and she couldn't help but lean forward... the fuzzy, red glint was clearer now, almost as if a kind of tendril of suspended desert-red dust was rising between the mutilated joints of the man's hand . . .

Orando didn't realise she'd been holding her breath, in the excitement of observing a case that would give her not only a great leap in her professional career but probably a popular non-fiction book as well.

She breathed in.

A few moments later, her fingers twitched. Unlike Broward, her fingers were long and she had nails. Sensibly-varnished, well-trimmed nails. But nails, nevertheless.

There was an itch on her chest. A really, annoying, deep-seated itch along her sternum. She started to scratch, just with one hand. But the itch could not be assuaged.

"Help," groaned Orando. Broward was forgotten. There was only the itch. "I need... I need help!"

She ran out of the room. Scratching with both hands, nails digging deep into her own flesh, long streaks of blood spreading across her blouse, the pearls in her necklace washed red before her frantic scrabbling broke the string and they fell, to go rolling across the floor.

A puff of ochre dust went with Orando, twining in and out of her mouth and nose with every inhalation and exhalation, as she ran sobbing and scratching, out to the lawn where all the patients and staff from Building Three were beginning to gather...

Three minutes later, McIndoe appeared out of breath and trembling in Broward's room. He was not in his orderly's uniform. The hood of his tracksuit was up, pulled over an unusually long-billed cap, completely hiding his face. He had a bag of tools in his left hand, the end of the kitchen blowtorch he'd used to spoof the fire detectors just visible.

He stopped when he saw Broward sitting up on the bed, all the straps broken or undone, trailing by the sides. The old inmate was hunched over, cradling himself.

Broward's stubby, remnant fingers were finally still. Not twitching, not scratching. At rest.

But they were red, the old man's hands were red, soaked to the wrists with his own blood.

McIndoe froze in the doorway. The fire alarm was still whooping, rising and falling, but in the moments between its wails he realised the sound he'd unconsciously been hearing for a few minutes was now identifiable.

Screaming.

Screams, coming from outside the double-glazed security windows, coming from the lawn between the buildings. The designated evacuation area.

There was often screaming in the hospital, but this was different. McIndoe had never heard such screams, never heard so many people screaming, all at once.

"I couldn't . . ." muttered Broward. "I couldn't hold it in. Seventeen years, and It knows, It knows. Halloween."

He looked up at McIndoe, his gaze older and more defeated than anyone's the attendant had ever seen.

"The itch . . . the itch . . . I just had to scratch."

"What . . . what is *It*?" asked McIndoe. He didn't even really know what he was saying, what good it would do to know. He'd hated himself for staying away, and he hated himself for coming back and trying to do something, and most of all he hated himself for being too late. He should have got Broward into the sphere earlier, no matter what it took.

"I don't know," whispered Broward. "I've never known. Something ancient, something terrible. People knew it before, but we've forgotten. All Hallow's Eve. Old Scratch. You'll see. I'm sorry, McIndoe. I'm sorry, sorry . . ."

"You tried," said McIndoe. "Hell, whatever's happening isn't your fault."

"Not that," whispered Broward. "I'm sorry for *you*. *It* will be back here soon."

"Yeah," said McIndoe. He shrugged wearily, knowing that this time he'd irretrievably fucked everything up. His life insurance was paid. The grandkids would make it, maybe they'd even do better without him along to try and guide them. "Don't worry. Like I said, you tried. I saw that, every time. You fought. I'm almost seventy, I could drop dead any moment. Not your fault."

"*It* comes back when it's had enough. Looking to be reborn again, to hide and grow," whispered Broward. "*It* likes a familiar place. Familiar. *It* was called that, sometimes. In my family..."

He leaned over as if in great pain and when he straightened up, there was a pair of sharp surgical scissors clutched between his palms, stubby fingers folded over to keep it tight. "I'm so sorry, McIndoe, but I...I can't do it any more. *It* has to go to family, and you're the closest I got. The itch...oh, the itch—"

McIndoe lunged, but he was too late. Broward had shoved the scissors as hard as he could into that itchy spot, right under his sternum. He was already good as dead. All the orderly could do was help him lie back, as the blood blackened the old man's chest and his eyes became dull. Curiously, his face continued to hold an expression McIndoe had never seen before. The attendant had seen plenty of men die. He'd never seen one look relieved before.

The orderly sat down in the chair next to the bed. The screaming was fainter. He could hardly hear it now. Just isolated, fading wails and cries under the constant up and down whooping of the fire alarm, and the sharp, frantic beeping of the monitors that had detected the absence of Broward's pulse and blood pressure.

Air moved in the corridor outside, a wind whistling through, though there were never windows open here, no way for a breeze to get in. The door creaked and moved a few inches. McIndoe tensed, trying to remember the words of a prayer he hadn't said since he was a very young man, lying wounded in the mud. It had been hot and very humid then. Now it was cold, air-conditioned cold, but he was sweating and he wanted to move but he couldn't.

There was a red glint in the air, the hint of dust carried on the wind, or a flight of tiny red insects flying all together like a little cloud, coming straight at McIndoe, straight at his chest...

McIndoe screamed as a white-hot wire thrust through his heart and out his back. He clutched at his chest, frantically lifted his tracksuit top and the T-shirt beneath. But there was no wound, and the pain was gone as quickly as it had come.

He stared at his breastbone. It looked no different than before. His skin was wrinkled and old, a few remaining hairs wiry and white. McIndoe thought it looked like someone else's chest, but he'd always thought that, at least since he was sixty.

Now it didn't just look different. His skin *felt* different. Like there was something there, something just under the skin, though it was not visible.

It *was* a little itchy. Just in the middle. Only a little bit now, but it was bad enough. Hard to imagine how much worse it would be in seventeen years...

McIndoe automatically moved to scratch, but stopped himself. His face set hard, and he sat for a while, thinking. Then he got up and found the tool bag where he'd dropped it on the floor.

There was a big screwdriver in there, would serve as a chisel, broad enough to sever a finger at the joint. And he had a hammer. The floor would be his workbench, and there were plenty of bandages close by he could use to stem the blood.

Painkillers too, but he didn't think he'd use them.

The pain would be a good distraction.

A distraction from the itch.

THANA NIVEAU

To Drown the World

THANA NIVEAU was born to the wail of the Wendigo and the whisper of warp engines. So it is no surprise that her literary aspirations have combined both the mythic and the speculative, gaining her publication in *Black Static*, *Interzone* and numerous anthologies. Her fiction has been reprinted in *Best New Horror* many times.

She has also been twice short-listed for the British Fantasy Award, for her debut collection *From Hell to Eternity* and her story 'Death Walks *en pointe*'.

Niveau is a Halloween bride, sharing her life with fellow writer John Llewellyn Probert in a crumbling Gothic tower filled with arcane books and curiosities. And toy dinosaurs.

"I had just written a story called 'Octoberland', set in Houston, where I grew up," explains the author. "It reawakened so many memories and feelings and, while dark, was an extremely nostalgic writing experience. I wanted to explore those feelings again with another place from my childhood—Galveston. I was reminiscing about it with my brother, and he told me about a recurring nightmare he used to have about the causeway. It became Evan's nightmare in the story.

"Horror is a great medium for exploring worst-case 'what if?' scenarios, and I've always been a huge fan of eco-horror. Toxic waste, pollution and nuclear power have created everything from Godzilla to man-eating worms and giant bunnies. But humans are ultimately the *real* monsters, and we're engineering our own downfall. The idea that there are still climate change deniers out there, in spite of all the scientific proof of what we've done to the planet, is bewildering.

"I confess I'm a little obsessed with the idea of a drowned Earth, and my darkest self sees something poetic in that being our ultimate fate."

E VAN HAD NEVER liked the causeway. He didn't like the water, and he certainly didn't like driving this close to it. It was only two miles from the mainland to Galveston Island, but it felt much longer. As a child, the drive had seemed endless to him. But then, all journeys had seemed endless when he was trapped in the back seat with his twin sister, Lea.

He always tried to see it through her eyes—the causeway, the water, even the island itself. And he always failed. The bay was a dull greenish-grey, matching the colour of the polluted Houston sky. But somehow Lea saw beauty in it. The sea and its creatures had fascinated her since their very first trip to the beach.

Evan still remembered it vividly, every detail. The huge ships gliding by out in the Gulf of Mexico, the seagulls wheeling overhead, occasionally diving down to snatch food from family picnics or steal fishermen's bait. There was the staccato *whirrrr* of fishing lines being cast, and the sloshing of waves where the water met the land. And there were the smells. Fish, sea air, barbecue and coconut suntan lotion.

Evan had been sitting on a pile of soft sand, using a plastic spade and bucket to build a castle. In his mind he could see exactly how he wanted it to look, but reality fell some considerable way short of fantasy. The disappointment was crushing. When his clumsy fingers refused to sculpt the delicately crenellated parapet exactly how it should be, he stood up and kicked the whole mess over, deciding it was more fun to be a giant destroying it instead.

The army men he'd placed inside (he'd decided they were time travellers) were helpless against the onslaught of his stomping feet. The largest tower collapsed, burying them in an avalanche of sand. One soldier managed to escape, crawling bravely towards the moat before the rest of the castle met a similar fate. It was fun playing the villain, but after a while Evan began to feel bad for his victims. He hurriedly rescued them from the sand and sent them back to their time machine so they could go home.

Behind him Lea was laughing brightly, and when he turned he saw her running towards the lapping waves. They pawed restlessly at the shore, foaming and frothing like boiled, sour milk. Lea tripped and went sprawling in the wet sand, staring around her in amazement. After a while she sat up. Then she reached down and plucked something from the sand. She held it up with a kind of hushed reverence, as though she'd found a sacred artefact.

Evan didn't want to go close to the water, but he was too curious about what she'd found. What if it was part of some pirate's treasure? A gold doubloon or pieces of eight?

But something seemed bent on thwarting all his wishes that day. It was only a seashell.

Lea looked up as he drew near, her eyes wide with excitement. "Look, Evan," she whispered. "It's alive!"

He peered closer and saw that she was right. A mass of wriggling legs emerged from the mouth of the shell. But there wasn't anything special about that.

"It's just a hermit crab," he said with a shrug, all wisdom and experience at the grand age of seven. Seven and nine minutes, he always told grown-ups. Those nine minutes were important.

The shell was almost as large as Lea's hand, and the reddish legs of the creature stretched out, waving in the air inches from her nose. Evan watched, curiously unnerved by the sight. A sudden strange image came to him of her popping the crab into her mouth, shell and all. In his mind he could even hear the sound it would make as she crunched it up, could practically *taste* it. He shuddered, banishing the unwelcome thought.

"It was something else once," Lea said in a strange voice.

"Huh?"

"Somebody threw it away, threw it in the sea. And it became this."

Now she was really creeping him out. She was holding the crab so close to her eyes she was in danger of being blinded by the squirming legs. There was a keenness to her scrutiny that disturbed him, something in her gaze that seemed old and knowing. She was suddenly like another person.

After a while she set the crab down and watched as it scuttled away, vanishing into the white foam of the waves. Lea looked up at Evan, her expression serious. He had the unpleasant sense that some kind of exchange had taken place, some silent communication.

Then the water surged, splashing and soaking her, and she erupted into delighted squeals and giggles as she flung herself into the surf. His sister was back, and whatever had replaced her for a moment was gone.

Evan had never forgotten that strange encounter, and the memory returned with every trip he made to Galveston to see her. They'd both been weird kids, and weird kids grew up to be weird adults. But lately her e-mails and texts had reached a new level of what could only charitably be called eccentric.

Lea was a field ecologist, buried deep in research on global warming. She'd developed a sudden interest in fossils, asking Evan to go to the Natural Science Museum and photograph all the Cambrian arthropods he could find there. Such arbitrary requests were nothing new, and he didn't really think anything of it. He'd dutifully done as she asked, and found himself enjoying the little excursion as he imagined her there with him. It felt like the old days, when she still lived in Houston, and they got to see each other more often.

He'd e-mailed her the pictures, but never heard back. That wasn't unusual either. She was easily distracted and she often got lost in work, especially when intriguing tangents presented themselves.

However, when he'd texted her a few days later to ask if she was happy with his photos, the response was baffling.

Thought Anomalocaris or Marrella but not. Archaean Era??

Before?? Maybe from protoplanets. Must show—come see!

He recognised the first name. It was one of the fossils he'd seen at the museum. Other than that, the message might as well have been in Klingon. They never bothered with full sentences when texting, but this was even more pared-down than usual. He'd called her back, but wasn't able to get a straight answer about what she wanted to show him. Just that it was incredible and he had to come.

He was at the highest point of the span now, the stretch of road furthest from the water. Ironically, it was the part that made him the most nervous. He could never banish from his mind the intrusive image of the bridge collapsing, of his car plummeting into the churning grey water, gravity pulling him down, down, down.

"It's only about ten feet deep there," Lea had once reassured him. "You could easily swim to the surface and get to the shore."

Easy for her to say. She was more at home in the water than on land. For Evan the very idea of his head being submerged was enough to trigger a sense of panic.

But he knew exactly what to do if his car ever did go in the water. He'd rehearsed it in his mind countless times to drill it in. First he'd unlatch the seatbelt, then try the electric window. If it worked, he'd lower it an inch and let the water slowly trickle in. If the electric window didn't work, he'd climb over the seat and use one of the old-fashioned cranks on the back windows. As the water filled the car, he would stay calm and focus his mind, and as soon as the level reached his chin, he'd take a deep breath, crank the window down the rest of the way and swim out. He could hold his nose and kick his way ten feet to the surface, he was sure of that. Once there he could float or dog-paddle to the pillars of the causeway and wait to be rescued.

Lea had laughed at his escape plan, but only until she realised he was serious. Then her expression had changed to one of pity.

"I could teach you to swim," she'd told him more than once. "Then you wouldn't be so afraid of the water."

"I'm not afraid of the water. I'm afraid of what's *in* the water."

"But there's nothing to be afraid of."

"Oh right, let me guess—the sharks are more afraid of me than I am of them?"

"You're statistically more likely to be struck by lightning than attacked by a shark."

"Fat lot of good those statistics will do me if I'm the unlucky bastard who gets the shark instead of the lightning."

It was a conversation they'd had so many times they could have recited each other's dialogue. He had never even told her the full truth—that it wasn't sharks he was really afraid of. What he saw waiting for him in the water was something else entirely, something with long, clutching arms that would pull him under. Something that would *claim* him.

Galveston was no pristine Caribbean resort with crystal-clear lagoons where you could see everything swimming around your feet. In the dark, briny water of the Gulf of Mexico, there was no way of knowing what had just brushed against your leg, or what you might step on down there.

Lea loved to dive beneath the surface, and those momentary disappearances when they were little had caused Evan intense distress. Quite apart from the irrational fear that she would never surface again, he lived in dread of her grabbing his ankles and dragging him down. She'd done it once in a motel swimming pool, and that was bad enough. But the idea of vanishing beneath those umber waves himself filled him with horror.

At the top of the span he looked to his left to see the railway line that ran parallel with the modern road. It was the original causeway, over a century old and apparently still used by trains, although Evan had never seen one there. In fact, he'd never even seen the drawbridge lowered. As kids he and Lea had always hoped to race a train to the island, but it was not to be.

The raised drawbridge was another thing Evan didn't like, although he couldn't have said why. Perhaps it was the way the two halves resembled a gaping mouth, like an alligator made of concrete and steel. The new causeway had no drawbridge; the arch was high enough for boats to pass underneath. But that didn't stop him imagining the road suddenly lifting up in front of him, all the traffic smashing headlong into the unyielding wall. It was only once he had finally crested the hill that he could relax.

One night he dreamed he saw a train. The two causeways were much closer together, and the new one was only wide enough for his car. The guard rails were missing. He heard the whistle of the approaching locomotive and looked up to see it racing along the tracks. Coming straight towards him. It was going too fast and he was going too slow. There was nowhere for him to go as the train jumped the tracks, its line of cars buckling as it twisted in the air. It came down on the narrow causeway and smashed through, plunging into the water like a sea serpent. Evan tried to brake, but the road followed the train's trajectory, slanting down towards the waves. He woke up just before he fell in.

It had all felt so real, so horribly inevitable, and he couldn't help reliving the nightmare every time he passed the drawbridge. Once he reached the island, his heart rate would go back to normal. He could see whatever it was Lea wanted to show him and they could have a nice lunch. Before that, though, he had to pass one final landmark: the sunken boat.

It had been there for as long as he and Lea could remember. The little fishing boat lay off to the right, among the reeds in the shallows at the edge of the shore. Only a piece of the hull remained now, and the masts jutted from the water like bones. In time there would be nothing left of it at all, and Evan felt an inexplicable pang of sadness at the thought. It was probably an eyesore for most, detritus that had never been cleared away. But, as eerie as it was, it was a fixture of the island for him and Lea.

At last he could see palm trees, and the bay gave way to wetlands as he neared the end of the causeway. A heron was stalking through the saltgrass of the marsh. He was safe on dry land once more and he made his way along the main road, catching glimpses of the Gulf down the streets to his right. As he passed the iconic mansion known as Bishop's Palace, it suddenly struck him that, in all the years their family had been visiting Galveston, they had never taken the tour inside.

He reached Lea's street and parked outside the little beach house she called home. She'd paid far too much for it, using most of the money from their inheritance. Then she'd squandered even more painting it a vibrant emerald green, only for the colour to fade within a couple of years. Sand, salt and sun were no friend to little wooden boxes. Now the house looked sickly, as did so many others around it. They were like film sets, places built to look like houses, but never actually meant to be lived in.

Still, he had to concede that it had a sort of charm. A slender palm tree grew in front, its trunk curved in a graceful arc. And the vibrant pink bougainvillea that swamped the porch was in full bloom, almost obscuring the little sign that said MERMAID CROSSING. Evan had bought it for her as a joke in one of the tourist shops along the Strand, never imagining she'd hang it up. But he liked that she had.

He'd driven all the way with the car's AC cranked up high, wishing it was actually possible to make himself cold enough that the stifling heat might be tolerable. He shut off the engine and braced himself, then stepped out into the steam bath of the island. It was only May and it was already over 100 degrees.

Before he had even closed the car door, Lea was pelting down the wooden stairs and running towards him, arms outstretched. He couldn't help but smile at her exuberance as she flung herself at him in a fierce embrace, the impact causing him to swing her around. One of her flip-flops came off and landed on the hood of his car and they both laughed.

"Wow, it hasn't been that long, has it?"

"It's been ages!" she lamented.

"Yeah, well, you *could* come see *me*, you know."

She didn't reply.

"Never mind," he said softly.

He always suggested it. She never responded. And he never pushed it.

As claustrophobic as the island and the water and the causeway made him feel, the mainland made her feel even worse. She didn't own a car, and the one time she had braved the journey to his place in a taxi—at his invitation and expense—she'd been like a small terrified animal that had spent its whole life in a cage and didn't know how to cope in the outside world. It had been awful to see. He'd driven her back himself the same night.

But she was happy here. She was living in the world that had always fascinated her, and the Gulf of Mexico was her backyard. There were shops and restaurants along the seafront, including Casa Mare, a shabby-chic little café where they usually ate when he visited. It was only a ten-minute walk away, but as far as Evan was concerned, in the stifling heat of a Texas summer, it might as well be ten miles. But he was willing to endure it for her.

He smiled at Lea and she mirrored his expression. She looked like a vintage movie star in her enormous shades and sun hat. And the white bikini-top and cut-offs made her tanned skin appear even darker. Everything about her radiated health and happiness. Physically anyway.

"You've gone totally native," Evan said. Next to her he looked pale and anaemic. No one would ever guess they were twins.

He armed sweat off his forehead as he closed the car door. The sun blazed overhead and he could feel the heat of the driveway through his sandals. Summers here were notoriously brutal, sweltering and sticky with humidity. Even so, houses like Lea's often didn't have air-conditioning. He never understood how she could stand it.

She smiled as she retrieved her flip-flop. She didn't bother to put it back on, and he winced at the sight of her bare foot on the scorching pavement. He remembered how the blacktop in the school playground used to turn soft in the heat, and the swings and monkey bars were too hot to touch.

Lea took his arm and pulled him towards the house. "Come on," she said. "I can't wait to show you!"

At the top of the stairs she kicked off her remaining flip-flop and dropped the other one beside it on the porch, leaving Evan behind to remove his sandals. Sand gritted under his bare feet as he stepped inside and he made a face. The floor was always sandy. He didn't know why she even bothered with the Buddhist no-shoes thing at all.

He tried to pull the front door closed, only for it to bang against the frame and bounce open again. It was hanging crookedly askew, wrenched off its top hinge.

"Lea, your door is . . . "

But she had vanished into the back.

He peered at the busted hinge for a moment longer before edging back inside, where it was cooler. The ceiling fan was on, listlessly stirring the heavy air. He pulled the chain to make it turn faster.

He didn't need to be told to help himself to coffee. Lea always managed to time it perfectly with his arrival. The aroma was heavenly, but it did little to mask the stronger smell of the sea that permeated the house through the open windows. There was a brisk breeze, but the air itself was like liquid salt. Lea said she found the scent of fish comforting, but to Evan it just smelled like the dumpsters outside a seafood restaurant.

He downed the coffee, sighing with pleasure at the invigorating taste. It was only in the past year that she'd finally gotten it right. Lea never drank coffee herself, so brewing the perfect pot for her brother had always been something of an experiment. He peeked in the cabinet to see what he was drinking and was surprised to find an expensive designer brand he never would have splurged on for himself. But he wasn't going to complain or tell her she shouldn't have. After years of suffering through her lesser efforts, this tiny luxury was only fair.

It took him a moment to register what was odd about the cabinet. Then it clicked. There was nothing to eat. Just a half-empty bag of rice and a couple of cans of tuna, nothing that looked like proper food. His curiosity got the best of him and he decided to look in the refrigerator, only to recoil at the stench. He slammed the door. Whatever was in there was well past its sell-by date. He had a sudden image of rotting bait and buckets of chum sitting out in the heat.

Well, maybe she just ate out all the time. Or she hadn't gone to the store yet for provisions. Maybe it was too hot even for her. He decided not to say anything. Not about the fridge anyway. He was definitely going to ask about the front door.

He was pouring another cup of coffee when she reappeared, bearing a long shallow plastic box, the kind you stored things in under the bed. She set it on the kitchen table and waved him over. "They're sleeping," she said in a theatrical whisper.

"You know your door is broken?"

She either didn't hear him or didn't care.

"Lea," he said. "Hello? What happened to your door? How long has it been like that?"

She looked up, distracted and annoyed that he was focused on something else. "How long has what—oh, the door. I don't know. Couple of months. The last tropical storm."

"Are you serious? Lea, do you have any idea how dangerous that is? Anyone could come in here! Or any*thing*! Look, all my tools are in the car. Let me just get them and I'll—"

"Leave it!"

He froze, silenced by the ferocity in her voice. He stood staring at her, too stunned to speak.

After a while she forced a little laugh. "Sorry. I just . . . I really want you to see this. Please?"

Her girlish plea made him relent. And her insistence had actually piqued his curiosity. With a final glance at the door, he crossed to the table and peered into the container. She might have just taken it from the oven, there was so much heat coming off it. Presumably she kept it on the back porch and had only brought it in to spare him the horror of the inhospitable temperature outside. But she'd only saved him from the heat, not the smell. If anything, it was worse than what was in the fridge. He wrinkled his nose and resisted the urge to pinch it shut.

The water was murky, but he could make out the shapes of several tiny pale creatures floating within, each about the size of a grain of rice. They didn't appear to be moving, not of their own volition. The water was still sloshing gently from the movement of the box and the creatures were rocked with the current.

Evan didn't know what to say. He wasn't even sure what he was supposed to be looking at. Frankly, he was far more concerned about the door.

"Now watch," Lea said. She dipped her fingers into a little plastic container and sprinkled some brown flakes into the warm, cloudy water. Nothing happened.

Evan opened his mouth to tell her the things looked dead to him, but she shushed him before he could speak. He sighed and turned his attention back to the water.

After a few moments he thought he saw one of them twitch, just a whisper of movement. Lea's little gasp told him this was the reaction she'd been expecting. Another creature jerked and darted across the water, leaving a tiny V-shaped wake behind it. One by one the others began to stir, scurrying around in the water. He could make out the flicker of tiny legs.

Lea looked overjoyed, but her excitement was way out of proportion to what had just occurred.

"So . . . " he ventured, "you gave fish food to some bugs and they woke up and swam around?"

Her expression hardened, and she stared at Evan as though he were a stranger. "They're not bugs," she snapped.

For a moment it seemed like she wasn't going to explain further, and he felt like the rug had been pulled out from under him. He'd clearly offended her, but he was totally in the dark. "Look, I'm sorry, but I have no idea what I'm supposed to be seeing here. You're the expert. You tell me what's so amazing about it."

"They're alive," she said, her eyes shining.

"I can see that. And?"

"They shouldn't be."

Evan was beginning to wonder whether this was some kind of practical joke. He'd driven all the way out here for *this?* He raised his eyebrows enquiringly, waiting for her to elaborate.

"Do you know what was in that water before?" She gazed down at the box.

"Judging from the smell, quite a lot of dead fish?"

Lea shook her head. "Nothing alive or dead. Nothing organic at all. It's just water from the Gulf." She peered closely into his eyes, as though anticipating a breakthrough on his part. "Polluted water from the Gulf," she added.

Evan was tiring of the game. He pulled his T-shirt away from where it had stuck to his chest and stood beneath the fan. "You're going to have to spell it out for me," he said wearily.

She dropped into a chair with a sigh. "Sorry. I forget sometimes you're not actually here with me."

He frowned at the odd admission, but he knew what she meant. He talked to her also when he was on his own. Only in his case there was no answering voice. He suspected Lea had a version of him with her all the time, who listened to her manic chatter and understood it. His eyes flicked again to the broken door.

"Just start at the beginning," he urged, tilting his head back to feel the breeze on his face.

"Yes. Okay. The beginning." She seemed to notice his discomfort for the first time. She got up and went to the fridge, and he braced himself for the smell. But instead she opened the door to the freezer, filled a glass with ice cubes and handed it to him.

He rubbed the glass gratefully across his forehead and over the back of his neck. No wonder she was so scattered; the heat was probably cooking her brain. He noticed that the sky had darkened with clouds. Rain would only increase the appalling humidity, but at least it might cool things down a little.

"Do you remember the first time we went to the beach?" Lea asked.

"I've never forgotten it."

"Do you remember that little Vietnamese girl?"

He nodded. He'd never forgotten her either.

After the weirdness with Lea and the crab, Evan had gone back to the sand, determined to build a new castle. Suddenly a scream rang out, as piercing as a siren. Sleeping sunbathers bolted upright, staring around, looking for the source of the cries.

The little girl had been splashing in the shallow water not far from Lea, and she had stepped on a piece of glass. Except it was more than just a piece of glass. It was half a broken liquor bottle, the kind a thug might use to carve-up someone's face in a bar fight. The glass had gone straight through her foot like a huge, vicious fang, and the girl was screaming at the top of her lungs as she lay where she'd fallen.

It was as though someone had yelled "Shark!" Her screams brought everyone out of the water at full-pelt, even Lea. When the grown-ups realised what had happened, they clustered around the girl and her parents, who were shouting for someone in the gawking crowd to call an ambulance.

There wasn't much the lifeguard could do, and the bottle was wedged so far into the girl's foot he advised them to leave it for the ambulance crew to remove. Or the surgeon in the hospital she was destined for.

Evan shuddered. "Yeah, I remember her."

"Well, the same thing happened to me a couple of weeks ago."

At his look of horror she was quick to add, "Oh, not as bad as her, don't worry. I got back here and managed to get all the glass out of my foot. At least I thought I did. I'm writing about the impact of climate change on the barrier islands, so I've been doing some tests on the water. Do you know how polluted the Gulf of Mexico is?"

Evan held up his hands. "Focus, Lea."

"Yeah, sorry. Okay, so a couple of days later, my foot got infected and I realised there were still some pieces of glass in it. I thought soaking it in seawater might help, so I did that."

Evan had forgotten all about his own discomfort. "What? Why didn't you go to a doctor?"

She shrugged. "No insurance. Besides, I didn't think it was that big a deal. Anyway, I fell asleep with my foot in one of those containers, and when I woke up I was fine. The water was all bloody and there were little shards of glass at the bottom, and my foot was healed." Lea returned to the table and looked down at the things swimming in the box. "The next day, they appeared."

Evan followed her gaze and watched the creatures. They were livelier now, and there was something oddly focused about their movements. It bothered him.

"They should have pulled that bottle out of the girl's foot," Lea mused, sounding far away. "They should have given it back."

He didn't like the glazed look in her eyes, the awe in her voice. She sounded like someone who'd joined a cult.

"What are you telling me?" he asked cautiously.

She lifted her head, a smile playing across her features. "I took something from the ocean. So the ocean took something from me. And together we made something new."

It had to be the heat making her crazy. That or the infection had been worse than she thought. He heard the echo of her voice all those years ago.

It was something else once. Somebody threw it away, threw it in the sea. And it became this.

Evan turned away. He set the glass of melting ice cubes on the counter and looked out the window. The leaves were wet and he realised it had been raining for some time. The rain drummed on the roof like impatient fingers, but it couldn't drown out the seagulls or the churning surf. The smell of rotting fish was starting to make his head spin. From here the water looked like chocolate milk, and he felt nauseated at the thought of his sister immersing herself in it day after day. How could they be so different? How could they look at that stretch of beach and see such entirely different worlds?

He rubbed his temples as he tried to think of what to say. Dredging his memory unearthed another unpleasant nugget of weirdness, and the pieces began to fall into place.

When they were kids, the beach and dunes had always been littered with trash, especially cans, bottles and those plastic yokes that held six-packs together. There was one day in particular when it seemed as if a garbage truck had overturned. They'd been about ten, Evan guessed, walking along the shore looking for seashells when they saw what looked like a plastic bag half-buried in the sand. It billowed a little in the breeze.

But as they drew nearer they realised it was a jellyfish. Lea immediately grabbed a long piece of driftwood and speared the creature's body, hoisting it high in the air.

Evan dodged away from her. "What are you doing?"

"I'm putting it back where it belongs," Lea stated matter-of-factly. "In the sea."

Evan shuddered. A dead jellyfish was just as dangerous as a living one, still capable of burning you with its stinging tentacles.

"I think you should leave it where people can see it."

But Lea wouldn't be deterred. She held the stick high overhead and the jellyfish dangled above her like a flag. She looked like a knight carrying a banner into battle as she marched towards the water's edge.

Evan held his breath, waiting for the creature to fall, to drop onto her head. Or slide down the stick onto her hands.

Perhaps it wasn't dead. He didn't like the way the gelatinous body resembled a huge, glazed eye. Was it watching him now?

"The sea gets lonely," Lea said. "If I put it back, she might turn it into something else."

These were ideas she had been obsessing over her whole life. How could Evan not have seen it? All at once he felt the crushing weight of guilt. He knew her better than anyone. He should have come out here more often, pushed aside his own neurotic fear about the stupid causeway. Instead he'd let her isolate herself on this island, in this squalid little shack, where her hold on reality had only gotten more slippery as the years went by.

He pictured her holed-up in here while a hurricane lashed the trees outside and threw thirty-foot waves against the seawall. The island was already sinking as the sea levels rose. How long would it be before the foul waters swallowed the whole house? She said the door had been busted since the last tropical storm. He shuddered to think who or what might have been able to just waltz right in while she slept. If she slept at all. Maybe she just sat up all night staring into buckets full of toxic waste, waiting for creatures to pop out and say hi. Maybe the open door was an invitation for something to come in from the sea.

There was a click as the ice cubes shifted in his glass, and he felt as though someone had dropped one down the back of his shirt. He didn't think those flakes she had dropped into the water were fish food. The heat, the smell, the sickening realisation... All at once he felt dizzy. His stomach lurched, and his voice was little more than a hoarse croak as he told her he needed the bathroom.

He rushed from the kitchen and got there just in time to fall to his knees before the toilet. He hadn't eaten anything that morning, and last night's beer tasted horrible on the way back up. After a few wretched heaves, he flushed the toilet and confronted his haggard reflection in the mirror. He ran the faucet and splashed cold water in his face and over his head, wishing the refreshing sensation would never end.

"You okay in there?" Lea called.

"I'm fine! Just... the heat, you know? I'll be out in a few minutes."

He listened as she padded away. Then he opened the door and slipped quietly down the hall, into her bedroom. There was something he needed to see. The rain was coming down harder, and a gust of wind rustled some loose papers somewhere in the room. It sounded like claws.

Her laptop sat on a little table against the wall. It was open, and a screensaver was dancing over the cracked screen. Evan tapped the trackpad and a document appeared. He assumed the confusing text that greeted him was a table with equations or chemical formulae. He scrolled to the beginning and began to read.

The Poisoned Wellspring: The Real Impact of Climate Change on the Ocean

4.56 billion years ago an immense cloud began to coalesce, spin and collapse under its own gravity in a process known as cold accretion. This solar nebula was the origin of our solar system. The orbiting chunks of rock and ice eventually became the four inner planets, and in what was still the infancy of the Earth, oceans began to form. Saltwater seas have dominated our planet for 3.5 billion years and they are the source of all life here. All *indigenous* life.

But just as intergalactic elements influenced the birth and development of our sun and planets, so too has Earth's dominant species played a part in the development of other forms of life.

Between 50% and 80% of all life on Earth exists in the ocean, but of the 1.5 million species that are known, there are potentially 50 million as yet undiscovered.

More statistics followed, with detailed information on mankind's impact on the planet's ecosystems, the melting of the ice caps and the rising sea levels. She speculated about the existence of distant planets with no land masses at all, where aquatic life could flourish.

He began to skim, but he was brought up short by the word "sea-monkeys". After a moment's confusion, he saw she was describing the process by which the little brine shrimp were awakened from their dormant, desiccated state by adding "instant life eggs" to their environment. He couldn't help but smile at the memory of the sea-monkey tank they had kept when they were little. It was probably many kids' introduction to the concept of false advertising.

But his smile vanished as Lea began describing her own similar process of reviving life forms from a cryptobiotic state.

The combination of global warming and pollution has created a reaction chamber for these organisms, most of which have been inactive for billions of years. Now many more are beginning to awaken.

As he read on, it became clear that she wasn't talking about the fossilised remains of prehistoric species; she was talking about life that had come from elsewhere in the universe, organisms trapped inside the rocks and space dust that had formed the solar system. They had survived the journey and the incomprehensibly long sleep, and now mankind's contamination of the planet was actually aiding in their re-birth.

One phrase bothered him especially: "most of which have been inactive." Was she seriously suggesting that aliens had been living among us for aeons?

"Oh, Lea," he said softly.

As it went on, the paper began to lose its objectivity, and its way. He caught the word "mermaid" at one point, but couldn't find the context for it. Several times she referred to the ocean as though it was alive itself and consciously nurturing both the creatures and the toxins inside it. There was her familiar theme about replacing what had been taken from the water so that it could transform. She talked as though the ocean itself wanted to transform, to drown the world. To reclaim it.

He saw a list of dates and numbers, with vague descriptions of the things he had seen flitting in the container. Something about the process of stimulating them had seemed oddly familiar to him at the time, but he hadn't made the connection with sea-monkeys. He knew almost nothing about the science behind this stuff, but if there were some 50 million unknown species in the ocean, then surely it made more sense that Lea had discovered one of those rather than something that travelled here from the far distant stars. Something that could be awakened just like those little brine shrimp.

Other odd phrases caught his eye as he continued to scroll through.

Eutrophication of the water triggered the Late Devonian mass extinction, wiping out three-quarters of all life on Earth. Now, as a result of the levels of pollution, a similar over-abundance of nutrients in the water is causing other species to thrive. One creature's poison is another's sustenance. And we are their "instant life eggs". As the sea levels rise, so will they.

It was all beginning to sound sinister and apocalyptic. And his heart twisted as he realised it went on like that, page after page of escalating madness. Evan couldn't take any more. He closed the laptop gently, and rested his hand on its warm surface before turning away, only to flinch at the sight of the room before him.

It was a shambles. The open window had allowed both rain and seawater to saturate the wall beneath it. Books and papers lay scattered across every surface, spilling onto the floor. Figurines had been blown off the shelves by the wind and never put away.

The bed was unmade, the sheet thrown back. And what he saw there made his skin crawl. It was full of sand. Not just a few grains either. She must have scooped up buckets of it and dumped it in her bed. Tears pricked his eyes and he turned to go, but a flicker of movement made him stop.

He didn't want to look, but he forced himself to move closer to the bed. There was something moving in the sand. A chill went through him as he realised not just what he was seeing, but what he had been hearing.

These were larger than the ones she had woken for him, and entirely translucent. She had mentioned crabs and sea-spiders in her paper, and they resembled both as they clambered through the wasteland where she slept. Each was about the size of his hand, with a soft, segmented body and rounded flaps down each side that looked more suited to swimming than crawling on land. Two long spines extended backwards from the head, and the creatures tracked his movement as he inched closer to the bed. As one, they scuttled towards the edge of the mattress, stretching their antennae towards him.

Outside, the storm sounded like a woman screaming.

He'd seen enough. He rubbed away the prickling sensation on the back of his neck, steeling himself as he returned to the kitchen.

Lea was standing over the container as if she'd never moved, still watching in fascination as the little creatures swam back and forth in patterns that she probably believed were attempts to communicate.

"Come on," he said, taking her gently by the arm. "We have to go."

She blinked in surprise. "What do you mean? You just got here. I thought we were going to have lunch."

He silently blessed her for providing the means to a perfect lie. "Exactly. I haven't eaten anything all day and I'm starved."

She looked puzzled as he took out his car keys. "But Casa Mare is so close. We can walk—"

"It's raining, silly. Can't you hear it?"

She looked up and he saw her register the sound. She smiled, but it was a pale imitation of the one she'd shown earlier, when he'd first arrived. That seemed like years ago.

He slipped his sandals on in the doorway. "It's okay," he said. "I don't mind driving. Besides, I wanted to go to the Strand anyway."

"Oh. Okay."

It was all he could do not to wilt with relief at her trusting compliance. As he led her down the stairs, through the rain and into the car, he felt like the villain in some old movie, luring the wide-eyed heroine to the asylum. Well, she could curse his tactics later, but there was no question that he had to get her away from this place. Away from the house, the water, the island. Most of all away from those . . . things.

They were both drenched by the time they were settled in the car. Lea had thrown a flimsy shirt over her bikini-top, but she didn't even seem to notice that she was still barefoot. Evan said nothing. He wasn't even sure where to take her. There was probably a hospital in Galveston, but he didn't know where it was and, in any case, he wanted her off the island.

The sky had darkened, and the car rocked from side to side as the wind threw waves of rain against it. This was more than just a monsoon. There hadn't been any weather warnings on the radio as he was driving over. But then, as always, he had been preoccupied.

He retraced the route he had taken to get to her house, hoping she was too out of it to notice he wasn't going in the direction of the Strand. The windshield wipers were having a hard time keeping up with the deluge, and when he glanced down a side street he saw white-capped waves leaping in the Gulf. Surely it was some trick of the light that made them look as high as the houses.

Lea didn't say a word, and her silence was even more disturbing than her fervent rambling. He'd expected her to freak out when she realised he was lying about where he was taking her. Instead, she was simply gazing out the passenger window. She was watching the same violent storm he was, but nothing about it seemed to faze her.

Evan was terrified. It was one thing to hold the car steady driving through gale-force winds on a road on the island, quite another to have to make it across the causeway in such conditions.

It's only two miles, he reminded himself. That was true, but reaching the mainland wasn't going to make the storm magically abate. Once there, he'd still have the problem of what to do with his sister.

One thing at a time.

When the causeway finally came into view, he felt light-headed. But he put his foot down and barrelled ahead, refusing to look at anything but the line of road in front of him. He couldn't maintain the speed for long, as the route was clogged with slow-moving traffic. He wanted to scream with frustration as he was forced to slow to a crawl.

The palm trees on either side were whipping back and forth, bent double in the fury of the storm, ready to snap like matchsticks any second. Then they were past them, past the salt marsh, and out over the open water. The bay rippled around and beneath the causeway like a black carpet.

"The boat."

Lea's voice was so soft he wasn't sure she had even spoken.

"What boat?"

He risked a glance at her and saw she was looking off to his left. As though exploiting his lapse in attention, the car swerved a little, pushed by a powerful gust of wind. He clutched the steering wheel and regained control, holding it steady as they edged further out onto the causeway.

"The sunken boat. It's gone."

Her words chilled him to the core. He desperately wished he could just jam his foot down on the accelerator, push the car up to 100 and rocket past all the other vehicles. Being trapped in this snail's pace with them was maddening. He had to outrun the storm. He also couldn't shake the feeling that it wasn't just the storm that was chasing them.

He was approaching the top of the span, the point he hated the most. Thunderheads loomed over the bay and the water appeared to be boiling. Huge curtains of rain swept across the lines of cars. Lightning carved a jagged path through the black clouds, and a deafening crack of thunder followed instantly.

The noise made Lea jump and she suddenly sat up, her eyes wide as she stared around, seeming to realise for the first time where they were. "Evan? What are you doing?"

His fingers contracted, clutching the steering wheel tightly as he tried to will the traffic to move, to drive, to get off the causeway. He tried to make himself smile for her sake. "I'm taking you to my place," he said. "We'll be safe there."

She stared at him for a moment, her expression fearful. "You can't take me away from here. The sea won't let you. It's part of me now."

He shook his head, wishing he could tune out her words. The traffic had come to a standstill at the crest of the hill, and the position gave him a view he would rather not have had. Horns blared as people became frantic, but they were trapped just like Evan was.

Lea continued, her voice calm, her eyes shining with unnatural intensity. "I gave myself to the water. I've been drinking it. And they've been drinking *me*."

Her words made him feel sick. The rain had become hail, battering the windshield like pebbles. It was all he could do to stay calm as dark waves rose below the causeway, surging high enough to send spray up onto the road. Stranded fish flopped on the concrete.

"Go, go, go," he urged the other drivers. "Please move!"

"It won't let you leave," Lea said again.

"Well, I'm damn well going to try!" he shot back.

But there was no way out of the gridlock. Occasionally he was able to creep forwards a few inches, but there was clearly some obstacle at the far end. Around him he saw people start to panic, abandoning their cars and running, stranding everyone else behind the roadblock of deserted vehicles. A man and woman pulled their two small children out of the Volkswagen stalled beside him and fled down the causeway.

Another bolt of lightning ripped the sky apart with an explosion that made Evan cover his ears. He watched in helpless horror as the leaping waves gained strength, until one massive surge crashed over the causeway and swept the family over the side. His stomach plunged.

Above them the clouds had massed together, fusing into an enormous storm-wall, sharply pointed at one end. Evan knew the danger signs. Anyone who'd grown up here would recognise that formation. They had no choice but to run.

"Come on, Lea, we have to get out of here before—"

But it was too late. The tornado dropped out of the cloud like a spike. It slammed straight down onto the railway, wrenching apart the girders of the drawbridge and sending them flying in all directions. The impact was deafening, almost drowning out the shrieking of the wind. It felt like an earthquake, and cracks began scurrying across the causeway. The road buckled, undulating impossibly, the motion sending stalled cars sliding and slamming into one another. Evan tried not to watch as people were trapped between them.

The waves didn't discriminate. They took both people and vehicles, pulling them off the road and into the watery hell below. For a split-second he remembered his escape plan and had to bite back a deranged laugh at the thought of calmly winding down the window and swimming free of the maelstrom.

The tornado coiled and twisted, and at first it seemed to be dancing away from the causeway. Then, as though changing its mind, it paused. And turned.

That was all the motivation Evan needed. He shouldered the door open against the pressure of the wind and grabbed Lea's hands, dragging her out of the car. The strength of the wind was unbelievable. It was like trying to push through a brick wall.

Lea shouted something, but he couldn't hear her over the noise of the storm. He'd always been told that a tornado sounded like a freight train. And it did. It was the train from his nightmare, the one that jumped the track and smashed into the causeway.

Waves leapt and crashed around them as Evan tried to run, yanking at Lea to get her to move. But she refused to go. He grabbed her in desperation and shook her, screaming her name. But she only gazed at him impassively, the picture of calm acceptance. He heard her next words clearly, and he had to wonder if she had even spoken aloud at all.

"If you take something from the ocean, it will take something from you."

His heart sank as he realised she was referring to herself. He made a last attempt to pull her along the road, but she seemed to have the weight of the whole island behind her. He felt her hand slip from his, and before he could grab her again, a column of water rose from the vortex at the base of the tornado. It climbed higher and higher, a boiling wall of liquid darkness, until it reached the height of the causeway before arching and falling, raining down on Lea like a giant hand.

Evan screamed as Lea vanished from sight and the force of the splash slammed him into the crash barrier. He scrambled to his feet and ran to the side, clinging to the guard rail as he looked down into the waves. But Lea was gone. There was nothing down there but churning black water.

He was too overwhelmed to notice at first, but the wind had died down. The tornado had thinned to a dancing string and was only stirring up the smallest waves.

Evan stared down into the sea, searching in desperation for any sign of Lea. As the choppy surface smoothed into a flat grey plane, a swirl of terrible colour moved in the darkness below. Something was taking shape. It had a strange, unnatural gleam, like a spill of oil. It grew in size as it rose towards the surface, and he thought he saw the flick of a large tail.

Evan stood frozen at the edge of the ruined causeway, trembling. He remembered the word he'd seen in her paper that he couldn't find a context for. Now he thought he understood. If flakes of Lea's dried blood had revived those alien creatures, what might her whole body awaken when fed to the poisoned ocean? What might she become herself?

He continued to watch as the humanoid shape darted beneath the surface, and something in its oily rainbow sheen felt like a message. But what it might be saying, he couldn't begin to guess.

STEPHEN JONES & KIM NEWMAN

NECROLOGY: 2017

DEPRESSINGLY, IT WAS another record year for significant losses in the genre. Along with a number of major authors and artists, we also saw the passing of no less than four cast members from the recent revival of TV's *Twin Peaks*, three memorable Hammer heroines, two great American horror directors, a pair of Hollywood Tess Trueharts, an iconic secret agent with a license to kill, and far too many good friends and colleagues . . .

AUTHORS/ARTISTS/COMPOSERS

American scriptwriter and TV producer **Alan M. Surgal** died on January 3, aged 100. His few credits include Arthur Penn's surreal *Mickey One* (1965) and 'The Canterville Ghost' episode of *Robert Montgomery Presents*, starring Cecil Parker.

British fanzine editor **Peter Weston**, who co-founded the Birmingham Science Fiction Group in 1971, died of complications from cancer on January 5, aged 73. From 1963-73 he published the Hugo Award-nominated periodical *Zenith* (aka *Speculation*), and later produced two issues of *Prolapse* before the magazine went on hiatus for twenty-three years and returned in 2006, changing its title to *Relapse* three years later. In the eary 1970s Weston helped launch

Novacon and organised three Speculation Conferences. He chaired Seacon '79, the 1979 World Science Fiction Convention in Brighton, and was Fan Guest of Honor at Noreason, the 2004 Worldcon in Boston. He also edited three volumes of the *Andromeda* SF anthology series in the 1970s, and his 2004 memoir was titled *Stars in My Eyes: My Adventures in British Fandom*.

American light fantasy and religious artist **James Christensen** died after a long battle with cancer on January 8, aged 74. A painter and sculptor whose art appeared on many SF and fantasy books from the 1970s onwards, some of his highly-detailed work was collected in *A Journey of the Imagination: The Art of James Christensen*, co-written with Renwick St. James. The pair also collaborated with Alan Dean Foster on the 1996 children's fantasy *Voyage of the Basset* and the annotated collection of Mother Goose verse, *Rhymes & Reasons*, published the following year. A member of The Church of Jesus Christ of Latter-day Saints, where he served as a bishop, Christensen won the Chesley Award three times.

British author **Hilary** [Denham] **Bailey** (aka "Pippin Graham"), who was married to author Michael Moorcock from 1962-78, died on January 11, aged 80. She reportedly co-wrote the 1969 novel, *The Black Corridor*, credited solely to Moorcock, and edited volumes 7-10 of the *New Worlds* anthology series (the first with Charles Platt). As a literary novelist, she wrote a number of books that were pastiches or sequels to other works, including *The Strange Adventures of Charlotte Holmes: Sister of the More Famous Sherlock*, *Frankenstein's Bride* and *Miles and Flora: A Sequel to Henry James' The Turn of the Screw*.

British fan **Vicky Stock**, who was involved in the committees of the Birmingham SF Group and the British Fantasy Society/ FantasyCon, died of breast cancer the same day, aged 37.

American best-selling novelist, screenwriter, producer and director **William Peter Blatty**, whose seminal 1971 demonic possession novel *The Exorcist* directly inspired the blockbuster movie, various sequels and a TV series, died of multiple myeloma on January 12, aged 89. Blatty's novel spent fifty-seven consecutive weeks on the *New York Times* best-seller list. He won an Academy Award for his screenplay for *The Exorcist* (1973), and he wrote and directed the film versions of his novels *Twinkle Twinkle "Killer" Kane!* and *Legion*, as *The Ninth Configuration* and *The Exorcist III*, respectively. His other books include *Demons Five Exorcist Nothing: A Fable*, *The Exorcist for the 21st Century* and the 2001 memoir *If There Were Demons Then Perhaps There Were Angels: William Peter Blatty's Own Story of The Exorcist*. Blatty was a recipient of the HWA Bram Stoker Award for Life Achievement in 1998.

British music and film critic, political theorist and blogger **Mark Fisher** (aka "K-punk") committed suicide on January 13, aged 48. He had been battling with depession for a long time. Fisher's insightful criticism ranged across such topics as M.R. James and H.P. Lovecraft to *Sapphire & Steel* and *The Terminator*. His books include *The Weird and the Eerie* (2016) and he contributed to *Fact* magazine, *The Wire* and *Sight & Sound*. In 2009 he co-founded the publishing imprint Zero Books with Tariq Goddard.

Dutch SF and fantasy fan, editor and translator **Annemarie van Ewijck** (aka "Annemarie Kindt") died on January 15, aged 73. She edited the semi-prozine *Holland SF* for nineteen years.

British author **Emma** [Christina] **Tennant** (aka "Catherine Aydy") died after a long illness on January 20, aged 79. Her many books feature genre elements, including *The Time of the Crack* (aka *The Crack*), *The Last of the Country House Murders*, *The Bad Sister* (filmed in 1983), *The Ghost Child*, *Two Women of London: The Strange Case of Ms Jekyll and Mrs Hyde*, *The Magic Drum: An Excursion*, *Faustine* and *Heathcliff's Tale*. From 1975-78 she edited the magazine *Bananas*, where she published such authors as Angela Carter, J.G. Ballard and John T. Sladek. Tennant also scripted the 1990 TV mini-series *Frankenstein's Baby*.

British comics artist **John Watkiss** died of cancer the same day, aged 55. Amongst the titles he worked on were DC Comics' *The Sandman*, *Sandman Mystery Theatre*, *Starman* and the 2006-07 revival of *Deadman*, along with various *Conan* comics for Dark Horse. Watkiss was also a storyboard artist, best known for his contributions to Disney's animated *Tarzan*, *Atlantis: The Lost Empire* and *Treasure Planet*.

American bookseller and fan **Larry Smith** (Laurence C. Smith) died of a dissected aortic aneurysm on January 20, aged 70. He co-chaired a number of conventions, including the 2010 World Fantasy Convention in Columbus, Ohio.

British SF fan **Mike Dickinson** died of lung cancer the same day, aged 69. He had been in poor health since being hit by a car a year earlier. He co-chaired the 1979 Eastercon (Yorcon) in Leeds with David Pringle, and was Toastmaster at Yorcon II in 1981. Dickinson's fanzines included *Adsun*, *Sirius* (with Alan Dorey), *Bar Trek* (with Lee Montgomeries) and *Spaghetti Junction* (with Jackie Gresham), and he edited three issues of the British Science Fiction Association's *Vector* in the late 1970s.

American screenwriter **Andy Ruben** died of a stroke on January 23, aged 67. After working as an assistant editor on Tobe Hooper's *Eaten Alive*, he teamed up with his wife (1979-92), director Katt Shea, to co-script *Stripped to Kill*, *Stripped to Kill 2: Live Girls* and *Dance of the Damned*. Ruben also wrote and directed *Club Vampire* starring John Savage.

American comics writer, artist and scriptwriter **Jack Mendelsohn**, who worked for DC and EC comics, died of lung cancer on January 25, aged 90. He co-scripted The Beatles' *Yellow Submarine* (1968) and worked on numerous cartoon TV shows, including episodes of *Sabrina and the Groovie Goolies*, *The New Scooby-Doo Movies*, *Spider-Man and His Amazing Friends* ('The Bride of Dracula!'), *Toxic Crusaders* and *Teenage Mutant Ninja Turtles*.

Veteran American comics artist **Dan Spiegle** died on January 28, aged 96. He began his career in 1949 drawing *Hopalong Cassidy*, and went on to illustrate such TV tie-ins as *My Favorite Martian*, *Space Family Robinson*, *The Green Hornet*, *The Invaders* and various *Scooby-Doo* titles. Spiegle also contributed to *Korak Son of Tarzan*, *Boris Karloff Tales of Mystery* and *Grimm's Ghost Stories*, plus graphic adaptations of Disney's *Son of Flubber*, *Mary Poppins*, *Herbie Rides Again*, *Return from Witch Mountain* and *The Black Hole*. Later work included DC's *Secrets of Haunted House*, *House of Mystery* and *Blackhawk*, Marvel's *Tarzan of the Apes*, *The Hunchback of Notre Dame* and *Who Framed Roger Rabbit*, and Dark Horse's *Indiana*

Jones series. In 1972 he co-created the "Doctor Spektor" character with Donald F. Glut for *Mystery Comics Digest.*

American screenwriter **John** [Thomas] **Gay** died on February 4, aged 92. His many credits include George Pal's *The Power, No Way to Treat a Lady, The Hunchback of Notre Dame* (1982), *Around the World in 80 Days* (1989 and 1999 versions) and *Summer of Fear* (1996). Gay also wrote the one-man play *Diversions and Delights*, which starred Vincent Price as Oscar Wilde. It premiered in San Francisco in 1977 and toured around more than 300 cities over the next three years.

The body of 71-year-old American writer, critic and essayist **Edward** [Winslow] **Bryant** [Jr.] was found at his home in Colorado on February 10. He had been ill for a long time and died in his sleep. The Nebula Award-winning author began publishing SF and horror stories in 1970, and his short fiction was collected in *Among the Dead and Other Events Leading Up to the Apocalypse, Cinnebar, Wyoming Sun, Particle Theory, Neon Twilight, Darker Passions, The Baku: Tales of the Nuclear Age, Trilobyte* and *Predators and Other Stories.* With Harlan Ellison he co-wrote *Phoenix Without Ashes* (1975), a novelisation of Ellison's script *The Starlost,* and he co-edited the anthology *2076: The American Tricentennial* with Jo Ann Harper in 1977. Bryant also wrote reviews, convention reports and essays for *Locus* and other magazines. He appeared in Somtow Sucharitkul's low-budget movies *The Laughing Dead* and *Ill Met by Moonlight,* while a short story was adapted for an episode of TV's *The Hidden Room* and the 2008 movie *While She Was Out,* starring Kim Basinger.

Italian-born artist **Gino D'Achille** died the same day, aged 81. After moving to the UK in the mid-1960s, he began painting book covers for such publishers as Ballantine, Ace Books, DAW Books, Granada/Grafton and Pan Books. His many credits include various titles in John Norman's "Gor" series, H.P. Lovecraft and August Derleth's *The Lurker at the Threshold,* Ron Goulart's *Vampirella: Bloodstalk,* Tanith Lee's *The Storm Lord* and *The Birthgrave,* Peter Tremayne's *The Vengeance of She,* Michael Shea's *The Colour Out of Time* and, most notably, eleven volumes in Ballantine's series of Edgar Rice Burroughs' "Mars" books.

American artist and author **Dahlov Ipcar** (Dahlov Zorach) died on February 10, aged 99. She wrote and illustrated more than thirty children's books, and her adult fantasy trilogy consisits of *The Warlock of the Night*, *The Queen of Spells* and *A Dark Horn Blowing*. Ipcar had her first solo exhibition at the Museum of Modern Art in New York when she was just twenty-one years old.

Canadian-born TV screenwriter and producer **Howard** [Michael] **Leeds** died in Los Angeles on February 11, aged 97. Leeds created and executive produced the SF sitcom *Small Wonder* (1985-89) and contributed scripts to *Bewitched* and *The Ghost & Mrs. Muir*. He also produced the latter show, along with *My Living Doll*.

Japanese *manga* writer and artist **Jirô Taniguchi** died the same day, aged 69. His time-travel fantasy *Harukanaru machi e* was filmed in 2010 as *Quartier lointain*.

British SF fan and bookseller **Dave Holmes** died of cancer on February 13, aged 61. He began selling books for Roger Peyton and Rod Milner's Birmingham store Andromeda Bookshop in the 1970s, and later started up his own mail-order store, Magic Labyrinth, in Leicester. Holmes used his position as a book dealer to promote the careers of many up-and-coming authors.

American wargame and role-playing designer and developer **Loren Wiseman** died of a heart attack on February 14, aged 65. He co-founded the Game Designers' Workshop in 1973, and helped developed such SF games as *Traveller*, *Space 1889* and *Twilight 2000*. In 2004 Loren was inducted into the Adventure Gaming Hall of Fame.

Hungarian-born SF fan **Thomas Endrey** died in mid-February, aged 77. He moved to the US in 1956 and attended many conventions. In the late 1990s he was assistant editor of Andrew I. Porter's magazine *Science Fiction Chronicle*.

British-born artist and designer **Alan Aldridge** died in Los Angeles on February 17, aged 78. From 1965-67 he was art director at Penguin Books, creating surreal and psychedelic covers for their SF books by Robert A. Heinlein, J.G. Ballard, Harry Harrison, Clifford D. Simak, Frank Herbert, William Hope Hodgson and others. After going freelance, he published the best-selling art book *The Butterfly Ball and the Grasshopper Feast* (with William Plomer, filmed in

1977), *The Penguin Book of Comics* (with George Perry) and the novel *The Gnole* (with Steven R. Boyett and Maxine Miller), along with designing the iconic logo for the Hard Rock Cafe and illustrating two volumes of Beatles lyrics. *The Man with Kaleidoscope Eyes: The Art of Alan Aldridge* was a 2009 retrospective. The artist also worked as a production designer on the animated films *Faeries* and *The Wind in the Willows* (1987).

American screenwriter and novelist **Hank Searls** (Henry Hunt Searls, Jr.) died the same day, aged 94. His 1964 SF novel *The Pilgrim Project* was filmed four years later as *Countdown*, and he also wrote the novelisation of *Jaws II*.

84-year-old American movie historian and critic **Richard [Warren] Schickel** died on February 18, following a series of strokes. The film critic for *Time* magazine from 1965-2010, he also wrote for *Life* and the *Los Angeles Times Book Review*. His many books include *The Disney Version: The Life, Times, Art and Commerce of Walt Disney*, along with biographies of Douglas Fairbanks, Sr., Cary Grant, D.W. Griffith, James Cagney, Gary Cooper, Marlon Brando, Clint Eastwood, Woody Allen, Elia Kazan, Humphrey Bogart, Charles Chaplin and Steven Spielberg. Schickel also recorded many DVD commentaries and wrote, produced and directed a number of documentaries, including *The Horror Show* (1979) and *The Harryhausen Chronicles* (1998).

American children's author and poet **Nancy [Margaret] Willard** died on February 19, aged 80. She won the Newbery Award for her 1982 poetry volume *William Blake's Inn*, and her other books include *Sailing to Cythera and Other Anatole Stories*, *Things Invisible to See*, *Firebrat*, *Sister Water*, *The Ballad of Biddy Early* and *Pish Posh Said Hieronymous Bosch*, the latter illustrated by Leo and Diane Dillon.

American writer and editor **Susan Casper**, the wife and companion of editor Gardner Dozois for forty-seven years, died in her sleep on February 24, aged 69. She had been ill for some time. She made her fiction debut in Charles L. Grant's anthology *Fears* (1983), and published a number of short stories (often in collaboration with her husband and Jack Dann). Casper's collaborations with Dozois were collected in *Slow Dancing Through Time* (1990), and the pair co-edited the 1988 horror anthology *Ripper!*, *Up the Rainbow: The Complete Short Fiction of Susan Casper* and the novel *The Red Carnival* appeared posthumously.

British artist **Vic Fair**, who created the movie posters for Hammer's *Countess Dracula* and *Vampire Circus*, died of complications from Alzheimer's disease and diabetes the same day. He was 78. Fair's other posters include *Theatre of Blood*, *Death Line*, *It's Alive!*, *The Devil's Rain*, *Vampyres*, *Legend of the Werewolf*, *The Uncanny*, *The Man Who Fell to Earth*, *Death Weekend*, *Harlequin* and many others, along with unused designs for Hammer's *Frankenstein and the Monster from Hell* and *The Legend of the Seven Golden Vampires*, *Dragonslayer*, *The Adventures of Baron Munchausen*, *The Clan of the Cave Bear*, *The Emerald Forest* and the Bond film *A View to a Kill*. Fair also designed the UK poster for the Stephen King adaptation *Graveyard Shift*, painted by Les Edwards. He retired in the late 1980s.

British publishing editor **Georgina Hawtry-Woore**, the wife of SF author Paul McAuley, died of cancer on February 27, aged 50. After working in bookselling and at the David Grossman Literary Agency, she joined HarperCollins in 1995 as an editorial assistant and was promoted to editor five years later. She moved to Century and Arrow in 2002, eventually becoming senior editor at the Cornerstone imprint. An award for self-published writers was re-named in her memory by Words for the Wounded, a literary organisation in aid of wounded and disabled veterans.

Author and musician **Avalon Brantley** died on March 5. She was in her mid-30s. Her stories were published in anthologies from such literary small presses as Ex Occidente Press, Egaeus Press, Mount Abraxis and The Swan River Press. Her only novel, *The House of Silence*, was inspired by the work of William Hope Hodgson and published posthumously by Zagava in 2017. Her short fiction was collected in *Descended Suns Resucitate*, and she co-authored the prose and poety collection *Transcensience* with her partner Lockett Hollis. She also contributed a number of essays on Russian symbolist writers to Tartarus Press' periodical *Wormwood*.

American comics artist **Dave Hunt** (David Hunt) died of cancer the same day, aged 74. He worked as a penciller and inker for both

Marvel and DC on such titles as *Captain America, Fantastic Four, The Amazing Spider-Man, Superboy, Wonder Woman* and *Scooby-Doo*, and he also contributed to such Disney titles as *Darkwing Duck, The Little Mermaid* and *Beauty and the Beast*.

Influential American underground comix artist and writer **Jay [Patrick] Lynch** (aka "Jayzey Lynch") died on March 5, aged 72. Best known for such titles as *Bijou Funnies, Bazooka Joe* and the comic strip 'Nard n' Pat', he later collaborated on the children's books *Otto's Orange Day* and *Otto's Backwards Day* with Frank Cammuso.

American-born screenwriter **Julian Zimet** died in Rome, Italy, on March 9, aged 97. As "Julian Halevy" he scripted *Psyche 59, Crack in the World, Horror Express* (with Christopher Lee and Peter Cushing) and *Psychomania* (aka *The Death Wheelers*).

American underground comix artist **Skip Williamson** (Mervyn Wilton Williamson, Jr.) died of renal failure on March 16, aged 72. He had been suffering from heart disease and diabetes. Williamson's work was published in *Bijou Funnies, National Lampoon, High Times* and other titles. He was the art director of *Gallery* and *Hustler*, and he illustrated Arthur C. Clarke's satirical SF story 'When the Twerms Came' for *Playboy*.

Legendary comics artist and illustrator **Bernie Wrightson** (Bernard Albert Wrightson, aka "Berni Wrightson"), who co-created the character "Swamp Thing" with writer Len Wein for DC Comics in 1971, died of brain cancer on March 18, aged 68. He began his career in the 1960s, working for such magazines as *Amra, Squa-Tront, Trumpet* and *Spa-Fon*, and he made his professional comics debut in 1969 with 'The Man Who Murdered Himself' in DC's *House of Mystery*. He went on to work with all the major comics publishers, and in 1975 joined the artists' collective "The Studio", along with Barry Windsor-Smith, Jeff Jones and Michael Kaluta. His collections include *Badtime Stories, The Berni Wrightson Treasury, Berni Wrightson: A Look Back, Back for More, The Mutants, The Reaper of Love and Other Stories, The Monstrous Collection* and many others, while his 1983 adaptation of Mary Shelley's *Frankenstein* still stands as a pinnacle of his skill. He illustrated editions of Stephen King's *Cycle of the Werewolf, The Stand* and *Wolves of Calla*, along with a graphic version of the movie *Creepshow*. Wrightson also contributed conceptual art to a number of movies, including *The Faculty*, *Galaxy Quest*, *Thir13en Ghosts*, *Reign of Fire*, George R. Romero's *Land of the Dead*, Frank Darabont's *The Mist* and Stuart Gordon's unproduced adaptation of H.P Lovecraft's *The Shadow Over Innsmouth*.

American-born Canadian TV scriptwriter and producer **Denis McGrath** died of cancer in Toronto on March 23, aged 48. He worked on such series as *Spacebar*, *Starhunter*, *Blood Ties*, *SGU Stargate Universe*, *Bitten*, *Continuum*, *Aftermath* and *Creeped Out*.

Award-winning Canadian novelist **Marie Jakober** died on March 26, aged 75. Her books include the 1976 SF novel *The Mind Gods: A Novel of the Future* and such historical fantasies as *The Black Chalice*, *Even the Stones* and *The Demon Left Behind*.

Italian musician and composer **Alessandro Alessandroni**, best known for his distinctive whistle on Ennio Morricone's theme for *Fistful of Dollars* and other Westerns, died the same day, aged 92. His composing credits include the movies *The Devil's Nightmare*, *The Mad Butcher*, *Lady Frankenstein*, *Very Close Encounters of the Fourth Kind* and *Killer Nun*. Alessandroni and his wife, singer Giulia De Mutiis, also provided the vocals for the song 'Mah Nà Mah Nà', which was heard on *The Muppet Show* and elsewhere.

American academic and SF critic **Mike Levy** (Michael M. Levy) died of cancer on April 3, aged 66. His reviews appeared in *Publishing Weekly, The New York Review of Science Fiction* and elsewhere, and he edited *Extrapolation* from 2006 onwards. Levy was also an editorial board member of *The Journal of the Fantastic in the Arts*, and he co-wrote the 2016 study *Children's Fantasy Literature: An Introduction* with Farah Mendlesohn.

Reclusive American horror fan **Persephone Longueuiel**, aged 50, died in a San Diego house fire with her 68-year-old bedridden mother, Elizabeth, on April 4. A former manager of the Comic Kingdom store in Hillcrest, she co-wrote stories and designed puzzles with Jay Allen Sanford for various magazines and comic books. Longueuiel also owned an extensive horror memorabilia collection that included signed and collectible books and original TV scripts. Fire officials described the inside of the burned-out home as "semi-hoarder conditions".

American children's author **Patricia C.** (Carwell) **McKissack** died on April 7, aged 72. She co-authored "The Clone Codes" SF trilogy (*The Clone Codes, Cyborg* and *The Visitor*) with John McKissack and Fredrick L. McKissack, and her short fiction is collected in *A Piece of the Wind and Other Stories to Tell* and *A Dark-Thirty: Southern Tales of the Supernatural*.

Roy Millenson, whose only SF story, "183rd Congress" appeared in the May 1954 issue of *Science Fiction Adventures*, died of cerebrovascular disease on April 9. He was 95.

American author **V.** (Victoria) **E.** (Estelle) **Mitchell** [Gustafson] died on April 13, aged 62. She wrote the tie-in novels *Star Trek: Enemy Unseen, Star Trek: Windows on a Lost World, Star Trek the Next Generation #22: Imbalance* and *Star Trek the Next Generation Starfleet Academy: Atalantis Station*. Three of her short stories are collected in the self-published chapbook *Ekaterin and Other Stories*.

Japanese *anime* artist and animator **Norio Shioyama** died with his wife in a high-rise apartment fire the same day. He was 77.

American author and screenwriter **William Hjortsberg** died of pancreatic cancer on April 22, aged 76. His 1978 novel *Falling Angel* was filmed a decade later by Alan Parker as *Angel Heart*. He also wrote the novels *Gray Matters* and *Nevermore* (featuring Edgar Allan Poe, Houdini and Sir Arthur Conan Doyle), and the collection *Tales & Fables*, and he scripted Ridley Scott's fantasy movie *Legend* (1985).

American-born author and musician **Patrick Meadows** died on the island of Majorca, Spain, the same day, aged 83. During the late 1960s and early '70s he had one story published in *Analog Science Fiction/Science Fact* (which also became the title story for the 1970 anthology *Countercommandment and Other Stories*) and four in *The Magazine of Fantasy and Science Fiction*. Meadows also contributed a painting to *Spectrum 9: The Best in Contemporary Fantastic Art*. From 1969 until 2008 he was co-founder and director of Majorca's International Music Festival of Deià.

American academic, critic and reviewer **Roger C.** (Clark) **Schlobin** died on April 25, aged 72. His genre studies include *A Research*

Guide to Science Fiction Studies (with Marshall B. Tymm and L.W. Curry), *The Literature of Fantasy: A Comprehensive Annotated Bibliography of Modern Fantasy Fiction, Andre Norton: A Primary and Secondary Bibliography* and *Phantasmagoria: Collected Essays on the Nature of Fantasy and Horror Fiction*. Schlobin also had two stories published in anthologies, and he wrote the novel *Fire and Fur: The Last Sorcerer Dragon*.

73-year-old American author and editor **Grania Davis** (Grania Eve Kaiman) died on April 28 after losing consciousness in a movie theatre. She was married to author Avram Davidson from 1962-64, and collaborated with him on *Marco Polo and the Sleeping Beauty* and *The Boss in the Wall: A Treatise on the House Devil* (reprinted in *Best New Horror* #10). Following Davidson's death in 1994, she co-edited the collections of his stories *The Avram Davidson Treasury: A Tribute Collection* (with Robert Silverberg), *The Investigations of Avram Davidson* (with Richard A. Lupoff), and *The Other Nineteenth Century: A Story Collection, ¡Limekiller!* and *The Ennead: The Romaunt of Vergil Magus: The Scarlet Fig; Or, Slowly Through a Land of Stone* (all with Henry Wessels). Davis' own books include *Dr Grass, The Rainbow Annals, The Great Perpendicular Path* and *Moonbird*, while her short fiction was collected in *Tree of Life, Book of Death: The Treasures of Grania Davis*. She also co-edited the anthologies *Everybody Has Somebody in Heaven: Essential Jewish Tales of the Spirit* with Jack Dann and *Speculative Japan: Outstanding Tales of Japanese Science Fiction and Fantasy* with Gene Van Troyer.

Davis was briefly involved with author Philip K. Dick, and the writer's third wife, **Anne R. Dick** (Anne Browning Williams), died the same day, aged 90. The couple were married from 1959-68, and her memoir *The Search for Philip K. Dick* was published in 2010.

American art and book collector Dr. **Howard Frank** died of complications from a bacterial infection on May 1, aged 75. A recipient of the Department of Defence's highest civil honour, the Presidential Distinguished Service Medal, for his expertise in information technology and contributions to the development of the Internet, he and his wife Jane published two books about their legendary art collection, *The Frank Collection: A Showcase of the*

World's Finest Fantastic Art and *Great Fantasy Art Themes from the Frank Collection*. Frank also contributed a number of articles about artists to *Realms of Fantasy* magazine.

Pioneering British comics historian and writer **Alan Austin** died of cancer on May 10, aged 62. He edited the 1970s fanzine *Fantasy Unlimited* (later *Comics Unlimited*) and in 1983 co-published the first *Comic Guide for Great Britain* with Justin Ebbs and Gary Fox. For many years Austin ran the comics store Heroes in Islington, London.

American SF author **Louis** [Henry] **Charbonneau** died in Canada on May 11, aged 93. His books include *No Place on Earth*, *Corpus Earthling*, *The Sentinel Stars*, *Psychedelic-40*, *Down to Earth*, *The Sensitives*, *Barrier World* and the movie novelisation of *Embryo*. Two 1960s episodes of TV's *The Outer Limits* were based on his work.

British comics artist **Edmund Bagwell** died of pancreatic cancer on May 14, aged 50. His strips appeared in such titles as *Black Axe*, *Marvel Comics Presents* ('Nick Fury'), *Crisis* and *2000 AD* ('Judge Dredd', 'Cradlegrave' and 'Tharg's Future Shocks').

Belgian comic book artist and writer **Pierre Seron** (aka "Foal") died on May 24, aged 75. He is best known for his long-running series *Les petits hommes* (The Little Men).

Renowned British anthologist, scholar and bookseller **Richard** [Lawrence] **Dalby** died of complications from diabetes on April 28, aged 68. One of the most learned authorities on supernatural and children's fiction, he edited many anthologies, including *The Sorceress in Stained Glass & Other Ghost Stories* (for which he rediscovered a "lost" story by M.R. James), *Dracula's Brood: Rare Vampire Stories by Friends and Contempories of Bram Stoker*, *Ghosts and Scholars: Ghost Stories in the Tradition of M.R. James* (with Rosemary Pardoe), *Ghosts for Christmas*, *Chillers for Christmas*, *Tales of Witchcraft*, *Horror for Christmas*, *Vampire Stories*, *Shivers for Christmas* and *Twelve Gothic Tales*, along with various volumes of *The Virago Book of Ghost Stories* and *The Mammoth Book of Ghost Stories*. Dalby also compiled a number of single-author collections for The Ghost Story Press, Ash-Tree Press and Sarob Press, amongst other imprints, and he was a regular contributor to the *Book & Magazine Collector*.

American children's book author and illustrator **Geoffrey Hayes** died on June 2, aged 69. He was working on a graphic-novel fairy-tale, *Lovo and the Firewolf*, at the time of his death.

Australian illustrator turned novelist **Arthur** [Richard] **Mather** died on June 4, aged 91. He co-created and drew Atlas Publications' *Captain Atom* comic (1948-54) and later went on to write such techno-thrillers as *The Mind Breaker*, *The Duplicate* and *The Pawn*.

British author and poet **Helen Dunmore**, a Fellow of the Royal Society of Literature, died of cancer on June 5, aged 64. Her books include the "Ingo" series and the ghost novel for Hammer, *The Greatcoat*. Dunmore also had stories published in four 1990s anthologies edited by Tony Bradman, including *Incredibly Creepy Stories*.

Eisner Award-winning American comics writer **James Vance**, best known for scripting Tekno Comix's *Mr. Hero the Newmatic Man*, created by Neil Gaiman in the mid-1990s, died of cancer the same day, aged 64. His other credits include *Kings in Disguise* and its sequel *On the Ropes*, along with *Aliens: Survival*, *Predator: Homeworld* and three issues of *Batman: Legends of the Dark Knight*.

American author and Professor Emeritus of the City University of New York, **Morton N.** (Norton) **Cohen**, died on June 12, aged 96. He wrote biographies of Lewis Carroll, H. Rider Haggard and Rudyard Kipling.

American business executive **Jim Galton** (James E. Galton), who was the president and CEO of Marvel Entertainment Group from 1975-91, and who is credited with saving the company from bankruptcy, died the same day, aged 92. Galton was also president of the paperback imprint Popular Library from 1968 until he was fired by the company's new owner, CBS.

American author **John Dalmas** (John Robert Jones) died on June 15, aged 90. He published his first SF story in *Analog Science Fiction/Science Fact* in 1970, and he went on to write a number of novels in different series, including *The Yngling*, *Fanglith*, *The General's President*, *The Lizard War*, *The Lantern of God*, *The Lion of Farside* and *The Second Coming*, amongst others. Dalmas' short fiction is collected in *Otherwhens, Otherwheres: Favorite Tales*.

American academic **William F. Touponce**, who co-founded the Center for Ray Bradbury Studies at Indiana University and *The New Ray Bradbury Review*, died the same day, aged 68. He also wrote books on Isaac Asimov and Frank Herbert.

Italian author, screenwriter, editor and translator **Sergio Altieri** (aka "Alan D. Altieri") died of a heart attack on June 16, aged 65. Known as the "Italian Master of the Apocalypse", his books include *Dark City*, *City of Shadows*, *Last Light*, the award-winning *Kondor*, the historical "Magdeburg" trilogy (*The Heretic*, *The Fury* and *The Daemon*) and the "Terminal War" trilogy (*Juggernaut*, *Magellan* and the forthcoming *Maelstrom*). Altieri was editorial director of a number of series for Mondadori from 2006-11, and he translated the first two volumes of *Prelude to Dune* by Brian Herbert and Kevin J. Anderson, George R.R. Martin's "Song of Ice and Fire" saga, and *The Dominator of Darkness*, a 2012 collection of the best stories by H.P. Lovecraft. He also worked for producer Dino De Laurentiis as a script editor on such movies as *Conan the Destroyer* and *Blue Velvet*.

American role-playing games designer and author **Stewart Wieck** died of a heart attack on June 22, aged 49. With his brother Steve, Wieck began self-publishing the fanzine *Arcanum* while still in high school, soon retitling it *White Wolf* as a tribute to Michael Moorcock. In 1991 the brothers formed the White Wolf Game Studio with Mark Rein-Hagen, publishing *Vampire: The Masquerade* and creating the *World of Darkness* and *Mage: The Ascension*. Stewart Wieck wrote a number of novels in the "World of Darkness" universe, including titles in the *Vampire: The Masquerade*, *Mage: The Ascension*, *Werewolf: The Apocalypse*, *Wraith: The Oblivion* and *Hunter: The Reckoning* series. He resigned from White Wolf in 2010 to set up Nocturnal Games.

British children's author [Thomas] **Michael Bond** CBE, the creator of Paddington the bear, died following a short illness on June 27, aged 91. He wrote the first of many Paddington books, *A Bear Called Paddington*, in 1958 while working as a cameraman at the BBC. The marmalade-loving character from Peru has been adapted for TV and, more recently, the movies (Bond made a brief appearance in *Paddington* [2014], and he also created the 1970s chidren's TV series *The Herbs*).

American author and editor **William L. (Lawrence) Hamling** died on June 29, aged 96. He was the managing editor of the pulp magazines *Amazing Stories* and *Fantastic Adventures* from 1948-51 and editor and publisher of the digest magazines *Imagination* (1951-58) and *Imaginative Tales* (1955-58). His fiction appeared in *Amazing Stories*, *Fantastic Adventures*, *Mammoth Detective*, *Mammoth Western*, *Imagination*, *Spaceways*, *Science Fiction Adventures* and other titles. In 1955 Hamling also founded and began editing the slick men's magazine *Rogue*, and four years later he started publishing paperback books under various imprints through his Greenleaf Publishing Company. These included many adult titles (often under pseudonymous bylines) by authors such as Robert Silverberg, Harlan Ellison, Philip José Farmer, Marion Zimmer Bradley, Robert Bloch, Donald E. Westlake and Kurt Vonnegut. Hamling was a member of First Fandom and was married to science fiction author Frances Deegan Yerxa Hamling.

American author **William Sanders** died on June 30, aged 75. His books include the alternate history *Journey to Fusang* and the collections *Are We Having Fun Yet?: American Indian Fantasy Stories* and *East of the Sun and West of Fort Smith*. As "Will Sundown" he wrote the novels *Pockets of Resistance* and the sequel *The Hellbound Train*. He won the Sidewise Award for two alternate history stories, and he edited *Helix SF* with Lawrence Watt-Evans from 2006-09.

British TV presenter and journalist **Barry [Leslie] Norman** CBE, the son of film and TV director Leslie Norman, died of lung cancer and pneumonia the same day, aged 83. From 1972-98 he presented the BBC's popular *Film* review programme, along with other movie-inspired series, many of which he also scripted. Although Norman was not a fan of horror films (he considered David Cronenberg's *Shivers* the worst film he'd ever seen), he did write a science fiction novel, *End Product* (1975), and for a number of years he scripted Wally ("Trog") Fawkes' satirical newspaper strip *Flook* in *The Daily Mail*. He also had his own brand of pickled onions, based on an old family recipe.

69-year-old Californian bookseller and SF fan **Dwain** [George] **Kaiser** was shot to death in the apartment above his store, Magic Door Used Books in Pomona, on July 3. Police arrested a 17-year-old who, with his mother, were longtime housemates of Kaiser and his wife. A member of the Los Angeles Science Fiction Society since 1965, Kaiser edited a number of fanzines, including *Astron*, *By Strange Unseen Gods*, *Nimrod*, *Nonstop Fun is Hard on the Heart* and *No Time, No Energy & Not Much to Say*.

Joan B. Lee (Joan Clayton Boocock), Marvel Comics' writer-editor Stan Lee's English-born wife for nearly seventy years, died of complications from a stroke in Los Angeles on July 6, aged 95. She contributed voice work to the 1990s TV cartoon series *Fantastic Four* and *Spider-Man*, and she had a cameo as herself in *X-Men: Apocalypse* (2016). Stan Lee publicly credited his wife for supporting him early in his career, when he was trying to create superheroes that readers could care about.

American "Golden Age" comics and newspaper artist **Bob Lubbers** (Robert Bartow Lubbers) died on July 8, aged 95. In the early 1950s he drew the *Tarzan* strip and went on to illustrate *The Saint*, *Secret Agent X-9* and *Li'l Abner*. Lubbers also worked for DC and Marvel, and some of his work was collected in 2001 in *Glamour International: The Good Girl Art of Bob Lubbers*.

Canadian playwright and short film-maker **David Widdicombe** died the same day, aged 55. His 2000 play *Science Fiction* won the Canadian Aurora Award.

92-year-old American comics artist **Sam Glanzman** (Samuel Joseph Glanzman) died on July 12, following surgery after a fall. He entered the comics industry in 1939 and created the character of "Fly-Man" for Harvey Comics. For Dell Comics he drew the movie tie-in *Voyage to the Bottom of the Sea* and *Kona Monarch of Monster Isle*. Glanzman illustrated issues of *Tarzan* for Charlton Comics, and he co-created *Hercules: Adventures of the Man-God* (1967-69) for the same company. He also worked on various war titles for Charlton, DC and Marvel.

American SF author **Jeff** [Gustav] **Carlson** died of lung cancer on July 17, aged 47. His books include the trilogy *Plague Year*, *Plague*

War and *Plague Zone*, and the series *The Frozen Sky, Betrayed* and *Blindsided*. He also wrote the stand-alone novel *Interrupt*, and his short fiction is collected in *Long Eyes and Other Stories*.

"Fabulous **Flo**" **Steinberg** (Florence Steinberg), who began her career as one-half of the fledgling Marvel Comics with Stan Lee in 1963, died of complications from a brain aneurysm and metastatic lung cancer on July 23, aged 78. During the 1960s she was not only Lee's secretary, but also the company's receptionist and fan liaison. Steinberg left Marvel in 1968 and set up her own independent/underground imprint, Big Apple Comix, in 1975.

Science fiction fan and radio presenter **Alan Dorey**, who was chairman of the British Science Fiction Association (1979-85) and co-edited the magazines *Vector* (1979-85) and *Matrix* (1982-84), died the same day, aged 59. Dorey was also part of the original *Interzone* collective in the early 1980s.

American-born Canadian author H. (Henry) **A. Hargreaves** died on July 27, aged 89. He published his first SF story in 1963 in *New Worlds*, and his short fiction is collected in *North by 2000* (expanded as *North by 2000+*).

American music composer **Daniel** [James] **Licht** died of cancer on August 2, aged 60. Best known for his award-winning work on all eight seasons of Showtime's serial-killer TV series *Dexter* (2006-13), his many other credits include *Atrapados, Children of the Night, Amityville 1992: It's About Time, Children of the Corn II: The Final Sacrifice, Severed Ties, Ticks, Amityville: A New Generation, Necronomicon: Book of the Dead, Children of the Corn III: Urban Harvest, Hellraiser: Bloodline, Thinner, Bad Moon, Brave New World, Legion of Fire: Killer Ants!, Don't Look Under the Bed, Cabin by the Lake, Soul Survivors* (2001), *King Solomon's Mines* (2004), *Beneath the Dark, Ghostmates* and an episode of TV's *Monsters*. Licht also contributed the music scores to the video games *Silent Hill: Downpour* and *Silent Hill: Book of Memories*.

British-born Australian SF author [Herbert] **Jack Woodhams** died on August 3, aged 85. His first short story appeared in *Analog Science Fiction/Science Fact* in 1967, and he went on to publish three novels, *The Authentic Touch, Looking for Blücher* and *Ryn*, and the collection *Future War*.

American bookseller **Roger Carlson** died of heart failure on August 4, aged 89. His wonderful labyrinthine store, Bookman's Alley, situated in an old carriage house in Evanston, Illinois, was featured as a setting in Audrey Niffenegger's best-selling 2003 novel, *The Time Traveler's Wife*. Carlson opened the bookshop in 1979 and ran it until 2013, when declining health forced him to sell.

British scriptwriter **Victor** [Francis] **Pemberton** died in Spain on August 13, aged 85. Best known for his 1968 *Doctor Who* script 'Fury from the Deep', which introduced the Time Lord's "sonic screwdriver", he also wrote episodes of the children's shows *Timeslip* and *Ace of Wands*, and the TV movies *Tales from the Thousand and One Nights* (1981) and the 1983 Edgar Wallace adaptation *The Case of the Frightened Lady*. Pemberton novelised his *Doctor Who* script.

British book editor and romantic novelist **Diane** [Margaret] **Pearson** died on August 15, aged 85. She began her career at Jonathan Cape Ltd. and was senior editor at Corgi/Transworld for thirty-eight years, where she first began publishing Terry Pratchett's "Discworld" books in paperback.

American space artist **Kim Poor** died of complications from the neurodegenerative disease ataxia/Machado-Joseph on August 16, aged 65. His paintings appeared on the covers of such magazines as *Analog*, *Asimov's* and *Omni*, and his work was also used in the TV series *Babylon 5*, *Alien Nation* and *SeaQuest DSV*. In 1982, Poor founded the International Association for Astronomical Artists with fellow artists Michael Carroll and Rick Sternbach.

Award-winning British author, poet and editor **Brian W.** (Wilson) **Aldiss** OBE died in his sleep on August 19, the day after his 92nd birthday. His first SF story was published in 1954, and his debut novel *Non-Stop* (aka *Starship*) appeared four years later. He published more than 100 books, including the novels *Hothouse*, *Greybeard*, *Earthworks*, *An Age* (aka *Cryptozoic!*), *Report on Probability A*, *Barefoot in the Head*, *The Malicia Tapestry*, *Moreau's Other Island* (aka *An Island Called Moreau*), *Dracula Unbound* and the "Heliconia" trilogy. His short fiction is collected in *Space Time and Nathaniel*, *The Canopy of Time*, *No Time Like Tomorrow*, *The Airs of Earth* (aka *Starswarm*), *Best SF Stories of Brian Aldiss* (aka *Who Can Replace* *a Man?*), *The Saliva Tree and Other Stange Growths* (the title story is a homage to both H.G. Wells and H.P. Lovecraft), *Neanderthal Planet, Last Orders and Other Stories* and *New Arrivals Old Encounters*, amongst other titles. The non-fiction study *Billion Year Spree: The History of Science Fiction* was later revised and updated with David Wingrove as *Trillion Year Spree, Hell's Cartographers* was co-edited with Harry Harrison, and *Bury My Heart at W.H. Smith's: A Writing Life* was an autobiography. Aldiss also co-edited six volumes of *The Year's Best Science Fiction* (1968-73) and four other anthologies with Harrison, and titles he also edited include *Penguin Science Fiction, More Penguin Science Fiction, Yet More Penguin Science Fiction, Space Opera, Space Odysseys, Evil Earths, Galactic Empires* and *The Folio Science Fiction Anthology*. His novel *Frankenstein Unbound* was filmed by Roger Corman in 1990, while his short story 'Supertoys Last All Summer Long' was the basis for Steven Spielberg's *A.I. Artificial Intelligence* (2001), which had been developed years before by Stanley Kubrick. A frequent guest of honour at conventions, Aldiss' many awards include the Hugo and Nebula. He was made SFWA Grand Master in 2000, and in 2013 he was a Special Guest at the World Fantasy Convention in Brighton, where he received the Convention Award along with William F. Nolan.

Scottish author **Gordon** [Maclean] **Williams**, best known for his 1969 novel *The Siege of Trencher's Farm*, which was infamously filmed by Sam Peckinpah as *Straw Dogs* (1971), died on August 20, aged 83. Williams also wrote the 1970s science fiction trilogy *The Micronauts, The Microcolony* and *Revolt of the Micronauts*, which began life as an unfilmed treatment for James Bond producer Harry Saltzman, and the horror novel *The Bornless Keeper* (as "P.B. Yuill"). With footballer Terry Venables he created the novel and TV detective "Hazell", and his 1967 novel *The Man Who Had Power Over Women* was also filmed.

American scriptwriter **Thomas** [Edward] **Meehan**, who won Tony Awards for his Broadway stage musicals *Annie, The Producers* and *Hairspray*, died on August 22, aged 88. He scripted the movies *One Magic Christmas*, Mel Brooks' *Spaceballs*, and *Elf: Buddy's Musical Christmas*, and co-wrote the libretto for Lorin Maazel's production of *1984* at the Royal Opera House. Meehan also co-executive produced the 2008-09 cartoon TV show *Spaceballs: The Animated Series*.

American author and publisher **Howard Kaminsky** died on August 26, aged 77. He began working in publishing in the 1960s, eventually rising in 1972 to President and Publisher of the Paperback Library imprint (which he soon changed to Warner Books). He went on to head Random House and William Morrow/Avon in the 1980s. Kaminsky also co-scripted the 1974 horror movie *Homebodies*, and with his wife, Susan Stanwood (who died in 2005), co-wrote a number of thrillers under the pseudonyms "Brooks Stanwood" and "Arthur Reid". Their first collaboration, the 1979 horror-mystery novel *The Glow*, was made into a TV movie in 2002.

American playwright **Bernard Pomerance**, whose best-known work was the 1979 Tony Award-winning play *The Elephant Man*, died of cancer the same day, aged 76. David Lynch's 1980 movie of the same name was not an official adaptation of Pomerance's work, although it shared many similarities.

Syd Silverman, who was the owner and publisher of the movie trade magazine *Variety* for more than thirty-five years, died on August 27, aged 85. He was the grandson of Sime Silverman, who founded the title in 1905, and took over *Variety* when his father Sidne Silverman died in 1950. In 1987 Syd Silverman sold the magazine and its companion, *Daily Variety*, to Cahners Publishing.

91-year-old British film historian **Peter S. Haigh** also died in August. For many years he was the editor of the monthly *ABC Film Review*, a promotional magazine for the ABC cinema circuit.

American science fiction writer and editor **Jerry [Eugene] Pournelle**, believed to be the first author to write a published novel on a word processor (in 1977), died of heart failure on September 8, aged 84. He had just returned from Atlanta's annual Dragon Con and mentioned in an online blog that he had contracted a cold or flu on the trip. Dr. Pournelle spent years working in the aerospace industry, and he published his first SF story in *Analog* in 1971. His books include the "CoDominium" space opera series: *A Spaceship for the King*, *West of Honor*, *The Mercenery*, *Exiles to Glory*, *Prince* *of Mercenaries* and the collection *High Justice*, along with later collaborations with S.M. Sterling and Larry Niven. Niven was the author Pournelle most often collaborated with, and the pair worked together on the novels *The Mote in God's Eye, Inferno, Escape from Hell, Lucifer's Hammer, Oath of Fealty, Footfall, The Burning City* and *Burning Tower*. He also collaborated with Niven and Michael Flynn on *Fallen Angels*, with Charles Sheffield on *Higher Education*, and with Roland J. Green on two sequels to his 1979 novel *Janissaries*. Along with a number of non-fiction books, Pournelle also edited many anthologies, including the "Endless Frontier" series (1979-92), the "There Will Be War" series (1983-90), the "Imperial Stars" series (1985-86) and the "War World" series (1988-94), mostly with John F. Carr, and the "Far Frontiers" series (1985-86) with James Baen. In 1973 he was the first winner of the John W. Campbell Award for Best New Writer, and he served as president of the SFWA from 1973-74.

Influential American comics writer and editor **Len Wein** (Leonard Norman Wein) died on September 10, six months after the death of his "Swamp Thing" co-creator, artist Bernie Wrightson. Wein, who was 69, also created the character of "Wolverine" with John Romita, Sr. and Herb Trimpe for Marvel Comics, revived the X-Men in 1975 with artist Dave Cockrum (co-creating "Nightcrawler", "Storm", "Colossus" and "Thunderbird"), and edited Alan Moore and and Dave Gibbons' *Watchmen* at DC. Amongst many other titles, he also worked on DC's *The House of Mystery, House of Secrets, The Witching Hour, The Phantom Stranger* and *Jonah Hex*; Marvel's *Tower of Shadows, Chamber of Darkness, Creatures on the Loose, Dracula Lives* and *Werewolf by Night*; Skywald's *Nightmare* and *Psycho*; Gold Key's *Boris Karloff Tales of Mystery, Star Trek* and *The Twilight Zone*, and Dark Horse's *Conan: The Book of Thoth*. Wein scripted episodes of various cartoon TV shows and co-wrote a number of comic-book novelisations, including *Mayhem in Manhattan* featuring Spider-man (with Marv Wolfman), *Stalker from the Stars* featuring the Incredible Hulk (with Ron Goulart writing as "Joseph Silva") and the movie tie-in to *Swamp Thing* (with David Houston). In 2008 he was inducted into the Will Eisner Comic Book Hall of Fame.

Veteran "Disney Legend", animator, designer, scriptwriter and songwriter [Francis] **Xavier Atencio**, died the same day, aged 98. A Disneyland "Imagineer" from 1965-84, best known for writing the songs 'Yo Ho (A Pirate's Life for Me)' and 'Grim, Grinning Ghosts (Otherworldly Concerto)' for, respectively, the theme rides Pirates of the Caribbean and the Haunted Mansion, he also worked in various capacities on the movies *Pinocchio, Fantasia, The Shaggy Dog* (1959), *Babes in Toyland* (1961), *The Misadventures of Merlin Jones* and *Mary Poppins* (1964).

Comedic Swedish actor, author, scriptwriter, songwriter and director **Hans** [Folke] **Alfredson** died on September 10, aged 86. His books include the 1996 alternate history novel *Attentatet i Pålsjö Skog* (*The Pålsjö Woods Attack*).

Iconic American monster movie artist **Basil Gogos**, best known for his colourful covers for Forrest J Ackerman's *Famous Monsters of Filmland* magazine in the 1960s and '70s, died of a probable heart attack on September 14, aged 78 (although some sources vary ten years either way). He had been suffering from Parkinson's disease for several years. Born in Egypt of Greek ancestry, he moved to America to study art and began painting covers for Western paperbacks and working for men's adventure magazines. He also contributed covers to such publications as *Screen Thrills Illustrated, Spacemen, Creepy, Eerie, The Spirit* and *Monsterscene*, along with trading cards, posters, fine-art prints, T-shirts and CD covers for such rock musicians as Rob Zombie and The Misfits. *Famous Monster Movie Art of Basil Gogos* was published by Vanguard Productions in 2005.

British book and magazine collector **Andy England**, who built the shelves for, and often helped out in London's Fantasy Centre bookstore, died on September 22, aged 63.

American author **Harvey** [Jay] **Jacobs** died of a sudden bacterial infection on September 23, aged 87. He had been diagnosed with brain cancer a short time earlier. His first SF story was published in *Tomorrow* in 1951, and his short fiction was collected in *The Egg of the Glak and Other stories* and *My Rose & My Glove: Stories (Real and Surreal)*, while his 1977 novel *American Goliath: Inspired by the*

True, Incredible Events Surrounding the Mysterious Marvel Known to an Astonished World as the Cardiff Giant was nominated for a World Fantasy Award.

American pianist and composer **Caesar Giovanni** died the same day, aged 92. He composed the piano solos heard in the *Thriller* TV episode 'The Terror in Teakwood' (based on the story by Harold Lawlor), and he also contributed to the soundtracks of such movies as *House of Usher* (1960), *Master of the World*, *The Cabinet of Caligari* (1962), the American version of Mario Bava's *Black Sabbath*, *The Comedy of Terrors*, *Seven Days in May*, *Wait Until Dark*, *The Power*, *Beneath the Planet of the Apes* and *Soylent Green*.

American author and scriptwriter **Harvey Jacobs** died of a bacterial infection and cancer on September 23, aged 87. From the late 1950s onwards, his short stories appeared in such magazines and anthologies as *Playboy*, *Mademoiselle*, *New Worlds*, *The Magazine of Fantasy and Science Fiction*, *Omni*, *The Year's Best S-F: 11th Annual Edition*, *Satan's Pets*, *More Little Monsters*, *The Book of Cats*, *More Wandering Stars*, *Blood is Not Enough*, *Strange Dreams*, *Snow White Blood Red*, *Twists in the Tale: Cat Horror Stories*, *Black Swan White Raven*, *The Mammoth Book of Comic Fantasy*, *Silver Birch Blood Moon* and *The Forsaken: Stories of Abandoned Places*, and were collected in *The Egg of Glak and Other Stories* and *My Rose & My Glove: Stories (Real and Surreal)*. During the late 1980s, Jacobs also scripted a number of episodes of TV's *Tales from the Darkside* and *Monsters*.

American author **Kit Reed** (Lillian Hyde Craig) died on September 24, aged 85. She had been diagnosed with glioblastoma, an aggressive type of brain tumour, several months earlier. Her first SF story appeared in *The Magazine of Fantasy & Science Fiction* in 1958, and her often satirical and transgressive novels include *Magic Time*, *Little Sisters of the Apocalypse*, *Thinner Than Thou*, *The Baby Merchant*, *The Night Children*, *Enclave*, *Son of Destruction* and *Mormama*. As "Kit Craig" she wrote a number of psychological thrillers, while her 1986 horror novel *Blood Fever* was published under the name "Shelley Hyde". Reed's darkly humorous short fiction is collected in *The Killer Mice*, *Other Stories and . . . The Attack of the Giant Baby*, *The Revenge* *of the Senior Citizens, Weird Women Wired Women, Seven for the Apocalypse, What Wolves Know* and *The Story Until Now,* amongst other titles. Similarities between her 1976 short story, 'The Attack of the Giant Baby' and the 1992 Disney sequel *Honey, I Blew Up the Kid* resulted in a lawsuit and a "special recognition" credit as part of the settlement.

American author **Digby** [Robert] **Diehl**, a former editor-in-chief at publisher Harry N. Abrams, editor of *The Los Angeles Times' Sunday Book Review* (1975-78) and a founding member of the National Book Critics' Circle, died of complications from Alzheimer's disease on September 26, aged 76. He also co-wrote and edited a number of celebrity autobiographies, and he was the author of the 1996 volume *Tales from the Crypt: The Official Archives.* Diehl was featured in the documentaries *Tales from the Crypt: From Comic Books to Television* (2004) and *Tales from the Crypt: A Tall Tales Panel—A Dissected Look at Tales from the Crypt Season 3* (2006).

American horror fan and film collector **Hugh** [Marston] **Hefner**, the founder of *Playboy* magazine and star of E! reality TV show *The Girls Next Door,* died of cardiac arrest on September 27, aged 91. Credited with sparking the sexual revolution of the 1950s and '60s with his groundbreaking men's magazine (which, besides creating the "Playboy Centerfold" and "Playboy Playmate", was also a high-paying fiction market for such writers as Ray Bradbury, Stephen King, Robert Bloch, Roald Dahl, Kurt Vonnegut, Harlan Ellison, Margaret Atwood, Richard Matheson, Charles Beaumont, Doris Lessing, Isaac Bashevis Singer and many others), Hefner became an iconic figure and a multi-millionaire, with a string of Playboy Clubs around the world. He had a life-long interest in movies, especially horror and science fiction, and he executive produced such films as *Macbeth* (1971) and *The Fiendish Plot of Fu Manchu,* the TV documentary *Lon Chaney: A Thousand Faces,* and numerous softcore *Playboy* videos. Hefner also made cameo appearances in *Citizen Toxie: The Toxic Avenger IV* (as the President of the United States) and an episode of *Get Smart.*

British-born American author and practicing witch **Raymond Buckland**, who founded his own "Seax-Wica" movement and operated various museums of witchcraft over the years, died the same day, aged 83. His 1990s "Committee Against Evil" fiction series comprised the novels *The Committee* and *Cardinal's Sin*, and he also wrote the "Bram Stoker Mysteries" *Cursed in the Act*, *Dead for a Spell* and *A Mistake Through the Heart*. Credited with introducing the Gardnerian tradition of witchcraft into the United States in 1964, Buckland's numerous non-fiction books on the subject include *Buckland's Complete Book of Witchcraft*, *Wicca for Life: The Way of the Life—From Birth to Summerland*, *Scottish Witchcraft & Magick: The Craft of the Picts*, *Doors to Other Worlds: A Practical Guide to Communicating with Spirits*, *The Witch Book: The Encyclopedia of Witchcraft Wicca and Neo-Paganism* and the *Llewellyn's Magical Almanac Annual* series, and he contributed the essay 'Witchcraft the Religion' to Kurt Singer's anthology *Tales from the Unknown*.

Japanese-born SF author and astrophysicist **Yoji Kondo** died on October 9, aged 84. As "Eric Kotani" he co-wrote the "Island Worlds" series (including *Act of God*, *The Island Worlds* and *Between the Stars*), *Delta Pavonis* and *Legacy of Prometheus* with John Maddox Roberts, *Supernova* with Roger MacBride Allen, and the TV tie-in *Star Trek Voyager: Death of a Neutron Star* with Dean Wesley Smith. Kondo also edited *Requiem: New Collected Works by Robert A. Heinlein and Tributes to the Grand Master* under his own name.

American author **Elizabeth Gilligan** (Elizabeth Murphy) died of cancer on October 10, aged 55. During the 1990s she wrote a column for *Midnight Zoo* and started publishing fiction. Her "Silken Magic" trilogy comprises the novels *Magic's Silken Snare*, *The Silken Shroud* and *Sovereign Silk*, and she edited the 2016 anthology *Alterna-Teas*.

Indian-born British rock guitarist and thriller author **Glover Wright** (Geoffrey Glover-Wright, aka "Buddy Britten" and "Simon Raverne"), a former executive at The Beatles' Apple Music, died in Jersey on October 11. His novels, which were often based around religious conspiracies, included the SF-themed *The Hound of Heaven* and *Aurora*.

American author **Julian** [Clare] **May** (aka "Judy Dikty"), best known for her best-selling "Saga of the Pliocene Exile" series in the 1980s (comprising the novels *The Many-Colored Land*, *The Golden Torc*,

The Nonborn King and *The Adversary*), died on October 17, aged 86. Her first SF story, 'Dune Roller', was published with her own illustrations in *Astounding* in 1951 and later filmed as *The Cremators* (1972). During the late 1970s and early '80s May wrote a number of children's monster movie tie-ins under the name "Ian Thorne" for Crestwood House, including *The Wolf Man*, *Dracula*, *Frankenstein*, *The Mummy* and *The Creature from the Black Lagoon*. Her other books include *Black Trillium*, *Blood Trillium* and *Sky Trillium* with Marion Zimmer Bradley and Andre Norton, along with the "Galactic Milieu" sequence, the "Rampart Worlds" series, and the "Boreal Moon Tale" trilogy. May authored nearly 300 books in numerous genres and under many pseudonyms, including *A Gazeteer of the Hyborian World of Conan* as "Lee N. Falconer". She published a SF fanzine in her late teens, chaired the 1952 World Science Fiction Convention in Chicago, and was married to editor and publisher T.E. Dikty from 1953 until his death in 1991.

Australian music composer **Dudley** [George] **Simpson**, best known for composing the incidental music for BBC-TV's *Doctor Who* from 1964-80, died on November 4, aged 95. He composed the theme music for such series as *The Tomorrow People*, *Blakes 7* and *Super Gran*, along with the music for episodes of *Out of the Unknown*, *Moonbase 3* and *Tales of the Unexpected*. Simpson also contributed (uncredited) to the 1973 horror movie *The Legend of Hell House*. He made a cameo appearance as an orchestra conductor in the fourth episode of the *Doctor Who* serial 'The Talons of Weng-Chang'.

American author **G.** (Gregory) **B.** (Bernard) **Banks** died of pneumonia on November 7, aged 51. He had been suffering from the brittle bone disease, osteogenesis imperfecta. Banks wrote the novels *Revolution Z* and *Three Hours to the Apocalypse*, and his short fiction is collected in *Phoenix Tales: Stories of Death & Life*, *Into the Every: Tales of Magic and Science* and *Scairy Tales: 13 Tantalizing Tales of Terror*.

British fan and editor **Carl T.** (Trevor) **Ford** died of complications from cystic fibrosis on November 13, aged 53. From 1983-90 he published the British Fantasy Award-winning small press magazine *Dagon*, initially inspired by the *Call of Cthulhu* RPG. He also edited one issue of *Unrated: Cinema of the Extreme*, and his short story 'Many Happy Returns' appeared in *The Fourth Black Book of Horror*.

Argentinean-born music composer and conductor **Luis** [Enríquez] **Bacalov** died in Italy on November 15, aged 84. His credits include *The Witch* (1966), *Ghosts Italian Style*, *Maniac Killer*, *La maschera* and the theme for *Night of the Zombies* (aka *Virus*).

British author and former *Best New Horror* contributor **John Gordon** died of complications from Alzheimer's disease on November 20, the day after his 92nd birthday. His supernatural and horror novels—often written for adolescent readers—include *The Giant Under the Snow*, the Jamesian *The House on the Brink*, *The Ghost on the Hill*, *The Waterfall Box*, *The Edge of the World*, *The Quelling Eye*, *The Grasshopper*, *Ride the Wind*, *Secret Corridor*, *Blood Brothers*, *Gilray's Ghost*, *The Flesh Eater*, the award-winning *The Midwinter Watch*, *Skinners*, *The Ghosts of Blacklode* and *Fen Runners*. Gordon set much of his fiction in The Fens area of eastern England, and his superior short stories are collected in *The Spitfire Grave and Other Stories*, *Catch Your Death and Other Ghost Stories*, *The Burning Baby and Other Ghosts* and the retrospective *Left in the Dark: The Supernatural Tales of John Gordon*.

American author **M.** (Mary) **M.** (Margaret) **Justus** died of metastatic cancer on November 22, aged 58. Her historical SF and horror novels include the "Time in Yellowstone" series (*Repeating History*, *True Gold* and *Finding Home*) and the "Unearthly Northwest" series (*Sojourn* and *Reunion*).

American librarian and biographer **Harold** [Wayne] **Billings** died on November 29, aged 86. He wrote three books about author M.P. Shiel: *M.P. Shiel: A Biography of His Early Years*, *M.P. Shiel: The Middle Years 1897-1923* and *An Ossuary for M.P. Shiel: The Final Years 1923-1947*. Billings also wrote a number of supernatural short stories.

American investigative reporter and horror author **Leslie H.** (Hunter) **Whitten** died of complications from sepsis on December 2, aged 89. His novels include *Progeny of the Adder* (1965, which may have inspired *The Night Stalker*), *Moon of the Wolf* (aka *Death of a Nurse*, filmed for TV in 1972), *The Alchemist* (as by "Les Whitten") and *The Fangs of Morning*. An enemy of President Richard M. Nixon, Whitten was spied on by the CIA and arrested by the FBI while he was working as a Washington journalist.

American illustrator **Joe Wehrle, Jr.** (Joseph J. Wehrle, Jr.) died on December 10, aged 76. His artwork appeared on the covers of *Planets and Dimensions* and *The Revised H.P. Lovecraft Bibliography* (both Mirage Press) and *Prince Zaleski and Cummings King Monk* and *The Princes of All Lands* (both Arkham House), and in such magazines and one-shots as *If*, *Galaxy*, *Whispers* (Karl Edward Wagner's 'Sticks'), *REH Two-Gun Raconteur*, *The Digest Enthusiast*, *Readers Guide to the Cthulhu Mythos*, *The Hannes Bok Memorial Showcase of Fantasy Art* and *Ec'h-Pi-El Speaks* (a posthumous collaboration with Virgil Finlay). Wehrle also had a few stories pubished in *Weirdbook* and elsewhere.

Veteran American animator and layout artist **Bob Givens** (Robert Herman Givens) died on December 14, aged 99. Credited with redesigning the first model sheet of "Bugs Bunny" for the 1940 short *A Wild Hare*, he worked on numerous Warner Bros. cartoon shorts (including *Ghost Wanted* and *Transylvania 6-5000*). Givens' later credits include *Daffy Duck's Movie: Fantastic Island*, *The Duxorcist*, *The Night of the Living Duck*, *Daffy Duck's Quackbusters* and the cartoon TV series *Ghostbusters* (1986) and *She-Ra: Princess of Power*.

Japanese *anime* writer **Michiru Shimada** died on December 15, aged 58. His many credits include the *Little Witch Academia* TV series (2017).

American SF writer **Roger Lee Vernon**, whose death was erroneously reported in 1980, actually died the same day, aged 93. His collection *The Space Frontiers* appeared in 1955 and he followed it with a novel, *Robot Hunt*, four years later. He finally returned to the genre in 2010 with the novel *The Fall of the American Empire – 2013: A Remembrance of Things Future*, and followed it with another novel, *The Plant God*, and a second collection, *If?????: In the World of "If" All Futures Are Possible*.

American comedy scriptwriter and producer **Lawrence J. Cohen** died on December 17, aged 82. With Fred Freeman he co-wrote five episodes of TV's *Bewitched* and the 1976 movie *The Big Bus.*

62-year-old American fan **Rick Sullivan** (Rickie P. Sullivan), who edited, published and was head writer for 110 issues of the influential New Jersey horror fanzine *Gore Gazette* (1980-94), died on December 18. Sullivan also fronted the horror-themed punk group, The Creeping Pumpkins.

French comics artist **Annie Goetzinger**, whose work includes the 1980s masked heroine "Félina" (with writer Victor Mora), died on December 20, aged 66.

American music composer, conductor and accordion player **Dominic** [Carmen] **Frontiere** died on December 21, aged 86. A former head of music at 20th Century Fox and Paramount Pictures, his credits include *Incubus* (1966), *Hang 'Em High, Revenge!, Probe, Hammersmith is Out, Haunts of the Very Rich, The House of Seven Corpses, A Name for Evil, Cleopatra Jones and the Casino of Gold, Don't Go to Sleep* and *Kingdom of the Spiders.* On TV, Frontiere composed the theme and incidental music for the first season of *The Outer Limits* (including the unsold pilots 'The Unknown' and 'The Ghost of Sierra de Cobre'), and he also worked on *The Invaders, The Flying Nun, The Immortal* and *Search.*

Scottish comics artist **Jim Baikie** (James George Baikie) died on December 29, aged 77. Amongst the strips he worked on were 'The Monkees' and 'Star Trek' in *Look-In*, 'Judge Dredd' and Alan Moore's 'Skizz' in *2000AD* and 'New Statesman' in *Crisis.* He also contributed to *Clive Barker's Nightbreed* for Epic, *Star Wars: Empire's Ends* for Dark Horse Comics, and *Batman, The Spectre* and *Electric Warrior* for DC Comics.

American pulp expert, collector, writer and publisher **Joel** [Jay] **Frieman** was found in his New Jersey apartment, having died on or around New Year's Eve. He co-edited the fanzines *Deeper Than You Think* (1968-69) with business associate Robert Weinberg and *Pulp* (1970-81) with Weinberg and Steve Riley. Frieman also contributed introductions to a number of reprints of Norvell W. Page's novels about "The Spider", one of several Popular Publications characters he bought the rights to in 1979 under his Argosy

Communications banner, and in 2017 he launched a new graphic series of *The Spider* under his own Argosy Comics imprint.

PERFORMERS/PERSONALITIES

American actress, former beauty pageant contestant, and fitness and nutrition expert **Francine York** (Francine Yerich), who starred in Ted V. Mikels' cult favourite *The Doll Squad*, died of cancer on January 6, aged 80. Trained in acting by Jeff Corey and mentored by Jerry Lewis, her other movies include *The Nutty Professor* (uncredited, 1963), *Space Probe Taurus*, *Mutiny in Outer Space*, *Curse of the Swamp Creature*, *I Love a Mystery* (1973), *The Centerfold Girls*, *Time Travelers* (1976) and Mikels' *Astro Zombies M3: Cloned*. On TV York appeared in episodes of *Shirley Temple's Storybook*, *My Favorite Martian*, *My Brother the Angel*, *Batman* (as The Bookworm's henchwoman), *Lost in Space*, *The Wild Wild West*, *I Dream of Jeannie*, *Land of the Giants*, *Bewitched*, *Future Cop*, *Jason of Star Command* (as "Queen Medusa"), *Lois & Clark: The Adventures of Superman*, and the failed 1969 Irwin Allen pilot *City Beneath the Sea*. She was film director Vincent Sherman's companion for the last nine years of his life.

Veteran Indian actor **Om Puri** OBE died of a heart attack the same day, aged 66. He appeared in many films in his native country, and was also in the Hollywood movies *Wolf*, *The Ghost and the Darkness*, *Code 46* and *The Lovers* (aka *Time Traveller*).

72-year-old American character actor **Gary Bayer** died of prostate cancer in Jerusalem, Israel, on January 6. He appeared in the movies *Eyes of Laura Mars*, *All That Jazz*, *Starflight: The Plane That Couldn't Land* (aka *Starflight One*), *Creator* and *Psycho III*, along with an episode of TV's *Highway to Heaven*.

Pioneering American stuntwoman and former circus acrobat **Paula Dell** (Paula Unger) died on January 9, aged 90. She began her movie career in Disney's *Son of Flubber* in 1963, and she also did stunt work in *Earthquake*, *Death Race 2000* (1975), *Logan's Run*, *Freaky Friday* (1976), *Once Bitten* and *Mystery Men*.

Italian-born Canadian character actor and comedian **Tony Rosato** (Antonio Rosato) died of a heart attack on January 10, aged 62. He appeared on TV in episodes of *RoboCop*, *Highlander*, *F/X: The Series*, *Eerie Indiana* and *Relic Hunter*, and he was also in the movies *The Haunting of Lisa* and *Sicilian Vampire*.

India-born **Nickola Sterne** (Pamela Violet Rown-Robinson) died in London on January 11, aged 102. She had small roles in the BBC-TV serials *The Quatermass Experiment* (1953) and *Quatermass II* (1955), and the 1984 post-apocalyptic *Play for Today* 'Z for Zachariah'.

American TV actor, comedian and cartoonist **Dick Gautier** (Richard Gautier), who appeared as "Hymie" the robot on TV's *Get Smart* from 1966-68 and reprised the role in the 1989 spin-off movie, *Get Smart, Again!*, died of pneumonia in an assisted living facility on January 13, aged 85. A regular on the superhero comedy series *Mr. Terrific* (1966-67), he also appeared in episodes of *Bewitched*, *The Flying Nun*, *Kolchak: The Night Stalker* ('The Werewolf'), *Good Heavens*, *Wonder Woman*, *Man from Atlantis*, *Fantasy Island*, *Happy Days* ('Welcome to My Nightmare'), *Knight Rider*, *Freddy's Nightmares* and *The Munsters Today*. Gautier also voiced a number of animated TV shows, and he replaced Adam West as Batman in a public service announcement about equal pay for women, appearing alongside Burt Ward as Robin and Yvonne Craig as Batgirl.

British actor **Philip Bond**, the father of actress Samantha Bond, died while on holiday in Portugal on January 17, aged 82. His TV credits include episodes of *The Voodoo Factor*, *Doctor Who* ('The Daleks'), *Sherlock Holmes* ('The Hound of the Baskervilles' with Peter Cushing), *The Champions*, *The Avengers* and *Doomwatch*.

73-year-old American adult film-maker, actor, porn advocate and historian **William Margold** died of a heart attack while hosting a live radio show the same day. He appeared in *Flesh Gordon*, *Dracula Sucks*, *Carnal Encounters of the Barest Kind*, *Pleasure Dome*, *Sex Drive 2020*, *Debbie Does the Devil in Dallas* (as "The Devil"), *Voodoo Lust: The Possession*, *Nympho Zombie Coeds* and *Hackin' Jack vs. the Chainsaw Chick 3D*, and he also worked in a production capacity on *Star Virgins*, *The Devil in Miss Jones 5: The Inferno* and many other adult movies. Margold founded or co-founded the X-Rated

Critics Organization (XRCO), Fans of X-Rated Entertainment (FOXE) and the charity group Protecting Adult Welfare Foundation (PAW).

American actor **Miguel** [José] **Ferrer**, the eldest child of actor José Ferrer and singer Rosemary Clooney, died of throat cancer on January 19, aged 61. He portrayed FBI Agent "Albert Rosenfield" in both the original 1990s TV series of *Twin Peaks* and the 2017 revival, as well as the spin-off movie, *Twin Peaks: Fire Walk with Me*. Ferrer's other movie credits include *Star Trek III: The Search for Spock*, *RoboCop* (1987), *Badlands 2005*, *DeepStar Six*, *The Guardian*, *Project: ALF*, *Justice League of America* (1997), the Stephen King adaptation *The Night Flier*, *Brave New World* (1998), *Sightings: Heartland Ghost*, *The Manchurian Candidate* (2004), *Hard Ride to Hell* and *Iron Man 3*. A regular on the brief 2007 revival of *Bionic Woman*, he also appeared on TV in episodes of *Tales from the Crypt*, *3rd Rock from the Sun*, *Night Visions* and *Medium*, along with the 1994 mini-series of King's *The Stand*, and contributed voice work to many animated shows and films. During the 1970s, Ferrer played drums and sang in bands with *Lost in Space* actor Billy Mumy.

Japanese actor **Hiroki Matsukata** (Hiroki Meguro), who starred in the 1966 fantasy *The Magic Serpent*, died of brain lymphoma on January 21, aged 74. He later turned up in Takashi Miike's existential *Izo*.

American actress **Mary Webster**, who co-starred with Vincent Price and Charles Bronson in AIP's 1961 Jules Verne adaptation *Master of the World*, died on January 23, aged 81. She also appeared in episodes of TV's *Men Into Space* and *The Twilight Zone* before retiring from the screen in 1963.

British character actor **Gorden** [Irving] **Kaye**, best known for his starring role in the BBC-TV sit-com *'Allo 'Allo* (1982-92), died in a care home the same day, aged 75. He had been suffering from dementia, and in 1990 the actor underwent emergency brain surgery after being involved in a car accident during a severe storm. Director Terry Gilliam cast Kaye in his films *Jabberwocky* and *Brazil*.

British leading man Sir **John** [Vincent] **Hurt** died of complications from pancreatic cancer on January 25, aged 77. He began his acting career on TV in the early 1960s, and his movie credits include *The Pied Piper* (1972), *The Ghoul* (with Peter Cushing, 1975), *Spectre*, *The Shout*, *Watership Down*, *The Lord of the Rings* (1978), *Alien* (replacing Jon Finch), *The Elephant Man*, *The Plague Dogs*, *1984*, *After Darkness*, Disney's *The Black Cauldron* and *The Tigger Movie*, *Jake Speed*, *Spaceballs*, *Frankenstein Unbound* (based on the novel by Brian Aldiss), *Monolith*, *Dead Man*, *Contact*, *Lost Souls*, *The Skeleton Key*, *V for Vendetta* (based on the graphic novel series by Alan Moore and David Lloyd), *Perfume: The Story of a Murderer*, *Indiana Jones and the Kingdom of the Crystal Skull*, *Outlander*, *Melancholia*, *Immortals*, *Only Lovers Left Alive*, *Snowpiercer* and *Hercules* (2014). Hurt appeared as "Professor Trevor 'Broom' Bruttenholm" in *Hellboy* and *Hellboy II: The Golden Army*, recreating the character for *Hellboy Animated: Blood & Iron*, and he played "Mr. Ollivander" in *Harry Potter and the Philosopher's Stone* (aka *Harry Potter and the Sorcerer's Stone*) and *Harry Potter and the Deathly Hallows: Part 1* and *Part 2*. On TV, he appeared in the eponymous role in Jim Henson's *The Storyteller* (1987-88), voiced "General Woundwort" in the animated *Watership Down* series (1999-2000), and starred in a disppointing 2010 version of M.R. James' *Whistle and I'll Come to You*. He was also in episodes of *Masters of Science Fiction* (Harlan Ellison's 'The Discarded'), *The Labyrinth* and *Merlin* (as the voice of The Dragon), and he turned up as the "missing" "War Doctor" in the *Doctor Who* special 'The Day of the Doctor' (opposite Matt Smith and David Tennant's Time Lords).

Emmy Award-winning American actress and production executive **Mary Tyler Moore**, who starred in TV sitcoms *The Dick Van Dyke Show* (1961-66), *Mary Tyler Moore* (1970-77) and *Rhoda* (1974-77), died of cardiopulmonary arrest due to pneumonia the same day, aged 80. Her other TV credits include episodes of *Steve Canyon* and *Thriller*, along with the 1976 musical special *Mary's Incredible Dream* (in which she appeard as the Devil, amongst other roles).

Armenian-American leading man **Mike Connors** (Krekor Ilevado Ohanian, aka "Michael Connors" and "Touch Connors"), who starred as the eponymous Los Angeles private detective in CBS-TV's *Mannix* (1967-75), died on January 26, aged 91. He had been diagnosed the week before with leukaemia. He appeared in Roger Corman's *Day the World Ended* and *Swamp Women*, along with *The Ten Commandments*, *Voodoo Woman*, *Kiss the Girls and Make Them Die*, *Nightkill* and *Too Scared to Scream* (which he also produced). Connors' TV credits included episodes of *One Step Beyond* and *Alfred Hitchcock Presents* (1989), and the 1984 half-hour SF sitcom pilot *Earthlings*, and he was also the voice of "Chipacles" in ten episodes of *Hercules* (1998-99).

American actress and former model **Barbara Hale**, best-remembered as legal secretary "Della Street" in the *Perry Mason* series (1957-66) and TV movies (1985-95), died of complications from COPD (chronic obstructive pulmonary disease) the same day, aged 94. She arrived in Hollywood in 1943 and was put under contract with RKO Radio Pictures, initially making uncredited appearances in a number of movies, including Val Lewton's *The Seventh Victim*, until working her way up to bigger roles. Hale was in the 1978 movie *The Giant Spider Invasion* and two episodes of TV's *Science Fiction Theatre*. She also appeared in an episode of *The Greatest American Hero* and a number of the *Perry Mason* tele-movies (including *Perry Mason: The Case of the Sinister Spirit*) alongside her son, actor William Katt.

American stage and screen actor **Stephen Joyce** also died on January 26, aged 85. He was in *A Stranger is Watching* and appeared on TV in episodes of *Alfred Hitchcock Presents*, *The Outer Limits*, *Invasion* and the mini-series *The Dark Secret of Harvest Home*, based on the novel by Thomas Tryon.

American stage actor and singer **Bob Holiday** died on January 27, aged 84. He originated the lead role in the musical *It's a Bird, It's a Plane, It's Superman!* in 1966, and played Clark Kent and the Man of Steel in 129 performances on Broadway. Holiday also appeared as Superman in a couple of TV commercials before retiring from show business in the 1970s and founding a successful home-construction business.

British stage and screen actor **Alec McCowen** CBE (Alexander Duncan McCowen) died on February 6, aged 91. He appeared in Hammer's *The Witches* (aka *The Devil's Own*), Alfred Hitchcock's

Frenzy and the rival Bond movie *Never Say Never Again* (as "Q").
He was also in an episode of *Orson Welles' Great Mysteries* on TV.
American leading man **Richard** [Lawrence] **Hatch**, who starred
as "Captain Apollo" in the ABC-TV series *Battlestar Galactica* (1978-
79), died of pancreatic cancer on February 7, aged 71. He was also
in *Charlie Chan and the Curse of the Dragon Queen* (as "Lee Chan,
Jr."), *Prisoners of the Lost Universe*, *Unseen Evil* (aka *The Unbelievable*),
InAlienable, *Season of Darkness*, *Alien Hunger*, *Starship II: Rendezvous
with Ramses*, *The Enchanted Cottage* (2016), *Asylum of Darkness*
and *Chatter*. On TV Hatch appeared in episodes of *The Sixth Sense*
and *Fantasy Island*, and he played "Tom Zarek" in the revided
Battlestar Galactica series (2004-09). Between 1997 and 2005 he is
credited as co-writer on seven *Battlestar Galactica* tie-in novels,
along with Christopher Golden, Stan Timmons, Alan Ridgers and
Brad Linaweaver, and in 1999 Hatch created a trailer for a possible
sequel to the series entitled *Battlestar Galactica: The Second Coming*.
   American adult movie actress **Jody Maxwell** (Jody Marie Hogsett),
who starred in the 1977 movie *The Devil Inside Her* and appeared
in the 1980 science fiction porn *The Satisfiers of Alpha Blue*, died
of cancer on February 12, aged 71. She also wrote articles for
numerous adult magazines, and her 2004 autobiography was titled
My Private Calls. She later became a public school teacher, and was
inducted into the Legends of Erotica Hall of Fame in Las Vegas in
2006.
   American professional wrestler **George** "The Animal" **Steele**
(William James Myers), who played Tor Johnson in Tim Burton's
biopic *Ed Wood* (1994), died of kidney failure on February 16. He
was 79.
   British-born Canadian character actor **Chris Wiggins**
(Christopher John Wiggins), who starred as "Jack Marshak" on TV's
Friday the 13th: The Series (1987-90), died of complications from
Alzheimer's disease on February 19, aged 87. His film credits include
The Neptune Factor, *Welcome to Blood City*, *Murder by Decree*, *An
American Christmas Carol*, *Virus* and *Mazes and Monsters*. He also
appeared in episodes of TV's *The Unforeseen*, *Purple Playhouse*
('Sweeney Todd, the Demon Barber of Fleet Street'), *Faerie Tale*

Theatre, *RoboCop*, *Earth: Final Conflict* and *ReGenesis*. In the 1960s Wiggins was the voice of "Thor" and "Don Blake" on the cartoon series *Mighty Thor* and *Captain America*, and the voice of "Will Scarlet" on *Rocket Robin Hood*. He also worked on many other animated series and movies.

Another Canadian character actor, **Richard McMillan**, died of thyroid cancer the same day, aged 65. He appeared in *The Legend of Gator Face*, *Shadow Builder*, *Universal Soldier II: Brothers in Arms* and *Universal Soldier III: Unfinished Business*, *The Day After Tomorrow*, *Cube Zero* and *The Fountain*, along with episodes of TV's *Are You Afraid of the Dark?*, *Forever Knight*, *PSI Factor: Chronicles of the Paranormal*, *F/X: The Series*, *Eerie Indiana*, *Goosebumps*, *Animorphs*, *Earth: Final Conflict*, *Lost Girl* and *Todd and the Book of Pure Evil*. In 2006, McMillan portrayed the wizard "Saruman" in the musical stage production of *The Lord of the Rings* at Toronto's Princess of Wales Theatre.

American character actor **Warren** [Lindsay] **Frost**, who portrayed coroner "Dr. Will Hayward" in ABC-TV's *Twin Peaks* (1990-91) and one episode of Showtime's 2017 revival, died after a long illness on February 19, aged 91. He was in *War of the Colossal Beast*, *Slaughterhouse-Five*, the obscure *Satan's Touch* (1984) and *Psycho IV: The Beginning*. His scenes as Dr. Hayward were deleted from *Twin Peaks: Fire Walk with Me*. Frost was also in episodes of TV's *Quantum Leap*, *Beauty and the Beast* (1989), *Intruders* and the 1994 mini-series *The Stand*, based on the novel by Stephen King. Frost's son Mark co-created *Twin Peaks* with David Lynch.

American stuntman and stunt co-ordinator **Trevor Habberstad** died of gastric cancer the same day, aged 27. He worked on *Face/Off*, *Spider-Man*, *Peter Pan* (2003), *Lady in the Water*, *My Bloody Valentine* (2009), *Hot Tub Time Machine*, *The Last Airbender*, *X-Men: First Class*, *Captain America: The First Avenger*, *In Time*, *Battleship*, *The Amazing Spider-Man*, *The Dark Knight Rises*, *Iron Man 3*, *After Earth*, *Star Trek: Into Darkness*, *Divergent*, *X-Men: Days of Future Past*, *Teenage Mutant Ninja Turtles* (2014), *Ant-Man*, *X-Men Apocalypse*, *Doctor Strange* and *Passengers*, along with episodes of TV's *Revolution*, *Teen Wolf* and *Agents of S.H.I.E.L.D.*

American bit actor **Peter Iasillo, Jr.**, who made a career out of playing homeless people, died of cancer on February 21, aged 63. He made his screen debut as a zombie in George A. Romero's *Day of the Dead* (1985) and was also in *Igor and the Lunatics*, *Spookies*, *Street Trash*, *Killer Dead* (aka *Non-Vegetarian Zombies from Outer Space*), *Skinned Deep* (with Warwick Davis and Forrest J Ackerman!), *HellBilly 58* and an episode of TV's *Gotham*.

61-year-old American leading man **Bill Paxton** (William Archibald Paxton) died of a stroke on February 25, following heart surgery. The actor's family subsequently filed a wrongful death lawsuit against the hospital and surgeon who performed the "high-risk" procedure. After beginning his career working in the art department on such films as *Death Game* and *Galaxy of Terror*, he turned to acting and appeared in *Night Warning* (aka *Butcher, Baker, Nightmare Maker*), *Deadly Lessons* (aka *Highschool Killer*), *Mortuary*, *Streets of Fire*, *Impulse*, *The Terminator*, *Weird Science*, *Aliens*, *Near Dark*, *Slipstream*, *Brain Dead*, *Predator 2*, *The Vagrant*, *Boxing Helena*, *Monolith*, *Future Shock*, *Mighty Joe Young* (1998), *Frailty* (which he also directed), *Spy Kids 2: Island of Lost Dreams*, *Spy Kids 3: Game Over*, *Club Dread*, *Thunderbirds* (as "Jeff Tracy"), *The Colony*, *Edge of Tomorrow* and *The Circle*. Paxton was also in episodes of TV's *The Hitchhiker* and *Tales from the Crypt*, and he portrayed "John Garrett" in the first season of *Agents of S.H.I.E.L.D.*

British actor and former American basketball player **Neil Fingleton**, who portrayed the giant "Mag the Mighty" on HBO's *Game of Thrones*, died of heart failure the same day, aged 37. Britain's tallest man at seven feet, seven-and-a-half inches, Fingleton also appeared in *X-Man: First Class*, *47 Ronin*, *Jupiter Ascending* and a two-part episode of TV's *Doctor Who* (as the "Fisher King"). He was also used as the motion-capture actor for the eponymous villain in *The Avengers: Age of Ultron*.

American character actor **Michael M. Ryan** died on March 1, aged 87. He played policemen in both *The Strangler* (with Victor Buono) and *Remo Williams: The Adventure Begins* (aka *Remo: Unarmed and Dangerous*).

80-year-old Puerto Rican-born actress **Miriam Colon** [Valle] died of a pulmonary infection in New York City on March 3. She appeared in *The Possession of Joel Delaney*, along with episodes of TV's *One Step Beyond*, *Shirley Temple's Storybook*, *Alfred Hitchcock Presents* and *Highway to Heaven*.

Robert [Jolin] **Osborne**, the on-air host of Turner Classic Movies since it began in 1994, died after a long illness on March 6, aged 84. As an actor, he had small roles in *Psycho* (1960) and an episode of TV's *One Step Beyond*, and appeared in a regional stage production in Seattle of *Night Must Fall* with Jane Darwell. He became a journalist on the suggestion of actress Lucille Ball, which led to a column at *The Hollywood Reporter* from 1983 until 2009. He was also the official historian of the Academy of Motion Picture Arts and Sciences and produced a series of books about the history of the Academy Awards. Osborne received a star on the Hollywood Walk of Fame in 2006.

American professional football player **"Sugarfoot" Anderson** (Ezzrett Anderson) died in Calgary, Canada, on March 8, aged 97. He appeared in half-a-dozen movies, mostly uncredited, including the 1952 "Bomba, the Jungle Boy" adventure, *African Treasure*.

American actress **Mary Menzies**, who portrayed "Isabella" in Roger Corman's *The Pit and the Pendulum* (1961), died the same day, aged 88. She also appeared, uncredited, in *Jane Eyre* (1943).

British stage and screen actress **Ann Beach**, who made her film debut in *The City of the Dead* (aka *Horror Hotel*, with Christopher Lee), died on March 9, aged 78. Her other credits include episodes of TV's *The Rivals of Sherlock Holmes*, *BBC Play of the Month* ('Rasputin') and *Tales of the Unexpected*.

British character actress **Jane Freeman** (Shirley Ann Pithers), who co-starred in 274 episodes of the TV series *Last of the Summer Wine* (1973-2010), died of lung cancer the same day, aged 81. She also appeared in the BBC's 1982 production of *Ghost in the Water*, based on the book by Edward Chitham.

British character actor **Tony Haygarth** (George Anthony Haygarth), who played "Milo Renfield" in the 1979 movie of *Dracula*, died of complications from Alzheimer's disease and vascular dementia on March 10, aged 72. He was also in *Britannia Hospital*,

The Bride, Dreamchild and *Ghostboat*. On TV, Haygarth starred in the title role of Nigel Kneale's seven-part SF comedy *Kinvig* (1981), and he appeared in episodes of *The Ghosts of Motley Hall*, *The Omega Factor*, *Dead Ernest*, *Space Precinct*, *Chiller* (Stephen Gallagher's adaptation of Peter James' novel *Prophecy*), the 1992 series of *The Borrowers* and its sequel, *The Return of the Borrowers*.

British character actor **John Forgeham** (John Henry George Forgham), who appeared with Tony Haygarth in the 1982 TV movie *Ivanhoe*, died the same day from internal bleeding after a fall. Aged 75, he was also in Nigel Kneale's *The Stone Tape*, and *Sheena*. Forgeham's TV credits include episodes of *The Avengers*, *Tales of the Unexpected* and Dennis Potter's *Cold Lazarus*. The first of his three wives was actress Georgina Hale.

Veteran American Western stuntman-actor **Jimmie Booth** (Walter Booth), died on March 16, aged 92. He had small roles in AIP's *Master of the World* (with Vincent Price), *High Plains Drifter*, *Treasure of Matecumbe*, *Star Trek: The Motion Picture* and numerous episodes of TV's *The Wild Wild West*.

American actor and novelist **Lawrence Montaigne** who appeared as both a Vulcan and the first Romulan seen in the original *Star Trek* series, died on March 17, aged 86. After making his screen debut as an uncredited soldier in *The Beast from 20,000 Fathoms* (1953), his other movies include *Captain Sinbad*, *The Satan Bug*, *The Power*, *The Psycho Lover*, Disney's *Escape to Witch Mountain* and Wes Craven's *Deadly Blessing*. On TV he was in episodes of *The Outer Limits*, *The Time Tunnel*, *Batman* (as the Joker's robot "Mr. Glee"), *The Invaders*, *The Man from U.N.C.L.E.*, *Voyage to the Bottom of the Sea*, *The Flying Nun* and Irwin Allen's 1969 pilot *City Beneath the Sea*. In a 2012 interview, the actor revealed that if Leonard Nimoy had left *Star Trek* to star in *Mission: Impossible*, Montaigne would most likely have replaced him as "Mr. Spock".

Legendary rock 'n' roll guitarist, singer and songwriter **Chuck Berry** (Charles Edward Anderson Berry) died on March 18, aged 90. His music and songs were heard in *Threads*, *Back to the Future*, *Teen Wolf*, *Back to the Future Part II*, *Men in Black*, *Hearts in Atlantis*, *The Santa Clause 2*, *The Shaggy Dog* (2006), *Arthur and the Invisibles*,

Blood: The Last Vampire, and TV's *The 4400*, *Scream: The TV Series* and *You Me and the Apocalypse*. Stephen King's novel *Christine* includes heading excerpts of Berry's lyrics.

American actor **Tony Russel** (Antonio Pietro Russo, aka "Tony Russo"/"Tony Russell"), who starred in a number of European movies in the 1960s, died the same day, aged 91. His credits include *Secret of the Sphinx*, *The Wild Wild Planet*, *The War of the Planets*, *The Invasion of Carol Enders* and *The Mystic Warrior*, along with an episode of *Rod Serling's Night Gallery* on TV.

American actress **Sally Kemp** died of cancer on March 21, aged 84. She appeared in *The Invasion of Carol Enders*, *Planet Earth*, *Spellbinder* and *Communion*.

American leading lady and singer **Lola Albright** (Lois Jean Albright, aka "Lola Deem"), who was a regular on the TV series *Peter Gunn* (1958-61) died on March 23, aged 92. She co-starred in the SF movie *The Monolith Monsters*, and on TV Albright appeared in episodes of *Tales of Tomorrow*, *Alfred Hitchcock Presents*, *The Alfred Hitchcock Hour*, *The Man from U.N.C.L.E.* (aka *The Helicopter Spies*, with John Carradine), *Cimarron Strip* ('The Beast That Walks Like a Man') and *The Incredible Hulk*. She was married to actor Jack Carson from 1950-57.

American actor **Lee Farr** (Leon Farb), who co-starred in TV's *The Detectives* (1959-60), died of cancer the same day, aged 89. He also appeared in episodes of *The Veil* (aka *Jack the Ripper*, hosted by Boris Karloff) and *The Invaders*.

Canadian-born actress **Jill Foster** [Florence Jill Hancock], who portrayed Darrin's secretary "Betty" (with various surnames) in the 1960s ABC sitcom *Bewitched*, died on March 24, aged 86. She also appeared in an episode of the obscure 1950s Canadian anthology TV series *The Unforeseen*. Foster was married to *Bewitched* scriptwriter Bernard Slade from 1953 until her death.

American actress, comedienne, singer and dancer **Chelsea Brown** (Lois Brown), who was a regular on TV's *Rowan & Martin's Laugh-In* from 1968-69, died of pneumonia on March 27, aged 74. She was in *Head* (with The Monkees), AIP's *The Thing with Two Heads*, and *The Return of Captain Invincible* (with Christopher Lee), along with an episode of *The Flying Nun*.

British actor **Ronald** [Charles Andrew] **Hines** died on March 28, aged 87. His credits include *House of Mystery* (1961) and *Sherlock Holmes and the Leading Lady* (with Christopher Lee as Holmes), along with episodes of *Out of the Unknown*, *The Avengers*, *Late Night Horror* (Robert Aickman's 'The Bells of Hell'), *Shadows of Fear*, *The Rivals of Sherlock Holmes*, *Doomwatch*, *Dead of Night*, *Star Maidens*, *Shadows* and *Jack the Ripper* (1988).

72-year-old Austrian-born actress **Christine** [Maria] **Kaufmann**, who posed nude for *Playboy* in 1999 at the age of 54, died of leukaemia in Germany the same day. She began her movie career in 1952, and her credits include AIP's *Murders in the Rue Morgue* (1971) and *Die Ängste des Dr. Schenk*. The first of her four husbands was Tony Curtis (1963-68), who she began dating when she was 16.

Hong Kong martial arts actor, stuntman and film-maker **Phillip Ko** [Fei] died of prostate cancer on March 30, aged 67. He appeared in numerous movies, including *Ghost Cat* (1980), *The Boxer's Omen*, *Seeding of a Ghost*, *Sex Beyond the Grave*, *Ninja Terminator*, *Magic Crystal*, *Cannibal Curse*, *Ultracop 2000* and *Shadow Mask*.

Mexican leading lady and former child actress **Alma Delia** [Susana] **Fuentes** [González] died on April 2, aged 80. She appeared in the movies *Los murciélagos*, *El ángel y yo* (with Tin-Tan), *Doctor Satán*, *Pánico*, *La isla de los dinosaurios* and *Blue Demon: destructor de espias*, along with the 1962 TV series *Las momias de Guanajuato*. Fuentes retired from the screen in 1970, and in her later years lived almost destitute with her pets in the garage of a delapidated mansion in Naucalpan, Mexico.

American actor **Steve Sandor**, who starred in the 1983 SF Western *Stryker*, died on April 5, aged 79. His other credits include the movies *The Ninth Configuration* and *Fire and Ice*, along with episodes of TV's *Star Trek*, *Matt Helm*, *Tales of the Unexpected*, *The Six Million Dollar Man*, *Fantasy Island*, *Knight Rider* and the animated *Superman*. He retired from the screen in the late 1990s.

American actor and insult comedian **Don Rickles** (Donald Jay Rickles) died of kidney failure on April 6, aged 90. He appeared in AIP's *X: The Man with the X-Ray Eyes*, *Muscle Beach Party*, *Bikini Beach*, *Pajama Party* (as "Big Bang, the Martian") and *Beach Blanket*

Bingo, along with John Landis' vampire comedy *Innocent Blood*. He voiced the grouchy character of "Mr. Potato Head" in the *Toy Story* films and video games, and he also worked on the animated movie *The Magic Sword: Quest for Camelot*. On TV, Rickles was in episodes of *The Twilight Zone*, *The Addams Family*, *The Munsters*, *The Wild Wild West*, *I Dream of Jeannie*, *Get Smart* and *Tales from the Crypt*.

British actor **Tim Pigott-Smith** OBE (Timothy Peter Pigott-Smith) died on April 7, aged 70. He appeared in the films *Clash of the Titans*, *The Hunchback of Notre Dame* (1982), *V for Vendetta*, Tim Burton's *Alice in Wonderland* (2010) and *Jupiter Ascending*, and was a voice artist on *The Little Vampire 3-D*. Pigott-Smith's TV credits include episodes of *Doctor Who* ('The Claws of Axos' and 'The Masque of Mandragora'), *Ghosts* and *Dr. Terrible's House of Horrible* ('Voodoo Feet of Death'). He also appeared on Broadway as "Dr. Watson" in the 1974 Royal Shakespeare Company's production of *Sherlock Holmes*, and in 1994 he was in a stage production of *The Picture of Dorian Gray*.

American actor **Peter** [Franklin] **Hansen** (aka "Peter Hanson") died on April 9, aged 95. One of his earliest movie credits was co-starring in *When Worlds Collide* (1951), and he was also in *Dragonfly* and episodes of TV's *Space Patrol*, *Science Fiction Theatre* (as six different doctors or professors!), *Men Into Space*, *The Outer Limits*, *The Man from U.N.C.L.E.* and *Starman*.

Mexican actress **Margarita Isabel** [Morales y Gonzalez], who co-starred in Guillermo del Toro's *Chronos* (1993), died of emphysema the same day, aged 75.

American actor and comedian **Charlie Murphy** (Charles Quinton Murphy), the older brother of Eddie Murphy, died of complications from leukaemia on April 12, aged 57. He was in *Night at the Museum*, *Unearthed* and *Frankenhood*.

Japanese actress and singer **Peggy Hayama** (Kotakari Shigeko, aka "Pegî Hayama") died of pneumonia the same day, aged 83. She appeared in the 1973 TV series *Ultraman Taro* and voiced the hero's mother.

American character actor [George] **Clifton James**, who portrayed comedy Southern Sheriff "J.W. Pepper" in the James Bond movies

Live and Let Die and *The Man with the Golden Gun* (both with Roger Moore), died of complications from diabetes on April 15, aged 96. His other credits include *The Werewolf of Washington*, *Superman II*, *Whoops Apocalypse*, and episodes of TV's *The Six Million Dollar Man*, *Highway to Heaven* and *Monsters* (Gahan Wilson's 'Leavings').

French actress and former fashion model **Yvonne** [-Thérèse-Marie-Camille Bédat de] **Monlaur**, who memorably starred as the naïve schoolteacher who released David Peel's vampire Baron Meinster in Hammer's *The Brides of Dracula* (1960), died of cardiac arrest on April 18, aged 77. She was also in *Circus of Horrors*, *The Terror of the Tongs* (again for Hammer, with Christopher Lee), *License to Kill* (1964) and *Skies Above*. She retired from the screen "for personal reasons" in the late 1960s.

93-year-old American supporting actor [Howard] **Trustin Howard** (aka "Slick Slavin") died of complications from a fall on April 20. He appeared in *The Atomic Kid*, the Edward D. Wood, Jr.-scripted *The Bride and the Beast* and *Invasion of the Star Creatures*.

British character actor **Patrick** [Arthur Oliver] **Westwood** died on April 21, aged 92. His film credits include *He Who Gets Slapped* (1947) and Roger Corman's *Pit and the Pendulum* (with Vincent Price and Barbara Steele). Westwood was a regular on *The Indian Tales of Rudyard Kipling* (1964), and also appeared in episodes of TV's *The Quatermass Experiment*, *Alfred Hitchcock Presents* (A.M. Burrage's 'The Waxwork'), *One Step Beyond*, *The Twilight Zone*, *The Avengers*, *Department S* ('The Duplicated Man') and *Space: 1999*.

Uruguayan-born actor **Gustavo Rojo** (Gustavo Adolfo Krefeld Sarandí Rojo y Pinto) died in Mexico on April 22, aged 93. Best remembered for his role as "Carlos" in *The Valley of Gwangi* (1969), he also appeared in *Tarzan and the Mermaids* (with George Zucco), *The Evil Forest*, *The Death Ray of Dr. Mabuse* and *A Witch Without a Broom*. The second of Rojo's three wives was actress Erika Remberg.

American actress **Erin** [Marie] **Moran**, who starred as "Joanie Cunningham" in the TV sitcoms *Happy Days* and the short-lived spin-off *Joanie Loves Chachi*, died of complications from throat cancer the same day, aged 56. She was also in the movies *Galaxy of Terror* and *Not Another B Movie*.

American actress and former beauty pageant contestant [Betty Jane] **Kathleen Crowley**, who co-starred in *Target Earth* (1954), died April 23, aged 87. Her other credits include the movies *The Flame Barrier* and *Curse of the Undead*, and episodes of such TV shows as *Kraft Theatre* ('Jane Eyre'), *Thriller* and *Batman*. She retired from the screen in 1970.

American tough-guy actor **Don Gordon** (Donald Walter Guadagno) died on April 24, aged 90. He made his movie debut in 1949, and his credits include *Zero Population Growth* (aka *Z.P.G.*), *The Return of Charlie Chan*, *The Final Conflict*, *The Beast Within*, *The Exorcist III* (aka *Legion*) and *The Borrower*. On TV he appeared in episodes of *Space Patrol*, *The Twilight Zone*, *The Outer Limits*, *Voyage to the Bottom of the Sea*, *The Wild Wild West*, *The Invaders*, *The Bionic Woman*, *Lucan*, *The Powers of Matthew Star*, *Automan* and *Knight Rider*. Actresses Helen Westcott and Nita Talbot were two of Gordon's four wives.

64-year-old Canadian-born actress **Glory Annen** (Glory Anne Clibbery), who co-starred in Norman J. Warren's *Prey* and *Outer Touch* (aka *Spaced Out*), died of complications from diabetes in London, England, the same day. She also turned up in *Marquis de Sade's Justine* (aka *Cruel Passion*, 1977) and *Supergirl* (1984), and was featured in the 1999 documentary *Evil Heritage: Independent Film-Making & the Films of Norman J. Warren*.

Mexican-born actor **Eric Mason** (Ernesto Benitez Macias) died in California on April 26, aged 90. He was in *Grave of the Vampire*, *Scream Blacula Scream* and *Kiss of the Tarantula*, along with episodes of TV's *The Six Million Dollar Man*, *Wonder Woman*, *Buck Rogers in the 25th Century*, *Fantasy Island* and *Voyagers!.*

Veteran American serial queen **Lorna Gray** (Virginia Mae Pound, aka "Adrian Booth") died on April 30, aged 99. She appeared with Boris Karloff in Columbia's *The Man They Could Not Hang* before moving to Republic, where she memorably starred as the beautiful villainess "Vultura" in the serial *Perils of Nyoka* and appeared as the heroine in the serial *Captain America* (1944). Her other credits include *Beware Spooks!* and *Valley of the Zombies* before she retired from the screen in 1951.

American actor **Vincent Baggetta**, who starred in NBC's *The Eddie Capra Mysteries* (1978-79), died on May 2, aged 72. He also appeared in *Embryo* and *The Man Who Wasn't There*, along with episodes of TV's *The Twilight Zone* (1963) and *Freddy's Nightmares*.

British character actor **Moray** [Robin Philip Adrian] **Watson** died the same day, aged 88. He made his screen debut in the BBC serial *The Quatermass Experiment* (1953), and his other TV credits include episodes of *The Avengers*, *Catweazle*, *Doctor Who*, *Tales of the Unexpected*, *Worlds Beyond*, *Star Cops* and *Tales of Mystery and Imagination*, hosted by Christopher Lee (1995).

Israeli leading lady **Daliah Lavi** (Daliah Lewinbuk) died in North Carolina on May 3, aged 76. Discovered by Kirk Douglas, the striking actress appeared in *The Return of Dr. Mabuse*, *The Demon* (1963), Mario Bava's *The Whip and the Body* (aka *Night is the Phantom*, with Christopher Lee), *Ten Little Indians* (1965), *The Silencers*, *Casino Royale* (1967), *Jules Verne's Rocket to the Moon* (aka *Those Fantastic Flying Fools*) and *Some Girls Do*. In the 1970s she had a career as a pop singer in Germany.

Scottish-born actress and former beauty queen **Quinn O'Hara** (Alice Jones), who co-starred as "Sinistra" in AIP's *The Ghost in the Invisible Bikini* (with Boris Karloff and Basil Rathbone), died of "multiple medical issues" in Los Angeles on May 5, aged 76. Her other movie credits include Larry Buchanan's remake of *Day the World Ended*, *In the Year 2889*, and *Cry of the Banshee* (with Vincent Price). O'Hara also appeared on TV in episodes of *The Man from U.N.C.L.E.*, *UFO* and *Fantasy Island*. She later became a nurse working with senior citizens.

American actor-stuntman **Jerry "Jack" Catron** (Jerry Eugene Catron) died on May 6, aged 85. During the 1960s he appeared in episodes of TV's *The Twilight Zone*, *Voyage to the Bottom of the Sea*, *The Man from U.N.C.L.E.*, *Bewitched*, *It's About Time*, *The Green Hornet*, *Batman*, *The Time Tunnel*, *Star Trek* and *Land of the Giants*.

German-born actor **Curt Lowens** (Kurt Löwenstein), who co-starred in *Werewolf in a Girls' Dormitory*, died of complications from a fall in Beverly Hills on May 8, aged 91. A Holocaust survivor and member of the Dutch resistance, who was often cast as a Nazis, he also appeared in *The Mephisto Waltz*, *Firefox*, *The Entity*, *Mandroid*, *Necronomicon: Book of the Dead*, *Invisible: The Chronicles of Benjamin Knight*, and episodes of TV's *Tarzan*, *Matt Helm*, *The Six Million Dollar Man*, *Wonder Woman*, *Man from Atlantis*, *Battlestar Galactica* (1979), *Galactica 1980*, *The Greatest American Hero*, *V*, *Knight Rider*, *Alien Nation*, *Monsters* (Robert Bloch's 'Reaper'), *Babylon 5* and *Flashforward*.

American actor and singer **Kenny Miller** died of pneumonia the same day, aged 85. He appeared in AIP's *I Was a Teenage Werewolf* (in which he performed the song 'Eeny, Meeny, Miney, Mo') and *Attack of the Puppet People*, along with the 1976 horror movie *Blood Stalkers* and an episode of TV's *Flash Gordon* (1954). His autobiography, *Surviving Teenage Werewolves, Puppet People and Hollywood*, was published in 1999.

Greek actress and punk singer **Mary Tsoni** committed suicide on May 8, aged 30. She suffered from severe depression. Tsoni's credits include the zombie movie *Evil* and its sequel, *Evil: In the Time of Heroes*.

American leading man **Michael Parks** (Harry Samuel Parks), who starred in and sang the closing theme song for the TV series *Then Came Bronson* (1969-70), died on May 9, aged 77. His body was buried at sea. Parks' movie credits include *The Werewolf of Woodstock*, *Distant Early Warning*, *The Savage Bees*, *Night Cries*, *The Evictors*, *Nightmare Beach*, *Sorceress* (1995), *From Dusk Till Dawn*, *From Dusk Till Dawn 3: The Hangman's Daughter* (as "Ambrose Bierce"), *Bullfighter*, *The Dead One* (2007), *Grindhouse* (aka *Death Proof* and *Planet Terror*), *We Are What We Are* and *Tusk*. On TV, he also appeared in episodes of *The Alfred Hitchcock Hour*, *Fantasy Island*, *War of the Worlds*, *Twin Peaks* and *SeaQuest 2032*.

American singer and actress **Lena** [Mary Calhoun] **Horne**, whose best-known song was 'Stormy Weather', died the same day, aged 92. Her movie credits include *Cabin in the Sky*, *I Dood It* and *The Wiz* (as "Glinda the Good"). Reportedly, MGM often shot her musical numbers so that they could be easily cut out of films in more racially insensitive areas of the U.S.

San Francisco flower-seller **Al Nalbandian** died on May 9, aged

95. He also had small roles in *The Mad Room*, *Invasion of the Body Snatchers* (1978), *Wacko*, *Peggy Sue Got Married*, *So I Married an Axe Murderer*, *James and the Giant Peach* and an episode of TV's *Captain Z-Ro*.

British character actor [Albert] **Geoffrey Bayldon**, best remembered for playing the title sorcerer in the children's TV series *Catweazle* (1970-71) and the creepy "Crowman" in *Worzel Gummidge* (1979-81), died of respiratory problems on May 10, aged 93. He was also in Hammer's *Dracula* (aka *Horror of Dracula*) and *Frankenstein Must Be Destroyed*, and Amicus' *The House That Dripped Blood*, *Tales from the Crypt* and *Asylum*, along with *The Adventures of Alice* (as the "White Knight"), *Casino Royale* (1967, as "Q"), *Scrooge*, *The Frighteners*, *Gawain and the Green Knight*, *Alice Through the Looking Glass* (1973, as the "White Knight" again), *The Slipper and the Rose: The Story of Cinderella* and *The Monster Club*. On TV, Bayldon appeared in the 1966 serial of Wilkie Collins' *The Woman in White* and episodes of *The Avengers*, *Journey to the Unknown*, *Once Upon a Time* ('Frankenstein'), *Orson Welles' Great Mysteries*, *The Tomorrow People* ('Into the Unknown'), *Space: 1999*, *BBC2 Playhouse* ('The Mind Beyond: The Man with the Power'), *Doctor Who* ('The Creature from the Pit'), *Sherlock Holmes and Doctor Watson*, *Tales of the Unexpected*, *Star Cops*, *The Return of Sherlock Holmes*, *The Storyteller*, *Prince Caspian and the Voyage of the Dawn Treader* (1989) and *The New Adventures of Robin Hood* (as "Merlin"). The actor also hosted the 2012 documentary *Amicus: House of Horrors*, and he portrayed the Doctor in two audio adventures of *Doctor Who*, 'Auld Mortality' and 'A Storm of Angels'.

American tough-guy actor **Powers** [Allen] **Boothe** died in his sleep of pancreatic cancer-related cardiopulmonary arrest on May 14, aged 68. His movie credits include *Southern Comfort*, *Red Dawn* (1984), *The Emerald Forest*, *By Dawn's Early Light*, *Mutant Species*, *Frailty*, *Sin City* and *Sin City: A Dame to Kill For*, and *The Avengers*. On TV, Boothe appeared as head Hydra honcho "Gideon Malick" in Season 3 of TV's *Agents of S.H.I.E.L.D.*, and he was the voice of "Gorilla Grodd" in the animated *Justice League* and *Justice League Unlimited* series.

Russian-born actor **Oleg** [Borisovich] **Vidov** died of cancer on May 15, aged 73. He defected to America in 1985 and had small roles in *2090* and *Wishmaster 2: Evil Never Dies*. From 1992-2007, Vidov and his wife Joan distributed the Soyuzmultifilm Studio animation library around the world.

American actress **Anne Kimbell** (Anne Banks), who starred in *Monster from the Ocean Floor* (1954) produced by Roger Corman, died on May 16, aged 84. She appeared in *Port Sinister* and the "Bomba, the Jungle Boy" adventure *The Golden Idol* before moving to Britain and retiring from the screen in 1958.

Australian-born character actress, artist, gallerist and film director **Clytie Jessop** (Clytie Lloyd-Jones), who memorably appeared as the ghost of "Miss Jessel" in *The Innocents* (1961), died in London on May 18, aged 88. Her only other acting credits are Hammer's *Nightmare* and Amicus' *Torture Garden*, both for director Freddie Francis (who shot the earlier film). In 1971 she held a benefit exhibition entitled 'Ozject D'Art' at her gallery in Chelsea to help the editors of *Oz* magazine, who were then facing obscenity charges.

American actress, socialite, fashion model and philanthropist **Dina Merrill** (Nedina Marjorie Hutton) died of complications from Lewy Body dementia on May 22, aged 93. On TV she appeared as "Calamity Jane" in three episodes of the 1960s *Batman*, along with episodes of *Rod Serling's Night Gallery*, *The Hardy Boys/Nancy Drew Mysteries* ('A Haunting We Will Go') and *Tales of the Unexpected*. Merrill was also in movies *Anna to the Infinite Power*, *Twisted*, *Fear*, *Suture*, *Mighty Joe Young* (1998) and *The Glow*. On Broadway she co-starred in a 1975 revival of Patrick Hamilton's play *Angel Street*. The daughter of Wall Street financier E.F. Hutton and cereal heiress Marjorie Merriweather Post, Merrill's first husband was an heir to the Colgate-Palmolive fortune. Her second husband was actor Cliff Robertson (1966-89) and, following their divorce, she married an investment banker who purchased RKO Pictures, which she managed. It was estimated that she was the richest actress in the world.

British leading man Sir **Roger** [George] **Moore**, who starred as "Simon Templar" in TV's *The Saint* (1962-69) and portrayed the second movie "James Bond" seven times, died in Switzerland on May 23, after a short battle with cancer. He was 89. Moore's suave and sexist Bond was featured in *Live and Let Die*, *The Man with the Golden Gun* (with Christopher Lee), *The Spy Who Loved Me*, *Moonraker*, *For Your Eyes Only*, *Octopussy* and *A View to a Kill*, and the actor also appeared *in The Man Who Haunted Himself*, *Sherlock Holmes in New York* (as Holmes) and *The Man Who Wouldn't Die*. On TV, Moore directed one of the best episodes *of The Saint*, 'The House on Dragon's Rock' (1968), and he also appeared along with his successor in the role, actor Ian Ogilvy, in a feature-length pilot for another series of *The Saint*, which was finally released in 2017. He authored two books about playing 007: *Roger Moore as James Bond: Roger Moore's Own Account of Filming Live and Let Die* (1973) and *Bond on Bond* (2012), while his 2008 autobiography was titled *My Word is My Bond*.

American TV actor **Jared** [Christopher] **Martin**, who starred in the science fiction series *The Fantastic Journey* (1977) and *War of the Worlds* (1988-90), died of pancreatic cancer on May 24, aged 75. His other credits include episodes of *Rod Serling's Night Gallery*, *Logan's Run*, *The Six Million Dollar Man*, *Project U.F.O.*, *Wonder Woman*, *The Incredible Hulk*, *Fantasy Island* and *Knight Rider*. Martin was also in the movies *Westworld*, *Rome 2072 A.D.*, *The Sea Serpent* and Lucio Fulci's *Aenigma*.

Serbian stuntman-actor and special effects supervisor **Dragomir Stanojevic-Bata Kameni** died the same day, aged 75. His credits include *Possession* (1981), *Strangler vs. Strangler* and *The Magic Snowman*.

Italian actor **Toni Bertorelli** (Antonio Bertorelli), who played "Conte Dracula" in the contemporary comedy *Zora the Vampire* (2000), died after a long illness on May 26, aged 69. He was also in a 2008 TV movie of *Pinocchio* starring Bob Hoskins.

American stuntman-actor **Vince Deadrick, Sr.** died on May 27, aged 84. He worked on the Bond movie *Diamonds Are Forever*, *Sisters of Death*, *The Beastmaster*, *Space Hunter: Adventures in the Forbidden Zone*, *Angel* (1984), *Ninja III: The Domination*, *Avenging Angel*, *D.A.R.Y.L.*, *Short Circuit*, *The Golden Child*, *The Dead Pool*,

Ghostbusters II, Indiana Jones and the Last Crusade, Total Recall (1990), *Bedazzled* (2000), *Timecop: The Berlin Decision* and *Pirates of the Caribbean: The Curse of the Black Pearl*, along with such TV series as *The Man from U.N.C.L.E., Star Trek, The Ghost and Mrs. Muir, Man from Atlantis, The Six Million Dollar Man* and *Star Trek: Enterprise.*

American actress **Elena** [Angela] **Verdugo** died on May 30, aged 92. One of the last links with the Universal horror movies of the 1940s, she co-starred with Lon Chaney, Jr. in both *House of Frankenstein* (1944) and *The Frozen Ghost* (1945). Her other film credits include the "Jungle Jim" adventure, *The Lost Tribe*; the final "Charlie Chan" mystery, *The Sky Dragon*; and the "Bomba, the Jungle Boy" adventure, *The Lost Volcano*; plus *Thief of Damascus* (again with Chaney, Jr.) and *Day of the Nightmare.* Verdugo's first husband was screenwriter Charles R. Marion.

British actress and glamour model **Molly Peters** (Mollie Peters), who had a brief screen career in the 1960s, including playing the nurse seduced by Sean Connery's James Bond in *Thunderball*, died the same day. She was 75. Her movie career ended after a disagreement with her agent.

American actor **Wendell Burton**, who voiced the title character in *You're a Good Man, Charlie Brown* (1973)—a role he recreated from the original stage musical—died of brain cancer on May 30, aged 69. He later became a Christian minister in his native Texas.

American actor **James** [Paul] **Burnett** died the same day, aged 48. He was in *Transcendence, Maze Runner: The Scorch Trials* and an episode of TV's *From Dusk Till Dawn: The Series.*

Danish actress **Mimi Heinrich** died on May 31, aged 80. She appeared in Denmark's two most famous genre movies, *Reptilicus* (1961) and *Journey to the Seventh Planet* (1962).

British TV actor **Roy Barraclough** MBE, who played "Alec Gilroy" in the ITV soap opera *Coronation Street* (1972-98), died after a short illness on June 1, aged 81. His rare film appearances include *The Slipper and the Rose: The Story of Cinderella*, and he was in Mark Gatiss' 2013 adaptation of M.R. James' *The Tractate Middoth.* Barraclough also co-starred as the pompous "Mr. Cobbledick" in the children's series *Pardon My Genie* (1972-73), and he was also in an episode of *Woof!*.

British character actor **Peter** [John] **Sallis** OBE, best-known to modern audiences as the voice of the hapless inventor "Wallace" in the stop-motion *Wallace & Gromit* films (including *The Curse of the Were-Rabbit* and *A Matter of Loaf and Death*), died on June 2, aged 96. He made his screen debut in a 1947 version of *A Midsummer Night's Dream* and went on to appear in *Stranger from Venus*, *Cinderella* (1958), *The Adventures of Alice* (1960), *The Mouse on the Moon*, *Scream and Scream Again* (with Vincent Price, Christopher Lee and Peter Cushing), *Wuthering Heights* (1970), *Frankenstein: The True Story* and *Full Circle* (aka *The Haunting of Julia*, based on the novel by Peter Straub), along with Hammer's *The Curse of the Werewolf* and *Taste the Blood of Dracula* (again with Lee). A regular on TV's *The Ghosts of Motley Hall* (1976-78), Sallis was also in episodes of *Strange Experiences*, *The Invisible Man* (1959), *The Avengers*, *Doctor Who* ('The Ice Warriors'), *Catweazle*, *Mystery and Imagination* ('Sweeney Todd'), *The Moonstone* (1972), *The Rivals of Sherlock Holmes*, *The Clifton House Mystery* and *Tales of the Unexpected*. In 1965 he originated the role of "Dr. Watson" in the Broadway musical *Baker Street*, co-starred in the British production of Frederick Knott's play *Wait Until Dark* (1966-67), and was featured in a 1968 BBC Radio production of *The Day of the Triffids*.

Polish-born actor **Stefan Gryff**, who played the police inspector in *The Legend of the Werewolf* (1975) opposite Peter Cushing, died in Britain on June 3, aged 78. He also appeared in episodes of TV's *The Avengers*, *The Champions*, *Whoops Apocalypse* and *Hammer House of Mystery and Suspense*.

American actor and producer **Roger** [LaVerne] **Smith**, who co-starred in TV's *77 Sunset Srip* from 1958-63, died of complications from Parkinson's disease on June 4, aged 84. He had also suffered from the muscle-nerve disorder myasthenia gravis for many years. In the 1957 Lon Chaney biopic *Man of a Thousand Faces* Smith portrayed Creighton Chaney (Lon Chaney, Jr.) opposite his mentor James Cagney. He was married to actress and singer Ann-Margret since 1967.

British actor, puppeteer, mime and ventriloquist **Andy Cunningham** (Andrew Cunningham), best known for the BBC children's TV series *Bodger and Badger* (1989-99), died of cancer on June 5, aged 67. He was also the (uncredited) puppeteer for "Ephant Mon", Jabba the Hutt's head of security, in the second *Star Wars* sequel, *Return of the Jedi* (1983).

Sultry American 1950s B-movie actress **Helene Stanton** (Eleanor Stansbury) died on June 7, aged 91. Given her stage name by Hollywood columnist Louella Parsons, her movie credits include *Jungle Moon Men* (with Johnny Weismuller) and *The Phantom from 10,000 Leagues*, before she retired from the screen in 1957. Stanton was the seventh (1949-53) of nine wives of former silent film actor Kenneth Harlan.

American actress **Glenne** [Aimee] **Headly**, who played "Tess Truehart", the girlfriend of Warren Beatty's detective in *Dick Tracy* (1990), died of complications from a pulmonary embolism on June 8, aged 62. Her other movie credits include Woody Allen's *The Purple Rose of Cairo*, *Making Mr. Right* (with her then-husband John Malkovich), *Paperhouse* (based on the YA novel by Catherine Storr) and *The Circle*. Headly co-starred in Hulu's half-hour comedy SF series *Future Man* (2017), which was dedicated to her memory.

American actor **Adam West** (William West Anderson), who portrayed TV's "Batman" in the eponymous 1966-68 ABC series and various spin-offs, died after a short battle with leukaemia on June 9, aged 88. On June 15, the city of Los Angeles shone the Bat-Signal on City Hall as a tribute to the actor. One of West's earliest movie appeareances was an uncredited role in the Boris Karloff movie *Voodoo Island* (1957), and he was also in *Robinson Crusoe on Mars*, *Batman: The Movie*, *The Eyes of Charles Sand*, *Poor Devil* (with Christopher Lee), *Warp Speed*, *Time Warp*, *One Dark Night*, *Zombie Nightmare*, *Doin' Time on Planet Earth*, *Omega Cop*, *Maxim Xul*, *An American Vampire Story*, *Seance*, *Monster Island* (as "Dr. Harryhausen"), *Tales from Beyond* and *Angels with Angels* (as "Alfred, the Butler"). On TV, he also starred in the series *The Last Precinct* (1986) and was a regular on *Black Scorpion* (2001), and he appeared in episodes of *The Outer Limits* (1964), *Bewitched*, *Off to*

See the Wizard, Rod Serling's Night Gallery, Fantasy Island, The Flash (1990), *Tales from the Crypt, Lois & Clark: The New Adventures of Superman* and *Goosebumps*, and he was a regular voice on *Family Guy* as "Mayor Adam West" (2000-17). He recreated his iconic role as Batman in *Legends of the Superheroes* and the animated series *The New Adventures of Batman, Tarzan and the Super 7, SuperFriends: The Legendary Super Powers Show, The Super Powers Team: Galactic Guardians, The Simpsons*, and the full-length *Batman: Return of the Caped Crusaders* and *Batman vs. Two-Face*. The actor also voiced "The Gray Ghost" on an episode of *Batman: The Animated Series*, "Mayor Grange" in *The Batman* and "Thomas Wayne" in *Batman: The Brave and the Bold*. West's 1994 autobiography was aptly titled *Back to the Batcave*.

British character actor **Sam Beazley**, who played "Professor Everard", who lived inside his portrait in *Harry Potter and the Order of the Phoenix* (2007), died on June 12, aged 101. In the mid-1930s he was part of John Gielgud's theatre company and appeared in the actor's acclaimed London stage productions of William Shakespeare's *Romeo and Juliet* and *Hamlet*. Following a poor review, he abandoned acting to run an antique shop. He finally returned to the profession when he retired at the age of 73.

American actress **Deirdre** [Michelle] **Berthrong**, who began her brief 1970s career playing one of the nude schoolgirls in the shower in *Carrie* (1976), died the same day of pneumonia, aged 64. She also worked as an assistant to director Jack Bender on the TV movie *Deadly Messages*.

Best remembered for her romantic attachments with three of the original members of the Rolling Stones (Brian Jones, Keith Richards and Mick Jagger), Italian-born actress and model **Anita Pallenberg** died of complications of hepatitis C in England on June 13, aged 75. She appeared as "The Great Tyrant" in Roger Vadim's *Barbarella*, was in Abel Ferrara's *4:44 Last Day on Earth*, and turned up as the Devil (opposite Marianne Faithfull's "God") in a 2001 episode of the BBC sitcom *Absolutely Fabulous*.

Henry J. Deutschendorf II, one of the twin boys who played "Baby Oscar" in *Ghostbusters II* (1989), committed suicide by hanging on June 14, aged 29. The nephew of the late country singer John Denver, he had suffered from a schizoaffective disorder for many years.

American actor, comedian, scriptwriter and TV producer **Bill Dana** (William Szathmary), best known for his Hispanic character "Jose Jiminez" (who became the mascot for the original seven Mercury astronauts), died on June 15, aged 92. He scripted the 1966 animated movie *Alice in Wonderland or What's a Nice Kid Like You Doing in a Place Like This?* and the 1980 *Get Smart* movie, *The Nude Bomb*. As an actor, he appeared in episodes of *Batman* (as Jiminez), *The Man from U.N.C.L.E.*, *Get Smart* and *Fantasy Island*, along with William Castle's *The Busy Body*, and *The Nude Bomb*.

American actor, producer and director **Stephen Furst** (Stephen Fuerstein), who played Centauri "Vir Cotto" in *Babylon 5* (1994-98) and *Babylon 5: Thirdspace* (1998), died on June 16. Aged 63, he had suffered from diabetes for many years. Furst was in the movies *The Unseen* (1980), *Silent Rage*, *Class Reunion*, *The Day After*, *Little Bigfoot 2: The Journey Home*, *Path of Destruction* and *Basilisk: The Serpent King*, the TV special *ALF Loves a Mystery*, and an episode of *Faerie Tale Theatre*. He also executive produced the low budget movies *Warbirds*, *Cold Moon* (based on the novel by Michael McDowell and directed by his son, Griff Furst), *Atomic Shark* and *Trailer Park Shark* (also directed by his son), and directed *Stageghost*, *Dragon Storm*, *Path of Destruction* and *Basilisk: The Serpent King* (the latter two as "Louie Myman"), along with episodes of *Babylon 5* and the short spin-off series *Crusade*.

British TV character actor **Brian Cant**, best remembered as the narrator of such popular children's series as *Camberwick Green*, *Trumpton* and *Chigley*, died of Parkinson's disease on June 19, aged 83. He also appeared in episodes of *Legend of Death*, *Doctor Who* and *The Hunchback of Notre Dame* (1966).

American actor **Howard Witt**, who portrayed the title character in the 1980s Disney TV movies *Mr. Boogedy* and *Bride of Boogedy*, died on June 21, aged 85. He was also in *Revenge of the Stepford Wives* and episodes of TV's *The Incredible Hulk* and *Once a Hero*.

American professional football player turned actor **Keith** [James]

Loneker died of cancer on June 22, aged 46. He appeared in *Lakeview Terrace*, *Destination Planet Negro*, *The Vault*, and the short *Scary Film*.

Veteran American stuntman-actor **Loren Janes** (Loren Lapham Janes, Jr.), who co-founded the Stuntmen's Association with Dick Geary in 1961, died of complications from Alzheimer's disease on June 24, aged 85. He began his career in the mid-1950s and his numerous credits include *Jupiter's Darling*, *Cult of the Cobra*, *Darby O'Gill and the Little People*, *Snow White and the Three Stooges*, *Planet of the Apes* (1968), *Beneath the Planet of the Apes*, *Planet Earth*, *The Terminal Man*, *Earthquake*, *Logan's Run*, *King Kong* (1976), *The Swarm*, *Escape from New York*, *The Sword and the Sorcerer*, *Halloween III: Season of the Witch*, *Hysterical*, *The Dead Zone*, *Repo Man*, *Back to the Future*, *Fright Night*, *Short Circuit*, *Masters of the Universe*, *Dead Heat*, *C.H.U.D. II: Bud the Chud*, *The Abyss*, *Hook*, *The Silence of the Hams*, *Wild Wild West*, *Megiddo: The Omega Code 2* and *Spider-Man* (2002), along with episodes of TV's *Star Trek* and *Search*.

American character actor **Skip Homeier** (George Vincent Homeier, aka "Skippy Homeier") died of spinal myelopathy on June 25, aged 86. His credits include *The Ghost and Mr. Chicken*, *The Wild Wild West Revisited* and episodes of TV's *Suspense*, *Science Fiction Theatre*, *Alfred Hitchcock Presents*, *One Step Beyond*, *The Outer Limits*, *The Addams Family*, *Voyage to the Bottom of the Sea*, *Star Trek*, *Circle of Fear*, *The Bionic Woman*, *The Six Million Dollar Man*, *Project U.F.O.*, *The Incredible Hulk* and *Fantasy Island*. He retired fom the screen in the early 1980s.

56-year-old Swedish actor **Michael Nyqvist** (Rolf Åke Mikael Nyqvist), who starred as "Mikael Blomkvist" in the original *The Girl with the Dragon Tattoo* (2009), two sequels, and the mini-series *Millennium* (2010), died of lung cancer on June 27. His other credits include *London Voodoo* and the TV series *Zero Hour*.

British actress **Joan Winmill Brown**, who played the maid "Mary Wells" during the April-July run of a 1951 touring stage production of *Dracula* starring Bela Lugosi, died on June 29 in Hawaii. She was 95. Brown had a few small film roles and also appeared in the BBC series *Epitaph for a Spy* starring Peter Cushing. Between

1948-49 she was the secret girlfriend of Robert F. Kennedy, who installed her in a flat in Kensington, and she later moved to America and became a follower of Billy Graham's evangelical "Crusade".

Iconaclastic British actor, poet, playwright, scriptwriter, painter and sculptor [John Henley] **Heathcote Williams** died of lung disease on July 1, aged 75. He appeared in Derek Jarman's *The Tempest* (1979, as "Prospero"), *Slipstream, Orlando, WSH: The Myth of the Urban Myth, Alice in Wonderland* (1999), *Nostradamus, City of Ember* and the TV mini-series *The Odyssey* and *Dinotopia*.

American actress and author **A'leisha Brevard**, who was one of the first people to undergo sexual reassignment surgery in the US in the early 1960s, died of pulmunary fibrosis the same day, aged 79. Born Alfred Brevard Crenshaw, she appeared as the female creature in *Bigfoot* (starring John Carradine) and was also in *The Female Bunch* (with Lon Chaney, Jr.), an episode of TV's *Rod Serling's Night Gallery*, and the two *Legends of the Superheroes* specials (as "Giganta").

Popular Italian comic actor **Paolo Villaggio**, best known for his trademark character "Fantozzi", died of complications from diabetes on July 3, aged 84. His credits include *Dottor Jekyll e gentile signore* (as "Dr. Jekyll" and "Mr. Hyde"), *Fracchia contro Dracula, Sogno mostruosamente proibiti* and *InvaXon: Alieni in Liguria*.

Former British professional wrestler turned actor and stuntman, "Tiger" **Joe Robinson** (Joseph Robinson), died the same day after a short illness, aged 90. He appeared (uncredited) in Hammer's *The Two Faces of Dr. Jekyll* (aka *Jekyll's Inferno*), Mario Bava's *Erik the Conqueror, Tartar Invasion, Taur the Mighty, Thor and the Amazon Women*, and the James Bond film *Diamonds Are Forever*. Robinson and his brother Doug gave actress Honor Blackman her first lessons in judo and karate for her role as "Cathy Gale" in TV's *The Avengers*, and they co-authored her 1965 volume *Honor Blackman's Book of Self-Defense*.

German-born actress **Solvi Stübing** (aka "Silvia Stubing") died in Italy on July 3, aged 76. She appeared in *Secret Agent Super Dragon, Battle of the Amazons, Strip Nude for Your Killer* and *Deported Women of the SS Special Section*.

American actor **Ji-Tu Cumbuka** (aka "Jitu Cumbuka") died of vascular disease on July 4, aged 77. He was in the movies *Blacula*, *Dr. Black Mr. White*, *Mandrake* (as "Lothar"), *Death Ray 2000* and *Covenant*. On TV, the actor co-starred in the sci-spy series *A Man Called Sloane* (1979-80) and appeared in episodes of *Rod Serling's Night Gallery*, *The Six Million Dollar Man*, *Faerie Tale Theatre*, *Knight Rider*, *Alien Nation* and *Murder She Wrote* ('Night of the Tarantula'). He basically retired from the screen in 1994.

74-year-old British actress **Carol Lee Scott** (Carol Waterman), who was best known as the wicked witch "Grotbags" on children's TV, died of cancer the same day. She originated the character on the ITV series *Emu's World* (1982-84) and continued it through three more series before developing her own show, *Grotbags*, which ran from 1991-93.

New Zealand-born character actor **John Karlsen** died on July 5, aged 97. He worked in Europe for most of his career, and his many credits include *Battle of the Worlds* (with Claude Rains), *Werewolf in a Girl's Dormitory*, *The Witch's Curse*, Federico Fellini's *8½*, *Crypt of Horror* (aka *Terror in the Crypt*, with Christopher Lee), *Crack in the World*, *The Amazing Doctor G*, Michael Reeves' *The She Beast* (with Barbara Steele), *Modesty Blaise* (1966), *The Christmas That Almost Wasn't*, *Mission Stardust*, *Fenomenal and the Treasure of Tutankamen*, *Spirits of the Dead*, *La bestia uccide a sangue freddo*, *Bill & Ted's Excellent Adventure*, *The Church*, *Roger Corman's Frankenstein Unbound* and *The Order* (aka *The Sin Eater*).

69-year-old American actor **John [Currie] Slade** was killed in an automobile accident on July 7. He had small roles in *976-EVIL*, *Black Magic Woman* and an episode of TV's *Voyagers!*

Italian leading lady and former fashion model **Elsa Martinelli** (Elsa Tia) died of cancer on July 8, aged 82. She co-starred in Roger Vadim's *Blood and Roses*, Orson Welles' *The Trial* and *The 10th Victim* (based on the story by Robert Sheckley).

American actor **Nelsan Ellis** (Nelson Leon Ellis), who played "Lafayette Reynolds" on the HBO series *True Blood* (2008-14), died the same day, aged 39. The actor had been trying to quit an alcohol addiction, and it is thought that alcohol withdrawal complications may have led to his heart failure. In Charlaine Harris' book series, short-order cook Lafayette was killed off, but he survived in the TV show because he was such a popular character. Ellis was also a regular on Season 5 of CBS' *Elementary*.

American voice actor, voice director, sound recordist and producer **Wally Burr** (Walter Story Burr) died on July 9, aged 93. His credits include such cartoon TV series as *The All-New Super Friends Hour* and *Super Friends* (as "The Atom"), *The Transformers*, and the English-language versions of the *anime* movies, *Fist of the North Star* and *Akira*. Burr also co-produced the 1970 TV movie *Sole Survivor* featuring William Shatner.

American stuntman-actor **John** [Hagen] **Bernecker** died of accidental blunt force trauma on July 13, after an accident on the set of AMC's *The Walking Dead*. The 33-year-old suffered massive head injuries after falling more than twenty feet onto concrete, and had been on a hospital ventilator. Bernecker had small roles in *Monsterwolf*, *Goosebumps*, *The Last Witch Hunter*, *Logan* and episodes of TV's *True Detective*, *Salem* and *The Parallax Theory*. He performed and co-ordinated stunts on a number of other movies and TV shows, including *Jonah Hex*, *Vampires Suck*, *Mysterious Island* (2010), *Dylan Dog: Dead of Night*, *Green Lantern*, *Creature* (2011), *Battleship*, *Abraham Lincoln: Vampire Hunter*, *Universal Soldier: Day of Reckoning*, *Looper*, *Escape Plan*, *Percy Jackson: Sea of Monsters*, *The Hunger Games: Catching Fire*, *Teenage Mutant Ninja Turtles* (2014), *The Hunger Games: Mockingjay—Part 1* and *Part 2*, *Fantastic Four* (2015), *Invisible Sister*, *The 5th Wave*, *Teenage Mutant Ninja Turtles: Out of the Shadows*, *Ozark Sharks*, *Black Panther* and *Avengers of Justice: Farce Wars*, along with episodes of *The Vampire Diaries*, *Scream Queens*, *Into the Bad Lands* and *The Magicians*.

89-year-old American actor **Martin Landau**, who won an Academy Award for his portrayal of Bela Lugosi in Tim Burton's biopic *Ed Wood* (1994), died of "unexpected complications" during a hospital visit on July 15. He was also in *The Fall of the House of Usher* (1979), *Meteor*, *Without Warning*, *The Return*, *Alone in the Dark*, *The Being*, *The Return of the Six Million Dollar Man and the Bionic Woman*, *Cyclone*, *By Dawn's Early Light*, *Firehead*, *Sliver*, *12:01* (based on the story by Richard A. Lupoff), *The Adventures of Pinocchio* and *The*

New Adventures of Pinocchio, Merry Christmas George Bailey, The X Files, Sleepy Hollow, City of Ember and *Dark Horse*. On TV, Landau starred with his then-wife, Barbara Bain, in the series *Mission: Impossible* (1966-69) and *Space: 1999* (1975-77), and he was also in episodes of *Wanted: Dead or Alive* ('The Monster'), *Shirley Temple's Storybook* ('The House of the Seven Gables'), *The Outer Limits, The Twilight Zone* (both the original and 1980s revival), *The Alfred Hitchcock Hour*, the 1964 pilot for *The Haunted* ('The Ghost of Sierra de Cobre), *The Wild Wild West, The Man from U.N.C.L.E.* ('The Bat Cave Affair', as a Lugosi-like villain), *Get Smart* and *Alfred Hitchcock Presents* (1987). The actor was reportedly Gene Roddenberry's first choice to play "Mr. Spock" on *Star Trek*, but turned the role down. In the mid-1980s, Landau portrayed the title role in a troubled national tour of the Broadway production of *Dracula*.

British character actor **William Hoyland** died the same day, aged 73. He appeared in *Assault* (aka *In the Devil's Garden*), the Bond film *For Your Eyes Only* and *Hellboy*, along with episodes of TV's *Thriller* (1975), *Invasion: Earth* and *Life on Mars*.

British character actor and playwright **Trevor Baxter**, who played "Professor George Litefoot" in the 1977 *Doctor Who* serial 'The Talons of Weng-Chang', died on July 16, aged 84. The actor also appeared in *The Hunchback of Notre Dame* (1997) and *Sky Captain and the World of Tomorrow*, along with a 1961 BBC Schools series of *Doctor Faustus* and episodes of *Adam Adamant Lives!, Mystery and Imagination* ('The Body Snatcher' and 'Feet Foremost'), *Thriller* (1975), *The New Avengers* ('The Eagle's Nest' with Peter Cushing), *The Dark Side of the Sun, Maelstrom* and the 1988 mini-series *Jack the Ripper*. Baxter later reprised his role of Professor Litefoot in the audio dramas *Doctor Who: The Companion Chronicles: The Mahogany Murderers* and the series *Jago & Litefoot* (with Christopher Benjamin), and in 2003 he adapted Oscar Wilde's novella *The Picture of Dorian Gray* for a touring stage production.

Canadian character actor **Harvey Atkin**, a regular on TV's *Cagney & Lacey* (1981-88), died of cancer on July 17, aged 74. His movie credits include *Cries in the Night* (aka *Funeral Home*), *The Last Chase, The Incubus, Visiting Hours, Mindfield, Around the World in*

Eighty Days (1990) and *Back to the Beanstalk*, while on TV he appeared in episodes of *The New Avengers, Seeing Things, Alfred Hitchcock Presents* (1989), *My Secret Identity, RoboCop, Goosebumps* and *Big Wolf on Campus*. The voice of "King Koopa" in the *Super Mario Bros.* cartoons, Atkin was also a voice artist on such animated shows as *A.L.F., Swamp Thing, Beetlejuice, Little Shop, Wish Kid, The Adventures of Tintin* (1992), *Tales from the Cryptkeeper, The NeverEnding Story* and *The Ripping Friends*, amongst many others.

American actor, stuntman and songwriter **Red West** (Robert Gene West) died of an aortic aneurysm on July 18, aged 81. A friend and former bodyguard to Elvis Presley and a member of the singer's inner circle "Memphis Mafia", West appeared in small, often uncredited roles in *Journey to the Center of the Earth* (1959), *Shock Treatment* (1964), *The Navy vs. the Night Monsters, The Wild Wild West Revisited, Raw Nerve, Natural Born Killers, The P.A.C.K., I Still Know What You Did Last Summer* and *Vampires Anonymous*, along with episodes of TV's *Get Smart, The Six Million Dollar Man, Battlestar Galactica* (1978), *Knight Rider, The Greatest American Hero* and *The Twilight Zone* (1986). West also appeared and performed stunts in the CBS series *The Wild Wild West*, and his son, John Boyd West, played him in the 1993 *Quantum Leap* episode 'Memphis Melody—July 3, 1954'.

Likeable French actor **Claude Rich** died on July 20, aged 88. His many credits include *The Burning Court* (based on the novel by John Dickson Carr), *Le vampire de Bougival*, François Truffaut's *The Bride Wore Black*, Alain Renais' *Je t'aime je t'aime*, *Asterix and Obelix Meet Cleopatra* and *The Mystery of the Yellow Room* (2003, based on the novel by Gaston Leroux).

71-year-old American actor **John** [Matthew] **Heard** [Jr.] was found dead from a heart attack in a California hotel on July 21. He was recovering from minor back surgery at the time. Heard appeared in the remake of *Cat People* (1982), *C.H.U.D., Too Scared to Scream, The Milagro Beanfield War, The Seventh Sign, Big, Locusts, The Legends of Nethiah, Sharknado* and *Living Among Us*. On TV he was in episodes of *Tales from the Darkside, Alfred Hitchcock Presents* (1985), *American Masters* ('Edgar Allan Poe: Terror of the Soul'), *The Outer*

Limits (1995), *Touched by an Angel*, *Battlestar Galactica* (2006), *Cavemen*, *Tim and Eric's Bedtime Stories*, *The Lizzie Borden Chronicles* and *Elementary*. The actor was married to Margot Kidder for six days in 1979.

British actress **Deborah Watling**, best remembered as companion "Victoria Waterfield" in the BBC's *Doctor Who* (1967-68), died after a short battle with lung cancer the same day, aged 69. As a child, she co-starred as "Sally Wilson" in the TV series *H.G. Wells' The Invisible Man* (1958-59), and she was also in episodes of *The Wednesday Play* ('Alice') and *Out of the Unknown*, and the 50th anniversary spoof *The Five(ish) Doctors Reboot*. The actress appeared with her father, character actor Jack Watling, in the *Doctor Who* serials 'The Abominable Snowman' and 'The Web of Fear'.

American character actor and Texas cattle rancher **Jimmy Clem** (James Melvin Clem) died on July 22, aged 84. He appeared in a number of regional films written and directed by Charles B. Pierce, including *The Town That Dreaded Sundown*, *The Evictors* and *Boggy Creek II and the Legend Continues* . . .

Welsh actor **Hywel** [Thomas] **Bennett**, who portrayed the murderous "Mr. Croup" in the BBC series of Neil Gaiman's *Neverwhere* (1996), died on July 25, aged 73. He retired from acting in 2007 after being diagnosed with a congenital heart defect. Bennett co-starred with Hayley Mills in the psycho-thriller *Twisted Nerve* and the Agatha Christie adaptation *Endless Night*, and his other film credits include *Percy*, *Alice's Adventures in Wonderland* (1972), *Artemis 81*, *Murder Elite*, *A Mind to Kill* and *Deadly Advice* (as "Dr. Crippen"). On TV, he made his acting debut in the 1965 *Doctor Who* episode 'The Death of Time', and went on to appear in episodes of *The Twilight Zone* (1986), *Virtual Murder*, *Cold Lazarus* and the revival of *Randall & Hopkirk (Deceased)*. Bennett's first wife (1970-88) was *Ready, Steady, Go!* presenter Cathy McGowan.

Prolific American voice actress **June Foray** (June Lucille Forer) died of cardiac arrest on July 26, aged 99. In a career that spanned more than seven decades she worked—often uncredited—on numerous cartoon shorts, movies and series. Amongst her many credits are *Red Hot Riding Hood*, *Cinderella* (1950), *Trick or Treat* and *A-Haunting We Will Go* (as "Witch Hazel"), *Peter Pan*, *Visit to a Small Planet*, *The Man Called Flintstone*, *How the Grinch Stole Christmas!* (1966), *Frosty the Snowman*, *Horton Hears a Who!* (1970), *The Phantom Tollbooth*, *Daffy Duck's Movie: Fantastic Island*, *Scooby Doo Meets the Boo Brothers*, *Who Framed Roger Rabbit*, *Daffy Duck's Quackbusters*, *Little Nemo: Adventures in Slumberland*, *DuckTales the Movie: Treasure of the Lost Lamp*, *Tiny Toons' Night Ghoulery*, *Space Jam*, *Looney Tunes: Back in Action* and *The Legend of Sasquatch*, along with such TV shows as *Rocky and His Friends* (as "Rocket J. Squirrel"), *The Flintstones*, *The Twilight Zone*, *Bewitched*, *It's About Time*, *Lost in Space*, *Off to See the Wizard*, *Scooby Doo Where Are You!*, *Get Smart*, *The Incredible Hulk*, *Spider-Man and His Amazing Friends* (as "Aunt May Parker"), *Teen Wolf*, *The Real Ghostbusters*, *DuckTales*, *Tiny Toon Adventures*, *Weird Science* and *Duck Dodgers*, amongst numerous other titles. In 1954, Foray appeared with Boris Karloff in the movie *Sabaka*.

American child actor **Leonard "Percy" Landy**, who starred in a number of "Our Gang"/"Little Rascals" short films, such *as Hide and Shriek* and *Aladdin's Lantern* (both 1938), died the same day, aged 84.

American actress **Patti Deutsch** (Patricia Deutsch), who was a regular on TV's *Rowan & Martin's Laugh-In* (1972-73), died of cancer on July 26. Deutsch appeared in an episode of *The Girl with Something Extra*, and she later became a voice actor in *Jetsons: The Movie*, *Tarzan* (1999), *The Land Before Time VII: The Stone of Cold Fire*, *Monsters Inc.*, and episodes of TV's *The Spooktacular New Adventures of Casper* and *Time Squad*.

American actor, Pulitzer Prize-winning playwight, author and musician **Sam Shepard** (Samuel Shepard Rogers III) died of complications from amyotrophic lateral sclerosis (aka Lou Gehrig's disease) on July 27, aged 73. His movie credits include *Resurrection*, *Purgatory*, *Hamlet* (2000), *Stealth*, *The Return* (2006) and *Midnight Special*, and he narrated the 2006 version of *Charlotte's Web*. Shepard also wrote and directed the horror Western *Silent Tongue*. He lived with actress Jessica Lange from 1982-2009.

American actor, documentary film-maker and certified sex coach

Robert Dunlap died the same day, aged 74. He appeared in episodes of TV's *Far Out Space Nuts*, *Lucan*, *Wonder Woman*, *The Greatest American Hero*, *Voyagers!* and *Automan*.

American TV actor **Peter Canon** (Peter Cannon), who played a Gestapo Lieutenant in the 1968 *Star Trek* episode 'Patterns of Force', died on July 28, aged 84. He also appeared in episodes of *Bewitched*, *The Monkees* ('The Devil and Peter Tork'), *Get Smart*, *Land of the Giants* and *The Six Million Dollar Man*.

Canadian-born actress **Treva Frazee** died of complications from Alzheimer's disease in Florida on July 30, aged 94. She had small roles in the 1973 horror movie *The Severed Arm* and episodes of TV's *The Ghost & Mrs. Muir* and *The Immortal*.

Acclaimed French actress and singer **Jeanne Moreau** died on July 31, aged 89. Her credits include Orson Welles' *The Trial* (based on the novel by Franz Kafka) and *The Deep*, François Truffaut's *The Bride Wore Black* (based on a novel by Cornell Woolrich), *Hu-Man*, *Until the End of the World* and *Ever After: A Cinderella Story*. On TV, Moreau starred in an episode of *Shades of Darkness* ('Agatha Christie's The Last Séance'). The actress was married to director William Friedkin from 1977-79.

American actress and former model **Nancy Valentine** (Annette Valentine) died the same day, aged 89. Discovered by Howard Hughes, she began her movie career in the late 1940s and her credits include *The Black Castle* (with Boris Karloff and Lon Chaney, Jr.), *Night Slaves* and an episode of TV's *Thriller* (Robert Bloch's 'Yours Truly, Jack the Ripper'). From 1949-52, Valentine was married to Jagaddipendra Narayan Bhup Bahadur, the Maharaja of Cooch-Behar in India, who was 22 years her senior. She retired from the screen in the early 1970s.

British actor [Timothy Sydney] **Robert Hardy** CBE, who played Minister of Magic "Cornelius Fudge" in four "Harry Potter" movies, died on August 3, aged 91. He was also in *A Midsummer Night's Dream* (1959), *Berserk* (with Joan Crawford), the 1971 M.R. James adaptation *The Stalls of Barchester*, the psychic detective pilot *The Incredible Robert Baldick: Never Come Night*, Hammer's *Demons of the Mind*, *Dark Places* (with Christopher Lee), *Psychomania* (aka

The Death Wheelers), *Gawain and the Green Knight* (1973), *Mary Shelley's Frankenstein* (1994), *The Lost World* (2001), *The Gathering*, *Harry Potter and the Chamber of Secrets*, *Harry Potter and the Prisoner of Azkaban*, *Harry Potter and the Goblet of Fire* and *Harry Potter and the Order of the Phoenix*. On TV, Hardy appeared in episodes of *The Veil* (with Boris Karloff), *Mystery and Imagination* (Vernon Lee's 'The Phantom Lover'), *Strange Report*, *Supernatural* (1977), *Buck Rogers in the 25th Century*, *Shades of Darkness* (Elizabeth Bowen's 'The Demon Lover'), *Screen Two* ('Northanger Abbey'), *The Case-Book of Sherlock Holmes*, *Gulliver's Travels* (1996) and *The 10th Kingdom*. While studying at university in Oxford, his tutors included J.R.R. Tolkien and C.S. Lewis.

American leading man **Ty Hardin** (Orison Whipple Hungerford, Jr., aka "Ty Hungerford"), who starred in the Western TV series *Bronco* (1958-62), died the same day, aged 87. He was also in *Berserk* with Robert Hardy, along with *The Space Children*, *I Married a Monster from Outer Space* and *Image of the Beast*. Hardin was married eight times, and in the 1970s he founded a Christian right-wing anti-establishment militia that stockpiled illegal weapons until raided by FBI and ATF agents.

British actress **Maggie Rennie** (Margaret McGrath), the second wife (1946-60) of actor Michael Rennie, died on August 5, aged 98. During World War II she was named the "Windmill Theatre's Blonde Bombshell of the Blitz" by *Life* magazine. On TV Rennie appeared in episodes of *The New Adventures of Charlie Chan*, *Thriller* (1974) and *Hammer House of Mystery and Suspense* ('Mark of the Devil').

Japanese actor-stuntman **Haruo Nakajima**, who performed inside the "Godzilla" ("Gojira") bodysuit in every movie from the original *Godzilla* (1954) to *Godzilla vs. Gigan* (1972), died of complications from pneumonia on August 7, aged 88. His numerous other credits include *Tômei ningen*, *Godzilla Raids Again*, *Half Human*, *Rodan*, *The Mysterians*, *The H-Man*, *Varan the Unbelievable*, *The Human Vapor*, *Mothra*, *The Last War*, *Gorath*, *King Kong vs. Godzilla*, *Matango*, *Atragon*, *Mothra vs. Godzilla*, *Dogora*, *Ghidorah the Three-Headed Monster*, *Frankenstein Conquers the World*, *Invasion of Astro-Monster*, *The War of the Gargantuas*, *Godzilla vs. the Sea Monster*,

King Kong Escapes, Son of Godzilla, Destroy All Monsters, Latitude Zero, All Monsters Attack, Yog: Monster from Space, Godzilla vs. Hedorah and *Tidal Wave*. Nakajima also appeared in various *Ultraman* TV episodes.

Tony Award-winning Broadway singer and actress **Barbara** [Nell] **Cook** died of respiratory failure on August 8, aged 89. During the 1950s she appeared on TV in productions of *Babes in Toyland* and *Hansel and Gretel*, along with an episode of *Alfred Hitchcock Presents*.

American actor, scriptwriter, producer and director **Joseph Bologna** died of pancreatic cancer on August 13, aged 82. He appeared in *Transylvania 6-5000* (1985), *Not Quite Human* and *Alligator II: The Mutation*. On TV Bologna was the voice of "Dan Turpin" on the animated *Superman* (1997-98) show.

American stunt performer [Sequana] **Joi "SJ" Harris** was killed on August 14 when a second-unit low-speed motorcycle stunt went wrong on the Vancouver, Canada, set of *Deadpool 2*. The 32-year-old road racer had successfully completed her first movie stunt five times, but died on a sixth attempt when her motorcycle accidentally hit a kerb and Harris was thrown through a glass window.

Welsh actress **Jennifer Daniel** (Jennifer Williams) died in London on August 16, aged 81. Best known for co-starring in the Hammer horrors *The Kiss of the Vampire* and *The Reptile* (both opposite Noel Wellman), her other film credits include a 1958 version of *A Midsummer Night's Dream*, and a 1992 adaptation of *Wuthering Heights*. On TV, Daniel appeared in the BBC's two-part *Beauty and the Beast* (1961), and episodes of *One Step Beyond, Hamlet* (1961), *Suspense* ('Virus X'), *Adam Adamant Lives!, Doomwatch, Thriller* (1973) and *The Boy Merlin*. She was married to the actor Dinsdale Landen from 1959 until his death in 2003.

American character actor **Jon Shepodd** (Hugh Goodwin) died in England the same day, aged 91. In a screen career that only lasted a decade, his credits include *What Ever Happened to Baby Jane?* and episodes of TV's *The Adventures of Fu Manchu, Men Into Space* and *The Alfred Hitchcock Hour*.

American actor-stuntman **Sonny Landham** (aka "Tex Miller"/"Bill Ashley"), who played Native American tracker "Billy Sole" in *Predator*

(1987), died of congestive heart failure on August 17, aged 76. Landham, who had a reputation for heavy drinking and volatile behavious, appeared in a number of adult films in the 1970s, and he was also in *Blood Bath* (1976), *Southern Comfort, Poltergeist, Northstar, 2090, Disintegration* and *Mental Scars*. He also did stunt work in *Love at First Bite*.

Veteran British entertainer Sir **Bruce Forsyth** (Bruce Joseph Forsyth-Johnson) died of bronchial pneumonia after a long illness on August 18, aged 89. He began his career in music halls, but was best known as a presenter of various game and variety TV shows in a showbusiness career that spanned eight decades. Forsyth also appeared in Disney's *Bedknobs and Broomsticks* and played the title character in 'The Canterville Ghost', a 1966 episode of TV's *Mystery and Imagination*.

Legendary entertainer **Jerry Lewis** (Jerome Joseph Levitch) died of the heart condition ischemic cardiomyopathy on August 20, aged 91. The American actor, comedian, singer, producer and director co-starred with nightclub, radio and on-screen partner Dean Martin in the horror comedy *Scared Stiff* (1953), a remake of the Bob Hope movie *The Ghost Breakers* from the same director. Lewis' other credits include a cameo in *Road to Bali, Artists and Models, Li'l Abner, Visit to a Small Planet, Cinderfella, The Nutty Professor* (which he also co-wrote and directed), *Way . . . Way Out, Slapstick of Another Kind* and *Arizona Dream*. He also turned up in an episode of TV's *Batman* (1966), and voiced "Professor John Frink, Sr." on an episode of *The Simpsons* ('Treehouse of Horror XIV'). Lewis was also credited as executive producer on the 1996 remake of *The Nutty Professor* starring Eddie Murphy, which he later regretted, and the sequel *The Nutty Professor II: The Clumps*, and he voiced his original character(s) in a 2008 cartoon sequel, also titled *The Nutty Professor*. In 1995, the actor became the highest-paid performer in Broadway history for his role as the Devil in a revival of *Damn Yankees*, and he directed a 2012 stage adaptation of *The Nutty Professor*. DC Comics' *The Adventures of Jerry Lewis* ran from 1957 until 1971.

French actress **Nicole** [Suzanne Fernande] **Besnard**, who had a brief movie career in the 1950s, died the same day, aged 89. Her credits include Rene Clair's 1950 film *Beauty and the Devil*, which was another version of the "Faust" story.

German singer and actress **Margot Hielscher**, who appeared in the 1982 film *Doktor Faustus* starring Jon Finch, also died on August 20, aged 97.

American actor and comedian **Jay Thomas** (Jon Thomas Terrell) died of cancer on August 24, aged 69. A regular on ABC's *Mork & Mindy* as "Remo DaVinci" (1979-81), his other TV credits include episodes of *Walt Disney's Wonderful World of Color* (Blake Edwards' 'Justin Case'), *Freddy's Nightmares*, *Fantasy Island* and *Joan of Arcadia*, and he voiced "Ares" in the animated series *Hercules* (1998-99) and the spin-off *Hercules: Zero to Hero*. Thomas was also in the movies *C.H.U.D.*, *Encino Woman*, *Dragonfly*, *The Santa Clause 2*, *The Santa Claus 3: Escape Clause*, *Horrorween* (featuring Donald Trump) and *Life Tracker*.

Former child actor, journalist and publicist **Boots LeBaron**, who had an uncredited role as one of the shell people in *One Million B.C.* (1940), died of heart disease on August 25, aged 85. LeBaron was Manager of Entertainment for the first Universal Studios Tours, and he later worked as the Unit Publicist for the 1983 movie of Stephen King's *Cujo*.

Greek actor and novelist **Takis Emmanuel** died on August 26, aged 84. A star in his native country, he also appeared in a number of international movies, including *The Magus*, *On Her Majesty's Secret Service* and *The Golden Voyage of Sinbad* (as "Achmed"). Emmanuel retired from acting in the mid-1980s to become an author.

Suave American actor **Richard** [Norman] **Anderson**, who played "Oscar Goldman" in both *The Six Million Dollar Man* (1974-78) and *The Bionic Woman* (1976-78) TV series and spin-offs, died on August 31, aged 91. His other credits include the SF classic *Forbidden Planet*, *Curse of the Faceless Man*, *Seven Days in May*, *Seconds*, the second "Kolchak" movie *The Night Strangler*, *The Six Million Dollar Man: Wine Women and War*, *The Six Million Dollar Man: The Solid Gold Kidnapping*, *The Stepford Children* and *The Return of the Six Million Dollar Man*. Anderson also appeared in and co-produced two later reunion TV movies, *Bionic Showdown: The Six Million*

Dollar Man and the Bionic Woman and *Bionic Ever After?*. On TV he was in episodes of *Captain Midnight*, *Thriller* (1960), *The Alfred Hitchcock Hour*, *The Man from U.N.C.L.E.*, *The Green Hornet*, *The Invaders*, *The Wild Wild West*, *Land of the Giants*, *Darkroom*, *Knight Rider*, *Automan*, *Fantasy Island*, *Alfred Hitchcock Presents* (1988) and the 1967 pilot *Ghostbreakers*. His first wife was Carol Lee Ladd, the step-daughter of actor Alan Ladd, and his second wife, Katharine Thalberg, was the daughter of actress Norma Shearer and Hollywood producer Irving Thalberg. Both marriages ended in divorce.

American actor, stand-up comedian and scriptwriter **Shelley Berman** (Sheldon Leonard Berman) died of complications from Alzheimer's disease on September 1, aged 92. He appeared in the obscure 1955 horror movie *Dementia*, *Every Home Should Have One* (aka *Think Dirty*), *Beware! The Blob* and *Teen Witch*. On TV, Berman was in episodes of *The Twilight Zone*, *Bewitched*, *The Man from U.N.C.L.E.*, *The Girl from U.N.C.L.E.*, *Get Smart*, *Knight Rider*, *The Munsters Today*, *What a Dummy*, *Monsters*, *Dead Like Me* and *Pushing Daisies*. His 1959 live record, *Inside Shelley Berman*, was the first comedy album to be certified gold (with more than 500,000 sales) and was the first non-musical recording to win a Grammy Award. He was also the first stand-up comedian to perform at Carnegie Hall.

American actress and acting coach **Elizabeth Kemp** died of cancer the same day, aged 65. She was in *He Knows You Are Alone* (1980), *The Clairvoyant* (1982) and the TV movie *Murderous Vision*.

Tough-looking Italian character actor **Gastone Moschin**, who portrayed comedy police sergeant "Aloisius Thorpe" in *The Weekend Murders*, died on September 4, aged 88. His other film credits include *Operazione Vega*, *Spy in Your Eye* and *Mr. Superinvisible*, and Moschin also appeared with Erika Blanc in an adaptation of 'The Fall of the House of Usher' on the 1979 TV series *I racconti fantastici di Edgar Allan Poe*.

Veteran Japanese character actor and UFO enthusiast **Yoshio Tsuchiya** died on September 5, aged 90. He appeared in *Godzilla Raids Again*, *Throne of Blood*, *The Mysterians*, *The H-Man*, *Varan the Unbelievable*, *Battle in Outer Space*, *The Human Vapor*, *Matango*,

532 STEPHEN JONES & KIM NEWMAN

Frankenstein Conquers the World, *Invasion of the Astro-Monster*, *The Killing Bottle*, *Son of Godzilla*, *Destroy All Monsters*, *Yog: Monster from Space*, *Godzilla vs. King Ghidorah* and *Inferno* (2005), along with episodes of TV's *Urutora Q* and *Ultraman*.

American actress and model **Barbara Flicker** (Barbara Joyce Perkins), a former personal assistant to Doris Day and the widow of TV writer and director Theodore J. Flicker, died on September 6, aged 85. She appeared in her husband's brief *Night Gallery* segment 'Junior' in 1971.

35-year-old American actor **Blake Heron** was found dead in his Los Angeles home on September 8. The cause of death was revealed five months later as an accidental drug overdose (including the opoid fentanyl). Former child actor Heron played a recurring character on the USA Network's 1999-2000 series *Good vs Evil* (aka *G vd E*), and his other credits include an episode of *Early Edition* and the 1996 TV movie *Trilogy of Terror II*.

American actor **Harry Landers** (Harry Sorokin), who played "Dr. Ted Hoffman" on TV's *Ben Casey* (1961-66), died on September 9, aged 96. A discovery of Bette Davis and a self-confessed "rebel-rouser", he was also in the movie *Phantom from Space*, along with episodes of *Captain Video and His Video Rangers*, *Tales of Tomorrow*, *World of Giants*, *Alfred Hitchcock Presents* and *Star Trek*. Landers worked for three months in small roles on Cecil B. DeMille's *The Ten Commandments* (1956), earning more money than either John Carradine or Vincent Price.

American character actor **Harvey Levine**, who appeared in *Mannequin*, *King B: A Life in the Movies* and an episode of TV's *The Wild Wild West*, died of lung cancer the same day, aged 78.

American actor **Mike Hodge**, who had a recurring role in the BBC/CTW children's TV series *Ghostwriter* (1992-93), died on September 10, aged 70. Hodge was also in the movies *The Shaman*, *Blue Steel*, *Dr. Jekyll and Ms. Hyde* and *Office Killer*.

American actor **Damu King**, who had a small role in the obscure horror-comedy *Guess What Happened to Count Dracula?* (1971), died of heart failure on September 13, aged 86. He also appeared in a number of blacksploitation movies in the 1970s.

American tough-guy character actor and musician **Frank Vincent** [Gatuso, Jr.], who played mob boss "Phil Leotardo" on HBO's *The Sopranos* (2004-07), died of complications during heart surgery the same day, aged 80. He also appeared in episodes of *The Young Indiana Jones Chronicles* and *Stargate: Atlantis*, along with the TV movie *NetForce*. Vincent was the basis for a character in Alan Roberts' *Killogy*, a series of graphic novels set during the zombie apocalypse.

American leading man **Stuart Moss** died of a heart attack on September 13, aged 79. He appeared in episodes of TV's *Star Trek*, *The Invaders*, *The Six Million Dollar Man* and *Beyond Westworld*, along with the movies *Doctor Death: Seeker of Souls*, *The Bat People* and *Conspiracy of Terror*.

Gaunt American character actor, singer and musician **Harry Dean Stanton** (aka "Dean Stanton"), best remembered for his role as the engineer "Brett" in *Alien* (1979), died on September 15, aged 91. He was also in *Death Watch*, John Carpenter's *Escape from New York*, *Christine* (based on the novel by Stephen King), *Repo Man*, *Red Dawn*, *UFOria*, Disney's *One Magic Christmas*, *Dream a Little Dream*, *Twin Peaks: Fire Walk with Me*, *The Green Mile* (another King adaptation), *Alien Autopsy* and *The Avengers*. Stanton's TV credits include episodes of *Inner Sanctum*, *Alfred Hitchcock Presents*, *The Wild Wild West*, *Faerie Tale Theatre*, *The Jim Henson Hour* ('Monster Maker'), *Alice* (2009) and the 2017 revival of *Twin Peaks*.

Danish actress **Bodil Miller** (Jørgensen), who was featured in the Danish version of *Reptilicus* (1961), died on September 16, aged 89. She was briefly under contract with Universal in the early 1950s.

British actress **Suzan** [Maxine] **Farmer** died of cancer on September 17, aged 75. Her genre credits include Hammer's *The Devil-Ship Pirates*, *Dracula—Prince of Darkness* and *Rasputin the Mad Monk* (all with Christopher Lee), along with *Monster of Terror* (aka *Die, Monster, Die!*, with Boris Karloff), *Where the Bullets Fly*, *Persecution* and the comedy short *Talk of the Devil*. On TV, Farmer appeared in episodes of *Sherlock Holmes* (1965), *Out of the Unknown*, *UFO*, *Thriller* (1975), *Blakes 7* and *Leap in the Dark*. She retired from the screen in 1980. Farmer was married to actor Ian McShane from 1965-68.

American character actor **Ben Hammer**, who often played authority figures, died on September 18, aged 92. He was in *Johnny Got His Gun* (based on the novel by Dalton Trumbo), *Invasion of the Bee Girls*, *Haunts*, *The Beastmaster* and *Mannequin*. On TV, Hammer appeared in episodes of *One Step Beyond*, *The Six Million Dollar Man*, *Gemini Man*, *Holmes and Yo-Yo*, *The Incredible Hulk* and *Highway to Heaven*.

Former American pro-football player and actor **Bernie Casey** (Bernard Terry Casey) died on September 19, aged 78. He was in the movies *Gargoyles*, *Dr. Black Mr. Hyde*, *The Man Who Fell to Earth*, *It Happened at Lakewood Manor* (aka *Ants!*), the "alternate" Bond movie *Never Say Never Again* (as CIA agent "Felix Leiter"), *Amazon Women on the Moon*, *Bill & Ted's Excellent Adventure*, John Carpenter's *In the Mouth of Madness* and *Vegas Vampires*. On TV, Casey's credits include episodes of *The Alfred Hitchcock Hour* (1985), *Time Trax*, *Star Trek: Deep Space Nine*, *SeaQuest 2032*, *Babylon 5* and the mini-series *The Martian Chronicles*, based on the stories by Ray Bradbury.

American middleweight boxing champion **Jake LaMotta** (Giacobbe LaMotta), who was portrayed by Robert De Niro in *Raging Bull* (1980), died the same day of complications from pneumonia, aged 95. La Motta turned up in small roles in *Confessions of a Psycho Cat* and *Maniac Cop* (he was the uncle of the movie's director, William Lustig).

British character actor and political campaigner **Tony Booth** (Anthony George Booth) died of complications from Alzheimer's disease on September 25, aged 85. He appeared in *The Return of Mr. Moto*, *Corruption* (with Peter Cushing), *Neither the Sea Nor the Sand* (aka *The Exorcism of Hugh*) and an early episode of TV's *The Avengers*. Booth was married four times and the father of eight daughters, including Cherie Booth, who is married to former Prime Minister Tony Blair.

80-year-old Czech actor **Jan Triska** died the same day from injuries he sustained after falling from Prague's iconic Charles Bridge two days earlier. His credits include *The Death of Tarzan* (1963), *The Return of the Man from U.N.C.L.E.: The Fifteen Years Later Affair*,

The Fantastic World of D.C. Collins, 2010, Apt Pupil, The Omega Code and *Lost Souls,* along with episodes of *Fantasy Island, Quantum Leap, Highlander* and *Highlander: The Raven.*

American character actor and singer **Barry Dennen** died on September 26, aged 79. He had suffered a brain injury following a fall at his home three months earlier. Best known for playing "Pontius Pilate" in the original Broadway production and 1973 movie of *Jesus Christ Superstar,* he was also in *Madhouse* (with Vincent Price and Peter Cushing), *The Shining* (1980), *Shock Treatment* (1981), *The Dark Crystal, Superman III, What Ever Happened to Baby Jane?* (1991) and *Liquid Dreams.* Dennen's TV credits include episodes of *Batman, Monster Squad* (as "Mr. Mephisto"), *Wonder Woman* (as "Adolf Hitler"), *Amazing Stories, Tales from the Darkside, Hard Time on Planet Earth, The Munsters Today, They Came from Outer Space, The Comic Strip Presents...* ('Demonella', which he co-scripted with Paul Bartel) and *Weird Science,* and he was also a prolific voice actor in cartoon shows and video games. In the early 1960s Dennen was instrumental in developing the singing career of Barbara Streisand, whom he was in a turbulent relationship with at the time.

Veteran Hollywood actress **Anne Jeffreys** (Annie Jeffreys Carmichael), who played the detective's girlfriend "Tess Truehart" in *Dick Tracy* (1945) and *Dick Tracy vs. Cueball,* died on September 27, aged 94. She also appeared in the movies *Tarzan's New York Adventure, I Married an Angel, Zombies on Broadway* (with Bela Lugosi) and *Genius at Work* (with Lugosi and Lionel Atwill). On TV, Jeffreys starred as the ghostly "Marion Kerby" alongside her husband Robert Sterling in the 1953-55 CBS series of *Topper,* and she was in episodes of *The Man from U.N.C.L.E.* ('The Abominable Snowman Affair'), *Tarzan* (1967), *Fantasy Island, Battlestar Galactica* (1979), *Buck Rogers in the 25th Century, Mr. Merlin* and the 1967 pilot *Ghostbreakers.*

American character actress **Marietta Marich** (Marietta Cox), who appeared as "Luda Mae Hewitt" in *The Texas Chainsaw Massacre* (2003) and *The Texas Chainsaw Massacre: The Beginning* (2006), died of complications from an aortic dissection on September 28, aged 87. Her other credits include *Children of the Corn: The Gathering* and *House of Good and Evil*.

Avuncular British stage and screen actor **Benjamin** [John] **Whitrow** died the same day, aged 80. He was in *Brimstone & Treacle*, *Fairy Tale: A True Story*, and episodes of TV's *Tales of the Unexpected* and *Bonekickers*.

American actress **Elizabeth** [Ellen] **Baur**, who was a regular on TV's *Ironside* from 1971-75, died after a long illness on September 30, aged 69. She began her career with small parts in *The Boston Strangler* and a 1968 episode of *Batman*. Her other credits include an episode of *Fantasy Island*.

Legendary American rock singer, songwriter and guitarist **Tom Petty** (Thomas Earl Petty) died of cardiac arrest from an accidental prescription drug overdose on October 2. He was 66. Petty had numerous hits with Tom Petty & the Heartbreakers and as a member of The Traveling Wilburys, while as an actor he appeared in the movies *Made in Heaven* and *The Postman*.

American actor-stuntman **Ben Bates**, who portrayed the "Arcane Monster" in Wes Craven's *Swamp Thing* (1982), died on October 4, aged 84. He was actor James Arness' stunt double for more than twenty years, and his credits also include an episode of TV's *Gemini Man*.

Japanese character actor **Yoshio Tsuchiya** died on October 5, aged 90. His many credits include *Godzilla Raids Again* (aka *Gigantis the Fire Monster*), *Throne of Blood*, *The Mysterians*, *The H-Man*, *Varan the Unbelievable*, *Battle in Outer Space*, *The Human Vapor*, *Attack of the Mushroom People* (aka *Matango: Fungus of Terror*), *Frankenstein Conquers the World*, *Invasion of the Astro-Monster* (aka *Monster Zero*), *The Killing Bottle*, *Son of Godzilla*, *Destroy All Monsters*, *Yog: Monster from Space*, *Rouge* (1984), *Godzilla vs. King Ghidorah* and *Inferno* (2005), along with episodes of the TV series *Ultra Q* and *Ultraman*.

British actor **Trevor** [Gordon] **Martin** died the same day in Bulgaria, aged 87. On TV he appeared in episodes of *Sherlock Holmes* (1965) and *Doctor Who*, and he was the voice of "The Beast" in the 1983 fantasy movie *Krull*. In 1974 Baxter became the first actor to portray the Time Lord on stage, in Terrance Dick's play *Doctor Who and the Daleks: Seven Keys to Doomsday* at London's Adelphi Theatre. He reprised the role for Big Finish's 2008 audio adaptation.

Former British professional boxer **Terry Downes** died on October 6, aged 81. He portrayed the hunchbacked servant "Koukol" in Roman Polanski's *Dance of the Vampires* (aka *The Fearless Vampire Killers*) and was also in *A Study in Terror* and *Dr. Jekyll and Mr. Hyde* (1980).

Acclaimed French actor **Jean** [Raoul Robert] **Rochefort** died on October 9, aged 87. He appeared in Luis Buñuel's surreal *The Phantom of Liberty*, *Death Rite*, the comedy *Frankenstein 90* (as "Victor Frankenstein"), *L'Atlantide* (1992), *Barracuda* (1997), *RRRrrrr!!!*, *Astérix and Obélix: God Save Britannia* and the 2004 TV mini-series *Frankenstein* (as the blind hermit). Rochefort was also the voice of the title character in Philippe Druillet's animated *Nosferatu* (2002). The actor became seriously ill while making Terry Gilliam's *The Man Who Killed Don Quixote* and the movie was eventually abandoned, as detailed in the fascinating documentary *Lost in La Mancha* (2002).

American character actor **Don Pedro Colley** died of cancer on October 11, aged 79. His credits include *Beneath the Planet of the Apes*, George Lucas' *THX 1138*, Disney's *The World's Greatest Athlete* and *Herbie Rides Again*, *Sugar Hill* (as "Baron Samedi"), *Quest of the Delta Knights* and *Piranha* (1995), along with episodes of TV's *The Wild Wild West*, *Rod Serling's Night Gallery*, *Search*, *The Bionic Woman*, *Space Academy* and *Fantasy Island*.

British character actor **Trevor** [Mills] **Byfield** (aka "Ziggy Byfield") died of pneumonia the same day, aged 73. He appeared in *The Wolves of Willoughby Chase* and Hammer's *Beyond the Rave*. On TV, Byfield had recurring roles in the supernatural sitcom *So Haunt Me* (1992-93) and the children's show *The Ghost Hunter* (2001), and was also featured in episodes of *Metal Mickey* and *Urban Gothic*. Byfield joined the original stage production of Richard O'Brien's musical *The Rocky Horror Show* when it transferred from a tryout at London's Royal Court in 1973 to the Classic Cinema, Chelsea, followed by a long run at the King's Road Theatre. Byfield played the dual role of "Eddie" and "Dr. Everett Scott" for a year, before taking over the part of "Dr. Frank N. Furter" from Tim Curry. He reprised the role for a tour of Japan in 1975, where his version of the song, 'Sweet Transvestite' ("from Transsexual, Transylvania"), was released as a single.

British actor **Roy** [Louis] **Dotrice** OBE, who co-starred as "Jacob 'Father' Wells" in the CBS-TV series *Beauty and the Beast* (1987-90), died on October 16, aged 94. Born on Guernsey, in the Channel Islands, he appeared in the films *A Midsummer Night's Dream* (1959), the ill-fated SF musical *Toomorrow*, Amicus' *Tales from the Crypt*, *Eliminators*, *Suburban Commando*, *Like Father Like Santa*, *Alien Hunter* and Guillermo del Toro's *Hellboy II: The Golden Army*. The actor also dubbed Harvey Keitel's voice in the SF movie *Saturn 3*. On TV, Dotrice's credits also include episodes of *Late Night Horror*, *Tales of Unease*, *The Rivals of Sherlock Holmes*, *Space: 1999*, *The Wizard*, *Tales from the Darkside* (Scott Edelman's 'My Ghostwriter—the Vampire'), *Faerie Tale Theater*, *Nightmare Classics* ('Carmilla'), *Earth 2*, *Babylon 5*, *Strange Luck*, *Tales from the Crypt*, *Hercules: The Legendary Journeys* (as "Zeus"), *Sliders*, *Touched by an Angel*, *Angel* and *Game of Thrones*. He was cited in the *Guinness Book of World Records* for his voice work on the first five audio book versions of George R.R. Martin's *A Game of Thrones*, for voicing the greatest number of characters (224) by a single person in an audio book (which have a combined running time of more than 200 hours). All three of Dotrice's daughters are actresses.

Award-winning British comedian **Sean Hughes** (John Hughes) died the same day, aged 51. He was being treated for cirrhosis of the liver. Hughes appeared in Neil Jordan's *The Butcher Boy* and the BBC-TV version of *Gormenghast* (2000).

Canadian character actor **John** [Francis] **Dunsworth**, who played town historian "Dave Teagues" on Syfy's *Haven* (2010-15), also died on October 16, aged 71. His credits include *Lizzie Borden Took an Ax* and episodes of *Lexx: The Dark Zone* and *Lexx*.

American actor **Brent Briscoe**, who played "Detective Dave Macklay" in the 2017 revival of David Lynch's *Twin Peaks*, died on October 18, aged 56. He had been hospitalised with internal bleeding and heart complications following a fall. Briscoe also appeared in *Modern Vampires*, *The Thirteenth Year*, *The Green Mile*, Lynch's *Mulholland Drive*, *Spider-Man 2*, *The Messengers*, *The Dark Knight Rises*, *Beneath* and *Zombeavers*, along with an episode of TV's *Medium*.

Argentine actor **Federico Luppi** (Federico José Luppi Malacalza), a favourite with Guillermo del Toro, died of a subdural haematoma on October 20, aged 83. Luppi starred in the director's *Cronos* and *The Devil's Backbone*, and also appeared in *Pan's Labyrinth*. Luppi was also in *Phase 7* and the forthcoming *Necronomicón*.

British character actress **Rosemary [Anne] Leach** died after a short illness on October 21, aged 81. She began her screen career in 1960 and appeared in such films as *The Mystery of Edwin Drood* (1993), *Whatever Happened to Harold Smith?*, *The Great Ghost Rescue* and *May I Kill U?*. On TV, the actress was in episodes of *Sherlock Holmes* (1965), *Judge Dee* ('The Haunted Pavilion'), *Bedtime Stories*, *Worlds Beyond*, *The Tomorrow People* ('The Living Stones'), *Chiller*, *Frighteners* and Stephen Volk's *Afterlife*. In 1996, Leach acted in a stage production of Emlyn Williams' play *Night Must Fall* at London's Theatre Royal, Haymarket.

American actor **Robert Guillaume** (Robert Peter Williams), best known as the voice of "Rafiki" in Disney's *The Lion King* and numerous spin-offs, died of complications from prostate cancer on October 24, aged 89. He was in *The Kid with the Broken Halo*, *The Meteor Man*, *Merry Christmas George Bailey*, *13th Child* and Tim Burton's *Big Fish*. The actor was a regular on the TV sitcom *Soap* (1977-80) and starred in the spin-off *Benson* (1979-86), and he also appeared in episodes of *Cosmic Slop*, *Touched by an Angel* and *The Outer Limits* (1998). Guillaume became the first black actor to play the title role in Andrew Lloyd Webber's *The Phantom of the Opera* when he replaced Michael Crawford in the initial Los Angeles run of the stage musical.

American actor **Jack Bannon** (John James Bannon), the son of B-movie actor Jim Bannon, died on October 25, aged 77. He was in *What Ever Happened to Aunt Alice?*, the TV movie *Perry Mason: The Case of the Sinister Spirit*, and episodes of *The Man from*

U.N.C.L.E., *The Invaders*, *Rod Serling's Night Gallery*, *Gemini Man*, *The Six Million Dollar Man*, *Future Cop* and *Nearly Departed*.

Former Hollywood child actress **Juanita Quigley** (aka "Baby Jane") died on October 29, aged 86. Her credits include Universal's *The Man Who Reclaimed His Head* (1934, with Claude Rains and Lionel Atwill), Tod Browning's *The Devil-Doll*, *The Blue Bird* (1940), *The Lady and the Monster* and the short *Cinderella's Feller*. She retired from the screen in 1951 to become a nun, but later renounced her vows and married a former priest.

American actor and singer **Ned Romero**, who co-starred as "Sgt. Joe Rivera" in the TV series *Dan August* (1970-71) and spin-off movies, died on November 4, aged 91. He was also in *House IV* and *Children of the Corn II: The Final Sacrifice*, and guest-starred (often as native Americans) in episodes of *Get Smart*, *The Munsters*, *Star Trek*, *The Six Million Dollar Man*, *Land of the Lost* (1974), *Bigfoot and Wildboy*, *The Incredible Hulk*, *Galactica 1980*, *Star Trek: The Next Generation*, *Seven Days*, *Star Trek: Voyager*, *Roswell* and *The Invisible Man* (2001).

Glamorous German leading lady **Karin Dor** (Kätherose Derr) died in a nursing home on November 6, aged 79. In July the previous year she had suffered a fall while on holiday, and her condition steadily worsened. Dor starred in such genre movies as *The Invisible Dr. Mabuse*, *The Carpet of Horror*, *The Strangler of Blackmoor Castle*, *Room 13*, *The Secret of the Back Widow*, *The Face of Fu Manchu* (with Christopher Lee), *The Sinister Monk*, *Die Nibelungen, Teil 1— Siegfried* and *Teil 2—Kriemhilds Rache*, the James Bond movie *You Only Live Twice*, *The Blood Demon* (aka *The Torture Chamber of Dr. Sadism*, with Lee again), *Assignment Terror* (aka *Dracula Versus Frankenstein*) and *Dark Echo*. Her first husband (1954-68) was director Harald Reinl, who was thirty years her senior and featured her in many of his films.

Irish actor **Scott Fredericks** (Frederick Wehrly) died the same day, aged 74. He appeared in two 1970s series of *Doctor Who* ('Day of the Daleks' and 'Image of the Fendahl'), along with *See No Evil*, Amicus' *From Beyond the Grave*, *Sherlock Holmes and the Baker Street Irregulars* and an episode of TV's *Blakes 7*.

Muscular American leading man and producer **Brad Harris** (Bradford Jan Harris) died on November 7, aged 84. He began his career in Hollywood in the mid-1950s, but his career took off in the early 1960s after he moved to Europe. He portayed the eponymous *peplum* heroes in *Goliath Against the Giants*, *Samson* and *The Fury of Hercules*, before moving on to the long-running "Kommissar X" spy series (co-starring Tony Kendall) and such other titles as *The Three Fantastic Supermen*, *King of Kong Island*, *Supermen*, *The Mad Butcher* (with Victor Buono), *Zambo King of the Jungle*, *The Mutations* (which he associate produced), *Lady Dracula* (which he wrote the original story for), *The Beast in Heat*, *Hercules* (1983) and *Shiver* (2012). Harris was also in an episode of TV's *The Incredible Hulk*.

American character actor **Charles Tyner** died on November 8, aged 92. He often played villains and slimeballs, and his credits include *Lilith*, *The Stalking Moon*, Alfred Hitchcock's *Family Plot*, Disney's *Pete's Dragon* (1977), *Evilspeak*, *Deadly Messages* and *Pulse*. On TV Tyner appeared in episodes of *The Incredible Hulk*, *Highway to Heaven* and *Diagnosis Murder* ('The Blair Nurse Project').

Urbane American character actor **John Hillerman** (Jack Ben Hillerman) died on November 9, aged 84. He was in *Sweet Sweet Rachel*, *High Plains Drifter*, *Audrey Rose* and *Hands of a Murderer* (as "Dr. John Watson"). On TV, Hillerman was a regular on the CBS series *Magnum P.I.* (1980-88) as the butler "Higgins", and he also appeared in episodes of *The Sixth Sense*, *Wonder Woman* ('Wonder Woman vs Gargantua') and the 1989 mini-series *Around the World in 80 Days*. Despite his clipped English accent, Hillerman was actually born in Texas.

Italian actor **Ray Lovelock** (Raymond Lovelock) died of cancer on November 10, aged 67. He was in *Queens of Evil* (and sang the theme song), *The Living Dead at the Manchester Morgue* (aka *Don't Open the Window*), the *giallos Autopsy* and *Murder-Rock: Dancing Death*, and *House of Shadows*.

Austrian leading lady **Erika Remberg** (Erika Crobath) died in Spain the same day, aged 85. Born in the Dutch East Indies (now Indonesia), she began her film career in 1950 and co-starred in

Circus of Horrors and *Cave of the Living Dead*. She married actors Gustavo Rojo (who pre-deceased her by seven months) and Walther Reyer, and director Sidney Hayers.

British character actor **Keith Barron**, who co-starred with Christopher Lee and Peter Cushing in *Nothing But the Night* (1973), died after a short illness on November 15, aged 83. He also appeared in Amicus' *The Land That Time Forgot* and *At the Earth's Core* (with Cushing again in the latter), and *Police 2020*. Barron also had a small role in *The Elephant Man* (1980), but his scenes were cut from the final film, and he narrated the UK trailer for Hammer's *Countess Dracula*. On TV he was in episodes of *The Avengers*, *Out of the Unknown*, *Randall and Hopkirk (Deceased)*, *Strange Report* ('Report 8944: Hand—A Matter of Witchcraft'), *Thriller* (1975), *The New Avengers*, *Leap in the Dark*, *Tales of the Unexpected*, *Doctor Who*, *The Case-Book of Sherlock Holmes* ('The Last Vampyre'), *Midsomer Murders* ('The Straw Woman') and *Johnny and the Bomb*, and he narrated the 1982-83 anthology series *West Country Tales*.

French character actor **Robert Hirsch** died on November 16, aged 92. His film credits include *The Hunchback of Notre Dame* (1956) and *Shock Treatment* (1973).

American actor **Earle Hyman** died on November 17, aged 91. Best known as the voice of "Panthro" in the *Thundercats* (1985-89) cartoon series, he was also in the movie *The Possession of Joel Delaney* and an episode of TV's *The Wide World of Mystery* ('And the Bones Came Together').

American actor turned TV prolific sitcom director **Peter [DuBois] Baldwin** died on November 19, aged 86. He appeared in *The Space Children*, *I Married a Monster from Outer Space*, Riccardo Freda's *The Ghost* (with Barbara Steele), *The Weekend Murders* and episodes of TV's *Man Into Space* and *The Outer Limits*. Baldwin directed the 1978 TV pilot *Space Force* and episodes of *ALF*, *CBS Summer Playhouse* ('Shivers') and *Sabrina the Teenage Witch*.

American actress **Della Reese** (Delloreese Patricia Early), who co-starred as the celestial "Tess" in CBS' *Touched by an Angel* (1994-2003), died the same day, aged 86. She was also in the movies *Psychic Killer*, *Emma's Wish*, *Christmas Angel*, *Me Again*, *Dear Secret Santa* and an episode of TV's *Picket Fences*. Reese was ordained as a minister in the 1980s and formed her own church, Understanding Principles for Better Living.

Scottish character actor **John Carlin** also died on November 19, aged 88. He appeared in *Holocaust 2000* and *Around the World in 80 Days* (1989), along with episodes of *The Adventures of Don Quick, Sexton Blake and the Demon God, Leap in the Dark, Luna* and *She-Wolf of London*.

83-year-old American cult leader and aspiring singer and song-writer **Charles Manson** (Charles Milles Maddox), whose "Family" of hippie groupies murdered actress Sharon Tate, the heavily-pregnant wife of director Roman Polanski, and several others in the summer of 1969, died the same day in a California hospital following gastrointestinal bleeding. In 1971, Los Angeles prosecutor Vincent Bugliosi used his "Helter Skelter" theory (based on The Beatles' song) to convict Manson and several female followers of seven murders. Manson was subsequently convicted of two other killings. Initially sentenced to death, which was later commuted to life imprisonment, his parole requests were repeatedly denied. He was portrayed by Steve Railsback in the movie *Helter Skelter* (1974) and Jeremy Davies in the 2004 mini-series *Helter Skelter*, Gethin Anthony in the TV series *Aquarius* (2015) and Evan Peters in several 2017 episodes of *American Horror Story: Cult*, and Michael Reed MacKay in *Summer Dreams: The Story of the Beach Boys*.

1970s teenage heartthrob, American actor and singer **David [Bruce] Cassidy**, died of organ failure on November 21, aged 67. He had struggled with alcoholism for most of his life, and in February he annnounced that he was suffering from dementia and would retire from performing. The son of actor Jack Cassidy, from 1970-74 Cassidy starred in ABC-TV's *The Partridge Family* with his real-life stepmother Shirley Jones. He later turned up in episodes of *Fantasy Island, Tales of the Unexpected, Alfred Hitchcock Presents* (1988) and *The Flash* (1991), along with the time-travel comedy movie *The Spirit of '76*. At his most popular, David Cassidy was the world's highest-paid live entertainer. Despite that, he filed for bankruptcy in 2015.

British character actor **Rodney Bewes** died the same day, aged 79. Best known for co-starring with James Bolam in the BBC sitcoms *The Likely Lads* (1964-66) and *Whatever Happened to the Likely Lads?* (1973-74), he was also in *Alice's Adventures in Wonderland* (1972), *Jabberwocky* and Disney's *The Spaceman and King Arthur* (aka *Unidentified Flying Oddball*), along with two episodes of *Doctor Who* ('Resurrection of the Daleks').

German character actor, scriptwriter and producer **Peter Berling** died in Rome, Italy, on November 21, aged 83. He co-wrote the 1978 *giallo The Rings of Fear* and appeared in *The Long Swift Sword of Siegfried*, *Tex and the Lord of the Deep*, *The Name of the Rose*, *Haunted Summer* and *Angel of Death*.

American character actor and Florida breakfast TV host **Dan Fitzgerald** (Daniel Louis Fitzgerald) died the same day, aged 88. He had supporting roles in such movies as *Mako: The Jaws of Death*, *The Final Countdown*, *Island Claws*, *Eyes of a Stranger*, *Invasion U.S.A.* (1985), *Whoops Apocalypse* and *Nightmare Beach*, along with two episodes of TV's *Superboy* (1991).

American actress **Carol** [Ann] **Vogel**, who starred in the Andy Milligan movies *Depraved!* and *The Ghastly Ones*, was found dead in a field behind her house on November 22, aged 75. She had been reported missing by her family two days earlier. Her other credits include episodes of TV's *Wonder Woman*, *The Phoenix*, *Automan*, *Highway to Heaven* and *Starman*. From 1979-84 Vogel was married to actor Jared Martin, who died six months before she did.

Veteran American character actor **Rance Howard** (Harold Engle Beckenholdt), the father of actors Clint and Ron Howard and the grandfather of Bryce Dallas Howard, died on November 25, aged 89. His numerous credits include Bert I. Gordon's *Village of the Giants*, *Locusts* (1974), *The Kid with the Broken Halo*, *The Fantastic World of D.C. Collins*, Disney's *Splash*, *Cocoon*, *Creator*, *Innerspace*, *B.O.R.N.*, *The 'Burbs*, *Limit Up*, *Universal Soldier*, *Wishman*, *Ticks*, *Ed and His Dead Mother*, Tim Burton's *Ed Wood* and *Mars Attacks!*, *Bigfoot: The Unforgettable Encounter*, *Children of the Corn III: Urban Harvest*, *Independence Day*, *The Sender*, *Small Soldiers*, *Psycho* (1998), *How the Grinch Stole Christmas*, *D-Tox* (aka *Eye See You*), *Legend of the Phantom Rider*, Tobe

Hooper's *Toolbox Murders* (2004), *Sasquatch Mountain*, *Grizzly Park*, *Audie & the Wolf*, *Within*, *Jonah Hex*, *InSight*, *Rosewood Lane* and *The Lone Ranger* (2013). On TV, Howard was in episodes of *Rod Serling's Night Gallery*, *Battlestar Galactica*, *Mork & Mindy*, *Superboy*, *Quantum Leap*, *Tales from the Crypt*, *Beyond Belief: Fact or Fiction*, *Babylon 5*, *Angel*, *Ghost Whisperer* and the revival of *The X Files*.

American actor **Julio Oscar Mechoso** died of a heart attack the same day, aged 62. He appeared in *Flight of the Navigator*, *Virus*, *Jurassic Park III*, *Planet Terror*, *Rise: Blood Hunter* and *Inheritance*, along with episodes of TV's *Quantum Leap*, *Touched by an Angel*, *Good vs Evil*, *Ghost Whisperer*, *Invasion*, *Flashforward* and *From Dusk Till Dawn: The Series*.

American actress **Heather** [May] **North**, best known as the voice of "Daphne Blake" in TV's *Scooby Doo, Where Are You!* and various spin-offs from 1970 until 1997, died on November 29, aged 71. She was also in an episode of *Circle of Fear* ('Elegy for a Vampire', based on a story by Elizabeth Walter). In 2003, North reprised her role as Daphne for the animated movies *Scooby-Doo and the Legend of the Vampire* and *Scooby-Doo and the Monster of Mexico*.

American comedy actor and singer **Jim Nabors** (James Thurston Nabors), who played TV's gormless "Gomer Pyle" on *The Andy Griffith Show* (1962-64) and his own sitcom *Gomer Pyle: USMC* (1964-69), died of immune system deficiencies in Hawaii on November 30, aged 87. He had had a liver transplant in 1994. Nabors also starred in the SF sitcom *The Lost Saucer* (1975-76), and his other credits include two episodes of *Off to See the Wizard* and the 1973 pilot *The Addams Family Fun House*. In 2013, at the age of 82, he married his longtime partner, former firefighter Stan Cadwallader, in a same-sex ceremony in Washington State.

American character actor and singer **Clifford David** died the same day, aged 89. His credits include *Hamlet* (1964), *Resurrection*, *Bill & Ted's Excellent Adventure* (as "Beethoven"), *The Exorcist III* (aka *Legion*), *Signs* and an episode of TV's *Great Ghost Tales*.

British character actor **Alfie Curtis** also died on November 30, aged 87. He had small roles in the first *Star Wars* (in the Mos Eisley Cantina sequence) and *The Elephant Man*.

Popular French singer and actor **Johnny Hallyday** (Jean-Philippe Léo Smet) died of lung cancer on December 5, aged 74. A national treasure in his native country, where he was known as the "French Elvis Presley", Hallyday appeared in *Diabolique* (1955), *Malpertius*, *Terminus* and *Crimson Rivers 2: Angels of the Apocalypse* (with Christopher Lee). He sold more than 100 million records in France alone, where he had thirty-three #1 hit singles.

American actor, producer and director **Conrad Brooks** (Conrad Biedrzycki), best remembered for his role as a policeman in Edward D. Wood, Jr.'s infamous *Plan 9 from Outer Space* (1959), died after a short illness on December 6, aged 86. Brooks also appeared uncredited in such other Wood productions as *Glen or Glenda* and *Bride of the Monster* (both with Bela Lugosi), as well as *Night of the Ghouls* and *The Sinister Urge*. Brooks was also apparently an extra in *The Mad Magician* (starring Vincent Price), and he also had small roles in *The Beast of Yucca Flats, A Polish Vampire in Burbank, Deathrow Gameshow, Curse of the Queerwolf, Puppet Master III: Toulon's Revenge, Test Tube Teens from the Year 2000* and Tim Burton's biopic *Ed Wood*. In the early 1990s, thanks to the release of several *Plan 9* documentaries around that time, Brooks became something of a cult figure, and he went on to appear in numerous no-budget independent movies such as *Conrad Brooks vs. the Werewolf, Bikini Drive-In, Little Lost Sea Serpent, Baby Ghost, Toad Warrior, The Saturn Avenger vs. the Terror Robot, Rollergator, Guns of El Chupacabra* (aka *Crimes of the Chupacabra*), *The Ironbound Vampire, Ice Scream, Alien Agenda: Under the Skin, Dead Students Society, I Woke Up Early the Day I Died* (based on an unproduced outline by Ed Wood), *Hollywood Mortuary, The Masked Strangler, Silent Scream* (1999), *The Atomic Space Bug, The Vampire Hunter's Club, The Monster Man, Max Hell: Frog Warrior, Raising Dead, Bikini Planet, Zombiegeddon, Minds of Terror, Corpses Are Forever, Dr. Horror's Erotic House of Idiots, Brain Robbers from Outer Space, Super Hell, 2020: An American Nightmare* (which he also co-produced), *Tomb of Terrors, Shadows in the Woods, Skeleton Key, Zeppo: Sinners from Beyond the Moon!, Super Hell 2, The Girl, Skeleton Key 2: 667 Neighbor of the Beast, Skeleton Key 3: The Organ Trail, Celluloid Bloodbath: More*

Prevues from Hell, Psychotic State, Super Hell 3: Dreams of Horror, Plan 9, Bite School, Movie Night 2, Pitfire of Hell, Killer Waves, Midnight Massacre, Subconcious Reality, Don't Let the Devil In, Skeleton Key 3 Part 2 and *Toilet Gator*, along with several other titles which may or may not have been filmed and/or released. In 1960, Brooks wrote, produced, directed and appeared in the short film *Mystery in Shadows*, and later in his career he produced, directed and was featured in *Out of This World, Blood Slaves of the Vampire Wolf, Jan-Gel: The Beast from the East, Jan-Gel 2: The Beast Returns, Jan-Gel 3: Hillbilly Monster, Gypsy Vampire, Gypsy Vampires Revenge* and *Gypsy Vampire: The Final Bloodlust*, most of which he also scripted.

Native American character actor **Steve Reevis** died on December 7, aged 55. His credits include *Grim Prarie Tales* and *Monsterwolf*.

American character actor **George Touliatos** died on December 8, aged 87. He was in *Virus, Prom Night* (1980), *The Last Chase* and *Firebird 2015 AD*, along with episodes of TV's *Seeing Things, The Twilight Zone* (1989), *The Ray Bradbury Theatre* ('The Long Years'), *Forever Knight, The X Files, M.A.N.T.I.S., Sliders, The Outer Limits* (1995), *Strange Luck, The Sentinel, Dead Man's Gun, Stargate SG-1* and *Supernatural*.

British leading lady **Suzanna Leigh** (Sandra Anne Eleen Smith) died of liver cancer in Florida on December 11, aged 72. The goddaughter of actress Vivien Leigh (from whom she took her stage name), she appeared as an uncredited extra in George Pal's *Tom Thumb* (1958) before going on to star in Amicus' *The Deadly Bees, Deadlier Than the Male*, Hammer's *The Lost Continent* (1968, based on the novel by Dennis Wheatley) and *Lust for a Vampire, The Fiend* (aka *Beware My Brethren*), and the comedy *Son of Dracula* (1974). The actress also appeared in an episode of TV's *Journey to the Unknown*, and she starred with Elvis Presley in the musical *Paradise, Hawaiian Style* (1966). Her 1998 autobiography was entitled *Paradise, Suzanna Style.*

British children's TV presenter **Keith "Cheggers" Chegwin** died of the lung condition idiopathic pulmonary fibrosis (IPF) the same day, aged 60. A recovered alcoholic, he had been a heavy smoker all his adult life. As a child actor, Chegwin starred in the Children's Film Foundation (CFF) movies *The Troublesome Double* and *Egghead's Robots* as inventor "Paul 'Egghead' Wentworth". He went on to host such popular TV shows as *Record Breakers* (1976-80), *Multi-Coloured Swap Shop* (1976-82), *Cheggers Plays Pop* (1978-86) and *Saturday Superstore* (1982-87), and in 2004 he appeared in four episodes of the game show *I'm Famous and Frightened*, set in a "haunted" castle. Chegwin's other film credits include Roman Polanski's *Macbeth, Aladdin and the Forty Thieves* (1984), *Whatever Happened to Harold Smith?*, *Shaun of the Dead* and *Kill Keith*, and he was also in a 1975 *The Tomorrow People* serial on TV. The younger brother of DJ and *Top of the Pops* presenter Janice Long, his first wife was co-presenter Maggie Philbin.

American stuntman/supporting actor **Louie** (Nicholas) **Elias** died on December 13, aged 84. The older brother of actor James Stacy and a former professional football player, his numerous movie credits include *War of the Colossal Beast, The Incredible Mr. Limpet, Dr. Goldfoot and the Bikini Machine, Batman: The Movie, Planet of the Apes* (1968), *Sssssss, Westworld* (1973), *The Man with Two Brains, B.O.R.N., Solar Crisis* and *Dick Tracy* (1990), along with episodes of TV's *The Twilight Zone, The Outer Limits* (as the titular alien in the episode 'Behold Eck!'), *Batman, Get Smart, The Wild Wild West, Star Trek, Future Cop, The Six Million Dollar Man, Logan's Run* and *Knight Rider*.

American leading lady and former model **Darlanne Fluegel** died on December 15, aged 64. She had been diagnosed eight years earlier with early onset Alzheimer's disease. Fluegel's credits include *Eyes of Laura Mars, Battle Beyond the Stars, Fatal Sky* (aka *Project: Alien*), *Pet Sematary II, Slaughter of the Innocents, Scanner Cop, Relative Fear* and *Darkman III: Die Darkman Die*, along with 1986 episodes of TV's *The Twilight Zone* (Stephen King's 'Gramma') and *Alfred Hitchcock Presents*. She retired from the screen in 1996.

British actor [David] **Jeremy Wilkin** died on December 19, aged 87. Best known for his voice work on such Gerry Anderson TV puppet series as *Thunderbirds* (as "Virgil Tracy"), *Captain Scarlet and the Mysterons* (as "Captain Ochre"), *Joe 90* and *The Secret Service*, he also starred in the SF serial *Undermind* (1965) and appeared in episodes of *UFO*, *Doctor Who* ('Revenge of the Cybermen'), *The New Avengers* and *Blakes 7*. Wilkin's film credits include *Curse of the Fly*, *Thunderbirds Are GO*, *Thunderbird 6*, *Doppelgänger* (aka *Journey to the Far Side of the Sun*), *The Spy Who Loved Me* and *Hyper Sapien: People from Another Star*.

American actor **Richard Venture** (Richard Charles Venturella) died the same day, aged 94. He was in *Dark Intruder*, *Man on a Swing*, *The Dark Secret of Harvest Home*, *Looker* and *Series 7: The Contenders*, plus episodes of TV's *The Powers of Matthew Star*, *The Adventures of Brisco County Jr.* and *Now and Again*.

Canadian leading lady **Heather Menzies** [-Urich], who portrayed runner "Jessica" in CBS' short-lived *Logan's Run* TV series (1977-78), died of brain cancer on December 24, aged 68. She also starred in *Sssssss*, Joe Dante's *Piranha* and *Captain America* (1979). The actress had a small role in *Endangered Species*, and appeared in an episode of *The Six Million Dollar Man* before retiring from the screen in 1990. Menzies posed nude in the August 1973 issue of *Playboy*, and she was married to actor Robert Urich from 1975 until his death in 2002.

British actress, model and singer **Luan Peters** (Carol Hirsch) died the same day, aged 71. Best known for her roles in the Hammer horrors *Lust for a Vampire* and *Twins of Evil* (with Peter Cushing), she was also in *The Flesh and Blood Show*, *Vampira* (aka *Old Dracula*) and *The Devil's Men* (aka *Land of the Minotaur*, again with Cushing). Peters also appeared on TV in episodes of *Randall and Hopkirk (Deceased)*, *Strange Report* and *Doctor Who*, and starred in the unsold pilot *Go Girl* (aka *Give Me a Ring Sometime*), in which she played a crime-fighting go-go dancer. As "Karol Keyes" she released a number of pop singles in the late 1960s, and followed them up with a few more in the 1970s under her own name. She also fronted the band 5000 Volts on *Top of the Pops*, replacing actual singer Tina Charles.

American character actress **Florence Schauffler** (Florence Cornelia Brown) also died on December 24, aged 97. Best known for her role as the old witch, Haggis, in *Pumpkinhead* (1988), she was also in *Stranded* and the TV movie *Goddess of Love*.

American voice actor and radio producer **Dick Orkin** (Richard Orkin) died of a stroke the same day, aged 84. He created and starred in the syndicated superhero spoof radio serial *Chickenman* in 1966, and he produced, co-scripted and voiced the title character in the 1988 animated version of Oscar Wilde's *The Canterville Ghost*.

Rugged American leading man **Thomas** [O'Driscoll] **Hunter** died on December 27, aged 85. He worked in Europe for many years, where he starred in a number of spaghetti Westerns, along with *The Vampire Happening*, *Madness—Gli occhi della luna* and *Equinozio*. Hunter also co-scripted *The Final Countdown* (1980).

American actress, singer and vaudeville performer **Rose Marie** [Mazetta] died on December 28, aged 94. Best known for co-starring as "Sally Roberts" in the TV sitcom *The Dick Van Dyke Show* (1961-66), she began her screen career in the late 1920s as "Baby Rose Marie". By the age of five, she had her own musical radio show on NBC. Marie was in *Bridge Across Time* (aka *Terror at London Bridge*, scripted by William F. Nolan), *Witchboard*, *Sandman*, *Shriek If You Know What I Did Last Friday the Thirteenth* and an episode of TV's *The Monkees* ('Monkees in a Ghost Town' with Lon Chaney, Jr.). The actress also supplied the uncredited voice of "Norma Bates" in Gus Van Sant's 1998 remake of *Psycho*. According to her twitter account, she had read all Stephen King's books and was a big fan of the author.

Welsh-born leading lady **Peggy Cummins** (Augusta Margaret Diane Fuller) died in London on December 29, aged 92. She had suffered a stroke. Cummins began her screen career in 1940 and co-starred in Jacques Tourneur's classic 1957 movie *Night of the Demon* (aka *Curse of the Demon*, based on "Casting the Runes" by M.R. James). Her other film credits include *Moss Rose* (with Vincent Price and George Zucco) and the Ealing comedy *Meet Mr. Lucifer*. She retired from the screen in the mid-1950s.

American character actor **Bob Morrisey** died of complications from Alzheimer's disease the same day, aged 71. He was in *Total Reality*, *Don't Look Down* and episodes of TV's *Nowhere Man*, *The X Files*, *Millennium*, *Sliders*, *The Outer Limits* (1999), *3rd Rock from the Sun*, *Good vs Evil*, *Buffy the Vampire Slayer*, *The Invisible Man*

(2001), *Angel, Roswell, Star Trek: Enterprise, Invasion* and *Flash-forward.*

Canadian-born actress and operatic singer **Gale Sherwood** (Jacqueline Nash) died in Florida on December 31, aged 88. She was the nightclub partner of singer Nelson Eddy from 1953 until his death in 1967. In a brief screen career, Sherwood played a female Tarzan in PRC's *Blonde Savage* (1947) and portrayed "Morgan Le Fay" in a 1955 TV movie of Mark Twain's *A Connecticut Yankee,* co-starring Boris Karloff. She retired from acting that same year.

Irish character actress **Doreen** [Sheila Elsie] **Keogh** died the same day, aged 91. Best known for her recurring role as barmaid "Concepta Hewitt" in the TV soap opera *Coronation Street* (1960-67), she was also in the 2005 zombie comedy *Boy Eats Girl.*

FILM/TV TECHNICIANS

Scottish-born film and theatre producer **Bill Marshall** (William T. Marshall) died of cardiac arrest in Toronto, Canada, on January 1, aged 78. He co-scripted and produced the 1970 movie *Dr. Frankenstein on Campus* (aka *Flick*). In 1976 he co-founded the Toronto International Film Festival with Henk Van der Kolk and Dusty Cohl.

British TV director **Rodney Bennett** died on January 3, aged 81. He began his career in the early 1970s, and his credits include episodes of *Dead of Night, Doctor Who, The Legend of King Arthur* and *Tales of the Unexpected.*

American production designer and art director **Joel Schiller** died on January 17, aged 86. Amongst the many movies he worked on are *The Road to Hong Kong* (uncredited), *Rosemary's Baby* (1968), *The Illustrated Man, A Reflection of Fear, Man on a Swing, The Muppet Movie, Charlie Chan and the Curse of the Dragon Queen, Megaforce* and *Slapstick of Another Kind.*

Pioneering British TV producer and director **David** [Edward] **Rose** died on January 26, aged 92. He began his career at the BBC, where he produced the 1977 dramatisation *The Witches of Pendle.* He subsequently became a senior commissioning editor and later head of drama at Channel 4, where he produced *Artemis 81* (featuring Sting and Ingrid Pitt) and oversaw the channel's "Film on Four" slate of productions until 1990.

British cinematographer **Frank Tidy** died of complications from dementia on January 27, aged 84. His credits include *Spacehunter: Adventures in the Forbidden Zone, One Magic Christmas, Slipstream, The Butcher's Wife, Through the Eyes of a Killer* (based on the story 'The Master Builder' by Christopher Fowler), *Chain Reaction* (1996) and *The Christmas Secret*.

American TV and movie director **Robert Ellis Miller** died the same day, aged 89. He began his career in television in the early 1950s and directed episodes of *Matinee Theatre* ('The Canterville Ghost'), *Shirley Temple's Storybook* and *The Twilight Zone*.

Academy Award-winning American sound engineer **Richard [Raleigh] Portman** died on January 28, aged 82. He worked on *Willy Wonka & the Chocolate Factory, Silent Running, Hammersmith is Out, The Day of the Dolphin, Chosen Survivors, The Nine Lives of Fritz the Cat, Young Frankenstein, The Town That Dreaded Sundown* (1976), *Star Wars, High Anxiety, Quintet, Resurrection, Delusion, Timerider: The Adventure of Lyle Swann, Something Wicked This Way Comes, Splash, Frankenweenie* (1984), *Baby: Secret of the Lost Legend, The Black Cauldron, The Great Mouse Detective, The Wraith, Hyper Sapien: People from Another Star, The Monster Squad, Made in Heaven, She's Back, Ghosts Can't Do It, Dark Angel* (aka *I Come in Peace*), *Cast a Deadly Spell, The Hand That Rocks the Cradle, Brainscan, Wolf* and the Stephen King adaptation *Dolores Claiborne*, along with two episodes of TV's *Tales from the Crypt*. Portman was reportedly indirectly responsible for inspiring the name of the "R2-D2" robot in the *Star Wars* series.

American movie preservationist and cineaste **David H. Shepard** died of cancer on January 31, aged 77. During the 1960s he was hired as curator of the newly-formed American Film Institute and went on to work with the Directors Guild of America and such distributors as Blackhawk Films, Kino Lorber and Lobster Films, Paris. Through his company Film Preservation Associates, Shepard helped restore most of the silent films available in today's video market, including Fritz Lang's *The Spiders*, *The Hunchback of Notre Dame* (1923), *The Thief of Bagdad* (1924) and *The Lost World* (1925), to name only a few.

British production designer and art director **Roy Forge Smith** died on February 6, aged 88. He began his career working at the BBC and his many credits include the movies *The Amazing Mr. Blunden*, *Monty Python and the Holy Grail*, *Jabberwocky*, *The Hound of the Baskervilles* (1978), *The Last Chase*, *Curtains*, *Love at Stake*, *The Kiss*, *Bill & Ted's Excellent Adventure*, *Warlock*, *Teenage Mutant Ninja Turtles* (1990), *Teenage Mutant Ninja Turtles II: The Secret of the Ooze*, *Teenage Mutant Ninja Turtles III*, *Dracula: Dead and Loving It*, *RocketMan* and *The Seventh Stream*, along with the first two seasons of CBS-TV's *Ghost Whisperer*.

British-born American TV producer and scriptwriter **Bruce Lansbury** (William Bruce Mageean Lansbury), the younger brother of actress Angela Lansbury, died on February 13, aged 87. The many series he worked on include *The Wild Wild West*, *The Fantastic Journey*, *Wonder Woman*, *Buck Rogers in the 25th Century*, *The Powers of Matthew Star* and *Knight Rider*, along with the TV films *Escape*, *Bell Book and Candle* (1976), *World War III*, *The Return of the Six Million Dollar Man and the Bionic Woman* and *I'm Dangerous Tonight*. Lansbury also executive produced the 1984 horror movie *Initiation*.

American cinematographer **Gerald Hirschfield** died the same day, aged 95. His credits include *Fail-Safe*, *Child's Play* (1972), *W*, *Young Frankenstein*, *The Ultimate Warrior* and *The Car*, plus episodes of TV's *Johnny Jupiter* and the 1954 pilot *Mandrake the Magician*.

Japanese film-maker **Seijun Suzuki**, who directed everything from mysteries (*The Sleeping Beast Within*) to operatic fantasies (*Princess Raccoon*), died on February 13, aged 93. As an actor, he appeared in more than twenty films, including the 1999 horror movie *Enbalming*.

German-born British director **Michael [John] Tuchner** died on February 17, aged 82. His credits include the 1982 TV movie of *The Hunchback of Notre Dame* starring Anthony Hopkins, *Back to the Secret Garden* and two episodes of *Tales of the Unexpected*.

American costume supervisor and designer **Stephen Lodge** died on February 26, aged 74. His credits include the TV movies *Revenge!* (1971), *Visions…*, *Something Evil*, *The Horror at 37,000 Feet*, *Snowbeast* and *The Strange Possession of Mrs. Oliver*, plus the series *Korg: 70,000 B.C.* (1974) and *Jason of Star Command* (1979). Lodge also worked as an actor, a producer, a stuntman and scriptwriter, coming up with the original story for *Kingdom of the Spiders* (1977) with Jeffrey M. Sneller.

American producer **Fred** [Robert] **Weintraub**, best known for *Enter the Dragon* (1973) and various other martial arts movies, died of complications from Parkinson's disease on March 5, aged 88. His other movies include *Invasion of the Bee Girls*, *The Ultimate Warrior*, *Trial by Combat* (aka *A Dirty Knight's Work*), *The Pack*, *The Devil's Arithmetic* (based on the novel by Jane Yolen), *Endangered Species* (2002) and *Dream Warrior*. His 2011 autobiography (written with David Fields) was entitled *Bruce Lee, Woodstock and Me: From the Man Behind a Half-Century of Music, Movies and Martial Arts.*

Legendary Hollywood producer **Jack H.** (Henry) **Harris** died on March 14, aged 98. His credits include *The Blob* (1958) starring Steve McQueen, *4D Man*, *Dinosaurus!*, *Equinox* (featuring author Fritz Leiber, Jr.), *Beware! The Blob*, John Landis' *Schlock*, John Carpenter's *Dark Star*, *Ape*, *Eyes of Laura Mars*, *Prison Ship* (aka *Star Slammer*) and the 1988 remake of *The Blob*. Harris also co-produced the 1960 Argentinean TV *series Obras maestras del terror*, three episodes of which were cobbled together into the Edgar Allan Poe movie *Master of Horror* (1965).

British-born director **Robert** [Frederick] **Day** died in Washington state on March 17, aged 94. He began his career in the mid-1950s, and he directed *Grip of the Strangler* (aka *The Haunted Strangler*, starring Boris Karloff), *Corridors of Blood* (with Karloff and Christopher Lee), *First Man Into Space*, *Tarzan the Magnificent* (with John Carradine), *Tarzan's Three Challenges*, Hammer's *She* (with Lee and Peter Cushing), *Tarzan and the Valley of Gold*, *Tarzan and the Great River*, *Ritual of Evil*, *The Big Game* and *The Initiation of Sarah*. On TV, Day's credits include episodes of *Tarzan* (1966), *The Avengers* (including 'Never Never Say Die' with Lee and 'Return of the

Cybernauts' with Cushing), *The Invaders*, *Circle of Fear* ('Time of Terror', based on the story by Elizabeth Walter), *The Sixth Sense*, *Logan's Run* and *Lucan*. He retired in the early 1990s, and his second wife was American actress Dorothy Provine.

American exploitation screenwriter, producer and director **Radley** [Henry] **Metzger** (aka "Harry Paris"), best known for such adult movies as *The Opening of Misty Beethoven*, died on March 31, aged 88. He began his career distributing European erotic movies in America and working as an editor on *The Flesh Eaters* (1964) and *The Beach Girls and the Monster* (uncredited). Metzger's most mainstream credit is the 1978 remake of *The Cat and the Canary*.

Disney "Imagineer" **George F. McGinnis** (the last to be personally hired by Walt Disney himself) died on April 6, aged 87. He designed many of the attractions for Disneyland, Walt Disney World and EPCOT, including Space Mountain. McGinnis also designed the robots in the 1979 movie *The Black Hole*.

British television producer and director **Christopher** [Thomas] **Morahan** CBE died on April 7, aged 87. His credits include a 1958 version of *Arsenic and Old Lace* starring Dave King and Peggy Mount. Morahan was head of plays at the BBC from 1972-76 before joining the National Theatre in 1977 as deputy to Peter Hall.

German cinematographer **Michael Ballhaus** died on April 11, aged 81. He shot Francis Ford Coppola's version of *Bram Stoker's Dracula*, *Wild Wild West* (1999), *What Planet Are You From?* and *The Legend of Bagger Vance*. His uncle, actor Carl Balhaus, appeared in Fritz Lang's *M* (1931) as the man who marked Peter Lorre with the sign "M".

American movie producer **J.** (Jeffrey) **C.** (Christian) **Spink** died from an accidental drug overdose on April 18, aged 45. Hs credits include *The Ring*, *The Butterfly Effect*, *The Ring Two*, *The Butterfly Effect 2*, *Insanitarium*, *The Butterfly Effect 3: Revelations*, Joe Dante's *The Hole*, *I Am Number Four*, *Zombeavers*, *Curve* and *Rings*, along with the ABC-TV series *Kyle XY*.

British-born Australian comedy scriptwriter and producer **Chris Bearde** died of a heart attack in California on April 23, aged 80. In the late 1960s and early '70s he was a resident writer for such shows as *Rowan & Martin's Laugh-In* and *The Sonny and Cher Comedy Hour*, and Bearde directed the 1983 horror spoof *Hysterical* starring the Hudson Brothers.

Academy Award-winning American screenwriter, producer and director [Robert] **Jonathan Demme** died of complications from oesophageal cancer and heart disease on April 26. He was 73. Demme began his career in the early 1970s, working for Roger Corman on such films as *Angels Hard as They Come* and *The Hot Box*, and he made his directing debut in 1974 with the women-in-prison movie *Caged Heat* (featuring Barbara Steele). His later credits include the Oscar-winning *The Silence of the Lambs*, *Beloved* and the 2004 remake of *The Manchurian Candidate*. Demme also had a supporting role as an actor in *The Incredible Melting Man* (1971).

American businessman **Stanley Weston**, who created the G.I. Joe action figure in 1963 and was a pioneer of the licensing and merchandising industry, died on May 1, aged 84. He sold the G.I. Joe concept to Hasbro, who turned it into a hugely successful toy line and TV and movie series, and he later helped created the 1980s animated TV show *Thundercats*.

Yoshimitsu Banno (Yoshimitsu Sakano), who scripted and directed the revisionist 1971 movie *Godzilla vs. Hedorah* (aka *Godzilla vs. the Smog Monster*), died of a subarachnoid haemorrhage on May 7, aged 86. He began his film career as an assistant director on Akira Kurosawa's *Throne of Blood*, and co-wrote and performed the same role on *The Last Days of Planet Earth*. In later years he was credited as an executive producer on *Godzilla* (2014) and the sequel *Godzilla: King of the Monsters* (2019), along with the 1982 animated Japanese version of *The Wizard of Oz*.

American make-up artist **Ron Berkeley**, who was closely associated with actors Richard Burton and Elizabeth Taylor, died on May 9, aged 86. He worked with the couple on such movies as *Doctor Faustus* (1967), *Hammersmith is Out*, *Bluebeard* (1972), *Night Watch*, *Exorcist II: The Heretic*, *The Medusa Touch*, *Absolution* and *Lovespell*, and his other credits include *The Time Machine* (1960), *The Manchurian Candidate* (1962), *The 7 Faces of Dr. Lao* and John Landis' *Innocent Blood*.

American production executive **Brad Grey** (Bradley Alan Grey) died of cancer on May 14, aged 59. He began his career as a production consultant on the 1981 horror movie *The Burning*, coming up with the original story with producer Harvey Weinstein and director Tony Maylam. Grey went on to executive produce such films as *What Planet Are You From?*, *Scary Movie* and *Charlie and the Chocolate Factory*. He was Chairman and CEO of Paramount Pictures from 2005-17.

American designer, engineer and documentary film-maker **Jacque Fresco** died on May 18, aged 101. He helped design the models for the 1953 SF movie *Project Moon Base* and an episode of TV's *Caprica*, and with Ken Keyes, Jr. he imagined a 21st century cybernetic society in the non-fiction book *Looking Forward* (1969).

American producer and director **Maury Dexter** (Morris Gene Poindexter) died on May 28, aged 89. His credits include *The Day Mars Invaded Earth* and *House of the Damned*. He was also an assistant director on the TV series *Highway to Heaven* (1984-89).

American cinematographer **Fred J. Koenekamp**, who shared an Academy Award for *The Towering Inferno* (1974), died of complications from a stroke on May 31, aged 94. After working as a camera operator on *The Outer Limits*, his credits include *Doc Savage: The Man of Bronze*, *Embryo*, *The Swarm*, *The Amityville Horror* (1979), *It Came from Hollywood*, *The Return of the Man from U.N.C.L.E.: The Fifteen Years Later Affair*, *The Adventures of Buckaroo Banzai Across the 8th Dimension*, *Alice in Wonderland* (1985), *The Return of the Shaggy Dog* (1978), *14 Going on 30* and *Splash Too*, along with ninety episodes of TV's *The Man from U.N.C.L.E.*

British-born film editor **Bill Butler** died in California on June 4, aged 84. He was nominated for an Oscar for his work on Stanley Kubrick's *A Clockwork Orange* (1971), and his other credits include *Vampira* (aka *Old Dracula*) and *Chameleon*.

American costume designer **Rita Riggs** died on June 5, aged 86. She worked with Alfred Hitchcock on both *Psycho* and *The Birds*, and her other credits include *The Legend of Hillbilly John* (based on stories by Manly Wade Wellman), Georges Franju's *Shadowman* and *Bad Moon*.

British film director **Cyril Frankel** died on June 7, aged 95. After appearing as a schoolboy extra (alongside author R. Chetwynd-Hayes) in *Goodbye Mr. Chips* (1939), he began directing documentaries in the early 1950s before moving on to such movies as Hammer's *Never Take Sweets from a Stranger* and *The Witches* (aka *The Devil's Own*). Frankel also directed episodes of TV's *The Avengers*, *The Champions* (including the pilot), *Randall and Hopkirk (Deceased)*, *UFO* and *Hammer House of Mystery and Suspense* (aka *Fox Mystery Theater*), and he was also a creative consultant on *Randall and Hopkirk (Deceased)*.

Carolyn Cronenberg (Carolyn Marcia Zeifman), the wife of director David Cronenberg, died in Toronto, Canada, on June 19, aged 66. She worked in various capacities on some of her husband's movies, including *Rabid* and *The Brood*.

British make-up and special effects designer **Simon Sayce** died after a long battle with cancer on June 20. Best known for creating Lemarchand's iconic Lament Configuration puzzle box for Clive Barker's *Hellraiser* and the sequel, *Hellbound: Hellraiser II*, he also produced David Cronenberg's mask for Barker's *Nightbreed*. His other credits include *The Unholy*, *The Lair of the White Worm*, *I Bought a Vampire Motorcycle* and *Extremity*.

American supervising sound editor and sound designer **David Lewis Yewdall** died of pancreatic cancer on July 4, aged 66. He worked on numerous movies, including *Deathsport*, *Piranha* (1978), *Humanoids of the Deep*, *Battle Beyond the Stars*, *Escape from New York*, *Halloween II* (1981), *Galaxy of Terror*, *The Thing* (1982), *Halloween III: Season of the Witch*, *Twilight Zone: The Movie*, *Wavelength*, *The Dead Zone*, *Christine*, *Amazons*, *The Philadelphia Experiment*, *Dreamscape*, *Transylvania 6-5000*, *Black Moon Rising*, *April Fool's Day*, *Sorority House Massacre* (1986), *Flicks*, *A Nightmare on Elm Street 3: Dream Warriors*, *Evil Dead II*, *Munchies*, *Near Dark*, *Flowers in the Attic* (1987), *The Unholy*, *Out of the Dark*, *Elvira Mistress of the Dark*, *Purple People Eater*, *The Punisher* (1989), *Halloween 5*, *Predator 2*, *Nemesis*, *Return of the Living Dead III*, *Philadephia Experiment II*, *Evolver*, *The Fifth Element*, *Starship Troopers*, *Phantoms*, *Fortress 2*, *Terror Tract* and *Sasquatch Mountain*.

American production designer and art director **Thomas E. Sanders** died of cancer on July 6, aged 64. He worked on *Hook*, *Bram Stoker's Dracula* (1992), *Red Riding Hood* (2011), *After Earth*, *Crimson Peak* and *Star Trek Beyond*. Sanders also directed one episode of TV's *Tales from the Crypt* ('About Face').

Tony Award-winning American dance choreographer **Danny Daniels** died on July 7, aged 92. He worked on such movies as *Zelig* and *Indiana Jones and the Temple of Doom*.

Oscar-nominated British film editor [Elizabeth] **Clare Douglas** died on July 9, aged 73. Her credits include *The Aerodrome*, *Cold Lazarus* and the 1976 *Doctor Who* serial 'The Masque of Mandragora'.

67-year-old Czech-born producer **Evzen** [William] **Kolar** died after a short illness in Los Angeles on July 11. He worked as a production manager on *To All a Goodnight* and the Bond film *Never Say Never Again*; as an assistant director on *Terror on Tour* and *Home Sweet Home*; as a production assistant on *Crawlspace*, and as an associate producer on *Masters of the Universe*.

American-born screenwriter, producer, editor and director **George A.** (Andrew) **Romero**, who revolutionised the zombie genre with the groundbreaking and hugely influential *Night of the Living Dead* (1968), died of lung cancer in Toronto, Canada, on July 16, aged 77. Romero continued his zombie series with *Dawn of the Dead* (1978), *Day of the Dead* (1985), *Land of the Dead*, *Diary of the Dead* and *Survival of the Dead*, and his other credits include *Season of the Witch* (aka *Jack's Wife*), *The Crazies* (1973), *Martin*, *Creepshow* (scripted by Stephen King), *Monkey Shines*, *Two Evil Eyes* (with Dario Argento), *The Dark Half* (based on the novel by King) and *Bruiser*. He also wrote *Creepshow 2* (based on stories by King) and a segment of *Tales from the Darkside: The Movie*, and executive produced the anthology TV series *Tales from the Darkside* (1984-88), *Dead Time Stories: Volume 1* and *Volume 2*, the 1990 remake of *Night of the Living Dead*, and the 2019 remake of *The Crazies*. Romero directed the music video for 'Scream' by The Misfits, and he had cameos in a number of his own films, along with playing an FBI agent in *The Silence of the Lambs* and appearing in the 2006 movie *Dead Eyes Open*. His short story 'Clay' was anthologised in

Modern Masters of Horror edited by Frank Coffey, while his comic book mini-series *Toe Tags Featuring George A. Romero* was published by DC Comics in 2004 and *Empire of the Dead* appeared from Marvel Comics in 2014. At the time of his death, Romero was developing *Road of the Dead*, to be directed by Matt Birman.

Legendary Disney "Imagineer" **Martin A.** "Marty" **Sklar** died on July 27, aged 83. While still a student at UCLA he began editing *The Disneyland News* in 1955, joining the company full-time the following year and working closely with Walt Disney to promote and develop the theme parks and attractions. During his liftetime Sklar attended the opening of every Disney theme park around the world, and he wrote the books *Disney: Dream It! Do It!: My Half-Century Creating Disney's Magic Kingdoms* (2013) and *One Little Spark!: Mickey's Ten Commandments and The Road to Imagineering* (2015).

American film editor **Eric** [James] **Zumbrunnen** died of stomach cancer on August 1, aged 52. He worked on numerous music videos, plus the movies *Being John Malkovich*, *Where the Wild Things Are*, *John Carter* and *Her*. Zumbrunnen also appeared in *Alien Beach Party Massacre*.

American film producer, writer and director [Willard] **Tobe Hooper**, best known for his iconic breakthrough movie *The Texas Chain Saw Massacre* (1974), died on August 26, aged 74. His other credits include *Eaten Alive* (aka *Death Trap/Slaughter Hotel*), *Salem's Lot*, *The Funhouse*, *Poltergeist*, *Lifeforce*, *Invaders from Mars* (1986), *The Texas Chainsaw Massacre 2*, *Spontaneous Combustion*, *I'm Dangerous Tonight*, *Night Terrors*, *Body Bags* (with John Carpenter), *The Mangler*, *Crocodile*, *Shadow Realm*, *Toolbox Murders* (2004), *Mortuary* (2005) and *Djinn*. On TV he directed episodes of *Amazing Stories*, *Freddy's Nightmares*, *Haunted Lives: True Ghost Stories*, *Tales from the Crypt*, *Nowhere Man*, *Dark Skies*, *Perversions of Science*, *Prey*, *The Others*, *Night Visions*, *Taken* and *Masters of Terror* (Richard Matheson's 'Dance of the Dead' and Ambrose Bierce's 'The Damned Thing', both scripted by Richard Christian Matheson). Hooper received a producer credit on the sequels/reboots *The Texas Chainsaw Massacre* (2003), *The Texas Chainsaw Massacre: The Beginning*, *Texas*

Chainsaw 3D and *Leatherface*, and he made cameo appearances in *The Texas Chainsaw Massacre 2*, *Spontaneous Combustion*, *Sleep-walkers* and *Body Bags*. With Alan Goldsher he co-authored the 2011 novel *Midnight Movie*, which featured the director as the main character.

South Korean director **Ki-duk Kim**, who co-wrote and directed *Yongary Monster from the Deep*, died on September 7, aged 82.

37-year-old **Chris Jones**, the British-born writer and director of the 2016 fantasy movie *The Death and Life of Otto Bloom*, died in Australia the same day.

Acclaimed British Shakespearian stage and film director Sir **Peter** [Reginald Frederick] **Hall** died of pneumonia on September 11, aged 86. He had been diagnosed with dementia in 2011. The founder of the Royal Shakespeare Company and a former director of the National Theatre, his stage productions include adaptations of William Shakespeare's *A Midsummer Night's Dream* (1959, 1962 and 2010) and *The Tempest* (1974), George Orwell's *Animal Farm* (1988) and Noël Coward's *Blithe Spirit* (2004). Hall also twice directed *A Midsummer Night's Dream* for the screen (1959 and 1968). The first of his four wives (1956-65) was French actress Leslie Caron.

The body of 47-year-old assistant location manager **Carlos Muñoz Portal** was found the same day with multiple gunshot wounds in an abandoned car on a dirt road near the rural town of Temascalapa, Mexico. He had been scouting locations for the next series of Netflix's *Narcos*. Amongst the movies he worked on were *Resident Evil: Extinction*, *Elysium* and the James Bond film *Spectre*.

American scriptwriter, director and producer **George Englund** (George Howe Ripley) died of complications from a fall at his home on September 14, aged 91. He began his career as an actor, starring in an episode of TV's *Lights Out* based on a story by John Collier. Englund also directed the surreal musical Western *Zachariah* (1971), loosely inspired by Hermann Hesse's novel *Siddhartha*, and produced the post-apocalyptic drama *The World, the Flesh and the Devil*. He was married to Cloris Leachman (1953-78) and co-authored the actress' 2009 autobiography.

American exploitation and adult film-maker C. (Charles) **Davis Smith** (aka "Charles Lamont") died on September 20, aged 87. He worked (often with Doris Wishman) as a writer, editor, producer and director on numerous low budget movies, including *The Girl from S.I.N.*, *The Amazing Dr. Jekyll*, *The Amazing Transplant*, *A Night to Dismember* and *Each Time I Kill*.

Two-time Oscar-nominated American cinematographer **Harry** [Alfred] **Stradling**, Jr. died on October 17, aged 92. He began his career working as an assistant camerman on such films as *Gaslight* (1944) before becoming a camera operator. As a director of photography, his credits include *The Mad Room*, *Nightmare Honeymoon*, *Damnation Alley* and *Prophecy*. He retired in 1988. His father, Harry Stradling, Sr., won an Oscar for his black and white photography on *The Picture of Dorian Gray* (1945).

Italian exploitation screenwriter and director **Umberto Lenzi** (aka "Humphrey Humbert", "Bert Lenzi", "Humphrey Logan", "Henry Milestone" and "Harry Kirkpatrick") died on October 19, aged 86. Lenzi worked in all genres, and his films include *Samson and the Slave Queen*, *The Spy Who Loved Flowers*, *Paranoia* (1969), *So Sweet . . . So Perverse*, *Seven Blood-Stained Orchids*, *Man From Deep River*, *Spasmo*, *Eyeball*, *Eaten Alive!*, *Nightmare City* (aka *City of the Walking Dead*), *Cannibal Ferox* (aka *Make Them Die Slowly*, initially banned in more than thirty countries), *Ironmaster*, *Ghosthouse*, *The House of Witchcraft*, *The Hell's Gate*, *House of Lost Souls*, *Hitcher in the Dark*, *Nightmare Beach* and *Black Demons*. He retired in the early 1990s.

Oscar-winning, German-born cinematographer **Walter** [Israel] **Lassally** died in Crete, Greece, on October 23, following complications from surgery. He was 90. Lassally shot *The Day the Fish Came Out*, *To Kill a Clown*, *Happy Mother's Day Love George*, *Memoirs of a Survivor* (based on the novel by Doris Lessing) and *The Mysterious Stranger*.

British costume designer **John Mollo**, who won an Oscar for his work on *Star Wars* (1977), died on October 25, aged 86. He also worked on the sequel, *The Empire Strikes Back*, plus *Alien*, *Outland*, *Greystoke: The Legend of Tarzan Lord of the Apes*, *The Jungle Book*

(1994) and *Event Horizon*. An expert in European and American military apparel, Mollo's look for Darth Vader was influenced by First World War trench uniforms and Nazi helmets.

Pioneering television director **Paddy Russell** (Patricia Mary Russell) died on November 2, aged 89. She began her career as a BBC stage manager on such programmes as Nigel Kneale's *The Quatermass Experiment* (1953) and *Nineteen Eighty-Four* (1954, starring Peter Cushing). In 1963 she became one of the first female directors in British TV, and her many credits include the 1972 serial *The Moonstone* (based on the novel by Wilkie Collins), along with episodes of *Doctor Who* ('Pyramids of Mars', 'Horror at Fang Rock' etc.), *Out of the Unknown*, *Late Night Horror* (Richard Matheson's 'No Such Thing as a Vampire' and John Burke's 'The Corpse Can't Play') and *The Omega Factor*.

American producer and agent **William Frye** died on November 3, aged 96. Best known for his classic television series *Thriller* (1960-62), hosted by Boris Karloff, he also produced the TV movies *The Screaming Woman* (based on the story by Ray Bradbury) and *The Victim*. Frye was instrumental in getting Bette Davis to star in *What Ever Happened to Baby Jane?* (1962).

54-year-old Welsh technician **Mark Milsome** died while shooting a night-time car stunt for the BBC/Netflix in Ghana on November 18. He worked in the camera department in various capacities on *Wuthering Heights* (1992), *Dark Waters*, *Mary Reilly*, *Photographing Fairies*, *Ritual* (originally the third *Tales from the Crypt* movie), *The Dark* (2005), *Dracula* (2006) and *Skellig*, along with episodes of TV's *Sherlock* and *Game of Thrones*.

Chinese film producer **Mona Fong** (Meng-Lan Li) died in Hong Kong on November 22, aged 83. A former singer, her many credits include *Hex vs. Witchcraft*, *Corpse Mania*, *Gu*, *Hex After Hex*, *Human Lanterns*, *The Enchantress*, *Demon of the Lute*, *Seeding of a Ghost*, *Sex Beyond the Grave*, *The Mad Monk* and *Out of the Dark*. She was married to studio executive Sir Run Run Shaw from 1997 until his death in 2004.

British-born film editor and director **Anthony Harvey** died in Southampton, New York, on November 23, aged 87. As an editor he worked on Stanley Kubrick's *Dr. Strangelove or: How I Stopped Worrying and Love the Bomb*, and went on to direct *They Might Be Giants* and *Svengali* (1983).

French screenwriter, director and novelist **Alain** [Rene Sando] **Jessua** died of pneumonia on November 30, aged 85. His films include *Shock Treatment* (1973), *Frankenstein 90* and *The Colors of the Devil*.

Prolific German screenwriter, producer and director **Ulli Lommel** (Ullrich Manfred Lommel, aka "Patricia Devereaux"/"Bianco Pacelli"/"Mario Van Cleef"/"Steven Sondberg"/"The Green River Band") died of heart failure on December 2, aged 72. A frequent collaborator with Rainer Werner Fassbinder and Andy Warhol, his many credits (in various production capacities) include *Tenderness of the Wolves*, *The Boogey Man* (starring John Carradine), *Brain Waves*, *Olivia*, *Boogeyman II*, *The Devonsville Terror* (starring Donald Pleasence), *Stangers in Paradise*, *Return of the Boogeyman*, *Lethal Orbit*, *Bloodsuckers* (1997), *Zombie Nation*, *Zodiac Killer*, *Green River Killer*, *The Raven* (2006), *Diary of a Cannibal*, *Curse of the Zodiac*, *The Tomb* (2007), *Borderline Cult*, *Dungeon Girl*, *Baseline Killer*, *Killer Nurse*, *Absolute Evil*, *Nightstalker* (2009), *Manson Family Cult* and *Boogeyman: Reincarnation*. Lommel also acted in his own and others' movies. He was married to his leading lady, actress Suzanna Love, from 1979-87.

American producer **Howard Gottfried** died of complications from a stroke on December 8, aged 94. A champion of unpredictable screenwriter Paddy Chayefsky, he produced Ken Russell's *Altered States*, Brian De Palma's *Body Double* and Burt Kennedy's *Suburban Commando*.

British director **Paul** [Anthony] **Annett**, best known for Amicus' werewolf mystery *The Beast Must Die* starring Peter Cushing, died on December 11, aged 80. His other film credits include *The Witching of Ben Wagner*, and he also directed episodes of TV's *Dead of Night* (1972), *Hammer House of Mystery and Suspense*, *The Adventures of Sherlock Holmes* and *Tales of the Unexpected*.

British director **Peter** [John] **Duffell** died on December 12, aged 95. Best known for Amicus' *The House That Dripped Blood* (1971, with Christopher Lee and Peter Cushing), his other credits include episodes of TV's *The Avengers* ('The Winged Avenger'), Hammer's *Journey to the Unknown*, *Strange Report* ('Report 8944: Hand—A Matter of Witchcraft'), *Tales of the Unexpected* and *Space Precinct*. Duffell also worked as an uncredited second-unit director on *Superman* (1978). His 2010 autobiography, *Playing Piano in a Brothel: Memoirs of a Film Director*, featured a Foreword by Christopher Lee, who described him as "The most underrated director we have had in Britain for a very long time".

American movie producer **Martin** [Nelson] **Ransohoff**, who discovered actress Sharon Tate and introduced her to her future husband, Roman Polanksi, died on December 13, aged 90. With Edwin Kasper, he formed the production company Filmways Television in 1952, which produced such popular shows as *Mister Ed* (1958-66) and *The Addams Family* (1964-66). Ransohoff's movie credits include *Eye of the Devil* (aka *13*), Polanski's *Dance of the Vampires* (aka *The Fearless Vampire Killers or: Pardon Me, But Your Teeth Are in My Neck*), *A Midsummer Night's Dream* (1968), *Castle Keep*, *Hamlet* (1969), *Catch-22*, *See No Evil* and *Nightwing*.

American production designer and art director **Thérèse DePrez** died of breast cancer on December 19, aged 52. Her credits include *Severed Ties*, *The Refrigerator*, *Summer of Sam*, *Dark Water*, *The Return*, *Mr. Magorium's Wonder Emporium*, *Black Swan* and *Stoker*.

American camera operator **Albert Bettcher** died on December 21, aged 97. He began his career as an uncredited first assistant cameraman on such movies as *Bell Book and Candle*, *The Three Stooges in Orbit*, *The Three Stooges Go Around the World in a Daze* and William Castle's *13 Frightened Girls* and *Strait-Jacket* before he became a camera operator on ABC-TV's *Batman* series. He then went on to work on *Battle for the Planet of the Apes*, *The Terminal Man*, *King Kong* (1976), *The Fury*, *Star Trek The Motion Picture*, *Blade Runner*, *Brainstorm* (1983), *All of Me*, *Howard the Duck*, *My Stepmother is an Alien* and the 1967 *Batgirl* TV pilot.

Academy Award-winning American film editor **Jerry Greenberg** (Gerald B. Greenberg) died after a long illness on December 22, aged 81. He worked on *They Might Be Giants*, *The Happy Hooker*,

Apocalypse Now, Dressed to Kill, Body Double and *Inspector Gadget.*

Oscar-winning, German-born movie editor **Thomas Stanford** died in Santa Fe, New Mexico, on December 23. He was 93. Stanford edited *Suddenly, Last Summer* (1959) and *The Legend of the Lone Ranger.*

USEFUL ADDRESSES

THE FOLLOWING LISTING of organisations, publications, dealers and individuals is designed to present readers and authors with further avenues to explore. Although I can personally recommend many of those listed on the following pages, neither the publisher nor myself can take any responsibility for the services they offer. Please also note that the information below is only a guide and is subject to change without notice.

—The Editor

ORGANISATIONS

Australasian Horror Writers Association (*www.australasian-horror.wordpress.com*) is a non-profit organisation that was formed in 2005 and provides a community and unified voice for Australasian writers of dark fiction, fostering the evolution of the genre within Australia. AHWA is the first point of reference for writers and fans of the dark side of literature in Australia, New Zealand, and the Pacific Islands. It spreads the acceptance and understanding of horror literature to a wider audience, and in doing so gains a greater readership for established and new writers alike. They also publish the magazine *Midnight Echo*, and offer opportunities to be published, mentor programmes, critique services, competitions and giveaways, opportunities to interact with other writers, publishers, artists and other key members of the community, genre news on the Australian scene, and links to horror-related and writing resources. E-mail: *australasianhorror@gmail.com*

The British Fantasy Society (*www.britishfantasysociety.org*) was founded in 1971 and publishes the *BFS Journal*, featuring articles and reviews, and *BFS Horizons*, which is devoted to fiction and poetry, along with occasional exclusive publications only available to members of the Society. Run by volunteers, the BFS offers an e-newsletter, free entry into the BFS Short Story Competition, free specialist writing workshops, discounted membership of FantasyCon and organised open nights and book launches. For yearly membership see the website for details.

The Horror Writers Association (*www.horror.org*) is a non-profit organisation of writers and publishing professionals around the world, dedicated to promoting dark literature and the interests of those who write it. HWA was formed in the late 1980s and today has more than 1,250 members—making it the oldest and most respected professional organisation for horror writers. One of HWA's missions is to encourage public interest in and foster an appreciation of good horror and dark Fantasy literature. To that end, they offer the public areas of their website, they sponsor or take part in occasional public readings and lectures, they publish a blog and produce other materials for book-sellers and librarians, they facilitate readings and signings by horror writers, and they are dedicated to recognising and promoting diversity in the horror genre. As part of the organisation's core mission, they also sponsor the annual Bram Stoker Awards® for superior achievement in horror literature at the annual StokerCon. E-mail: *hwa@horror.org*

SELECTED SMALL PRESS PUBLISHERS

The **Alchemy Press** (*www.alchemypress.co.uk*).

American Fantasy Press (*www.americanfantasypress.com*), 919 Tappan Street, Woodstock, Illinois 60098, USA.

BearManor Media (*www.bearmanormedia.com*), PO Box 1129, Duncan, OK 73534-1129, USA.

Black Dog Books (*www.blackdogbooks.net*), 1115 Pine Meadows Ct., Normal, IL 61761-5432, USA. E-mail: *info@blackdogbooks.net*

Borderlands Press (*www.borderlandspress.com*), POB 61, Benson, MD 21018, USA.

Cemetery Dance Publications (*www.cemeterydance.com*), 132-B Industry Lane, Unit #7, Forest Hill, MD 21050, USA. E-mail: *info@cemeterydance.com*

Chthonic Matter (*www.chthonicmatter.wordpress.com*).

The **Clive Barker Archive** (*www.clivebarkerarchive.com*). E-mail: *philandsarah@clivebarker.info*

Cōnfingō Publishing (*www.confingopublishing.uk*), 2 Stonecroft, Parkfield Road South, Manchester M20 6DA, UK. E-mail: *tim@confingopublishing.uk*

Copper Dog Publishing LLC/MoonDream Press (*www.copperdogpublishing.com*), 537 Leader Circle, Louisville, CO 80027, USA.

Crystal Lake Publishing (*www.crystallakepub.com*).

Cutting Block Books/Farolight Publishing (*www.cuttingblock-books.com*), PO Box 1521, Winchester, VA 22604, USA.

Cycatrix Press/JaSunni Productions, LCC (*www.jasunni.com*), 16420 SE McGillivray Blvd., Ste 103-1010, Vancouver, WA 98683, USA. E-mail: *jasunni@jasunni.com*

Dark Cloud Press (*www.darkcloudpress.com*).

Dark Minds Press, 31 Gristmill Close, Cheltenham, Glos. GL51 0PZ, UK. E-mail: *mail@darkmindspress.com*

Dark Regions Press LCC (*www.darkregions.com*), PO Box 31022, Portland, OR 97231, USA.

Dim Shores (*www.dimshores.com*), PO Box #3092, Citrus Heights, CA 95611-3092, USA.

Earthling Publications (*www.earthlingpub.com*), PO Box 413, Northborough, MA 01532, USA. E-mail: *earthlingpub@yahoo.com*

FableCroft Publishing (*fablecroft.au*).

Fedogan & Bremer Publishing LLC (*fedoganandbremer.com*), 3918 Chicago Street, Nampa, Idaho 83686, USA.

Flame Tree Publishing (*www.flametreepublishing.com*), 6 Melbray Mews, Fulham, London SW6 3NS, UK. E-mail: *info@flametreepublishing.com*

Franklin/Kerr Press (*www.franklinkerr.com*), 349-L Copperfield Boulevard #502, Concord, North Carolina 28025, USA.

Gehenna & Hinnom Books (*gehennapublishinghouse@gmail.com*), 205 South 25th Avenue B, Hattiesburg, MS 39401, USA. E-mail: *cpdunphey@gmail.com*

Great British Horror Books/Black Shuck Books/KnightWatch Press (*www.greatbritishhorror.com/www.blackshuckbooks.co.uk*), "Hillbrow", North-bourne Road, Deal, Kent CT14 0LA, UK.

Hersham Horror Books (*silenthater.wix.com/hersham-horror-books#*).

Hippocampus Press (*www.hippocampuspress.com*), PO Box 641, New York, NY 10156, USA. E-mail: *info@hippocampuspress.com*

JournalStone (*www.journalstone.com*).

McFarland & Company, Inc., Publishers (*www.mcfarlandpub.com*), Box 611, Jefferson, NC 28640, USA.

Necro Publications (*www.necropublications.com*), 5139 Maxon Terrace, Sanford, FL 32771, USA.

Nightjar Press (*nightjarpress.weebly.com*), 63 Ballbrook Court, Wilmslow Road, Manchester M20 3GT, UK.

Night Shade Books (*www.nightshadebooks.com*), 307 West 36th Street, 11th Floor, New York, NY 10018, USA.

Nunkie (*www.nunkie.co.uk/theatre-shows/*).

Parallel Universe Publications (*paralleluniversepublications. blogspot.co.uk/*), 130 Union Road, Oswaldtwistle, Lancashire BB5 3DR, UK.

Perpetual Motion Machine Publishing (*www.pmmpnews.com*), Cibolo, Texas, USA. E-mail: *darkmoonhorror@gmail.com*

Pro Se Productions, LLC (*www.prose-press.com*), 133 1/2 Broad Street, Batesville, AR 72501, USA. E-mail: *editorinchief@prose-press.com*

PS Publishing Ltd/Drugstore Indian Press/PS ArtBooks Ltd/ Stanza Press/PSi/The Pulps Library/Electric Dreamhouse (*www.pspublishing.co.uk*), Grosvenor House, 1 New Road, Hornsea HU18 1PG, UK. E-mail: *editor@pspublishing.co.uk*

Quantum Corsets (*www.quantumcorsets.co.uk*). E-mail: *contact@ quantumcorsets.co.uk*

The Refuge Collection (*www.ozhorrorcon.com*). E-mail: *Dillonstephen@ hotmail.com*

Sarob Press (*sarobpress.blogspot.com*), La Blinière, 53250, Neuilly-le-Vendin, France.

Savoy Books (*www.savoy.abel.co.uk*), 456 Wilmslow Road, Withington, Manchester M20 3BG, UK. E-mail: *office@ savoy.abel.co.uk*

Shadow Publishing (*www.shadowpublishing.webeasysite.co.uk/*), Apt. #19 Awdry Court, 15 St. Nicolas Gardens, Birmingham, West Midlands B38 8BH, UK. E-mail: *david.sutton986@btinternet.com*

Shadowridge Press (*www.shadowridgepress.com*).

Sinister Horror Company (*www.sinisterhorrorcompany.com*).

Spectacular Optical Publications (*www.spectacularoptical.ca*), 53 Delaney Crescent, Toronto, Ontario M6K 1P9, Canada.

Subterranean Press (*www.subterraneanpress.com*), PO Box 190106, Burton, MI 48519, USA. E-mail: *subpress@gmail.com*

The Swan River Press (*www.swanriverpress.ie*), Dublin, Ireland. E-mail: *brian@swanriverpress.ie*

Tartarus Press (*www.tartaruspress.com*), Coverley House, Carlton-in-Coverdale, Leyburn, North Yorkshire DL8 4AY, UK. E-mail: *tartarus@pavilion.co.uk*

Telos Publishing (*www.telos.co.uk*), 5A Church Road, Shortlands, Bromley, Kent BR2 0HP, UK.

Undertow Publications (*www.undertowbooks.com*) Michael Kelly Editor, 1905 Faylee Crescent, Pickering, ON L1V 2T3, Canada. E-mail: *undertowbooks@gmail.com*

Valancourt Books (*www.valancourtbooks.com*).

SELECTED MAGAZINES

Ansible is a highly entertaining monthly SF and fantasy newsletter/gossip column edited by David Langford. It is available free electronically by sending an e-mail to: *ansible-request@ dcs.gla.ac.uk* with a subject line reading "subscribe", or you can receive the print version by sending a stamped and addressed envelope to Ansible, 94 London Road, Reading, Berks RG1 5AU, UK. Back issues, links and book lists are also available online.

Black Static (*www.ttapress.com*) is the UK's premier horror fiction magazine, produced bi-monthly by the publishers of *Interzone*. Six- and twelve-issue subscriptions are available, along with a lifetime subscription, from TTA Press, 5 Martins Lane, Witcham, Ely, Cambs CB6 2LB, UK, or from the secure TTA website. E-mail: *andy@ttapress.com*

Classic Images (*www.classicimages.com*) edited by Bob King is a monthly newsprint publication for those who love old movies. Most issues contain material of interest to horror and SF fans, and subscriptions are available. 301 E. 3rd Street, Muscatine, IA 52761, USA. E-mail: *classicimages@classicimages.com*

Decidious Tales (*www.decidioustales.com*), Black Thunder Press, PO Box 175, Garberville, CA 95542, USA. E-mail: *deciduoustales@ gmail.com*

Finnish Weird (*www.finnishweird.net*), Helsinki Science Fiction Society, Itämerenkatu 22 B 21, 00180 Helsinki, Finland. E-mail: *tjerrman@pp.htv.fi*

The Ghosts & Scholars M.R. James Newsletter (*www.pardoes.info/roanddarroll/GS.html*) is a scholarly journal published roughly twice a year. It is dedicated to the classic ghost story and, as the title implies, to M.R. James in particular. Two-issue subscriptions are available from Haunted Library Publications, c/o Flat Two, 36 Hamilton Street, Hoole, Chester CH2 3JQ, UK. E-mail: *dandrpardoe@gmail.com*

Illustrators (*www.bookpalace.com*) is a beautifully designed and published full-colour periodical devoted to art and artists. The Book Palace, Jubilee House, Bedwardine Road, Crystal Palace, London SE19 3AP, UK. E-mail: *IQ@bookpalace.com*

Locus (*www.locusmag.com*) is the monthly newspaper of the SF/fantasy/horror field. Contact Locus Publications, 655 13th St, Suite 100, Oakland, CA 94612, USA. Subscription information with other rates and order forms are also available on the website. E-mail: *locus@locusmag.com*.

The Magazine of Fantasy & Science Fiction (*www.fandsf.com*) has been publishing some of the best imaginative fiction for six decades. Produced bi-monthly, single copies or an annual subscription are available by US cheques or credit card from: Fantasy & Science Fiction, PO Box 3447, Hoboken, NJ 07030, USA, or you can subscribe via the website.

Occult Detective Quarterly (*greydogtales.com/blog/occult-detective-quarterly/odq/*). E-mail: *occultdetectivequarterly@yahoo.com*

Pulp Horror/The Paperback Fanatic (*www.thepaperbackfanatic@sky.com*). Justin Marriott's excellent, if irregular, publications for those who love old and new books. E-mail: *thepaperbackfantatic@sky.com*

Rabbit Hole (*harlanellisonbooks.com/shop*) is a semi-regular newsletter issued to members of The Harlan Ellison Recording Collection. You can subscribe via the website or contact The Harlan Ellison Recording Collection, PO Box 55548, Sherman Oaks, CA 91413-0548, USA.

Redrum Recordz (*redrumrecordz.bandcamp.com/music*).

Rue Morgue (*www.rue-morgue.com*) is a glossy bi-monthly magazine subtitled "Horror in Culture & Entertainment". Each issue is packed with full colour features and reviews of new films, books, comics, music and game releases. Subscriptions are available from: Marrs Media Inc., 1411 Dufferin Street, Toronto, Ontario M6H 4CT, Canada, or by credit card on the website. E-mail: *info@rue-morgue.com*

Scream (*www.screamhorrormag.com*) is a glossy bi-monthly British news-stand magazine, described as "The horror bible for horror fans". It features news, reviews, articles, interviews and lots of ads about mostly new and classic movies, but it does also carry a book review column. Alan Clayton is the submissions editor at: *submissions@screamhorrormag.com*

Space and Time: The Magazine of Fantasy, Horror, and Science Fiction (*www.spaceandtimemagazine.com*) is published twice a year. Single issues and subscriptions are available from the website or from: Space and Time Magazine, 458 Elizabeth Avenue #5348, Somerset, NJ 08873, USA.

Supernatural Tales (*suptales.blogspot.com*) is a fiction magazine edited by David Longhorn, with subscriptions available via PayPal, cheques or non-UK cash. Supernatural Tales, 291 Eastbourne Avenue, Gateshead NE8 4NN, UK. E-mail: *davidlonghorn@hotmail.com*

Things in the Well (*www.thingsinthewell.com*). E-mail: *news@ozhorrorcon.com*

Weirdbook (*www.wildsidepress.com*) is a PoD revival of the iconic fantasy and horror magazine, edited by Doug Draa and published by Wildside Press LCC, 9710 Traville Gateway Drive, #234, Rockville, MD 20850, USA.

BOOK DEALERS

Cold Tonnage Books (*www.coldtonnage.com*) offers excellent mail order new and used SF/fantasy/horror, art, reference, limited editions etc. Write to: Andy & Angela Richards, Cold Tonnage Books, Poundwater, Farway, Colyton, Devon EX24 6EG, UK. Credit cards accepted. Tel: +44 (0)1404-871001. E-mail: *andy@coldtonnage.com*

DreamHaven Books & Comics (*www.dreamhavenbooks.com*) is open Tuesday through Saturday and also has a mail-order outlet, offering new and used SF/fantasy/horror/art and illustrated etc. with regular catalogues (both print and E-mail). 2031 E. 38th Street, Minneapolis, MN 55406-3015, USA. Credit cards accepted. Tel: (612) 823-6070. E-mail: *dream@dreamhavenbooks.com*

Fantastic Literature (*www.fantasticliterature.com*) mail order offers the UK's biggest online out-of-print SF/fantasy/horror genre bookshop. Fanzines, pulps and vintage paperbacks as well. Write to: Simon and Laraine Gosden, Fantastic Literature, 35 The Ramparts, Rayleigh, Essex SS6 8PY, UK. Credit cards and Pay Pal accepted. Tel/Fax: +44 (0)1268-747564. E-mail: *simon@fantasticliterature.com*

Hyraxia Books (*www.hyraxia.com*), Toft Cottage, 1 Beverley Road, Hutton Cranswick, East Yorkshire YO25 9PQ, UK. Specialist sellers of rare and collectible modern first editions, including many genre titles. They also buy books. Tel: +44 (0)7557-652-609. E-mail: *shop@hyraxia.com*

The Iliad Bookshop (*www.iliadbooks.com*), 5400 Cahuenga Blvd., North Hollywood, CA 91601, USA. General bookstore that has a very fine selection of new, used and rare books, with an emphasis on literature and the arts. Tel: (818) 509-2665.

Porcupine Books offers regular catalogues and extensive mail order lists of used fantasy/horror/SF titles via E-mail *brian@porcupine. demon.co.uk* or write to: 37 Coventry Road, Ilford, Essex IG1 4QR, UK. Tel: +44 (0)20 8554-3799.

Reel Art Collectibles/Horrorbles (*www.reelart.biz*), 6727 W. Stanley, Berwyn, Illinois 60402, USA. Nicely designed Chicago store selling movie material, classic comics, vintage toys and rare books. They also host celebrity signings and have regular warehouse sales. Tel: 1-708-288-7378. Facebook: *Reel Art, Inc.*

Terence McVicker Rare Books (*www.batsoverbooks.com/?page=shop/index*) is a mail-order business offering premium rare and collectible items—many H.P. Lovecraft and Arkham House-related. A weekly e-mail reader features additions, updates and news. E-mail: *info@batsoverbooks.com*

Ygor's Books specialises in out of print science fiction, fantasy and horror titles, including British, signed, speciality press and limited editions. They also buy books, letters and original art in these fields. E-mail: *ygorsbooks@gmail.com*

ONLINE RESOURCES

The Dark (*www.thedarkmagazine.com*) edited by Sean Wallace is a free monthly online magazine that is also available for digital download.

Fantastic Fiction (*www.fantasticfiction.co.uk*) features more than 2,000 best-selling author biographies with all their latest books, covers and descriptions.

Hellnotes (*www.hellnotes.com*) offers news and reviews of novels, collections, magazines, anthologies, non-fiction works, and chap-books. Materials for review should be sent to editor and publisher David B. Silva, Hellnotes, 5135 Chapel View Court, North Las Vegas, NV 89031, USA. E-mail: *news@hellnotes.com* or *dbsilva13@gmail.com*

The Horror Zine (*www.thehorrorzine.com*) is a monthly online maga-zine edited by Jeani Rector that features fiction, poetry, interviews and reviews. It is also available in a PoD edition and produces its own books.

Locus Online (*www.locusmag.com/news*) is an excellent online source for the latest news and reviews.

Nightmare Magazine (*www.nightmare-magazine.com/*) edited by John Joseph Adams is an excellent monthly online site for fiction (both new and reprint), interviews and podcasts.

Pseudopod (*www.pseudopod.org*), the premiere horror fiction podcast, continues to offer a free-to-download, weekly reading of new or classic horror fiction by a variety of voices. The site remains dedicated to paying their authors while providing readings for free and offering the widest variety of audio horror fiction currently available on the net.

SF Site (*www.sfsite.com*) has been posted twice each month since 1997. Presently, it publishes around thirty to fifty reviews of SF, fantasy and horror from mass-market publishers and some small press. They also maintain link pages for Author and Fan Tribute Sites and other facets including pages for Interviews, Fiction, Science Fact, Bookstores, Small Press, Publishers, E-zines and Magazines, Artists, Audio, Art Galleries, Newsgroups and Writers' Resources. Periodically, they add features such as author and publisher reading lists.

Tor.com (*www.tor.com*), publishes new fiction, articles, novel excerpts, artist galleries, reviews and a lot more.

Vault of Evil (*www.vaultofevil.wordpress.com*) is a site dedicated to celebrating the best in British horror with special emphasis on UK anthologies. There is also a lively forum devoted to many different themes at *www.vaultofevil.proboards.com*